I0650724

Formerly *Weird Tales*®
Summer 1994

ISSN 0898-5073
Cover by Ian Miller

THE OWL'S NEST

What's in a name?

Welcome to . . . precisely what, we will leave future bibliographers to figure out. If you're a long-time reader, you've probably noticed by now that this magazine's title isn't what it used to be, for this is Volume One, Number One, of *Worlds of Fantasy & Horror,* not *Weird Tales®* #309.

What is going on here?

We have come to an extremely amicable parting of the ways with Weird Tales, Ltd., the owners of the trademark *"Weird Tales®."* As a result, the fantasy magazine published by Terminus Publishing Company, Inc., has now changed its name to *Worlds of Fantasy & Horror.* Since we've re-started the volume and issue numbering, we expect that some collectors will classify this as "associational" with the classic *Weird Tales®.* The indexing tangle will be nowhere near that of some other titles in the field. Possibly purists will insist that the long history of *Weird Tales®* is no longer linear, but, as of 1994, forked.

So, *Worlds of Fantasy & Horror* it is. Nothing else has changed. All subscriptions will be honored. All rates (subscription, advertising, payment to authors and artists) remain the same. Frequency of publication remains the same (quarterly). As long as copies of back issues of *Weird Tales®* remain available, Terminus Publishing Company, Inc., will continue to sell them.

This change has given us the opportunity to stop and define precisely our aesthetic agenda (to use David Hartwell's elegant phrase). In other words, what is this magazine about?

The new title pretty well sums it up. This magazine celebrates the *imaginative* in fiction, with a shading toward the darker end of the spectrum. While our range remains, we modestly observe, wider than anybody else's, we are more likely to publish horror than whimsy, although whimsy, of course, is not to be ruled out. (The great advantage is that you, the reader, can never quite know how a story will turn out. In an all-horror magazine, it would be more obvious. Even monotonously so.) Our horror is usually (but not 100% of the time) *fantastic* horror. We admit that we are reacting against the movement which tries to play down the supernatural as much as possible, merge horror with crime fiction, and call the result "Dark Suspense." We

aren't Splatterpunk either, but then, who is these days?

We intend to publish all kinds of fantastic fiction. In a publishing scene where, conventionally, a story about, say, the dead returning to an apartment in contemporary New York is marketed as *horror,* while the same story about the dead returning to a haunted castle in lost Atlantis ten thousand years ago becomes *fantasy,* we at *WoF&H* do not recognize or care about such a distinction. We're not sure that "sword and sorcery" remains a valid label anymore; but if such a story comes along, sure, we can use it. Hopefully this issue gives some idea of our potential range.

In the future, we expect to assemble fewer Feature Author issues than we did in the past, but there will be some, notably *WoF&H* #2, which will showcase **Charles de Lint** with a brand new novella and short story by this outstanding author, plus an interview. We have stories on hand by Tanith Lee, Reginald Bretnor, Lord Dunsany, Ian Watson, Keith Roberts, Chet Williamson, and many more. Jason Van Hollander's *Weirdisms* series will be discontinued, but he promises us something new, *Pages from the Hell Book.* Allen Koszowski's *Classic Horrors* will continue. The next one illustrates "The Monkey's Paw."

So we hope you'll stay with us.

We are sorry to announce the death of one of our field's truly perennial figures, **Frank Belknap Long,** who passed away recently at age 90. Mr. Long's first professional story appeared in *Weird Tales* in 1924, after he had already come to the attention of the great H.P. Lovecraft in the amateur press. He contributed to most of the fantastic pulps of the '20s, '30s, and '40s. As a science-fiction writer, he was a prolific contributor to *Astounding Science Fiction.* He held various editorial posts in the '50s and '60s, wrote science-fiction novels under his own name and gothics under his wife's name (Lyda Belknap Long); and returned to the supernatural horror field, where his last work appeared in the early '80s. His memoir of Lovecraft, *Howard Phillips Lovecraft: Dreamer on the Night Side,* appeared in 1975. He was also a poet of distinction, but he will always be best remembered for the stories he wrote for the early *Weird Tales*, particularly "The Hounds of Tindalos" and "The Space Eaters," which contribute to Lovecraft's Cthulhu Mythos.

We also learned, via the British science-fiction newsletter *Ansible*, the distressing news that popular author and illustrator **Keith Roberts** is so gravely ill that he cannot now write or draw. Our sympathies go out to him. We very sincerely hope that he will again be able to do the creative work for which he is so justly praised. Meanwhile we are able to guarantee him another appearance in our pages, probably in our next issue, with the story we have in inventory. Roberts is the author of the classic *Pavane*, plus *The Chalk Giants, Kaeti and Company, Kiteworld, The Boat of Fate, Anita,* and many more. He is a superb writer, and worth seeking out.

We heard from various readers and would like to hear from more in the future. **Peni R. Griffin** comments at length:

"On the subject of writers with creeds, first touched on in Ian Watson's interview [. . .], I think there are probably two crucial points affecting the writer's output. The first point, obviously, is simply the writer's degree of talent and skill. C.S. Lewis and J.R.R. Tolkien succeed as well as they do because they were good writers, regardless of their religious beliefs. If they had been athiests, they would still have written good stories, albeit not the same stories. Martha Finley, author of the Elsie Dinsmore series, wrote lousy books; and they would have been just as lousy if she had chosen to preach atheism or Hinduism instead of the WASP-Christianity she did preach.

"For those whose talent is less than Lewis's and greater than Finley's (i.e., most of us!), a great deal depends on the security and honesty of the faith. The way to make a plot and characters work is to make them act as much like the real world as you can — meaning, of course, the real world the author lives in. A skeptical fantastic writer has it easy. She only has to ask herself, 'Okay, I've got an ordinary college student here in an ordinary college. What really happens if I throw in a guardian angel?' She reads up on guardian angels, consults her knowledge of human nature, decides what slant she wants, and she's got a story. But what about a Christian who really believes in guardian angels? How does he avoid the temptation to preach? Does his own reverence get in the way of a realistic portrayal of the angel or the college student? Knowing that prejudice against Chriatianity exists among fantasy fans, does he purposely restrain himself? Or does he worry about what will happen if his minister reads this story?

"The problem is even harder if you're a practicing pagan, and feel you've got to explain everything that happens in terms of the rituals, etc.; and it's hardest of all if you believe in a form of supernaturalism which is considered kooky or fraudulent, and which you either really want to push, or are trying not to doubt."

Publisher: **George H. Scithers**
Editor: **Darrell Schweitzer**
Managing Editor: **Carol Adams**
Art Director: **Michael W. Betancourt**
Assistant Editors:
Leslie Smith, Dainis Bisenieks,
Diane Weinstein, Don Keller, & Kyle Phillips
Computer Consultant: **David J. Williams III**
Of Counsel: **Matthew Wolfe**
Typesetter: **Owlswick Press**
Printer: **Associated Printers**

Manuscript Submissions:

Yes; we read unsolicited submissions — but **only** if they are in standard manuscript format. To survive, all editors insist on a few Rules: each submission must be in proper format and must include a return envelope addressed to you with enough postage affixed to bring the manuscript back to you. If you want us to discard the manuscript if not bought, tell us so; but then include a business-letter-size envelope *with postage affixed,* addressed to you, so we can send you our comments. No loose stamps, please!

We have a set of guidelines that cover manuscript format, what we're buying, the works; if you want a copy, send us a business-letter-size envelope, with postage affixed, addressed to you, and ask for those guidelines.

Proper manuscript format is also discussed in many reference works. Some of us have even written one: *On Writing Science Fiction: the Editors Strike Back!* by Scithers, Schweitzer, & John M. Ford; $19.50 in hardcovers, order from Owlswick Press, 123 Crooked Lane, King of Prussia PA 19406-2570.

Another excellent work from the same publisher is Barry B. Longyear's *Science-Fiction Writer's Workshop*: $9.50 in trade paperback. These prices include shipping and handling; in Pennsylvania, please include 6% sales tax.

We are not responsible for manuscripts in our hands or in transit. You **must** keep a copy of every manuscript you send out. You **must** put your name and address on the first page of every manuscript. Please: **no** binders, folders, or padded envelopes; and especially: **no** registered or certified mail for which we would have to stand in line at the post office!

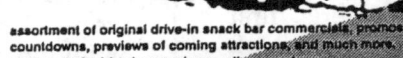
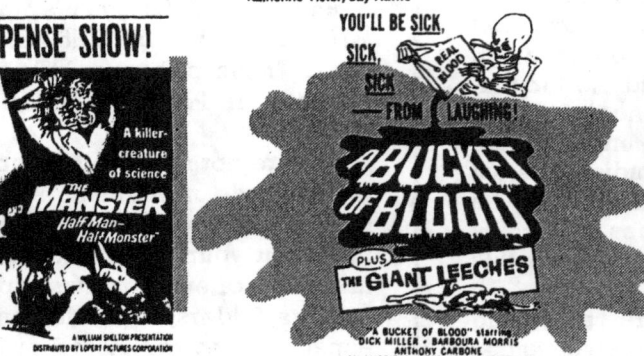

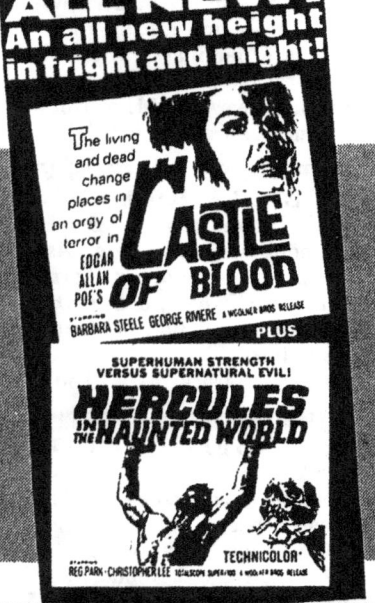
The Editors

7

"[. . .] As usual, you make it very hard to pick a best story this issue. [. . .] 'Mirror, Mirror' gets my vote for the top spot, because it's the one I keep remembering the first two weeks after reading it. Then 'Hollows,' because it does so many of the things I read fiction for. [. . .] My third vote is for 'Repairs,' because [. . .] who can resist the Electrolux as hero?"

Craig Thompson wants to encourage us to publish new work, something we hardly need encouragement in doing (but we appreciate hearing from him anyway) since just about everything we publish except the rediscovered Lord Dunsany stories (taken from British magazines of decades ago) *is* new. Perhaps he means we need to discover more new authors. Yes, we do. Our hottest "find" in recent years was Robert Deveraux, whose "Ridi Bobo" in #306 has been picked up for Ellen Datlow and Terri Windling's *The Year's Best Fantasy and Horror* anthology. The story wasn't Deveraux's first, but it was certainly an early one in what should be a long and brilliant career. (Bob's first novel, *Deadweight,* is now out from Dell Abyss.)

Christopher Dunn especially praises John M. Ford's "Troy: The Movie" as "a joy to read." **Richard J. Pearce,** along with several others, had good words for Steve Schlich's "Repairs," concluding, "In a field dominated by repulsive imagery, Steve has a heart. We should cherish such writers." **Loki,** who denies his Norse divinity but may be a relative of Henry VIII, defines a Weird Tale as "ominous and magical," a lovely phrase which we hereby steal (with credit given) to define the sort of tale we like to read.

Elaine Weaver says of Ian MacLeod's "The Dead Orchards," "I loved the dark, brooding atmosphere woven by Mr. MacLeod. It is this sort of story that makes *Weird Tales®* the legend that it is, for nowhere else can I find a story that I simply can't stop reading, even though it makes me squirm and mutter, 'Oh God'." Celebrated Arkham House poet, author of *Songs and Sonnets Atlantean,* **Donald Sidney-Fryer** had just seen his first issue of our magazine, and wrote to say, "I am quite frankly impressed! You've achieved what no other editor of WT in its various revived forms has managed to do: while still paying respect to the traditions of the magazine, as well as of the weird tale over-all, you have brought it up to date as a living entity, reflecting where we all are now in the '80s and '90s. This is *no mean feat."* We can only hope, now, that Don will like the magazine under its new title as much.

The Most Popular Story in our previous issue was, by a large margin, "The Persecution Machine" by Tanith Lee. Phil Parks's Goreyesque illustrations for that story were also singled out for special praise. Second place also went to Tanith Lee, for "Mirror, Mirror," and third to Ian MacLeod for "The Dead Orchards." Steve Schlich's "Repairs" gained many plaudits, as did Lee's "One For Sorrow." Ω

SHADOWINGS

by Douglas E. Winter

By Any Other Name

The worm turns.

Not long ago, a likeable, intelligent editor for one of the major New York publishers asked me to read the manuscript of a first novel. She hoped that I would offer some suitable words of wisdom for the book's cover — the ubiquitous "blurb." I agreed to read the novel, whose title and premise were enticing, but I withheld any promise to deliver a quotable quote. When I turned to the manuscript a few weeks later, I was mesmerized, caught up in an intense and certifiably weird *tour de force.*

I wrote to the editor and offered an enthusiastic paragraph, reporting that this was no ordinary book, but probably the most original and unnerving first novel that I had read in years. In concluding, I noted that here, at last, was what readers have been waiting for: A new horror for the Nineties.

I soon received a gracious call from the editor, thanking me for taking the time to help her with marketing that most problematic of commodities, a first novel; but then came a curious request. She wanted to use my impassioned remarks on the back cover of the book, but . . . would I agree to eliminate one word?

The word was *horror.*

Since the early 1980s, we have been besieged with this word. For better — and, more often, for worse — "horror" has come not only to define, but also to dictate, a *kind* of fiction. The writer whose best-selling novels brought new credence to the language of fear was labeled the "King of Horror." Publishers eagerly branded their products as "horror" through cover copy and publicity; some went so far as to use the word as an imprint. Magazines proclaimed their devotion to it. Entire shelves and sections in bookstores and libraries wore the name. A World Horror Convention was born. Writers gathered, like lost sheep, into a herd known as the Horror Writers of America. The word, the word: The horror, the horror.

In this sudden quest for identity, for a way of labeling whatever impulse had given readers and filmgoers the particular appetite for chaos that marked the fading 1970s, the moment was what mattered: for writers, notoriety and income; for booksellers and publishers, sales. Few considered the long-term consequences, and those who raised their voices were ignored, shouted down. We witnessed, in the name of "horror," a curious entropic journey into a limitless frontier, which soon resulted in a circling of the wagons, the claiming of a known and seemingly solid ground, around which signifying fences — names, covers, icons, styles — were erected to define, describe . . . and confine.

A fiction whose fundamental impulse was the creation of unease was being made safe for mass consumption. Soon a "horror" existed that was as recognizable as science fiction or the romance — and thus as capable of denigration. When, in the mid-1980s, Clive Barker put forward his battlecry: "There are no 'limits,'" he raged against the repressive force of *genre* as much as that of more obvious forms of censorship.

Little wonder that Stephen King, victimized by the ever-encroaching fences of his success, should write a compelling triptych — *Misery, The Dark Half,* and "Secret Window, Secret Garden" (in *Four Past Midnight*) — about bestselling writers haunted by their literary pasts. As a coda, King destroyed his trademark setting, the town of Castle Rock, in *Needful Things;* but whether he has succeeded in wiping the slate clean remains to be seen. Like Robert Bloch, for whom "Psycho" became an unshakable middle name, he will most likely reign eternal as the "King of Horror" whether he writes the long-rumored sequel to *Salem's Lot* or truly becomes his generation's Dickens.

The eternal debate about what constitutes "horror" proceeds from the misguided belief that a definition has significance to anyone but the middleman. A category is important to publishers and their distribution network, particularly the publishers whose reputations and finances depend upon placing a *kind* of product on the shelf; but consider the plight of these selfsame publishers who, after pushing a product called "horror" — with little regard for its quality, slowly but surely eroding the audience of interested readers — find that this product does not sell. Consider, too, the writing career that is staked on writing vampire novels. In a market gone batty, with endless titles sucking blood — and thus life — from the market, a disgruntled vampire writer told me recently that she was writing a "completely different kind of book." Oh, really? Yes . . . a werewolf novel.

This is a siege mentality, a refusal to look outside the nonexistent boundaries that have haunted the horror fiction of the past decade. When, in the late 1980s, the name "horror" lost its already suspect veneer, the inevitable next step was to turn inward, eating itself, in an effort to find cliques, movements, subgenres, some palpable (and, of course, marketable) means of distinguishing "us" from "them." Some writers, principally those made nervous by the word "horror" and its adolescent and visceral connotations, opted for the gentler sound of "dark fantasy." Others flirted briefly with something known as the "new horror"; and a repeated catchword was "cutting edge," which suggested rather dramatically that the blade of horror had indeed dulled.

When a handful of younger writers, encouraged by Barker's blood-spattered surge to fame, took the name "splatterpunks" in a mixture of pride and jest, they found both notoriety and derision as the latest "movement." (That most writers appearing in the *Splatterpunks* anthology resisted the editor's effort to pigeonhole and co-opt them is noteworthy, but did not prevent a forthcoming sequel, whose release in 1994 is about as far behind the curve as eight-track tape). While the original writers of "splatterpunk" worked from principle, their heirs, ever eager to distinguish themselves, worked only from a kind of delusional hope that the "shocking" would get them noticed: hence the semi-professional "sexpunks" whose obsession with genitalia is rivaled only by twelve-year-old boys. The latter crew, in particular, represents the lunatic child of inbreeding: genre begetting subgenre begetting sub-subgenre until sooner or later, its writers are not communicating to anyone but an initiated few — even though, as novels from *Rosemary's Baby* to *The Throat* confirm, the audience for horror numbers in the millions.

The long-rumored death of "horror" is thus a self-fulfilling prophecy; once given life, a category fiction of "horror" was doomed to die — consigned to the purgatory of specialty stores and specialty shelves where its fate is that of the romance or the western: to function as a certain kind of fiction for a certain kind of audience. The phone call from my editor friend was not unexpected: at last the implied has become explicit. Horror has reached, it would seem, the exalted stature of science fiction, trapped in a virtually inescapable ghetto of its own making: a place of the negligible, where entertainment has come home to die.

But horror, like its favorite creatures of the night, does not perish so easily. The doomsayers forget its persistence, its uncanny ability to mutate and survive, which ought to serve as the most powerful clue that this fiction is not easily consigned to a category — it exists, thrives, lingers, and occasionally triumphs because, unlike any other supposed kind of fiction, horror is an *emotion*.

When the name proves a hindrance, then, as my editor friend suggested, the simple solution is to change it.

The current catchphrase is "dark suspense" — horror indeed, but without the pejorative influence of its name. A literature of "dark suspense" is nothing new, given the likes of Jim Thompson, whose first novel, *Now and On Earth* (1994, Vintage/Black Lizard, $9.00), has been reissued this year with an introduction by Stephen King. But the lines have blurred; where once Thompson would have been classified as a crime writer (much as King's own *Salem's Lot* would probably have been published as a Crime Club novel if written in the 1950s), now he has stepped beyond that category — because the fundamental impulse of his fiction was horror.

Dell Books, which in recent years has strived to maintain the respectability of horror through its Abyss imprint, will soon introduce a "dark suspense" imprint known as Cutting Edge. Among the first releases is an unabashed horror novel, Tim Lucas's *Throat Sprockets* (1994, price not set) — a cunning, droll, obsessive satire that is truly a remarkable debut novel. I searched my bookshelves for apt comparisons, and soon realized that I could only invent them: Stoker's *Dracula* rewritten by J.G. Ballard, *Last Year at Marienbad* directed by Mario Bava. If his work is indicative of the quality of Dell's lineup, then we may well have an imprint as commanding as the late, lamented Black Lizard.

The penumbra of "dark suspense" seems also to embrace "terror," which once described psychological horror as made famous by Bloch and Thompson. One of their spiritual successors was V.C. Andrews, a critically maligned but immensely popular novelist whose dysfunctional family sagas were resonant with autobiography. Dead now for almost a decade, Andrews is abused shamelessly in *Ruby* (1994, Pocket, $5.95), courtesy of her estate, which commissioned Andrew Neiderman to ghost-write "in her tradition" while ignoring the unfinished manuscripts she left behind, which diverged from her publisher's expectations. There is no better paradigm for the pathos of genre: even in death, Andrews cannot escape its clutches.

In recent years, the word "terror" has been applied, with some justification, to the bestselling novels of Dean R. Koontz, which cleverly use the motifs of horror without invoking its supernatural or psychological tropes; but when it is found on the cover of Richard Christian Matheson's first novel, *Created By* (1993, Bantam, $21.95), there is either confusion or the proverbial nod and a wink: this taut walk down the Hollywood Boulevard of the 1990s is set firmly within the traditional territory of horror. In chronicling the disintegration of a cynical television producer/screenwriter whose blood-and-tits series makes "NYPD Blue" look like "The Muppet Show," Matheson terrorizes; but he cuts more deeply, opening psychological and metaphysical veins with the sharp prose style that also distinguishes his short fiction.

F. Paul Wilson's *The Select* (1994, Morrow, $22.00) is a breakout novel, the kind of book that needs no cover copy but stands ready to deliver . . . what? Ask the readers of John Grisham; for that matter, ask the readers of Stephen King. Once we step outside the confines of "horror" — or "terror," or whatever other words are used to sell this fiction — and thus step away from the audience for the black-jacketed paperbacks, we find an America that is eager to experience the range of emotion that we know as horror. *The Select* speaks to that audience; it is a transcendent thriller that, like a Timex, just keeps on ticking. Set for the most part in an enigmatic medical school whose corridors are as shadowed and sinister as any gothic castle, *The Select* has it all: a front-page plotline, breakneck pace, quirky yet canny characterizations . . . and horror. Like King or Straub or Barker before him, Paul Wilson has not left the field; he has elevated it.

As *The Select* suggests, another guise of horror is the "medical thriller," often identified with Robin Cook, a physician whose titanium-dense (and often mean-spirited) prose is nevertheless salesworthy because it plays into our profound distrust of modern science. Readers should spend their time instead with Steven Spruill, who writes the kind of novels Robin Cook would write if Robin Cook could write. In *My Soul to Take* (1994, St. Martin's, $22.99), Spruill unwinds the time-honored premise of the medical thriller — a female physician caught in a web of conspiracy — in such refreshing tones that he nearly reinvents the form. Combining timely themes — sexual harassment, espionage in the aftermath of the Cold War — with a compelling medical and moral quandary, Spruill puts the reader through a virtual kaleidoscope of fictional styles: descriptions of surgical procedures give way to visions of war-torn Kuwait, hard science fiction melts into CIA paranoia and then into unabashed horror.

A recent incarnation of horror is the "new gothic" — which, like splatterpunk, seeks by name and aesthetic stance to distinguish its peculiar wheat from *genre* chaff. Where the splatpack's selling point was an insistent dialogue about (and in too many cases, pandering to) sex and violence, the new gothic is a more clever and constructive proposition, invoking, of all things, horror's literary tradition in order to set itself apart from generic perdition. Thus Lewis Gannett's *The Living One* (1994, Plume, $10.95), which, if published at all in the 1980s, would have assuredly worn the mantle of horror in the style of Anne Rice, is transmuted into a "gothic thriller." Although the darling of academics, mainstream critics and dilettantes who prefer their fear dolloped out in fluted crystal (rather than, say, in splatterpunk's barfbags), the new gothic is a curious self-exile to a land of literary make-believe. Because its manifesto — that horror will always survive and prosper as literature — is a foregone conclusion, the implicit conceit is revealed: By whose imprimatur do these authors represent the literature of our time?

This is not to say that writers of the "new gothic" lack talent; it is abundant, for example, in the work of Patrick McGrath, and this should discourage, not encourage, a label. McGrath's latest novel, *Dr. Haggard's Disease* (1993, Poseidon, $20.00), is an impressive and discomforting ode to the disease that is passion. Resolutely retro, undeniably self-conscious, McGrath pursues the unspoken horrors that are anathema to supermarket bookracks: the intangible horrors of passivity, perplexity, and barely glimpsed profundity that — unlike the vampire — walk with us daily.

Although recently identified with the "new gothic," Joyce Carol Oates is a force unto herself, and has been for years. While Anne Rice has sustained a wider popular audience, Oates is more conscientious; she has eluded the million-seller madness by an insistent refusal to be conveniently packaged. She readily embraces the term "horror," although she favors the "grotesque" in describing her own dark fiction, and indeed this is both the subtitle of her welcome collection *Haunted* (1994, Dutton/Abrahams, $21.95) and the subject of its afterword.

The "new gothic" is a variant of the "old school" perspective of academe, whose proponents, like literary Luddites, eschew the modern (and especially the popular) and hold that horror's glory days lurk in the "weird fiction" of its past. Acolytes of weird fiction rely on the company of M.R. James and the Bensons for legitimacy, but tend to obsess about H.P. Lovecraft, often to the point of considering him *sui generis*, thus ignoring his rich knowledge of supernatural horror in literature — and the work of predecessors and contemporaries such as the remarkable Polish fantasist Stefan Grabinski (1887–1936), whose fiction has been translated at last in *The Dark Domain* (1993, Dedalus European Classics, $10.95).

For some time, the "weird fiction" clique embraced Ramsey Campbell as its contemporary savior, based upon his Lovecraftian roots and layered, at times baroque, narrative style. One wonders what these folks will make of Campbell's latest novel, *The Long Lost* (1993, Headline, England, £ 16.99), which is thoroughly modern, a suburban psychodrama that would play in Peoria, but not in R'lyeh. After a disappointing opening act in which a couple befriends a mysterious old woman, *The Long Lost* transcends its familiar plot — the social intruder motif of Fatal Attraction, The Hand that Rocks the Cradle, The Crush, The Temp, etc., etc., etc. — through gloriously obsessive set-pieces that are vintage Campbell. No other writer can so elegantly walk the tightrope of madness, and for these moments alone, *The Long Lost* is worthwhile.

A more likely rallying point for connoisseurs of the "weird" is the latest offering of short fiction by Thomas Ligotti, *Noctuary* (1994, Carroll & Graf, $18.95). From its brief introductory remarks (whose opening sentence — No one needs to be told about what is "weird" — is a fitting rebuff to those who would categorize) to its delightfully idiosyncratic stories, this book should be read by anyone who professes some ability to define "horror." Ligotti is pure magic: elusive, enchanting and endlessly entertaining.

Another promising writer of short stories is Elizabeth Massie, whose fiction has been collected in a limited edition chapbook, *Southern Discomfort: The Selected Works of Elizabeth Massie* (1993, Dark Regions, P.O. Box 6301, Concord, CA 94524, $5.95). Wry, witty and capable of the most sublime sorts of nastiness, Massie is drawn to characters who live in desperate isolation — the lost, the lonely, the lurking, those disturbing reminders of just how society prefers to view its outcasts. With photographs manipulated by H.E. Fassl, this slim volume is a rare find and worthy of immediate attention; but sadly, Massie is an admitted writer of horror fiction — not simply a good writer, but a great writer — and her commitment to the form finds her being published primarily in the hinterlands.

Perhaps she needs a gimmick; certainly that seems the case with *Sacred Prey* (1994, Truman Press, $19.95), a horror novel written by a "Scream Queen." Vivian Schilling, we are told, is the star of films we've never heard of named *Future Shock* and *Soultaker,* and peers out from her "Glamour Shots" author photo with a sly come-on that's the best thing between these particular covers. From its opening line — "The bayou moaned in the darkness like a vast creature hungry for life to feed the voices of its dead" — to its amazing cover, which proclaims that the book (despite its 1994 copyright and publication date) won the "1993 Gold Scroll Award for Outstanding Achievement in Literature" — this is indeed the malaprop of the macabre.

Let's put an end to this madness of believing in horror as a *genre*. The language of fear is the language of the *terra incognita* — the no-man's land, a place that is not yet a place. We encounter its discourse in our dreams, in religious frenzy, or when death brushes past, and we are denied the assurance of being ourselves — untouchable, unchangeable, immortal. This is not a language that may be packaged; nor is it one that may be marketed, at least for very long. When we are told what is horror, then inevitably we are told what is not horror; and soon we doubt, we disbelieve, we disagree.

What we are witnessing, then, is not the death of "horror," but the death of a *genre*. Horror will never escape us — indeed, our literary history is proof positive that fear is the only constant of storytelling. Great horror fiction is being published today; sometimes it wears other names, other faces, marking the fragmentation that precedes the meltdown of a sudden and ill-conceived thing that many publishers and writers foolishly believed could be called a genre. One hopeful result will be the departure of the bottomfeeders and lemmings, who will move along to writing the flavor of the new decade and allow the Tom Ligottis and Elizabeth Massies of this world more room to breathe and grow. Ω

Out of the aperture came two horrible shapes — two inhuman things with immense, clapping wings and glittering eyes. Hideous; enormous. *BATS!* "Stragella" by Hugh B. Cave

Allen Koszowski

THE MAN
IN THE WHITE MASK

by Darrell Schweitzer & Jason Van Hollander
illustrated by Jason Van Hollander

1594
Van Hollander

"Argue with me, boy!" Father screams. "Dispute! Let's hear the thunder of your words, the cannonfire of your dialectic! Something! God — !"

He dances on the hilltop. He writhes, his brain, his soul, his very being afire with the flames of Hell. Down below, the Spanish soldiers are preparing to burn our manor house, and this desecration, this utter desolation of beautiful things gathered over the lifetimes of countless ancestors, this erasure — Yes! Especially the loss of the laboratory, where the gross elements become precious essence; and the library, where error is confounded and truth discovered, where now the very wisdom of mankind is left to perish —

These are enough to make even the non-philosopher pause and reflect on the futility that surpasses all understanding.

"Explain! Explicate! Cite chapter and verse! Damn you, I gave you a mind! Use it!" Father shrieks. He lunges at me, nearly upsetting the wheelbarrow which is my lifeboat in this shipwreck of our lives.

You gave me little else, I want to say, but I cannot find the cruelty to do so. Father stumbles. He is on his knees before me, weeping like a penitent, his hands folded in what may genuinely be prayer.

"Please be quiet," I say softly. "They'll hear us."

"They are *much* too preoccupied," he hisses back.

Profundity! Only a master painter could capture the scene, vast and dark, with suggestions of shapes, here a hill, there, far away, a town, black clouds drifting overhead with galleon slowness, and down at the bottom a spark of light as the first firebrand is raised, handed over to the bristle-chinned commander, who harumphs to the massed soldiery.

And one more thing, an enigma, an intrusion: a tall, dark, masked person stands with us on the crest of the hill, motionless. Who is he? What business has he here? I try to ask. I point. But Father will not heed. His attention is elsewhere.

"*Tercios* mercenaries," he rants, "riff-raff, syphilitics. Spain's finest."

Torchlight flares the commander's armor. It is infernal, this glare — worse, theatrical. Every arquebus shares the same hellish gleam, every breastplate, morion. The eyes of Spain sparkle, a field of fiends disguised as men. Pikes scratch the sky.

Now the commander, in the manner of the Sovereign Lord of Hell, bawls out a tirade long and loud in his half-incomprehensible tongue. I can barely make out the words, drifting up to me like the sound of stormy surf. A military oration.

Who can doubt their valor? Who can question the mettle of Commander Bristle-Chin as he flings the fiery torch in through the window of our steep-gabled manse? Not once does he singe himself! So deftly does Bristle-Chin accomplish his task that he ceases to seem Satanic or even militaristic. His vanity has transformed him into an acrobat, a carnival monkey drunk with his own strut. He twirls delicately. His men laugh, shaking their weapons in

Darrell Schweitzer & Jason Van Hollander

a demonic clatter. Evil, they say, is exquisitely banal. Perhaps this ambassador from Hell was a tumbler or a strolling player before his soldiering days.

Throughout all this time, they never notice us, though we are in plain sight, so intent are the thousands of them on their piety, their devotions, for this, too, is an *act of faith,* like so many they have performed in our country of late.

Primus. The Beginning of My Education.

On this night, for the first time, my eyes are truly opened, and I begin to read the first page in the textbook of life.

And I weep from the absurdity of it all. Not out of grief, but because I cannot laugh, and, indeed, absurdly, my conscience requires that I should be doing *something.* As I watch our house take fire, as the fire grows into a vast and living architecture of reds and oranges, I feel a deeper emotion than I have ever experienced before, something new.

Absurdity. That we stand here, alive, while Father's great library flutters away, page by page, into the night. Certainly the Spanish soldiers looted the house before burning it, but the books were of no use to them.

I call him my father, but he is not, except in the sense that God is the Father of men. No carnal act produced such a misshapen creature as myself. I am a half-finished thing of clay and human tatters, grown in a dung-heap in the traditional manner, a *homunculus* which has spent its entire existence in a wheelbarrow, shaped like a youth from the head down to the mid-chest and completely formless thereafter, without legs or bowels or manhood; animate but immobile, my lower self forever wrapped in a blanket. The fact that Father saved *me* at the end rather than dumping me out and filling the wheelbarrow with his precious books confirms my suspicion that he created me in order to have someone to argue with and lost interest as soon as I had eyes and ears and mouth and feeble arms and hands to turn pages. Now sixty, he has no one else. His wife is gone. She never had any children, for all she used to wheel me about in this conveyance claiming me as her own, just to please him. But it was too much — even she felt the terrible, agonizing absurdity; and, lacking a sense of humor, she took one last adulterous fling, then died.

"God's prank," he calls me. He says it now. "God's prank."

"No, yours," I reply.

Below, the soldiers are singing bawdy songs. How merry we all are this night!

Aged, alone, crazed enough to argue with a lump of dirt which has no particular flair for theology, this mystical and heretical arguer, Cornelius de Bloot, has needlessly risked his life too many times. Years ago his questionable experiments and Protestant extremism caused him to be imprisoned for a day and a night. He was adjured to desist. *He was warned.* Alas, the infection of his doctrines has finally cost us our pigs and chickens and our

ancestral mansion . . . this Palace of Flame that we three refugees (Father, myself, and Odysseus the kitten, whom I cradle in my arms) now squint at.

It is a serious matter, a house-burning, the extermination of the accumulated resonances of all who have ever dwelt there. Yes, it was falling down anyway. There were no florins for repairs. The pettiest of petty nobles is my ignoble and servantless sire. Impoverished, he has lived like the most lumpish peasant, alone with the rumblings of his mind, arguing with me, his creation and mirror . . . wearing rustic garb patched beyond mending . . . with goose shit on our tables and books . . . while in every room he tested new heresies, exercised new schismatic theories, sought to bring about the alchemical marriage of the ethereal with the earthly; and the fumes of Hell, the teachings of Calvin and Luther, and the stinks from Father's furnace blackened the foundations long before the fires of Spain . . . but most of all I remember Yanna the ewe kissing me awake every morning. Dawn, viewed through Yanna's wool, was a fleecy nimbus. Never again will I smell her grass-sweet breath which made me yawn and forget, however briefly, the incompleteness of my nature.

A serious matter. These Spanish whoresons don't know how to take it seriously. They lack all rudiments of civilization.

"It is Pandemonium itself," Father sighs. "A palace of cinders."

Down below, valiant Bristle-Chin, the commander, impales a chicken on a lance — an egg-laying wonder named Peck-Peck — and hurls her into the fire. The bird squawks, *screams,* chars, her feathers going up in an explosive puff. The marauding gentlemen of Spain find this endlessly comical. Theirs is a crusade against Protestant chickens, and these sufferings are nothing compared to what torments the Devil has prepared for such heretical hens in the world to come.

I dig my nails into the sides of the wheelbarrow, stifling a scream. It is too painful, this comedy. Now Father is weeping softly, for Peck-Peck I think. By the light of Peck-Peck's demise, his teardrops are diamonds.

Not to be outdone, the other soldiers begin to toss kittens into the fire, siblings of Odysseus, whose religious opinions, likewise, are not what the Pope would want.

The commander makes another speech, completely unintelligible this time, no doubt apologizing for the meagre loot: a few murdered chickens, a wheel of cheese, and Yanna, whom they will doubtless rape.

The rooftree of the house snaps thunderously, and the whole structure collapses inward, releasing constellations of swirling sparks.

Secundus. A New Chapter in the Book of My Malformed Life.

Now Odysseus, Father, and I are wanderers indeed. I have a moment of prophetic vision. I foresee him dying somewhere on a road, or in a frozen marsh, blackened, stiff, while the kitten perishes in my hands and I remain as I am, forever, neither dead nor alive, washed by seasons of rain back into my original shapelessness.

Father takes up the handles of the wheelbarrow and turns away from the holocaust. Yes, in his eyes I see bleakness and wintery wastes.

"It's all your fault," I say, loud enough for him to hear.

"My conscience is my own," he rasps back; and his face seems a pale mask, still and white as Death.

But not quite. I compare him to the *other*. I realize that the enigmatic intruder is still with us: a tall, slender figure clad in gray rags, whose serenely beautiful face is like a mask carved out of finest marble. This one nods to me from behind Father, then turns back to watch the burning.

No, Father's face is merely weary. The *other* is white as Death. I name that other *Absurdity*. That he should be mere Death, the vulgar reaper out of some ridiculous peasant mystery play, is too much. No, he is the desolator of reason, the destroyer of all order, the sublime god of nonsense, Absurdity, the only fit companion on our journey which has just begun.

But Father does not see him. Poor Father. I must make him happy if I can. I was created to argue. That is my task.

"Father, does God demand that the soldiers of Philip make their war on chickens and cats? Is it truly the God of Love who demands that so many thousands of our Dutch countrymen be 'relaxed' to the Inquisition?"

"God is good, but Satan is everywhere!" Father exclaims. For once I am inclined to agree with him. There is no argument. With surprising agility, he carts me away from the scene, till the light of the inferno behind us fades like the setting sun. I scratch Odysseus' ears so he doesn't leap out. Purrs from the kitten; a wet nose presses my palm. All at once it occurs to me that Odysseus doesn't mourn his murdered brethren at all —

"This stupid animal is completely devoid of fellow-feeling!" I declare, amazed.

Replies the August Arguer: "Only mankind possesses compassion. By God's grace we have received this treasure."

"And I, Father — ?"

"All God-fearing men are adjured to love one another, to practice compassion, to grow in Christian virtue even as —"

"Even as do the Spanish invaders consider themselves men of righteous and Godly deeds. Truly Father, we are all of us actors in some formless play of our own making. God never enters into it."

"*Blasphemy!*" cries my heretical sire as he pushes faster. Within minutes he is deep into a scathing and learned rebuttal. He doesn't need his books. He can quote, transpose, rend, distort from the library of his own mind. So heated is this diatribe that I imagine the wax melting from my ears . . . and after a while I pass into a kind of daze, dreaming of fire while the wheelbarrow rolls and jolts over the frozen countryside. I grieve for the kittens, for Peck-Peck. Actors, all of them, in some rambling script God left half finished, even as Father left me . . . Overhead, the stars suggest freedom. The heavens are boundless, infinite. "God's mercy is infinite," I hear myself pray.

"But only for the worthy," Father pants, pushing me onward to the lightless horizon. The man in the white mask, Old Marble Face I jokingly label him, walks alongside me silently. Father cannot see him, or does not react if he does.

It is very strange.

Odysseus the kitten has slept peacefully all this while.

Tertius. Containing Life's Allegory.

Half an hour later Father is gasping for breath and we must halt at the edge of a town. A commotion nearby alerts us. Revellers, staggering drunkards. How very odd. "A *kermesse*?" I ask.

"Peasant louts. How can they go on with their merrymaking at such an hour?"

"Or in such times?"

"Political developments, I assure you, my son, never enter into the minds of these —"

A roisterous fellow with shit-stained breeches and a large, dead fish in his codpiece bumps into the wheelbarrow, rocking it. I grab hold of the kitten.

"I have been elected —" He hiccups. "— I have been elected the King of Beer. Truly, I am the heartiest guzzler of all . . . the very incarnation of Gambrinus . . ."

"Move, you clot of beer-foam! Make way for my son and myself !"

Bellows the outraged Monarch of Beer: "Why don't you throw yourself into a canal, you pillar-biting, bible-licking old turnip!"

Cursing righteously, thunderously, like Moses come down from the mountain to find the golden calf, Father turns the wheelbarrow and plunges into the sea of revellers. Their mood is, I apprehend, more desperate than truly joyous, as if only by celebration can they keep horror away. Perhaps so. Bodies collide with us from all sides. I flop backward, grab hold of the edge of the wheelbarrow, and pull myself upright once more. Odysseus, poor puss, yowls as buxom women leer and flounce their enormous breasts at us. I am amazed at the ampleness of their flesh. I only wonder how I would react if Father had made me a trifle more complete. But I can only be ashamed of my state, and play the rôle expected of me: a deformed beggar.

And again and again I glimpse my secret companion, the man in the white mask, flitting among the crowd, touching a whore on the shoulder, helping a sodden old man raise a stein nearly as large as he is to his lips, bumping a child backward into a rainbarrel with a flourish of an elbow. Our eyes meet, an understanding far deeper than words passes between the two of us. Suddenly we are fast friends, colleagues, fellow outcasts and outsiders.

What fools are these humans, these mortals.
Yes, holy fools, divine clowns.

I want to speak, to introduce my new-found friend to Father, but the masked one shakes his head, and is gone.

Then a fancy seizes me: we are strolling players on a tour — a cripple-thing, a crazy old man, a cat, and this *other*, who is the most brilliant of us all, the one who plays the heroic parts, handsome to the point of almost feminine beauty, lithesome, strong. Here we are — set out to traverse life's gaudy stage. We whisk through a maze of celebrants and tents and trestle-tables, none too clean. Once an aged knight is with us, clad in archaic, tarnished armor like something out of an exquisite masque. He is the last hero of the Round Table, I decide, sent to find the Holy Grail here in the kingdom of the wicked, unable to die until he finds it, infinitely weary, sure to inhabit the Earth until the end of time with only myself and the Wandering Jew for company. A fancy. My fate. Drunken faces drift out of the darkness and swirling smoke. ("Cripplebones! Beggarlegs!" If only they knew.)

We enter a forest, the babble behind us fading like the last lines of a bad play. Soon we are alone among black trees, alone with the newly risen, waning moon, with the gleaming, ice-covered branches, with the wind and the stars. From time to time I see my friend, the man in the marble-white mask, gliding between the tree trunks in utter silence. It is a comfort to have him there.

It is no more than a change of scenery, a rearrangement of the set as the play goes on, as we journey across the crowded stage — a senseless, passionate performance.

As if on cue, we reach a clearing where some genuine strolling players have pulled their wagon over by the side of the road. They laugh and wave as we pass. Such droll costumes! One woman is dressed like the crescent moon. This lunar maid throws a sugar cookie at me ("All for love!") and I catch it in my mouth like a clever dog, too polite to explain that since I have no stomach or bowels I really can't eat, and when I pretend too often the food putrefies within me and Father must pour water down my throat, shake me, and empty me out like a jug.

But, cookie in mouth, I grow wistful. Will I ever know love before I die? Will I ever truly live?

"What is life without love?" I mutter as the actors bow and curtsy.

Then one of them, a gangly angel with a gashed forehead, asks if we've seen "a man in a white mask" — a deserter from their troupe.

The cookie sticks in my throat. I cannot speak.

"No," Father replies. "What concern is it of mine if one of your fellow sinners wanders away? You will all wind up in the same place eventually. Meet him there."

The angel-actor shrugs. "Well, if you see him, run the other way, fast. He is mad. He thinks he is Grim Death himself." The actor touches his bloodied forehead. "He wields a hammer instead of a scythe, but with some skill nevertheless."

"You mock God by impersonating one of his angels," returns the Great Controversialist. "You deserve no less."

With an exaggerated bow this spindly-limbed angel bids us farewell. I am too distracted to reply. I think of my friend in the woods, pacing us on our journey for what reason I do not know. He cannot be a mere renegade actor, I am sure. That is not even absurd, merely ridiculous. The blow has addled the angel's wits, obviously.

My fantasies are too compelling for me to consider the matter further. I dream of the breasts of the moon-maid, and as I think on these shapely parts I hear a pitiful mewing and find that I'm squeezing and kneading poor Odysseus.

We pass briefly into the darkness again, through the forest, as I whisper tenderly to the frightened kitten; then we pass a haywain where, atop the haystack, two adolescents engage in fornication despite the cold. Moonlight silvers the boy's bobbing backside.

"The Devil will send them a letter of thanks," my cheerless Father says. I stifle a laugh. Then I regard myself with amazement. The excitement of the night, the stimulus, all this motion have changed me. I am becoming more human. How much I yearn for such Satanic commendations, Father can never know.

Onward. I look to left and to right for my friend in the white mask. I want to share my discovery with him. But there are only the black trees, passing one by one in the darkness.

Scant minutes later we overtake an old Jew clad in a skullcap and patchwork cloak. He falls in beside us. He warns us that Leyden Town swarms with pro-Spanish *Glippers*. Flanders is in decline, he says. The seaports are silting up, and Royalist atrocities occur daily. He identifies himself as an Antwerper, a follower of Erasmus. ("That bloated bladder of Humanistic pap!" opines my father, but the Jew only smiles.) Before he leaves us, this worthy son of Abraham warns us that the Spanish seek two fugitives, a *de vehementi* dogmatizer and his crippled son.

A little while later, in a field where corpses still smolder at a dozen stakes, Father and I pause to consider this description of ourselves. I wonder if fire would merely harden me like a piece of pottery, since I am made of clay, not flesh. But then Scripture clearly states that Adam and the sons of Adam were likewise made from clay.

Yet this woman-born clay does not harden. Even as we linger there, one of the corpses emits a noise. I raise a hand to my mouth to stifle a cry. But the corpse merely shifts in its scorched bonds, throwing sparks, like a log settling in a fireplace.

Heretics all.

Startled by our intrusion, sleeping crows awake and caw at us. They are waiting for morning, when their breakfast will be cooled enough to eat.

"We must find shelter," Father says. "We cannot go on. We must rest." But I don't want to rest. For all the loss of the house has pained me, for all the deaths of the chickens and cats have filled me with horror, the night has been an exciting one, filled with so many new sights and sounds and experiences. I am like a baby newborn, eager to be alive for the first time.

Absurdity. Beautiful absurdity.

He wheels me away. I glance back and see the man in the white mask standing among the charred corpses. Our eyes meet.

Soon, he says. *I shall join you very soon.*

Quartus. In Which Base Imposture Is Transmuted Into Golden Truth.

When we reach a certain furrowed field used as a mass grave by the Spaniards, Father announces that we are safe. No one comes there at night for fear of the countless, outraged ghosts of the slain. We will be safe there, for we, too, are outraged.

It is a great, frozen stewpot of a place, filled with bodies imperfectly buried. Limbs and heads jut from the earth. Armor and helmets glint in the moonlight. Old rusty pikes stand like a flourish of malnourished trees.

"How many Netherlanders lie here?" I ask, trying to be casual.

"God knows." Father taps the soil with his foot. "This is a crowded place. Soldiers of Orange, Walloons, victims of the Inquisition, some Spaniards, German mercenaries. Plague corpses. Thousands upon thousands."

"The triumph of Death," I hear myself remark, not really understanding what that means. Since I am not truly alive, how can I understand death? A vexing problem. Father and I will thrash it out sometime. But now —

Odysseus leaps from my lap, runs over to a leathery hand protruding from the soil, sniffs, and meows mournfully.

"We must pray for these poor souls," Father says.

And I wonder, too, whether or not a homunculus like myself even has a soul. I suspect not. I have more in common with Odysseus the kitten than with Cornelius de Bloot.

But he created me as an arguer:

"What good will your prayers do for the Dead? I say, let the living pray for the living!"

(Well argued, clay-thing. Where does that leave you, homuncular lump? I have no idea.)

"Such disrespect!"

I reach out my hand. Odysseus returns to my lap. "You and your valueless prayers. Think how much happier mankind would be if nobody prayed, ever. There would be fewer fires lit in this world." I am momentarily sentimental, stroking the cat. My eyes well up with teardrops; I see a blurry vision of Father opening and closing his mouth.

"You are no longer my son," says this watery replica after a few seconds.

"Was I ever?"

Father roars. I hurl the cat at his chest. Not to be outdone, he snaps off an arm from the frozen corpse of a *Schwartzreiter* pistoleer and whacks me across the shoulder with it. Odysseus scrambles for safety among a heap of skulls. Soon Father and I are pelting one another with clods of earth — I nearly spill myself reaching for more ammunition — and throughout the battle there is laughter from an intermediate distance.

A stranger, dressed in a cassock of indescribable blackness.

"Ho there," says he as Father flings a heavy boot at my ear.

"Whoever you are, the affairs of a father and his son are no concern of yours," the great theologian Cornelius de Bloot shouts in his most exasperated manner.

Heavy silence. Then the black-cassocked man in the crudely carven, wooden skull mask steps forward. He is but a ludicrous caricature of that fascinating *other.* "But this is my domain." The stranger's voice through the mask is soft, silken, infinitely reasonable. "I am the *Stadholder* of this melancholy place."

Stammers Father: "Some *Stadholder* . . . Who are you and why do you wear that ridiculous mask?"

"Lo, I am the Pontiff of Despair; and my throne is the throne of woe. I lead you now into the infernal city. Abandon all hope —"

Father snorts derisively.

"But your droll behaviors have cheered me somewhat," the stranger goes on. "Yonder is the *sanctum sanctorum* of my realm." He points to a heap of charred bones. "I yearn for such entertainers as yourselves; for my palace is hollow with echoes and lacks mirth."

"We are not strolling players!"

I point to the wooden mask and proclaim like a child who is being very clever, "I know you!"

"All men know of me in the end," comes the sepulchral reply, "but few seek me before their appointed time. Tell me, what brings you both into this darkness?"

Father clears his throat, as if about to make a speech. "I am Cornelius de Bloot, truth's dearest martyr, unafraid to lay bare my mind whatever the consequence! This runty baggage is my son, Adam."

"Very droll indeed!" (Can he possibly know? Is he going to count my ribs?) "A bag of nettles, your son. It seems he does not share your theological views."

This pretend-Death waves a white-gloved hand and begins to walk away. Father hefts the wheelbarrow and follows.

I call out, "Even so, we are both fugitives, heretical opinions being our alleged crime."

"You are betrayers, betrayed," the man in the wooden mask laughs. "But this sits well with me. It really does; for I am out of sorts with the tenor of the times and all religious disputes confound me. So tell me, Adam de Bloot, are you a Calvinist or a Catholic?"

Here is a sublime absurdity indeed. I am my

Father's mirror. I am an answerer, the lesser end of an endless dialogue in flesh and clay. I never thought of myself as actually holding a position —

"My beliefs are a personal matter."

Again, Father snorts. He huffs for breath. Surely the adventures of the night have fatigued him to his utmost limit.

"Yet you walk the same heretical path as your father," the masked impostor goes on, ignoring him.

I glance down at the blanket in my lap. Odysseus should be curled there asleep, but he is not. I don't know what has become of him. "I walk nowhere — It is only this affliction which binds me to my father and his opinions."

"Yes, but are you a Lutheran or Loyalist, Calvinist or Catholic?"

Ah, the banality of evil! For an instant I shudder, afraid this man is no more than an informer, an agent of the secret police. But I reject the notion as insufficiently fantastic.

"My son doesn't know which end he shits out of," Father gasps. (Exquisite! Droll, yes!)

Again the question floats from behind the crude wooden mask: *What are you, Adam de Bloot?*

"I don't know what I am," I hear myself answer.

"Truth is a sly response," the cassocked one laughs into my face, leaning so low that I can feel his hot breath through the mouth-hole of the mask. He stands up and continues his discourse. "Calvinists and Catholics. Both sects are committed to purely spiritual values. What a marvel that they fight like wild beasts in this purely material world. Ah well. Folly reigns over all."

He laughs at my father now, who seems exhausted of words and only turns his face away.

"Follow me to my castle. There, Cornelius de Bloot, we shall engage in learned conversation. What theories we may spin. We shall immerse our intellects in a sea of debates, and know the true and inner natures of God and Satan and Mankind. Let us sup on controversy. Let us gorge ourselves on dialectic —"

"And puke up —" But Father cannot think of any clever ending, and leaves the phrase dangling.

The other ignores this sudden and inexplicable failure of vocabulary in the Great Arguer. "What say you, Cornelius de Bloot?"

"Do you mock me?" is all Father can reply. Truly age and weariness have taken their toll.

"I offer you freedom from *this!*" The black-robed figure gestures dramatically to the mounds of corpses. I follow the sweep of his hand. Filling my gaze are the armies of the night, very still. "I offer you more than mere hospitality. An intellectual, spiritual haven awaits you."

"Ah," says Father. "We shall see what we shall see."

Absurdity! Priceless!

Quintus. Which Concludes Endearingly.

"We have come, at last," says the man in the white wooden mask (How primitive the workmanship of that mask — it looks like an enormous nutshell vaguely carven into a travesty of a human face, then painted white. It would frighten only an imbecile.), "to the heart of my empire, the very Castle of Unease, where we shall be nevertheless at our ease to dispute and wrangle and pull the truth out of falsehood like torturers with our tongs — or should I say tongues?"

He seems to pause as if awaiting applause for this feeble play on words, but neither Father nor I heed him. We are too amazed at what we see.

It is a Castle of Unease indeed. It must have taken the madman months to construct. How, then, could he have deserted his fellow players only this night? Perhaps he sneaked away on regular intervals to work on this imperial project. Or else thousands upon thousands of lunatics have labored here and died, adding their bones to the already impressive collection, contributing themselves to the very masonry —

The structure is a supernatural manifestation, surely, not the work of this self-deluded trespasser, but of a far, far greater architect.

Upended coffins form the walls. Human bones fill in the gaps, jut from the tops to form the battlements. A gate of cunningly joined bones swings in the night breeze. In silence, we three enter. (Where is Odysseus the kitten? I never do find out. No matter. He does not belong. Cats are never absurd.) Within, the facade of the Palace of Woe is even more incredible. Thousands of skulls, neatly arranged, grin down at us, forming windows, arches, walls. Twisted metal writhes among them, like wrought-iron ivy. The faint wind sings as it passes through. Moonlight gleams on bare bone, on frost, on ice.

In the center of a single, round chamber, the masked one takes his seat on a throne of human remains, whole bodies obviously thawed and shaped and refrozen into truly demented positions. Behind, hundreds of arms uprise like fronds. Before, skeletons lie on the floor in supplication. On either side, frozen pikemen in finest armor stand a guard of honor.

Father maneuvers the single wheel of my conveyance through human debris, crunching ribs, femurs, vertebrae.

"Father," I whisper, "I beg you. No more arguments, no more contradictions. Take us both away from here."

"I can only go forward," he says, "never back."

"Never back!" thunders our host, who has overheard our conversation.

"Besides," Father says meekly, "he has offered us shelter."

This is not absurdity now. It is not delicious, exhilarating. There is no trace of the imaginative in it. It is merely dreary humiliation, the pain of old age. The events of the night have broken my father's spirit. I resolve to arouse him, to make him whole once more, before it is too late and our mad guest loses patience with the uninspired dialectic.

Forward. Above and around me, the universe

spirals on its crazed path to some unknown end. But before me, a new horror. The wooden-masked one works some kind of lever, and a section of the floor slides away, revealing an open coffin, and there, peacefully composed, *is the corpse of the moon-maiden actress,* still in her amusing costume, her huge and fascinating breasts bare, frozen solid like curves of ivory. Only her forehead is marred by a congealed wound.

"I am king of this land," announces our host. "It is only fitting that I have a queen. Is it not so? Now dispute with me, Cornelius de Bloot!"

"I —"

"Come now! Deliberate! Explicate! Do something! Give me some words! What of freedom of conscience? Should laity read the scriptures? What of the two wills, divine and human, or is it just one? Is the Pope the successor to Peter or is he the Great Beast? Tell me!"

He leans forward on his hideous throne. For an instant it seems that there is nothing behind his mask at all except perhaps a faint candleflame. Then I am truly afraid, that this impersonator is not the real impostor at all, not the mad, renegade actor, but a *thing of spirit —*

I reach for his mask, but it is too far, of course. Father swats my hands down. To the Lord of Woe he says, "Sir, I think you insult me. Have a care."

"Better . . . Yes, better . . . but still it lacks fire. *Seigneur* de Bloot, a man of your erudition should not be ashamed to air his views *fully* and at *great length . . .*"

"As indeed I am not," says Father, suddenly standing rigidly upright, like a soldier at attention. Then he slumps again. "But I am very tired."

Oh, it is a pity, an agony, to see my father reduced thus! First and above all else he is an arguer, a debater, a thunderer of logic and invective. For him to fail, now, for him to *fail to appreciate the absurdity of our situation,* for him to express nothing at all in the face of this ludicrous fraud is more than the heart — even the clay heart — can bear. It is, yes, like death.

Our host, too, is disappointed. He descends from his throne. Something, a rat perhaps, scurries among the bones. Father falls to his knees in utter exhaustion, his hands folded, but he cannot pray. He is beyond even that. He gazes blankly at the frozen corpse of the actress.

The masked one walks among the rubbish by the edge of the open grave. He removes a blood-stained mallet from beneath his cassock, raises it to strike.

"Father!" I cry. "Father! *I have ceased to believe in God!*"

And he is himself again! He rises. He thunders. *"What?"* I repeat my fantastic charge; and, roaring like some enraged bull, he lunges at me. The mallet-stroke goes wild. Father and I tumble, wheelbarrow and all, into the grave, onto the frozen breasts of the moon-maiden.

Then Father is shouting, and the would-be Grim Reaper is hauling him up out of the grave by the ankles. I can barely move, so puny are my arms, so useless the distorted mass of my body. I lie on my back, atop my beloved moon-maiden, and flail my limbs uselessly in the air. But up above me, the battle is magnificent, as Father's opinions and deliberations and quotations of Holy Writ are like a cannonade, like a raging tempest, and his opponent can only stutter and squeal and bark like a dog while the two of them grapple, mind-to-mind, hand-to-hand. There's a wondrous glimpse of Father with his hands around the impostor's neck, the wooden mask askew, the face beneath an explosion of protruding eyes and tongue and inferior scholarship.

Ah Father!

It is only much later that, slowly, painfully, I wriggle out of the grave like some crippled worm, my hands bloody, my arms and shoulders all but screaming from the exertion.

I pause, wheezing, my breath coming in opaque puffs. Otherwise the room is silent. The darkness of the night has faded into the gray of first light.

There I espy the forms of the crazed impostor, dead, his neck broken, and Father, likewise dead and glassy-eyed, heaved backward by the dying man's last desperate effort, dangling three feet above the floor, impaled on a pike held by one of the frozen corpse-guards.

The impostor's face is quite ordinary, craggy and unshaven.

Then something moves. I turn with effort and behold the man in the white mask, the true one, my companion of the road. He glides over the corpse-and-bone rubble like a cloud. He bows before me. His mask is more beautiful, more delicately featured than I have ever seen it before. It glows from within, as if the pale sun is rising inside his head.

"You are *Absurdity!*" I croon. "You are the spirit of all things incongruous. You are the ruler of our age!" There, I have said it. It is my first, my only original opinion. I am no mere foil for Father's arguments now.

The other is startled. He shakes his head, sadly. I swear it. Sadly.

"I am Death," he says. "Did you not know me? I am the messenger of endings."

"No, you are absurd. Life is likewise absurd. You cannot be Death; Death makes perfect sense!"

"Does it?" He touches Father's face, closing his frozen eyes. "Does absurdity then make perfect sense?"

I lack any reply. Were this a debate, he would be the victor.

"I am your admirer! Your disciple!" Even as I say it, I don't know what that means. The words merely come.

"Yes," he says. "You are."

Miracle of miracles: Death himself gives me life, for he has stolen so many and can surely spare one for a little while. He shapes me with his cold hands, forming the lower part of my body in every detail, fashioning legs and feet, helping me upright, explaining to me as he works that I have been able to see him all this while because I was neither truly alive nor dead, whereas human beings may only glimpse him at the appointed hour, when their doom is upon them. I, lump of clay, vegetable product of a dung-heap, *homunculus*, have therefore been a visionary, a kind of prophet. My eyes have been open all along, while those of men remained closed. I have seen far more deeply into the nature of things than any other.

But now I have become a man, and this vision fades. I can barely discern him at all, only a suggestion of shadow, a movement like a wisp of smoke, and the glowing white mask floating in the air, illuminating the gloomy interior of the bone-palace.

His whisper is like the wind. "Now, go forth, my creation, my ally, and live truly as men live. You are strong. You are lustful. You shall seize riches and lands, and be reckoned great among your kind. You shall send many into my kingdom, as tribute. Go now, and the world shall tremble at your tread. Go."

I pull the impostor's cassock off his body to cover my nakedness, and go.

Much later, at the edge of the death-fields, I look back. Mist rises out of the frozen earth at the touch of the sun. I see them for a moment, heading in solemn, silent procession back into the fading night, into the dark lands: Death in his glowing white mask, bearing an hourglass and a scythe; and the impostor, crestfallen and penitent in his underwear with his crude mask dangling from his neck; the actress with her moon-shaped costume and naked breasts; and Father, animate, waving his arms, leaping up and down, *arguing* furiously, shouting theology, dialectic, all manner of heresy no doubt — *arguing* with Death himself.

He is magnificent, my Father, and definitely absurd. At this moment I love him very much.   Ω

OUR HERO BATTLES THE MONSTER SLIME

Although it *was* a dark and stormy night
Our Hero felt no numbing touch of fear,
For he'd been trained since birth that he was Right,
That Right makes Might, especially in a fight,
And so his conscience and his mind were clear.

    He said, "My strength is as the strength of ten
    Because my heart is pure!" He never thought
    Heredity might be a factor then,
    Nor training, when, with scores of lesser men,
    He learned the lessons well that he'd been taught.

He faced the Monster Slime with cheerful heart,
He knew he wouldn't lose for he was Strong,
His Lance and Sword would cut the Slime apart,
He'd take a cart and trundle home its heart,
And celebrate his Triumph. He was wrong.

    The Monster snapped in twain the Lance and Sword,
    And shucked him from his armor like a clam,
    Consumed the armor daintily, ignored
    The Magic Sword and, looking rather bored,
    Relaxed into a pile of moldy jam.

The Monster sighed, "I wish these Heroes knew
That Monster Slimes have hearts that are pure, too!"

— John S. Davis

AT DIAMOND LAKE
by William F. Nolan
illustrated by Allen Koszowski

"I don't understand why you won't go," his wife said. "I just don't understand it."

"We'll go to Disney World," Steve told her. "They say it's a real kick."

"To Hell with Disney World!" she said sharply. "I want to go up to the lake."

"No, Ellen."

"Why no?"

"It's too damn cold up there in the fall."

"And this summer, when I wanted us to go up for the Fourth of July, you said it would be too damn hot."

He shrugged. "I'm going to sell it. I've got it listed with a realtor."

"Your father dies and leaves you a beautiful redwood house on Diamond Lake and you won't even let me *see* it!"

"What's to see? A lake. Some woods. An ugly little cabin."

"It looks charming in the scrapbook photos. As a boy you seemed so *happy* there."

"I wasn't. Not really." His eyes darkened. "And I'm not going back."

"Okay, Steve," she said. "You can spend *your* vacation at Disney World. I'm going to spend *mine* at Diamond Lake."

Ellen worked as an artist in a design studio; Steve was vice president of a local grocery chain. For the past five years, since their marriage, they had arranged to share their two-week vacations together.

"You're being damned unreasonable," he said.

"Not at all," she told him. "What I want to do seems perfectly reasonable to me. We have a cabin on Diamond Lake and I intend to spend my vacation there. With or without you."

"All right, you win," he said. "As long as you're so set on it, I'll go with you."

"Good," she said. "I'll start packing. We can drive up in the morning."

It took them most of the day to get there. Once they left the Interstate the climb into the mountains was rapid and smooth; the highway had been widened considerably since Steve was a boy. When his father had bought property on the lake and built a cabin there, the two-lane road had been winding and treacherous; it those early days the long grade to Crestline, five thousand feet up, had seemed endless. Now, their new Chrysler Imperial swept them effortlessly to the summit.

"We need something special to celebrate with," Ellen said as they headed into the heavily wooded area. "I want to get some champagne. Isn't there a shopping center near the lake?"

"The village," Steve said, his hands nervously gripping the wheel. He'd been fine on the trip up, but now that they were here . . . "There's a general store at the village."

"Are you okay?" she asked him. "You look sick. Maybe I'd better drive."

"I'm all right," he said.

But he wasn't.

Coming back was wrong. All wrong.

A darkness waited at Diamond Lake.

The village hadn't changed much. A boxy multiplex cinema had been added, along with a sports clothing store and a new gift shop. All in the same quaint European motif, built to resemble a rustic village in the Swiss Alps.

Ellen bought a bottle of Mumm's at Wade's General Store. Old man Wade was long dead, but his son — who'd been a tow-headed youngster the last time Steve had seen him — was running the place. Looked a lot like his father; even had the same type of little wire glasses perched on his nose, just the way old Ben Wade used to wear them.

"Been a long time," he said to Steve.

"Yeah . . . long time."

Afterward, as Steve drove them to the cabin, Ellen told him he'd been rude to young Wade.

"What was I supposed to do, kiss his hand?"

"You could have smiled at him. He was trying to be nice."

"I didn't feel like smiling."

"Can't you just relax and enjoy being up here?" she asked him. "God, it's *beautiful!*"

Thick pine woods surrounded them, broken by grassy meadows bearing outcroppings of raw granite, like dark scars in a sea of dazzling fall colors.

"Do you know what kind of flowers they have up here?"

"Dad knew all that stuff," he said. "There's lupine, iris, bugle flowers, columbine . . . He liked to hike through the woods with his camera. Took color pictures of the wild life. Especially birds. He loved scarlet-topped woodpeckers."

"Did you walk with him?"

"Sometimes. Mostly, Mom went, just the two of them, while I'd swim at the lake. Dad was really at his best in the woods, but we only came up here twice after Mom died. When I turned fourteen we stopped coming altogether. I tried to get him to sell the place, but he wouldn't."

"I'm glad. Otherwise, I'd never have seen it."

"I'll be relieved when it's sold," he said darkly.

"Why?" she turned to him in the seat. "What makes you hate it so much?"

He didn't answer. They were passing Larson's old millwheel and Steve had his first view of Diamond Lake in fifteen years — a glitter of sun-bronzed steel flickering through the trees. A chill iced his skin. He blinked rapidly, feeling his heart accelerate.

He should never have returned.

The cabin was exactly as he remembered it — long and low-roofed, its redwood siding in dark contrast to the white, crushed-gravel driveway his father had so carefully laid out from the dirt road.

"It looks practically *new!*" enthused Ellen. "I thought it would be all weathered and worn."

"Dad made sure it was kept up. He had people come out and do whatever was needed."

He unlocked the front door and they stepped inside.

"It's lovely," said Ellen.

Steve grunted. "Damp in here. There's an oil stove in the bedroom. Helps at night. Once the sun's down, it gets real cold this time of year."

The cabin's interior was lined in dark oak, with sturdy matching oak furniture and a fieldstone hearth. A large plate-glass window faced the lake. On the far shore, rows of tall pines marched up the mountainside. A spectacular panorama.

"I feel like I'm inside a picture book," said Ellen. She turned to him, taking both of his hands in hers. "Can't we try and be happy here, Steve — for just these two weeks? *Can't* we?"

"Sure," he said, "we can try."

By nightfall, he'd conjured a steady blaze from the fireplace while Ellen prepared dinner: mixed leaf salad, angel hair pasta with stir-fried fresh vegetables and garlic, and apple tart with vanilla ice cream for dessert.

She ended the meal with a champagne toast, her fire-reflecting glass raised in salute. "Here's to life at Diamond Lake."

Steve joined her; they clinked glasses. He drank in silence, his back to the dark water.

"I'll bet you had a lot of friends here as a boy," she said.

He shook his head. "No . . . I was mostly a loner."

"Didn't you have a girlfriend?"

His face tightened. "I was only thirteen."

"So? Thirteen-year-old boys get crushes on girls. Happens all the time. Wasn't there anyone special?"

"I *told* you I wasn't happy here. Do we have to go on and on about this?"

She stood up and began clearing the dishes. "All right. We won't talk about it."

"Look," he said tightly. "I didn't want to, but I *did* come up here with you. Isn't that enough?"

"No, it isn't enough." She hesitated, turning to face him. "You've been acting like a miserable grouch."

He walked over, kissed her cheek, and ran his right hand lightly along her neck and shoulder. "Sorry, El," he said. "I'm letting this place get to me and I promised myself I wouldn't. It's just all this talk about the past."

She looked at him intently. "Something bad happened to you up here, didn't it?"

"I don't know," he said slowly. "I don't really know *what* happened . . ."

He turned to stare out of the window at the flat, oily-dark expanse of lake. A night bird cried out across the black water.

A cry of pain.

The next morning was windy and overcast but Ellen insisted on a lake excursion ("I have to see what the place is like.") and Steve agreed. There was an outboard on his father's rowboat and the sound of the boat's engine kicked echoes back from the empty cabins along the shore.

They were alone on the wide lake.

"Where *is* everybody?" Ellen wanted to know.

"With the summer people gone, it's pretty quiet. Too cold for boating or swimming up here in October."

As if to confirm his words, the wind increased, carrying a sharp chill down from the mountains.

"We'd better head back," said Ellen. "This sweater's too thin. I should have taken a jacket. At least *you* were smart enough to wear one."

Steve had turned away from her in the boat, his eyes fixed on the rocky shoreline. He pointed. "There's someone out there," he said, his tone intense, strained. "On that dark pile of boulders."

"I don't see anyone."

"Just *sitting* there," Steve said, "watching us. Not moving."

His words suddenly seemed ominous, disturbing her. "I don't see anyone," she repeated.

"Christ!" He leaned toward her. "Are you blind? *There* . . . on the rocks." He was staring at the distant shore.

"I see the rocks, but . . . Maybe the wind blew something over them that looked like —"

"Gone," he said, not listening to her. "Nothing there now."

He pushed the throttle forward on the outboard and the boat sliced through the lake surface, heading for shore.

A hawk flew low over the wind-scalloped water, seeking prey.

The sun was buried in a coffin of dark gray sky.

It would be a cold night.

At one A.M., under a full moon, with Ellen sleeping soundly back at the cabin, Steve had crossed the lake to the boulders. He felt the cold knifing his skin through the fleece-lined hunting jacket; the wind had a seeking life of its own.

He was able to ignore the surface cold; it was the *inner* cold that gripped him, viselike. A coldness of the soul.

Because he knew.

The motionless figure he'd seen sitting here on these humped granite rocks was directly linked with his dread of Diamond Lake.

And, just as he had expected, the figure reappeared — standing at the dark fringe of pine woods. A woman. Somewhere in her twenties, tall, long-haired, with pale, predatory features and eyes as darkly luminous as the lake water itself. She wore a long gown that shimmered silver as she moved toward him.

They met at the water's edge.

"I knew you'd be back someday," she said, smiling at him. Her tone was measured, the smile calculating, without warmth.

He stared at her. "Who are you?"

"Part of your past." She opened the slim moonfleshed fingers of her right hand to reveal a miniature pearl at the end of a looped bronze chain. "I was wearing this around my neck the last time you saw me. You gave it to me for my twelfth birthday. We were both very young."

"Vanette." He whispered her name, lost in the darkness of her eyes, confused and suddenly very afraid. He didn't know why, but she terrified him.

"You kissed me, Stevie," she said. "I was a shy little girl and you were the first boy I'd ever kissed."

"I remember," he said.

"What else do you remember," she asked, "about the night you kissed me, here at the rocks? It was deep summer, a warm, clear evening with the sky full of stars. The lake was calm and beautiful. Remember, Stevie?"

"I . . . I can't . . ." His tone faltered.

"You've blocked the memory," she said. "Your mind dropped a curtain over that night. To protect you. To keep you from the pain."

"After I gave you the necklace," he said slowly, feeling for the words, trying to force himself to remember, "I . . . I *touched* you . . . you didn't want me to, but I —"

"You raped me," she said, and her voice was like chilled silk. "I was crying, begging you to stop, but you wouldn't. You ripped my dress, you hurt me. You hurt me a lot."

The night scene was coming back to him across the years, assuming a sharp focus in his mind. He remembered the struggle, how Vanette had screamed and kept on screaming after he'd entered her virginal young body . . . but then the scene ended for him. He could not remember anything beyond her screams.

"I wouldn't be quiet and it made you angry," she told him. "Very angry. I kept screaming and you punched me with your fists to make me stop."

"I'm sorry," he said. "So sorry. I . . . I guess I was crazy that night."

"Do you remember what happened next?"

He shook his head. "It's . . . all a blank."

"Shall I tell you what happened?"

"Yes," he said, his tone muted, dreading what she would say. But he *had* to know.

"You picked up a rock, a large one," Vanette told him, "and you crushed my head with it. I was unconscious when you put me in your father's boat . . . *that* one." She pointed to the rowboat that Steve had used to cross the water. "You rowed out to the deep end of the lake. There was a rusted anchor and some rope in the boat. You tied me, so I wouldn't be able to swim, and then you —"

"No!" He was breathing fast, eyes wide with shock. "I didn't! Goddamn it, I *didn't!*"

Her voice was relentless: "You pushed me over the side of the boat into the water, with the anchor tied to me. I sank to the bottom and didn't come up. I died that night in the lake."

"It's a lie! You're alive. You're standing here now, in front of me, alive!"

"I'm here, but I'm not alive. I'm here as I would have been if I'd been able to grow up and become a woman."

"This is all —" His voice trembled. "You can't really expect me to believe that I'd ever —"

"— murder a twelve-year-old girl? But that's exactly what you did. Do you want to see what I was like when they took me from the lake . . . after the rope loosened and I'd floated to the surface?"

She advanced. Closer, very close.

"Get away from me!" Steve shouted, taking a quick step back. "Get the Hell away!"

A little girl stood in front of him now, smiling. The left side of her head was crushed bone, stark white under the moon, and her small body was horribly

swollen, blackened. One eye was gone, eaten away, and the dress she wore was rotted and badly ripped.

"Hi, Stevie," she said.

Steve whirled away from the death figure and began to run. Wildly. In panic. Using the full strength of his legs. Running swiftly through the dark woods, rushing away from the lake shore and the thing he'd left there. Running until his breath was fire in his throat, until his leg muscles failed. He stumbled to a panting halt, one hand braced against the trunk of a pine. Drained and exhausted, he slid to his knees, his labored breathing the only sound in the suddenly wind-hushed, moonlit woods. Then, gradually, as his beating heart slowed, he raised his head and . . . oh, God, oh Christ . . .

She was there!

Vanette's ravaged, lake-bloated face was *inches* from his — and her rotted hand, half mottled flesh, half raw gristle and bone, reached out, delicately, to touch his cheek . . .

Two years later, after Ellen had sold the lakefront property and moved to Florida, she fell in love with a man who asked her what had become of her first husband.

Her reply was crisply delivered, without emotion. "He drowned," she said, "at Diamond Lake." Ω

THE VAMPIRE LOVER, OR THE BITER BIT

His lips were full and red and tasted sweet,
His skin was soft and white, his arms were strong
As hardened steel, his fingers and his feet
Were tapered, graceful, sensuous and long,
And when he spoke, his voice was like a song
Of endless love from which she could not part.
And when he flew she wished to fly along,
But as he slept she staked him through his heart.
Then dragged him down the stairs and in her cart
She drove his body to a crossroads near.
With cross and garlic and a silver dart
She sealed his buried coffin, left him here.

Why did she love him and yet cause his Death?
She could not stand his awful bloody breath.

— **John S. Davis**

DESERT PURSUIT

They've followed me for days. I hear the sound
Of running feet on hardened desert sand.
My breath rasps painfully. I dodge around
Each spiny plant that crowds this lonely land.
No time for food, no water close at hand,
I suck on pebbles, still my mouth is dry.
The sun is setting soon, I understand,
And in the darkling starlight I will try
To lose the natives from my trail, or die.
I could not figure out just how they knew,
When we first met, what kind of Thing am I,
They saw, they feared, but now the chase is through.

I think I'll turn, run back to meet them soon.
For now my Change begins, with the full moon.

— **John S. Davis**

THE EARTH IS MADE OF STARDUST, AND SO IS THE LIFE THEREON

by Morgan Llywelyn
illustrated by Janet Aulisio

I only believe what I see with my personal eyes, and not always then.

So when that fellow Whatsisname caught the first fairy in North America and it was ultimately exhibited in the Museum of Natural History, I stood in line with about a million other New Yorkers to get a look at it. Some were frankly sceptical. A few, first-generation immigrants from the look of them, could not hide their expressions of superstitious fear. yet even when a cold rain started to fall no one left the line. We stood there shuffling our feet and blowing our noses, lured by some forgotten magic from outgrown childhoods.

When I finally reached the head of the line I found a dense crowd solidified around the hermetically sealed glass case in the main gallery. I am six feet tall and play a mean game of racketball, so like any experienced Manhattanite I shoved my way through until I was right at the front, next to the case.

Then I stopped and stared like the rest.

The creature in the case could not possibly be real. It sagged wearily atop an obviously plaster toadstool and I was about to turn away with a snort of disgust when it opened its eyes and looked straight at me.

Electricity sparked up my spinal column.

This particular fairy had eyes the colour of amethysts. On this particular day. It's one of the mysteries of their race that eye colour changes according to mood. Continuing to look at me, the fairy unfolded her gossamer wings. She lifted into the air, hovered briefly, then drifted to the front of the case until she was no more than a foot away from me.

Beauty and grace! Once you've seen a living fairy, those words take on new meaning. She was perhaps three inches tall, slim as a twig, with a touchingly heart-shaped face holding perfect features in miniature. Silver-gilt hair rippled down her back between butterfly wings. A gauzy, shimmering robe containing all the hues of the rainbow rose and fell above tiny, exquisite breasts with every breath she drew.

According to one of the many explanatory notices I had read while waiting in line, purified oxygen was piped directly into the case through a series of chemically treated filters.

She breathed. She was real, all right. And she was looking at me, I swear it. She gave off a gorgeous opalescent glow.

"Move along, buddy, so the other folks can have a look." A beefy guard broke my trance and forced me to pass on toward the exit. Looking back over my shoulder I caught one glimpse of her still watching me, with the palms of her tiny hands pressed against the glass.

Next day I managed to be at the head of the line when the Museum opened.

You could say I had a professional interest. Show me a biogenetic reconstructionist who is not fascinated by the prospect of a live fairy and I'll show you a decapitation victim.

The second time I saw her it was as if she'd been waiting for me. She came to the front of the case at once. She seemed slightly thinner than yesterday; the tiny features looked pinched, somehow. And her glow was a trifle dimmer, with a faint yellow tinge.

"She's sick," I heard someone in the line mutter. "I read they're all getting sicker every day. Ironic, isn't it? We finally discover there really are fairies, only to have them go extinct on us?"

Within days of the original find, almost five hundred of her kind, both male and female, had crept from fissures in the earth in places as dissimilar as a garden in upstate New York and the slums of Mexico City. The earliest ones were put on exhibit due to public demand, but subsequent finds were being held in those odd little "fairy stations" the scientists were building in a frantic effort to create a habitat that would keep them alive. Because they were dying, all of them. Slowly, but obviously.

No one knew how long it took a fairy to die. We had never believed in them anyway.

There was one exception, perhaps, to that statement. The Russians insisted they had known about them all along. They claimed to have found over seven hundred within the dissolving borders of the Soviet Union, and insisted theirs were smaller than ours and had more sparkle. Yet even they had found no way to communicate with the creatures, and theirs were dying as surely as ours. According to all reports, the first fairy mortality might be expected within a matter of days.

Affixed to the glass case in front of me was a plaque labelling the fading beauty within as "Tinkerbelle." Purely a guess, of course. I wondered what her real name was — surely nothing so prosaic for a creature woven out of moonbeams.

I wondered what it was like for her living in there with the phony toadstools and the yellowing ferns and our doctored oxygen hissing in upon her.

When she put her little hands against the glass again I quickly pressed my fingertips to them from the other side. At once the guard was on me like ugly on an ape, making me move back.

Tinkerbelle stuck her tiny tongue out at him and my heart turned over. Then she unfolded her polychrome wings — you could see light through them — and drifted back to her toadstool.

What I was seeing was impossible. A humanoid, no matter how small, could not fly.

Science has explained that it is also impossible for bees to fly, as they are aerodynamically unstable.

Explain that to a bumblebee.

Tinkerbelle folded herself gracefully into a sitting position and stared out at me. The electricity ran up my spine again.

Bemused, I left the Museum and went to work. Don would be awaiting my report.

Futureforms Unlimited paid me a handsome stipend to sit around drinking coffee out of styrofoam cups thinking up new ways to play God. The discovery of the fairies should be sufficient to spark off thousands of new ideas, as Don told me when he gave me the time off to visit the Museum. He wouldn't go himself, of course. Doncaster Turley wouldn't stand in line to view the Second Coming.

I refuse to call him my immediate superior because that would make me his immediate inferior, which I am not. Don is a narrow, sallow man with a face like a rat-trap and an insatiable appetite for blowsy blondes. To give him credit he was one of the founders of Futureforms, but his only real interest was in its profit potential, as I knew very well. He was Management and I was Talent and there was an insuperable chasm between us.

"Is this fairy something we could profitably duplicate?" Don asked in that nasal, supercilious voice of his that never failed to irritate me.

I looked dubious. "Enormously complex nervous system, just for starters," I told him. "I couldn't hazard a guess at it without having done a micro-dissection, and once they begin dying no one's going to let us have one for our experiments. Compared to the big boys, we're just a shoestring outfit run out a former dry-cleaning plant."

"You don't have to be insulting, Mooney." I was supposed to call him Don, as if we were friends, but he insisted on calling me by my last name instead of Mike, or Michael, in order to avoid us seeming too friendly. Typical.

I gave him a disgusted look. Don couldn't tell the difference between an insult and reality. Maybe for him they were the same.

"If this fairy thing proves to be as profitable as I think it could be," he went on, "no one will call us a shoestring lab any more. What would you need to start growing fairies in a test tube?"

"Are you serious?"

"Of course I am. The potential is enormous. Every parent in America would want one for the kiddies."

I longed to take a poke at him. The idea of hordes of spoiled little rug-rats pulling wings off creatures like Tinkerbelle and breaking their fragile limbs made me sick to my stomach.

"I have my own project," I reminded him, "one that is potentially more valuable to the whole human race."

"Idealized crap. Developing bio-forms to carry antigens into bone marrow."

"It might just mean a breakthrough in AIDS research someday."

"And it might not. Besides, grants to small firms for medical research are drying up in the current economic climate, or hadn't you noticed? I suppose not; that sort of thing is my worry. And I tell you, Mooney, if we don't find some good way to make a profit soon we're going to go under. These fairies could be the very thing. Get on it. If you need one for a model, how about the one you saw at the Museum?"

"They'd never let us borrow her."

"Who said anything about borrowing? You just don't understand how the world really works, do you? I know people who know people. A bribe here, a favour called in there . . . you'll have your fairy. We'll make it look as if she wanted to crawl off somewhere and die, and managed to escape while the guards weren't looking."

I wanted no part of it. Yet I could not resist the thought of being able to hold her, actually hold her, in my hands.

I'll say this for Doncaster Turley. He had a gift for bribery and theft. It only took him a few days to have it all set up. With a smirk on his face, he informed me, "Operation Fairy Rescue is a go, Mooney. Think of it as a service you're performing, a humane service. Did you ever perform a humane service for a fairy before?" he added with a sickening snigger.

Since the advent of real fairies, an appreciable percentage of our population had been forced to seek alternative pejoratives for another segment of the population in order to avoid confusion. In this as in many other things, Don was totally insensitive.

I liked women, actually, but he wouldn't know that. He had no interest in anyone's feelings but his own.

Before we stole (make that before I stole, because Don would of course have me do the dirty work) Tinkerbelle, I made one final trip to the Museum to survey the situation. The crowds had thinned considerably by the time I arrived, shortly before closing, and I was able to walk all the way around the case, studying the fixture. It's a sign of the times that a fairy had to be exhibited behind bulletproof glass.

Tinkerbelle followed my movements, drifting gracefully around the inside of the case. Whenever I let myself look at her our eyes met. I wished there was some way I could tell her what was going to happen and reassure her. She looked so pale, so much weaker than when I had first seen her.

She would never survive the sort of treatment necessary if she was to serve as a genetic model for Don's get-rich-quick scheme.

Sometime after midnight I returned to the Museum. In accordance with the arrangements Don had made, a strategic and rarely-used door was left unlocked. I had a map showing rooms and corridors marked with the times when guards patrolled, and the locations of the electric-eye sensors. I also had wire cutters and sufficient knowledge to disable the most critical alarm systems along my route.

Doncaster Turley, I decided, was a bank robber manqué. Nevertheless I was terrified every step of the way. I fully expected the guards to grab me, heroically resisting whatever inducements they had been offered. If I had not been so worried about Tinkerbelle I would have abandoned the whole idea and run like Hell.

When I reached her exhibit I found a soft light burning to one side of the case. She lay curled up beneath a plume of fern, as if she was asleep. But as I drew near she was on her feet instantly, eyes wide in surprise.

Her eyes were ruby that night.

Motioning her to stand back, I prepared to go to work on the case. Don had given me an assortment of tools and told me how to get it open, then how to damage it from the inside so it would look as if the fairy had escaped on her own. People would accept that, he said. They were still uncertain as to what a fairy could and could not do.

She seemed to understand my gesture and moved away from the area where I was working. Sweat rolled down my back, though the Museum gallery was cool. Every sound made me start. I had no taste for crime, I quickly discovered. But I could not go away and leave her there.

When at last the case was open Tinkerbelle and I looked at each other with mutual uncertainty. I leaned toward her and held out my hand, palm up. She gazed at it, then at my face. At last, with a tiny sigh, she stepped onto my palm.

She weighed no more than a dream.

With infinite gentleness I lifted her and conveyed her to my jacket pocket, which had been specially lined with silk. She understood its purpose at once and slipped inside. I finished what I had to do, then hurried away from the despoiled exhibit. My heart was hammering so loud they could have heard me in Queens.

From time to time I slipped one finger into the pocket and felt it grasped by two tiny hands. Once she rubbed her cheek against my finger, as a kitten would do.

I had no intention of turning her over to Futureforms Unlimited. While Don had been making his arrangements I had been making some of my own, just in case we were really able to pull it off.

I hadn't quite believed we would, to tell the truth. But then I hadn't believed in fairies, either. Now I had one in my pocket and I was determined to take care of her or die in the attempt.

Which I surely would if Doncaster Turley caught me making off with something he believed was now the ill-gotten but potentially profitable property of Futureforms Unlimited.

© JANET AULISIO DANNHEISER 1994.

Morgan Llywelyn

31

If you had just stolen a fairy, where would you go?

Where would you go if your name was Michael Mooney and you had a grandmother from County Cork, who filled you with soda bread and stories about the Good People?

Tinkerbelle was in one pocket; in the other I had a ticket for a one-way flight on Aer Lingus, to Shannon, Ireland.

We stopped by my apartment long enough to collect my suitcase containing some clothes and the things that really mattered to me: my parents' wedding certificate in its frame, a small trophy I'd won as part of a championship baseball team in high school, a couple of books by Loren Eiseley and a signed edition of *The Martian Chronicles*. A pair of earrings that once belonged to a girl I'd loved and lost. A tattered snapshot of Cocoa Bean, beloved dog of boyhood. My passport.

I offered Tinkerbelle a drink made of honey and distilled water, held out to her in a teaspoon that looked like a basin beside her face. She took a minute sip, to please me more than anything, I think. I did not know what to feed her. The fairies were reputed to be possible omnivores, but it was very difficult to get any of them to eat. Part of their sickness, probably.

When she was safely tucked back into my pocket we set off for Kennedy Airport.

In one night I had thrown away my whole life and begun a new one. I felt numb.

To my relief, apparently Tinkerbelle did not show up on the security screen as a dangerous weapon as we were being examined on our way to Departures. The thought had crossed my mind. She was Mystery.

Thirty-five thousand feet above the Atlantic, while I was waiting for the flight attendant (a gorgeous green-clad girl from County Donegal) to bring me a much-needed drink, I felt a tiny convulsion in my pocket. Glancing around to make sure no one was watching, I pulled it open and peered inside.

Tinkerbelle looked up at me, red-faced and obviously embarrassed. She, who could fly on her own wings, was being desperately airsick in my pocket.

The in-flight film was a dazzling, adventure-filled saga utilizing partial animation, astounding special effects, and taken from one of Anne McCaffrey's books about dragons, but I found I could not concentrate on it, though I am a McCaffrey fan from 'way back.

Reality stranger than fiction was curled up in my pocket.

In spite of my grandmother, I had never been to Ireland before. Shannon Airport was something of a culture shock. Though totally modern it was tiny by comparison with the labyrinthine airports of New York and Atlanta, and no one in the place was screaming or shoving.

Furthermore, in the windows of the airport giftshop I saw paperback books about Irish fairies and folklore.

I purchased an assortment of maps, knowing I must find a place remote enough that Tinkerbelle and I could escape the pursuit I anticipated. My flight attendant had mentioned that Donegal was "empty," and I liked the idea of a wild coastline and green silences. We would have enough to live on for quite sometime, until Tinkerbelle either died or I felt it was safe to return home. I had prudently withdrawn my savings and cashed my securities, and had a small fortune in traveller's checks safely tucked inside a money belt around my midriff.

From my first look at Ireland, however, I felt such a precaution was a bit extreme. I saw no one who could, by the wildest stretch of the imagination, be mistaken for a New York mugger. The native Irish are incredibly gentle people.

Collecting my luggage, I made my way out of the terminal in hopes of finding a cabstand. I had the names of several nearby hotels, and an assortment of Bed and Breakfast places that were reputed to be clean, welcoming, and reasonable. But first of all I needed a drink. I needed to find a real Irish pub.

Stepping from the bright, dry atmosphere of the terminal, I found myself on an expanse of concrete pavement glistening with mist, and more mist hung thick in the air, seeping into the pores of my skin with a curiously soothing sensation. It was like being wrapped in cotton wool.

An unmarked and rather battered sedan at the curb proved to be a taxicab, driven by a redfaced man in a shabby suit. He cheerfully relieved me of my luggage, looked me over with a practiced eye, and remarked, "Sure and flyin' is thirsty work, so it is."

"You've got it," I told him, sinking back into my seat with a feeling of relief at having my mind so clearly read.

Hurrying away from the sterility of the airport, he drove me through glorious countryside to what he called "me local," a small, plastered building at the intersection of two otherwise deserted country roads. "Take yer time," he said as we pulled up in front. "I'll be here when ye come out." He did not turn off the meter for the simple reason that he had never turned it on.

Ireland is different, I told myself.

When I opened the blackened oak door, the warm, beery pub atmosphere billowed out to greet me. The central feature was not the bar but a massive stone fireplace wherein an incongruously small pile of something like dark bricks was smouldering, giving off incredibly sweet smoke. Peat, I thought, sniffing deeply and remembering my grandmother's description. The dried earth of Ireland; haunting, evocative.

A cluster of men was ranged along the bar as if they had been in place for weeks. They moved aside companionably to make room for me. One or two nodded, unafraid to acknowledge my existence.

Not like New York at all. Ireland was obviously very different.

"I'd like a Scotch, please," I said to the barman. "With water on the side."

"Ye'll be wantin' ice with it," he announced. "Ye bein' American an' all."

"How did you know I'm American?"

He grinned. "Yer accent. And yer shoes."

When had the man had time to notice my shoes — during the few seconds it had taken me to walk across the floor?

"Not that they aren't grand shoes," he added as if afraid of offending me. "I wouldn't say no to a pair o' them meself, so I wouldn't." He reached for the Scotch.

The man nearest me at the bar, a small, wizened fellow in a checkered cloth cap, said, "Ye can't buy yer first drink in Oirland yerself. Keep yer wallet in yer pocket, lad, it's no good to ye yet." He slapped the bar with his hand. "None o' that foreign drink now, Aidan. Give yer man a pint and pull another fer meself. Next shout's on you," he added, winking at me.

"A pint" proved to be a larger-than-a-pint glass of Guinness stout, dark and rich as black velvet and collared with creamy foam. The first drink was heaven, the second was better. My benefactor tactfully shrunk away from me to allow me to enjoy it in peace.

"How did you know I had just arrived?" I asked him.

"And wasn't Paddy Spellissy after bringin' ye in the taxi? He always brings 'em here from the airport. Better for business than the day after Lent is Paddy Spellissy."

The smell of the burning peat permeated the atmosphere.

I felt a stirring in my pocket. Surreptitiously, I pulled it open the smallest bit and peered in. Tinkerbelle was looking up at me. Her eyes were huge, and the exact colour of emeralds.

Her glow was decidedly brighter.

I wished I could take her out and let her see this place. I wished she had been able to perch on my shoulder in Paddy Spellissy's taxi and watch the flowered fields and the grey stone walls roll by as Paddy unerringly avoided the traffic-laden highway and took us through picturebook countryside.

I wished . . .

I took another big swig of Guinness.

"Pulls the best pint between here and Ennis," my host confided, nodding at the barman. Then in the same breath he asked disarmingly, "And what are ye carryin' in yer pocket yerself?"

Startled, I could not help glancing down. The glow was escaping from my pocket and lighting up my jacket almost to the shoulder.

Exhausted, jet-lagged, giddy with tension, I had just drunk a pint of Guinness much too fast. Before I could stop myself I said, "A fairy."

The man's eyebrows wriggled violently upward in search of the brim of his cap. "Ye don't say now."

A palpable hush fell over the pub.

I was appalled at my indiscretion. No streetwise New Yorker ever gave away any vital information about himself to strangers in bars. I had only been

in Ireland less than an hour and already I had made a dangerous admission.

Muttering something about a joke, I prepared to slide off the barstool and leave before I made matters worse. Then I discovered a fresh pint had magically materialized in front of me. The man in the cap was holding another and looking at me expectantly.

Next shout's on you, he had said.

Embarrassed, I dug in my wallet and produced a sheaf of the Irish pound notes for which I had exchanged American dollar bills at the airport. With an air of long practice the barman extracted the sum required, giving me more change than I expected.

I could hardly walk out immediately. So I drank the pint. The man in the cap kept me company, swallow for swallow. Mid-glass he remarked, "I'm after seein' the fairies meself when I was a wee chiseler." He sighed. "Donkey's years ago, it was."

From the expression on his face I could not tell if he was pulling my leg or not. The silence in the pub was unnerving. Every face was turned toward us. "Did you?" I asked politely.

"Absolutely. And now yer after tellin' me ye have one in yer pocket. All the way from Amerikay, is it?" Before I could draw back he reached out and touched the pocket. The glow pulsed so strongly it was reflected on his face. He jerked his hand back and made the sign of the Cross on his chest. Every man in the pub did the same. "Jesus Mary and Joseph," someone said.

There was an expression on their faces I could not identify. Bringing their drinks with them, they formed a circle around me.

One said, "Bedad, but yer killin' em over there, aren't ye? Poisonin' the soil. Poisonin' the water. Anyone could have told ye what would happen." He shook his head.

Another added, "Why do ye think none of 'em have come crawlin' outta the earth of Oirland to die? Because our soil and water are still mostly clean, so they are."

"Do you mean you still have fairies living here?"

The man in the cap shot me a look of such pitying contempt that I regretted the question. "It's the poison that sickens 'em and drives 'em out of hiding places that have sheltered their kind for thousands of years. Turn yer one there loose in Oirland and it wouldn't die at all. Not unless yer bring in yer rotten pollution on us, God preserve and protect us."

The men in the pub, barman included, crossed themselves again.

"If you are certain of all this why haven't you said something to the authorities?" I demanded to know.

"The authorities." A hawkfaced man with broken teeth and impossibly blue eyes snorted. "We don't have much time for the authorities here. We've been interfered with too much, too long. We mind our own business and keep the head down. But it's a shame against God what you're doing to his Creation."

Leaning around the hawkfaced man's shoulder, another man intoned in a rich whiskey bass, "The Earth is made of stardust, and so is the life thereon."

His words rang like bells. It was my first experience of the sweet wild poetry that emerges unbidden when the Irish gather.

"It is for a fact," agreed the man in the cap. "Stardust, to be treated like somethin' special, not poisoned so yer man in the Big Smoke can buy himself another Merc."

"Big Smoke? Merc?"

"City. Mercedes. Fancy cars, all that class of thing."

I wondered what class of thing these men drove. I recalled seeing only a pack of rusty bicycles leaning against the wall outside as I came in. None of them had been chained to anything.

A new glass of Guinness sat on the bar in front of me.

The thickset, darkhaired man nearest the fireplace began singing, eyes closed, glass in hand, in a clear sure tenor with a faintly nasal undertone that carried the sound of antiquity. He sang as if he stood alone on a windswept cliff a thousand years ago. The men around me turned their attention to him, or to their own drinks. Nothing more was said about fairies.

"Have a crisp." Someone offered me a small bag of potato chips. Another Guinness arrived. A second singer took up when the first left off. Someone else bought me the best toasted ham and cheese sandwich I had ever tasted.

When at last I emerged from the pub Paddy Spellissy was waiting for me, settled comfortably behind the steering wheel of his taxi and reading the *Irish Times* in the deathless twilight of a summer evening. The air was pure and sweet and green with growing things. I drew it into lungs that had never smelled the untainted breath of Creation before.

There was an energetic stirring in my pocket. Looking down, I saw Tinkerbelle's head pop out. She gazed around, looked up at me with bright emerald eyes, smiled broadly for the first time (revealing teeth that really were tiny pearls), then snuggled down again, content.

The entire front of my jacket was drenched with stardust.

I got into the taxi. "Take us anywhere," I directed Paddy Spellissy.

"Take us home." Ω

IMPROBABLE BESTIARY: THE OTHER

If life is a banquet, I wasn't invited.
And yet uninvited I nonetheless came.
The feast was prepared, and the music delighted;
'Tis pity the guest-list excluded my name.
The laughter grew loud whilst the revels increased,
Yet I hungered while gentlemen ate.
For I am the Other, ignored at the feast,
And I watch in the dark . . . and I wait . . .

The music runs faster, the revelries flourish,
The ladies sup wine till their bodices burst.
And where in this feast is the food that will nourish
My hunger? The drink that will silence my thirst?
No guest in this hall — not the first, nor the least —
Deigns to spare me a crust from his plate.
For I am the Other, who starves at the feast,
And I watch in the dark . . . and I wait . . .

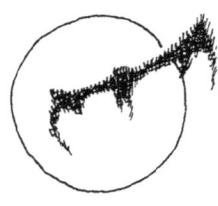

And now there is silence, and dancers grow cold
And the wine lingers warm in the cask.
On the table are goblets of crystal and gold;
I ignore them, and bend to my task.
The hunger within me at last is released
In this harlequinade of the dead.
For I am the Other, who came to the feast,
And I waited, and watched . . . *and I fed.*

— F. Gwynplaine MacIntyre

IMPROBABLE BESTIARY: THE VAMPIRE

Robots get rusty and Ghouls smell revolting.
Werewolves are musty and Harpies keep moulting.
In all the array of the damned and the doomed,
The Vampire alone is impeccably groomed.
Trolls are disgusting and Goblins are grimy.
Mummies want dusting and Swamp Things are slimy.
Of all the undead and the dread and depraved,
The Vampire alone is well-bred and behaved.

His cape is black satin, his bearing is suave.
His blood-lines are Latin, his accent is Slav.
He casts no rude shadow, he throws no reflection;
The Vampire's as regal and proud as the Sphinx.
His manners (while drinking your blood) are perfection;
He makes you feel *glad* to get stuck for the drinks!
When choosing a victim, he first stops to check
And says: "Pardon my fangs; may I *please* bite your neck?"

Man-Eating Plants tend to play with their food.
Huge Mutant Ants are inclined to be rude.
Unlike all the other unnatural terrors,
The Vampire alone doesn't show up in mirrors.
Sentient Fungoids are frequently rotting.
Blood-Sucking Zombies are constantly clotting.
Of all the perverse and profoundly profane,
The Vampire keeps going all night . . . in this vein.

— F. Gwynplaine MacIntyre

A PLAY FOR THE JADED
by Ramsey Campbell

A schoolroom. It contains a blackboard on whose ledge rests a stick of chalk. The room occupies half of the stage, which is divided by a wall containing a door. On the other side of the wall is a flowerbed from which protrudes a trowel. Between the schoolroom and the audience is a locked box with holes bored in it. Sounds of clawing and thumping as of something trying to escape are heard from the box.

The schoolteacher enters and chalks the name **Jack** on the board. On this cue, **Jack** appears from the rear of the auditorium and makes his way to the stage.

Teacher: "This is Jack."

The teacher writes *Jill,* and **Jill** joins **Jack** on the stage.

Teacher: "This is Jill."

Jack and **Jill** stand on either side of the box and face the audience.

The teacher chalks the word *owl* on the board and hands the key of the box to **Jack,** who unlocks it. **Jill** reaches in and produces an owl which she dangles upside down by its legs while showing it to the audience. The owl flaps and hoots, as should the audience.

Teacher: "This is an —"

Jack and **Jill** in unison: "Owl."

The teacher chalks the word *fowl* on the board.

Teacher: "The owl is a —"

Jack and **Jill** in unison: "Fowl."

The teacher chalks *howl* on the board. (The timing of what s/he writes and of what s/he then says ought to give the audience time to anticipate how the word is going to figure in the action.)

Teacher, speaking directly to the audience: "Shall we make the owl howl?"

Jack and **Jill** nod eagerly. **Jack** grasps one leg of the still inverted owl while **Jill** keeps hold of the other. They pull in opposite directions, very slowly. The owl begins to screech.

Teacher, in the tone of someone teaching an important lesson: "A screech owl cannot howl."

Jack and **Jill** continue to pull. The teacher chalks the word *bowel.*

Teacher: "See the owl's —"

Jack and **Jill** are too taken aback by what they've done to respond. The teacher repeats the cue more loudly and raps the word on the blackboard while s/he stares at the auditorium. Once members of the audience have responded, **Jack** and **Jill** repeat the word as if it causes them some distress.

Jill: "That bowel is foul."

The teacher's expression makes it clear that the pupils are not supposed to anticipate words. As the teacher angrily chalks *foul* on the blackboard, **Jack** lets go of the leg he's holding, and the remains of the owl swing towards **Jill,** who cries out and drops the object.

The teacher swings round and having seen what's happened, paces toward **Jill.** When s/he's close enough to touch her s/he points at the mess on the floor, then returns to the board and chalks the word *trowel.*

Teacher: "**Jill** must dig with a —"

Jack, delighted: "Trowel."

Jill trudges to the flowerbed and begins to dig. She grimaces at the audience.

Jack, more delighted than ever: "See her scowl."

The teacher turns slowly and stares at **Jack** with hideous menace, but **Jack** doesn't notice. *Scowl* is chalked on the board. **Jill** continues to dig until the hole is several feet long and a couple of feet wide.

Jack, puzzled: "That's a big hole for an owl."

The teacher shares an evil grin with the audience. **Jill** is standing in the hole and wiping her forehead with the back of her hand. The teacher chalks up *towel.*

Jill to **Jack:** "Towel."

Jack to audience: "Hear her growl."

The teacher's expression makes it clear that if there had been any hope of a reprieve for **Jack**, there certainly isn't now. While **Jack** saunters offstage the teacher chalks *growl* and then, after a short pause, *jowl*.

Teacher to audience as if sharing a secret: "Is the towel for Jill to mop her jowl?"

The teacher's delivery ought to be sufficient answer in itself. If anyone in the audience calls out a response, the teacher may stare hard at them as if identifying them for future reference. **Jack** returns and takes a towel to **Jill**. It has obviously been pulled off a roller — it's quite narrow, but several yards long. He teases her, offering it to her and snatching it away, before she is able to grab it from him.

Jill mops her face and gazes after **Jack** as he moves away. He goes to the owl and grins wickedly at the audience. Squatting down, he separates the body from its contents. He doesn't notice that **Jill** is tying a noose in one end of the towel, which she then conceals in the earth at the side of the hole. The teacher watches.

Jill: "Owl."

Jack winks at the audience. He hides the entrails in one hand before picking up the owl. The teacher chalks up the word *yowl* on the board as **Jack** walks innocently up to **Jill**. **Jack** drops the owl in the hole and then stuffs the contents of the owl down **Jill**'s collar. He's so overcome by mirth at the result that he can't move from where he's standing — that's to say, in the noose concealed by the earth.

Teacher to audience: "Shall we make Jack yowl?"

This question may be repeated more than once. When the audience seems sufficiently enthusiastic about the prospect, **Jill** slips the noose over **Jack**'s ankles and pulls it tight. He falls on his back at the edge of the hole. As he tries to push himself upright, **Jill** wraps the other end of the towel around his wrists and pulls it tight before tying his arms behind his back. He's now lying on his side by the hole.

The teacher writes *bowel* on the board, and then *trowel*. He takes his time about this and about asking the next question.

Teacher to audience: "Shall Jill trowel his bowel?"

The teacher shouldn't be satisfied with less than full encouragement. When the appropriate business has been performed the teacher speaks again.

Teacher to **Jill**: "Feed Jack his bowel."

Jill sets about this operation. As **Jack**'s protests become less coherent, the teacher poises the chalk at the blackboard.

Teacher: "Jack, that sound is a —" [writing the word while speaking it] "— vowel."

Once **Jack** is gagged, Jill stands back to admire her handiwork. His struggles grow weaker and eventually cease, and she pushes him into the hole. Throughout this action the teacher waits at the blackboard with the chalk poised to write another word. When **Jill** has finished, the teacher gazes about the audience, locating those people who were vociferous earlier, and then chalks the word *prowl*.

Teacher: "Prowl, Jill, prowl."

Jill surveys the audience. Her experiences have obviously turned her brain. She advances towards one or more of the members of the audience identified by the teacher, then rushes at whichever of them first responded to the teacher's prompting. Flourishing part of her victim as she goes, she dashes out of the auditorium.

The teacher looks satisfied with a job well done, and calls the theatre staff to clear the auditorium. As the audience leaves, the teacher shouts after them.

Teacher: "Now Jill is on the prowl."　　　　Ω

SPRING

Trapped in the frozen earth
Hands sweetly pressed against
Slumbering flowers,
Fanged lips smile.
Waiting for the thaw,
Dreaming of spring.

— **Kathleen Youmans**

HOLLOW BONES
by D. Christine Benders

This is my skin.

I've gotten used to it, but I can see you're uncomfortable. That's okay; I don't mind. Well, actually, I do mind. It used to be a nice, rich, brown color. You can't really see through it, it just looks as if you could. I agree it's disconcerting, but as I said, I've gotten used to it.

Please come in. You're in already, so I guess it's redundant for me to say so. I usually do anyway. It makes people more comfortable somehow. Don't mind if I don't rise. I tire easily.

I used to keep my door locked. Now I don't bother; I don't have anything worth stealing. Besides, now that they've taken an interest in me, unwelcome guests don't stay long.

I suppose I should have guessed Claire sent you. She sends most of the people who come: sometimes social workers, sometimes researchers. No, not psychiatric, parapsychic. Of course, sometimes it's hard to tell which kind it is without asking. They tend to look a little alike; earnest, you know, concerned.

Not to offend, but which are you?

I see.

I do have other friends, but they don't send people. Come to think of it, they don't really visit anymore either. Claire does. She's good that way.

It isn't kindness, not the sending people part; she wants me to move out and hopes someone will talk me into it. She worries about me. She's a good friend, if a bit insistent at times. I don't know why I should move out, I'm comfortable here.

I don't know if she's coming today. She doesn't tell me. Did she tell you? No? I'm not surprised. I still have the dinner she cooked me yesterday, so she might not come today.

This is Claire's sweater. It fits me beautifully, doesn't it? It's only mine on loan, until I can get energy up to go shopping. It's just I've lost so much weight in the last few months, nothing of mine fits. I look like a little kid playing dress-up; even my pants fall off me.

You should sit down. Over there. I have straight-backed chairs if you prefer, though I suggest you not use the one with the rush bottom; it looks more comfortable than it is. The wing chair is nice. If you like rockers, I have a bentwood and a recliner. Take your choice; but make sure you're comfortable. We have to wait now, and it's hard to wait if you're squirming in your chair.

I don't know how long. Used to be I'd wait forever; sunset to sunset, until the days ran together. Not any more. Now it seems they aren't ever far away. Sometimes they come while I'm walking down the street.

I'm not sure how I first knew. It took a long time before I understood. At first things around me kept moving; kept not being where I'd left them. I used to think it was someone playing pranks, then I thought I was going crazy.

The first one I saw; John. I thought he was a burglar. I didn't think to call the cops; just grabbed a frying pan and tried to brain him. The pan went right through him. He just looked at me, kind of interested, kind of hurt. Then he walked through that wall over there.

I told Claire about it.

She was fascinated. She started dropping by, nearly every day. Then she started bringing people; mediumistic manifestations, one of them said. It sounded like a disease. We made jokes about the fourth-floor walk-up sideshow. Later, I think Claire got scared, so she didn't come as often, but she kept sending people.

But that was early days; I couldn't hear them then. I could just see them. Some of them were not nice to look at. Still aren't. The really horrible ones don't show up often, which is a blessing.

Outside, it took a while longer. I'd known about them inside the apartment here for a while; a month, maybe more, I'm not sure. Then I started seeing them on the street.

By their eyes. Their eyes gave them away. You know, you walk down the street, ride the bus; people's eyes just slide off you. People don't establish eye contact; but *they* do. They see you, they look at you, they dare you to look back; no, they demand you look back.

I don't go out often any more, just to buy food, and sometimes not even then. Claire does most of my shopping. She cooks for me too. She makes a big pot of something and then I just have to heat what I need. It helps now that I'm so tired all the time.

I only go out when I absolutely have to, and then only at night. It's easier not to see them at night. They need so much. And there are so very many of them. It isn't easy, being needed. Here in my apartment it's a little easier to limit who I deal with. It's very important to set limits while I can.

Regulars? I suppose you could say so. There's Berthe and John; they're here often. There are others; I can't name them all.

Periodicity. What a word.

It isn't timing, exactly, it's more like groupings. If John is here, then Bevis and Ainsley may show up. Then again, maybe not.

No. There are no rats; nor mice either. Not even roaches. They don't like this floor. They may not even like the building, I haven't checked. I think I still have neighbors.

I don't? Oh.

John takes care of my laundry. It's good of him. Berthe means to do the washing, but it's beyond her; not enough substance. I don't like to remind her of her condition. I'm fond of her, I hate to see her upset. I think John is in love with her a little, but he'd never admit it. She says laundry is women's work; it's beneath him. He says he's stronger than she is, so it's only fair he should do the work. It's a regular discussion for them; I don't get involved.

Yes, that's John. You can say hello if you like. He won't speak, but he'll smile at you. He isn't shy, not the way you mean. He says you people with solid bones are all deaf. It's a joke. I tell him *my* bones are solid; he says they won't be for long.

He doesn't speak to Claire either.

I don't think Berthe will come, she tends to be shy. Even Claire's only seen her a couple of times.

I hope you don't need the bathroom, he'll do the wash there. He can manage the taps, but the machine confuses him. He says the taps are decadent, but he hasn't suggested I get a pump put in. It's a good thing I don't go through many clothes in a month, the shower rod would never hold up. . . .

Please don't scream. It's only the Hamilton boys. They aren't really dangerous. Intense, yes. Demanding, yes. Hard to resist, yes. They used to be ladies' men, long ago. Sometimes, there's a certain glitter in their eyes; but they've never done anything awful to me. Still, you shouldn't scream. I think it gives them ideas.

I call them boys; they're brothers. Ainsley is rather a dear, if a little trying sometimes. His memory is quite good, and his manners are always superior; courtly, old-fashioned. I'm just glad he brings his brother instead of his father. According to Ainsley, his father, the Colonel, has no use for persons of color. It would make visits awkward.

Ainsley, on the other hand, claims to have always had a love of dark women. He always looks at me meaningfully when he says that. I think it's sweet.

I apologize for Bevis. His memory isn't nearly as solid as Ainsley's; he remembers his brother and little else. Unfortunately, his body remembers perfectly well; not at all a nice death. Wouldn't you agree?

Yes, of course they can see you. They can always see you. Didn't you understand? You can see them because I'm here; otherwise you wouldn't. No, the blood won't drip on you; Bevis isn't nearly strong enough for that to happen.

Ainsley is a different matter. You might even be able to feel when he kisses your hand. I always can. I didn't before, but I can now.

Ainsley's a great one for kissing. He's very romantic. He says people with solid bones know nothing about passion. Of course, he doesn't have any bones. I mentioned it once; he was quite put out. He said passion was in the mind. He makes a good case for his view. I used to worry, but as I mentioned to Claire, he can't get me pregnant.

I'm sorry. Claire thought it was funny when I said it to her. So did Ainsley; he said he planned to keep trying. I was just trying to explain; I didn't mean to embarrass you.

Yes. They change. They do change. Everyone does, or they die.

Yes, I suppose they couldn't exactly die again, could they? But they could cease. At least, they could get to where I couldn't see them any more than you usually do.

John's changed. He sees walls where he didn't used to, and I don't think he ever did laundry before he started doing mine. And Berthe, I'm fairly sure she never argued with a man before in her life; or ever thought of falling in love. Bevis: it's hard to say about Bevis, he's so nearly not here. But Ainsley now, Ainsley. I could be wrong, but it seems to me he's getting stronger.

I think maybe they all are.   Ω

D. Christine Benders

A TALK WITH FRED CHAPPELL
by Darrell Schweitzer

Worlds of FANTASY & HORROR: When you accepted your World Fantasy Award [at the World Fantasy Convention, at Calloway Gardens, Georgia, Halloween weekend, 1992] you described the experience as being like a homecoming. So, could you start out by explaining that? What were the beginnings of your interest in the fantasy field?

Chappell: In fact, it's very much like a homecoming indeed as we sit in a deserted bar at the Calloway Inn and look through the glass window there and see L. Sprague de Camp and his lovely wife pacing up and down as they wait for a taxi to the airport, I expect. I recall that the first time I saw Mr. de Camp was in 1951, at the New Orleans World Science Fiction Convention. So it's a full circle for me.

I was quite an active fan from 1950 until about 1954 when I went off to college and had to become interested in other things, other kinds of books, in the struggle to stay in school. And so I developed other literary interests, and when I began publishing my own writing I published very different work from science fiction or fantasy. So, now that my last volume of short stories, *More Shapes Than One* has been so well received by fantasy readers, I feel that I've come back to the people I grew up with, so to speak.

WoF&H: But you started out trying to write fantasy and science fiction.

Chappell: That's correct.

WoF&H: You've mentioned submitting things to fanzines in the early '50s. How much did you actually publish back then?

Chappell: Actualy I published a great deal in fanzines at the time. I published in one called *Sirius*. I'm sorry but I can't remember the editor's name. I also published a lot with an editor named Sheldon Deretchen, until he became an ardent Marxist. Politics bored me. But I also published quite extensively in Bob Silverberg's *Spaceship*, in fanzines — boy, it's hard to pull up names at this point — edited by Joel . . . somebody. But in most of the well-known fanzines of the time. I think I published in Charles Riddle's famous *Peon*. I was quoted in Lee Hoffman's *Quandry*.

WoF&H: Was this fiction, non-fiction, or what?

Chappell: I did a little bit of non-fiction. I tried to write science articles and I still have no aptitude for that. I published a fair amount of poetry in fanzines, but mostly fiction. Short stories.

WoF&H: Are any of them ones you'd want to see the light of day again?

Chappell: [Laughs.] I'm not ashamed of having written them. I'm a little ashamed that they're so patently terrible. But I don't have to apologize for that. I wrote then the best that I could write. That's my practice now. I did publish a couple of stories under a pen name in professional magazines, not because I was trying to hide my identity, but because I thought that was a romantic thing to do. *Now,* because I don't like those stories, I don't give that pen name away. Somebody'll dig it up, I am sure, but I hope not.

WoF&H: So you went away and served an apprenticeship in other types of literature. So, could you tell us about your subsequent career? What happened next?

Chappell: I published six novels. I've published about twenty books of poetry and fiction — that includes novels and short stories — over a period of thirty years. I published my first novel in 1963 with Atheneum. I moved to Harcourt Brace following an editor, Hiram Haydn. I've always stayed with editors rather than publishers. I've been in and out of mainstream literature, mostly as a poet. I have a reputation for poetry, I expect, if I have a reputation, but maybe also for fiction. I've won the requisite number of awards and prizes. Of course, my real career is teaching college.

WoF&H: Before your very recent work, what the fantasy reader knew you best for was a book called *Dagon*, which seemed to come out of nowhere around 1968 at a time when only the immediate minions of August Derleth were writing anything having to do with Lovecraft or the Cthulhu Mythos — and suddenly *Dagon* happened. How did it come about?

Chappell: It came in my mind to write it, and so I wrote it. My publisher had no notion of what I was doing or what it was about. I didn't enlighten him. He had never heard of H.P. Lovecraft, and I didn't tell him, because I knew it would do no good as far as marketing went and nobody needed to know it. I figured it would have a very obscure, short-lived career in the United States, which, as a matter of fact, at first, it did. Then it won the most prestigious of French literary prizes. It won the *Prix de Meilleur des Livres Etrangers,* the Best Foreign Book Prize, from the French Academy, and has had a Continental reputation since then. It's now still in print in a wonderfully gaudy mass-paperback edition from St. Martin's Press with a cover that is the kind of cover that you dream of for a book you've written when you are fourteen or fifteen years old, but then when you get to be thirty-four or forty years old you hide it from your mother.

WoF&H: How was this book received by your regular mainstream readership?

Chappell: Insofar as I had one, they were just puzzled, but not entirely puzzled because my other books were also rather strange to them. I've never published any work but one that didn't have some touch of fantasy or irrealism in it — and *that* one had a science-fiction fan club active in the middle of it. So most of my readers kind of expected oddness. But my first novels were very difficult, hard metaphysical exercises. They weren't very attractive to readers. This was because that was the kind of book I wanted to write. Then after a certain period I figured I'd had enough of that and I wanted to write a more popular book, one that would sell pretty well and would pay my poetry publisher back. He was obviously going to lose money publishing my poetry. So I thought I'd write him a novel that would sell some copies. So I wrote a more humane novel, and, sure enough, it worked out pretty much as we'd predicted.

WoF&H: Did your mainstream or academic colleagues regard your involvement in fantasy as a bad habit to be apologized for?

Chappell: They didn't understand it in the least, to tell the truth. They didn't understand it so thoroughly that I had received no comment on it at all. Writers in the academy rarely receive any direct comment on their work. You have to be Brett Easton Ellis to get any comment from your colleagues. Nobody reads your work because they all have their own concerns. They all have their own careers to pursue. When a book comes out, they say "Congratulations," if they remember to, and that's the end of it. But after I got some reputation, my fiction was looked at with some favorable regard, and critical articles began to appear, so they figured it must be all right, because people are writing about it. The one credential a writer can establish in academia is that the scholars are writing about your work. That's about the size it. [Laughs.]

WoF&H: How do you feel about that? Is it rather like being stuck in a museum while you're still alive?

Chappell: It's kind of like receiving a lifetime achievement award when you're thirty-five. You figure it's all over but the tombstone.

WoF&H: I am thinking of one instance I know of: a teacher who was actually fired from a university job when they found out he was writing science fiction, back about 1950.

Chappell: I'm not surprised but I'm sorry to hear it. The prejudices of academe are so well known that they don't need to be remarked on by me today. We have to admit that the prejudices of the science fiction and fantasy community are pretty well known too. The fans don't read much outside their field. They don't care for what we would call mainstream poetry. But I don't mind. As far as I'm concerned, a story is a story is a story, and if a story is good enough, it will reach readers of any persuasion.

WoF&H: What is the attraction of the fantastic for you? It seems you've stuck with it even when you weren't immediately rewarded for doing so.

Chappell: It was the most attractive thing to me when I was at that age we read everything, when childhood is one long series of books interspersed with boring other things you have to do. My chosen reading was science fiction and fantasy. The reason for this was that, growing up in a small mill town in northwestern North Carolina, I had very little access to mainstream literature that was of any interest to me at all. Of the other genre literature around, detective stories, westerns, love pulps, that sort of thing, only science fiction seemed exciting or interesting. I learned a great deal from it and owe a great deal to it. I learned how to write by reading science fiction pulp magazines. Also, at the same time, I learned how not to write.

WoF&H: Are you still a reader and collector of this sort of thing? The reason I ask is that it's clear in "The Somewhere Doors," which is a story about a science fiction writer, that you had a copy of the August 1936 *Astounding* on your desk as you wrote it.

Chappell: I'm not a dedicated collector. In fact I shouldn't admit this, but I have a whole attic full of terrific pulp magazines from the 1930s. I have an especially large collection of *Astounding* and *Famous Fantastic Mysteries,* which I have not taken care of. They're falling into sawdust. Every time I think about them, a red blush of shame creeps up the back of my neck and over my ears. But life is full of things one should take care of and doesn't.

WoF&H: At what point did you discover H.P. Lovecraft?

Chappell: I discovered him through the letter columns of the pulp magazines, in *Famous Fantastic Mysteries.* One of the great things about the pulp magazines of the era was the letter columns. There was a real give-and-take between the readers and the editors — and the writers to some extent — in those days, which was not only interesting to read, but rather comforting for a reader to come to and find that other people read these things too, that it must be all right, that people who can actually write letters also read these magazines.

Famous Fantastic Mysteries had a letter column in which people kept requesting again and again that they reprint some stories by an H.P. Lovecraft. They rarely did so — almost never, and so this was very intriguing. Well, Victor Hugo's comment that nothing is so interesting as a wall on the other side of which something is happening springs to mind. It intrigued me so much that when I finally did read my first Lovecraft story, I was rather disappointed, because of course nothing could live up to the expectations that these accolades had aroused. But then when I read some other, better stuff, I found that he held up for me. He still holds up for me. The best stories still remain in my mind. I esteem them almost as highly as any other literature I know of.

WoF&H: In your collection *More Shapes Than One,* there is a definite impression of H.P. Lovecraft in story after story. Can you define that special something about him?

Chappell: The thing he worked hardest on, which seems to be his forté, was atmosphere. He claimed that the supreme achievement available to horror fiction was the creation of atmosphere. The landscapes that he created in fiction remain as vivid in my mind as many real landscapes I've seen, and certainly as vividly as many of the paintings I've seen. Outside of that, the use of recondite or forbidden knowledge seemed particularly wonderful. A great many writers use that, but Lovecraft uses it with wonderful force and appeal. Where he was not good is exactly in the places he knew he was not good, in the creation of character and in the construction of plots. Sometimes these are not the things we most value in a writer.

WoF&H: In your story entitled "Weird Tales" you did something I've always wanted to see someone do in a Cthulhu Mythos story. The last two lines are written from the point of view of someone living in a time *after* the Old Ones have won and repossessed the Earth. The rest of us are wondering why, if they're so powerful, they haven't won long ago.

Chappell: It seemed to me that if I could end the story correctly, it would treat all the Mythos stories of Long and Derleth as well as Lovecraft as being reportage rather than fiction — disguised reportage in order to save their lives. That's what I wanted to pull off with it. As far as I know, you are the only reader to point out in print that the story takes place *in the future.* But that's not revealed until the last words of the story.

WoF&H: I was getting entirely tired of the sort of Mythos story that goes: Scholar discovers mouldering book, then is eaten by Things. I once wrote a parody in which the Old Ones win, just to get it all over with.

Chappell: Yes, I've seen the parody. It was inevitable that someone would write it, and I thought you did a good job. I must say that there are some interesting details that Lovecraft scholars might like to know. One of my dearest friends in the early '70s was the great Southern poet Allen Tate, who, as it happened, was a close friend of Lovecraft's associate, Samuel Loveman, in those years. Well, not a close friend, I shouldn't say that, because he did not *like* Samuel Loveman, but he gave me all sorts of personal information about Loveman — who is really an obscure figure in American literature — and so I was able to use that as background. I felt I had access to a kind of information not many people would have. All the quotations that are in documents in the story are real. Those came from Hart Crane's letters or from H.P. Lovecraft's letters.

WoF&H: If you ever got to meet H.P. Lovecraft, what would you say to him?

Chappell: Thanks a bunch, kid. I owe you one. [Laughs.]

WoF&H: What brought you back to writing more fantasy, all of a sudden in the past few years?

Chappell: That's not exactly true, the "sudden" part. If anybody had world enough and time and wanted to paw through my earlier fiction, he would see that even the realistic novels shade into fantasy, then shade back out again. I try to make this seamless, but I don't draw a distinction between what is real and what is imagined. It seems to me that what is real *is* what is imagined, that we can only know the world as we imagine it. Our problem is not that we imagine too much, and therefore become unreal, but that we don't imagine fully enough, and don't understand the reality that's out there.

WoF&H: In the sense that we don't create the world by imagining it. We *recognize* the world by imagining it.

Chappell: We discover the world by imagining it.

WoF&H: But there are those who try to shape the world by imagining it. It seems to me that they tend to get hit by something hard and sharp fairly soon.

Chappell: That's absolutely true. It's one of the first signs of maturity, when we first realize that what we dreamed about and hoped for ain't gonna be it. But that's not a fundamental or serious mistake. That's just a mistake of youth and of incomprehension. Sooner or later the real mistake is always going to be not daring to imagine fully or surprisingly enough.

WoF&H: So this would make fantasy a kind of training for coping with reality.

Chappell: Yes, I think it is a method of coping with reality or trying to comprehend reality. Actually, in order to cope with reality, it takes willpower, which is not something that fantasy is very good at developing.

WoF&H: There'd also a type of realism whose virtue is being completely realistic, and any intrusion of fantasy renders it false or dishonest. That too is a method of coping with reality.

Chappell: I agree with that. I would not want to be reading one of Hemingway's stories and find that magical transformations suddenly begin to take place. That would ruin the story and ruin the vision of reality that Hemingway's stories set up. On the other hand, I would not like to read a Marquez story or a Borges story in which there was just plodding detail after plodding detail. There are some writers who are very good at that, and there are some writers who are not good at it.

There is a great deal of talk, and there has been for some while, about Magic Realism, but that's always really been with us. I would recommend to any fantasy reader that he might have a look at a novel by Emile Zola, the inventor of naturalism, called *The Sin of Father Mouret,* because there's where the mythic and the fantastic are developed straight out of the the most raw, naturalistic basis for fiction that you can imagine. And yet, it's still realistic and still fantastic at the same time. It's very powerful.

WoF&H: A most intriguing contrast is the recent film *The Fisher King,* which hints at fantasy all the way through, but the whole honesty and validity of it is precisely that there is *nothing* fantastic at the end. It's a story about coping with delusions.

Chappell: Some psychological studies are like that, like de Maupassant's stories. "The Horla," for example. Or Fitz-James O'Brien's "What Was It?" These are stories which start out seeming to be fantastic, but are actually portraits of a sensibility or of a diseased mind. Behind the fantasy is a terrible reality. Poe invented this mode. He was probably the best at it.

WoF&H: You've at least touched on that. But one of the things that's so impressive about *More Shapes Than One* is the range. A couple of the stories are science fiction. Some are purely whimsical, the one about the highway blocked by a symbolist poem waiting to to be written —

Chappell: I enjoy writing humor when I can. It's very difficult. I know it is the hardest thing for me to write. Perhaps it is for other folks too. But I enjoy it because readers enjoy it. I give a lot of readings, and people are so happy to have a humorous story read to them rather than a grim story that leaves them depressed. You sign more books when you have a humorous story, I think. [Laughs.]

WoF&H: But a lot of humor dates in a way that grim things don't.

Chappell: That's because some humor depends on topical elements.

WoF&H: However, I suspect that those who deliberately write for immortality do not achieve it.

Chappell: [Laughs.] I think that's probably true. If we do, how the hell would we know?

WoF&H: Or be able to enjoy it? But to change the subject, what are you writing now?

Chappell: I have a book of poems out, if anyone's interested in that, called *C*, that is, the Roman numeral *One Hundred.* After that comes a book with a very hot title. *Plow Naked,* it's called, but it's a book of essays on modern poetry. And after that, I hope to do another book of fantastic short stories. I have about half of them written and a satiric novel about philosophy.

WoF&H: What are your writing methods like?

Chappell: I write everything out longhand. Even the novels I write in longhand. When I am writing fiction, I try to write two pages a day, which will amount to about twelve hundred words. The next day, I go over it and I rewrite those pages, sometimes extensively, sometimes not so extensively, and then launch in after that to the next pages, which goes on until I'm halfway through a novel. After that I can't do it, because the bulk would be too much. I'd spend the whole day rewriting and rereading. So when I've got half the book, I just go writing straight on. Then I do an enormous amount of revision, constantly. If a young writer wants to make his living writing, I'm the worst model he could follow. I will rewrite stories time and time and time again. Even after they're published I sometimes revise them.

I determined early on that I did not want to make

my living writing. I wanted the freedom of what I wrote. I wanted to be able to write poetry in freedom. So I decided to acquire another profession, besides the writing, so I can keep on writing, but also have fun.

WoF&H: This is a very important point. A writer shouldn't quit his day job until holding it literally costs him money. Otherwise you may be forced into over-production and end up imitating yourself. Suppose somebody said, "Here's five million dollars. I want you to write five sequels to *Dagon.* Don't give me this stuff about not having anything to say. Just do it." What would you do then?

Chappell: I would have to say, "No." I would love to write more Mythos stories, but none having to do with *Dagon.* By the way, I've got to tell you, *Dagon* was not a fantasy book I put out, a horror book I wrote just for the fun of it. It was a different book for me. It was very personal. It caused me a great deal of personal anguish. I had to live through that book. My first two novels I had written in fairly short order, but that one caused me a lot of troubles. I think it's a real failure. My ambitions were much too large for such a short book. I wanted to make it very powerful and very concrete, hard. That was probably the wrong approach. I could not write that book again. It's all I can do to reread it.

WoF&H: But other people seem to like it, or it wouldn't still be in print.

Chappell: Perhaps one of the reasons that they like it is because it cost me so much. I suppose you can tell that this is a genuine book. The writer cares about this book, whatever kind of botch he made of it.

WoF&H: Surely there are some books which are more admirable for their ambition than for what they actually achieve. A very, very competently rendered nothing is still nothing.

Chappell: Yes, but sometimes I just love competent nothings. One of my favorite writers is P.G. Wodehouse, for example. There is nothing terrible about works which are competent nothings. On the other hand, I do admire more works by writers like Faulkner and Lovecraft and Poe because they tried to go — to boldly go — where no man has gone before.

WoF&H: Surely this is what writing is all about: following your obsessions.

Chappell: Yes. I think it has to be more than obsessions. It has to be a kind of *vision* of what we think or hope or dread is out there, rather than what one person has to get off his chest, but I'm not sure that I'm equipped to distinguish between the two.

WoF&H: Maybe we only find that out after we read what we've written.

Chappell: Yes, and after it's published and some decades have gone by.

WoF&H: That's a pretty good ending line. Thanks, Fred.

Chappell: Thank you.   Ω

LONDON BURNING
by Jeff VanderMeer
for Anne Kennedy
illustrated by Vincent diFate

Caroline Bancroft walked past the many cots of the Children's Ward on Montgomery Central's third floor, stopping at the last cot, the one which faced the wall, the one which held Rebecca.

Rebecca was a five-year-old girl who had lost her arms and legs to the German bombs. The child's face was not that of a porcelain doll; nor did it have the ruddy toughness which distinguished so many of London's survivors. No, the child's skin seemed translucent and Caroline had the irrational fear that, were she to touch the child, under the harsh glare of hospital lamps, her hand might well slide *through* the body.

The only anchors, the only hints of solidity beyond the fixtures of flesh and blood, were the eyes, which stared at the far wall, at a point between ceiling and floor. A frigid gaze, the pupils the color of deep water, frozen over and motionless.

"Rebecca, won't you please say something?" she asked the girl, as she did every morning. "Just so we know you're all right?"

Caroline had a hundred more important duties than making a child speak, but the eyes — cold and dead and blank — hypnotized her.

Rebecca kept her silence. Caroline sighed and went about cleaning the child's body: disposing of waste from the catheter, washing the pale skin with wet cloths, and massaging the memory of arms and legs, the seamless, stitched-up places that reminded Caroline of stocking dolls she had made when she was young.

"Come *on*, Rebecca," she said, after she had fed the child. "Speak to me!"

No response.

According to the doctors, Rebecca hadn't suffered brain damage, but there she lay, unmoving, alive in a straitjacket of flesh.

Caroline pulled the sheets up to Rebecca's neck.

"When I was your age, my Dad used to take me for walks through Hyde Park on Saturday afternoons. Did you ever feed the ducks at Hyde Park, Rebecca? When we got back, my Mum would have rhubarb pie waiting for our tea."

Caroline pushed back Rebecca's hair, fixed it with a pin, tucked it into a braid.

Yes, rhubarb pie, and more recently — before he'd been called up — George had come by her parents' house, the smile that passed between them conveying knowledge of secret meetings at his flat. After tea, they'd go over to a pub and drink gin and lime, see a flick with George's buddies.

The theatre was empty now, one wall having fallen in during a Luftwaffe attack. And most of George's friends were also in the army, or dead.

Strange, she thought, straightening the sheets, how one vision could lead to another, until it was like the pack of cards in *Alice in Wonderland*. She was conscious now of the warm, humming sounds of the hospital, the quiet tread of feet in the hall, the fan blades which swished above her head.

"I have to go, Rebecca."

Was the child even now turning over memories in her mind, examining them like the dolls within dolls?

"I really have to go."

Caroline rose to her feet.

"Please try tomorrow, dear. I know you can hear me."

Then she was through the door, sweating, breathing heavily, as though she had run up to the eighth floor and back.

No one seemed to understand her helplessness — the helplessness which became irritation, then fear, because she could not reach a little girl. (And the fear beneath the fear. If she could not heal Rebecca, then . . . No, it was too terrible to think of.)

Once, she had tried to tell her mother. She described men screaming, chunks torn from their legs, their groins, the smell of rotting flesh thick and cloying. The spray of blood from a man with glass in his throat. The nakedness, the flash of white belly, sodden with ash and mud. And her mother wrapped her in a smothering hug, said, "It's all right, dear," and didn't understand. Didn't connect.

George would have understood, but she couldn't be sure because his hopelessly dated postcards with their mandated cheeriness had never responded to *her* letters, in which she had told the truth — about how alone she felt, about conditions at the hospital.

Finally, at dusk, uniform still flecked with blood and grime, Caroline found herself out on the streets, walking for home. The undamaged blocks closest to the hospital reminded her of a time before war, when the houses had boasted sparkling clean porches, the greens, browns, and yellows bright, the paint not peeling or burnt away. Then it was just London again, Hyde Park and Piccadilly and *home*. London fading into Autumn.

The farther she walked, the worse the neighborhoods became . . . here, gangs of ragged boys ran from house to house, turning up treasures in the ruins: a brass candlestick or a girdle or someone's toothbrush.

More than the boys or the fires or the dazed look on people's faces, there were the cats: persians, tabbies, calicos and mixed breeds. Many had lived in the foundations and although bombs had reduced the buildings to caricatures of ash and cement and glass, the cats had somehow survived. Now the streets crawled with strays, scattered only by the occasional lorry. Some strays were rumored to have feasted on their dead owners. Even after the war, Caroline would remember the sensation of being watched by a hundred feline eyes, some carrying still other eyes in their mouths.

In her nightmares, George stared at her, and she was unable to help him.

For a moment, memories of George before the war spilling out like unframed family portraits, she found it difficult to breathe, to move, but she controlled her panic, forced it down.

She took a wrong turn. Then another, and another, until, thoroughly lost, bumping into people, she stopped walking, almost sank to her knees.

She had happened upon a street which had once been an outdoor marketplace. Now it lay deserted, the wooden tables splintered and up-ended. A lukewarm breeze blew scraps of cloth and newspaper across the sidewalk. A last faint scent of fresh fish and vegetables made her mouth water.

Turning to her left, she saw a woman in a robe walking away from her. Patchwork scenes had been woven into the robe; the bright blues and reds and yellows, which should have been garish, lent the woman a fevered elegance.

"Excuse me," Caroline said to the woman's back. No response. No break of stride.

"Excuse me," Caroline said, louder, hurrying to catch up. But the woman began to walk faster.

"Excuse me," she shouted when the gap had widened to forty feet. "Excuse me, but do you know the way to Fordham Street?"

At the sound of Caroline's voice, the woman broke into a run.

"Wait! Please!" Caroline shouted.

The woman ducked into an alley.

Caroline ran to the alley's mouth, saw nothing but deserted pavement ahead. She hesitated for a moment, debated turning back, realized she had no hope of retracing her path, and continued forward.

Alert for the slightest movement, Caroline found her steps growing heavy. She began to sweat. The sky glimmered slate-gray and a heady smell, like petrol, hung in the air. Everything was too dark, too hot. A cat brushed against her ankles, mewling. Her movements began to mimic the frantic fluttering of the moths which circled the few functional shop lights, the frenetic clawing of the cats as they tried to catch the moths. How stupid she had been!

Sirens wailed. Her heart caught in her throat. The scream, rising and falling, forced calm upon her. The all-too-familiar searchlights of anti-aircraft de-fenses began to eclipse the sky. Caroline heard the hum of bombers.

The whistling, tumbling song of the bombs as they fell unfroze her legs. She ran forward, looking for shelter. Beside a pile of rubble, she saw a tobacconist's, but the side wall had fallen in. The steps of a nearby clock tower were blocked by wood and stone. Panicked, she spotted two girders which had fallen at an angle to each other. She dove beneath them, bruising her legs. She covered her head with her arms. She snuggled as deep into the concrete as possible. She waited, trembling.

The ground shivered, sent knives deep into her spine, wrenched the breath from her mouth. But the ground did not break beneath her. The bombs had hit farther away than she feared. Thunder rolled over Caroline, dust coating her as debris sprayed up around the sanctuary. Flames roared and flared, crackling wood not twenty meters away.

Slowly, fearfully, ears ringing, she unbent and touched her feet, her legs — then head, shoulders, belly. No injuries, only the dust, which she brushed from her uniform without success.

She rose slowly, like an old woman, and looked around her. To her surprise, buildings stood, ragged as curtains, draperies of façades which glowered with fires or with shadow, propped up by no discernible means. The clock tower caught her eye. The hands were dark and twisted, but most of the bricks had stayed in place.

Then she saw the woman in the patchwork robe.

At first Caroline just stared, her skin prickling. She wanted to pinch herself to make sure she was awake, alive, watching.

Beneath the clock tower, the woman danced on a raised slab of concrete, lit by flame and the tracers of anti-aircraft fire. Her hair was streaked with dust. Beyond the hair and the outlined nose, mouth, chin, Caroline could see only the silhouette and the dance. The dance began as a formal waltz, in step with an invisible partner; so much in step, cohesive, that Caroline squinted, wondering if she had missed a man in the darkness, perhaps hugging the clock-tower wall.

But the dance soon changed, became angry — fast and flickering as the flames, choreographed for warfare. The hands cut the air like those of a flamenco dancer, but faster, so much faster that her body appeared to be moving in several directions at once, the legs with their own purpose, the arms and torso separate creatures twisting, twisting, almost twisting free.

The sirens began to wail again, along with a louder, insistent hum, and she realized a second strike was two minutes, one minute, away. Stumbling over rubble, Caroline ran toward the woman.

"Take cover!" she shouted.

The woman continued to dance, more fiercely than before, using the robe as a weapon, with a snap and a curl which warned, *stay away!*

Caroline cleared the slab's edge with one jump.

Her momentum carried her into the dancer. They fell. Caroline winced as she scraped her side, then winced again when the woman punched her in the stomach. By the time the surprise wore off, the dancer had gotten in two stiff kicks. It took Caroline almost twenty seconds of grappling to finally pin the woman down, then hoist her, still squirming, over her shoulder. She staggered back to the shelter, where she dumped her burden without ceremony.

The bombs hit, closer, and both women shook with the tremors. Caroline's stomach lifted and fell, her body jolted off the ground.

The shaking subsided again. The fires provided some illumination, and Caroline — her breath coming in fish-like gasps — watched the dancer cough as she propped herself into a sitting position. She crossed her legs. The robe had fallen open, revealing her breasts, and she wrapped it tightly about herself. Where before she had seemed to Caroline like an expanding, multi-limbed demon, now she had contracted into herself, small and defenseless.

"You hurt me." Caroline's voice was dry with dust.

A dazed expression widened the dancer's face. A rough face, in the fire's light, as if a talented sculptor had done a hurried clay sketch of a striking woman. The jaw was too set, the cheekbones too unyielding. Her lipstick had smeared, so that red slashed across the chin and, above, to the lower part of the nose.

"You stupid girl. Why? Why?"

The voice, deep and husky, conjured up images of gypsy caravans, tarot cards, and thick Mediterranean stews. The incomprehension in the question made Caroline stumble over her reply. As if she had to justify the action.

"You would have died." She slapped dust off her body. "You felt the tremors."

The woman laughed, a hacking sound, as she tried to clear her lungs of dust.

"Let them come! I danced for them."

"That's insane!"

The woman shrugged. She leaned toward Caroline, who flinched. "Don't be scared. What is your name? I can't read your tag."

"Caroline Bancroft," she said, blood rising to her face. She wanted to hit the woman for her rudeness. "I'm sorry. I'm sorry, but you've a strange idea about suicide —" Her voice cracked; she swallowed, continued in what she hoped was a calm tone: "Why not just take some pills or cut your throat? It's so much more precise than doing a striptease for the Luftwaffe."

A chuckle followed by high-strung laughter, as if some internal cog had come undone.

"Why are you laughing?" Caroline demanded. A flurry of giggles. She kicked out at the dancer. "Stop it! It's not funny."

"But it is funny, child," said the woman, controlling her hysteria. "Much funnier than what others have said."

"Others? Do you mean the curfew Wardens?"

The dancer took a cigarette from a pocket in her robe, used a lighter on the tip, blew toward Caroline's face.

"Not polite, are you? Not bred on politeness. You ask my name, first. Ask my name."

Caroline sighed, settled back against a girder.

"What is your name?"

"My name is Moriah, Moriah Wisenman." She proffered a cigarette. "You want one? No? Then I have two." She stuck the second in her mouth, lit it. "As for dying, when I was very young, Rabbi Spevack took me aside and said, 'Moriah, always put yourself in God's path and he will reward you. Never make your own path, for that is the path to unhappiness.' I think he was drunk." She took a long drag. "I found these on a dead man." A laugh. "Imagine that! A dead man with smokes. As if he needed them."

"I've heard about people like you," Caroline said, determined to ignore anything that stank of sickness, of insanity.

"What sorts of things?" The voice trembled with uncertainty, or eagerness.

"That you're a crazy old woman!"

The savagery of her response surprised her. She was shaking, actually shaking with rage, she realized from afar, a part of her that had escaped the war, escaped the deaths . . . or been numbed beyond feeling by them. Her thoughts darkened as they turned back to George.

Moriah slapped her across the face. It stung. It brought the anger out onto her features, contorting them.

"I want to die, child," hissed Moriah. "That's my choice." She looked out at the raging fires, the fountains of flame. "I used to dance on the West End. I used to have a husband."

Caroline looked at the ground, her eyes wet. This, she realized (breathe deeply, try to relax) was shell shock. This was post-bomb trauma. The emptiness. The panic. The anger. Had Rebecca gone through this? Was her numbness now due to the bombs?

Moriah plucked the cigarettes from her mouth, extinguished them in one fluid, cruel scrape against concrete.

"Let me tell you why I want to die."

"You're crazy," Caroline said, putting her hands over her ears. "I don't want to listen to a crazy woman."

Moriah roughly pulled Caroline's hands away. "Listen to me! I didn't have to slap you. I could have stuck my cigarette in your eye. You deserved it. I'm going to tell you about a Vision."

"I don't understand."

"At night, I dream of true events. I fly above the Earth, looking down on all the people. The wind blows like glass through my robes and the trees are needles in my skin."

. . . but I cannot control my flight. I can only follow a path set for me. I always dip lower. So low,

so near, the world no longer seems so clear, clean, or undivided.

In my Vision, I fly over a work camp somewhere in eastern Europe. The snow is three, four feet deep, but naked men and women stand out in the cold. Soldiers, too, with swastikas on their helmets, wearing thick coats. They chat about the war, the Russian front. It is so cold I can feel it in my joints.

Beyond the soldiers: the barbed wire and bonfires of the camp. The camp is never more than wire and smoke in the dream. I cannot taste it, hear it, smell it . . . as though it has already faded from the senses into memory.

"I would have gone ice skating today," one soldier says to another, in German. I can hear that voice even now. We should be out ice skating.

Today, the men and women have formed two lines, their lips blue, their eyes dull and straight-ahead. One of the officers comes over, begins to shoot the first line. The second line of workers stands behind the first, watching.

The officer doesn't always shoot them in the head. Sometimes in the stomach. Sometimes the legs. A casual act. A daily routine. Until, finally, the whole line is dead or dying. Quietly. In the blood-clotted snow.

In the dream, I am among them, shot in the stomach so I die slowly.

I watch as the soldiers round up the workers from the second line, bring them back to camp. The bodies, our bodies, remain behind, sprawled and orderly, eyes staring into nothing and nowhere. Why bother with a proper burial?

And so the few of us who are still dying and not dead have some cold comfort: beneath us are others from the days, the weeks, before — frozen, the fingers reaching through the layers of snow, perhaps touching the arms of the newly dead. The roots of this field are fingers, their touch the only eyes for the blinded. I am a corpse. I am a corpse among many corpses, my hands moving ever so slowly toward the light, searching for the brittle fingers of another.

Silence.

Caroline, glancing over at Moriah, saw that she had drawn herself up into a fetal position, the eyes locked on a field of the dead. She reminded Caroline of Rebecca, looking so small, with the gaze so focused and mature.

Moriah's hands shook as she lit a cigarette.

"I've had this ability since the bombs killed my husband and leveled our house. I was unconscious for five days. When I woke, I could see into the minds of the dying. I have died half a hundred times, Caroline."

"They can't be true dreams," Caroline managed to say. "They just can't be. They're nightmares."

"They are real."

"So you try to kill yourself each night."

She shrugged. "One more death? It is not so bad. The bombs gave me this gift. They will take it away from me." *Gift* with a hiss, like a curse.

In the dark, in the flames, they stared at each other, Caroline wearing a puzzled expression.

"Listen," whispered Moriah. "I can hear the bombs again."

They waited in silence as the hum came closer, coupled with the familiar whistle. Caroline watched the religious intensity on Moriah's face, the tight jaw and cocked head. Then the clock tower exploded. The sky blossomed orange. Caroline shrieked from the heat. Under the roar and weight of impact, her skin seemed on fire.

She managed to pin Moriah to the floor as the woman tried to wriggle past her. Debris rained down on their shelter and gouts and torrents of flame shot up. The acrid, acid smell of bombs stabbed through her nostrils. Moriah kicked. Moriah bit. Caroline held on until the body beneath her went limp. The bombs fell and fell and fell, shaking Caroline until all sensation or memory of sensation was gone. She lost hold of Moriah, but it didn't matter: no one could have moved more than a few meters under the onslaught. The rain of rocks and wood made her deaf.

All she could do was make believe that the houses still stood, that people would be bustling about happily in the streets when she opened her eyes, that they would not be pulling corpses from the rubble in the morning.

Later, after the all-clear, the sun was coming up and, incredibly, a light rain had begun to fall. Fires sizzled in the ruins and cats blinked and shook themselves and went about their business with an air of mild reproach.

Caroline raised herself from the wreckage, every muscle, every bone aching. She bled from shrapnel cuts on her arms and legs. Her face was black with soot. Slowly, she began to stumble over the debris, not exactly sure where she was going, and not really caring.

Moriah had vanished.

The soldier came with the photograph six days later, an infantryman who reminded Caroline of George. He came in the evening, grunted greetings from beneath his black raincoat hood, handed her the envelope, and disappeared into darkness.

There seemed to be no urgency involved in opening the envelope, so she put it on the mantel. She was so tired from her rounds — a sour ache she could feel in her bones when she walked — that she simply took off her sweaty uniform, and curled up in bed. Let the bombs come. She no longer cared.

The next morning, she opened the envelope as she sat in the kitchen eating porridge. Light from the kitchen window blurred the features and Caroline had to stare at the photograph for several seconds before she recognized George. He stood in front of a vast stone paw, his hair disheveled. Dunes curved off into the distance.

George smiled, but his eyes had been reduced to pinpricks by the black-and-white photo.

The image had a sharpness, a neatness of composition, which confounded her. On the back had been scrawled, "Hope you are safe and well. An American newsman friend took this. Home soon. I hope. Love, George." The date was four months stale.

When the message began to sound like gibberish, she stopped re-reading it and put it in a box with all the other letters. Someday soon they had to stop coming. They had to.

At the very bottom of the stack was an official letter from the army, dated three months before. It related the circumstances of George Harrington's death, in combat, body irretrievable. George's mother had forwarded it to her.

Then she fled the apartment.

At 11:00 P.M. that night, Caroline pulled back the sheets on two more of the dead. One was a pilot, his face a welter of bone and eyeball and gray matter. A sickly-sweet smell rose from his corpse, diluted only by the sterility of the sheets.

The body he escorted was Moriah's, her eyes closed, her robe of many colors wrapped tightly around her body. The lighting made Moriah paler than alabaster.

Caroline's throat tightened. For the first time in six days, she felt her features constrict in a display of emotion: an ache, a scream, a laugh? She did not know which, but she clenched her jaw against the impulse.

Hands shaking, she opened the robes to reveal pristine flesh beneath, from neck to breasts to thighs. Not a scratch. Caroline ran her hands over the body, searching for a wound, an indentation, anything which might hint at a cause of death; she found nothing but unbroken skin.

As she began a second inspection, Caroline found her eyes drawn unwillingly to the face. Without the smear of lipstick, Moriah did not look mad at all. Just tired. Surely she was only asleep, not dead, *not looking so perfect.* Caroline's stomach almost betrayed her. She swallowed several times.

Her hands, superbly trained, had continued the interrogation. She discovered a sliver of metal, no thicker than a needle, lodged in Moriah's neck.

Later, in a stolen hour of solitude, Caroline found herself again mouthing a litany to a child who seemed not to hear her. Only this time, tears scalded her cheek as she sat with Rebecca.

"What are you looking at?" She shook Rebecca's shoulder. "Say something, damn you!"

Rebecca stared at the wall.

She released Rebecca. She shuddered, bowed her head, and looked up at the wall through her tears. A shock ran through her body. The convulsion surprised her with its intensity, in the way her nerve ends caught fire.

For she did see now, finally, as Rebecca saw, as Moriah had seen, that the wall was not made of plaster, but of bones, skeletons stacked atop each other, the skulls crushed and compressed, the legs fragile as bird wings. A layered field of the dead. She saw George and Moriah, and many others, so many she did not recognize, but who had surely passed through her hands at the hospital.

She let out a sharp, barking laugh. Even as she watched, with the new eyes the bombs had given her, even as she thought herself mad or damned with the Sight, her shoulders slumped, a score of muscles untensing. Here were dozens who could not be saved, already beyond any salvation she could give them.

It would take all her strength just to save herself.

Ω

PAST LIVES

She started out as a dinosaur turd.
That life over, but well lived,
she became a now-extinct type of wild carrot.
Then she was an early mammal, just two inches long,
not very cute, but toothy. Oops. Bad karma
cut her down until she was a rock
in a comet that only visited the sun
once every ten thousand years.

Humans were there the nth time she got back,
but did she get a shot at that? No,
she was a rock in a pasture wall, sandstone.
It wore away, finally, kicked by small boys
into thousands of pebbles, each too small,
for a soul of her caliber.

Life as a blacksnake ennobled her soul,
so next she got to be a richly illuminated
Book of Hours, done for the Countess Mervielle.
In that life, she was soul-mate
to a brilliant sword lost to the Saracens.
Alas, they never actually met,
but knew and loved each other by fame.
The book and the sword lived well
into later centuries, crumbling slowly,
until her soul, dying strengthened and virtued,
was born into a '65 Cadillac, handsome with fins.
In that life she was male, and her love
(who had been a sword) was a loom owned
by a Navaho weaver with tuberculosis.

They were both junked. And now she sits
before me, a fine PC full of service
glorifying man and God whenever she can.
I've lost track of her lover.
Perhaps in some later life she'll live on an Ashram,
human at last, or be a Philosopher King,
or a program for tracking tornadoes,
or a snail, or a dolphin, or nothing at all.

— **Mary A. Turzillo**

LEAVE THEM WHERE THEY LAY
by Valerie Stiller

We buried everything. Especially if it was dear to us, we wrapped it gently in tissue, lovingly placed it in its little box, and buried it. Not too deep, just enough to hide it from other prying ten-year-old fingers, easy enough for our own tiny ten-year-old hands to dig back up. Anything with a lid would do: an old cigar box, or those little plastic treasure chests that bubble gum once came in. We liked to hide things — things that were important to us. We would bury jewelry, doll clothes, food — there was more candy planted in my backyard than tulip bulbs.

Jennie and I weren't close, but for a few weeks that summer we became great friends. Back then, you changed best friends like partners in a square dance. Each new coupling brought a special secret to share, and Jennie and I had our Troll secret. Nobody but us knew where they were buried. They were monstrously small, hideous creatures. Perpetually naked, standing on short, stumpy legs, exposing their oversized navels and lack of sexual characteristics. Their only distinguishing feature was their Troll hair — burnt orange, smoky black, or angry red; that's how you could tell yours from mine. They all had topaz glass eyes which never wavered, never cracked. Forget Barbie and her Playboy figure, her smart designer clothes. Trolls captured our imaginations, my generation's blue Smurfs.

We took these outcasts from a pretty doll world and gave them a new home in the earth of the backyard. Like Egyptian kings and queens, they were wrapped in Troll finery, pink tissues, and bows. Their resting place was tombstoned with a concrete square, **Prop. LILY**. A gas line or town property marker, it made a great name for our club.

"Hey, are you back for good? On your own?" The annual Fourth of July barbecue on our block brought everyone out, the air electric with fireworks smacking overhead, colors illuminating the sky religiously, feverishly. Little kids ran about, armed with sparklers like assault weapons, wanting to play like the big kids, holding the streaming candles at arm's length.

"The kids and I moved back; Pete's in Chicago." I didn't want to pry into Jennie's life, to dig up too many painful feelings. It didn't seem right, somehow; I didn't belong there. I had kept my distance from all my old friends. "You ever see Bobbie or Denise? I haven't; been four or five years now."

"No," she said, "we weren't that close. I always thought you and I were the best set of friends, you know." She smiled.

Why does it take twenty years to admit these things? I never knew she felt that way; I felt guilty and warm all at the same time.

We walked in the dimness of evening, the **rat-ta-ta-tat** of firecrackers snapping in the distance, the air smelling of barbecues overcooking frankfurters and hamburgers. Chains of Chinese lanterns draped the patios and the streets, our block had orgied into one large party, everyone sharing everything. Like all old friends do who don't know each other well enough now to ask about their lives, we reminisced. No chance of bringing up today's fresh reality in favor of yesterday's gentle fantasy. We unearthed the past, finding the memories more inviting and less painful than trying to become new friends all over again.

"Do you remember the beauty contests? The Swing Championship of 1969? The Skateboard Finals?" I still have the scar on my knee from not using the skateboard.

"And Prop LILY, remember? Those poor Trolls buried for what, twenty years? Naked and all, where did we put them?"

My mind saw the four-inch concrete brick that signaled where our childhood treasure was buried.

"Probably rotted away by now pretty good. Or maybe a dog dug it up and ate the damn things."

Jennie's adult cynicism of things that couldn't be reborn once they died hit me. Her angry hopelessness, seeing the past through the limited possibilities of the present, knowing you couldn't have things the way they once were. It's a shame it takes so long to realize it.

Still, we had given power to those Trolls, power from our girlish love. Maybe they had survived the pressures of twenty years, safe and calm in their little box. I pulled a torch out of the neighbor's lawn.

"I think I remember where we put it, between the Dixons' and the Shafts' houses. Let's go."

Jennie led the way; her memory proved better than mine. Like a Girl Scout she found the path, now overgrown by wild berry bushes and forsythia. We stomped along, not worrying about the dark, not worrying about the scratchy bushes or branches pulling at our hair. Staking a claim, I shoved the torch into the ground, marking the land for ours. We sank to our knees, digging with both hands to find the marker bearing our name, looking under the poison ivy, behind the bleeding red flowers.

"Do you see it yet?"

Our shadows danced behind us. The air smelled acrid, like too many firecrackers were popping in one place, too many old leaves were scratching our palms.

"Oh there, see it!" Jennie sounded young and sweet, like a ten-year old spying an ice cream truck down the block. We encircled the square concrete block with our hands, digging out the letters with a stick, the **Prop. LILY** name telling everyone we belonged there.

"Doesn't look like anyone's been here in years. Everything's too overgrown to have been disturbed." I was thankful that no one had come along and moved the earth, found our Troll graveyard, released our past without so much as a glance backward.

"I think they're buried just below the marker, here." I dug my hands into the soil, soft and warm like summer earth should be, receptive to flowers and new life. We pawed away at it, bringing scoops of dirt up and up.

She felt it first.

"Wait, I've got it."

We paused and looked up. Jennie had lost the hardness of a thirty-year-old woman with two kids. I wondered if the years had dropped off my eyes too, leaving a little girl in bell-bottom pants and a mod shirt sitting in my place. We grasped hands and incanted; the words came back: "The Prop LILY Club is called to order. Members only on these grounds." The torch blew behind us, the ivy grew taller on the trees.

In the hole, a small brown top rose hump-backed in the soil.

"It's still intact!" The soil had turned cooler, more fragrant like deep rich coffee beans and my mom's clothes drawers. We lifted out the little plastic chest, once trimmed in fake gold with a make-believe padlock painted on its front.

"I don't remember what else we put in here. I know we buried the Trolls, but did we put in anything else, like jewelry or food or money?" We were whispering, my hair had risen on the back of my neck; the night air had stopped moving.

"I don't know, but I do know my Troll's name is Sam. Sam the Troll." That was important, to remember and be able to call him by name after twenty years; he'd feel special. Jennie placed the little chest on the ground and rubbed her hands together. Two large white firebursts exploded over our heads, falling like snow dissolving in the sky, making a whining noise as they dropped, melting into the night.

The lid snapped off its hinge. A few fat water bugs crawled out but no worms at least; I hated worms. The tissue paper had crumbled away, and one small beige foot popped up in the casket.

"Sam," Jennie murmured, "is that you?"

The firecrackers shouted around us, **blam blam blam**, as she lifted his little carcass out of the box. "Man, those ugly things don't change much, do they?" She held the little body up high in the light; he made abnormal shadows on the ground, his red hair a flame, ten feet long, his belly round and pregnant with twenty years of earth, his topaz eyes gleaming at the arrival of his former mistress.

"Oh, he's perfect!"

He was: not a blemish, no holes from being chewed in the night, no hair loss. Like magic, like a Troll, he had remained intact. Sam could have stayed in his chest for a hundred years and his topaz eyes would still beam fire at us, his large ears would still hear us coming and his outstretched arms would await our grasp, no matter how long we were away.

I looked down. Where was my Troll? Wasn't she in the box with her husband? Samantha had black hair, like mine, usually braided, neat, ladylike, tied with a pink bow. But there was no Troll in the box, just some fake jewelry, a cool Peace symbol, and two pieces of faded paper.

Jennie was overwhelmed with Sam; she held him, wiped away the moisture on his face, combed his hair with her fingers. I opened the note.

This box and its contents are the property of Jennie Passus and Veronica Futoras. Do not take or touch; this is ours, forever and for always.
The Prop LILY Club, May 2, 1971.

Old. I opened the other note. Jennie was walking Sam on the ground, telling him to stretch his legs a little as they were probably cramped. His naked little body made soft footprints on the turned earth; he waddled back and forth, looking like an Indian relic in an archaeological dig. I smiled at her in her adolescent fervor and read the paper in my hand. The handwriting was small and uncomfortable: it didn't look familiar.

Sam, I have gone out to explore. Sorry you won't come with me; I'll miss you. If they ever come back, tell them I've gone to find them. Tell them I understand, and I will be back. I promise you I will.
Samantha. April 12, 1993.

I looked at Jennie, so blissful with her Troll. The dampness had seeped into my jeans; my legs were cold; the shadows behind Sam grew tall and round, like a shadow upon a shadow. The leaves rustled; the firecrackers became more insistent, blowing fast in strings of five and ten.

I wanted very much to bury Sam again, bury him so someone would be here when Samantha returned, not us, just Sam, just the way things were before we dug up our history and played it back again. I wanted very much to put the box back in the ground and leave it there. Leave it for another twenty years, so Samantha could find it looking the same, untouched. Let her find Sam, and he'd tell her we came back for her, but she was gone.

And I didn't want Samantha showing up at my door like an old friend, making me feeling guilty and warm at the same time.

I looked around at the small graveyard we had inadvertently made, dark and lonely, surrounded by tall shapes with sounds hidden in the corners. It was our fault; we should have left them undisturbed, overgrown and buried, like memories are supposed to be. Why does it always take twenty years to discover these things?

The Fourth of July spoke loudly, shoving the night in our faces, a whining red flare burst in the sky, screaming as it fell down on us. Then the night stood still — it could have been 1973 or 1993. I looked into the empty box and wished we had either left the past alone, or had never left it at all. Ω

NEIGHBORHOOD WATCH
by Duncan Adams

It was rumored that Ms Simms was a whore, but I found it hard to believe. She certainly had the looks, but her general demeanor was far too lady-like, and not at all street-wise. It was Ted, our oldest resident, who introduced her at our weekly neighborhood watch meeting.

"Ms Simms has moved into number thirteen," he announced. "And I'm sure we're all happy to welcome her to Saint Mary's Park."

The assent was less than enthusiastic. Most of the residents were far older than Ms Simms and I, and they'd obviously heard the gossip about her morals. Miss Pinchette avoided even a grunt by blowing her nose delicately at the appropriate moment.

"Shall we bring the meeting to order?" said Ted, breaking the embarrassed silence. "Anyone anything to report? Anything suspicious?"

"We *must* do something about the dogs," said Miss Pinchette. "And the cats," she added, glancing at Ms Simms with seemingly equal revulsion.

"Cats are one thing, dogs another," said Ray. "When I was on the force, we learned that the law doesn't expect cat owners to be able to confine them. . . ."

"Yes, yes, yes," interrupted Miss Hinchcliffe, our retired headmistress. "It's dogs we're more concerned about. I thought we put young Darren in charge."

"Yes, you did," I said hurriedly. "I've scared quite a lot off, but there's a problem. It's the timing, you see. Whenever I'm available, the dogs are nowhere to be found. But I'm keeping my eyes open."

"He's doing the best he can," said Ted dismissively. "Anything else?"

"Courting couples," said Miss Pinchette. "I found one of those . . . those . . . rubber things . . . it made me feel quite faint, I can tell you. . . ."

"No need to worry on that score," said Ray. "Caught them at it only last night. They won't be back in a hurry, no fear."

"Anything else?" said Ted, preparing to wind up the meeting.

"Actually, yes." It was Ms Simms, raising her hand as though she were back at school. "But I'm not sure I should say anything, what with me being new and all."

"We're all equal here," said Ted. "We're only interested in keeping the neighborhood up to scratch. Fire away, young lady."

"Well, I was wondering about the drugs. . . ."

"Drugs!" I was on my feet, fists clenching and unclenching, rage in my voice.

"Steady on, lad," said Ted, pushing me back into my seat. "Young Darren had a bad experience with drugs," he explained to Ms Simms. "*Very* bad. But none of us likes drugs. Tell us what you know."

"Well," she hesitated, "it was early this morning, about one-thirty I guess. I heard voices in the trees behind my place, where the developers have just started excavating, and I went to investigate. . . ."

"Dashed brave of you," said Ray.

"Actually, I kept well out of sight, but I heard every word that was said. There were three blokes, and they were setting up a big deal. Two kilos of crack, they said, and it's to be tomorrow night, same time, same place. I think crack's that awful cocaine stuff. Anyway, I was going to tell the police. . . ."

"No point," said Ted. "They never listen."

"He's right," agreed Ray. "I used to be a copper myself, and I know. We've got to deal with this ourselves."

"Count me in," I said. "In spades!"

For technical reasons, I never rise until just after midnight. Nor do any of the other residents. I can usually hear the last echoes of the twelfth chime of Saint Mary's clock as I sit up in my grave.

The others rose swiftly too. As always, we had little energy on first awakening, but there were ways to remedy that, and since we had a lot to do, that was our first priority.

Jasper used to be an electrical engineer, and he's one of our most useful residents. We clustered around him, laying our faintly shimmering hands on his insubstantial head, feeding him as much of our energy as we dared to spare. Only his right arm became solid, but it was enough.

We made our way to where the grave diggers had left their mechanical excavator. Jasper's reinvigorated arm was sufficient to start it, and then to manoeuvre it over the precise location required. Soon, there was a sizeable hole. Jasper climbed down and continued the excavation by hand until the main electric cable that fed the church was exposed.

Sparks flashed briefly, and Jasper straightened his back triumphantly.

One at a time, we reached into the hole and touched the nail Jasper had thrust through the cable. I'd only done this a couple of times before, and I found it unnerving. It was hard enough getting used to being a ghost, but the semi-solid, pseudo-ectoplasmic phase was rather irritating. Like being made of half-set jelly. We can change our shapes if we want, but mostly we stick to what we were like in our latter incarnate years, and that's what we did that night.

"Ms Simms!" exclaimed the Misses Pinchette and Hinchcliffe in unison. "Really!"

Ted coughed, then turned away. Ray, Jasper, and all the other men, myself especially included, ogled. "Lord," gasped Jasper. "Ain't that somethin'?"

All doubts concerning her occupation vanished as, her drab respectability defiantly discarded, Ms Simms pirouetted gaily. She wore black, skin-tight boots reaching halfway up her thighs, giving way to black fishnet tights and a skimpy leather one-piece jerkin out of which her breasts threatened to leap. Spiked bracelets gripped her wrists, and she held a thick bull whip loosely in one hand. "This is my *punishment* outfit," she said. "It seemed appropriate."

"Come on, everyone," said Ted, vainly trying to avert his eyes from Ms Simms. "We've got things to do. Not much time, you know. Go to it, Darren."

So, for the moment, the spell was broken. I knew my job, and I went about it quickly. Down by the stream, in the older part of the graveyard, the church railings had rusted badly, and as I pulled and twisted, a dozen sharply-pointed metal spears were soon lying by my feet. Gathering them up, I rejoined the others, and distributed them. Ms Simms said "thank you" so sexily that my ectoplasmic knees trembled with excitement.

Then we hid in the undergrowth behind Ms Simms's grave, and waited.

It was just after one that we heard the cemetery gate squeak open. Although there was only a half moon, the sky was clear, and the two men fumbled their way between the graves.

"Shush now," whispered Ted unnecessarily. "Everyone quiet."

As they entered the uncleared land behind Ms Simms's grave, the two men lit a torch, and stopped in the clearing Ms Simms had told us about. From their conversation, it was obvious they were waiting for the third man. The one with the crack itself. Although I'd been heavily into the drug scene, I didn't know either of them. I had been a user, not a pusher, and neither of them had ever sold me anything.

But the third man, when he arrived, was entirely different. I forgot all about Ted's carefully formulated plan when I saw the familiar features of Eddie (Pothead) Manton, local pusher, and my most hated enemy.

"You!" he gasped as I crashed out of the brambles. "But I thought you were dead!"

I've got to give Ted and Ray their due; they acted fast. Even the Misses Pinchette and Hinchcliffe were in the ring of angry ghosts who surrounded the three criminals, goading them into a huddle with the spears. Ted and Ray pulled me away from Pothead, my nails gouging his throat as they forced my fingers away.

"That bastard sold me bad H," I shouted. "That's what killed me! I wouldn't *be* here if it weren't for that bastard!"

"Take it easy, son," said Ray, still holding me. He waited until I stopped struggling, then said: "If I let you go, will you keep your hands off him?"

I reluctantly agreed, and he released me.

"Now you three listen to me," said Miss Pinchette, waving her railing at the three trembling men. "This is a decent neighborhood, and before we let you go, you have to promise never to come back. . . ."

"Bullshit!" I shouted, pointing at Pothead. "This man *kills* people. We can't just let him go!"

That caused a great debate. Since the other two weren't known killers, we released them after making them give appropriate promises, but we hung on to Pothead. Then he began to gibber and plead, and I think it was partly because we were losing power and becoming rather ghostly again. We could still brandish the railings, though, and that kept him under control.

"As ye sow, so shall ye reap," said Mortimer, our resident cleric, and the one I thought would have been most opposed to taking the law into our own hands. "The vengeance of the Lord must be visited upon him."

"I agree," said Ray. "As a policeman, I've seen the misery drugs cause. You've only got to look at young Darren here — dead at nineteen."

Soon after that, the argument wasn't *whether* we should kill him, but who would actually do it. As we argued, Pothead begged, pleaded, promised to reform, shat himself, begged a lot more, and generally made a pathetic exhibition of himself.

"No, not you, Darren," said Ted when I immediately volunteered. "This is justice, not vengeance. If we're going to execute him, then it must be done dispassionately."

"Let me," said Ms Simms huskily. "Punishment is my specialty."

There was a strange silence as we all considered the implications of her offer.

"Yes, but how?" said Ted when no one objected.

"Leave it to me," she said, slinking up to Pothead, then cracking her whip right in front of his terrified eyes. "Run, you coward!" she shrieked. "Run for your life!"

As he took to his heels, we all thought she was allowing him to escape, but we soon realized otherwise. It was a cruel cat-and-mouse game, and it was one she couldn't lose. Whereas Pothead scrambled frantically over and around the gravestones, Ms Simms simply flowed through them. After only a brief few seconds of unimpeded flight, she appeared in front of him, cracking her whip, and screaming at him in a demoniac manner. Even we ghosts were afraid of her, and it soon became very clear that something other than simple retribution was driving her.

Sobbing, Pothead collapsed on a crumbling grave, his breath rasping, chest heaving, and eyes bulging. Ms Simms was metamorphosing into something softer, and as she dropped her whip we saw she was now dressed in a frilly silk negligée. At first, Pothead hardly seemed to notice, then he relaxed a little as he saw how unthreatening she had become.

"This is how *he* liked me to look," she said softly. "He was one of my best clients. Would you like to know who he was?"

Pothead made no reply, but tried to burrow down into the gravestone, away from Ms Simms and the rest of us.

"Oh, my gosh," gasped Ted as Ms Simms slipped the negligée over her head, then let it fall to the ground. The Misses Hinchcliffe and Pinchette turned away, but the rest of us stood gazing at the heavenly body exposed to our view. Only Pothead seemed unimpressed.

"Wouldn't you like to know who he was?" coaxed Ms Simms, her bare feet making crunching sounds in the ornamental marble chippings as she advanced on him. "Don't you think I have the most divine body? *He* thought so. Do you know who he was?"

"No," wheezed Pothead. "Please let me go."

"Take off your clothes," she demanded, her long legs either side of him as she gazed down at him aloofly.

There were a few moments of awkward scrabblings, then he lay naked and scrawny on the grave, the divine Ms Simms above him. "Please let me go," he whimpered.

She bent her knees, straddling him, her face only inches from his. "He liked to nuzzle my neck," she said, presenting her white neck to Pothead's lips. "Go on, kiss it!"

Pothead's lips touched the ectoplasm, tasting the dead flesh, then recoiling. "He was on acid," said Ms Simms. "But I didn't know it. He must have thought he was a vampire or something, because he bit straight through my jugular. Like Darren, I don't like pushers."

"Oh, my God," sobbed Pothead.

"Not out of vengeance, Ms Simms," implored Mortimer, but it made no difference.

Two huge canine fangs sprang from Ms Simms's lips, and as Pothead shrieked, she drove them into his neck. There was a wet, sucking sound that went on for a few seconds as Pothead's legs thrashed uselessly around, then he went very still. Ms Simms lifted her head, wiping the gore from her mouth with the back of her hand. "Glad I'm not a vampire," she said as Mortimer crossed himself. "It's quite unpleasant really."

No one commented.

"What do we do now?" asked Mortimer, his voice hushed. "Shall we put him in the hole where the electric cable is? I could read the burial service, and then we could just fill him in."

"Oh yes, that's a *great* idea," said Ray. "And what do we do tomorrow night when he applies to join the neighborhood watch? Eh?"

"Sorry," said Mortimer. "I didn't think."

"He's not staying here," said Miss Pinchette, glancing disdainfully at Ms Simms. "We need altogether a better class of person."

"We just leave him," said Ray. "He'll be found tomorrow when the gravediggers come. Probably be cremated, I should think. There'll be another vampire scare, but what can they do? Drive stakes through our hearts? Big deal!"

"Dawn's not far off," said Ted, looking at the sky. "We'd better be getting back."

I lingered with Ms Simms for a short while after they went. The power from the cable had now completely ebbed away from us; we were tangible to each other, of course, but not to the living world.

"Perhaps you'd like to come back to my place," I suggested. "I can't offer you any coffee or anything. . . ."

"No, you can't," she said wistfully. "But I noticed you had some rather interesting marble chippings by your headstone."

"Interesting marble chippings?" I said, puzzled.

"Silly boy," she said as she gripped my arm. "Come on, let's go."   Ω

CHAUNT OF THE GRAY MAN

Grey my horse
and grey my mantle
Grey the hour of my coming.
Grey my horse
and grey my mantle.
Grey my hounds that course beyond,
Mine is the name
spoken in whispers,
Mine is the song
that the starving sparrow sings.

Grey the grass
and grey the forest.
Grey the leaves at my passing.
Grey the grass
and grey the forest.

Grey the sun and grey the moon.
Mine is the name
spoken in whispers.
Mine is the song
that the starving sparrow sings.

Grey my hand
and grey my visage.
Grey the clouds and grey the wind.
Grey my hand
and grey my visage.
Grey the flesh that I have touched.
Mine is the name
spoken in whispers.
Mine is the song
that the starving sparrow sings.

— t. Winter-Damon

THE DWARF HOLÓBOS & THE SWORD HOGBITER

by Lord Dunsany
illustrated by Frank Kelly Freas

Now the King of the Bad Countries went to war with the King of the Birch Lands, because of his golden whiskers, which he was wishful to seize. And the army of that first king marched westwards until it came to a forest. And his name was Thlog. A hundred men they were, and they came to the dark forest, where night fell early; and when the night was come they camped under the beeches. And the stars sailed slowly over the tops of the trees, and the blackbirds sang and it was dawn and the army awoke. "So far so good," said the captains in the morning. "We are well on our way to the Birch Lands. But now we must enquire more particularly of the way, lest we miss the frontiers of the Kingdom of Birchlands and meet with the army of some kingdom with which our master is not at war." And to this end they were all agreed, and to that end sent out scouts.

Now there was a cottage in that forest in which an old woman dwelt with her son, who was a charcoal-burner. And the scouts came to the door, and knocked thereon, and the young man opened it and saw the soldiers and called out with delight to his mother that soldiers had come; for he had never seen soldiers before. And they asked him to tell them the way to the Kingdom of Birchlands.

But he answered that there were no roads through the forest, so that none in the forest knew the way to anywhere, excepting only the witches; so that in order to find the way they must go to the house of a witch. So they asked him where they might find the house of a witch, and he said, "In the deeps of the forest." And they asked him to show them the way to the deeps of the forest, and he took his hat and his staff and away they went.

Now the way to the deeps of the forest was easily found, for they only needed to go where the trees grew thicker and thicker, and when they came to where the trunks were so close together that a man could only barely pass between tree and tree, they were there. And they all looked round for a while and could see nothing, and then one of them smelt smoke and, walking in the direction of the smell, they came to a cottage older and odder than aught they had seen before. The walls were of gnarled trunks, and twisted beams made its door, and the windows were of dark and bubbly blue through which one could no more see in than one can see to the floor of the ocean. "This," said one of the scouts, "must surely be the house of a witch."

"That is so," came the voice of the witch from inside the cottage.

And the door slowly opened, and an old witch appeared. And one of the scouts asked her respectfully if she were a witch.

"So it is believed by the wise," she said, "and feared by the foolish, and known to the beasts of the forest, who keep their counsel."

"Then will you please tell our army the way to the Kingdom of the Birchlands," the scout asked her.

"And for what purpose do you seek the way to that kingdom?" the witch asked him.

"We go to smite off the golden whiskers of the king of that land," he replied. "For our king is at war with him and would have his whiskers, and has promised his eldest daughter's hand in marriage to whoever will bring those golden whiskers back."

"Know you," replied the witch, "that those whiskers can only be severed by the sword Hogbiter, and by no other weapon soever?"

"We knew it not till you told us," the scout replied.

"It is so," said the witch.

"Then be so courteous," they said, "as to tell us the whereabouts of the sword Hogbiter, that we may come by it and strike off the golden whiskers, and that one of us may be given the hand of the king's daughter."

"It lies upright," she said, "in the heart of the oldest oak in the forest."

"And where may that be?" they asked her.

"In the deeps of the forest," she said, "not far from here. You'll know it by its size."

Impatiently then the scouts set off through the forest to find the oldest oak. But the young charcoal-burner, whose name was Igdrathion, stayed behind with the witch, for he mused that it was one thing to find the largest oak, and another to cut it down. So he said to her as soon as the scouts were gone, "Good Madam Witch, pray tell me how one may cut through that oldest oak."

"Ah-ha," she said. And in the silence that followed her remark they soon heard the sounds of chopping, for the scouts had found the oak and were hewing it.

"The oak," said the witch, "is thicker than any rich man's house, and their little swords will not reach the centre thereof in a year."

"And what may reach it sooner?" asked young Igdrathion.

"Only the axe," she replied, "of the dwarf Holóbolos."

"And where does he dwell?" he asked her.

"He dwells where none may find him," she said, "but by calling his name aloud in the depths of the forest, at dawn when the blackbirds sing."

"And for what will he chop?" said he.

"For the sheer love of chopping," she said; "and for my sake, if you mention my name."

"And your name, Madam Witch?" he asked her.

"The enchantress Lirila," she replied.

And Igdrathion thanked her gratefully, and went back to his mother's cottage. And all that day the sound of the chopping of swords was heard from the trunk of the oldest oak.

And early the next day Igdrathion went out of the cottage before the blackbirds sang and all was still in the forest, and it appeared yet to be night, and suddenly one wild, clear voice rang out, so wild and shrill Igdrathion knew not what it could be; but before it ceased, and while yet his wonder lived, the chorus of all the blackbirds broke out and joined it, and he knew it was only the voice of the first of the blackbirds. And, standing there while they sang, he called aloud the name of the dwarf Holóbolos.

And the dwarf answered with an unearthly grunt, and came waddling towards Igdrathion out of the undergrowth. He was six foot eight, not in height, for he was a dwarf, but across the breadth of his shoulders. And he carried an axe in the shape of the moon when it is five days old. And Igdrathion called out to him in the dark of the wood, "For the sake of the enchantress Lirila." And the dwarf answered, "For that I will do all things."

And Igdrathion said to him, "I would have you chop."

And Holóbolos answered, "Chopping I love above all things."

"Let us haste, then," said Igdrathion, "and we will go to the oldest oak in the forest. For there is an army in the forest and they seek to cut it down."

"They will not cut down that oak," said the dwarf, "for a year."

"How long will it take you to cut into the middle of it?" asked Igdrathion.

"Ten minutes," the dwarf replied.

"Then there is time," said Igdrathion. "Shall we go to the oak tonight while the army is sleeping?"

"We will," grunted Holóbolos.

"There is time to spare," repeated Igdrathion. "How shall we spend it?"

"In sleep," said Holóbolos, "the sleep from which you awakened me." And he rolled back among the bracken and hazels and saplings, and grunted three times and was asleep again. And faintly there tapped through the forest the sounds of the swords on the oak. But Igdrathion went back to his mother's cottage.

"What are you going to do with the dwarf Holóbolos?" said his mother, for she had heard the grunts of the dwarf.

"He is going to get me the sword Hogbiter," he replied, "from the heart of the oldest oak."

"And what are you going to do with the sword Hogbiter?" she asked him.

"I am going to smite off the golden whiskers that grow on the King of the Birch Lands," he answered.

"And what do you want with those whiskers?" she said.

"The army want them," he told her, "the army that came to the forest."

And still the old woman would not let the matter drop, but went on with her questions. "And what use has the army," she asked, "for the golden whiskers that grow on the King of the Birch Lands?"

"Much use," he said. "For they take them back to their king, who has promised to whoever shall bring them to him, the hand of his daughter in marriage."

"The hand of his daughter!" she said. "And shall it go to one of them?"

"To whom else?" said Igdrathion.

"Why not to you, if she be worthy of you," his mother replied.

But no such fancy had come to Igdrathion.

"Should I marry the dawn?" he said. "Or one of the stars?"

"Aye," she replied. "If they were worthy of you."

And while he wondered, she spoke thus: "See now, the golden whiskers that grow on the King of the Birch Lands are among the seven wonders of the world that are next after the first seven. Moreover they are the prop and pillar of Birchlands, and the envy of the Bad Countries. When, therefore, they are smitten off from the head of that king, the power of Birchlands will fall and its army will all surrender. But if they go up against Birchlands with weapons that cannot smite away its prop and support they will never overcome Birchlands, but will be overcome by it. Aid them not therefore, but bide your time, and see what may be won by means of the sword Hogbiter."

And Igdrathion said no more, but silently thought of the King of the Bad Countries' daughter.

Now the day wore away as other days, and there came the hour when the birds are singing and dwarfs awake from sleep and witches come out of their houses. And Igdrathion heard the sound of the chopping of oak grow fainter till it had ceased. And as soon as the silence was heavy all round the oak in the distance, Igdrathion went to the undergrowth and awoke the dwarf Holóbolos, and together they went through the forest; and they went quietly, as foxes go, and all that prowl in the night, and so came to the oldest oak.

"There it stands," said Igdrathion.

And the dwarf Holóbolos said nothing, but only took one long breath and lifted the axe that was the shape of the moon on its fifth day. The handle was all of iron, but the great head was of steel, and shone like the moon on water. He lifted it and poised it there for an instant, and the whole vast breadth of the dwarf rippled as he brought the axe-head down, and it entered the oak as a shovel enters snow. For the next ten minutes the dwarf shovelled the oak, and the smooth edge of the axe shone still as bright as the moon, and no dint or scratch whatever was seen upon it.

And then at the end of ten minutes, from one of his hail of blows the great axe came back with a gash cut into its shining face, as though it were a slice of melon that had been beaten against a knife. And the dwarf looked at it and knew that he had stricken against the sword Hogbiter, because there was nothing else upon Earth that could dint his axe. "Lo!" he said. "We have come on the sword Hogbiter."

"Be careful, I pray you," requested Igdrathion, "not to harm the sword with your axe."

"There is nothing," said the dwarf, "that can harm Hogbiter, but the comet that shall be the end of the world, if it hits the sword fair in the middle; and the time of the comet is not yet."

"And when will the comet come?" asked Igdrathion.

But the dwarf had turned away from him back to his work, and was shovelling the oak away from around the sword Hogbiter. So five more minutes passed; and at the end of that time the sword fell clear of the oak.

"What shall we do now?" said Igdrathion. For though he had the sword, there was a whole army in the forest, and all looking for that same sword.

"She'll know," said the dwarf Holóbolos, and he pointed to where the house of the witch was hid in the deeps of the forest. So Igdrathion took the sword and went to the witch's house, with Holóbolos ambling behind him. The sword was long and straight, and not gross like the axe, and sapphires were shining dimly in the hilt, and the straight blade shone like a beam of stormy sunlight, and it was a joy to behold.

And when they came to the house of the witch among the boles of the beeches, and Igdrathion had knocked on the door and the door opened and the witch appeared in the doorway in her black cloak, the dwarf Holóbolos abased himself kneeling, with his forehead and all his huge breadth on the ground. And Igdrathion bowed and said, "Madam enchantress, I have the sword Hogbiter here. What shall I do with it?"

And she said, "Keep it."

And he said, "What of the army?"

And she turned to the dwarf Holóbolos, still prostrate among the mosses, and said to him, "What are its ways? For I know little of military things."

And he raised his head from the earth and said, "The scouts that work at the oak will be relieved, and others will cut tomorrow."

"Then" said she, "you must hide another sword in the oak and cover it up as well as you may, and let them take it and fight the King of the Birch Lands with that, and not with the sword Hogbiter.

"And where, O enchantress," said the dwarf Holóbolos, "shall we find another sword?"

And the enchantress smiled and said, "There came a knight once to this forest and came to my house, and forgot the world and had no longer any care for its ways, and left his sword here when he went. Here it is, and you may leave this sword in the tree."

So the dwarf and Igdrathion thanked her and went away with the two swords. And she went back into her cottage and shut out the glow of her candlelight from the forest, and Igdrathion and Holóbolos hurried away in the dark, for they wished to hide the sword in the oldest oak before light should come to the forest and the army wake and return to the tree.

"The scouts," said Holóbolos, as he piled in their places again the huge blocks that he had smitten out of the oak, "will boast that they cut in further than they did, and the new ones that will cut on the morrow, when they find their work going easily, will give the credit of it to their own industry."

So he piled up the fallen blocks in the gap in the oldest oak round the sword that the knight had forgotten, and Igdrathion watched him dimly, for it was night, while an owl observed him shrewdly from one of the high branches. And long before the first blackbird knew of the dawn, the work was finished, although untidily, and when the scouts marched up to the tree in the morning they set to their work of chopping without observing too closely that it had all been chopped already. And so they came to the sword, and a good sword of its kind, but not magic.

And the first thing that Igdrathion did when he got back to his mother's house was to cut two strips of leather out of a hide the length of the sword, and he laid them together and his mother stitched them, and there was the scabbard. And his mother made him a belt of another strip and fastened the scabbard to it, and he put the belt around him and was ready to travel. Then he said farewell to his mother and to the dwarf Holóbolos, and set out for the Bad Countries, while the army marched off with its sword, going the other way. And going the other way they came to the border of Birchlands, but Igdrathion saw the sunset shine on the spires of the palace of the king that had sent them to war.

Now Igdrathion knew well enough, as he walked over the bright grass of the Bad Lands, that he was only a woodman, dressed in the smoky garb of a charcoal-burner. Yet he knew that he had only to draw the sword Hogbiter for its flash to illuminate him, and so to dazzle the eyes of any regarding him that they would scarce notice his charcoal-burner's clothes. And so, in spite of his garb, he walked with an air, which was noticed by the small creatures that hid in the grass, so that they knew that he went on a journey of which great things were to come.

But Igdrathion knew not what was to come. He only knew that the hand of the eldest princess of the House of the Bad Countries was to be given to him who should bring to the King of those lands the golden whiskers of the King of the Birch Lands. But what manner of woman she was he did not know, scarce knowing if she were human or divine, or if she was among vast unattainable forces such as precipices, icebergs, or the aurora that shone to the north. Therefore he had determined to go and look, a thing that he dared to do now that he had beside him the sword Hogbiter. And as the sun went under the rim of the Bad Countries, and the light went out of the grass like a smile that has faded, but the spires of the palace shone still, and flashed and rejoiced and twinkled, Igdrathion came to the palace gates, whence the long shadows were gone.

Now it so chanced that it was the custom of the eldest princess of that kingdom to sit with her maids in a balcony overlooking the evening at the hour when the moths were about and the odour of flowers arose and the birds sang and the west was a glory, for she greatly cared for these things. And sitting among her maids Igdrathion saw her, gazing into the evening. And the princess looking down from her balcony chanced to see him then, a youth untroubled as yet by time, and unfamiliar with cities. And he, looking up, perceived her glowing among her maidens, but had not yet seen her eyes, although a glow came from them along the shades of the evening. And still, though he saw her beauty, he was not sure as yet whether it was all human beauty, or of things remote though earthly.

But at that moment, the eldest princess, whose name was Bourodilla, said to her maidens, "He has a sword. Perchance he brings us news of the war. Go therefore one of you and ask him what news there be, and if there have been battles yet."

So one of her maidens slipped back through the window and through three rooms of the palace and ran out and found Igdrathion. And to him she said, "Princess Bourodilla would know what news you have on the war that the army is waging."

And he said to the maiden, "I will tell the princess."

And she said to him, "That is not necessary. But tell me what news there be, and I will tell the princess."

And he made answer, "The talk of armies is not for maidens. But I will bring to the princess myself the report of the going up of the army and all its doings."

And when she found that she could not shake him and that he would not deliver his report to her, the maiden brought him with her to the palace, through the great doorway and up the stairs and through three rooms and out on to the balcony where the Princess Bourodilla sat, beautiful in the evening, and the moths sailed to and fro.

And he saw that she was beautiful, but so were the maidens round her. Then she moved her head and turned her eyes towards him, and in all the full glow of them he knew then what beauty was. And the glow of that beauty flashed in on his mind more suddenly than the glow of dawn through the forest, stealing among still branches over the dew in spring to gleam upon the anemones, but there was the same serenity, waking in him the same wonder, and the light was in them such as came to the forest, when he felt that such a light had never come there before, whether dawn brought it every day or not; and he waited for her to speak, as he sometimes waited to hear the chorus of blackbirds before the forest woke. That her eyes were blue he did not so much notice, as that he was held in their light, as the sunlight holds the forest when all its life is awake. And as birds soared up to the sunlight and butterflies woke and flowers opened and shone, so there awoke in him new thoughts and new inspirations, and he dreamed of adventurous quests and of what he would do with the sword.

"Whence are you?" she said to him.

And he said, "From the forest."

"And is the forest fair?" she asked.

"Fair," he said, "as the loveliest shell from which men gather pearls in the deeps of the fairest sea."

"Fair as a pearl?" she said.

"No. Fair as a shell," he said, "from which the pearl has been taken."

And she knew he meant that, though the forest was fair, it lacked the beauty at which he was gazing now.

"And is the army enjoying its war?" she asked.

And he told how the army had marched on through the forest, and how there burned in each man the hope to seize and smite off the golden whiskers that grew on the King of the Birch Lands. But of the sword Hogbiter he said nothing.

"Would you like to seize those whiskers?" she said to him then.

When she said this the sword Hogbiter throbbed in its sheath, for the magic that was in the sword could understand words. But Igdrathion said nothing, not knowing what words could say, and stood

THE DWARF HOLÓBOS & THE SWORD HOGBITER

there gazing and thought of the sword and dreamed of what it might do. And dreaming still he bowed and turned away, and went from the balcony and through the rooms and down the stairs and away out of the palace, the tips of whose spires were still darting their twinkling rays over Bad Lands.

Now as soon as it was light on that day on which Igdrathion went to the palace of the King that ruled over Bad Lands, the army of that King away in the forest woke early, and twenty of its men were sent to the oldest oak, and there they chopped and found the sword as I said, though it was not the true sword Hogbiter. And it was not yet noon when they got it out of the tree; and they brought it to their captains, who, believing it to be Hogbiter, marched away with it triumphant towards the country of Birchlands.

And they marched for the rest of the day and for most of the next day, sleeping two more nights in the forest, but in the light of the third day's morning they found a country beyond the forest, wide and sunny and open, in which white trees were shining. And on the next day after that, whether it was by luck or careful planning who shall say, for none may wholly estimate the part that luck plays in war, they came to the country of Birchlands, fair and bright in the morning. Fair and bright it shone, an open and sunny downland, and afar on a fold of the downs its little capital stood.

Then the Chief Captain drew the sword that he deemed was Hogbiter, and all the captains drew their swords and the soldiers lowered their pikes, as the army spread out from its line of march and assumed the line of battle; and in this guise, this stern array, they advanced against the city wherein its king ruled over Birchlands. And, as they advanced, the army of Birchlands gathered along the walls, and flashes gleamed in the city, like the flash of lightning reflected on to the clouds when the storm is far away. These flashes that shone, though dimly, now and then from the city, arose from the activities of the King when he saw his capital threatened, and the magic that began to glow in his whiskers.

Some fighting there was at the gates when the army arrived, but it was little more than a skirmish, because the main defence of the city, and all that land, lay behind the wall of the palace; it was the redoubtable, unbreakable, magical, golden whiskers that grew on the head of the King. There are many heavy tomes of magic lore in the world, bound in dark, old leather and locked with hasps, and not all of them have I read; wherefore I cannot say whether those whiskers or the axe of the dwarf Holóbolos were stronger. I believe that they were of an exactly equal magic, and that, though it was certain that the axe of Holóbolos could not cut them, yet they could never gnash the axe of Holóbolos.

But certain it is that no other weapon on earth could equal the hardness of the golden whiskers, and only one could sever them, and that one was not the sword the Chief Captain bore, as he now advanced on the King, who stood before his throne with his magic shining. And on these whiskers now the army of Birchlands had fallen back fighting, as an army falls back on the ramparts of some great defence which is to hold back an enemy for a day and brighten history for ages. And the army of the Bad Countries wavered before those whiskers, but the Chief Captain advanced alone, gripping the sword that he believed to be Hogbiter.

And the King of the Birch Lands stood there before him dressed in his suit of armour, hardened by labour of dwarfs through days and nights to make it proof against any blow of a sword. All but his whiskers and mouth and eyes were covered with armour, and even over his mouth and eyes there were bars of steel, forming a grid through which no sword could pass; only his whiskers were completely bare, for them, being harder than any armour in all the world, he left glittering outside the steel; and there they shone, making all the armour bright, and the magic of them, unencumbered by armour, exerted its influence freely over all the ways of the city; and the opposing army could feel the force of it, as a traveller feels the strength of a mighty wind blowing down from a mountain. This the Chief Captain felt, as all the rest, but he raised aloft the sword that he deemed

Hogbiter and brought it crashing down on the golden whisker that grew on the left of the King.

Though I speak of a wine-glass cast to a marble floor, or a flower-pot hurled at a garden wall in anger, or ice of a lake that is broken by rocks of an avalanche, yet will I not avail to give any picture of how that sword was shivered on touching the golden whisker. And the King of the Birch Lands smiled under his armour, and the golden whiskers gleamed. And in the gleam of the golden whiskers the host of the King of the Bad Countries was discomforted, and the power of the magic that blew against them grew stronger, and they drew back and the armies of Birchlands poured after them. Thus was the army defeated which went up against Birchlands, and whether by magic or fighting no historian cares, but only that there was defeat, come how it may, and that victory was with the Birch Lands. Then the army of the Bad Countries retreated, and came again to the forest and marched back through its dimness and home to its barracks, telling all, and truly telling them that they were only defeated by magic; though how they were defeated no chronicler cares.

Now, while this army did half a day's march after finding the false sword, Igdrathion did a day's march in the other direction; and, marching back by night, he was only half a day's march behind them next day at dawn. Round about dawn he rested; then he ate oatcake that he had in a wallet and drank at a stream and started later than the starting of the army, but travelled more swiftly than they, as a man alone does travel. A glimpse or two he had of birds disturbed and a few cattle running, but no other sign he saw of the routed army. In the early morning of the day after the battle he came to a gate of the city from which their king ruled Birchlands, and flags flew from every tower in honour of victory, and carillons were ringing in every spire. The gate was open and the sentries rejoicing, and Igdrathion went in between them unmolested, and unmolested he walked up the city's widest way. None heeded him in his russet dress, nor heeded Hogbiter hidden in strips of hide.

And so unhindered he came to the marble steps of the palace, and up their brightness he walked and came to the main door, which was opened to let the melody of musicians flow from the court and rejoice the popular streets with their music in honour of victory. And while the courtiers danced he marched on alone and came to the King of the Birch Lands, who sat high on his throne, letting the magic of his golden whiskers flow forth to mellow his realm. And the King was still in the armour in which he had won his victory, and the golden whiskers came glittering out through two slits in the helmet, and shone as rivulets in a golden dawn flowing over boulders of iron.

And Igdrathion said, "It is war," and stepped up to him, lifting the sword Hogbiter. And the King of the Birch Lands drew his sword at the same time, and lifted it up to parry, but lifted it idly, and smiled as he lifted it, a smile that was hidden in the dark of his helmet; but the golden whiskers glowed as though they shared to the full with their king his belief that nothing could ever prevail against them. And as they shone like two increasing dawns, brightening the palace and the ways of the city beyond, Igdrathion smote with his sword at the one on the left, and Hogbiter went through the sword which the King held up to parry, as a well-swung scythe will go through the stalk of a daffodil, and went on and came to the whisker and went through that also, and stopped on the armour across which the whisker flowed, for no more force was left in it after the tremendous achievement of severing what could be severed by no other sword in the world.

As the whisker fell Igdrathion lifted his sword again and with a backhanded stroke smote off the right-hand whisker, which had no longer even a sword to guard it, vain though that guarding would be. And as he struck through this whisker the other one fell to the marble with the clatter as of the fall of great engines of iron, and the fall of the right-hand whisker resumed their reverberations; and a glow went out of the palace and out of the city, and over all the kingdom of Birchlands there came a moment like the moment at which the sun has gone under the earth and the light over all the land, for that was the light of the sun, but from the kingdom of Birchlands itself its own glow was gone, for the magic with which it shone was gone with the golden whiskers. And with the loss of that magic a listlessness fell on the army, and the courtiers ceased to dance and rejoicings died in the streets and all the musicians stopped in the midst of their music.

And Igdrathion gathered up the golden whiskers, and their magic which had opposed him was now with him, for magic has no care as to whom it serves. And he walked out of the palace holding the golden whiskers, and a glow was all about him as he went. Some there were who might have raised a sword against Hogbiter, but when they saw the sword rejoicing in Igdrathion's right hand, and the golden whiskers glittering in his left, they knew, and could even feel, there was too much magic for man. Moreover, the magic now in his left hand was the very magic that had ruled that kingdom for ages, for the golden whiskers that grew on their king were hereditary.

So Igdrathion marched away, and even dogs fled from his coming, fearing the magic they felt in the golden whiskers, or else in the sword Hogbiter. More than the golden whiskers he did not take, for he lived a long while ago, a simple mind, the child of a simple age, waging a simple war. It was still in the early morning as he marched away from the city, and when noon was over those lands he was far away, going blithely, singing a song. So he passed through the country of Birchlands, until before sunset there darkened the distant horizon the low line of the forest. It was time already to rest, but he marched on, though tired, so as to sleep in the forest, for its dark glades were as home to him. And night fell and the stars were bright ere he reached the edge of the forest, and he marched but a short way in and lay down and slept on the bracken.

When dawn came to the forest and the chorus of birds awoke him, Igdrathion felt a glow in his heart, which shone from his high achievement, before he even saw the rays of the sun. Then he ate a meal from his wallet and, rising up, set off to look for the dwarf Holóbolos. And far he marched to find him, and the sun went under the branches, and again he lay down on the bracken and slept till the blackbirds sang. Now this being the hour at which the dwarf might be summoned, he called him many times by his uncouth name, till the monstrous form of Holóbolos crawled out of the bracken.

"What brings you now?" asked Holóbolos.

"Gratitude," answered Igdrathion. "For your axe obtained for me Hogbiter, and with Hogbiter, lo, I have won the golden whiskers."

And he showed those unbendable, unbreakable whiskers to the dwarf, glimmering bright in his hand. And Holóbolos drew a little back with his axe, saying "Let them not touch my axe, lest they blunt its blade."

For though a great gash was in it, from its meeting with Hogbiter, the rest of the edge was sharper than other earthly things, excepting only that sword. And Igdrathion drew back the whiskers as Holóbolos had requested. And now there were met together the four hardest things in the world, which were firstly the sword Hogbiter, then the two golden whiskers that had grown on the King of the Birchlands, and very close after these the axe of Holóbolos.

"Whither now?" said Holóbolos.

"First to the witch to thank her," Igdrathion replied; "to the great enchantress Lirila. Then to my mother's cottage, and then to the palace of Bad Lands."

"I would stay in the bracken," muttered Holóbolos. "For chopping is sweeter than travelling, and the forest fairer than cities."

But Igdrathion said farewell to him, and set out, and came soon to the house of the witch, and knocked at her door to thank her and to tell her that he had come by the golden whiskers. But this she knew before he knocked at her door, for the glow of them shone through the crannies, and magical things know well all other magical things, and she knew that the glow was that of the golden whiskers.

"Keep them outside," she said, as she opened the door, "for there is some magic in my poor house, but none that is able to stand against that of the golden whiskers, and they would but blunt my magic and tarnish its brightness."

So he kept outside with the whiskers and thanked her from there. And then he went to his mother's cottage, and found her there by her fire in an old brown chair carved out of a bole of oak, and showed her the golden whiskers, and for her son's sake she admired them and said they were fine whiskers,

although she had no need of magic herself, thinking the simple things of the forest enough. And she gave him a meal of eggs that her hens had laid, and of vegetables grown in her garden under the oaks. And she asked him whither he was going now, and he said to the King of the Bad Lands to give him the golden whiskers, and she warned him against that king.

But he took no heed of the warning, for he said, "He has promised the hand of his eldest daughter to whoever shall bring him the golden whiskers that grew on the King of the Birchlands. So what else can he do?"

But the old woman knew and trusted the ways of the forest and all that went therein, and had little trust in the folk that lived in the lands that lay beyond the frontier of beech and oak. Nevertheless, with a high unclouded heart Igdrathion, having said farewell to his mother, set off for those very lands and, travelling all day in the shade of the mighty branches, saw sunset glowing again on the spires of the palace where sat King Thlog on his throne and reigned over Badlands. And it was again the hour when the Princess Bourodilla was wont to sit in her balcony, with her maidens about her, looking out on the ways of the city through the mellow glow of the evening; and she saw Igdrathion coming along those ways, with the sword Hogbiter in its sheath beside him, and the golden whiskers glittering in his hand and bringing a brightness to the shade of the ways that had lately lost the sun. And she said farewell in her heart to her father's gleaming spires and to all the ways of his city.

And Igdrathion went up to the gate of the palace and the sentries would have stopped him, but he raised the golden whiskers to shine in their faces, and the magic that was in those whiskers troubled them. So he passed through the sentries and entered the palace and strode on with the glow and the magic going before him, and soon he stood before the King of those lands, King Thlog himself in glory upon his throne. And now he said to the King: "Behold, the golden whiskers."

And King Thlog received them graciously. And when the King had received the golden whiskers from Igdrathion kneeling before him, and said no more, Igdrathion reminded him of his eldest daughter and the promise that he had made. But the King of the Bad Lands had forgotten his promise. And, when nothing the young man said could bring it back to his memory, Igdrathion arose and drew out from its rustic sheath the long sword Hogbiter, that no other sword could scratch, and the magic that was in the whiskers was weaker than what there was in that sword. And the King held up the golden whiskers against him, and they glowed, but they glowed in vain against the sword Hogbiter.

And the King opened his mouth to speak fiercely, but when he saw that the whiskers glowed in vain he forgot what it was he would say, but kept his mouth open still while he tried to remember, and open it still remained while Igdrathion strode away. He strode away through the rooms that led to the balcony where the Princess Bourodilla was seated among her maidens, looking out on the evening. And as he went he pondered what he would say. But when he came to the balcony, and the princess's eyes were upon him, looking into his face, he said nothing; nor did the Princess Bourodilla speak, and her maidens were dumb beside her. And together they went from the palace, he holding the sword Hogbiter aloft in his right hand, she leaning on his left arm, and none who saw the long flash of the bright sword Hogbiter stopped him.

Together they went away to the deeps of the forest, to found a kingdom there, whereof he and she were king and queen for such a long time that no historian uses less than many large pages on which to tell of their happy and glorious reign, and the memorable things that the forest saw in their era. Their palace was built for them by the dwarf Holóbolos, partly of standing trees where the beeches grew most close in the deeps of the forest, and partly of the great boles that he cut with his axe near by and placed erect between them, dragging them to their places from where he cut them, alone. And all this he did with inconceivable swiftness, for he cut the oaks and the beeches with his axe as another man cuts poppies and corn with a scythe. And, when he had clamped them together, he laid the planks of the floor, which he cut with his axe from the oaks, as another man with a knife cuts slices out of a cheese.

And when the walls and the roofs and the stairways had been all hurled into their places by the might of the dwarf Holóbolos, and the power of his swift axe, the enchantress Lirila came out of her cottage and entered the new palace and made the smaller things that a palace needs, by enchantment, either directly by the power of her spells, or by calling up from the forest spirits of which we know nothing, to weave the tapestries and hang the arras, and clothe the floors with carpets of fair design.

Certain it is that for the fireplaces and chimneys she called up from the deeps of the forest certain gnomes. And all this building was done by the strength of the dwarf and the magic of the enchantress and the industry of the gnomes, with inconceivable swiftness. Some say that it took days to build this palace, while others write merely of hours. Certain it is that this palace was fair, and that Igdrathion and the Princess Bourodilla lived happily there for as long afterwards as there is any record, and their children and their grandchildren became a dynasty.

Of the glories of that palace and its fountains, and the gardens that glowed about it under the oak tress, of the spring that blessed them and the summer in which they dreamed, and the autumn that touched the beeches with an unearthly glory, of the dawns and the noons and the sunsets that saw these things, and the butterflies that rejoiced in them, of the creatures that haunted the forest and left their haunts to wonder at them, and of the mellow years that passed over them and left them lovelier yet, let poets sing.

Enough for me to say that between Birchlands and Badlands there arose a kingdom happier than each, at which both of them looked in awe. And the King of the Bad Countries went to war no more with Birchlands, for he dreaded the sword of Igdrathion, the unbreakable sword Hogbiter, which lurked in the forest between them; and the magic that glowed in the whiskers that were won in the war with Birchlands was fading slowly away; every dawn they were weaker, and weaker still in the evening, like an old clock nobody winds, which is running slowly down.

But gradually as the coming out of the stars, first one, then three, then hundreds all in a rush, and then millions, the golden whiskers grew again on the head of the King of the Birch Lands. Ω

CHILL AROUND THE CABIN

Today,
on the dirt trail
in the woods around my house
I found bones.
Piled, picked at
crowned by a canine skull:
a heaped carcass whitened by the sun
like evergreen limbs
by a cloak of
ice and snow.

Thought it was a stray dog by day
but presently in the night
I hear its voice:
a piercing moan mixed with the wind
swaying trees
and rocking clouds against the moon.

The wolf died hungry
in my pasture
and now, dwelling between
the breezes it howls,
scratches and rattles my windowpane
with chill, crystal claws
that slice at my cabin door
seeking the warm hearth
and steamy meat within.

— John R. Harford

NORM LITTMAN'S 15 MINUTES
by A.R. Morlan and John S. Postovit
illustrated by Rodger Gerberding

"The day will come when everybody will be famous for 15 minutes."
— *Andy Warhol*

"I don't know what he was about. He was a mystery. But I still miss him."
— *James Rosenquist, on Andy Warhol's death in 1987*

"THURSDAY, April 16, 1981
. . . I'm in this period where I think, What is it all about? You do this and what does it mean, and you do that and what does it mean?"
— *Andy Warhol*
The Andy Warhol Diaries

Click! wurrrrr . . . .
The Wanna-Be was back in the gallery. I didn't even need to turn around anymore, like I did on the first couple of days of the exhibition, to know that *he* was back, snapping pictures. But not pictures *of* the pictures, like everyone else was doing. It was kinda hard to tell just *what* the Wanna-Be was aiming his camera at. I mean, he'd have this 35 mm pointing at the stuff *between* the stuff on the walls, or at the line where the carpeting met the white-painted walls. Sorta like a kid who picks up his Dad's Nikon and spends half an hour playing *paparazzo* with imaginary movie stars, until Dad comes home and whupps the stuffing out of the kid's cushions for messing with an expensive camera. And never mind what the old man's gonna say when the pictures get developed.

That's what the Wanna-Be reminded me of, even though he was way too old to be playing with a fancy-schmancy camera like film grew on trees and he'd raked himself a big pile.

All it was was **Click! wurrrrr . . . .**, move on to the next empty space between things, then pause to drop in some more film when the roll was full. The Wanna-Be had this little plastic shopping bag, the crinkly white kind with the self-handles like they give you in the grocery store (unless they run low and try to sneak one of those old paper bags on you, then grump a lot when you insist on a plastic one anyhow), and I could see the outlines and vague colors of the 35 mm film boxes inside. He had *that* bag slung over his left arm. On the other arm, he had a couple more bags, ones with the college logo on them, from the little gift shop Dean Yarrow's wife and her art-fart crowd run during exhibitions at the college gallery.

The stuff in his grocery store bag never changed, but he had different stuff in his art gallery bags every night. Postcards, sweatshirts with the frat and sorority letters on them, those little pottery gimcracks the ceramics students turn out by the kilnful — every night there was something new weighing down his right arm.

Tell the truth, I really didn't notice what the Wanna-Be had bought himself on the first night of the exhibition, 'cause there were just too many Wanna-Be's running around who looked more or less like the camera-toting Wanna-Be so that you needed a score card to keep them all straight. There were the girl ones, and the black ones, and the ones who got the glasses or the white wig all wrong, and the ones who couldn't keep their yaps shut and kept spouting, "Hi, I'm Andy Warhol, and for fifteen minutes we'll *all* be famous."

When I walked into the gallery that night, February 20, it was like that picture of the Campbell's soup cans come to life, only instead of can after can of red and white labels, it was like face after face of Warhol. All pale wigs and big glasses and black turtlenecks. One of the few folks who did look different was Dean Yarrow's wife, and *she* looked like the soup can picture I was just talking about. It was her dress. A webby papery thing, sorta like a hospital gown but with no sleeves and no slit up the back, and piped with black all around the armholes and neck. Printed all over with soup cans, 'cept for the horizontal gold and white stripes on the bottom. It was a Campbell's give-away back, oh, in '67 or '68. Cost two labels and a buck. But on Dean Yarrow's wife, the cans looked like the ones you'd buy at a warehouse outlet, after some kid stocking shelves slipped on a grape and dropped the whole case of soup.

"*Norm,*" the Dean's missus gushed, waddle-crinkling over to where I was standing, "You *must* bring in some of those Brillo boxes from that closet of —" She was practically gleeful — gleeful, that's what you call it. 'Course, why wouldn't she be, here in the boonies of Wisconsin in a fly-speck college on the opening night of an Andy Warhol exhibit that *she'd* arranged. Buku expensive for a college gallery that usually exhibited local-yokel artists or students. But she'd managed to get a giant grant from the state. "Bringing art to the *people,*" that's what she'd been gushing all night.

So . . . it pleased me no end to tell her that I'd tossed out the last box of Brillo, even though I had a whole fresh *case* of them sitting in the cramped room where I store my janitorial supplies. I use it — the Brillo — to rub lime deposits off the rest room faucets. Water's pretty hard up this way in Wisconsin.

Mrs. Yarrow sighed, and I smelled those horrible cheese-nut whahoozies on her breath, the puffy things she bakes up every time there's a new show in the gallery. The ones people take, bite into, and then hide somewhere narrow and dark and out of sight. Now that's a job worse than acting as a "security person" (Mrs. Yarrow's fancy talk) for whatever traveling exhibit is housed in the campus gallery — cheese-nut whahoozie hunting. And the art-farts who come to these exhibits are tip-top whahoozie-hiders. And if you don't find one of them suckers within two days the gallery stinks worse than the football team's locker room.

Just to get even with Mrs. Yarrow for baking up those smelly puffs — again — I added, "Nope, no Brillo left in this building. Want I should run to the store and buy some?"

Mrs. Yarrow crinkled her fat cheeks and nose until her red-framed glasses rode up above her plucked eyebrows. "Oh, *no*, Norman, not *tonight*! This is a very ex*pensive* collection — Warhol's still *very* hot, you know," she confided, which was about as astounding as saying that the walls around us happened to be painted *white*. That's what I *really* hate about Dean Yarrow's wife — she acts like a person is an intellectual moron if he isn't glued to *Masterpiece Theatre* during supper, or doesn't read *Smithsonian* magazine while taking a crap. Heck, *I* knew who Andy *Warhol* was. I'd seen the reports on the news when they auctioned off his stuff, and I'd bought those *People* magazines with his diary excerpts in them. Actually, the only time I've been kinda confused on all this artsy-schmartzy stuff was the time when I brought along a pen and piece of paper when they had that George Segal exhibit. How was I supposed to know that there's an actor *and* an artist with the same name? (If you can call dummies covered with white gauze bandages or whatever the heck he used on them *art* . . . .)

But art critic or not, I knew me one thing about art — once the artist goes to the big palette in the sky, all those Japanese businessmen start checking over their bank accounts, just panting for when the auction of the painter's stuff will begin.

And *that* night, I didn't even think that the exhibit was anything to start hyperventilating over, even with the guy being five years dead and the room filled with all those Wanna-Be's. I mean, all there was was pictures of *Coke* bottles, and Liz Taylor with way too much make-up. And one of a guy wearing a James Dean tee shirt, only instead of one picture being worth, like, maybe ten words, there were just four pictures, all alike, and stacked together.

I thought I knew what it was like being a fly, all those multiple images swimming around me as I strolled around the gallery, to make sure no one took anything off the walls and rolled it up in a back pocket. Kind of a stupid job, when you think on it, but it gives me an excuse to wear a sports jacket and tie a few nights a month, not to mention the extra bucks on the paycheck. And it makes Mrs. Yarrow and the rest of the art-tarts happy.

When I couldn't take looking at the pictures anymore, or at the Wanna-Be's (now why can't Madonna paint — I'd go for a room full of girls in those bustier things), there were framed sayings some of the art students had lettered hanging around the gallery — "The whole thing is work. Everything is work" ". . . a sphinx without a secret" "Great, great, great" "Sex and parties are the two things you still have to actually be there for" and "In the future, everyone will be famous for 15 minutes."

I supposed it was stuff Warhol had said, or that people said about him. From the looks of the hangers-on flitting about the gallery, there were a lot of folks who thought that tonight was when their 15 minutes were coming due. There had been a rumor buzzing around campus that the MTV News crew was following this mini exhibit of Warhol's stuff around, but if they were, someone must've tipped 'em off about the cheese-nut whahoozits, 'cause they never did show up.

The throngs of Wanna-Be's thinned out the night after the big opening. That was when I noticed the old, picture-shooting Wanna-Be. I suppose he was there before, but like I said, it was fly-eye time that first night. And while the old guy wasn't the only wigged and bespeckled person toting a camera, he was the only one who both took pictures *and* kept his lip zipped. The being quiet part didn't bother me none, but the pictures part did. It was kinda weird, how he just bobbed through the gallery, not even looking at "his" artwork, only pausing to take pictures of the nothing between the something. Not a peep out of him, only **Click! wurrrrr** . . . . and sometimes the soft crunch of his hand rooting around in that plastic grocery bag.

But to me, the ironic thing was that nobody paid him any mind. Like his get-up made him invisible, even though the twerps on the campus newsrag stopped nearly every *other* Wanna-Be for some words of wisdom to print in the next issue. I don't think it was him being really old — easily senior citizen discount age — that made them all shy away from him, because there were a couple of other older men sporting silver-white wigs hanging around the gallery. And him being quiet didn't seem to be the problem — if a Wanna-Be wasn't yakking, one of the little skirts on the paper staff would pester him or her into at least repeating the "15 minutes" bit.

Maybe it was the determined way he took his pictures. No, not determined . . . *fated*'s more like it. Sorta like he was saying, Don't bug me, I *gotta* be doing this.

Thinking it over, it seems that I really took an interest in the old guy because of his cheekbones. They proved that he was a Slav, like Warhol was. (I'd read or heard someplace that his real name was Warhola, which is about as Czech as you can get. Being Czech on Ma's side, I know Slav cheekbones when I see 'em. I don't have Horvokas, Husas, Horacks and Smetanas on my family tree for *nothing*.)

And the Wanna-Be sorta looked like Warhol, only older, which made sense when you figure that if Warhol hadn't of died five years ago, he really would be in his sixties. Anyhow, judging from those pictures in *People,* Warhol looked like something he'd silkscreened — all broad areas of tone, with no definition. (I'm not as blind as Mrs. Yarrow thinks I am — I *do* notice more in life than wrestling and which TV dinner I pop in the oven. I just like to drive her nuts by not bragging about what I know.)

Wasn't easy to follow the Wanna-Be, though. Just when I'd stroll closer for a better look at him (and to sniff out any half-chewed cheese-nut whahoozies), he'd take a left or right and wander past me, off for the opposite end of the gallery. A few seconds later I'd hear him, **Click**ing and **wurrrrr**ing behind me — *right* behind me, which made me start and turn around real quick.

But like I said before, after a while I got used to it, and didn't jump in my clothes when he came up behind me. Funny thing, how he always had plenty of stuff from the art gallery shop, but I never noticed *when* he bought it. Like his bags filled by osmosis whenever he passed by the shop itself.

By the third day of the exhibit, the 22nd, I noticed a few new things about the Wanna-Be. He still wore the "uniform" that all the Wanna-Be's wore — black sweater, dark jeans, penny loafers, big glasses, wig, and camera — but there was something odd *under* his dark turtleneck. Big lumps near his collarbones, like giant-size warts or moles, all in a semi-circle. None of the others had had those bumps under their sweaters. And they moved; when he turned his head one time, they all shifted along with his neck.

That's when it dawned on me — he'd swiped something. From the gift-shop, most likely, since all the artwork here was square, flat, and bigger than he was. No wonder he was distant, and did the camera thing. Shoplifter tricks. At last, a chance to do some real security work —

"Hey. You. Bud. With the camera." I was trying to sound authoritative, but it came out like Leslie Nielsen playing "bad cop" on *Police Squad.* At least the guy didn't laugh. He turned around, took a picture of something beyond my left shoulder, and asked, "Me?" only it wasn't like a question, exactly. Real flat, expressionless voice. Behind his glasses, his eyes were very brown and kinda flat, like tiny contact lenses held cupped-side out, so all I saw was dark pooled inside, with no reflection of me.

"Uh . . . I'm the security guard, and I . . . uh, noticed something under your sweater —" I was talking kinda low, so no one (Mrs. Yarrow in particular) would hear me make an ass of myself in front of a gallery visitor, in case the guy *did* have warts or something. Ones that shifted.

"Oh. You mean this?" Letting the camera swing on its strap, the Wanna-Be patted his collar bones, pulling the knit close to the lumps. In the even white light, I saw the fuzz-dulled gleam of precious stones. A necklace, with rocks that didn't come from any tacky-schmacky faculty-run college gift shop.

Feeling like a grade-A prime asshole, hoping that nobody'd noticed what I'd done, I mumbled, "Sorry, Bud . . . I wasn't sure —"

"I don't like to show them off," the guy droned, his voice barely rising above the low rumble of conversation around us, "but I like to just have them with me." He didn't say any more, but didn't move, either. Like the ball was in my court and it was time to dribble.

"Uh . . . well, that's okay, Bud. Just my job, y'know. Otherwise they don't think they get their money's worth."

"I like money too," the Wanna-Be said solemnly. Over his dark-jacketed shoulder, I saw a picture Warhol'd done. Money. Lots of dollar bills. It figured; this guy was an *expert* Warhol Wanna-Be.

More silence, the kind that just aches to be filled. It was like the guy had this vacuum aura around him, so unnatural I just *had* to fill it up. Like this guy had taken the ". . . sphinx without a secret" bit to heart.

Around us, the sporadic groups of visitors ebbed and flowed, and I think I heard Mrs. Yarrow jabbering around a mouthful of whahoozies, but — and it gets strange here — it was like the Wanna-Be and I were alone in the gallery. Spooky (I'd read about the real Warhol having a boyfriend and all), yet sort of reassuring, too. He wasn't threatening in his silence, like the jocks who've had one too many and block my way in the halls come night time, so I have to mop around them. It was like . . . even as he was there, he wasn't *there.* Not like other people, when they're complete. I mean, I couldn't see *through* him, nothing like *that,* but . . . well, he just wasn't *complete.* Least not without a person having to add something to him. Shovel something into the void.

"Ummm, yeah. Money's good. You've got a point there. Uh, Bud, you a student here? An artist? I notice you been coming here every —"

"This is my show." Self-assured, yet not bragging, either. I waited for the "15 minutes" bit, but he didn't say it. Just stared with those brown, brown eyes, like he was and wasn't interested in me. Uncomfortable, remembering about Warhol kissing all those celebrity guys, I scratched the back of my neck until I noticed that his bag of film was mainly full of used film in the little grey and black holders, the kind kids here use to store pot in, plus the opened boxes.

"Hey, Bud, you're gonna have some processing bill for all those."

A nod of the silver-wigged head. I saw wisps of greying hair peeping around the bottom edges. Little shadows pooled in the deep pores on his slightly bulbous nose. Only color on his face was the shiny part inside his lips. The guy was unnerving — in one way he looked realer than real, with every pore, whisker and flake of dead skin high-lighted, yet . . . in another way he wasn't real at all. Like those resin people statues they had here once.

Mrs. Yarrow was laughing at something — Dean Yarrow's lucky that there are no male hyenas in Wisconsin. The Wanna-Be turned to stare at her with all the involvement of a pigeon looking around for something to splatter. Like one thing's as good as the next. Snapped her picture, too. That caught Mrs. Yarrow's attention; she turned and mouthed, *Get back to work* to me, then turned back to whoever she'd been jabbering at.

The Wanna-Be was gone by the time I turned my head. So I walked around some more, until the gallery closed, and I could do my real job, janitorial work.

After hanging my jacket and good shirt on a bent nail in my "office," I got to work, vacuuming the gallery walls and carpet, with that stupid industrial machine that doesn't pick up lint unless I leave my back on every inch of nap. (Why the Dean won't spring for an upright is beyond *me*.) The vacuum makes enough noise to make a buffalo deaf at twenty miles, so at first I didn't hear anything as I worked, but when the long hose attachment got all twisted around, I had to shut off the motor — and nearly jumped out of my jeans when I heard that **Click! wurrrrr** . . . . from across the room. The old Wanna-Be was standing next to the Liz Taylor picture, his pale face and hands sorta leeching *into* the wall behind him, I hesitated before yelling, I mean it was such a *strange* illusion. Like the wall was wearing clothes . . . .

Then I came to my senses. "Hey, Bud! What the fuck you *doing*?"

In answer, he snapped a picture of me, grungy tee shirt and all.

"*Hey!* Knock it *off*, Bud! If anyone sees you in here, my ass is burnt brown grass . . . gallery's closed, Bud. Time to shove off —"

(Funny, he *wasn't* in the gallery when I shut the door —)

"This is where I belong."

"Oh . . . you mean you came with the show. Like the other guy," I said, thinking of the representative of the collection who was staying with the Yarrows.

"This is my show." Just like he said it before.

Well . . . the guy wasn't *damaging* the art, and I figured he'd paid to come every night. And wearing a necklace under his clothes wasn't a *crime* —

"Uh . . . what I'm asking is, do you *belong* here? It's okay with the Dean's wife?"

"Tina?" That clinched it for me; he knew her first name. Few of the students knew Mrs. Yarrow's first name. (The woman doesn't *look* like a "Tina.") So he *had* to be one of her artsy-smartsy cronies, maybe a companion of the guy who travelled with the exhibit. *I* wasn't privy to her "inner circle."

"Then I guess it's all right if you stay. But only until I'm done working, okay? And don't *touch*

anything," I pleaded, as I turned on the vacuum. His silvery-wigged head woggled absent-mindedly as he went about taking pictures of whatever it was he saw that I couldn't.

Actually, it was kinda nice having someone to keep me company as I worked. I mean, being a janitor suits me fine most of the time, 'cause I'm not much of one for conversation or going out with the guys. I like my wrestling on TBS and USA, and I like my TV dinners extra hot so the steam rises up so thick I don't have to really look at how much of a dump my apartment is. Like the line about the cobbler's kids needing shoes. I'm the janitor with the sloppy house. But it's mine, and no one ever comes over, so who's the wiser, right?

I like being alone, but the being lonely part's the killer.

But most folks are twits anyhow, so usually I'm happy alone . . . yet, for some reason, it was getting to me that night, until I noticed the Wanna-Be in the gallery with me. I guess that's why I got a little panic-filled when I turned around and noticed that he'd left the gallery. "Easy come, easy go," I muttered, and kept on working, until I half-heard something strange, yet familiar, out in the hall beyond the gallery, before it branches off into the student lounge. Not the sound of his camera, but the sound of *my* stuff in the "office" being moved around.

The Wanna-Be *was* rooting in my stuff, shoving aside cartons of liquid cleaner and old buckets, mumbling "Great, great," as he pawed over my cleaning supplies. As I watched him from the doorway, he finally found what he'd been after — the boxes of Brillo Mrs. Yarrow had wanted for the exhibit. (I'd seen pictures of those big Brillo boxes Warhol did, after he'd died — and they weren't in this exhibit. I guess Mrs. Yarrow thought nobody'd notice if they were kinda small.)

The old guy quickly pulled the boxes out and stacked them against a corner of the tiny room, then snapped a picture. I waited until he **wurrrrr**ed the film forward before shouting, "You deef, Bud? I *said* DON'T TOUCH ANYTHING!"

I suppose I shouldn't have done that, blowing up at someone who knew Mrs. Yarrow by first name, and probably could get me fired, but he was grubbing in *my* space. I mean, I don't have much in life, but it was mine, my little corner of this big, indifferent world, and it's all I'm ever going to have at my age, so him playing with the Brillo boxes was important. Something I couldn't let just go by.

"Oh. This is your stuff. You were cleaning my stuff, so I —"

"You Wanna-Be's are all alike, aren't you Bud? *You*'re nothing, so you latch onto something bigger and better than you just so the *impression* of somebody great rubs off, huh? Wanting to be someone is one thing. Doing it's another. Shit, I wanna be famous, too, but if I am, I want it because of *me*, understand?"

He just stared at me with those flat brown eyes,

not agreeing or disagreeing. Empty. Waiting for me to spout off. Which I did:

"Trouble with you is, you kinda do look like this Warhol, and that makes you think you *are* him. Run around snapping pictures of nothing, standing around like a *sphinx* —"

"Truman said that about me. We weren't anything alike, really —"

"Who?" The real Warhol knew half the universe, so I didn't remember which "Truman" he was talking about.

"*Capote*. He said that. About me. I puzzled him —"

"Oh *c'mon* already. Quit talking about dead guys." It was funny, but I wasn't as mad anymore, even though the Wanna-Be was obviously trying to get to me by *not* seeming to want to get to me.

"Truman dead . . . know what? I know he is, but I don't believe it because he wasn't around when it *happened*. Like I wasn't." He half-smiled at that, a sad, knowing little smile that looked copied off some advertisement.

"You cop that line from one of Warhol's books?" I leaned against the doorway and patted my pockets for a cigarette. He nodded, but added, "I got it from *me*. It's written in one of my books, if you care to look it up —"

Shaking out my match, I said through a haze of smoke, "Which one, the diary or the one from '88? That party book —" I'd read about that one in a Sunday edition of some newspaper.

"No and no. *The Philosophy of Andy Warhol*. My book," he insisted, and it was then that I noticed that his detachment was chipping away bit by bit. Even his eyes lost some of that flat shine; I could see *in* them a little. And what I saw looked kinda *lonely*. A look I knew from my own mirror.

"Really? So that mean's I'm talking to a stiff, right?"

"Do I look like one?" A real question at last. I noticed that he was sweating; my "office" adjoins the pump room, which heats the gallery.

"Nah," I drawled, as he took off his jacket. Man, was he skinny. He moved stiffly; under his sweater I noticed he had on more than the hidden necklace. A corset or brace of some kind, around his middle. I saw that painting of Warhol they showed on CBS's Sunday news show with Charlie Kuralt, the one of his scars from when that nutty dame shot him. Whoever this guy *was*, he had *everything* down pat. Patter than pat . . . . But the guy seemed so earnest, so . . . *driven*, I couldn't bear to be mean anymore.

"Hey, Bud, whatever you want to be called —"

"Some people called me 'Drella whether I liked it or not . . . but Bud's good —"

" 'Drella-Bud, whatever, you up to sharing a 'bach dinner? I have some sandwiches, nothing fancy, but . . . and some cookies —"

"Mint ones?" He actually looked eager.

"No . . . Oreos. But they're double stuff ones —"

"Okay . . . ."

So we sat on cartons and shared my meager bachelor's feast. I know the guy had to have bukus of money, to afford that necklace and all that film, but Hell, he looked *hungry*. And it was my food, not Mrs. Yarrow's putrid cheese-nut whahoozits. I mean, pawing through my stuff or not, he didn't deserve *that* kind of punishment.

As we ate, I talked. About how I could kill the kids when they rammed whole rolls of toilet paper into the johns, and how Mrs. Yarrow's art-fart crowd got on my nerves, and how I wasn't in any rush to come home at night, save for needing a place to sleep. I talked way too much, but the Wanna-Be didn't mind. He just chewed and nodded and listened to me, like I was ten times more powerful than Dean Yarrow or the college president, even. Like I *mattered*. The only time he spoke to me was when I said that I didn't really understand "his" artwork (I was humoring the guy by then, saying this or that was "his" creation, or "his" words.)

"I don't know if anything I did *is* art, even though, on one level, it's *all* art. I mean, people bought my stuff because of who I wa— am, and because their friends all bought it . . . it got to the point where I never could be sure *why* they bought it. But if my art *is* like, *art*, I guess it's because *everything* is art, if you think about it." He picked up his sandwich bag, holding it my eye level. "I guess this is art, same as my silkscreens in there. You're art, just like Marilyn or Mao. I guess *I'm* art, too," he added with a self-depreciating chuckle.

"No kidding," I mumbled around my bologna on rye.

"Some people claimed I was my own best creation . . . and I am. Thirty years ago, I didn't know what to do, what to paint . . . I had no *ideas*. Then I looked at a can of soup and realized it could be art. Art for everyone. You go to the store, and there's art all around you. If it is designed, that's a form of art . . . but no one had put it out *as* art before. That's why I collected everything. Good, bad, whatever. In its own way, it was art —"

"Auctioned off for a pretty penny, too —"

"Because I saw it as art . . . no, I know that it sold high because of *me*, period. I may be dead, but I'm not *obtuse* —"

Since he'd brought up the subject, I took a stab at finding out something which had been bothering me. Even if he was a fake.

"Yeah, well, since you're . . . uh, *dead*, what's it like?"

"Now or when it happened?" I didn't like the look in his brown eyes. For a second I was afraid he might really know the truth — and tell me.

"Uh . . . whenever."

"I don't remember what it felt like when it *happened*. I was asleep. But now . . . it's actually an awful lot like it was before. You just *are*, without remembering exactly when you knew it. You go around, but things aren't much better than they were in life. People act nicer when it comes to remembering you, sometimes nicer than they were when you were alive. But not much is different. It's something like going to a party where everyone is so accustomed to seeing you around they don't notice you even if you are there!"

I smiled to myself, Guy's *gotta* be a fake. Spouting platitudes and pop philosophy . . . Just like the *real* Warhol did, I thought with a little discomfort, like a stifled burp.

"— I was so famous, everybody knew me, so now nobody notices me," he was saying, as he gathered up his crinkly bags from where he'd placed them by his feet while he ate.

"You're not *going*?" I asked, too fast.

"'Fraid so . . . I have other places to be. Other showings of my work. I follow it," he finished simply. I suppose my face betrayed me, or something, for he handed me the grocery bag full of exposed film.

"This is for the food. The cookies were very good. Now I have to go get some tea. I saw a restaurant down the road." With that he was gone; jacket under one arm, gift shop bags under the other, a skinny short silver-wigged old man trotting briskly down the hall.

I started to call after him, but didn't. I'm *not* lonely.

Least not in front of a stranger.

It wasn't until he was gone that I realized there was something odd about the bag of film — it was too heavy. Peering in the white bag, I saw the Wanna-Be's camera nestled among the round rolls of exposed film. I was so busy yakking I didn't see when he slipped it in the bag.

I don't take pictures myself, so I don't know an F-stop from my a-hole. But I knew where I could get those rolls of film developed.

For free.

Being a janitor, I do a lot of walking around the campus at night. Past a lot of rooms which should be locked come day's end but aren't. And sometimes when I clean a classroom I find more than dirty blackboards, if you get my drift. One kid in particular is a real Romeo, carries on like the world's his oyster and there's no such thing as AIDS. After I stumbled on him in six different rooms with as many different girls, the kid got this strange notion he *owed* me something for me keeping my yap shut. Me, I figure it's his life and his business if he wants to be an irresponsible little geek, so I never took him up before on his offer of "anything, any favor you *want*, Norm" — but the punk *is* a photography minor . . . .

And he didn't bat an eye when I dumped the bag of film in the darkroom the next day (I wasn't a *chump* — I took out the camera) and come evening, close to the time when I was getting ready to patrol the exhibit, Mr. Sexy came trotting down to my "office," panting, "Mister *Litt*man, wait'll you see *these!*"

"Don't tell me, they're all blank, right?" I adjusted my jacket collar. Romeo pushed a manila envelope into my hand, saying, "No *way* . . . why didn't you tell me you were this good? Makes me feel like a piker —"

I ripped open the envelope and pulled out twenty glossy sheets covered with tiny strips of pictures.

"What's this shit? I wanted individual pictures —"

"Contact sheets. I didn't know which ones you'd want enlarged or how big —"

I held the sheets up to the light. Even with the pictures being so tiny, I knew right off what I was looking at — it was like, yet wasn't like the works I'd been casually guarding in the gallery for the past few days.

Somehow, the Wanna-Be hadn't been photographing blank walls *or* the view over my shoulder . . . but he wasn't taking pictures of anything which existed in the gallery, either. In fact, I doubt that the things he'd been snapping pictures of could ever look like that in real life.

There must've been over a hundred images, small, but not so small that I couldn't help but see that they were all Andy Warhol's *artwork*. Not bad copies, not even good copies. *His* stuff. I *felt* it.

Except . . . *except* . . . I'd never met the real Andy Warhol, yet there was a picture of *me* among the 1990 model cars, new cereal and dog food boxes, soda bottles and soup cans, *dozens* of other things.

Me, with a lavender face and flat-looking, brightly colored hair and eyes, colors that clashed in a special way unique to Warhol, just like the ones on the Marilyn and Liz pictures in the gallery.

These were real, *new* Warhol works. Not copies, not something his assistants at that "Factory" studio of his churned out. There was just this *touch* to everything. Not copies, like that pattern on the soup can dress Mrs. Yarrow had. I don't know much about high art, but sometimes knowing isn't the same as *knowing,* in the gut. A hundred little things I half-understood told me my hunch was right — the way the colors went together, the simple flat shadings, the odd strings of detail here and there. And the choice of images — like he said in my "office," this *was* art for everyone.

Even a schlump like me. There were pictures of my "office." My mop bucket. My peg board of tools and electrical tape. My folded lunch bag. And the funny, wonderful thing was, no matter how much he'd doubted himself, this really *was* art. Simple things, stuff I'd considered ugly, even, but when he let me see through his eyes, even my homely belongings were *beautiful*.

I don't know why, but my eyes teared up. Drops of moisture beaded on my eyelashes as the kid said, "Tell me which ones you want copied, 'kay, Norm? Gotta get going," but I didn't turn around until after he left. When I moved my head, the light made the tears in my eyes shimmer, in rainbow colors — and I saw the world through different eyes. A *dead* guy's eyes, to be honest.

My can of Comet was breathtaking. My mop glowed. The hallway beyond my door was something out of a fairy tale — the kind I hadn't believed in for years.

I glanced at the sheets again. The pictures were

true Warhols . . . but how he'd painted or silk-screened or what*ever*ed them, let alone snapped pictures of them, was beyond me. Especially in a gallery showing an exhibit of his work five years after his death —

Suddenly, I shook the envelope. I heard film stock rattling inside. Mr. Horny-Toad had put in the negatives . . . but he'd never see them again, that's for sure. Heart doing the rhumba in my chest, I stashed the negatives and contact sheets in my "office," locked it, and hurried to the gallery. Just in *case* —

But he wasn't there. No more **Click! wur-rrrr** . . . . No Wanna-Be's at all, in fact. Everyone gave up on MTV showing up. Even Mrs. Yarrow was moping in a pink pants suit.

And me? I wandered around the exhibit, intoxicated. It all makes so much *sense*. I wanted to hug myself — it's all so clear, so plain, yet so lovely. Everything is art, all around me. Not just the Warhol works, but everything. The biggest damn art gallery in the world *is* the world. And we're all part of the exhibit.

I finally felt important, like *my* 15 minutes had come. And I'd earned them, every last second of them.

But in the middle of all this, I realized that I couldn't just hog all I'd discovered, either. There are a lot of schlumps like me out there, who are just so blind — and the irony was, even the Wanna— even *Warhol* didn't really realize what he'd *given* to everyone.

The exhibit was closing the next day; more people showed up to help the guy who traveled with the exhibition cart up everything and take it to the next stop on the tour. I showed up early for work, just so I could talk to them, and *show* them. At least that's what I was thinking, that I *had* to share this with the world — both the art and the Warhol-running-around part, but . . . I suppose I should've known what would happen if I tried to tell it in *order* —

Before I showed them the contact sheets, I explained the part about the Wanna-Be, working up to his payment for our meal, and up to that point the exhibit guys were looking like "Uh, *huh, sure*" at each other, but when I mentioned how the camera made the bag heavy —

"Do you have this camera *with* you?" the guy who'd been staying with the Yarrows asked me, his pale eyes glittering. That glitter should've warned me . . . .

Like a dummy, I showed them the camera. And one of the younger guys, who'd actually met Warhol before 1987, began shaking.

"This is one of *his* cameras," he whispered, in this voice that made *"his"* sound like it should've been in capitals, like God or something. "This is the one he bought at Saks in '85, I was with him when he bought it, see, here's the little nick in the casing — I have a *picture,* of him and Jerry Hall, and Andy was carrying this —"

You guessed it. Warhol *did* own that camera. I

saw the picture of him, it and Jerry Hall. And the fingerprints were there. *His.* They actually checked, only later on. *That* day, they didn't care about my story about how I got it; they said, "What matters is that it has been *found*!" like they'd stumbled across the Holy Grail in a back alley. Which maybe wasn't all that far from the truth. Least as far as I'm concerned.

The weird thing was, no one was interested in the contact sheets. Oh they looked, with a little magnifying glass set in a round black case, and said, "Nice work," and "Playful anachronisms," and then forgot all about them. There was publicity to arrange, and the auction to organize. I even got a share of the money . . . after they verified that I really *didn't* steal the camera that no one had actually reported missing in the first place. After all, they keep finding stuff in Warhol's closets and studio anyhow.

And I even got my 15 minutes. On MTV News, all the other news services, too. A nine second segment, played umpteen times on umpteen networks. I suppose it all adds up to fifteen minutes. I don't really care about *that* though. It was nice while it lasted, but life goes on, right?

Once all the hoo-haa died down, and Mrs. Yarrow got over her snit over *me* being in the news, and not her in her soup can dress, I took my negatives to the 24 hour photo service down in Eau Claire. The one where they have specials each month, like a free set of second prints, or poster-sized blow-ups of your choice. I picked a month when they gave out free prints, the 4 × 6 ones, too.

When I picked out the ones I like best, I waited until they had the poster special and had five made up. My Brillo boxes, a 1990 Mercedes Benz, my mop bucket, a white Persian cat, and the one of me. In my grungy tee. Not that I'm *vain*, but there was some scribbling on the bottom of the picture, like Warhol had signed the print plus added a message too. And I wanted to see what those words were.

And when my posters were ready, I didn't unroll them until I got home. I was all soda fizz and antacid tablets in water when I got to the one of me, and read the words written in a sprawling, loose handwriting:

I never said the 15 minutes were consecutive, did I?

> *your friend in loneliness and art*
> *Andy Warhol*
> *"Bud"*

It made me sad, realizing I was right, you know. About him being lonely. But at least he's got his art, to follow around, and watch over. Just like I have *my* art now, all around me where I work, and where I live.

So like now, when I watch wrestling, I don't have to have my TV dinners so hot any more. I like the art on my walls, *my* Warhol exhibition — "bringing great art to the people," all right. Sometimes, I wonder how he is, and wonder if he's glommed onto any of his old cameras. If he did, I hope whoever gets the film appreciates it, and is smart enough to keep the camera a secret to himself, or herself.

It's funny, but I miss the guy, even though he left an awful lot of himself here with me. Funny duck, but okay, too. Least he never — you know — came on to me. I think he just enjoyed my company, if what he wrote is true. For a long time, I thought I'd never know for sure if he was just being nice or what, but now I guess I will get to know after all.

I've seen the schedule of exhibits for next year. Mrs. Yarrow wangled another big grant, and got the forty-seven car paintings and drawings he did for the Daimler-Benz people, which he left unfinished when he died. I know that his works are scattered, and shown in a lot of other cities, too, at the same time as Mrs. Yarrow's exhibit, but . . . you never know, do you?

Just in case, I bought a box of cookies. Mint ones. And I've been putting tea in my thermos.
'Cause I *like* it . . . .   Ω

THE LONGEST BOUGH

When rooftops and chimneys disappear
And the bosky wood begins,
The road veers sharply to the left
And the roadside bramble thins.

There at the top of a naked hill
A gaunt old elm tree stands,
Withered by worse than nature's blight:
Accursed by human hands.

For one night under a bloody moon
And the light of baleful stars
A crazed lynch mob dragged an innocent man
From the safety of sheltering bars.

They kicked and pushed him up the hill
And pummeled him till he bled,
And the longest bough of the old elm creaked
With the weight of the hapless dead.

All who joined in that hideous crime
Have paid full price since then.
Some died in anguish; some without sign
Have dropped from the world of men.

But deep in the night, when the bloody moon
And the baleful stars hang chill,
The longest bough of the old elm tree
Creaks with its burden still.

— Stanley McNail

BLIND
by Joyce Carol Oates
illustrated by Denis Tiani

Sometime during the night which is a terrible dark here in the country on moonless nights the electricity went off.

I was wakened by it, I think. I was asleep, and suddenly wakened. A low rumbling sound like the sound of collapse. Arid a harsh pelting rain drumming on the roof over my head which is a low ceiling and a low roof of rotting shingles close over my head. And blown slantwise against the windows so I sat up terrified hearing the hiss! hiss! of the rain seeking entry.

I did not speak to *him,* nor even wake *him.*

Let the old fool slumber, let them all sleep. Snoring and snuffling and a rattle in their throats. At that age, what can you expect?

I am not a tearful woman; in truth I am a strong and practical minded woman with the experience of years. Overseeing the household in our other house, and here — in our retirement. (*His* retirement: how is it mine?) Thus I am not fearful of storms except in a practical way; you must use your common sense in a household, one member of the household at least. Hearing the rain like that streaming down the window as it was streaming down the walls of the house vertical and plunging because the eaves' gutters had not yet been cleaned, and were overflowing; thus the water runs down the house to the old stone foundation and into the cellar, oh God. That was my fear. That, and not the storm itself. Because of course *he* had not gotten around to cleaning the gutters, no matter how I reminded him.

One day soon, now it was April at last in this cold windy place, I would drag the aluminum step-ladder out of the barn myself, to rid the eaves of rotted leaves and other debris to shame him. That old man. But I had neglected to do so, yet — and now, too late. And now the **hiss! hiss!** of the rain seeking entry.

It was then that I attempted to switch on the bedside light but the power was off. The room so utterly dark I could not see my hand in front of my face. Groping for the lamp, and almost knocking it over blundering against the shade, muttering to myself but to no avail the power was off. (Did *he* hear my distress? — snoring and snuffling the ratchety noise of phlegm in his throat? Never!) Several times during the winter the power had gone off, once it was off for eighteen hours, and when I telephoned to complain the girl said in a smirky little voice, The company is doing all it can, ma'am, power will be restored as soon as possible. And each time I called, the girl said in a smirky little voice, The company is doing all it can, ma'am, power will be restored as

soon as possible. Until at last I shouted into the phone, You're a liar! You are all liars! I pay for our electricity and we want better service! And there was silence, I believed I had gained the little snip's respect at last, but then said the smirky little voice, I could all but see the red lipstick pursing in mockery of decent respect for one's elders, Ma'am, I have told you — the company is doing all it can.

So in fury I slammed the receiver down. So hard, it clattered to the floor. Hairline cracks in the cheap plastic.

I tried then to see the time. Peering into the dark where the clock should be. But even the green-luminescent numerals were gone, it was so dark. But I judged (by the pressure on my bladder: I am wakened regularly each night by this discomfort) that it was between 3:00 A.M. and 3:30 A.M. The very middle of the night so you would know the electric company would be slow to get a repair crew out, and use that as an excuse.

I was breathing hard now, in exasperation and worry, and had to use the bathroom, and in this pitch dark! — swinging my legs (which are slightly swollen, the ankles especially) off the bed and rising unsteady on bare feet. Where were my slippers? — I groped for them, but could not find them.

I sighed and may have murmured to myself, as I acknowledge it is my habit to do, where once I addressed the cat and in other years the canary, *he* being deaf when it suited him, murmuring aloud, God have mercy! though from my tone you would judge God is no friend of mine any longer. Not for many years you may be sure. But *he* did not hear, slumbering on, no doubt lying on his back, his jaw drooping and a strand of spittle leaking across his cheek I did not doubt.

I am not a heavy woman, still less fat. I have grown a bit stout, which puts pressure on the legs and back. Sometimes I grow short of breath, as with natural impatience.

In my place, I tell my daughters, when rarely they call, you would be no different. Oh don't you tell *me!*

Slowly then, painstakingly I groped my way to the bathroom, for my bladder *was* pinched, and I was in near-distress. Had I shut my eyes I alight have been unerring, for the room, the entire house, is memorized in my mind, but I tried to see which is in such circumstances a mistake. Thus stubbing my toe, thus bumping against the bureau, groping for the door which did not seem to be where I knew it must be, but a few feet to one side. Panting, muttering to myself, for at my age you come to expect more respect from the world of objects if not from the world of humankind, but of course *he* did not hear, lost in selfish slumber.

Fortunately the bathroom is in the hall right outside the bedroom. So I had not far to go.

Inside, forgetting the lights were off, I fumbled for the wall switch, so strong is the force of habit.

I was able to use the toilet with little trouble, though. Noting that the bathroom was, I thought, darker somehow than the bedroom and the hall; though there is a window behind the toilet overlooking a steep-sloped roof and an old overgrown pasture. (Bathed in moonlight many times these past twelve years since moving to this place I had stood at the window, looking out. To see what? In expectation of what?) But now the window too was lost in darkness. Utter blackness. You would not have believed a window was there at all, except for the pelting rain, the noise and damp.

I flushed the toilet once, twice, a third time before the mechanism took hold. Cursing the plumbing as many times in the past, for something was always breaking down in this old house and who then would call the plumber? — and who make out the check, to pay the bill? And my daughters saying, Why do you nag Daddy, why don't you let Daddy alone you know his nerves poor Daddy they say, or used to say. As if the little fools knew —

Well it was my fault I suppose. Agreeing so readily in fact so vehemently to sell our old house, to move *here*. Leaving our house in the college town where we'd lived for forty-three years, to move *here*. This farmland and monotony of trees that held a memory for *him* (because when he was a boy, his family had taken him to visit some relatives here in the summer — happiest memories of his life he said) but not for *me*. Leaving my three women friends without saying goodbye because they'd slighted me, took me for granted and I would not tolerate it, so moving away was my revenge and I took it. And too late to regret it now.

I groped my way back to bed in the terrible black, hearing the rain louder than before, that **hiss!** against the windowpanes and drumming on the roof. *He* wasn't snoring so loud now, or the wind was loud enough to drown him out; he'd never stirred when I got out of bed. I could have had an attack or fit or fallen down the stairs in the pitch black and would he take notice? — don't make me laugh. Lowering myself into bed, and the box springs creaked. Still, *he* never stirred.

So I tried not to think about the rain, and the cellar. The over flowing eaves. I tried to calm my mind seeing waves of black water move toward me, shallow waves, where I might rise, and float, as I'd learned to float at the pool, on my back; what a surprise I could float so easy and feel no fear when the younger women had trouble, the skinny ones had the worst time of all. When it's so easy. You just give yourself up to it. And float.

But my mind wouldn't rest. It was like knitting — the steely needles clicking and flashing.

All the years *he* locked himself away in his study

not to be disturbed typing over his lecture notes, always the same lecture notes, working on his scholarly articles, his single book — the source of some ancient Greek tragedy no one ever read who hadn't been assigned to. Well we were proud of him I suppose, his wife and daughters I suppose, there is natural pride in us all thus we must be proud of something I suppose! And of course his salary as a professor of classics supported us, I grant that. Poor fool sucking on that pipe of his not knowing what it was, he sucked. None of them do. and when he was forbidden actual smoke he sucked on the unlit pipe like a baby with a rubber nipple, now that *is* pathetic. They held the retirement party in the classics common room, just sweet red wine and cheese cubes on toothpicks, a few toasts, the chairman praising and *him* rising to thank, tears gleaming in his eyes while the younger professors exchanged smirks and even the senior professors, next to go, swallowed yawns like swallowing pits almost too big to go down. Now that was funny to observe!

All toasts to Professor Emeritus, and *him* raising his wine glass so solemnly. Never knowing. Poor vain fool never guessing what it was the first thing to come into *my* mind, about that occasion.

Yet, then, in a weakness of my own, seeking revenge on [my only friends, I let him talk me into moving out here.

His retirement: how is it mine?

I tried to sleep but the rain continued hard as before, and the thunder began to come nearer like something huge rolling across the countryside aimed for this very house so my eyes flew open in terror as the thing, it was a gigantic round object, *rolled over the house and away across the fields to disappear. But no lightning! Not before, or after. The night was dark as any night I had ever seen.*

Now I tried to wake *him*. Seized his shoulder, shook *him*.

Wake up! help us! Something terrible has happened!

My voice climbed high as a mad soprano's yet had no effect on *him*. In this pitch black I could not see *him*, not so much as a blur,

Yet I was certain it must be *him*, my husband of fifty-one years lying beside me slack and heavy as a bag of fertilizer, the mattress sagging beneath him. I groped feeling his whiskery jaws, his thin hair and the bony skull beneath. I groped feeling his eyes, which were wide open like my own.

Myron! What is it! What has happened to you!

Yet he lay there unmoving. And now a dank sickish odor arose from the bedclothes pinching my nostrils hard.

I realized I had not heard his breathing for some minutes. That snoring-snuffling, that rattle in his throat.

Anger rose in me in clots like phlegm. Sucking that pipe of his not knowing what he sucked, hadn't the doctor warned him! — and I, and his doting daughters, warned him!

But, no: Professor's mind was off in the ancient world, or poking about in the stars (for the Universe was one of his "interests.")

Wake up! Wake up! Wake up! How dare you leave me, at such a, time! — and I struck his shoulder hard, with my fist.

Did *he* groan, or was it my imagination? — drowned out in any case by a sudden swelling of thunder again, rolling over the countryside and the house so I whimpered for mercy like a child. And still there was no lightning, not the briefest of flashes!

Which was not natural, I knew. For thunder must be preceded by lightning, for thunder is precipitated by lightning splitting the sky in pieces, that fact I knew.

Unless the sound was not of thunder at all but something else?

Suddenly I was in the grip of a panic seizing me from the outside as from the dark, I pushed *him from me as of no further use, for had he* known who I was, or so much as looked at me these many years? — the thought coming to me, *No one can help anyone now, this is the dark of the very beginning, and the end.*

That would have been about 4 A.M., by my subsequent calculations. At the time, in my panicked state, in the first knowledge that *he* was dead, and that I should get help, I was not able to absorb the significance of such wisdom. Knowing only that I was alone, oh and so terrified! my heart beating like a wild creature's so terrified! That *he* had abandoned me at the very start of this siege, this terror abroad in the world beyond my knowledge.

I climbed out of our common bed desperate to be gone as from a grave.

The ceiling was leaking? — the bedclothes were damp, something sticky on the coverlet. That foul sickish-sweet odor in the air despite the fresh smell of the rain. Oh I blamed *him!* I blamed *him!* Fumbling for the telephone in the dark, overturning a lamp, and I shrieked, oh I screamed, and began sobbing like a young bride having lost *him,* whose face I had not truly seen for a long time, though not so long a time as *he* had not seen mine.

Once, my elder daughter had discovered me, in the kitchen of our old house in University Heights, and said, shocked, Why Mother, why Are you crying? — and I hid my face from her young eyes murmuring in anger and shame, Because your father and I are no longer husband and wife, we have not loved each other in twenty years, and my daughter drew in her breath sharply as if she had heard an obscenity from this middle-aged woman, her mother's lips; and said, Oh Mother! — I don't believe that! — turning away from me in distaste for she meant instead, as they all mean, the children who spring from our bodies and stride away quick and brisk as they can, I don't want to hear such a thing from *you.*

And now *he* was dead, and I must get help, except, on my hands and knees groping for the fallen telephone, I understood that, if he was dead, it was

for the same reason that the power was out; if the power was out, it was for the same reason that he was dead — thus beyond all human help.

And did I want strangers coming into this room, even should they be able to find this house, this room, in the pitch-black night?

My fingers scrambled against the coarse material of the carpet but I could not locate the plastic telephone, nor hear its dial tone which meant, I realized, that the telephone lines too were down; all communication with the outside world had ceased.

That foul sickish odor. *His. Him.* Suddenly it was unbearable, cooped up in here with *him.* A wildness came over me, that I had to escape.

I crawled on hands and knees in the direction of the door, whispering to myself yes! yes! like this! have courage! There was a kerosene lamp on the bureau, and matches, for just such emergencies; but I seemed to know that I would not be able to find it, still less light the wick with my trembling fingers.

So it was, on hands and knees trailing my nightgown stinking of the grave, I escaped.

Slowly, painstakingly, panting with strain, I descended the steep stairs into the dark.

So many steps! — I had never counted them before, and, descending them now, lost count at twenty.

I grasped the banister (which was not very steady) with my left hand and groped along the wall with my right hand. My eyes were dry of tears now and wide open staring seeing nothing below me except the dark, blunt and depthless as a smear of black paint. I understood that there was something mysterious about this dark which was like no other dark of my life.

I must see, I must have light to see.

I was desperate to get downstairs, to get the flashlight out of the cupboard; to light candles. In my haste I had forgotten my bathrobe, my slippers. I could not have said which year it was, nor where I was, which house this was of the houses I had lived in. Oh, a woman of my age, coarse gray hair trailing down between her shoulder blades, heavy flaccid breasts, hips, thighs, belly flaccid too, panting like a dog, and sweating, even on these drafty stairs sweating, barefoot and ungainly, how my former friends would stare in pity, how my daughters would sneer! Never do you dream as a young woman that, one day, this will be *you.*

The rain and the thunder continued, but still there was no lightning. Except for the pull of gravity I did not seem to be going *down* until suddenly, lowering a foot to the next step I discovered there was no next step, I had come to the end of the stairs.

I was trembling badly, crouched as if to ward off an attack. But the darkness was empty.

And here the foul odor of that upper room was dissipated. I could still smell it — it clung to my flannel nightgown, my hair — but less strongly. A sharp smell of rain and earth prevailed, a smell I associated with spring. The rains of spring, and the

thaw after the long winter. Each year the thaw seems to come later in the season, thus it is more welcome. On gusty days, when the Sun shines, such smells can make you feel as if you are *alive.*

I was clutching at the newel post trying to get my bearings. To my right was the parlor, to my left the kitchen. It was the kitchen I sought.

Like stepping off into black water then I groped in the direction of the kitchen yet colliding at once with a chair (but who had left a chair in such a place?) and knocking the side of my head against the sharp edge of something (a shelf? — *there?*), finally entering the kitchen knowing it was that room by the odor of cooking and grease and the cold linoleum beneath my feet.

Here too I fumbled for the light switch on the wall — so strong is the force of habit.

But no light of course. The darkness remained steady and depthless.

It crossed my mind here to attempt the telephone another time, for there was need to get help, a terrible need wasn't there? — though memory was blurred, as to exactly why. But the telephone, on the wall beside the sink, was on the far side of the expanse of floor black and fearful as deep water, and my bowels clenched at the risk. And *what if I was not alone? What if something waited for me to make a false move?* All unexpectedly I found myself at the refrigerator, the, door open, cold wafting out, ravenous with hunger; suddenly I reached blindly yet unerringly for a piece of frosted cinnamon coffee cake I had wrapped in cellophane yesterday morning, a quart container of mile, able to see in my mind's eye as I could not see in the dark. And shameless and trembling with animal appetite I stood there, the door open wastefully, devouring cake until the last crumb was gone and drinking milk so greedily some dribbled on my nightgown. Then, appetite sated, I felt the disgust of my behavior, and the folly, quickly shutting the door to conserve the precious cold.

The electricity being off, and who knows when it might be restored, perishables in the refrigerator and the freezer were in danger of spoilage. Of course a freezer will keep certain foods (for instance meat) for hours before defrosting begins but once the process starts it cannot be reversed, under threat of food poisoning.

I was in dread of being without food if the storm continued, if the roads were out and I dared not leave the house for days. For the telephone was of no use, for even should my call go through, I would be greeted by mockery and derision. I would be provoked,into screaming curses, and then they would know my name.

I had to have light, now in a panic ravenous for light as for food I groped my way to the cupboard where the flashlight was kept, amid the canisters and aerosol spray cans; but where was the flashlight? — had *he* misplaced it? — in my haste knocking an object to the floor where it shattered, a cup perhaps, shattering at my feet and now the added danger of stepping in broken glass with my poor bare feet, O God have mercy! So distraught now whimpering aloud *Why? why? help me!* seeking the lost flashlight I wondered if unknowingly in my past I had committed some terrible sin for which I must now be punished, some meanness or hardness of the heart committed not willfully perhaps but in the absence of will or conscious intention as in our blind lives we perform so many actions only half thinking, half *seeing* the effects of our behavior. And if so, may You forgive me!

(Yet I could not believe I had truly committed any such sin, for I remembered nothing. As if the electrical failure here had erased all memory too. As if, in absolute dark, there need be no time save absolute Now.)

And then in my desperation trying an adjacent cupboard, where the flashlight had never once been, I discovered it! — snatched it up at once and pushed the little switch with my thumb; but, though it clicked on at once, *there came no light.*

How was it possible? Was the battery dead? And yet, I had used the flashlight only recently, down in the cellar — in the dark alcove where my canned fruits are kept.

And yet: *there came no light.*

Sobbing aloud now in frustration and despair I took a step unwisely and my foot came down on a splinter of glass. Fortunately I had not put my full weight upon the foot, yet the cut stung, and was surely bleeding.

Carefully then as I could, trying to control my sobbing (for I am as I have said a practical-minded woman, the capable wife of this and previous households for beyond a half-century), I groped my way to the far side of the kitchen, located the counter beside the sink, the drawer beneath, where loose candles and matches were kept for such emergencies, and moving my lips in prayer to You for mercy (I, who had cast off in disdain my belief in You so many years ago!) struck matches, holding them with trembling fingers against a candle's invisible wick, and how vexing! how much trickier a task than lighting a candle you can see! finally after numerous clumsy attempts, I succeeded, I swear, for one of the matches *did* catch fire, and I smelled sulphur — but I saw *no flame.*

Then it was clear and irrefutable to me, what I had only suspected previously — that there was something mysterious about this dark, this night; something that made it unlike any other dark or any other night. For it was not the mere absence of light (which is of course derived from our Sun) but the *presence of dark itself thick and opaque as any matter.*

Thus I realized it could have no visible effect whether a match was "lighted" — whether a candle wick "burned." What would have been light under normal circumstances was immediately sucked away, vanished, as if it had no existence. For indeed it had no existence.

If I could bear this, till dawn — !

With dawn, surely all, would be well? (The storm seemed to be abating. Yet even if the rain continued, and the sky remained overcast, there *would* be light — for what evil force could withstand the strength of our Sun?)

I did not believe in God, but I believed in our Sun. Though never listening with much attention when *he* would prattle on reading to me out of one of his science magazines, the billion-billion-billion age of the Sun, or size of the Universe, or whether Time might be collapsed into something small enough to fit in my thimble! — as if, sighing with my house-wifely tasks, I had the patience for such.

How exhausted I was suddenly, my search for light so futile, and my dignity rent, I turned in haste to grope my way back out into the hall thinking in my confusion that I would climb the stairs and return to bed — not remembering in my confusion what it was that had usurped my bed, thus my sleep, how I abhorred it, what wickedness it sought to inflict upon me, and another time I stepped upon glass this time cutting my foot more severely. Fool! fool! fool! I cried feeling the blood slippery against the linoleum floor; yet, spared of seeing it, unexpectedly I seemed hardly to care.

I groped, stumbled, blundered my way into the hall, and into the parlor, sobbing aloud in anger, and if anything or anyone awaited me, in that dark smelling of mildew and dust (had I not cleaned in that room, vacuumed and polished, only last week?) I did not care in the slightest — I did not. So exhausted now that my legs were as water beneath me, I groped for the sofa, a handsome old leather sofa of *his* purchase as I recalled it, smooth to the touch but fine-cracked in places with age, and cold. But by now I did not care what sort of thing it was I lay down on. I wanted only to shut my eyes, and sleep.

And did I sleep, indeed? — was it sleep I slipped into, or a greater, bottomless dark, whimpering and moaning to myself, unable to find a position on the sofa that did not pinch my neck, distend my spine? — release formless terrors to my brain?

I did not dream. I "saw" nothing. Until waking at last to the Sun, I "saw" myself waking eager and smiling to the new day, a pale but unmistakable sunlight leaking through the lacy curtains of the parlor window — At last! at last!

Except, cruelly, this *was* a dream — and when I sat up blinking and dazed, I found myself staring into the dark, as before; the unchanged, hideous dark. For long minutes I simply could not grasp what had happened, where I was, for I was *not* in my bed, nor in any bed I knew; calling out, so great was my confusion, Myron! Myron! Where are you! What has happened to us!

And then, as if a black tide swept upon me, and swept me away with it, I remembered. I knew.

Should you track me to my hiding place supposing me, a woman of my age, alone, thus vulnerable, you would be mistaken. For the darkness in this place is so complete, none of you will ever penetrate it.

And I have driven in three-inch spikes, to seal the door from within.

I am in no danger of running out of provisions. I have stocked all I could of fresh and canned goods from the kitchen; I have here, in the cellar, dozens of jars of preserves — pears, cherries, tomatoes, rhubarb, even pickles; and there is an apple bin, and a sack of Idaho potatoes. Devoured raw, some foods are more delicious than cooked.

(The preserves I had prepared out of a need to keep busy, here in the country where I knew no one,, and cared to know no one. even as *he* went about shaking hands, smiling in *his* hope, poor fool, of being accepted as one of you. And which of us now stands vindicated?)

I am no longer fearful of the dark. For here, in this place, it is *my* dark.

When it was exactly, how many days (days? nights? now there is no distinction, the very words sound foolish) I understand what had happened and how, with no more delay, I must hide, I cannot recall — it may have been the equivalent of a month, it may have been only a few hours ago. In perpetual night, Time does not apply.

I do remember though long months through the preceding winter when the sky was overcast and the Sun, burning through, had a look of tarnished pewter; the many evenings the lights in the house would dim and flicker. My complaints to the power company fell on deaf ears — of course.

Then came the storm: the actual attack.

And when I woke to dawn it was to night though hearing certain but unmistakable sounds — the cries of birds close about the house — understanding that it *was* dawn; yet without the Sun.

And the rain had ceased. and the thunder. Groping to a window in what was the parlor I pressed both hands against the pane feeling, yes, the warmth of the Sun, it *was* the Sun, though invisible. As, earlier, there had been the struck flame of a match and a candle's burning wick. But the change was upon the world, *there could be no light.*

I had not time then to comprehend what had happened, what disaster of nature, knowing only that I must act quickly! Homeowners like myself would have to protect themselves against looting, burning, rape, and pillage of every kind — for the world would now divide itself into those *with* shelter and provisions and those *without.*

Those *with* a secure hiding place, and those *without.*

So I have barricaded myself here. In the cellar, in the dark,. I require no eyes.

I have memorized all this space by touch. Never can I be enticed to leave. Thus do not appeal to me, do not threaten me, do not even approach. I know nothing of *before* the catastrophe, and have no interest. Should any of you claim to be kin of mine, even to be my daughters, be advised: I am not the woman you once knew, *nor any woman at all.*

In *his* prattle *he* once marveled at certain dangers to the Earth from outer space, a warning, or was it a prophecy, that one day a malevolent celestial body (comet? asteroid?) would strike Earth with an impact equivalent to the release of numberless nuclear explosions, thus rocking Earth off its natural course, raising pulverized rock and dust to block all sunlight henceforth casting sinful mankind into perpetual night. If this is Your wish, so it is Your wish. It is the end of the old world yet not the end to those of us who were prepared.

Even now I hear sirens in the distance. I am sure that that foul, acrid smell is a smell of smoke.

But I have no curiosity; I have made my own peace.

As I've said I have provisions to last for many months — for the remainder of my life. I have food, and water; not water out of the well but water fresh enough for me, dank, earthy-smelling but plenteous here in the cellar darkness where it lies in some areas to a depth of four or five inches; and, when rain returns, it will trickle freely down the rock walls where I can lap it delightedly with my tongue. Ω

ROKURO-KUBI

by Reginald Bretnor
illustrated by Stephen E. Fabian

It was one of those nights at The Bilge Pump when all the science-fiction people — a lot of them from Berkeley and pretty weird — had taken not only most of the tables but also all but a couple of the seats at the bar, but as always there were a few scientists mixed in, to say nothing of stray travellers, soldiers of fortune (real and rambo-type), and one or two quiet friends of Captain Edmund Casebolt Crankshaw, who owns and, with his lovely Javanese mistress and Mickey, his huge Fijian bartender with the filed teeth, runs the place. In short, the atmosphere was just right for story-telling — usually the taller the better.

The Bilge Pump is down in the bowels of H.M.S. *Dryad,* which sank at her moorings when her crew deserted in mass during the Gold Rush, like so many other good ships now buried under San Francisco's waterfront. A few of her officers, however, managed somehow to keep her after-cabins watertight, so that when the *Dryad* House Hotel (famous or infamous, take your pick) was built over her, with her mizzen-mast still sticking up through the lobby, all you had to do to reach the Bilge Pump was walk down the companionway and there you were.

I spotted Crankshaw at his usual table, at the far end of the bar, but saw he was with a stranger and started for the bar. He spotted me. "Jackson!" he called. "Jackson Hendry! Come and join us. Here, this'll interest you."

As I seated myself, he introduced his companion Dexter Meerlo, Colonel Dexter Meerlo, a tall, very gaunt, very hard old man — several years, I guessed, beyond retirement. He was seated right in front of the semi-nude Dryad figurehead which had once graced the ship's prow.

Mickey, grinning ferociously, brought me my usual good scotch and water. Crankshaw was, as always, sipping Pusser's Rum, and Meerlo was drinking, of all things, warm *saké*. I must have raised an eyebrow because he smiled at me. "Spend enough time in Japan," he said, "and it begins to grow on you —" He smiled again. "— like the tea ceremony and the *kabuki* drama and so many of their women, like moss-covered stone lanterns, and the dripping cryptomerias in wet weather, and their temples and three-hundred-mile-an-hour trains, and pilgrimages and graveyards." He poured himself another cup of *saké*. "Yes, yes — especially the graveyards. Let's say nothing about what they own over here. It's not important."

"Not important?" I said incredulously.

"I don't think so. Not to them. Not in the long view. Their psychic roots are fastened so deeply in the past, in their dreadful civil wars, in the cruelties of those centuries of lawlessness — and, almost worse, the customs of the Tokugawa Shogunate — read the code of Tokugawa law. Think! Is this not true of so many great cultures? This memory of opposites? Think of Imperial Germany, in many ways Europe's most civilized country, but with the memory of the 16th century's horrible witchhunts, and the Thirty Years War and finally the Kaiser's war and Hitler's, and the Holocaust — and probably the loveliest music the world has ever known. And what of our past? What of democracy and the Rights of Man — and Hamburg and Dresden and Hiroshima and Nagasaki?"

I looked at Crankshaw.

"Listen," he said, "He may have a point."

The soft light from the ship's brass oil lamps in their gimbals — the only illumination that Crankshaw permitted there — shone from the burnished paneling and from the harsh planes of Meerlo's face, and he leaned forward over the table. "Edmund tells me you're an anthropologist," he said. "Well, if you will forgive my effrontery, I'll tell you a story. You cannot understand a people, a culture, until you understand their fears, their terrors, their ghosts and goblins. The night side of their lives. And do not think these things are not real! Never fall into that delusion."

He drank his *saké* down, poured more from the warmed pot. *"So,"* he said, "let us talk about Japan, about their night-fears, about the things that haunt their buried dead."

Again I glanced at Crankshaw, raised an eyebrow. Was *saké* having its treacherously subtle influence? He shook his head very slightly.

"First," Meerlo went on, "I must tell you that I was not a line officer."

"My error," Crankshaw interrupted with a smile. "I should have said *Doctor* Meerlo — Herr Doktor Colonel."

"Hardly. We didn't go in for such pomposities in the U.S. Army, but I did become a doctor, and I was commissioned during the Occupation — I'd been much too young for the War — and, partly because I spoke fairly good Japanese, I was assigned to a unit in a rather isolated Northern prefecture, one which had scarcely felt the war directly — not the way Tokyo and Osaka and Kobe felt it. But let me backtrack. I spent several years in Japan as a small boy, in the late 'twenties, and much of the time we lived in the old Tor Hotel on the Hill in Kobe, run by Swiss; and of course while we were there I managed to catch most of the childhood diseases that were prevalent; and — I can't imagine what possessed her to do it — my mother used to read aloud to me, usually Lafcadio Hearn's renditions of what the publishers were pleased to call 'Japanese Fairy Tales' — tales of the returning, vengeful dead, of shapechangers like the Cat of Nabeshima, of vampires. They gave me nightmares, but they also stimulated my interest in that dark side of Japan, so that later on I read things like James de Benneville's *Yotsuya Kwaidan* and *Bakemono Yashiki,* which are enough to give even an adult nightmares. If you want to get some idea of how dreadful ghostly Japan was and is, look at Kuniyoshi's ghost-prints." He called to Mickey to replenish the *saké* supply.

"Now don't misunderstand me. I love Japan. My wife was Japanese. My children are half Japanese and justly proud of it. *But*—" He paused, rapping the table-top for emphasis. "But love changes no realities. The Japanese nation is what it is, with its perfect aesthetics, its superb, refined arts, and all the horrors it has inherited — horrors which showed themselves at the Rape of Nanking, the Bataan Death March, in Cabanatuan and Bilibid Prison and in every area where a new generation of Japanese troops who believed themselves to be all-of-a-sudden samurai were turned loose. Yes, and there is a close relationship between such behavior and the nightside of which I spoke. I think Jung might have had a great deal to say about it — the mass subconscious, the heritage of those cruel centuries."

"We all share in it," said Crankshaw, "at least in our own. It varies. In Europe, the farther east and south you go, the more terrible the history of needless cruelty, of torture. In England, in the Scandinavian countries, it was — at least relatively — mild, but we are really no exception except in degree."

"That is true," said Meerlo. He looked at me. "Some anthropologist should study this. Have you read a book called *The Holographic Paradigm?* which speaks of the entire living universe as a hologram created by a universal mind — of which our own minds are a part? Could it be that we ourselves, with our heritage of fear and suffering, inflicted on us and *by* us on others — could it be that in the hologram it is we who bring the horrors of the night to life?"

"But do they really come to life?" I asked — I'm afraid very dubiously.

"Do they? Ask yourself — why is it that the same parts of Eastern Europe that nourished monsters like Vlad the Impaler and Elizabeth Bathory are especially noted for their vampires, their werewolves? I know little about those — but I do know what kind haunt Japan."

"You *know?*" I said.

"I *know*. My first overseas assignment, after my graduation and internship, when I joined as a first lieutenant, was to Japan. The occupation was about a year old, and everybody had long since stopped being nervous about it. I was assigned to a town called Nakazawa, not much more than a market town for the surrounding countryside. It was a town of ancient temples — a lot of them — and a few old, old feudal mansions, mostly in a sad state of disrepair, and a great warren of humbler dwellings, most of which had probably been burned down and rebuilt dozens of times in the old days, and endless graveyards. Are you familiar with Japanese cemeteries? With their lichened stones, and carved stone lanterns, and boulders with names and poems carved into their surfaces? All usually well cared for, carefully landscaped, their paths raked daily so that ancestors are honored and relatives and descendants not inconvenienced? Well, Nakazawa had one cemetery, near a temple abandoned and falling into ruin, which had not been cared for. It was on the outskirts, just up-river a few hundred yards from our HQ — a dismal, depressing place; even the ancient trees overlooking it seemed struggling simply to survive. The Japanese whom we hired, and others we had regular dealings with, didn't like to go anywhere near it, at least at night, and the only answer we could get out of them if we asked was *bakemono, bakemono,* meaning it was haunted. Most of us, of course, simply took this with a grain of salt, but we had one man — a QM sergeant named Jimson Tellis, from somewhere in the Southwest, who was dead certain all the talk was just a cover-up for something the Japanese didn't want us to find out.

"We had a strange set-up. Nobody could figure out why the Army had put us there, and what their reasoning was behind their choice of units. There was a QM warehouse and a small motor pool, all commanded by a captain who always seemed to be off somewhere inspecting something, and an engineer unit under a first lieutenant, and a short-handed company of infantry with another captain. We also had a Mormon chaplain — nobody could figure out just why because he was the only Mormon there. And of course there was my medical detachment, and what with one thing and another only too often I turned out to be the ranking commissioned officer — I guess because most of the others took every chance they could get to approve their own leave applications. Anyhow —"

But at that point, Captain Crankshaw interrupted him. "Forgive me," he said. "Did you see who just came in?"

"You mean that enormous fat man?"

"I do, and I'm afraid he'll almost certainly come over and announce he's joining us — and I really won't be able to say no because if we turn him down he'll start nagging those science-fiction people, who after all are having a good time. You see, he's a — well, the only way I can put it is that he's a queller of tales. He belongs to some organization that claims to investigate anything they don't consider normal *scientifically* — you know, ESP and UFOs and sea serpents and all that sort of thing — and he loves to get some of the science-fiction and fantasy types riled up. Of course, what he is is a dedicated debunker, in other words about as credulous as he can get. It takes a strange sort of mind to argue that a career shipmaster could mistake a school of porpoises for a sea monster."

"And I suppose he feels the same way about *bakemono?*"

"Oh, indeed yes."

"Well then, by all means ask him over." Meerlo smiled thinly. "I'll give him an earful."

But the newcomer needed no invitation. As soon as he spotted Crankshaw and the vacant chair at our table, he waved and headed toward us, red-faced and rumpled and puffing from his walk down the stairs. He was somewhere in his late fifties, with rather dim blue eyes and a funny little pursed mouth. "Aha!" he cried out. "Crankshaw, I see you're not alone!"

"We were in the middle of a story," replied Crankshaw.

"Good, good!" he said, ignoring the lack of welcome in the Captain's voice. "I'm Luther Hengist — *Professor* Luther Hengist, to be precise."

"Of economics, the *science* of economics," added Crankshaw, "and this is Colonel Meerlo, Colonel Dexter Meerlo, and I think you already know Jackson here."

Professor Hengist acknowledged our presence by rather perilously lowering his bulk into the chair, and waved to Mickey, who, looking thoroughly disgusted, brought him a Perrier.

"Now do go on with your story," he urged, with his tight little smile. "Just pretend I'm not here."

"I was talking about something that happened during the Occupation," said Meerlo. "I mentioned that this Sergeant Tellis thought all those stories of a haunted graveyard had to be a cover-up, to keep us from finding something out. He was out to make every buck he could, any way he could, and being a quartermaster he had access to all sorts of trading stock, some of it stuff almost worthless to us but which the Japanese needed desperately. Looking back at it, I realize that he had an uncanny eye where works of art were concerned — those that were almost valueless at the time but are now, in some cases at least, worth fortunes. God only knows what he managed to ship back to the states — bronzes and lovely old ceramics and fine iron kettles, scrolls and woodblock prints and temple bells and sacred statues. But what he wanted most was swords, and that of course was a different kettle of fish, for the Japanese had had to turn all their weapons in, swords and spears and the lot, so he had to do his wheeling and dealing with officers who'd managed to get one or two and NCOs in charge of local sword warehouses. Of course, he grabbed a lot of fine sword furnishings, guards, and the mountings of the hilt, some of them simply splendid, but it was the blades he was really after. He'd picked up a Japanese accomplice, a man named Mori — after what happened, we called him *Memento Mori* —"

I saw Hengist prick up his ears at that.

"This Mori," continued Meerlo, "was pretty well despised by his countrymen — under a different sort of Occupation, a Nazi or Soviet one, he'd have been a petty Quisling, but to us he was just a crooked little s.o.b. on the make — though sometimes now I wonder —"

He broke off. Mickey — telepathically aware? — brought him another properly warmed bottle of *saké*.

He raised his tiny cup. "Here's to *bakemono*!" he said, and we all — Hengist, to my surprise, included, probably because he had no idea of what *bakemono* meant — drank with him. "Well, Mori tipped him off to a General Inaba, one of the old generation of samurai generals, long retired, who had known that Japan could never win a war with the United States, with the free West. It was, especially from a Japanese standpoint, a tragic story. One of his sons had been killed in China during the 'thirties, the other early in their invasion of Malaysia. They were his only sons, there were no grandsons, and it was too late to follow the old custom of adopting a remoter relative. The same thing had happened to General Nogi during the Russo-Japanese War. In each case, that meant the end of their House, and that no one would be left to pay due reverence to the ancestors. Anyhow, old Inaba died only three months before the surrender and no one knew what had become of his swords — his family's swords, swords dating back through centuries, a great Heian Period *ō-dachi*, over five feet long and very possibly a National Treasure, a splendid *katana* by Rai Kunitoshi, another by Inouye Shinkai, certified to have cut through three men at the chest with one stroke in the sword-tester's yard, a *tantō* forged for a daimyo by Kawabe Masahide, and a few others. Those names may not mean anything to you, but they meant a great deal in Feudal Japan, and where money is concerned they'd mean a very great deal to today's collectors.

When old Inaba died, one or two very distant relations, one a naval officer, another a Buddhist priest, made hurried trips to Nakazawa, and saw to it that his ashes were buried in the family plot in that deserted graveyard. But the swords had simply vanished. What had become of them? Well, Sergeant Tellis thought he had the answer; maybe Mori hinted at it. He was sure the old man had had them buried with him, under or near the great, rough boulder with his name and death-poem carved into it. And he, Jimson Tellis, was going after them. They would, he said, be safely boxed and wrapped in many layers of covering, oiled and thoroughly waterproofed, and he was only waiting for a good soaking rain so the digging would be easier. The damned fool went around bragging about it, so finally nobody took him seriously. His CO called him an asshole, mentioned that desecrating graves was very definitely an Occupation no-no, then forgot it. It was another noncom, a Corporal Lammers from Arkansas, who finally came to me about it — at the last minute.

"It was a cold, wet miserable late evening. I was in my quarters and Lammers came pushing his way in past my Japanese servant, who was politely trying to keep him out. 'Doc — I mean *sir* —' he blurted. 'I don't know who the Hell else to talk to. Seems like there's no commissioned officers left except a coupla second looeys. Even the padre's off someplace. But sir, that goddam Jim Tellis is off his nut. He's got himself a pair of shovels and he swears he and Mori are on their way to that ol' graveyard to dig up Inaba's bones or whatever and get his swords, and sir, when the Japs here get wind of it and start kicking up a stink it's goin' to make MacArthur mighty unhappy. Sir, can't you do *something*?'

"Lammers had been my driver many times, and I knew he wasn't the sort to go off half-cocked, but still I hesitated. 'You're sure there's no other officer available?' I said.

" 'Not as I could locate, sir.'

" 'And just where in the graveyard is the old general's grave?'

" 'I found out, sir. It's up in the northwest corner, where the wall crumbles and runs almost to the river. I've got the captain's car and we can run it up the road to that hill above the northeast corner of the wall, turn off the engine, and coast almost clear down to it. Tellis is usin' a jeep, and he'll be able to drive clear down to the grave, but we'll have to walk after we reach the wall so's to sneak up on them. And sir —' He was really getting agitated. '— we'd best leave right away quick, or they'll have the place halfway dug up by the time we get there.'

"I saw the sense in that. I told him to get the car started up, phoned my own sergeant to tell him what I was up to, slipped into my cavalry mackinaw, and got in next to Lammers. We were on our way immediately."

Meerlo paused while Mickey replenished the supply of *saké*, brought Crankshaw some more Pusser's and me another scotch-and-water, and ignored Hengist's gesture towards his Perrier.

"It really was a wretched night. The rain had stopped, at least for a while, and though there was an almost full moon, it was hiding behind the windswept clouds as though ashamed to show its face. At the crest of the hill, Lammers shut off the engine, and we ghosted silently down the narrow path toward the wall's northeast corner. We probably would have mired down if we'd tried to drive any farther. We left the car without shutting its doors, and started walking, hugging the wall and trying to stay out of the mud. The trees, wind-whipped, showered icy water down on us. A third of the way, and we saw the jeep; apparently Tellis hadn't wanted to risk driving any farther. Another third, and we heard low voices and the sound of shovels digging into the sodden earth. And it was then we saw *it*. In the moon's erratic light it floated out of the trees and along the wall, perhaps six feet off the ground. We saw it momentarily, quite clearly; then a cloud hid it; then it showed again. It looked for all the world like a ghastly severed head, its pallor seemingly self-illuminated, a severed head trailing its gullet, its stomach, its sickly gut."

"*Rokuro-kubi!*" whispered Crankshaw.

"So you know?" said Meerlo.

Hengist chuckled. "Somebody must've thought it was Halloween," he commented.

Meerlo didn't even look at him. "We were frozen there, both of us. We saw it only too, too clearly. We saw its strangely yellow teeth, the shreds of hair clinging to its scalp, and what we hoped were not its eyes. There was no sound, none at all. It passed by. It disappeared. We did not, could not, move. After an interminable minute, we heard a single dreadful shriek, then frantic, running, stumbling feet, then somebody trying desperately to get the jeep's engine

started, finally succeeding, then the jeep, its engine screaming, slewing in the mud and finally passing us in its attempt to reach the road. There was only one man in it, and it did not look like Tellis. I really can't say how long we stood there paralyzed before we saw the thing come floating back. We stared at it. There was one difference. Now the stomach, which had first been flaccid, was distended. It passed us, moving more slowly than when it first appeared. Once more it vanished into the trees. Only then were we able to break the spell that held us, to move our limbs, to speak."

" 'Jesus H. Christ!' gasped Lammers. 'What was *that*?'

" 'We'd better go and see what's happened,' I told him, I'll admit very reluctantly. 'That wasn't Tellis in the jeep. Come on.'

"Like a good soldier, he followed my unenthusiastic lead. We made our way along the wall, pausing to look apprehensively over our shoulders. We reached the wall's end, where it was crumbling. We climbed over. Before us was the huge boulder which marked the general's grave, and in front of it, lying there contorted, was Sergeant Tellis. His eyes were wide. His face was a riven mask of horror. He was, of course, quite dead."

"The man died of terror, obviously," declared Hengist. "Of terror and his own ignorant superstitions. What he saw was in all probability some sort of child's balloon."

"Obviously?" Meerlo turned to me. "What do you think, Mr. Hendry?"

"There's certainly no shortage of such cases," I replied, "Belief and suggestion are a treacherous combination, but usually among primitives. Besides, no balloon the size of a man's head could possibly drag the appendages you described. There's no known gas, not hydrogen, not helium, that'd make it possible."

"More Perrier, bartender!" called Hengist irritably. Then, "Of course not, unless it was held up by wires. In that weather, among those dripping trees, they'd be quite invisible. Yes, it could very well have been a Japanese paper lantern with a face painted on it, pulled along back and forth. Someone had undoubtedly heard the man bragging."

"Do you think so?" Meerlo smiled.

"Think so? I'm certain of it!"

"There is a Japanese legend," put in Crankshaw quietly, "of a sort of vampire called a *rokuro-kubi*," which very closely resembles what you have described."

"Exactly!" crowed Hengist. "And that fellow Mori probably filled the sergeant's head with the idea."

Crankshaw shrugged. "Dexter," he said, "tell us what you did after you found him."

"I did the most difficult thing I've ever done. My craven instinct was to order poor Lammers to keep watch while I drove back and made the necessary phone calls — one to the closest MPs, one to our hospital in the much bigger city about fifteen miles away, and one to whoever was Tellis' ranking QM officer. But I managed to remember the responsibilities of rank, so I sent him to make the calls, giving him very precise instructions. We'd need an ambulance, I told him, and he was to forward my urgent request that they send their top surgeon, a Major Whitehead — I really emphasized that because I knew there'd have to be an autopsy, and the sooner the better.

"As I've said, Lammers was a good soldier. He actually protested that wouldn't it be better if he stayed and I went back? But I could see how relieved he was when I made it an order, and off he went like a bullet. I could tell by the sound of the car's motor that he was wasting no time.

"He made the calls in the order I'd stipulated, to get the ambulance and surgeon and the MPs on the way as fast as possible, but it still seemed like forever. I shivered there alone, leaning against the general's monument, and hoping against hope that nothing would come drifting, through the trees and the errant wisps of fog, towards me. Nothing did, and after a year or so, Lammers — God bless him! — arrived with another QM sergeant and a very young Engineer officer, neither of whom were any help. Then the ambulance arrived, and we got Tellis out of there, and later that night Major Whitehead and I performed the autopsy."

"And of course," said Professor Hengist, "you found nothing?"

"Oh, we found no evidence of violence," replied Meerlo, "— which by the way let that wretched Mori off the hook — he'd been found weeping next to the wrecked jeep — but one of our medics handling Tellis when they brought him in pointed out an odd circumstance. 'Major,' he said, 'there's one thing queer. Lift this guy's head. It doesn't weigh hardly anything at all.'

"We lifted it, and he was right, so of course there was only one thing to do. Reluctantly, reporting the procedure step by step, we opened up the skull."

"And — ?" scoffed Hengist.

"And it was empty," said Meerlo. "There was *nothing* in it, nothing except a stub of brain-stem and a little — a very little — spinal fluid. Naturally, we filed two reports. One attributed the death to traumatic shock and heart failure. The other was very detailed and remained highly classified."

"What nonsense!" Hengist snapped, rising to his feet uncertainly, looking around as though for the refuge of more congenial company. "Do you expect me to believe that? And without any evidence?"

"Evidence?" Meerlo looked him up and down contemptuously. "There was enough for us. Under his nose, on his upper lip, there was a single drop of blood. And —" He paused, shuddering suddenly. "— and I never have been able to forget that hideously distended stomach."

"I wonder —" said Captain Crankshaw quietly, after a long, silent moment. "I wonder what sort of ghouls and vampires and unspeakable night-things we can expect to haunt Germany and Soviet Russia, or Vietnam and Cambodia, or the remotenesses of China, or the wastes of Ethiopia? In the future, what will haunt *our* world?" Ω

ISSN 0898-5073

Spring 1995 Cover by Jason Van Hollander

Worlds of Fantasy & Horror is published 4 times a year by Terminus Publishing Co., Inc., 123 Crooked
Lane, King of Prussia PA 19406-2670. Single copies, $4.95 in U.S.A. & possessions; $6.00 by mail
elsewhere. Subscriptions: 4 issues (one year) $16.00 in U.S.A. & possessions; $22.00 elsewhere, in U.S.
funds. Publisher is not responsible for loss of manuscripts in publisher's hands or in transit; please
see page 5 for more details. Postmaster: send address changes to *Worlds of Fantasy & Horror,* 123
Crooked Lane, King of Prussia PA 19406-2670. Copyright © 1995 by Terminus Publishing Co., Inc.; all
rights reserved; reproduction prohibited without prior permission. Typeset, printed, & bound in the
United States of America.

THE OWL'S NEST

Welcome to *Worlds of Fantasy & Horror*, Volume One, Number Two, which may be easily confused with a Certain Other Magazine which Terminus Publishing Co., Inc., no longer publishes. For those of you who came in late, let us briefly recapitulate: Between 1987 and early 1994, Terminus published *Weird Tales*, a continuation of the greatest pulp fantasy magazine of all time, the celebrated journal in which Robert E. Howard, Ray Bradbury, H.P. Lovecraft, Fritz Leiber, and many others made their first impressions upon the literary world. There are nineteen Terminus issues, numbered #290–308. Our just-previous issue, *Worlds of Fantasy & Horror*, Volume One Number One, would have been *Weird Tales* #309, had not fate intervened.

Fate intervened in the form of a television offer, made to the *owners* of the *Weird Tales* title, Weird Tales, Limited, who, quite understandably, took the offer. In the process they had to pull in various franchise options, including ours. The parting of the ways was on extremely friendly terms, and we admit that if we were in their shoes, we'd have done the same thing.

The result was that our previous issue suddenly became *Worlds of Fantasy & Horror*. Why that title? Some of you have written in expressing a certain amount of dismay at the change. Well, we believe in candor. Here's the candid truth: there's no sign that anybody else is going to be publishing a magazine called You Know What any time in the immediate future. Nothing has been announced, and we aren't privy to any deals currently being made. So, it seemed perfectly fair for us to go for a title which is not only descriptive of the contents, but just happens to have a very familiar, big red 'W' in it.

The, idea of course, is that many readers will pick up this familiar-looking magazine and get it all the way home before realizing that it's not quite what it used to be.

But, you may ask, whom are we trying to fool?

The answer is, no one at all. Our intention is to reassure rather than to deceive. *Worlds of Fantasy & Horror* will continue to have the same editorial staff, the same physical appearance, the same departments, the same stories as before. Only five words — the title — are different.

This seemed a better way to make it through the transition than changing the title to, say, *The Innsmouth Squamous Necrophage Review*.

The future's still exciting in these pages: Future issues include stories by Tanith Lee, Avram Davidson, Ian Watson, and many of the other regulars. Jason Van Hollander, who produced this issue's resplendent cover, will be back with a new graphic feature, *Pages from the Hell Book*. Even your editor will be back with a sequel to the World Fantasy Award nominated "To Become a Sorcerer."

In Memoriam: Robert Bloch, 1917–1994

We deeply regret to announce the death of one of the fantasy field's all-time greats, Robert Bloch, who died recently at the age of 77. Bloch had the ability to make anyone jump with fright — or roll with laughter. He was a unique talent and personality and will be greatly missed. Faithful Terminus readers will remember our special Bloch issue of *Weird Tales*, #300, and subsequent Bloch stories in issues 301 and 302. We had hoped to publish him in our pages many more times in the future.

Robert Bloch was born in 1917. As a teenager, he began correspondence with H.P. Lovecraft, who encouraged his efforts at horror fiction and even made corrections and notes on Bloch's fledgling manuscripts. Bloch's first professional appearance was "The Feast in the Abbey," published in *Weird Tales* for January 1935. Before long he was continually demonstrating, as he did all his life, that horror and humor are often two sides of the same coin. One of his earliest stories, "The Shambler from the Stars," featured a sage author of weird fiction, who remarkably resembles Lovecraft and who comes to a bad end, devoured by extra-cosmic Things. It's a joke, and an effective story at the same time. Lovecraft then replied with one of his masterpieces, "The Haunter of the Dark," in which another fearsome Thing makes off with a much younger writer named "Robert Blake."

Bloch's humor is sometimes overlooked. He was a charming man, one of the funniest our field has ever known, always in demand as a speaker or toastmaster. He wrote overtly humorous fantasy for the pulps, such as the "Lefty Feep" series for *Fantastic Adventures,* which come as close to baggy-pants vaudevillian comedy as the fantasy genre ever has, and quite a few other stories, such as the oft-reprinted and once filmed, "The Cloak," which induces some very *nervous* laughter, as the protagonist, a ham actor playing a movie vampire, finds himself wearing a *real* vampire's cape.

Bloch also had the ability to make macabre jokes in straight horror stories, *strengthening* rather than weakening the horror as he did so. One of his celebrated punch lines was, "Cat got your tongue?" You'll have to read the story ("Catnip") to see precisely what the cat did. . . .

Robert Bloch was also, incidentally, the author of *Psycho,* the novel from which the Alfred Hitchcock film of the same name was derived. As he was explaining in interviews forever after, no, the shower scene wasn't his idea. It was a joke of a different sort in Rhode Island 1975, at the first World Fantasy Convention, when Bloch had just finished (humorously) explaining this again, the mayor of Providence came in and immediately complimented Bloch in the shower scene in *Psycho.* Later that same afternoon, when Bloch received the Life Achievement Award from the convention, he chortled, "I haven't had this much fun since the rats ate my baby sister!"

BLOCH WAS SUPERB became a byword in fanzines, a familiar tag-line, accurate and descriptive. He was indeed; he was a pioneer in many important ways: modernizing the supernatural horror story; leavening horror with macabre humor; and developing what might be called the pathological suspense novel, a crime novel from the viewpoint of an evil or diseased mind. Certainly such modern bestsellers as *The Silence of the Lambs* owe a lot to work Bloch did as early as the late '30s and early '40s ("Slave of the Flames," about a pyromaniac, and the classic "Yours Truly, Jack the Ripper") not to mention

STAFF

Publisher: George H. Scithers.
Editor: Darrell Schweitzer.
Managing Editor: Carol Adams
Art Editor: Diane Weinstein
Assistant Editors: Leslie Smith,
Dainis Bisenieks, Spencer Blum,
& Michael W. Betancourt
Computer Consultant: David J. Williams III.
Of Counsel: Matthew Wolfe

Typesetters: Owlswick Press
Printer: Morgan Publishing, Inc.

MANUSCRIPT SUBMISSIONS:

Yes; we read unsolicited submissions — but *only* if they are in standard manuscript format. To survive, all editors insist on a few Rules: each submission must be in proper format and must include a return envelope addressed to you with enough postage affixed to bring the manuscript back to you. If you want us to discard the manuscript if we don't buy it, tell us so, but include a business-letter-size envelope, addressed to you, with proper postage affixed, so we can send you our comments. No loose stamps, please!

Proper manuscript format is discussed in many reference works. Some of us have even written one: *On Writing Science Fiction: the Editors Strike Back!* by Scithers, Schweitzer, & John M. Ford; $19.50 in hardcovers, from Owlswick Press, P.O. Box 8243, Philadelphia PA 19101-8243. Another excellent work from the same publisher is Barry B. Longyear's *Science-Fiction Writer's Workshop:* $9.50 in trade paperback. These prices include shipping and handling; in Pennsylvania, please include 6% sales tax.

We are not responsible for manuscripts in our hands or in transit. You *must* keep a copy of every manuscript you send out. You *must* put your name and address on the first page of every manuscript. Please: *no* binders, folders, or padded envelopes; and especially: *no* registered or certified mail for which we would have to stand in line at the post office!

such novels as *The Scarf, The Dead Beat,* and *American Gothic.*

Yes, he was superb.

Editorial Book Reviews. Let us recommend a couple of volumes you might not otherwise know about:

The Smoke of the Snake by Carl Jacobi, published by Fedogan and Bremer, 1994. 208 pp. $28.00. Jacobi was one of the workhorses of the pulp era, producing many, many horror, weird-menace, mystery, and adventure yarns (and occasional science fiction). He was always competent, occasionally outstanding, and one of the more popular contributors to *Weird Tales* in its original incarnation. Three volumes of his short fiction were published by August Derleth's Arkham House. A fourth was planned, but then Derleth died and Arkham House veered in a radically different direction, becoming what it is today, a publisher of high-class, literary science fiction. Jacobi's "fourth Arkham" languished unpublished until now. Fedogan and Bremer have even tried to make it look as much like an old-style Arkham House book as possible. The contents, except for the title story, which appeared in *Top-Notch* in 1934, and "The Street That Wasn't There" (a science-fiction story written with Clifford D. Simak, from *Comet,* July 1941), were all published in the '70s and '80s, although they may have been written earlier. One is from the Terminus *Weird Tales,* #293. This collection is a must for fans of the Good Old Days. Order from: Fedogan and Bremer, 700 Washington Ave. S.E., Suite 50, Minneapolis MN 55414.

Miscellaneous Writings by H.P. Lovecraft, edited by S.T. Joshi. Arkham House, 1994. 568 pp. $29.95. Arkham House has not completely abandoned its horror-fiction roots, having recently published Ramsey Campbell's World-Fantasy-Award-winning omnibus, *Alone with the Horrors,* and reissued the works of H.P. Lovecraft in new editions, carefully corrected and restored by S.T. Joshi. This latest addition to the Lovecraft series is a work of monumental scholarship, collecting rare essays, satires, prose-poems, stories, and letters from a variety of largely unobtainable sources. The essays take up the bulk of the book and reveal sides of Lovecraft's genius, wit, erudition, and (mostly in the political section) occasional pig-headedness.

Here are the Old Gent's theories on writing fantastic fiction, his eccentric, antiquarian travelogues, his "commonplace book" of story-ideas, and much more. Those who believe that Lovecraft Knew the Real Truth about the occult were right: H.P.L. was virtually on his deathbed when he wrote the letter to Nils Frome included in this volume, which explains that supernaturalism is bunk — but all the more interesting in fiction as a result. Essential reading.

Scream For Jeeves, A Parody, by P.H. Cannon. Wodecraft Press, 1994. 85 pp. $7.50. Suppose H.P. Lovecraft had collaborated with P.G. Wodehouse? Well, just suppose . . . and the result was the retelling of certain famous Lovecraft terror tales as the adventures of Jeeves and Wooster. Life, one might conclude, as does Bertie, could well become "a hideous thingummy." Cannon, a noted Lovecraft scholar who also knows his Wodehouse, has brought off this stunt almost flawlessly in three tales. Our favorite is "Cats, Rats, and Bertie Wooster," in which the celebrated duo check into Exham Priory, which Lovecraft described at some length in "The Rats in the Walls." The afterword, which tries to draw serious links between Lovecraft, Wodehouse, and Conan Doyle, perhaps protests too much. The whole idea of the joke is the incongruity: Lovecraft and Wodehouse do *not* have much in common. That's why the juxtaposition works so splendidly. Order from Necronomicon Press, 101 Lockwood St., West Warwick RI 02893.

And, not so much a review as a shameless plug, we pass on to you without comment that The Borgo Press (P.O. Box 2845, San Bernardino CA 92406) has published in paperback for $16.00, in hardcovers for $26.00, **Speaking of Horror** by Darrell Schweitzer, a book of interviews with horror writers. The interviewees are: Robert Bloch, Ramsey Campbell, Tanith Lee, Dennis Etchison, Charles L. Grant, Thomas Ligotti, Brian Lumley, William F. Nolan, Manly Wade Wellman, Chet Williamson, and F. Paul Wilson.

Letters from Our Readers.

We didn't get many letters on anything other than the title-change. Artist **Denis Tiani** was among the most complimentary, praising, in particular, the Ian Miller cover, and remarking, "The new title may not carry with it the same historical weight as the old *Weird Tales,* but it's a good title and will, no doubt, go on to create its own historical weight." Then again, **Jeremiah McDonnell** suggested we couldn't have done worse if we'd called the new magazine *Printed Pages of Fear-Flavored or Magic-Flavored Oat-*

meal. He didn't say if he liked the stories. We hope he appreciated them more than we appreciate oatmeal.

Henry Wessells praised the diversity of the first issue, and asked, with inadvertently sad irony, "Where is Avram Davidson when we need him?" implying that a Davidson tale would be just the right spice to complete the recipe for an issue. Well, we have at least one more Davidson tale forthcoming; but Avram is, alas, dead, having passed away in early 1993. He was one of the underappreciated greats of fantasy fiction, a writer of unparallelled charm and wit. Damon Knight once suggested that Davidson was the best short-story writer since John Collier, and we cannot disagree.

Author **F. Gywnplaine MacIntyre** praised several stories, notably Ramsey Campbell's "A Play for the Jaded") as an example of that forgotten form, the "reading play," and also had very kind words for Morlan's and Postovit's "Norm Littman's 15 Minutes," then went on to suggest that, instead of "The Dwarf Holóbolos," he would rather have seen a Jorkens story by Lord Dunsany. Alas, the Dunsany stories that we are running come from a trove of hitherto-unknown and uncollected ones discovered in old (mostly British) magazines. There is one more Jorkens, but it is a mystery, not a fantasy. Of the more than one hundred stories discovered, actually, only about two dozen are both fantasy and worth the attention of a general reader, rather than a Dunsany scholar. You will be seeing a few more of them in these pages. We *did* feature one adventure of Dunsany's famous clubman in *Weird Tales* #306.

Long-time *Weird Tales* author **Hugh B. Cave** was so wonderfully surprised by Allen Koszowski's illustration of his 1930s classic "Stragella" that he said, "It goes into a frame and up on my workroom wall." But before Mr. Cave could chop up a copy of the issue, we put him in touch with the artist, about whom Mr. Cave writes, "I'm honored that he chose a tale of mine on which to demonstrate his remarkable talent."

The Most Popular Story.
We didn't receive enough votes to come to any conclusive ranking. Ramsey Campbell's "A Play for the Jaded," Duncan Adams's "The Neighborhood Watch," Lord Dunsany's "The Dwarf Holóbolos," and Reginald Bretnor's "Rokuro-Kubi" all drew at least one first-place vote.

Let us hear from you! Ω

The Editors

THE DEN

by S. T. Joshi

Is the horror boom over? It is, certainly, difficult to speak conclusively on the subject, but certain signs are unmistakable.

As I write, there is not a single book by Stephen King, Anne Rice, Clive Barker, Dean R. Koontz, or Peter Straub on the *New York Times* best-seller list; several major publishers have either entirely eliminated or severely reduced the number of horror titles they issue; horror magazines even in the small press are dying like flies.

Of course, each new work by King or Rice or Koontz does reach the best-seller list, sometimes the top of it (if Danielle Steel happens to be having a slow year), but even these books are staying on the best-seller list for shorter and shorter periods of time.

But if major publishers are shying away from horror, the small press is stepping in to fill the void. At a time when desktop publishing is becoming increasingly affordable, the enterprising small-press publisher need be able to dispose of only 500 or 1000 copies — sometimes even less — to make a modest profit, and not by producing artificially inflated "signed limited" editions. Whether the field in general will return to its pre-King state, where writers worked in obscurity, had day jobs, or wrote horror under the guise of suspense or science fiction, it is too early to say; but it is difficult to deny that, amidst the predictable masses of mediocrity and outright rubbish, some of the most distinctive and innovative work in the field is emerging from the small press.

TAL Publications (P.O. Box 1837, Leesburg, VA 22075) seems to be attempting to make a name for itself as the publisher of "erotic horror." To date it has issued several chapbooks, including books by Elizabeth Massie, Wayne Allen Sallee, and D. F. Lewis, none of which I have read.

What I *have* read is *Edward Lee's Quest for Sex, Truth and Reality* (1992), and I wish I hadn't. This is about the most talentless little book I have come upon in a long time: it reminds me of nothing so much as the stories high school students write to see who can gross each other out the most.

Marginally better — but only marginally — is Lucy Taylor's *Unnatural Acts* (1992). The three stories in this collection — as in Taylor's work generally — could only pass for horror in an age when anything with a little sex, blood, and violence can pass for horror.

Taylor has now issued two larger collections of stories with Silver Salamander Press (22926 NE Old Woodinville-Duval Road, Woodinville WA 98072), *Close to the Bone* (1993) and *The Flesh Artist* (1994). I hardly know what to say about these tales. Most of them are merely wild stories of bizarre sex with some bloodletting thrown in.

Any "message" they may contain is of the most fatuously obvious sort. Consider the title story of the second collection. Here we have a mad plastic surgeon who becomes obsessed with the women — or, more specifically, certain parts of them — he has operated on and takes to killing them out of a crazy sense of personal ownership. No one needs to be told what the underlying themes are — the possessiveness of men, the objectification of women, our society's emphasis on physical appearance, etc. etc.

This is all old stuff — we've heard it before, and Taylor's treatment is simply too undistinguished to be interesting. Those comparatively few tales where she ventures into fantasy, science fiction, or the supernatural would make good parodies if they were so intended. And repeated doses of Taylor's work lead not to revulsion or horror, but to boredom. It all starts sounding the same.

Norman Partridge's silly introduction to *The Flesh Artist*, where he compares Taylor's emergence to that of Clive Barker, unwittingly gets to the heart of the matter: Taylor, like Barker, is severely hampered by her chosen subject matter. She utterly fails to realise that this monotonous emphasis on aberrant sex and mindless violence — with its implication that the apex of horror is the harm that can be done to the physical body — only testifies to a staggering poverty of imagination. All she does to jolt the jaded reader is to increase the dosage of violence — but the end result is still tedium.

Writers like Edward Lee and Lucy Taylor have, of course, a built-in defense against negative criticism: they, like the splatterpunks, can take a weird sort of moral high ground and claim that objections to their work rest upon mere squeamishness or prudery. They can say that their stories are bold, confrontational, in-your-face, etc., etc. It never occurs to them to think that they may simply be bad writers.

Silver Salamander has done slightly better with Michael Shea's *I, Said the Fly* (1993), a horror/SF novella that was itself an expansion of an earlier short story. Here we are plunged into a world in which a strange alien invasion has resulted in "holes" in "electromagnetic informational flow-systems" around the world, the cause or purpose of which is not immediately evident. Engagingly written as it is, this story could have profited in being turned into a full-fledged novel, for its provocative conceptions require still more

by S.T. Joshi

elaboration for proper development. Shea is a veteran writer of science fiction, fantasy, and horror, one whose charmingly warped view of the world is peculiarly captivating.

Roadkill Press (Little Bookshop of Horrors, 10380 Ralston Road, Arvada CO 80004) has apparently gained some sort of reputation as the publisher of cutting-edge horror; but on the evidence of the three booklets I have read, I can't see how. Unlike the TAL booklets, the Roadkill Press pamphlets are not actually bad but merely mediocre and undistinguished.

Edward Bryant's *Darker Passions* (1992) contains three stories of mundane violence and menace, all written in a flat, toneless idiom that lulls one to sleep instead of producing unease. Dan Simmons, who has written a long-winded introduction to the book, makes a perfect clown of himself by comparing one of the stories to Hemingway's — as if writing one-sentence paragraphs and being sparing with the adjectives makes one a Hemingway.

Not Broken, Not Belonging is a story written by Randy Fox from a "concept" by Alan M. Clark. What this really means is that Clark drew some (quite striking) illustrations and wanted Fox to write a story around them; but the result is confused, fragmentary, and insubstantial. The story ends where it should begin, leaving a myriad of plot threads unresolved.

Rather more promising is Norman Partridge's collection, *Mr. Fox and Other Feral Tales* (1992). This volume has evidently attracted some attention, but only the title story — a convoluted and strangely beautiful tale of love and murder — is worth notice. Partridge too is fond of mingling sex and horror — or of turning sex into horror — but, thankfully, he can write. He strikes me as a somewhat less intense version of David J. Schow.

If *Mr. Fox,* in spite of the windy praise of its supporters, only showed an inkling of promise, then Partridge's first novel, *Slippin' into Darkness* (CD Publications {P.O. Box 18433, Baltimore MD 21237}, 1993) displays that promise fulfilled. This is one of the finest horror novels of the last decade — nearly as fine, perhaps, as Schow's *The Shaft* (1990), which by some incredible mischance has failed to receive an American edition. Although entirely non-supernatural, *Slippin' into Darkness* evokes an atmosphere of dreamlike weirdness by its fragmented narration and tough but strangely poetic prose.

Partridge also creates an illusion of the supernatural by the ghostly hovering of April Destino — a young woman who, gang-raped in high school, descends into prostitution and ultimately kills herself — over the entire scenario. She is already dead when the novel opens, but she is nevertheless the central character in the book, the character against whom each of the vividly realised figures — the four high-school jocks who raped her, the black man who filmed the rape and who becomes a shabby producer of child pornography films, the woman who was April's best friend in school but who betrayed her through jealousy — must define themselves.

This *tour de force* of a novel, whose entire surface action occupies exactly one day but whose flashbacks skillfully paint an affecting picture of high school life, is a relentless psychological portrait of people who showed youthful promise but have lapsed into mediocrity, amoral criminality, and humiliating failure.

As horrible as the rape of April Destino and her subsequent suicide are, the true horror of *Slippin' into Darkness* is the horror of wasted lives and futile violence. Although a profoundly depressing work, this novel is as compelling a read as any I have had in a long time. It is one of those very few books which one wishes would never end.

Necronomicon Press (101 Lockwood Street, West Warwick RI 02893) began its life in 1976 with the sole purpose of publishing the obscure writings of H. P. Lovecraft. Its founder, Marc A. Michaud, was for a long time content to fill this humble niche, but lately he has been branching out by publishing the obscure writings of other classic writers (William Hope Hodgson, Robert E. Howard, Clark Ashton Smith) and, most recently (under the editorship of Stefan Dziemianowicz), a series of small booklets of original fiction. The results are, in most cases, very pleasing to behold.

Three of the titles, to date, were — at least in part — initially designed as contributions to an anthology of sequels to or elaborations on Lovecraft's "The Shadow over Innsmouth," edited by Stephen Jones and scheduled for publication in 1990, the year of Lovecraft's centennial.

The plans fell through;, and, although I understand the volume is now to be brought out by Fedogan & Bremer, several of the tales have since appeared elsewhere.

Brian Stableford's *The Innsmouth Heritage* (1992), the first in the Necronomicon Press Fiction series, makes its indebtedness to Lovecraft's tale explicit in its very title. And yet, Stableford's tale avoids the pitfalls of most pastiches by being a genuine *extension* of the idea contained in the original. Most writers who take it into their heads to "pay homage" to some distinguished work in their field appear to find the pinnacle of success to be some half-baked rewrite of the story in question, as if the least flicker of a new idea were some sort of sacrilege.

Stableford takes the basic premise of Lovecraft's story — the mating of human beings and amphibians and the loathsome hybrids that result — and refashions it: the physical abnormalities of the town's denizens ("the Innsmouth look") are now interpreted as a genetic mutation. This is familiar ground for Stableford, whose *Sexual Chemistry: Sardonic Tales of the Genetic Revolution* (1991) also broached this theme; but here, I fear, the exposition is a trifle too clinical to carry much punch.

Lovecraft, for all the pseudo-science of his later tales, never failed to tell a rousing story — a narrative that achieved an almost unbearable cumulative effect by the steady augmenting of tension and suspense. Stableford's story appeals too exclusively to the intellect, and what emotional resonances it has derive largely from its allusions to Lovecraft's tale.

The next offering in the Necronomicon Press Fiction line, Steve Rasnic Tem's *Decoded Mirrors: 3 Tales After Lovecraft* (1992), also contains, in its first story, a contribution to Stephen Jones' abortive anthology. This tale, "Decodings," is a masterwork of suggestion that justifies the entire booklet; the other two tales are less distinguished.

Like Stableford's, these stories attempt to fuse Lovecraft's cosmic horror with the intimate, domestic horror that has dominated the field in the last several decades; the union of such antipodal approaches will always be uneasy and rarely successful, but in at least one instance Tem has turned the trick.

The third spinoff of "The Shadow over Innsmouth" is "Deepnet," the first of three tales in David Langford's *Irrational Numbers* (1994). Langford is primarily a science-fiction writer and, like Stableford, ingeniously takes the "Innsmouth heritage" of disease and decay into the

disturbingly near future: what would happen if the Innsmouth folk entered the computer age and began marketing video games and computer programs? Although, like Stableford's story, this tale lacks any overt climax or any real action to speak of, it manages to create a really unnerving effect in its quiet way.

The other two tales in the booklet are narrated a little too fragmentarily to carry a very potent effect, although there are points of merit in both.

As if to reassure readers that the Necronomicon Press Fiction series would not be merely a forum for Lovecraft pastiches, the next booklet, Scott Edelman's *Suicide Art* (1992), takes us into

a very different world — our own world of serial killers, child molesters, transexuals, and other phenomena that Lovecraft could not even have imagined.

The two tales in this booklet are certainly confrontational — the first one, "The Suicide Artist," quite literally so in its berating the reader for enjoying its account of child abuse, the second in its uncompromising tale of a transexual haunted by the penis he has had cut off — but would be more successful if Edelman could remedy the clumsinesses, awkwardnesses, and occasional illiteracies in his prose style.

I am not even sure the second tale is a horror story at all; its culminating scene presents what a Roman Catholic would no doubt find outrageously blasphemous, but to this hardened old unbeliever it seemed merely comical.

One can speak only with reverence of Ramsey Campbell, surely the leading horror writer of our time. His *Two Obscure Tales* (1993) ought to be considered a sort of pendant to his landmark story-collection *Demons by Daylight* (1973), for they were written shortly after most of the tales in that collection were set down. They are, to be sure, mighty obscure; and Campbell's brief afterword doesn't help matters much. Campbell himself sums up the matter by saying: "All one's fiction is to some extent about how one was at the age of writing it, and I can only be relieved I'm growing old."

If it were not enough that Necronomicon Press has convinced such luminaries in our field as Stableford, Tem, and Campbell to issue booklets, one of its latest offerings is by no less prestigious a mainstream writer as Fred Chappell. Chappell, of course, has had a long, if intermittent, love affair with Lovecraft and with horror fiction in general: his *Dagon* (1968) unquestionably ranks with Colin Wilson's *The Mind Parasites* (1967) as the most successful novel-length elaboration of Lovecraft's conceptions, and several stories in his recent collection, *More Shapes Than One* (1991), also feature takeoffs of Lovecraft.

The Lodger, a novelette published by Necronomicon Press in 1993, is a partial sequel to the short story "Weird Tales," a sort of historical fantasy in which the brief encounters between Lovecraft and Hart Crane are used as a springboard. In *The Lodger* we are introduced to a little-known member of this Crane-Lovecraft circle, a poet named Lyman Scoresby, who by means

of his poetry collection takes possession of a man of our time, much to the latter's irritation.

The Lodger is not a horror story, nor even a fantasy in any meaningful sense: it is a comedy and a satire, and an exquisite and hilarious one. As a poet and an academician, Chappell is both well qualified and well equipped to skewer the absurdities of modern poetry and modern academic scholarship. His tale is wholly delightful.

It may seem odd that none of the four stories in Donald R. Burleson's *Four Shadowings* (1994) is Lovecraft-inspired — for Burleson has for nearly two decades been one of the leading Lovecraft scholars in the world — but as a matter of fact very little of his bountiful fiction (a generous sampling is available in *Lemon Drops and Other Horrors* {Hobgoblin Press (Box 809, Bristol RI 02809), 1993}) is Lovecraftian. It is, however, on the whole relatively traditional — and this too is a little peculiar from a critic who has recently caused considerable controversy by venturing into some of the more arcane reaches of poststructuralism.

Burleson's tales are competent, elegantly written (a teacher's voice is described as "a ship of sound cutting through a fog of daydream"), occasionally quite revolting, and in general entirely satisfying.

Of the four stories in this booklet, the first and the fourth are the best. "A Student of Geometry" adopts a Campbellian approach (the volume is dedicated to Ramsey Campbell) in probing the cloudy mind of a young girl who can't seem to pay attention to her geometry lessons. (Burleson is, incidentally, a professor of mathematics.) The atmosphere, however, is less that of Campbell than that of, say, Conrad Aiken's "Silent Snow, Secret Snow." "One-Night Strand" treads exquisitely on the borderline between grisly horror and farce in its account of what a solitary traveler finds in the adjoining room of a motel.

It is worth pointing out that many of the Necronomicon Press booklets are enhanced by the superior artwork of Jason C. Eckhardt, Robert H. Knox, Allen Koszowski, and Stephen E. Fabian.

It must flatly be declared that the production standards of most of these books are not of professional calibre. TAL is the worst of the lot: its title page features the author, title, copyright notice, author's signature, and publisher's address all crammed together in a plain sans-serif type — apparently to save paper.

Almost all these publishers are in desperate need of a copy editor and some basic instruction in layout and design. Most of the authors (established professionals like Chappell, Stableford, Tem, Campbell, and others of course excluded) can't write grammatically to save their lives. Lucy Taylor is the worst of the lot: to choose some examples purely at random, it seems that she does not know how to spell the verb *breathe,* how to spell *Coney Island* or *Euripides,* does not know the difference between *effect* and *affect,* and is unsure how to spell the possessive case of *men* and *women.*

In terms of design, we have awful things like page numbers on the inside margins, type too large for the page dimensions, typos by the bushel, and the use of many different display fonts in a single book. ("Well, I paid for 'em when I bought PageMaker, so why shouldn't I use 'em?") Only the Necronomicon Press line consistently features a design, typeface, and artwork that come up to professional standards.

It is interesting to note how many of these publications (the Necronomicon Press pamphlets excluded) feature effusive introductions by the writers' friends — as if the authors (or publishers) could not risk allowing the works to stand on their own. This sort of mutual back-patting is getting very common in the horror field, and Ed Bryant must be ranked as one of the prime offenders: in introductions and reviews alike he so egregiously exaggerates the merits of mediocre writers as to make one lament the near-total lack of critical standards in the current horror market. (The real horror is the very distinct possibility that Bryant *actually likes* the stuff he praises.) All this is going to sound entirely ridiculous to future generations when nearly the whole of this material is mercifully swept into the dustbin of oblivion.

The small presses I have surveyed here are by no means the only ones in this field; indeed, I have by design ignored some of the more prestigious imprints such as Arkham House or Mark V. Ziesing, whose products both in literary merit and in physical appearance need fear no comparison with commercial publishers. Arkham House's editor James Turner consistently produces products of exquisite design, although most of his recent volumes are in the science-fiction field. Ziesing has just issued David J. Schow's *Black Leather Required* (1994), a landmark story collection by one of our leading writers.

I also do not wish to convey the impression that all work from commercial presses is distinguished while all, or nearly all, work from the small press is amateurish. The fact is that most of what the commercial presses publish is also pretty amateurish, and it now seems purely a matter of luck whether a given writer is published by the one or by the other.

Small press magazines are gamely making a go of it, even though a vast amount of what they contain is perfect rubbish. And yet, it certainly does seem as if quality eventually rises to the surface. Ramsey Campbell, T.E.D. Klein, Thomas Ligotti, Dennis Etchison, and many of the other leading writers in the horror field gained their start in the small press; Norman Partridge seems ready to join their company.

As for the others, they will remain where they are, and some of them may perhaps develop a twisted pride in being unacceptable to the mainstream; but all they will accomplish is to perpetuate the half-truth that the small press is the home of the has-been and the never-was. Ω

by S.T. Joshi

WHERE DESERT SPIRITS CROWD THE NIGHT

by Charles de Lint
Illustrated by George Barr

If your mind is attuned to beauty,
you find beauty in everything.

— Jean Cooke,
in an interview in *The Artist's
and Illustrator's Magazine, April 1993*

All I ask of you
Is that you remember me
As loving you
— traditional Sufi song

Each of us owes God a death.
— attributed to Humphrey Osmond

1

Sophie didn't attend the funeral. She hadn't met Max yet, couldn't have known that his lover had died. On the afternoon that Max stood at Peter's graveside under a far too cheerful sky, she was in her studio in Old Market, preparing for a new show. It wasn't until the opening, two months later, that they met.

But even then, Coyote was watching.

2   Sophie:

There is a door in my dreams that opens into a desert . . .

where the light is like a wash of whiskey over my vision;

where the colour of the earth ranges through a spectrum of dusty browns cut with pale ochre tones and siennas;

where distant peaks jut blue-grey from the tide of hills washing up against the ragged line the mountains make at the horizon, peaks that are shadowed now as the sun sets in a geranium and violet glory behind me;

where the tall saguaro rise like sleepy green giants from the desert floor, waving lazy arms to no one in particular, with barrel cacti crouching in their shadows like smaller, shorter cousins;

where clusters of prickly pear and cholla offer a thorny embrace and the landscape is clouded with mesquite and palo verde and smoke trees, their leaves so tiny they don't seem to grow from the gnarly branches as to have been dusted upon them;

where a hawk hangs in the sky high above me, a dark silhouette against the ever deepening blue, gliding effortlessly on outspread wings;

where a lizard darts into a tight crevice, its movement so quick, it only registers in the corner of my eye;

where an owl the size of my palm peers at me from the safety of its hole in a towering saguaro;

where a rattlesnake gives me one warning rattle, then fixes me with its hypnotic stare, poised to strike long after I have backed away;

where the sound of a medicine flute, breathy and soft as a secret, rises up from an arroyo, and for one moment I see the shadow of a hunch-backed man and his instrument cast upon the far wall of the gully, before the night takes the sight away, if not the sound;

where the sky, even at night, overwhelms me with its immensity;

where the stillness seems complete . . .

except for the resonance of my heartbeat that twins the distant drum of a stag's hooves upon the dry, hard ground;

except for the incessant soughing cries of the ground-doves that feed in the brushy vegetation all around me;

except for the low sound of the flute which first brought me here.

The sweet scent of a mesquite fire in the middle of a dry wash draws me down from the higher ridges. The ground-doves break like quail with a rushing thrum of their wings as I make my way near. A figure is there by the fire, sitting motionless, head bent in shadow. I stand just beyond the circle of light, uncertain, uneasy. But finally I step forward. I sit across the fire from the figure. In the distance, I can still hear the sound of the flute. My silent companion gives neither it nor my presence any acknowledgment, but I can be patient, too.

And anyway, I've nowhere else to go.

Given her way in the matter, Sophie would never attend one of her own openings. She was so organized and tidy that she never really thought that she looked like the typical image of what an artist should be and she always felt awkward trying to make nice with the gallery's clients. It wasn't that she didn't like people, or even that she wasn't prone to involved conversations. She simply felt uncomfortable around strangers, especially when she was supposed to be promoting herself and her work. But she tried.

So this evening as The Green Man Gallery filled with the guests that Albina had invited to the opening, Sophie concentrated on fulfilling what she saw as her responsibility in making the evening a success. Instead of clustering in a corner with her scruffy friends, who were doing their best not to be too rowdy and only just succeeding, she made an effort to mingle, to be sociable, the approachable artist. Whenever she felt herself gravitating to where Jilly and Wendy and the others were standing, she'd focus on someone she didn't know, walk over and strike up a conversation.

An hour or so into the opening, she picked a man in his late twenties who had just stopped in front of *Hearts Like Fire, Burning* — a small oil painting of two golden figures holding hands in a blaze of colour that she'd meant to represent the fire of their consummated love.

He was tall and slender, a pale, dark-haired Pre-Raphaelite presence dressed in somber clothes: black jeans, black T-shirt, black sports jacket, even black Nikes. What attracted her to him was how he moved like a shadow through the gallery crowd and seemed completely at odds with both them and the bright, sensual colours of the paintings that made up the show. And yet he seemed more in tune with the paintings than anyone else — perhaps, she thought wryly as she noticed the intensity of his interest in the work, herself included.

Hearts Like Fire, Burning, in particular, appeared to mesmerize him. He stood longest in front of it, transfixed, his features a curious mixture of deep sadness and joy. When she approached him, he looked slowly away from the painting and smiled at her. The expression turned bittersweet by the time it reached his eyes.

"So what do you think of this piece?" he asked.

Sophie blinked in surprise. "I should probably be asking you that question."

"How so?"

"I'm the artist."

He inclined his head slightly in greeting and put out his hand. "Max Hannon," he said, introducing himself.

"I'm Sophie Etoile," she said as she took his hand. Then she laughed. "I guess that was obvious."

He laughed with her, but his laugh, like his smile, held a deep sadness by the time it reached his eyes.

"I find it very peaceful," he said, turning back to the painting.

"Now that's a description I've never heard of my work."

"Oh?" He regarded her once more. "How's it usually described?"

"Those that like it call it lively, colourful, vibrant. Those that don't call it garish, overblown. . . ." Sophie shrugged and let the words trail off.

"And how would you describe it?"

"With this piece, I agree with you. For all its flood of bright colour, I find it very peaceful."

"It reminds me of my lover, Peter," Max said. "We were in Arizona a few months ago, staying with friends who have a place in the desert. We'd sit and hold hands at this table they had set up behind their house and simply let the light and the sky fill us. It felt just like this painting — full of gold and flames and the fire in our hearts, all mixed up together. When I look at this, it brings it all back."

"That's very sweet."

Max turned back to the painting. "He died a week or so after we got back."

"I'm so sorry," Sophie said, laying a hand on his arm.

Max sighed. "It doesn't hurt to talk about him, but God do I miss him."

You can say it doesn't hurt, Sophie thought, but she could see how bright his eyes had become, only just holding back a film of tears. The openness with which he'd shared his feelings to her made her want to do something special in return.

"I want you to have this painting," she said. "You can come pick it up when the show's over."

Max shook his head. "I'd love to buy it," he said, "but I don't have that kind of money."

"Who said anything about you having to pay for it?"

"I couldn't even think of . . ." he began.

But Sophie refused to listen. "Look," she said. "What would be the point of being an artist if you only did it for the money? I always feel weird about selling my work anyway. It's as though I'm selling off my children. I don't even know what kind of a home they're going to — there's no evaluation process beforehand. Someone could buy this painting just for the investment and for all I know it'll end up stuck in a closet somewhere and never be seen again. I can't tell you how good it would make me feel knowing that it was hanging in your home instead, where it would mean so much to you."

"No, I just couldn't accept it," Max told her.

"Then let me give it to Peter," Sophie said, "and you can keep it for him."

Max shook his head. "This is so strange. Things like this don't happen in the real world."

"Well, pick a world where it could happen," Sophie said, "and we'll pretend that we're there."

Max gave her a curious look. "Do you do this a lot?"

"What? Give away paintings?"

"No, pick another world to be in when you don't happen to like the way things are going in this one."

Now it was Sophie's turn to be intrigued. "Why, do you?"

"No. It's just . . . ever since you came over and started talking to me, I've felt as though we've met before. But not here. Not in this world. It's more like we met in a dream. . . ."

This was too strange, Sophie thought. For a moment the gallery and crowd about them seemed to flicker, to grow hazy and two-dimensional, as though only she and Max were real.

Like we met in a dream . . .

Slowly she shook her head. "Don't get me started on dreams," she said.

4   Sophie:

"There are sleeping dreams and waking dreams," Christina Rossetti says in her poem "A Ballad of Boding," as though the difference between them is absolute. My dreams aren't so clearly divided, not from each other, and not from when I'm actually awake either. My sleeping dreams bleed into the real world; actually, the place where they take place seems like a real world, too — it's just not one that's as easily accessed by most people.

The experiences I have there aren't real, of course, or at least not real in the way people normally use the word. What happens when I fall asleep and step into my dreams can't be measured or weighed — it can only be known — but that doesn't stop these experiences from influencing my life and leaving me in a state of mild confusion so much of the time.

The confusion stems from the fact that every time I turn around, the rules seem to change. Or maybe it's that every time I think I have a better understanding of what the night side of my life means, the dreams open up like a Chinese puzzle box and I find yet another riddle lying inside the one I've just figured out. The borders blur, retreating before me, deeper and deeper into the dreamscape, walls becoming doors, and doors opening out into mysteries that often obscure the original question. I don't even know the original question anymore. I can't even remember if there ever was one.

I do remember that I went looking for my mother once. I went to a place, marshy and bogled like an old English storybook fen, where I found that she might be a drowned moon, pinned underwater by quicks and other dark creatures until I freed her from her watery tomb. But I came back from that dreamscape without a clear answer as to who she was, or what exactly it was that I had done. What I do know is that I came back with a friend: Jeck Crow, a handsome devil of a man who, I seem to remember, once wore the physical appearance of the black-winged bird that's his namesake. Is it a true memory? I don't know, he won't say, and our relationship has progressed to the point where it doesn't really matter anymore.

I only ever see him when I sleep. I close my eyes and step from this world to Mabon, the city that radiates from Mr. Truepenny's, the bookstore/art gallery I made up when I was a kid. Or at least I thought I'd made it up. It was the place I went when I was waiting for my dad to come home from work, a haven from my loneliness because I didn't make friends easily in those days. Not having anyone with whom I could share the fruits of my imagination, I put all that energy into making up a place where I was special, or at least I had access to special things.

Faerie blood — courtesy of a mother who, Jilly is convinced, was a dream in this world, a moon in her own — is what makes it all real.

"Who was that guy you spent half the night talking to?" Jilly wanted to know as she and Sophie were walking home from the restaurant where they'd all gone to celebrate after the opening. Sophie had asked Max to come along, but he'd declined.

"Just this guy."

Jilly laughed. "'Just this guy.' Oh, please. He was the best looking man in the place and he seemed quite smitten with you."

Sophie had to smile. Only Jilly would use a word like smitten.

"His name's Max Hannon," she told Jilly, "and he's gay."

"So? This means you can't be friends?"

"Of course not. I was just pointing out that he's not potential boyfriend material."

"It's possible to be enamoured with someone on an intellectual or spiritual level, you know."

"I know."

"And besides, you already have a boyfriend."

Sophie sighed. "Right. In my dreams. That doesn't exactly do much for me in the real world."

"But your dreams are like a real world for you."

"I think I need something a little more . . . substantial in my life. My biological clock is ticking away."

"But Jeck —"

"Isn't real," Sophie said. "No matter how much I pretend he is. And Mabon isn't a real city, no matter how much I want it to be and even if it seems like other people can visit it. You can talk all you want about consensual reality, Jilly, but that doesn't change the fact that some things are real and some things aren't. There's a line drawn between the two that separates reality from fantasy."

"Yeah, but it's an imaginary line," Jilly said. "Who really decides where it gets drawn?"

They'd been through variations on this conversation many times before. Anyone who spent any amount of time with Jilly did. Her open-mindedness was either endearing or frustrating, depending on where you stood on whatever particular subject happened to be under discussion.

"Well, I'll tell you," Jilly went on when Sophie didn't respond. "A long time ago a bunch of people reached a general consensus as to what's real and what's not and most of us have been going along with it ever since."

"All of which has nothing to do with Max,"

Sophie said in an attempt to return to the original topic of their conversation.

"I know," Jilly said. "So are you going to see him again?"

"I hope so. There's something very intriguing about him."

"Which has nothing to do with the way he looks."

"I told you," Sophie said. "He's gay."

"Like Sue always says, the best ones are either married or gay, more's the pity."

Sophie smiled. "Only for us."

"This is true."

6   Sophie:

The desert dream starts in the alley behind Mr. Truepenny's shop — or at least where the alley's supposed to be. I'm in the back of the store with Jeck, poking around through the shelves of books, when I hear the sound of this flute. It goes on for awhile, sort of lingering there in the back of my mind, until finally I get curious. I leave Jeck digging for treasure in a cardboard box of new arrivals and step past the door that leads into the store's small art gallery. The music is sort of atonal, and the instrument appears to have a limited range of notes, but there's something appealing about it all the same. I walk down a long narrow corridor, the walls encrusted with old portraits of thin, bearded men and women in dresses that appear far too stiff and ornately embroidered to be comfortable. The heels of my shoes click on the wooden floor in a rhythmic counterpoint to the music I'm following. I stop at the door at the far end of the hall. The music seems to be coming from the other side of it, so I open the door and step out, expecting to find myself in a familiar alleyway, but the alley's gone.

Instead, I'm standing in a desert. I turn around to see that the door through which I came has disappeared. All that I can see on every side of me is an endless panorama of desert, each compass point bordered by mountains. I seem to be as far from Mabon as that city is from the place where my body sleeps.

"What is this place?" I say.

My voice startles me, because I didn't realize I was speaking aloud. What startles me more is that my rhetorical question gets answered. I turn to see the oddest sight: there's a rattlesnake coiled up under a palo verde tree. The pale colour of the tree's branches and twigs awakes an echoing green on the snake's scales which range through a gorgeous palette of golds and deep rusty reds. That's normal enough. What's so disconcerting is that the snake has the face of a Botticelli madonna — serene smile, rounded features enclosed by a cloud of dark ringlets. *The Virgin and Child with Singing Angels* comes immediately to mind. And she's got wings — creamy yellow wings that thrust out from the snake's body a few inches below the face. All that's lacking is a nimbus of gold light.

"A dreaming place," is what the snake has just said to me.

For all her serenity, she has an unblinking gaze which I doubt any of Botticelli's models had.

"But Mabon's already a dreaming place," I find myself replying, as though I always have conversations with snakes that have wings and human faces.

"Mabon is your dreaming place," she says. "Today you have strayed into someone else's."

"Whose?"

The snake doesn't reply.

"How do I get back to Mabon?"

Still no reply — at least not from her. Another voice answers me. This time it's a small owl, her feathers the colour of a dead saguaro rib, streaks of silver grey and black. She's perched on the arm of one of those tall cacti, looking down at me with another human face nestled there where an owl's beak and round eyes should be, calm madonna features surrounded by feathers. At least wings look normal on her.

"You can't return," she tells me. "You have to go on."

I hate the way that conversation can get snarled up in a dream like this: every word an omen, every sentence a riddle.

"Go on to where?"

The owl turns her head sharply away then turns back and suddenly takes off from her perch. I catch a glimpse of a human torso in her chest feathers — breasts and a rounded belly — and then she's airborne, wings beating until she catches an updraft, and glides away. A stand of mesquite swallows her from my sight and she's gone. I turn back to the rattlesnake, but she's gone as well. The owl's advice rings in my mind.

You have to go on.

I look around me, mountains in every direction. I know distance can be deceiving in the open desert like this, in this kind of light, with that immense sprawl of sky above me. I feel as though I could just reach any one of those ranges in a half-hour walk, but I know it would really be days.

I find my sense of direction has gone askew. Normally, I relate to a body of water. In Newford, everything's north of the lake. In Mabon, everything's south. Here, I feel displaced. There's no water — or at least none of which I'm aware. I can see the sun is setting towards the west, but it doesn't feel right. My inner compass says it's setting in the north.

I turn slowly in place, regarding the distant mountains ranges that surround me. None of them draws me more than the other and I don't know which way to go until I remember the sound of the flute that brought me here in the first place. It's still playing, a sweet low music on the edge of my hearing that calms the panic that was beginning to lodge in my chest.

So I follow it again, hiking through what's left of the afternoon until I don't feel I can go any further. The mountains in front of me don't seem any closer, the ones behind aren't any further away. I'm thirsty and tired. Every piece of vegetation has a cutting edge or a thorn. My calves ache, my back aches, my throat holds as much moisture as the dusty ground underfoot. I don't want to be here, but I can't seem to wake up.

It's the music, I realize. The music is keeping me here.

I've figured out what kind of flute is being played now: one of those medicine flutes indigenous to the Southwest. I remember Geordie had one a couple of years ago. It was almost the size of his Irish flute, with the same six holes on top, but it had an extra thumb hole around back and it didn't have nearly the same range of notes. It also had an odd addition: up by the air hole, tied to the body of the flute with leather thongs, was a saddle holding a reed. The saddle directed the air-jet, up or down against the lower reed and it was adjustable. The sound was very pretty, but the instrument had next to no volume. Geordie eventually traded it in for some whistle or other, but I picked up a tape of its music to play when I'm working — medicine flute, rattles, rainstick, and synthesizers. I can't remember the last time I listened to it.

After carefully checking the area around me for snakes or scorpions or God knows what else might be lurking about, I sit down on some rocks and try to think things through. I'd like to believe there's a reason for my being here, but I know the dreamlands don't usually work that way. They have their own internal logic; it's only our presence in them that's arbitrary. We move through them with the same randomness as the weather in our world: basically unpredictable, for all that we'd like to think otherwise.

No, I'm here as the result of my own interference. I followed the sound of the flute out the door into the desert of my own accord. I've no one to blame but myself. There'll be no escape except for that which I can make for myself.

I'm not alone here, though. I keep sensing presences just beyond my sight, spirits hovering in the corners of my eyes. They're like the snake and the owl I saw earlier, but much more shy. I catch the hint of a face in one of the cacti, here one moment, gone the next; a ghostly shape in the bristly branches of a smoke tree; a scurry of movement and a fleeting glimpse of something with half-human skin, half-fur or -scale, darting into a burrow: little madonna faces, winged rodents and lizards, birds with human eyes and noses.

I don't know why they're so scared of me. Maybe they're naturally cautious. Maybe there's something out here in the desert that they've got good reason to hide from.

This thought doesn't lend me any comfort at all. If there's something they're scared of, I don't doubt that I should be scared of it, too. And I would be, except I'm just too exhausted to care at the moment. I rest my arms on my knees, my head on my arms.

I feel a little giddy from the sun and definitely dehydrated. I came to the desert wearing only sneakers, a pair of jeans and a white blouse. The blouse is on my head and shoulders now, to keep off the sun, but it's left my arms, my lower back and my stomach exposed. They haven't so much browned as turned the pink that's going to be a burn in another couple of hours.

Something moves in the corner of my eye and I turn my head, but not quickly enough. It was something small, a flash of pale skin and light brown fur. Winged.

"Don't be scared!" I call after it. "I won't hurt you."

But the desert lies silent around me, except for the sound of the flute. I thought I caught a glimpse of the player an hour or so ago. I was cresting a hill and saw far ahead of me a small hunched shape disappear down into the arroyo. It looked like one of those pictographs you sometimes see in Hopi or Navajo art — a little hunched-back man with hair like dreadlocks, playing a flute. I called after him at the time, but he never reappeared.

I hate this feeling of helplessness I have at the moment, of having to react rather than do, of having to wait for answers to come to me rather than seek them out on my own. I've walked for hours, but I can't help thinking how, realistically, all that effort was only killing time. I haven't gotten anywhere, I haven't learned anything new. I'm no further ahead than I was when I first stepped through that door and found myself here. I'm thirstier, I've got the beginning of a sunburn, and that about sums it up.

The air starts to cool as the sun goes down. I take my blouse off my head and put it back on, but it doesn't help much against the growing chill. I hear something rustle in the brush on the other side of the rocks where I'm sitting and I almost can't be bothered turning my head to see what made the noise. But I look around all the same, and then I sit very still, hoping that the Indian woman I find regarding me won't be startled off like every other creature I've met since the owl gave me her cryptic advice.

The woman is taller than I am, but that's not saying much; at just over five feet tall, almost everyone I meet is taller than I. Her features have a pinched, almost fox-like cast about them, and she wears her hair in two long braids into which have been woven feathers and beads and cowrie shells. She's barefoot, which strikes me as odd, since this isn't exactly the most friendly terrain I've ever had to traverse. Her buckskin dress is almost a creamy white, decorated with intricate beadwork and stitching, and she's wearing a blanket over her shoulders like a shawl, the colours of which reflect the surrounding land-scape — the browns and the tans, deep shadows and burnt siennas — only they're much more vibrant.

"Don't run off on me," I say, pitching my voice low and trying to seem as unthreatening as possible.

The woman smiles. She has a smile that trans-forms her face; it starts on her lips and in her dark eyes, but then the whole of her solemn copper-col-oured features fall easily into well-worn creases of good humour.

I realize that hers is the first face I've seen in this place that didn't look as though it had been rendered by a Florentine painter at the height of the Italian Renaissance. She seems indisputably of this place, as though she was birthed from the cacti and the dry hills.

"Why do you think I would do that?" she asks. Her voice is melodious and sweet.

"So far, everybody else has."

"Perhaps you confuse them."

I have to laugh. "*I* confuse *them*? Oh please."

The woman shrugs. "This is a place of spirits, a land where totem may be found, spirits con-sulted, lessons learned, futures explored. Those who walk its hills for these reasons have had no easy task in coming here."

"I could show them this door I found," I start to joke, but I let my voice trail off. The crease lines of her humour are still there on her face, but they're in repose. She looks too serious for jokes right now.

"You have come looking for nothing," she goes on, "so your presence is a source of agitation."

"It's not something I planned," I assure her. "If you'll show me the way out, I'll be more than happy to go. Really."

The woman shook her head. "There is no way out — except by acquiring that which you came seeking."

"But I didn't come looking for anything."

"That presents a problem."

I don't like the way this conversation is going.

"For the only way you can leave in such a case," the woman goes on, "is if you accompany another seeker when their own journeying is done."

"That . . . that doesn't seem fair."

The woman nods. "There is much unfairness — even in the spirit realms. But obstacles are set before us in order that they may be overcome." She gives me a considering look. "Perhaps you are simply unaware of what you came seeking?"

She makes a question of it.

"I heard this flute," I say. "That's what I followed to get here."

"Ah."

I wait, but she doesn't expand beyond that one enigmatic utterance.

"Could you maybe give me a little more to go on than that?" I ask.

"You are an artist?" she asks.

The question surprises me, but I nod.

"Kokopelli," she says, "the flute-player you heard. He is known for his —" she hesitates for a moment "— inspirational qualities."

"I'm not looking for ideas," I tell her. "I have more ideas than I know what to do with. The only thing I'm ever looking for is the time to put them into practice."

"Kokopelli or Coyote," she says. "One of them is responsible for your being here."

"Can they help me get back?"

"Where either of them is concerned, anything is possible."

There's something about the way she tells me this that seems to add an unspoken "when hell freezes over," and that makes me feel even more uneasy.

"Can you tell me where I might find them?"

The woman shrugs. "Kokopelli is only found when he wishes to be, but Coyote — Coyote is always near. Look for him to be cadging a cigarette, or warming his toes by a fire."

She starts to turn away, but pauses when I call after her.

"Wait!" I say. "You can't just leave me here."

"I'm sorry," she tells me, and she really does seem sorry. "But I have duties that require my attention. I came upon you only by chance and already I have stayed too long."

"Can't I just come along with you?"

"I'm afraid that would be impossible."

There's nothing mean about the way she says it, but I can tell right away that the question is definitely not open to further discussion.

"Will you come back when you're done?" I ask.

I'm desperate. I don't want to be here on my own anymore, especially not with night falling.

"I can't make you a promise of that," she says, "but I will try. In the meantime, you would do better to look within yourself, to see if hidden somewhere within you is some secret need that might have brought you to this place."

As she starts to turn away again, I think to ask her what her name is.

"Since I am Grandmother to so many here," she says, "that would be as good a name as any. You may call me Grandmother Toad."

"My name's Sophie."

"I know, little sister."

She's walking away as she speaks. I jump to my feet and follow after her, into the dusk that's settling in between the cacti and mesquite trees, but like everyone else I've met here, she's got the trick of disappearing down pat. She steps into a shadow and she's gone.

A vast emptiness settles inside me after she's left me. The night is full of strange sounds, snuffling and rustles and weird cries in the distance that appear to be coming closer.

"Grandmother," I call softly.

I wonder, how did she know my name?

"Grandmother?"

There's no reply.

"Grandmother!"

I run to the top of another ridge, one from which I can see the last flood of light spraying up from the sunset. There's no sign, no trace at all of the Indian woman, but as I turn away, I see the flickering light of a campfire, burning there, below me in a dry wash. A figure sits in front of it. The sound of the flute is still distant, so I make the educated guess that it isn't Kokopelli hanging out down there. Grandmother's words return to my mind:

Look for him to be cadging a cigarette, or warming his toes by a fire.

I take one last look around me, then start down the hill towards Coyote's fire.

7

Sophie awoke in a tangle of sheets. She stared up at a familiar ceiling, then slowly turned her head to look at her bedside clock. The hour hand was creeping up on four. Relief flooded her.

I'm back, she thought.

She wasn't sure how it had happened, but somewhere in between leaving Grandmother Toad and starting down towards Coyote's fire, she'd managed to escape the desert dream. She lay there listening to the siren that had woken her, heard it pass her block and continue on. Sitting up, she fluffed her pillow, then lay down once more.

No more following the sound of a flute, she told herself, no matter how intriguing it might be.

Her eyelids grew heavy. Closing her eyes, she let herself drift off. Wait until she told Jeck, she thought. The desert she'd found herself in had been even stranger than the fens where she and Jeck had first met — if such a thing was possible. But when she fell asleep she bypassed Mr. Truepenny's shop and found herself scrambling down a desert incline to where a mesquite fire sent its flickering shadows along a dry wash.

8   Sophie:

"Little cousin," Coyote says after we've been sitting together in silence for some time. "What are you doing here?"

I can't believe I'm back here again. I would never have let myself go back to sleep if I'd thought this would happen. Still, I can't stay awake forever. That being the case, if every time

I dream I'm going to find myself back here instead of in Mabon, I might as well deal with it now. But I'm not happy about it.

"I don't know," I tell him.

Coyote nods his head. He sits on his haunches, on the far side of the campfire. The pale light from the coals makes his eyes glitter and seem to be two different colours: one brown, one blue. Except for his ears, his silhouette against the deep starry backdrop behind him belongs to a young man, long black hair braided and falling down either side of his head, body wrapped in a blanket. But the ears are those of the desert wolf whose name he bears: tall and pointed, tips quivering as they sort through the sounds drifting in from the night around them.

Wind in the mesquite. Tiny scurrying paws on the sand of the dry wash. Owl wings beating like a quickened breath. A sudden squeal. Silence. The sound of wings again, rising now. From further away, the soft grunting of javalinas feeding on prickly pear cacti.

When Coyote turns his head, a muzzle is added to his silhouette and there can be no pretending that he is other than what he is: a piece of myth set loose from old stories and come to add to the puzzle of my being here.

"So tell me," he says, a touch of amusement in his voice. "With your wise eyes so dark with secrets and insights lying thick about you like a cloak . . . what *do* you know?"

I can't tell if he's making fun of me or not.

"My name's Sophie," I tell him. "That's supposed to mean wisdom, but I don't feel very wise at the moment."

"Only fools think they're wise; the rest of us just muddle through as we can."

"I'm barely managing that."

"And yet . . . you're here. You're alive. You breathe. You speak. Presumably, you think. You feel. The dead would give a great deal to be allowed so much."

"Look," I say. "All I know is that I stepped through a door in another dream and ended up here. I followed this Kokopelli's flute-playing and Grandmother Toad told me I have to stay here unless I either discover some secret need inside me that can be answered by the desert, or one of you help me find my way back."

"Kokopelli," Coyote says. "And Grandmother Toad. Such notable company to find oneself in."

Now I know he's mocking me, but I don't think it's meant to be malicious. It's just his way. Besides, I find that I don't really care.

"Can you help me?" I ask.

"Can I help? I'm not sure. Will I help? I'll do my best. Never let it be said that I turned my back on a friend of both the flute-player and Nokomis."

"Who?"

"The Grandmother has many names — as does anyone who lives long enough. They catch on our clothes and get all snarled up in a tangle until sometimes even we can't remember who we are anymore."

"You're confusing me.

"But not deliberately so," Coyote says. "Let it go on record that any confusion arose simply because we lacked certain commonalties of reference."

I give him a blank look.

"Besides," he adds, "it was a joke. We always know who we are; what we sometimes forget are the appellations by which we come to be known. There are, you see, so many of them."

"I just want to get out of this place."

Coyote nods. "I must say, I have to admire anyone with such a strong sense of purpose. No messing about, straight to the point. It's refreshing, really. You wouldn't have a cigarette, would you?"

"Sorry, I don't smoke."

It's hard to believe that this is the same person who sat in silence across the fire from me for the better part of an hour before he even said hello. I wonder if archetypal spirits can be schizophrenic. Then I think, just being an archetype must make you schizophrenic. Imagine if your whole existence depended on how people remember you.

"I gave it up myself," Coyote says. Then he proceeds to open up a rolling paper, sprinkle tobacco onto it and roll himself a cigarette. He lights it with a twig from the fire, then blows a contented wreath of smoke up into the air where it twists and spins before it joins the rising column of smoke from the burning mesquite.

I'm beginning to realize that my companion's not exactly the most truthful person I'm going to meet in my life. I just hope he's more reliable when it comes to getting a job done or I'm going to be stuck in this desert for a very long time.

"So where do we start?" I ask.

"With metaphor?"

"What?"

"The use of one thing to explain another," Coyote says patiently.

"I know what it means. I just don't get your point."

"I thought we were trying to find your secret need."

I shake my head. "I don't *have* any secret needs."

"Are you sure?"

"I . . ."

"Are you sexually repressed?"

I can't believe I'm having this conversation. "What's that got to do with *anything?*"

Coyote flicks the ash from the end of his cigarette. "It's this whole flute-player business," he says. "It's riddled with sexual innuendo, don't you see? He's a fertility symbol, now, very mytho-poetic and all, but it wasn't always that way. Used to be a trader, a travelling merchant, hup-two-three. That hunched back was actually his pack of trading goods, the flute his way of approaching a settlement, *tootle-toot-toot*, it's only me, no danger, except if you were some nubile young thing. Had a woman in every town you know — they didn't call him Koke the Poke for nothing. The years go by and suddenly our randy little friend finds himself elevated to minor deity status, gets all serious, kachina material, don't you know? Becomes a kind of erotic muse, if you will."

"But —"

"Ah, yes," Coyote says. "The metaphorical bit." He grinds his cigarette out and tosses the butt into the fire. "Your following the sound of his flute — *his* particular flute, if you get my meaning — and well, I won't say he's irresistible, but if one were to be suffering for a certain particular *need*, it might be quite difficult *not* to be drawn, willy-nilly, after him."

"What are you saying? That all I have to do is have sex here, and I get to leave?"

"No, no, no, no. Nothing so crass. Nothing so obvious. At this point it's all conjecture. We're simply exploring possibilities, some more delightful than others." He pauses and gives me a considering look. "You're not a nun, are you? You haven't taken one of those absurd vows that cut you off from what might otherwise be a full and healthy human existence?"

"I don't know about nuns," I tell him, "but I'm outta here."

I stand up, expecting him to make some sort of protest, but he just looks at me, curiously, and starts to roll another cigarette. I don't really want to go out into the desert night on my own, but I don't want to sit here and listen to his lunacy either.

"I thought you were going to help me," I say finally.

"I am, little cousin. I will."

He lights his cigarette and then pointedly waits for me to sit down again.

"Well, you haven't been much help so far," I say.

"Oh right," he says, laying a hand theatrically across his brow. "Kill the messenger why don't you."

I lean closer to the fire and take a good long look at him. "Is there *any* relevance to anything you have to say?" I ask.

"You brought up Kokopelli. You're the one who followed the music of his randy little flute. You can't blame me for any of that. If you've got a better idea, I'm all ears."

He cups his hands around those big coyote ears of his and leans forward as well. I try to keep a straight face, but all I can do is fall back on the ground and laugh.

"I was beginning to think you didn't have any sort of a sense of humour at all," he says when I finally catch my breath.

"It's not that. I just want get away from here. When I dream, I want to go to Mabon — to where *I* want to go."

"Mabon?" Coyote says. "Mabon's yours? Oh, I love Mabon. The first time I ever heard the Sex Pistols was in Mabon. That was years ago now, but I couldn't believe how great they were."

Whereupon he launches into a version of "My Way" that's so off-key and out of time that it makes the version Sid Vicious did sound closer to Old Blue Eyes than I might ever have thought possible. From the hills around us, four-legged coyote voices take up the song and soon the night is filled with this horrible caterwauling that's so loud it's making my teeth ache. All I want to do is bury my head or scream.

"Great place, Mabon," he says when he finally breaks off and the noise from his accompanists fades away.

Wonderful, I think. Not only am I stuck with him here, but now I find out that if I ever do get out of this desert, I could run into him again in my own dreaming place.

9

"I've got to figure out a way to sleep without dreaming," Sophie told Jilly.

They were taking a break from helping out at a bazaar for St. Vincent's Home for the Aged, drinking tea and sharing a bag of potato chips on the back steps of the old stone building. The sun was shining brightly, and it made Sophie's eyes ache. She hadn't slept at all last night in protest of how she felt Coyote was wasting her time.

"Still visiting the desert every night?" Jilly asked around a mouthful of chips.

Sophie gave her a mournful nod. "Pretty much. Unless I don't go to sleep."

"But I thought you liked the desert," Jilly said. "You came back from that vacation in New Mexico just raving about how great it was, how you were going to move down there, how we were all crazy not to think of doing the same."

"This is different. All I want to do is give it up."

Jilly shook her head. "I'm so envious of the way you get to go places when you dream. I would *never* want to give it up."

"You haven't met Coyote."

"Coyote was your favorite subject when you got back."

Sophie sighed. It was true. She'd become enamoured with the Trickster figure on her vacation and had even named her last studio after a painting she'd bought in Santa Fe: Five Coyotes Singing.

"This Coyote's not the same," she said. "He's not all noble and mystical and, oh I don't know, mischievous, I suppose, in a sweet sort of a way. He's more like the souvenirs in the airport gift shop — fun if you're in the right mood, but sort of tacky at the same time. And definitely not very helpful. The only agenda he pursues with any real enthusiasm is trying to convince me to have sex with him."

Jilly raised her eyebrows. "Isn't that getting kind of kinky? I mean, how would you even do it?"

"Oh please. He's not a coyote all of the time. Mostly he's a man." Sophie frowned. "Mind you, even then he'll have the odd bit of coyote about him: ears mostly. Sometimes a muzzle. Sometimes a tail."

Jilly reached for the chip bag, but it was empty. She shook out the last few crumbs and licked them from her palm, then crumpled the bag and stuck it in the pocket of her jacket.

"What am I going to *do?*" Sophie said.

"Beats me," Jilly said. "We should go back inside. Geordie's going to think we deserted him."

"You're not being any help at all."

"If it were," Jilly said, "I'd join you in a minute. But it isn't. Or at least, we've yet to find a way to make it possible."

"He's going to drive me mad."

"Maybe you should give him a taste of his own medicine," Jilly said. "You know, act just as loony."

Sophie laughed. "Only you would think of that. And only you could pull it off. I wish there *was* some way to bring you over. Then I could just watch the two of you drive each other mad."

"You could always just sleep with him."

"I've been tempted — and not simply because I think it'd drive him away. He's really quite attractive and he can be very . . . persuasive."

"But," Jilly said.

"But I feel that as though it'd be like eating the fruit in fairyland — if I give in to him, then I'll never be able to get away."

10   Sophie:

So every night when I dream, I come to the desert and Coyote and I go looking for my way out. And every night's a trial. My night-nerves are shot. I'm always on edge because I never know what's going to happen next, what he's going to want to discuss, when or if he's going to put a move on me. We never do find Kokopelli, but that's not the worst of it. The worst thing is that I'm actually getting used to this: to Coyote and his mad carrying-on. Not only used to it, but enjoying it. No matter how much Coyote exasperates me, I can't stay mad at him.

And my desert time's not all bad by any means. When Coyote's being good company, you couldn't ask for a better friend. The desert spirits aren't shy around him, either. The aunts and uncles, which are what he calls the saguaro, tell us stories, or sing songs, or sometimes just gossip. All those strange madonna-faced spirits drop by to visit us, in ones and twos and threes. Women with fox-ears or antlers. Bobcat and coati spirits. Cottontails, jack rabbits, and pronghorns. Vultures and grouse and hawks. Snakes and scorpions and lizards. Smoke tree ghosts and tiny fairy duster sprites. Twisty cholla spirits, starburst yucca bogles and mesquite dryads draped in cloaks made of a thousand thousand perfectly-shaped miniature leaves.

The mind boggles at their variety and number. They come in every shape and size, but they all have that madonna resemblance, even the males. They're all that strange mix of human with beast or plant. And they all have their own stories and songs and dances to share.

So it's not all bad. But Kokopelli's flute-playing is always there, sometimes only audible when I'm very still, a Pied Piper covenant that I don't remember agreeing to, but it keeps me here. And it's that loss of choice that won't let me ever completely relax. The knowledge that I'm here, not because I want to be, but because I have to be.

One night Coyote and I are lying on a hilltop looking up at the stars. The aunts and uncles are murmuring all around us, a kind of wordless chant like a lullaby. A black-crested phainopepla is perched on my knee, strange little Botticelli features studying mine in between groomings. Coyote is smoking a cigarette, but it doesn't smell like tobacco — more like piñon. A dryad was sitting on an outcrop nearby, her skin the gorgeous green of her palo verde tree, but she's drifted away now.

"Grandmother Toad told me that this is a place where people come to find totem," I say after awhile. I feel Coyote turn to look at me, but I keep my own gaze on the light show overhead. So many stars, so much sky. "Or they come to consult spirits, to learn from them."

"Nokomis is the wisest of us all. She would know."

"So how come we never see anybody else?"

"I'm nobody?" the little phainopepla warbles from my knee.

"You know what I mean. No people."

"It's a big desert," Coyote says.

"The first spirits I met here told me it was somebody else's dreaming place — the way Mabon is mine. But they wouldn't tell me whose."

"Spirits can be like that," Coyote says.

The phainopepla frowns at the both of us, then flies away.

"Is it your dreaming place?" I ask him.

"If it was my dreaming place," he says, "when I did this —" He reaches a hand over and cups my breast. I sit up and move out of his reach. "— you'd fall into my arms and we'd have glorious sex the whole night long."

"I see," I say dryly.

Coyote sits up and grins. "Well, you asked."

"Not for a demonstration."

"What is that frightens you about having sex with me?"

"It's not a matter of being frightened," I tell him. "It's the consequences that might result from our doing it."

He reaches into his pocket and pulls out a condom. I can't *believe* this guy.

"That's not quite what I had in mind," I say.

"Ah. You're afraid of the psychic ramifications."

"Say what?"

"You're afraid that having sex with me will trap you here forever."

Am I that open a book?

"The thought has crossed my mind," I tell him.

"But maybe it'll free you instead."

I wait, but he doesn't say anything more. "Only you're not telling, right?" I ask.

"Only I don't know," he says. He rolls himself another cigarette and lights up. Blowing out a wreath of smoke, he shoots me a sudden grin. "I don't know, and you don't know, and the way things are going, I guess we never will, hey?"

I can't help but react to that lopsided grin of his. Frustrated as I'm feeling, I still have to laugh. He's got more charm than any one person deserves and when he turns it on like this, I don't know whether to give him a hug or a bang on the ear.

11

A week after her show closed at The Green Man Gallery, Sophie appeared on Max Hannon's doorstep with *Hearts Like Fire, Burning* under her arm, wrapped in brown paper.

"You didn't pick it up," she said when he answered the bell, "so I thought I'd deliver it."

Max regarded her with surprise. "I really didn't think you were serious."

"But you will take it?" Sophie asked. She handed the package over as though there could be no question to Max's response.

"I'll treasure it forever," he said, smiling. Stepping to one side so that she could go by him, he added, "Would you like to come in?"

It was roomier inside Max's house than it looked to be from the outside. Renovations had obviously been done, since the whole of the downstairs was laid out in an open concept broken only by the necessary support beams. The kitchen was off in one corner, separated from the rest of the room by an island counter. Another corner held a desk and some bookcases. The remainder of the room consisted of a comfortable living space of sprawling sofas and armchairs, low tables, Navajo carpets and display cabinets.

There was art everywhere — on the walls, as might be expected: posters, reproductions and a few originals, but there was even more three-dimensional work. The sculptures made Sophie's heartbeat quicken. Wherever she looked there were representations of the desert spirits she'd come to know so well, those strange creatures with their human features and torsos peeping out from their feathers and fur, or their thorny cacti cloaks. Sophie was utterly entranced by them, by how faithful they were to the spirits from her desert dream.

"It's funny," Max said, laying the painting she'd given him down on a nearby table. The two ocotillo cacti spirit statues that made up the centerpiece seemed to bend their long-branched forms towards the package, as though curious about what it held. "I was thinking about you just the other day."

"You were?"

Max nodded. "I remembered why it was that you looked so familiar to me when we met at your opening."

If her desert dream hadn't started up after that night, Sophie might have expected him to tell her now that he was one of its spirits and it was from seeing her in that otherworldly realm that he knew her. But it couldn't be so. She hadn't followed Kokopelli's flute until after she'd met Max.

"I would have remembered it if we'd ever met," she said.

"I didn't say we'd actually met."

"Now you've got me all curious."

"Maybe we should leave it a mystery."

"Don't you dare," Sophie said. "You have to tell me now."

"I'd rather show you than tell you," Max said. "Just give me a moment."

He went up a set of stairs over by the kitchen area that Sophie hadn't noticed earlier. Once he was gone, she wandered about the large downstairs room to give the statues a closer look. The resemblances were uncanny. It wasn't so much that he'd captured the exact details of her dream's desert fauna as that his sculptures contained an overall sense of the same spirit; they captured the elemental, inherent truth rather than recognizable renderings. She was crouched beside a table, peering at a statue of a desert woodrat with human hands, when Max returned with a small painting in hand.

"This is where I first saw you," he said.

Sophie had to smile. She remembered the painting. Jilly had done it years ago: a portrait of Wendy, LaDonna and her, sitting on the back steps of a Yoors Street music club, Wendy and LaDonna scruffy as always, bookending Sophie in a pleated skirt and silk blouse, the three of them caught in the circle of light cast by a nearby streetlight. Jilly had called it *The Three Muses Pause to Reconsider Their Night.*

"This was Peter's," Max said. "He loved this painting and kept it hanging in his office by his desk. The idea of the Muses having a girl's night out on the town appealed to the whimsical side of his nature. I'd forgotten all about it until I was up there the other day looking for some papers."

"I haven't thought of that painting in years," Sophie told him. "You know Jilly actually made us sit for it at night on those very steps — at least for her initial sketches, which were far more detailed than they had any need to be. I think she did them that way just to see how long we'd actually put up with sitting there."

"And how long did you sit?"

"I don't know. A few hours, I suppose. But it *seemed* like weeks. "Is this your work?" she added, pointing to the statues.

Max nodded.

"I just love them," she said. "You don't show in Newford, do you? I mean, I would have remembered these if I'd seen them before."

"I used to ship all my work back to the galleries in Arizona where I first started to sell. But I haven't done any sculpting for a few years now."

"Why not? They're so good."

Max shrugged. "Different priorities. It's funny how it works, how we define ourselves. I used to think of myself as a sculptor first — everything else came second. Then when the eighties arrived, I came out and thought of myself as gay first, and only then as a sculptor. Now I define myself as an AIDS activist before anything else. Most of my time these days is taken up in editing a newsletter that deals with alternative therapies for those with HIV."

Sophie thought of the book she'd seen lying on one of the tables when she was looking at the sculptures. *Staying Healthy With HIV* by David Baker and Richard Copeland.

"Your friend Peter," she said. "Did he die of AIDS?"

"Actually you don't die of AIDS," Max said. "AIDS destroys your immune system and it's some other illness that kills you — something your body would have been able to deal with otherwise." He gave her a sad smile. "But no. Ironically, I was the one who tested positive for HIV. Peter had leukemia. It had been in remission for a couple of years, but just before we went to the desert it came back and we had to go through it all again: the chemo treatments and the sleepless nights, the stomach cramps and awful rashes. I was sure that he'd pulled through once more, but then he died a week after we returned."

Max ran his finger along the sloped back of a statue of a horned owl whose human features seemed to echo Max's own. "I think Peter had a premonition that he was going to die and that was why he was so insistent we visit the desert one more time. He had a spiritual awakening there after one of his bouts with the disease and afterwards, he always considered the desert as the homeground for everything he held most dear." Max smiled, remembering. "We met because of these statues. He would have moved there, except for his job. Instead, I moved here."

Sophie got a strange feeling as Max spoke of Peter's love for the desert.

"Remember we talked about dreams at the opening?" she said.

Max nodded. "Serial dreams — what a lovely conceit."

"What I was telling you wasn't something I made up. And ever since that night I've been dreaming of a desert — a desert filled up with these." Sophie included all of the statuary with a vague wave of her hand. "Except in my desert they aren't statues; they're real."

"Real."

"I know it sounds completely bizarre, but it's true. My dreams are true. I mean, they're not so much dreams as me visiting some other place."

Max gave her an odd look. "Whenever someone talked about what an imagination I must have to do such work, Peter would always insist that it was all based on reality — it was just a reality that most people couldn't see into."

"And are they?"

"I . . ." Max looked away from her to the statues. He laid his hand on the back of the owl-man again, fingers rediscovering the contours they had pulled from the clay. "I should show you Peter's office," he said when he finally looked up.

He led her up to the second floor which was laid out in a more traditional style, a hallway with doors leading off from it, two on one side, three on the other. Max opened the door at the head of the stairs and ushered her in ahead of him.

"I haven't been able to deal with any of this yet," he said. "What to keep . . . what not . . ."

A large desk stood by the window, covered with books, papers and a small computer, but Sophie didn't notice any that at first. Her attention was caught and trapped by the room's other furnishings: the framed photographs of the desert and leather-skinned drums that hung on the walls; a cabinet holding kachina figures, a medicine flute, rattles, fetishes and other artifacts; the array of Max's sculptures that peered at her from every corner of the room. She turned slowly on the spot, taking it all in, until her gaze settled on the familiar face of one of the sculptures.

"Coyote," she said softly.

Max spoke up from the doorway. "Careful. You know what they say about him."

Sophie shook her head.

"Don't attract his attention."

"Why?" Sophie asked, turning to look at Max. "Is he malevolent? Or dangerous?"

"By all accounts, no. He just doesn't think things through before he takes action. But while he usually emerges intact from his misadventures, his companions aren't always quite so lucky. Spending time with Coyote is like opening your life to disorder."

Sophie smiled. "That sounds like Coyote, all right."

Her gaze went back to the cabinet and the medicine flute that lay on its second shelf between two kachinas. One was the Storyteller, her comical features the colour of red clay; the other was Kokopelli. The medicine flute itself was similar to the one that Geordie had traded away, only much more beautifully crafted. But then everything in this room had a resonance of communion with more than the naked eye could see — a sense of the sacred.

"Did Peter play the flute?" she asked.

"The one in the cabinet?"

"Mmm."

"Only in the desert. It has next to no volume, but a haunting tone."

Sophie nodded. "I know."

"He'd play that flute and his drums and rattles. He'd go to sweats and drumming nights when we were down there. I used to tease him about being a trying to be an Indian but he said that the Red Road was open to anyone who walked it with respect."

"The Red Road?"

"Native spiritual beliefs. I went with him sometimes, but I never really felt comfortable." He touched the nearest statue, an intricate depiction of a prickly pear spirit. "I love the desert, too, but I've never been much of a joiner."

"Did that disappoint Peter?"

Max shook his head. "Peter was one of the most open-minded, easy-going individuals you could ever have met. He always accepted people for what they were."

"Sounds like Jilly. No wonder they got along."

"You mean because of the painting?"

Sophie nodded.

"Peter never met her. I bought it for him at one of her shows. He fell in love with it on the spot — much as I did with the painting you gave me today." An awkward smile touched his lips. "I had more money in those days."

"Please don't feel guilty about it," Sophie told him, "or you'll spoil the pleasure of my giving it to you."

"I'll try."

"So did Peter have desert dreams?" Sophie asked. "Like mine?"

"He never told me that he had serial dreams, but he did dream of the desert. What are yours like?"

"This could take awhile."

"I've got the time."

So while Max sat in the chair at Peter's desk, Sophie walked about the room and told him, not only about the desert dream and Coyote, but about Mabon and Jeck and the whole strange life she had when she stepped into her dreams.

"There's something odd about Coyote referring to Nokomis," Max said when she was done.

"Why's that?"

"Well, everything else in your desert relates to the Southwest except for her. Nokomis and Grandmother Toad — those are terms that relate to our part of the world. They come from the lexicon of our own local tribes like the Kickaha."

"So what are you saying?"

Max shrugged. "Maybe Coyote was the woman who sent you looking for him in the first place."

"But why would he do that?"

"Who knows why Coyote does anything? Maybe he just took a liking to you and decided to meet you in a roundabout way."

"So was he Kokopelli as well?" Sophie asked. "Because it's the flute-playing that got me there in the first place."

"I don't know."

But Sophie thought perhaps she did. She stood before the cabinet that held Peter's medicine flute. It was too much of a coincidence — Max's sculptures, Peter's interest in the desert. The feeling came to her that somehow she'd gotten caught up in unfinished business between the two, neither quite willing to let the other go, so they were haunting each other.

She turned to look at Max, but decided she needed one more night in her desert dream before she was ready to bring up that particular theory with him.

"It feels good being able to talk about this with someone," she said instead. "The only other person I've ever told it to is Jilly and frankly, she and Coyote are almost cut from the same cloth. The only difference is that Jilly's not quite as outrageous as he is and she's not always talking about sex. Everything Coyote wants to talk about eventually relates to sex."

"And *have* you slept with him?"

Sophie smiled. "I guess there's a bit of Coyote in you, too."

"I think there's a bit of him in every one of us."

"Probably. But to answer your question: no, I haven't. I'll admit I've come close — he can be awfully persuasive — but I have the feeling that if I slept with him, I'd be in more trouble than I already am. I'd be trapped in those dreams forever and I can't see that being worth one night's pleasure."

Max shook his head. "I hate it when people try to divorce sex from the other aspects of their life. It's too entwined with everything we are for us to be able to do that. It's like when some people find out that I have HIV. They expect me to disavow sex. They tell me that promiscuity got me into this position in the first place, so I should just stop thinking about it, writing about it, doing it. But if I did that, then I'd be giving up. My sexuality is too much a part of who I am, as a person and as an artist, for me not to acknowledge its importance in my life. I may not be looking for a partner right now. I may not live to be forty. But I'll damned if I'll live like a eunuch just because of the shitty hand I got dealt with this disease."

"So you think I should sleep with him."

"I'm not saying that at all," Max replied. "I'm saying that sex is the life energy and our sexuality is how we connect to it. Whether or not you sleep with Coyote or anyone else isn't going to trap you in this faerie otherworld, or even get you infected with some disease. It's *why* you have sex with whoever you've chosen as your partner. The desire has to include some spiritual connection. You have to care enough about the other person — and that naturally includes taking all the necessary precautions.

"How often or with how many people you

have sex isn't the issue at all. It's not about monogamy versus promiscuity; it's about how much love enters the equation. If there's a positive energy between you and Coyote, if you really care about him and he cares for you, then the experience can only be positive — even if you never see each other again. If that energy and caring isn't there, then you shouldn't even be thinking about having sex with him in the first place."

12   Sophie:

So now I'm feeling cocky. I think I've got the whole thing figured out. Those first spirits told me the truth: this isn't my dreaming place. It's either Peter's or Max's, I don't know which yet. One of them hasn't let go of the other and whichever one of the two it is, he's trying to hang on to the other one. Maybe the desert belongs to Max and he doesn't know it. Maybe its his way of keeping Peter alive and I just tumbled into the place through having met him that night at my opening. Or maybe it belongs to Peter; Peter wearing Kokopelli's guise in this desert, calling me up by mistake instead of Max. He probably got me because I'm such a strong dreamer and when he saw his mistake, he just took off, leaving me to fend for myself. Or maybe he doesn't even know I'm here. But it's got to be one or the other and talking to Kokopelli is going to tell me which.

"No more fooling around," I tell Coyote. "I want to find Kokopelli."

"I'm doing my best," he says. "But that flute-player — he's not an easy fellow to track down."

We're sitting by another mesquite fire in another dry wash — or maybe it's the same one where we first met. Every place starts to look the same around here after awhile. It's a little past noon, the sun's high. Ground-doves fill the air with their mournful *coo-ooh, coo-ooh* sound and a hawk hangs high above the saguaro — a smudge of shadow against the blue. Coyote has coffee brewing on the fire and a cigarette dangling from the corner of his mouth. He looks almost human today, except for the coyote ears and the long stiff whiskers standing out from around his mouth. I keep expecting one of them to catch fire, but they never do.

"I'm serious, Coyote."

"There's people put chicory in with their coffee, but it just doesn't taste the same to me,"
he says. "I'm not looking for a smooth taste when I make coffee. I want my spoon to stand up in the cup."

He looks at me with those mismatched eyes of his, pretending he's as guileless as a newborn babe, but while my father might have made some mistakes in his life, raising me to be stupid wasn't one of them.

"If you'd wanted to," I say, "we could have found Kokopelli weeks ago."

The medicine flute is still playing, soft as a distant breeze. It's always playing when I'm here — never close by, but never so far away that I can't hear it anymore.

"You could take me to him right now . . . if you wanted to."

"The thing is," Coyote says, "nothing's as easy as we'd like it to be."

"Don't I know it," I mutter, but he's not even listening to me.

"And the real trouble comes from not knowing what we really want in the first place."

"I know what I want — to find Kokopelli, or whoever it is playing that flute."

"Did I ever tell you," Coyote says, "about the time Barking Dog was lying under a mesquite tree, just after a thunderstorm?"

"I don't want to hear another one of your stories."

13

But Coyote says:

Barking Dog looks up and the whole sky is filled with a rainbow. Now how can I get up there? he thinks. Those colours are just the paints I need for my arrows.

Then he sees Buzzard and he cries: "Hey, Uncle! Can you take me up there so that I can get some arrow paint?"

"Sure, nephew. Climb up on my back."

Barking Dog does and Buzzard flies up and up until they reach the very edge of the sky.

"You wait here," Buzzard says, "while I get those paints for you."

So Barking Dog hangs there from the edge of the sky, and he's hanging there, but Buzzard doesn't come back. Barking Dog yells and he's making an awful racket, but he doesn't see anyone and finally he can't hang on any more and down he falls. It took Buzzard no time at all to get to the edge of the sky, but it takes Barking Dog two weeks to fall all the way back

down — bang! Right into an old hollow tree and he lands so hard, he gets stuck and he can't get out.

A young woman's walking by right about then, looking for honey. She spies a hole in that old hollow tree and what does she see but Barking Dog's pubic hairs, sticking out of the hole. Oh my, she's thinking. There's a bear stuck in this tree. So she pulls out one of those hairs and goes running home to her husband with it.

"Oh, this comes from a bear, don't doubt it" her husband says.

He gets his bow and arrows and the two of them go back to the tree. The young woman, she's got an axe and she starts to chop at that tree. Her husband, he's standing by, ready to shoot that bear when the hole's big enough, but then they hear a voice come out of the tree:

"Cousin, make that hole bigger."

The young woman has to laugh. "That's no bear," she tells her husband. "That's Barking Dog, got himself stuck in a tree."

So she chops some more and soon Barking Dog crawls out of that tree and he shakes the dust and the dirt from himself.

"We thought you were a bear," the young woman says.

Her husband nods. "We could've used that meat."

Barking Dog turns back to the tree and gives it a kick. "Get out of there, you old lazy bear," he cries and when a bear comes out, he kills it and gives the meat to the young woman and her husband. Then he goes off, and you know what he's thinking? He's thinking, I wonder what ever happened to Buzzard.

14   Sophie:

"Was I supposed to get something out of that story," I ask "or were you just letting out some hot air?"

"Coffee's ready," he says. "You want some?"

He offers me a blue enameled mug filled with a thick, dark brown liquid. The only resemblance it bears to the coffee I'd make for myself is that it has the same smell. I take the mug from him. Gingerly, I lift it up to my lips and give it a sniff. The steam rising from it makes my eyes water.

"You didn't answer me," I say as I set the mug in the dirt down by my knee, its contents untouched.

Coyote takes a long swallow, then shrugs. "I

don't know the answer to everything," he says.

"But you told me you could find him for me."

"I told you I would try."

"This is trying?" I ask. "Sitting around a campfire, drinking coffee and smoking cigarettes and telling stories that don't make any sense?"

He gives me a hurt look. "I thought you liked my company."

"I do. It's just —"

"I thought we were friends. What were you planning to do? Dump me as soon as we found the flute-player?"

"No. Of course not. It's just that I want . . . I need to have some control over my dreams."

"But you do have control over your dreams."

"Then what am I doing here? How come every time I fall asleep, I end up *here?*"

"When you figure that out," Coyote says, "everything else will fall into place."

"What do you think I've been trying to do all this time?"

Coyote takes another long swallow from his mug. "The people of your world," he says, "you live two lives — an outer life that everyone can see, and another secret life inside your heads. In one of those lives you can start out on a journey and reach your destination, but when you take a trip in the other, there's no end."

"What do you mean there's no end?"

Coyote shrugs. "It's the way you think. One thing leads to another and before you know it you're a thousand miles from where you thought you'd be and you can't even remember where it was you thought you were going in the first place."

"Not everybody dreams the way I do," I tell him.

"No. But everybody's got a secret life inside their head. The difference is, you've got a stage to act yours out on."

"So none of this is real."

"I didn't say that."

"So what are you saying?"

Coyote lights another cigarette, then finishes his coffee. "Good coffee, this," he tells me.

15

"And these stories of his," Sophie said. "They just drive me crazy."

Jilly looked up from her canvas to where Sophie was slouching in the window-seat of her studio. "I kind of like them. They're so Zen."

"Oh please. You can keep Zen. I just want something to make sense."

"Okay," Jilly said. She set her brush aside and joined Sophie in the window-seat. "To start with, Barking Dog is just another one of Coyote's names."

"Really?"

Jilly nodded. "It's a literal translation of *Canis latrans*, which is Coyote's scientific name. That last story was his way of telling you that the two of you are much the same."

"I said sense," Sophie said. "You know the way the rest of the world defines the term?"

"But it does make sense. In the story, Coyote's looking for arrow paints, but after he gets sidetracked, all he can do is wonder what happened to Buzzard."

"And?"

"You were following this flute music, but all you can think of now is finding Kokopelli."

"But *he's* the one playing the flute."

"You don't know that."

"Nokomis told me it was either Coyote or Kokopelli who tricked me into this desert dream. And she told me that it was Kokopelli's flute that I heard."

Jilly nodded. "But then think of what Max told you about how out of context she is. You've got a dream filled with desert imagery, so what's a moon deity from the eastern woodlands doing there?"

"Maybe she just got sidetracked."

"And maybe she really was Coyote in another guise. And if that's true, can you trust anything she told you?"

Sophie banged the back of her head against the window frame and let out a long sigh. "Great," she said. "That's just what I needed — to be even more confused about all of this than I already am."

"If you ask me," Jilly said, "I think it's time you left Coyote behind and struck out on your own to find your own answers."

"You don't know how good he is at sulking."

Jilly laughed. "So let him tag along. Just take the lead for a change."

So that night Sophie put on the tape she'd bought around the time Geordie was messing around with his medicine flute. *Coyote Love Medicine* by Jessita Reyes. She lay down on her bed and concentrated on the sound of Reyes' flute, letting its breathy sound fill her until its music and the music that drew her into the desert dream became one.

Coyote's stretched out on a rock, the brim of his hat pulled down low to shade his eyes. Today he's got human ears, a human face. He's also got a bushy tail of which he seems inordinately proud. He keeps grooming it with his long brown fingers, combing out knots that aren't there, fluffing out parts that just won't fluff out any further. He lifts the brim of his hat with a finger when he sees me start off.

"Where are you going?" he asks.

"I've got an appointment."

From lying there all languid in the sun, with only enough energy to roll himself a cigarette and groom that fine tail of his, suddenly he bounds to his feet and falls into step beside me.

"Who're you going to see?" he wants to know.

"Kokopelli."

"You know where he is?"

I shake my head. "I thought I'd let him find me."

I hold the music of the medicine flute in my mind and let it draw me through the cacti and scrub. We top one hill, scramble down the dusty slope of an arroyo, make our way up the next steep incline. We finally pull ourselves up to the top of a butte, and there he is, sitting cross-legged on the red stone, a slim, handsome man, dark hair cut in a shaggy page-boy, wearing white trousers and a white tunic, a plain wooden medicine flute lying across his knees. A worn cloth backpack lies on the stone beside him.

For the first time since I stepped into this desert dream all those weeks ago, I don't hear the flute any more. There's just the memory of it lying there in my mind — fueled by the cassette that's playing back in that world where another part of me is sleeping.

Kokopelli looks from Coyote to me.

"Hey, Ihu," he says. "Hey, Sophie."

I shoot Coyote a dirty look, but he doesn't even have the decency to look embarrassed at how easy it was for me to track Kokopelli down.

"How do you know my name?" I ask the flute-player.

He gives me a little shrug. "The whole desert's been talking about you, walking here, walking there, looking everywhere for what's sitting right there inside you all the time."

I'm really tired of opaque conversations and I tell him as much.

"Your problem," he says, "is that you can't seem to take anything at face value. Everything you're told doesn't necessarily have to have a hidden meaning."

"Okay," I say. "If everything's going to be so straightforward now, tell me: which one are you? Peter or Max?"

Kokopelli smiles. "That would make everything so easy, wouldn't it?"

"What do you mean?"

"For me to be one or the other."

"You said this was going to be a straightforward conversation," I say.

I turn to Coyote, though why I expect him to back me up on this, I've no idea. Doesn't matter anyway. Coyote's not there anymore. It's just me and the flute-player, sitting up on the red stone of this butte.

"I didn't say it would be straightforward," Kokopelli tells me. "I said that sometimes you should try to take what you're told at face value."

I sigh and look away. It's some view we have. From this height, the whole desert is laid out before us.

"This isn't about Peter or Max, is it?" I say.

Kokopelli shakes his head. "It's about you. It's about what you want out of your life."

"So Coyote was telling me the truth all along."

"Ihu was telling you a piece of the truth."

"But I followed your flute to get here."

Kokopelli shakes his head again. "You were following a need that you dressed up as my music."

"So all of this —" I wave my hand to encompass everything, the butte, the desert, Kokopelli, my being here "— where does it fit in?"

"It's different for everyone who comes. When you travel in dream, you can bring nothing across with you; you can bring nothing back. Only what is in your head."

And that's my real problem. I know my dream worlds are real, but it's a different kind of real from what I can find in the waking world. I work out all of my problems in my dreams — from my mother abandoning me to my never seeming to be able to maintain a good relationship. But the solutions don't have any real holding power. They don't ever seem to resonate with the same truth in the waking world as they do in my dreams. And that's because I can't bring anything tangible back with me. I have to take it all on faith and for some things, faith isn't enough.

"Perhaps you expect too much," Kokopelli says when I try to explain this to him. "We are shaped by our experiences and no matter where those experiences occur, they are still valid. The things you have seen and done don't lose their resonance because you can only hold them in your memory. In that sense there is little difference between what you experience when you are awake or when you dream. Keepsakes, mementos, tokens . . . their real potency lies in the memories they call up, rather than what they are in and of themselves."

"But I don't always understand the things I experience."

Kokopelli smiles. "Without mysteries, life would be very dull indeed. What would be left to strive for if everything were known?"

He picks up his flute and begins to play. His music carries us through the afternoon until the shadows deepen and twilight mutes the details of the desert around us. Although I don't hear a pause in the music, at some point he's put on his pack and I look up to see him silhouetted against the sunset. For a moment I don't see a man, but a hunchbacked flute-playing kachina.

"Tell Max," he says, "to remember me as loving him."

And then he steps away, into the night, into the desert, into the sky — I don't know where. I just know he's gone, the sound of his flute is a dying echo, and I'm left with another mystery that has no answer:

If he was Peter, how did he know so much about me?

And if he wasn't, then who was he?

17

"I've been thinking a lot about the desert lately," Max said.

He and Sophie were having a late dinner in The Rusty Lion after taking in a show. They had a table by the window and could watch the bustling crowds go by on Lee Street from where they sat.

"Are you thinking of moving back to Arizona?" Sophie asked.

Max shook his head. "I probably will one day, but not yet. No, I was thinking more of the desert as a metaphor for how my life has turned out."

Sophie had often tried to imagine what it would be like to live with a terminal disease and she thought Max was probably right. It would be very much like the desert: the barrenness, the vast empty reaches. Everything honed to its purest essence, just struggling to survive. There wouldn't be time for anything more. She wondered if she'd resent the rich forests of other people's lives, if she knew her own future could be cut short at any time.

"I think I know what you mean," she said.

Max laughed. "I can tell by the way you look that you've completely misunderstood me. You're thinking of the desert as a hopeless place, right?"

"Well, not exactly hopeless, but . . ."

"It's just the opposite," Max said. "The desert brings home how precious life is and how much we should appreciate it while we have it. That life can still flourish under such severe conditions is a miracle. It's an inspiration to me."

"You're amazing, you know that?"

"Not really. We all know we're going to die someday, but we like to pretend we won't. Given the hand I've been dealt, I don't have the luxury of that pretense. I have to live with the reality of my mortality every day of my life. Now I could just give up — and I won't pretend to you that I don't have my bad days. But when I tested positive, I made myself a promise that I was going to dedicate whatever time I have left to two things: to fight the stigmas attached to this disease and to squeeze everything I can out of life."

The waitress came by with their orders then and for awhile they were kept busy with their meals.

"You look a little gloomy," Max said later, when they were waiting for their coffees. "I hope I didn't bring you down."

"No, it's not that."

"So tell Uncle Max what's bothering you."

"My problems seem so petty compared to what you have to put up with."

"Doesn't make them any less real for you, though. So 'fess up. Are you having man trouble again? We can be such bitches, can't we?"

"I suppose," Sophie said with a smile, then her features grew serious. "I just get tired of arguing. Everything starts out fine, but it always ends up with me having to adjust my life to theirs and I'm just not ready to do that anymore. I mean, I know there's going to be compromise in a relationship, but why does it always have to be on my side?"

"Compromise is necessary," Max agreed, "so long as you never give up who you are. That isn't compromise; that's spiritual death. You have to remain true to yourself."

"That's what I keep telling myself, but it doesn't make it any easier."

"Somewhere there is someone who'll love you for who are, not what they think you should be."

"And if there isn't?" Sophie said. "If I never connect with that person?"

"Then you'll be alone."

"Alone."

Sophie sighed. She was too familiar with what it meant to be alone.

"It's hard to be alone, isn't it?" Max said.

Sophie nodded.

"But better to be alone than to settle for less than what you need . . . less than what you deserve."

"I suppose."

"Here," Max said. He reached down under his chair for the package he'd carried into the restaurant when he'd arrived. "Maybe this'll cheer you up."

He put the package on the table between them. Sophie looked at him.

"What is it?" she asked.

"Open it up and find out."

Inside was one of Max's sculptures — a new one. Sophie recognized herself in one small figurine that made up the tableau, only she was decked out in a leather cap from which sprang a deer's antlers giving her a very mythic air. She stood in front of a saguaro on which was perched a tiny owl with a woman's face. Lounging on a rock beside her was a familiar figure in jeans, shirt and vest, coyote features under the cowboy hat. On the ground between them lay a medicine flute.

"It's beautiful," she said, looking up at Max.

"It's for you."

"I just —"

"Don't you even dare say you can't accept it."

"I just love it," Sophie said.

"Like I said," Max told her. "I've been thinking a lot about the desert lately."

"Me, too."

18   Sophie:

Sometimes when I'm in Mabon, walking its streets while my body's sleeping a world away, I'll get a whiff of smoke that smells like piñon and then somewhere in the crowd I'll spot a lean man who I swear has coyote ears poking up out his hair, but he's always gone before I can get close enough to be sure.

Coyote was right about one thing: the journeys we take inside our heads never end.

I never thought I'd say this, but I miss him. Ω

For Robin Hardy.

Note: The story of Coyote and the Buzzard is based upon traditional Kickapoo folklore.

A CHRISTMAS CAROL REVISITED:

MR ROBERT CRATCHIT MANY YEARS LATER

A grave has sheltered Scrooge for fifteen years
While I've amassed more wealth than he dared dream.
East-enders rent their doleful rooms from me
And labor for my gain from birth to bier.

My wretched wife lives on the coast of Spain
Where servants fear her hateful snarl and gaze.
Son Tim and I lost contact. Now in shame
I learn a pipe from China spares him pain.

Fools say the price I've paid for wealth is huge.
I'm rich! I need not listen to buffoons.
Yet sometimes when the shadows stalk my room
I wonder what dark dreams drove mad Old Scrooge.

— Lawrence Barker

THE STORY OF TSE GAH
by Lord Dunsany
illustrated by Rodger Gerberding

I know, now, that there are other lands than our land. I know that there are lands beyond the mountains. One of them is Tibet, another is China, and then there is Nepal. I know this, because I have seen the ambassadors from China and Tibet to our land, and an envoy came from Nepal. They came and stood in front of me. And I know many things besides these. I am going to write down all the things that I know, which were in the past, for they are all gone now, and all things are changing, so that I fear that the old things will come no more. The future I cannot see as I can see the past; yet it will come, and it will be just as much what was ordained as the past; but it is all strange and uncertain and I wish to think of it no more. The monks write of it, but I will write of the past.

Some things I remember separately from other things. I remember them clearly, but I do not remember when they occurred. Other things I remember being followed by others, and they by others again, so that I know when they were. I remember a garden with some very bright flowers, taller than I; and I remember a great white-and-green butterfly coming to one of them. But I do not remember when this was. I was with the women then. They had taken me to the garden of the palace. And they used to be with me in the palace, too. Sometimes I saw the monks, but they never came very close. Afterward I was taken away from the women, and I never saw them anymore, only the monks.

The women told me a little about Tse Gah — just that he was god of the mountains, and that his name was Tse Gah, and that he ruled over our land, and had made it, and spoke by thunder. But the monks taught me a great deal about Tse Gah.

I was frightened of Tse Gah, who had made the mountains. And one night while he spoke, and the lightning flashed also, I was very much frightened indeed, and the monks smiled. One of them standing quite close to me smiled so curious a smile that, strange though it is to write, it was that smile that taught me what I had never guessed. And it was a very strange thing to be taught.

Who reads this may think it very strange that I did not know, but I did not. Perhaps I was not taught it, but guessed from that smile when I was frightened of Tse Gah. I was five years old when I learned this. When I knew this, it accounted for everything. I knew now why the women were afraid of me. I had always known that they were, though I never knew why. All the monks frightened me; and they used to puzzle me, too, because I saw that they were a little more frightened of me. Now I knew why. It accounted, too, for the long memories that the monks had taught me to have. I was an earthly incarnation of Tse Gah, and could remember everything forever, even the making of the mountains.

The palace was all of wood and very dark. I used to sit nearly all day among many great pillars; some were gold and some were red, but they were all of wood. I had never been allowed any toys. But Then I found out that I was Tse Gah. I asked for toys. They looked at me and I think that they knew that I knew, for toys were brought. I asked for clay to play with, and I was brought clay. When it was placed before me, I played with it, and the monks watched me playing. I remembered what the women told me about Tse Gah's making the mountains. So I made little mountains. And the monks watched and nodded their heads.

After they brought me clay, I asked for more toys; and toys were brought — lovely ones. When I saw that they brought me toys whenever I asked for them, I asked for a horse. But they would not give me a horse, though I was Tse Gah. They would never let me walk far from the palace, and I very seldom left the palace at all. If I asked to go out to pick flowers, they brought me armfuls of flowers and strewed them before me, but they would not let me go and play in the garden by myself. When I did go to the garden, there were always three monks with me, sometimes four or five.

It was very dark in the palace, particularly in my part of it. My part of the palace was the temple. That is where all of the big pillars were. And it was full of gongs. Whenever I spoke, a monk would beat a gong and then call loudly what I had said. He used to call it in a ringing tone, and it seemed very grand. But he did not always repeat what I had said just as I had said it. Sometimes he would add things of his own, and often leave out things I had said, or alter them. If I complained of this, the gong would be beaten again, and I would hear my complaint being chanted, but not as I had said it.

I asked again for a horse, and the monk who beat the gong said I had asked for a dragon on which to ride over the land. When I saw that the monks would never give me a horse, I said that I would be Tse Gah no more, and that I would remember nothing that happened hundreds of years ago, and would make no more prophecies; for they used to make me make prophecies, and the monks always fulfilled them. And I said I would leave the thunder alone, and it could do what it liked.

Then all the monks in the temple looked at one another in a way that frightened me, but they said nothing. And one of them went away into a dark part of the temple where I had never been; and presently an old monk came out of the darkness, one I had never seen before. And all the monks, except him, went away. Then, when we were all alone, the old monk prostrated himself before me, but I was still very frightened. I did not know who he was, or why he had come.

I raised my hand, as I had been taught to do, to give him the blessing of Tse Gah. Then he seized my hand, and I found he had chains under his great, dark robe, and he fastened an iron band around my wrist, and a chain went from the band and he hooked the other end of the chain to a hook that there was on one of the pillars. Then he did the same with one of my ankles, fastening that chain to a hook on another pillar. Then he stripped off my clothing and brought out a thick bamboo, which was also hidden under his robes, and was as long as I, even longer. And then he began to beat me. He beat me with all his might. I cried out, but no one came. Then, I screamed louder, but nothing stirred in the temple; not even the gongs were sounded.

by Lord Dunsany

At first I cried out that I would curse him, and then I threatened him with thunder. But he still beat on. I have never known such pain. And then I cried so hard that I could not speak. When the pain grew so great that I could bear nothing more, I said that I would never again say I would not be Tse Gah, and that I would do whatever the monks told me, and remember my memories, and prophesy just as they said. Even then he still beat me. At last he stopped. And then he prostrated himself before me once more, and I gave him the blessing of Tse Gah, and he went away into the dark and I never saw him again.

Then the monks that had left me came back. I was still crying. I told them that I had been cruelly beaten. They said none could have beaten me. I said I had been chained up. They could see the chains. Then they unfastened the bands from my wrist and ankle and said that I must have been chained by some god from Tibet or China. No man, they said, could have done it. And they asked me to prophesy against the god that had chained me; and I did as they said. I always did as the monks said after that. They never gave me a horse.

The monks had great horns, longer than a man, that they used to blow to keep away devils. I used to hear them at night whenever I was awake, or it may have been the devils I heard, or perhaps both, the horns and the devils hooting against each other. They used to hoot if I went for a walk in the garden; and the farther away I walked, the more they hooted.

There used to be incense in the temple: they often burned it before me in brass bowls; it smelled very sweet and it made me sleepy. When I woke from the sleep that I had slept because of the incense, any words that I uttered before I was quite awake were written down in a book. These were prophecies. Gongs were beaten and they were read out. I never remembered what I said just as I was waking up after the incense, so I do not know if the prophecies that were read out were what I had said or not.

I used to want to play with other children, but none were allowed near me. No one was allowed to speak to me but the monks. Sometimes they would keep me in the temple for days. Sometimes there were services in the temple from morning till night, and all the time I had to sit on the altar. I grew very tired then. They would never let me go and play. Once there was a drought in the valley, and they prayed before me for a week. Then the rain came on the seventh day. I could not have sat on the altar any longer, if the rain had not come. I slept for three days and nights after that.

It was all gongs and horns and the darkness of the temple. One day was just like another. They taught me to read so that I could remember more easily the things that had happened hundreds of years ago. And they taught me to write, too. It was very hard to learn, but I am glad now. And then the revolution came. The people came up from the valley and killed the monks. There was great blowing of horns, but they killed them. They would have killed me, too, but I easily got away from them. I slipped from the temple when I saw them killing the monks. It was all over — blood. I got out through the door to the garden, and ran down the side of the mountain. I prophesied against the people of the valley as I ran, but it had no effect. I could hear their angry shouts as loud as ever, and the horns of the monks growing fewer.

Now I am going to do more. Am I not Tse Gah? The monks have taught me for years. Now I will do what they have taught. I am going to thunder. I have tried to do it before and I could not. But now I am going up to the highest peak. I have noticed that lightning strikes often upon the mountain-tops. It will be easier for me to thunder there. Then the people of the valley will know that I am Tse Gah. And I shall go back to the palace, and there will be no more monks there, and the people have killed them. And I shall have a horse.

The air is sultry now, and I feel that it will be easy to thunder. It is very sultry, and the sky is growing black. Now I have reached the peak. I will thunder and the people shall know. I will. I . . .   Ω

THE FOREVER TREES
by Charles de Lint

illustrated by Allen Koszowski

> If you understand, things are just as they are.
> If you do not understand, things are just as they are.
> — Zen saying

1

In the end, what she remembers isn't her name, not at first, who she was or even how and where she lived her life. What she remembers is this:

When I was a child I had this ability to simply go somewhere. It wasn't a good place or a bad place — just *another* place. I wouldn't hide there, but when I was there, I couldn't be found. I didn't have to walk there, I'd just be there, in that ghost place.

Sometimes now I think it was a part of me, a piece of my mind where I'd go when things were bad. But then I remember: I went there when things were good, too.

2

Tasha never stops thinking, thinking. She's a visual artist but her mind's always full of words, scuttling around inside her head like mice in an old house when the sun goes down, the eyelids are drawn, the shutters fastened, the body still sleeping, but that secret part of her where the spirit candle burns the brightest is busy-busy, talking to itself, remembering, dreaming. She paints because of those words.

It's like this: She sees colours for words, like a light mottled grey touched with soft green and purple for whisper. Free is a Prussian blue that goes on forever, acquiring a hint of violet just before it vanishes from sight. Cacti is a deep fuchsia, but cactus is a warm buttery yellow with streaks of olive green and greenish browns. New is the electric colour of a kingfisher's wing and ford is the coppery red of an old pen nib, but Newford is a grey with highlights of henna and purple.

Joe doesn't pretend to understand. He looks at her art. He knows that her paintings are fragments of stories, conversations, essays, all chasing down those mice in her head, trying to put them into some semblance of order, but he doesn't get the translation. All he sees is colour on the canvas, random patterns that make no sense even after Tasha reads them to him.

But it doesn't stop them from being friends.

They're just friends. Good friends.

"I don't want to exchange bodily fluids with you," she tells him once. "It always spoils things."

He wonders at the time if that's how she really meant to put it, or if she just liked the way the words looked as she said them, but he understands what she means. Sex is good. Sex is fun. There's no better place to be, he thinks, than in the middle of a relationship when most of the awkwardness is gone and you're still crazy about each other. But one person always loves the other more and the imbalance undermines the best of intentions and eventually it all falls apart. He's seen it happen. He's had it happen. Lovers have come and gone in his life, but Tasha's constant. She's not one of the guys, not even close. She brings out the best in him, the way a friend should, but too often doesn't. Asks hard questions, but doesn't answer them for him. Lets him work them out for himself. The way he does for her.

"Men always want to fix everything," she tells him another time, "and I can't figure out why. I'd settle for simply understanding things."

Gets to where he knows exactly what she means. She talks about men, he talks about women, they're generalizing, like you do, but they're not talking about each other. It's not that they're sexless. The gender thing is there, it's part of what endears them to each other, the insights they get into what each is not, but the attraction's strictly platonic. Which makes it all the more confusing when Joe finds himself thinking not about her, Tasha, his friend, but about the curve of her neck and the way her hennaed hair lies so soft against it, how she fills her sweater and jeans with perfect contours that he wants to explore, palm to skin, soft, she'd be so soft, so smooth, like silk, touching her would be like touching silk, but warm.

He'd give anything to taste her lips and all of a sudden everything's way too complicated and he wants to fix what's going on instead of understanding it.

3

To get to that ghost place, first I'd have to find the meadow. Summer growth slaps my knees as I follow the long slope up from the bottom of the hill where the hedge is an unruly thicket tangled up in heaps of gathered fieldstone. It's been years since the slope was ploughed, but not so long that the forest has resettled the open ground. The weeds are never too tall and there are always wildflowers in bloom, great stuttering sweeps of colour that twist and wind in spiraling paths up and down the slope of the hill. Sometimes there's a hawk, high up, floating in the sky, but I don't see it right away, rarely look for the grey-brown cut of its wings against the blue. As I make my way up the slope, my gaze is always on the forest.

It's a crown of trees on the crest of the hill, trunks and fallen snags slow-dancing around the granite outcrops, a hundred-acre wood, but Pooh doesn't live there and I'm not Christopher Robin. I wouldn't even want to be. I liked being a girl and I like being a woman.

Under the trees, the air is cool and dark and rich with the wet smell of old damp wood, of ferns and mushrooms and the moss that cushions my footfalls. Not far from where the edge of the meadow and the forest blurs, a natural spring bubbles up from a leak in the granite and trickles pell-mell through the leaf-mold and around the stones. The water hurries with a jigging and reeling rush that's long since cut a narrow cleft through the dark red earth as it ribbons its way down the slope. All the trees seem to lean down to listen to it as it goes by.

What kind of trees? I don't know. I never had a name for them. They're big, some of them. Bigger than redwoods. But gnarled like old oaks or elms. And kind. I can't really explain. There's a kindness about them. They always welcome me. I know they're older than the stars, thick with mystery and wind music rustlings and shadow. Written on their bark are the histories of ancient

times, long-lost, and a thousand forgotten stories that they must remember, but they always have time for me. Child, girl, woman. I only ever felt kindness in that hundred-acre wood.

Nim called them the forever trees.

4

So Joe's redefined their relationship, but Tasha doesn't know. She comes over that evening to watch a video with him and feels something different in the air. Innocent in a white T-shirt and snug jeans that make her seem anything but, she looks around his apartment to see what's changed. The bookcase still stands on one wall, its shelves stuffed with paperbacks, magazines and found objects like a tattered slipper or a chipped coffee mug that have been there so long they've acquired squatters' rights and would look out of place anywhere else. The sofa still faces the old cedar chest that holds Joe's TV set and stereo. The same posters are on the wall, along with the small reproduction of a Hockney print in its narrow metal frame. The same worn Oriental carpet underfoot. The two beers Joe brings from the kitchen are given temporary refuge on the same apple crate that usually serves as his coffee table.

Nothing's different, but everything has changed. Joe seems — not edgy, but he can't stop moving. His usual stillness has dissolved, leaving behind the bare bones of nervous energy that makes his fingers twitch, his toes tap. Tasha tucks a loose lock of red hair back behind her ears and sits down on the sofa. She leans back, draws her knees up to her chin, smiles over them at Joe who's hovering about in the middle of the carpet until he finally sits down as well.

The video he's picked is *Enchanted April.* They've seen it before, but tonight the holidaying women don't absorb him. He's constantly stealing glances at her until Tasha begins to wonder if she's got a bit of her dinner stuck to her chin or lodged in between her teeth. A scrap of egg noodle. An errant morsel of snow pea. She explores the spaces between her teeth with her tongue, surreptitiously gives her chin a wipe with the back of her hand.

When she puts her feet down for a moment to reach for her beer, Joe is suddenly right beside her. She turns to look at him, confused, their faces only inches apart. He leans closer. As their lips touch, all the clues Tasha hadn't realized were clues go tumbling through her mind, rearranged in their proper order, the mystery solved, the confusion now embracing what had brought this change to their relationship and how could she have missed it? But then she lets the confusion go away and enjoys the moment, because Joe's a better kisser than she had ever imagined and she finds she likes the feel of his back and shoulders as she returns his embrace, likes the press of his chest against her, especially likes the touch of his lips and the tingling that wakes in her belly as the tips of their tongues explore each other.

"This is nice," she murmurs when they finally come up for air.

Nice hangs behind her eyes, all chicory blue, like when the sun first pulls the petals awake, and speckled like a trout. The movie plays on, forgotten except for the flickering glow it throws upon their faces.

"It's weird," Joe tells her. "I just haven't been able to stop thinking about you." The parade of his words kaleidoscopes through her. "It's like we've been friends for what — eight, nine years? — and all of a sudden I'm seeing you for the first time and I can't believe that I've ever been the least bit interested in another woman."

It takes Tasha a moment to separate the meaning of what he's saying from the colours.

"Are you saying you love me?" she asks, not sure how she wants him to answer, for all that she's been thoroughly enjoying the intimacy of the past ten minutes.

Joe gives her an odd look, as though he hadn't thought things through quite that far. But then he smiles.

"I guess I am," he says.

The words wake a warm flood of colour in Tasha's mind, a mingling of rose and pale violet like a coneflower's bloom in the twilight.

"How do you feel?" he asks.

"I'm not sure," she says softly. "It's all so sudden. It's . . ." She can't find the colour to tell him what she feels because she's not sure herself, she puts a hand behind his head and draws his lips back towards hers. "Kiss me again," she murmurs just before their lips meet.

The words float in their colours through her mind but Joe doesn't need the invitation.

5

I guess I have to explain everything, don't I? Nim lives in the hundred-acre wood. At least I think she does, because that's the only place I've ever seen her. Actually, I'm not even sure she's a she. I just always think of her as female, but as I try to describe her I realize she's asexual, androgynous. No breasts, but no body hair or Adam's apple either. Her long curly hair is always filled with seeds and twigs and burrs, but it's still soft as duck down. Skinny, she's so skinny you'd think she was made of sticks, but her limbs are pliant. She's the first person I've ever met who's as double-jointed as me. Maybe more. And she hears colours, too.

"But not sounds," she said when we're talking about it one time. "Just words."

Like me.

6

Joe knows he's screwed up big time. Tasha stays the night and they sleep together. They don't make out, they just sleep together, but somehow that makes everything seem more intimate instead of less. He wakes up to find her lying there beside him, still asleep. He traces the contour of her cheek with his gaze, and he sees a

friend, not a lover, all the little fireworks have packed up and gone. He stills thinks she's beautiful, ethereal and earthy, all mixed up in one red-topped bundle, but desire has fled. Making love to her would be like making love to a relative.

She opens her eyes and smiles at him, her warmth washing over him in a gentle pulsing tide until the guilt he's feeling registers, the smile droops, worry flits across her eyes.

"What's wrong?" she asks.

"This is a mistake," he tells her. "This is a serious mistake."

"But you said —"

"I know. I . . ."

He can't face her. He's feeling bad enough as it is. The hurt that's growing in her eyes is going to devastate him. He gets out of bed and starts dressing, fast, doesn't even look to see what he's putting on.

"I've got to get to work," he says, for all that it's a Saturday morning. He combs his hair with his hands, give her an apologetic look. "We'll talk about it," he adds, knowing how lame it sounds, but he can't seem to do any better. "Later."

And then he's gone. Tasha stares at the door of the bedroom through which he's fled. She's sitting up in the bed, has the bedclothes pulled up to her chin but they don't do anything for the shivering chill he's left behind, the blank spot that seems to have lodged in the middle of her chest. It's hard to breathe, hard to think straight. Harder still when she starts to cry and she can't stop, she just can't stop.

7

The thing is, I don't ever have to come back if I don't want to. I could stay forever the way Nim does and never grow any older. What brings me back? It used to be my puppy — Topy. I'd come back for Topy, but then one day I let her stay and she's lived in the hundred-acre wood with Nim ever since. Nobody could understand why I wasn't sad that she'd run away, but they didn't understand that she hadn't run away for me. I could see her any time I wanted to. I still can.

What brought me back after that? I don't know. Different things. I like this world, but sometimes everything gets to be too much for me in it. Like it's hard just having simple conversations when you have to be constantly separating the meanings of what's being said from its colours. I can't argue with people. By the time

I've worked out what we're fighting about, everything's usually gotten way more complicated, gotten so tangled up and knotted that it'll never make sense again. At least not for me. The hundred-acre wood gives me a break from that. Give me a chance to catch my breath so that when I come back to this world I fit in a little easier.

Nim knows what I mean. She's never going back, she says. She wants to become a forever tree herself and sometimes, when I look at her, all twig thin with that wild bird's nest of hair on top, I think she's half-way there.

8

Tasha makes her way home, crawls into her own bed, pulls the covers over her head, but can't stop the chill, can't stop the tears. It hurts too much — not because Joe redefined the relationship and then, after she tentatively embraced its new parameters, he went and backed off. She enjoyed necking with him last night, but she wasn't exactly making a lifetime commitment herself. No, it's that he didn't stay to talk. To explain. She hasn't been betrayed by a lover she's just met; she's been betrayed by one of her oldest friends.

She waits for him to call, but the phone stays silent by her bed. Saturday night. All day Sunday. Maybe it's better that way. She's never been good on the phone. Without a face to concentrate on, without being able to watch the lips move, or absorb the subtext that resonates in eyes and facial tics and twitches, conversation too often turns into nothing more than a confusing porridge of colour.

So Sunday evening she gets out of bed, dresses, tries to fix her face so that it doesn't look as though she's been crying for most of the weekend, sets off for Joe's apartment. Dreading it. Already knowing it'll be a disaster when she attempts to filter word-sense from the colour flood of what they'll say to each other. But they've been friends too long for her not to try.

Friends, she thinks. Friends don't treat each other this way. Her ability to trust is undergoing a test of faith. Once the masks drop, anything could be waiting there. That's something she's always known. The shock is finding a mask where she didn't expect one to be. She'd never realized that Joe could have been wearing a mask all this time.

But friends make mistakes, she told herself, and she clung to those words, spoke them aloud.

Saw yellow ochre veined with madder and blues. The grey underbelly of a summer cloud, winging across it, a flock of magenta and yellow-gold flowers.

But the colours couldn't disguise the fear that no matter what happened tonight she was never going to be sure if Joe was wearing a mask or not. There was just no way to *know*.

9

I guess the hardest thing to explain is how the hundred-acre wood is a real place, that I really go there, that when I'm walking under the forever trees, I'm not here anymore. It's not like I've shut my eyes and gone to some place inside my head. That's what I thought it was at first. Well, not at first. When I first went, I was too young to even wonder about that kind of a thing.

My parents knew there was something wrong with me, but no one could figure out what it was. It wasn't until years later that anyone even came up with a name for my condition: Synaesthesia. Everyone just thought I was a slow learner, that the connections in my head weren't all wired the right way, which is true I guess, or I'd be like everybody else, right?

I didn't talk until I was five because it took me that long to realize that it was words people used to communicate with each other — not colours. Because I *was* communicating, you see. Right from the first. But it was with crayons and watercolour paints and nobody could understand what I was saying. When I finally started to use words it was like having to translate everything from a foreign language.

That's what so seductive about the hundred-acre wood. When I talk with Nim, I'm communicating directly with her. I don't feel like I'm muddling around with translations. I never get the feeling that she's impatient with the long pauses in our conversations because she hears and sees everything the same as me. When I show her one of my paintings she knows exactly what I'm saying with it — the same way that somebody else can read a page from a book.

I guess one day I'll go and I won't come back. I'll become a raggedy wild girl like Nim with twigs and burrs in my hair.

Maybe we'll both end up as forever trees.

Maybe that's where they came from.

Maybe we're both dryads — and we just haven't matured from tree spirits into proper trees yet.

The idea of it makes me smile

If we were forever trees, we'd have *really* slow conversations, wouldn't we?

10

Joe is not a bad guy. Like Tasha said, even friends make mistakes. He never wore a mask around her and that was part of the problem that night when he told her he thought they should be lovers *and* friends. Maybe he should have waited, kept it to himself a little longer until he'd really worked it out in his own head, dealt with it in a way that wouldn't have hurt Tasha before sharing his feelings with her. But maybe it took his sharing those feelings for him to work it out.

He knew it hadn't been fair to her, but he hadn't meant to hurt her. Not that night. Not when he fled the next morning. He'd just gotten confused, couldn't think straight, but he meant to make it right. He meant to call her and apologize for screwing up the way he had, screwing up big time, and he hoped she'd forgive him because maybe they weren't supposed to be lovers, but nothing in his life meant more to him than Tasha's friendship.

So he phones her, Sunday night, lets the phone ring and ring, but there's no answer. He keeps trying up until midnight, then he finally goes over to her apartment, lets himself in with the key she gave him so long ago, but she really isn't there, she wasn't just ignoring the phone, she really isn't home. But she isn't anywhere else either.

Days go by and she's never home, never at her studio, nobody has seen her, nobody ever sees her again.

Joe's sitting in his apartment, cradling one of Tasha's paintings on his lap, and he's remembering holding her one night when she's having a stress attack, when all the words turned into too many colours and everything inside her just shut down for awhile so that she didn't even know who or where she is; he's remembering what she told him that night, about a ghost place she can visit, a hundred-acre wood of forever trees. He believed she could go there, didn't ask for proof. That's what friends do — they accept each others' secrets and marvels and hold them in trust.

So Joe knows where Tasha has gone, running up a long meadowed slope with a wild girl and a puppy, vanishing into the embrace of a forest of forever trees, and he misses her, more than anything, he misses her, and what he regrets, what he regrets the most, is that he never asked her how to get there himself so that he could see her again. Ω

by Charles de Lint

CHANGE OF DIET

When Erma Jones sliced and ground dear Freddy up,
she summoned her elderly Aunt Jane to sup,
and offered her "roast pork," with gravy and peas,
and gave her some more to take home and freeze.
Jane broke a tooth, the poor old thing,
and swallowed what must have been Fred's wedding ring.

Next, finding her children a bit of a bore,
Erma had Auntie to dinner once more,
and cooked up this time a pair of meat pies,
with mushrooms and carrots stirred in with the eyes.
Auntie got sick, a blatant admission,
she'd started to form her own grim suspicion.

So Erma called Auntie one very last time.
Respected beyond even *hint* of a crime,
she never was stingy, ingracious, or mean,
but she dined *alone,* and *licked* her plate clean . . .
Then drab, dowdy Erma, our public librarian,
ended her days a strict vegetarian.

— Darrell Schweitzer

IMMORTAL BANQUET

The withered arm of Time has plucked the blooms
That crowned the brow of Love, and rent the ring
Of roses 'round Love's head. Decay consumes
The petals. Powdered grey flecks everything.
Thus shorn of blossoms, Love's skull draws
Its scalp in wrinkles that retract
And tighten. The first of all Time's laws
Would seem the *last:* the fatal fact
That life means death. Yet death begins rebirth:
Love's phantom sheds its flesh and rides the sky.
Below, its skeleton sinks deep in earth.
The gnarled old arm of Time grasps high —
But cannot seize the cloud as it encloses
In silken mist . . . gold-ruby roses.

— Steven Eng

Two Poems

THE KILLER SOUL

by Steven Rogers
Illustrated by Denis Tiani

Bellingham looked up from his comp screen when his door vid lit up. A metro patrolman in street-attack uniform stood outside his office. The young man looked all business — one burly fist was wrapped around the handle of his service weapon, the other on his pedestrian prod. He appeared to be no more than twenty, a grim-faced, square-jawed giant with a neck big enough for two heads. Bellingham slammed his own meathook fist onto the entry button and the door whooshed open.

The patrolman stepped into the doorway, his eyes narrowed. He glanced both directions before he entered the office — reflex action, Bellingham knew. This kid couldn't squat down to take a shit without first he looked twice around the toilet stall.

"Dale Dombroski," Bellingham growled. The patrolman tensed and stared hard at the middle of the room, at a dark spot Bellingham had programmed into the room's lighting twenty years before. Bellingham leaned back in his antique desk chair, lit a cigar. "So. You always walk into Lieutenants' offices with your hand on your weapon? Ya gonna shoot me? Hell of a way to make room for promotion, kid."

"Lieutenant Bellingham." Dombroski tensed a tiny bit more before he relaxed.

Good, Bellingham thought. The kid didn't *sound* startled. "That's me. Sit down, Dombroski, look around the room. I like pissant patrolmen to be comfortable before I ream their asses."

Dombroski didn't react to that. His eyes roamed the room, and Bellingham saw the kid's pupils widen when he noticed the file cabinet — *yeah, kid, real paper files*. Then the young officer saw the old computer, complete with functional keyboard and no vocamodum in sight. Finally, Dombroski looked upon Bellingham in all his seventy-two-year-old, thirty-pounds-over-the-department's-weight-for-height-limit glory, and frowned. "You can't ream my ass, sir," he said flatly. "You aren't in my chain of command."

Bellingham decided that he liked the kid right

then and there. *He's the one. Now if I can only convince him I'm not crazy.* "You're right, kid. I'm just a detective lieutenant. I can't criticize you. I eat lunch with the Goddamned patrol captain every day, but I can't criticize you. I can Goddamned make sure you ain't never promoted, that you work the Drunken Alley district until you retire, but I can't criticize you, you understand."

Dombroski gulped. "I've always wanted to work in the bureau, sir. Any . . . advice you would have for me would be greatly appreciated."

Bellingham nodded, blew smoke. "Good. Now I'll tell you a secret. I didn't call you in here to jump your shit. No siree. Matter of fact, I called you in here to give you laudits."

"Laudits, sir?"

"Laudits, Dombroski. Don't know the word? Look it up. Ask your Goddamned computer when you get into your skimmersquad tonight. Better yet, I'll tell you right now. Means you get an atta-boy, Dombroski. Is that neck genetically engineered, by the way?"

"This neck is Polish, sir, it had all the genes it needed. And my intelligence is two standard deviations above this country's norm, and that wasn't purchased either. I'm not conversant with twentieth century slang, sir. Is it a prerequisite to conversation with you?"

"No, Dombroski." Bellingham was unruffled. He pulled an ancient manila folder from his top desk drawer. "But it is useful knowledge if you're going to understand the background associated with a current case I thought you might be interested in working with me. The Lucinda Mandell homicide."

Bellingham proffered the folder and Dombroski's hand shook just a little as he snapped it up. *His hand won't shake like that again for twenty years, thirty if he's not a drinking man,* Bellingham thought. *You want this one bad, don't you kid. But if you don't believe what I'm gonna tell you — if you don't at least have an open mind . . . Well, if you don't, this case ain't yours, and I'll just make the arrest myself and keep looking for my replacement. But I'm tired, kid, real tired. I hope you do believe, Dombroski.*

"Sir?"

Bellingham's eyes leapt into focus. "Huh. Oh. Lapse of age, kid. I'll take a pill for it when I gets home. Read the file."

"This must be part of your lapse, sir. This file isn't the Mandell case — it's a girl named Thorton, and it happened in the nineties. I fail to see how a 49-year-old homicide could have any bearing —"

"I was 23 years old and worked for a department halfway across the country when I caught that son-of-a-bitch," Bellingham interrupted. "Two years out of recruit school, like you — college took a little longer then than it does now. Anyway, we had these serial murders, four of them. Thorton was the last. The killer's name was Donnie Morris. He jimmied this Thorton girl's lock, hid in her apartment. He did his cutting before he strangled her, had sex with her after. Then he left a line of poetry, handwritten, on her blood-drenched pillow. He wasn't a real imaginative guy. He'd treated all his other victims the same."

"Sounds much like the Mandell case, sir."

"It is the Mandell case, kid. Right down to the line of poetry on the victims' pillows."

"*Tender, pretty heart, I hold in my hands,*" Dombroski read from the file. "*Lovely whore, find you God, my true love in another dream.* Not much of a poet. But what does this have to do with Mandell? Says here this Morris guy got the death penalty, back when there was such a thing. Do we have a copycat connoisseur of old murders? Probably somebody who always wanted to be a cop."

"No," Bellingham snorted. "No copycat. Just a cat."

"Sir?"

Bellingham spun the vid screen around and punched up another old file — not as old as the paper one. "Morris died three years after his conviction. He wasn't interested in appeals like most of them were. Said he just wanted to get it over with. He missed the big Supreme Court ruling by six years. Now this one . . ." Bellingham brightened the screen. "This one came just after we got the felony DNA files on line. It happened when I was working in Dallas, just before I pulled up stakes and moved here. This guy didn't need a trial." Bellingham grinned into the screen. "He was shot dead during the arrest."

"The Louise Hopps case," Dombroski read the

title. "Suspect Vernon Lewis Borgan killed during arrest by Detective . . . David Bellingham."

"I was forty-nine," Bellingham said with a shrug, as though that explained everything. "And I was stupid. I had this idea that the animals, the real animals, mind you, should be put out of their misery. Throw all that money being spent on custody and appeals into treating little kids with violent potential. I figured that was the only way to get any real results. And I had Borgan dead to rights."

"Why are you telling me this?" Dombroski's hands made fists on the desk. "The statute of limitations for Misconduct in Public Office is only seven years, Lieutenant, but homicide —"

Bellingham leaned back and waved smoke away from his face. He stubbed out his cigar and turned on the air circulator. "It was a clean shoot, all on video," he said, his voice tight. *This kid's a real hero, ready to ride off on any tangent where he senses an injustice. Either that or he doesn't like me. Probably both.*

"But we're straying away from the point of this briefing." Bellingham tapped the top of the vid screen with his index finger. "This murder was identical. Borgan shorted out this woman's access lock — an early model without an alarm. Then he cut her when she came in, and strangled her, and did his thing. He left a line of poetry on her pillow, and it —"

"*Tender, pretty heart, I hold in my hands,*" Dombroski read once again. "*Lovely whore, find you God, my true love in another dream.* So what? So this Borgan guy read the same book as Donnie Morris did. And Lucinda Mandell's killer read the same book of poetry, too. It surely isn't the same man . . . unless you made a mistake on the DNA matching."

"No," Bellingham tilted his head and squinted up at the last wisp of his cigar smoke. "There was no error. Borgan did his killing right after the DNA files went on line. He didn't even know enough to use a rubbsuit, like our modern slimeskins do." As he spoke on his eyes clouded and his voice diminished. "He left blood. And semen. And skin and saliva and hair. Messy, messy case.

"That brings us to Lucinda Mandell. You were one of the initial officers on the scene, weren't you, Dombroski?"

"I was first," Dombroski nodded.

"And it was you who found that itsy-bitsy gob of skin in the alcove down the hall from Mandell's apartment. That's where the atta-boy comes in. For a bedroom murder, the evidence guys don't normally process niches twelve feet from the apartment entrance."

"I surmised he had to put on the gloves and the mask somewhere, sir," Dombroski explained. "The autoramp and the elevator were both too contaminated already, so I ignored them. Then I saw a fingernail clipping in the alcove — sir, the alcove was immaculate, and the building's Clean-O-Comp panel reading indicated that the autovac had been through that alcove not an hour before the homicide. And there was the fingernail clipping on the floor. I photo'd it and packaged it on the low probability that it might be valuable."

"You took a shot in the dark, Dombroski." Bellingham leaned forward. "And the shot hit home. DNA got the report back to me today. The fingernail and a little skin had been bitten off by its owner, a twenty-two-year-old white male named Holliss J. Bakker. And the skin fragment had trace elements on it, trace elements that spelled R-U-B-B-E-R gloves."

Dombroski smiled just enough to crinkle his eyes, and Bellingham suspected he was seeing an ear-to-ear grin.

"Mother Tee." the patrolman said quietly. Bellingham wondered if she was his patron saint. "Enough to convict him?" Dombroski's eyes suddenly narrowed."

"Not at all," Bellingham grunted. He pressed the print button for hardcopy of something he'd been fiddling with on the autofax. "What we have here is a search warrant, Dombroski, courtesy Judge Harold Franklin, complete with access code to Bakker's apartment. Now I'm gonna ask you one quick question under the Veracity Grid, and if you answer it right you're going to execute the warrant with me, and we're going to find enough evidence to call in an arrest warrant request, and we're going to put Mr. Bakker in prison for the rest of his natural life with no parole option." Bellingham gestured toward the Veracity Grid. "Now put your hands in the little wire gloves and look directly into the grid screen."

"You can't force me to take a Veracity Grid, sir," Dombroski bristled. "The union manual says —"

"You can read the Goddamned union manual in your squad in Drunken Alley while another uniform and I make the arrest, kid. This isn't a disciplinary action, it's something I want to know before I give you the Goddamned privilege of making a homicide arrest." Bellingham gestured toward the door. "It's your choice. That guy that

by Steven Rogers

beat you out for first place in your academy ratings, what's his name, Schmitt—Hell, I'll just go find him —"

"I should get up and walk out of here now," Dombroski glared at the floor. He then grimaced, stood, and walked to the Veracity Grid.

"They say it's kind of uncomfortable," Bellingham said.

"It is," Dombroski nodded. "At academy we practiced on each other. Come to think of it, all certified operators are schooled in pairs. You are certified, aren't you, sir?"

This kid just don't quit, Bellingham realized. *Good.* "Yeah, I'm certified. I grandfathered in when these machines first came out, 'cause I knew how to use the old polygraphs. And those were a lot harder to use correctly, even though they didn't pack a wallop like these things do."

Dombroski put his hands into the gloves slowly, settled onto the stool, and stared into the grid. Bellingham turned on the machine. Lime green lights winked as the machine scanned Dombroski's retina and decided it recognized him. His bio-norms showed up a second later, and the Veracity Grid sucked on Dombroski's hands.

"I have a theory, Dombroski," Bellingham said. "I think I made a mistake when I killed Borgan, and I think the state made a mistake when they killed Donnie Morris. Now I'm going to tell you my theory and you're going to tell me what you think of it."

"Is that all?" Dombroski's jaw set as he stared into the machine, and the machine stared into him. "Then go ahead. One quick question never hurt anyone, and besides, the effects of this machine aren't as uncomfortable as the media reports."

Bellingham shrugged. He could tell without watching the readouts that the kid was scared stiff. "So it isn't true what they say, that the Grid is like standing in your own puke and grabbing on to an electric fence?" Bellingham just couldn't resist one preliminary question.

The autoramp in Bakker's building was broken. Normally that would have been cause for Bellingham to grunt out ancient obscenities all the way up the elevator, but his homicide adrenalin and his pure delight at Dombroski's answer on the Grid kept him cheery. No, the kid didn't believe his theory. But he *could* believe it. Bellingham had been afraid he'd never find a qualified individual who *could* believe it.

"I wonder what the bacteria count in here is," Dombroski mused as the two cops stepped through the garbage in the hallway outside Bakker's door.

"I dunno, kid," Bellingham said slowly. He squinted at the access panel next to Bakker's door, then handed the warrant to Dombroski. "You punch in the code."

Dombroski quickly scanned the code and then punched it into the panel while Bellingham stood behind him. "No disrespect, sir, but you should have your vision checked if you can't read the numbers on the panel. They aren't all that small, you know." The door whooshed open.

"Well it's not so much my vision, Dombroski," said Bellingham. "It's just that Bakker has a pretty good knowledge of electronic locks. I figured he just might have booby-trapped his." Bellingham shrugged as Dombroski flushed. "Now we know."

Dombroski tapped the vid-corder in the center of his helmet as he stepped across the threshold into the apartment. Inside were more dirty walls and a lot of porno vids. An oil painting of an ugly old woman dominated the wall opposite the door, and her eyes followed Bellingham as he maneuvered around piles of dirty clothes and things he couldn't quite identify. The apartment was a two room setup, a bathroom and a large living-bedroom, with a kitchotility unit against one wall. A small water fouton covered with a dirty blanket filled the corner of the room where the eyes of the painting weren't visible — only because a massive vid unit blocked the view.

"That oil would be mamma," Bellingham said with a shudder. "Back in the nineties, Donnie Morris had an efficiency apartment like this, with a little waterbed and a big-screen TV blocking his mother's portrait. Tuna fish. Shit, this place even smells the same. Well, let's get to it. Bakker should be home from work in ninety minutes, and I want enough for an arrest warrant by then. We'll pop him as he walks in the door."

"And if we find nothing?" Dombroski asked. His attention was focused on a tiny hole in the wall over the door. "There is a security recorder fitted into this wall, sir. I wouldn't have expected it in this neighborhood, but it's equipped with a good pinhole lens. If we don't get enough to arrest him he's going to know we were here."

Bellingham shrugged. "If we find nothing, my theory is blown. I tell you, this guy keeps evidence. He's young and he's smug — he doesn't think we have a clue as to who he is. There'll be a rubbsuit here somewhere, and a knife with all the trace evidence we'll need. And there'll be a book like I told you about, kid. Mark my words."

"I hope so, sir." Dombroski frowned and began rifling the apartment's only closet.

Sixty minutes later they finished. Dombroski was smiling one of those tiny smiles again. "I still cannot say you aren't insane, Lieutenant. But your instincts are intact." The rubbsuit Dombroski had found in the closet was packaged neatly, alongside the smaller package which held the knife. Bellingham's field testing kit had indicated samples favorable in comparison with the standard skin samples that the evidence-techs had retrieved from Mandell's body.

"Not enough for conviction, until the lab confirms," Bellingham said into his Talk-O-Comp, "but probable cause for a warrant?"

The tiny screen of the Talk-O-Comp flickered as Judge Franklin nodded severely, and a notarized sheet of signed hardcopy rolled off Bakker's printer a few moments later. After a nod and a thank you to the judge, Bellingham signed off. He turned slowly and faced Dombroski.

"I tell you, there's a disc of poetry here somewhere. Maybe it's coded or something, but it's named *Windows of the Soul*. And inside is a poem that has been written before. The poem says —"

"Sir, this Bakker man will be here in twenty minutes. We've already determined that all the discs here are pre-recorded. The lab can look for one that makes reference to your poetry later, after the arrest. Let's get ready to take him."

Bellingham sighed and nodded. He could see any chance for belief fading from Dombroski's eyes. *I've won the battle, but I've lost the war,* Bellingham thought grimly. "Sure, kid. But be ready. On my prior, similar arrests over the years, our suspects have always been armed."

Bellingham had been right again, Dombroski realized. Bakker walked into his apartment with a nice Colt Lasarassist Nineteen Shot in hand, and Bellingham took an exploding dummie before Dombroski had a chance to nail the slime with his non-lethal. When Bakker awakened, Dombroski was standing on his hair.

"The shot you fired took my partner's head off." There was no emotion in the young metrotrooper's voice.

Bakker could only see his own reflected face in the cop's mirrored visor. He realized he'd not been bound, and there were no other cops in sight. He figured he knew what that meant. He looked up from the face and saw the cop's fat semi-auto Lasarassist pointed at the top of his head at point-blank range. A calmness came over Bakker, and he smiled, though the pain from having his hair pulled turned the smile into a wince. "God will protect my soul," he said to the trooper. "Go ahead and shoot."

"I don't think I'll be doing that," the patrolman sighed.

Bakker's body convulsed as he took another jolt from the non-lethal. The sound of sirens got all mixed up with the voice of the cop, saying, "You'll spend the rest of your long life in prison, Bakker. The rest of your life."

After his back-up officers bound and removed the suspect, Dombroski picked up the small book that had fallen from Bakker's pocket when he fell. "I'll package this as evidence myself," he said to the evidence tech.

The evidence man looked at the little book in Dombroski's hands. "Handwritten — your guy sure was strange. *Windows of the Soul.* What is it, poetry?"

Dombroski nodded. "Yeah. Bakker wrote it himself." *And I'm gonna need it someday, Bellingham, when I'm old and gray and overweight. We can keep this guy instead of killing him, but one day he'll die anyway. I hope you're back by then, Bellingham. I hope I can find you.* Ω

ART IMITATES, ALL TOO WELL

Higgledy-piggledy
Klarkash-Ton artisan
Mirrored wordSmithing in
Carvings & paint:

Arch-fiends from Averoigne,
Zombies of dead Zothique . . .
Who's game enough to peek?
Brother, I ain't.

— Ann K. Schwader

A TALK WITH CHARLES DE LINT

by Patricia Caven

The year 1984 saw the publication of Charles de Lint's first novel. Ten years and some 30 books later, his name has become synonymous with the fantasy explosion of the past decade. Nominated for several World Fantasy awards, vice-president of the Horror Writers Association of America, and recently named new reviewer-in-residence of *The Magazine of Fantasy and Science Fiction*, de Lint maintains a strong profile in the community.

We interviewed him at his home in Ottawa, Canada — the setting of so many of his early novels.

Worlds of Fantasy & Horror: When did you first decide you wanted to publish?

Charles de Lint: I never wanted to be a writer to begin with. I never thought about it. I always did write, but I was more interested in music. I chose the wrong kind of music to play. I chose Celtic music before there was anything like World Beat or any kind of a market for it.

I just kind of fell into publishing my writing, through a friend who suggested I send some stuff off and it got bought. It kind of made a little click in my head when I realized this is something I like to do; and if there's a chance that I can do something that I like to do *and* make a living at it, it was worth pursuing.

WoF&H: Which was your first novel sale?

de Lint: I sold three in the same week. Two to Ace, *The Riddle of the Wren* and *Moonheart*; and *The Harp of the Grey Rose* to Donning Starblaze.

WoF&H: What led you into writing fantasy?

de Lint: I've always been interested in fantasy. As a little kid reading *Bolk the Bear* books, *Wind in the Willows, Winnie-the-Pooh*, and all that kind of stuff, then eventually moving into folk and fairy tales. I've just generally had an interest in this type of thing all along.

Also, I got into traditional music because of all the folk tales and myths I was reading. I really liked the music, and it's always gone back and forth between the music and the fantasy. It goes from hand to hand too, like one feeds the other.

WoF&H: You began your career with high fantasy but have made your mark as a contemporary fantasist. Why the change?

de Lint: You have to understand that when you see the books come out they don't necessarily come out in the order I've written them; and you don't see everything I write, especially in those early years. I've gotten better in my craft, I suppose.

The difference between now and then is everything sells now, and I'm hoping it sells because it's good. But in the old days, I wrote about three or four high fantasy novels, and then I wrote one of those that was a combination of the two. High fantasy and the real world. It was actually my wife MaryAnn's suggestion. She's been very strong in my career and really good at pointing things out.

I think writers get lost sometimes in their own work. They lose any sort of objectivity whatsoever. She was the one who suggested when I tried this one book and it didn't work out, I should try it again. Then I did *Moonheart*. I just liked it, I just really liked it. It's interesting that it's often cited as a really innovative thing to do.

You know my feeling is that maybe it was innovative at the time it came out but it's part of a long tradition. I mean James Branch Cabell wrote contemporary fantasy; it's just not contemporary anymore. You can go all through the history of fantastic literature.

A lot of people wrote contemporary fantasy in their own time, so it's really just continuing the tradition.

WoF&H: Did your mystery reading influence your fantasy writing?

de Lint: I think everything I do, every bit of input I have influences my writing; from ordinary conversations to the music I'm listening to, to the fields of art.

I read very broadly. I haven't always read as broadly as I'm probably reading now, but I've never just read fantasy. I think that made it easier for me to write contemporary books, because I'd been reading them. More than the mystery novels, it's probably been thrillers. Having read a lot of them, *Moonheart* to me is basically just a thriller. A lot of the contemporary fantasy I've written are thrillers, they just have a fantasy element in them. Sometimes it's a larger one, sometimes it's a smaller one, whatever works for the story.

WoF&H: You've been called one of the fathers of contemporary fantasy. . . .

de Lint: I'd rather be considered the second cousin, I think. Father makes you feel so old.

WoF&H: Is it strange to see the elements that you brought to the forefront develop into archetypes of the field?

de Lint: One of the things that made it so interesting for me to write, was that I was writing something nobody else had written.

When I'm writing my first draft it's like reading a book to me. The work doesn't come until later on. That's another reason why some of my books were different at the time. No one was writing about the things I was interested in, and I wanted to see how it would turn out. What it would be like to mix up police procedural with Gypsy magic. What it would be like to have the Mafia mix with a Lord Dunsany sort of thing.

It is sad that it's become more common. I would rather see people doing their own thing. Not that I think they're ripping me off, I just think that they're taking the easy way out. I would like to see people be as innovative with it as I had to be with high fantasy.

Archetypes are useful because of what they are, but I think they can also lead you into not utilizing your potential to your fullest, whether it's as a writer or a reader. It's always been a frustration of mine.

The fact that someone reads Tolkien, which is great, and enjoys Tolkien, fine, and decides to write a Tolkien-type book because they're inspired by it. But rather than going back to the sources that Tolkien used, they use Tolkien as the source. It's at a point now where it is second, third, or fourth generation.

If you are going to base it on folkloric sources, there is such a wealth of material that can be utilized. It just blows me away that more people don't use it. There are people who do it. I see Native American stuff being used, but you know there's a whole world out there. I'd hate to think it's that people are too lazy to do the research or are not interested in those other cultures. The whole point behind science fiction and fantasy is we're interested in different things. I would like to think that we're more open to differences.

WoF&H: Another theme in your work is the Celtic myth? Do you think that's been overdone?

de Lint: There's nothing wrong with the Celtic myth. It's like the King Arthur interest many, many years ago. I thought it was dead, and then along came Parke Godwin with *Firelord* and Marion Zimmer Bradley with *The Mists of Avalon*. People who had something different to say. The same thing with Celtic material.

I think of that book by Ian MacDonald, *King of Morning, Queen of Day*. You never want to say, don't write Celtic fantasy, not if that means we're going to lose a book like that MacDonald.

WoF&H: How important is setting to your work?

de Lint: I don't like to write about places I haven't been. Because I live in Ottawa, I tend to write about Ottawa or around-about Ottawa, because I couldn't always afford to travel.

I travelled a lot as a kid, but I don't remember clearly enough of the details to be able to set something in those other places. Since then I've been able to do some travelling, but I still haven't spent enough time in various places to write about it.

For *Little Country* I spent time in Cornwall specifically to do research. I've done trips to New York or L.A., and I do see stories I would like to utilize that kind of a cityscape in, but I honestly couldn't. That's why the made-up city of Newford came into being. It was a chance for me to use my perception of these other cities. Newford has that big-city feel to it. Those stories kind of take on a life of their own.

WoF&H: Have you had a positive response to this creation?

de Lint: Very, very positive. I never even thought about doing a Newford collection like *Dreams Underfoot*. It was my editor at Tor who suggested it. They were buying two books but they specifically wanted a collection of Newford stories at the same time. That was the point when I realized that I actually *had* enough stories for a collection.

In fact, there's another collection coming out that I'm working on now. The working title for it is *The Ivory and the Horn*. I'm not sure I'm entirely happy with that title. We'll have to see.

But the really interesting thing about Newford is that it just grew. I think I'd written about seven or eight stories before I even realized I was enjoying the setting and these characters. That's when I started making notes on a rough map of the city, named it, figured out what kind of setting it was in, and have worked out the relationships between the characters more carefully.

The thing I like about the Newford characters

is that they're like a repertory company. I have this whole bunch of people, and when I have the kind of story I want to tell, lots of times one of them will fit in. It's as they say, "Oh, I could do that part." I enjoy that aspect of it.

WoF&H: Do you prefer writing novels to short stories?

de Lint: One of the things about doing short stories is that I do them in between my novel projects. Novels can be very long projects. The last one took up a year for a first draft. That doesn't include the research before or all the re-writing after. That's a big investment of time. So you tend not to experiment as much because if you do it for a living, and you screw it up, how are you going to pay your rent? So you tend to be a bit more cautious.

The short story is going to be a week's time to write. If you blow it, you've only lost a week. You can really cut loose with different writing styles, different ways of telling a story. I think that writing short stories has really helped my writing in general.

WoF&H: How do you write your books?

de Lint: I have to start at the beginning. I have to experience it the way the reader would experience it, because then I can tell if it works. I prefer to experience it the way the reader will.

WoF&H: A reader's writer . . .

de Lint: That's because I'm not writing. I'm reading when I'm writing. It really feels that way. It's like opening a book and finding out what happens next when I'm writing a first draft.

The dangerous thing about writing that way is you can end up with manuscripts that are 200 pages long and just dead-end. When that happens I usually back-track and start in a new direction. Some are just unsalvageable.

WoF&H: Have you been pleased with how your books have been presented?

de Lint: Let me put it this way. I'm very happy with my cover treatment in England. I have cover and copy approval written in my contracts, and they've been really good about it. In fact, they held back *Little Country* from its February release until September because the cover just wasn't appropriate, which was very good of them. They're contractually obliged to do so but it was good they went through all that.

Lots of times you'll find things supposedly in the contract, and they'll just ignore them. I'm also very happy with what's happening in North America with Tor, my current publisher.

All I could get in North America was cover

and copy consultation. Even though they're not obliged to do so by contract, they've bent over backwards to get my input on material and stuff like that, so I've been real lucky with them as well. I haven't disliked a single cover that's come out from Tor.

WoF&H: How important is the packaging?

de Lint: I think packaging is everything. That's what sells the book, unless you have a name.

If the package is inappropriate you're going to have one of two things happen. People are going to pick it up because they think it's something they'll like and it's not, or people who would like it are going to look at the cover and just pass it over.

You can't always have good art; I mean there aren't necessarily enough good artists in the world, but at least be appropriate.

I didn't like the cover for *Svaha*, but it was appropriate. It gave you the idea that it was a futuristic novel, and it had a lot to do with native stuff. You can't ask for more. I'm not trying to be a primadonna about it, I just really want it to send out the right message.

WoF&H: Do you have a tendency to structure your day to your writing?

de Lint: I have a tendency to structure everything in my entire life. I'm not Mr. Spontaneous. An optimum day for me would be to get up and get my writing done in the morning, then do research, correcting galleys, etc., later on in the afternoon. So that's sort of an optimum day.

But I think it's really important to have a life. I don't care what your job is, if you devote yourself entirely to it, you're going to get stale. I can't figure out people who don't have a life and they're writing all the time. What are they writing about? Where does the input come from after awhile?

WoF&H: Who are you reading now?

de Lint: I tend to get real tired of the same motifs that appear all the time in any kind of fiction book. At the moment in fantasy, it's the same thing over and over again.

Although I still like fantasy, I tend to look for writers who are doing different things in a fantasy element. Lots of times I find them in the mainstream. Someone like Thomas King. His novel *Green Grass, Running Water* is the best fantasy novel of 1993, yet I doubt very few people in the field will read the book. It's got everything a fantasy should have. Or people like Alice Hoffman. Her books now are more and more mainstream, but they will often have an element of the fantastic in them.

I'd also have to say that I tend to read more female writers than male. I'm not really sure why. It's just that I find that lots of times they're telling more interesting stories. Most of the history of story-telling in novels in the last hundred years has been from men, so we've pretty well got all their stories. We've heard them so often that women's voices are different because the stories they're telling are newer to us.

I also tend to drift towards native women writers or Hispanic women. It's not because I'm politically correct, it's because I want to be absorbed in what I'm reading, exposed to new things. I want to learn something new from a book. That's my criterion.

WoF&H: You often write from a female perspective. Are you comfortable there?

de Lint: I'd never realized I was writing so much from a female perspective. I started to think about it, and I realized that the reason I do so is the same reason I write about native people or gypsies. I find it's the best way to find out about someone else, and I'm really curious about what it would be like to be a woman or whoever I'm writing about. I'll often set a book from that point of view to try and find out. How successful I am, I have no idea.

I don't like stereotypes, and I like the idea of being able to combat stereotypes through my fiction. I think that everyone is capable of everything; of a resourceful woman being the hero and saving the day through her own pluck and ingenuity — without having to rely on someone else saving her.

If that sort of inspires people at all to go out and do something more for themselves rather than wait for others to do it for them, then I think that is a wonderful thing to do.

WoF&H: Would you write a novel centered around a gay character?

de Lint: Actually, the story I'm most proud of with gay characters appears in this issue.

The way I tell stories is how they're appropriate. This story is right for that. It deals with issues I wanted to deal with: the sexuality of people.

I think it's a terrible shame when someone is HIV positive or has AIDS, and our society expects them to have no more sexuality. It seems bizarre to me to tell someone they are being punished for that sexuality.

WoF&H: The new *The Encyclopedia of Sci-*

ence Fiction mentions you for *Svaha* only. "A kind of sweetish simplicity sometimes overloads his fantasy tales, especially the earlier ones." How do you respond to this?

de Lint: I'm not upset by the quote. The themes behind my books are really, really basic.

I try to write with a very optimistic frame of mind, because I think the world is a great place and I'd like to see it stay that way and get better. When I write about dark things, it's not because I'm trying to bring everybody down, it's just that I'm saying let's all look at this and fix it.

I do have a simplistic view. My themes are love and friendship and trust and sticking together. Things like the family unit is good, but it doesn't necessarily have to be blood relations; you make your own family. It's things like this, which I guess are thought of as simple, but to me they're the basics of our lives. That's what I'm interested in because I think that's what's important. When I'm doing my horror novels, I'm trying to do the same positive messages that I have in my other writing, but I just use a darker framework.

WoF&H: Why publish your horror under the pseudonym Samuel M. Key?

de Lint: The reason I sort of went ahead and did it, besides clearing up my inventory of books at Ace, was that I had gotten criticism from some people about my novel *Mulengro*; that they found it too graphic, too dark.

One of my beliefs is that if you're going to write a violent scene then you should write them very realistically. I don't think they should be made to look like they're fun. I think that puts a false image across.

When I do write a violent scene, I make it realistic, I make people hurt. And if they're hurt, they're going to hurt for the rest of the book. I want to disturb people, but I want to disturb them for the right reasons — because of an issue in the novel, because of something that has happened to a character. I don't want to disturb them because something is graphic, because it's the style of writing they don't like.

But unfortunately, for many years, my book covers haven't been very true to the story inside. It would look like a high fantasy but it would be contemporary fantasy. So *Mulengro* looked like everything else but it was a darker story. I just thought that when my horror books came out, who knows what kind of a cover they would put on it? People who normally read my fantasy would think it's just another inappropriate cover, and they'd be unpleasantly surprised. I don't want to do that to people. The whole thing just seemed like a good way to do it.

If I'd do it again, I don't know. One of the things about being a writer is that it's good to promote your name. The more often your name is around the better off you are; *Samuel Key* doesn't do anything for me in the sense of building my career. I don't have any more of his books planned at the moment, but who knows? It depends on my schedule and how my writing goes.

WoF&H: Do real issues have a place in fantasy? Can they be dealt with adequately in what's considered an escapist literature?

de Lint: I don't consider fantasy escapist literature. I think it can be but I think that for contemporary fantasy to work it has to deal with serious issues, otherwise it is trivial. I think it is important to talk about the problems we have. I would hate to think it trivializes the experiences. I would like to think that it's bringing more awareness to them. It's a real thin line in how you deal with it.

WoF&H: What do you think of this trend towards eroticism and sexuality in fantasy, which until recently has been almost parochial?

de Lint: It's more in the horror field that I've seen these various collections of erotic horror coming. It seems to be a big deal. Frankly, I don't find them very erotic because it seems to me most people figure that if you have sex with violence it's erotic horror. It doesn't work for me. Within fantasy, I don't know.

Sex has been part of mainstream literature for a very long time, so when it's in a story I don't particularly go, "Oh, this is very sexy." I don't think about it in those terms. I guess maybe it's just that people are trying to bring the genre more in line with the rest of the world's writing.

WoF&H: You've been asked to take over from Orson Scott Card as reviewer for *F & SF.* Are you looking forward to that?

de Lint: Yes, very much. It's always nice to have a bigger audience. To me, the way I review is like you're sitting down with a couple of friends and talking about books. That's the way I approach it. It's lovely to have a forum when I have something to get excited about. There's going to be stuff in there, the off-the-wall stuff, like Thomas King's last book. When stuff that good comes around, I'll definitely try and sneak them in.

WoF&H: What do you foresee in the future for fantasy?

de Lint: I'd like to see the writers be more honest with their material; putting more of themselves into it.

I'd like to see the views be broader, I'd like to see them utilize more influences than just the standard things. I'd like to see them take more chances. And those are all things I have to do myself.

WoF&H: What's coming up for you?

de Lint: The new novel is called *Memory and Dream,* and it's set in Newford. There's also *The Wild Wood,* part of Brian Froud's Faerielands series. It's set in Canada.

WoF&H: Is there anything you'd like to end with?

de Lint: No. Well, I'd just like to say that I really hope I finish my story in time for this issue. Ω

THE POLAR BEAR

The ghost of the white bear
Roams the night,
Crying and crying.

Blood stains fur bright
Red; drops to snow
And vanishes.

Vast pads leave no imprint.
His tribe is dead
Or dying.

The machines have come,
Lumbering through the Arctic waste,
Un-live-ing.
The birds are gone too,
And the soft-skinned seals,
And the singing whales
From the northern seas.

Only the inner ear can hear
Bird-song, whale-song
And the bear's cry,
Grown small and cold
In the vast night.

— **Margo Skinner**

PIPER'S WAIT
by Keith Roberts
illustrated by Stephen Fabian

There is a forest in England. It is an ancient place; there are mile on mile of trees, villages and towns that huddle to this day behind walls of living green. There are roads to serve those towns, modern roads that thrust their tarmac spears through what is still in part a wilderness; and vehicles go down those roads, cars and lorries and the yellow vans of commerce. Down and down, pushing always to the coast; across the heath, through the blazings of the rhododendrons, into the proud towns where the cranes work in their pairs and the ships come in from the salt sea.

Close to that forest's inmost heart lies a village that to this day still has no name. Some little distance off there is a glade, the trees that ring it gnarled and dark. A road runs by it, dropping through a little hollow before rising again to meet the endless woods. The road, and the clearing it skirts, share a name. That name is Piper's Wait.

For some years now the place has been a campsite. There the trailers come and the motor caravans, to set their brakes, erect their privies and their little striped awnings. There the dreadful batwinged women set about their suppers, bored children play dutifully with their frisbees and pingpong bats and wait to be called in. As night falls the little windows glow, one after the next, with their endless patternings of floral cloth, and all is peace. Or seemingly so; for just occasionally a family will couple up their rig, make all secure and slip quietly away. Because for some folk, when night falls the character of the glade appears to change. So they creep off, and their plastic cups and saucers do not rattle; for it is not good camping practice to allow such things to happen.

In the morning the ponies and cattle edge cautiously back to bully the tourists for their scraps; for they too, at night, seem to avoid the place. Why is unclear; though the old folk who live round about have been heard to mutter in their cups that beasts alone understand the whisperings of leaves.

The name of the glade has likewise caused debate among the idly curious. Letters have been written, to the cheerful magazines that guard the interests of such folk as caravanners; but to my knowledge no certain answer has been made. I know that answer; it was given me on a day lightless and flaring as the Piper himself knew. Once it was his secret, then it was mine; now, by your leave, I offer it to you. For secrets, like curses, are meant for handing on.

Once, in the long ago when men wore cowls and jerkins and sowed grain broadcast from baskets on their hips, there was a man they called the Piper. A very strange man he was too. None understood him; yet folk comprehended his every mood. Never had he been known to utter human words; and yet he spoke from dawn to sunset, on his flute. And when he played, folk somehow felt the meaning. Shrill sometimes was his music, shrill as the pain of knives; then it spoke of death and separation, the pain of loss and love. Sometimes it was soft, soft as the murmurs of a dreaming child; and then the hearers thought of times of plenty, of fulfillment and peace.

All who heard the Piper marvelled; but all privately shook their heads. For these things, sweet though they might be to the ear, were nonetheless spells; spells conjured from a tube of fretted wood. And no good comes, of dabbling with the dark.

The Piper was a tall man for his times; tall and slender, with deepest eyes of a curious dark blue. Some said there was unfriendliness in their gaze, others that there was much sadness and compassion; which latter view seemed more likely, for surely no man who sees the world and its folk as they truly are can for ever hold his spirit aloof. Whatever the truth though, what is certain is that the Piper never spoke. Some claimed he was incapable of speech; but that was not the case. His flute spoke for him; so he had never found a use for human words.

Sometimes he would play at Harvests Home,

and then indeed the dancing went the brisker; folk looked at each other with new eyes, saw virtues they might otherwise have missed, and loved afresh.

At other times, on heaths and barren moorlands, his flute spoke of darker things; then people would cringe and run, crouch closer to their cottage fires glad of stout bolts and bars. They would wonder then, with knuckles to their mouths, how he had acquired such skills; and of course with time the usual tales became current, the tales that are told of all such folk. He was under a curse; he had travelled to Fairyland to learn his piping from the Old Ones themselves; he had bartered his soul, his only gift from God. But the matter was never resolved. Sometimes, or so the rumours went, he played at the courts of Kings; and they would laugh with joy, showering him with gold, or creep shivering away, according to the mood he had laid on.

But those stories were likewise never confirmed; it must suffice that he came again and again to the green glades of the forest. There he would play and play, and the children would gather round to listen and laugh, and he would seem content. In time their elders would come, to

call him to their cottages; he would partake, smiling, of soup or gruel, and go his way.

Some claimed the Piper wasn't mortal; that he was a changeling, born of the Fairy Folk themselves. Some went further, speaking of him in hushed tones as they would speak of a god. He was mortal though; painfully so, as his tale will show. At one point only did the rumours near the truth; that was when they spoke of a curse.

Cursed he certainly was, and with the oldest fate of all; that he was born, that he was flesh and blood, and that he was aware. That awareness grew on him, as of course it grows upon us all; with it came responsibility. The responsibility he felt both to others and himself; for the things he saw so clearly had somehow to be given shape. And that was when his music had its birth, when he began to speak not with words but through his flute; because the things he saw were not capable of normal utterance.

He saw great kings, certainly; he saw women beautiful beyond dreams, he saw lovely girls in short white dresses, the like of which had surely never been. He saw machines that thundered along roads yet to be made. He saw the cargoes they carried, the foodstuffs and the wines; he saw

by Keith Roberts

the very lamps that lit their way, the jewel-strings of them stretching out for ever, amber and silver fires that burned high and without heat. All this he saw, and more. He saw the hearts of his dream-folk, and knew that men can never change. This his flute sang; which is perhaps why his listeners sometimes crept away appalled.

He came one day, unannounced as was his wont, to that village that has no name. He walked slowly, with many a pause, brow furrowed as if in intense thought; for he was troubled in his mind.

He had seen, more clearly than before, the strange low buildings of another age, each standing in its little plot of land. He had seen the trim-fenced gardens, the vehicles standing patient in their drives, the thin bright wands jutting talisman-fashion from the roof of every house. He shook his head as if to clear it; but the vision intensified rather than fading, till the cluster of wattle huts his human eyes recorded seemed themselves mere ghosts, threatening to flicker and vanish. He shook his head again, exerting all his will. His eyes blazed, till a child who would have spoken ran scampering in fear, and at last the unwanted vision began to fade; though a part of his mind still wondered what it might portend.

He made his way to the house of Jack the Fletcher; for Jack had sheltered him times enough before, he was always sure of a welcome at his hearth. The food he was given, plain but nourishing, cheered him, so that the dull mood into which he had fallen lightened by degrees. He sat in firelight and candlelight — for in his honour they had even lit priceless tapers — and listened to the talk of Jack, his family and his many guests and friends.

Once indeed he took the flute and gave them his new vision, or at least as much of it as seemed proper; but mostly he sat hands in lap, nodding and smiling as he heard their dreams. The dreams their lips spoke, the others that lay buried beneath the words.

Mostly though, and as the evening wore on it was increasingly noted, he listened to one young girl. Lissome she was and slight, dressed all in white and with May blossoms twined into her hair. Her bearing was modest, her manner becomingly shy; but her hands made deft shapes in the flamelight, and her voice to him had the lisp and tinkle of a brook. This was why his flute was quiet; indeed it was remarked of him later that he had never been known to pay so much attention to one person's speech.

Jack Fletcher discussed it at length, in the tavern where they drank their ale and mead and threw hand-arrows at a great wood board. But no conclusion was reached, save perhaps that voiced by Will the Tanner, a kindly, lonely man, who after much thought and considering his pot of ale said, "Thou need'st not have two flutes at once." Jack and his friends shook their heads uncomprehending; for they had already agreed among themselves that Will was a little touched in his wits. But the tanner was right. For the first time, the Piper had heard a music sweeter than his own.

What happened next was surprising. At least those of the villagers who discussed the matter owned themselves puzzled; and since the affair formed the main topic of conversation for weeks to come, that meant everybody save babies and the very sick. One would have thought that with such a radically new preoccupation the Piper would have remained if not within the village, at least in easy reach. Instead, he vanished; from the forest, from the region, some said from all the haunts of men.

Twice the crops were sown and gathered in; and still there was no word of him. Meanwhile, many things happened within the village itself; more in those two seasons, it seemed, than in the lives of many men. The girl, that slender stripling with her mane of brown and marvellous hair, became betrothed. The boy to whom she was promised was a sturdy lad, the son of a yeoman. Within the limitations of the time he seemed to have good prospects; for that class of person was then becoming discrete, aware of new strength. In the village though the old ways still held sway; to marry, the girl needed permission of her feudal lord. So to his hall she went, her family and the family of her loved one in attendance, to seek his blessing.

Now the lord was not a bad man, though sometimes it was said of him he wore his duties heavy. Also it was clear enough to him the high old days were done; the sheep had eaten the men that tended them. So his blessing was given, and that handsomely; wine casks were broached, the whole village bidden to a feast in the great house that stood apart, grandly, on a rising swell of land. All rejoiced, looking to better times, not least the families of the betrothed; but there was a rub in the matter. For his lordship had a son.

What passed between the young man and the erstwhile bride none could tell; but from that day, the very day of the betrothal, the rumours began, running like shadows, like ink blotches under the high bright sun. She was here, she was there; such a thing had taken place, such and such words had been said.

The villagers put their hands to their cheeks, widening their eyes with fear; which was understandable, for in those days all folk were strong for God. What is certain is that from that time on, the girl began to change. What had been graceful, proud, began to sag, deteriorate, to shamble in drunkenness down the street, to frighten the goats and chickens once herded with such care, make them run in fear.

Her own family disowned her, driving her from the door with blows; after which she slept where best she could. She drained the tosspots in the village inn; for none dared give her nay. Those eyes that had been modest, downcast, shy, were fiery, brown and dead. None cared to meet them; so folk stepped from her path, and held their peace as best they might.

At this point the Piper heard, from wherever he might have been. He returned to the village; the people were alarmed to see him one grey dawn, stalking the single street of the place as gaunt and ragged as a spectre. But none accosted him. He made his way to a small glade in the woods, a glade known only to him, and there he sat motionless a great while.

It was evening before his decision was reached; he rose and made his way to the house of the old lord, standing alone and frowning on its little hill. Once more he stared awhile; finally he looked up at the sky, filled now with a glowering, dusty light. He placed the flute to his lips and began to play. He made a tune the like of which even he had never wrought; and fortunate it was that there were no folk near, because the melody he conjured was not for human ears. It called to old things, things thought dead and certainly best forgotten, things from the start of Time itself.

Nothing happened at first; but the tune crept higher by insensible degrees, became a shrilling, an insistence. As it rose so the clouds massed, driving from the west. Finally the storm broke, with crash after ear-splitting crash. The lightning bolts struck the great house time and again, sending tiles spinning with the roof beams and the ties that held them, singeing the Piper's very clothes where still he stood and played.

Flames leaped up, dancing, setting the last timbers ablaze, the last stick of wood from the meanest kitchen chair. Finally, when all was consumed, the rain came, in silver rods that seemed to stand up from the earth. At that, the Piper lowered his flute; and he might or might not have smiled. He sat down on a stump of soaking wood and began, slowly and methodically, to pack the instrument away.

When he raised his eyes again a man was limping toward him, dimly visible against the banks of still-glowing ash. It was the old lord. His back was bowed, as if by the weight of years, and he carried a massive stick, on which he leaned continually for support. The Piper knew that now his home and treasures were burned he had little time to live; but his lip once more curled, because compassion was dead in him. The old man stared awhile; then he sat down on the drenched grass at the Piper's feet, and the other raised no hand to stay him. He fiddled with his stick; finally he said, "Why have you done this thing?" There was no anger in his voice; merely a great weariness.

The Piper made no answer. But the old man, the lord, read the reason in his eyes. He said, "It was for my son. It was revenge." The Piper turned at that, and spoke the first word he had ever been known to utter. He said, "Yes."

The other shook his head at that, and passed a hand across his face. He said gently, "But my son is dead, Piper. He has been dead this many a month."

The Piper looked at the ground between his feet. He was silent a long time; then he raised his head. It was full dark, so there was no reading the expression on his face. He touched his tongue to his lips, and used his second word. He said, "Why?"

The old man shook his head again. "I know your opinion of me," he said. "You artist, you Fairy, you rejector of normality, of pity; you shaper of patterns, you maker and unmaker of lives. But now you will hear me; and you will mark my words. Aye, even you; and that for the rest of Time." He paused. "Rear a child," he said. "Rear a daughter or a son. Then you will understand the pain of loss. You on your lofty pedestal, who can call the thunder and lightning to your bidding; become human if you dare. Be human for a day, an hour; then you can speak to me. Till then I spurn you, and all your kind; spurn you, and spit on your name."

Now the Piper was human, with all the passions of a mortal man; so the words struck him to the core. The other had risen; he reached to grip his sleeve. "How?" he cried, anguished.

"*How . . . ?*" But the old man in his turn would not relent. "This tale you contrapted in your mind," he said. "That you devised, to satisfy your pride. This saga of villains and excesses, so different from the truth. But you with your fine imagination, you the poet; you wouldn't be interested in that."

He shook his head once more; it seemed the only gesture left him. "My son went with the girl," he said. "I make no bones of it, as he made none. She placed enchantment on him, and he yielded. From humanity; that humanity you laud in song, and counter by your acts. For payment, she destroyed him. She took his health, his living and his mind. She sucked him dry, left him a shell; a shell for which he had no further use. Now you, at her behest, have destroyed what used to be his home." He drew a ragged breath.

"I am for death," he said. "We both know my time is short. But you will live; and for that life I pity you, Piper." He turned then to the retainers who waited, sorrowing, by the still-glowing ash; they took his arms, bore him silently to the village.

The Piper sat a long, long while, staring at the flute he still gripped in his hands. His fists tensed, as if he might break it to pieces; but the act could bring no relief, no act of destruction truly brings relief. He had found that already, to his cost and the cost of others. The fault lay square on him, not on a tube of harmless wood; so finally he rose. He stowed the thing carefully in his satchel and walked away.

He went to the house of the Fletcher, and Jack opened and regarded him. He was unsurprised; for the tale of the night's doings had been brought to him. He was a sturdy man, deep-chested and slow of speech; strong in the arm they said and weak in the head, though that was far from the truth. What was true was that he'd never found much use or need for thought. But thoughts came now, tumbling in baffling succession through his brain. He saw the man before him was much changed; and though he had no notion of what had truly passed, his compassion was aroused.

Who am I, he thought in his slow way, *to criticise another? Is it mine to blame? I fletch the arrows that are used in war. Is it mine to say whose heart they rest in, in France or Normandy or the Low Countries? No, that is for our lord the King; for his word it is, and his alone, that guides our host. If judgement is to be made in this, then it is a matter for God.* So he admitted the Piper, and gave him sanctuary for many days.

For his part the Piper sat quiet and watched, in the Fletcher's tiny workshop at the back of the cottage. His mind, that had been so full, now seemed empty; he relished, for a time, the release from thought.

He saw how the fine goose quills were prepared, how they were trimmed and angled to the shaft to make that shaft rotate. None knew, in those days, why it was better for an arrow to spin, why it would fly more true; that secret had not been wrested from the Lord. But Jack knew it for a fact, and facts were all he dealt in. The Piper even helped him for a time, when and where he could, sorting the bundles of shafts, spinning each on his thumbnail to find the straightest; till he understood, by this small hint and that, his time was come. Jack was tiring of him; his patience had been extended to its limit.

So he moved out. He built himself a hut on the far edge of the village; a small and humble place, for he needed nothing grand. Cranky it was and leaning, but it would serve his purposes. For timbers he searched the forest round about. He took fallen saplings, and branches dropped from trees; for he would assail no living thing. From Jack he borrowed a saw and adze; but some tasks remained beyond his power.

At first no one would help him, till the day two sawyers arrived; grim, dour men as silent as he. They halved the trunks for the great crucks, shouldered their saw and walked away. Next morning others of the village arrived to load the timbers onto carts, drag them to the appointed spot. Why they should do such a thing, the Piper could not understand. Perhaps through his music an answer could have been made; but his human mind was numbed. He furnished the house in the same rough manner, took in the gifts left for him; the sacks of grain and meal on which he would live. After which he took to sitting evenings in his doorway, watching the green forest and playing his flute. The tunes he conjured were gentle though; tunes of yearning and regret. No demands were in them; they raised no forces, either of the darkness or the light.

Most of all he played the song of sorrow; sorrow for all humankind, that makes its hearers weep.

Meanwhile the old lord died and was buried, as had been ordained. The site of the house he had lived in, the house he had shared with his broad-faced, curly-headed son, was shunned by sinners and the righteous alike; no word was spoken, either of praise or blame, and it seemed the affair was at an end. Though that of course was not to be.

The girl continued her hectic progress. Men saw her sometimes in the dusk, a white wraith flitting through the endless gloom of trees, poised brief against the harsh black boles of winter. The God-fearing would cross themselves, turn shuddering away; but others, as like as not, would follow. She walked unheeding through the summer rains, splashed knee deep, thigh deep if she chose, in the filthy mud of lanes.

Always she called, though never with her voice; always men came, for in truth few could resist her. The village grumbled, but to itself alone. In latter times perhaps she would have been brought to fire; but the folk of those days, for all their faults, were gentle. The people kept their counsel; for men are human after all, and their lives were harsh. Also, the best of wives grow fat with time.

The Piper watched and waited. Action, now, was foreign to him. He had made one grievous error; in the sight of God, he could not afford another. And of course the inevitable happened; finally, she came to him. A summer evening it was when she tapped his door, an evening rich with the scents of forest trees. She said in her little, tinkling voice, "Can I come in?"

He considered, carefully. For he must make no more hasty choices. Finally he said, "Yes." He stepped back from the entrance; for there were tears on her face and throat, and he could not turn her away. Also of course he saw the young child that she once had been, staring frightened from the backs of her almond-tilted eyes.

They talked a great time that first night, she sitting cross-legged on his bracken bed, her skirt modestly disposed. He saw the scars criss-crossing on her calves and ankles, the wounds of careless brambles. The flesh that had been sweet and perfect was marred for all time now; and once again his pity was aroused. She told him how she'd been sleeping on Jack the Fletcher's floor, how she had no place now to call her own, nowhere to lay her head and be at peace. For men had used her for their purposes, then turned her out of doors.

Behind the little room he lived in lay another. Tiny, not more than a cubicle; but it too had a bracken bed, and to one side, on a little table, stood a pitcher of pure spring water. What purpose he'd had in building the place not even the Piper could have said; but he opened the door, and showed it her. "This is yours," he said

in his harsh, rough voice, "for as long as you desire."

She ran to him then, crying and kissing. "I'll fetch my things," she said. "It won't take long, I haven't very much. All I want, now, is to be at rest. I've learned my lesson; but nobody else believes." So he gave her shelter, as shelter had once been given to him; and the village could talk and whisper as it chose. For his heart, at last, was radiant with joy.

He played for her later. He played the songs of peace and happiness, better, certainly, than even he had ever played them before; but to no avail. It seemed her mood had changed from the winsomeness of the afternoon, changed with the growing dusk. Her eyes were opaque again, and lifeless; it seemed she didn't hear the notes. It was then perhaps that the first flickerings of doubt assailed him; he laid the flute aside, busied himself with a frugal supper.

He sat and brooded after she had retired, sipping a little wine, staring at the single taper that was all he allowed himself. Once he looked in on her, quietly. She lay face down, her breathing steady and deep; the single coarsely-woven blanket had twitched aside, disclosing nakedness. He brooded down at her awhile; then stepped forward gently to adjust the covering. She moaned a little in her sleep, but did not wake.

He resumed his vigil. The taper had burned down; he lit another from it, placed it in the holder on the table. His eyes in the tiny pool of light were dark, unfathomable. Finally he took up the flute again. He sat with it a moment in his hands, turning it to see the spindled gleams reflect from polished wood. Then he set it to his lips.

The notes he made were soft, so as not to wake his charge; but they were nonetheless a summons. A summons, and a challenge; the first he had uttered for many weary months. Again and again, tirelessly, the call went out; but there was no response. The tree leaves whispered, round the little hut; a moth boomed and blundered, somewhere in the shadowed recesses of the roof. So he began again; for he had decided, and time alone would prove him right or wrong, that she was possessed, that by some device a demon had snared her soul, trapped it behind bars she could not break. That soul that had once been the world to him. Gently, beguilingly, using all his art, he called that demon to him. Nothing came of course; but he had hardly expected a result. Devils by all report are cunning; they'll not present themselves at the snapping of a pair of mortal fingers.

Nonetheless, the demon heard. The flush of dawn was showing above the trees before the Piper flung himself down wearily to rest; but it seemed his head scarcely touched the bracken before the hut shook to thunderous knockings. The door burst inward; instantly the room was filled with armed men. The King's own bodyguard, ridden hard from London.

"Where is the witch?" they shouted. "Her fame has gone abroad through all the land. Deliver her to us, Piper; for she must stand her trial."

He cried out at that, would have intervened; but a blow from a mailed fist stretched him half senseless on the floor. They straddled him contemptuously, standing on his hands; he could only rage and weep. They dragged her forth, her dress half ripped away, shrieking as if she was already damned. They sat her on a horse, bound her hands and feet. He called to her, desperate, and she gave one backward glance. His heart broke afresh at the contempt in it, the scorn; then she was gone, cantering through the leafy glades to answer for her crimes.

Once again, his brain seemed numbed. He bathed his stiffening fingers, stared unseeing at the broken knuckles; sat beneath an oak and watched the sun rise, the forest breezes move the sprays of leaves. Once a hind came, stepping delicate and shy; but so still was he that she had no fear. She browsed a while contentedly; then she too was gone.

The day wore on. Midges danced in the levelling beams of sunlight; finally the silence of the forest was broken. A troop of dancers appeared, tumbling between the trees, on their way to this village or that; the Moorish men, whom in another life the Piper had loved with all his heart. They clustered round him, jabbering anxiously, touching his wounded hands; and he rose wearily to prepare a meal, for no stranger had ever left his hut unfed.

They smiled, accepting; but when they came to dance their thanks, with their trews and napkins and bells, he silenced them with one note on his flute. They understood then; packed their things, and crept silently away.

Now that he was truly alone, the taunting began once more. He saw her at a thousand gentle moments; touching, kissing, patting others with her little hands. She flung her head back, combed her lovely hair; tucked her legs beneath her as she stared up at him, flamelight dancing on her solemn face. He heard her laughter, the tinkling of her voice; finally he fell into a species of trance. He saw a glade in the forest, a glade where few men came. She danced there for him, danced for him alone, swirled her skirt to show the perfection of her legs. He held his arms out, half started up; and on the instant the vision changed. He saw her pressed to grass, to earth; he saw her body jerk and tremble, heard her cry out. She locked her ankles above her partner's back; and the Piper's own shout woke him. He glared around him wildly, the demon's laughter still ringing in his ears; then comprehension came. It had been fantasy, all was fantasy; but he knew now where he must go.

He left the cottage with its door swinging free, for birds to roost in the rafters, dust to gather on the floor. He was done with housen, and the homes of men. He made his way to the glade that he had seen. By it ran a dipping, rutted track; and the trees about it were still.

He chose his spot with care; a grassy hollow between the roots of an ancient, spreading beech. He played the song he had played before, the song of summoning. He listened, head cocked slightly to one side; and then he played again. Midnight, and the flute still sounded, echoing eerily between the unseen trees; dawn, and the notes still sounded firm and clear. Through the day that followed he went on untiring; and for many days to come. And this was the Piper's Wait.

Here too of course the legends began. Because some said he sat ten years, some a hundred, some a thousand. But that was nonsense, because the Piper was still a mortal. Sometimes the notes seemed to falter, at others the sounds ceased altogether; then the villagers — those who had plucked the courage to creep within earshot — were sure the player had died, from hunger, exhaustion or cold. But always, somehow, the tune rose again, patient, indomitable. Because the Piper, now, was sustained by rage; a rage colder and more implacable than any he had known.

His course lay clear enough. Wrongs were to be righted, more than the wrong to the girl. Blood was on the demon's hands, and on his own; his good name had been blighted in the sight of God. For that the fiend would answer, if it took the rest of Time.

The shuddering villagers noted the strains of the flute had once more become raucous, harsh. Gone was the beguiling; the call was imperative now, not to be borne. Even they found themselves drawn closer, by some force beyond their will; their nerve broke finally at that, they fled to their huts, crouched in the dark to gabble hasty prayers, to thank their God, as in the old days, for padlocks and bars of oak.

As for the Piper, the visions burned now continuous and stark. He saw the blue-black roads slash into the forest, saw again the yellow vans that plied them. He saw the girl dance in a score of different garbs; while time and again the roaring in his ears became the noise of engines. The great trucks ground by day and night among the trees, up from the coast now, onward for ever to distant, boiling London. Other machines, greater and still more wonderful, sailed the very sky. All these things, he knew, would one day be; in a world cleansed of demons, cleansed of fear. Freed, perhaps, from the very shackles of death.

The demon came. What earthly form it took, no man could say. Nor did any dare to imagine. But one day, or one year, or one century, the Piper faced his enemy. The Wait was over.

What passed between them, again was never known. Perhaps they talked; though popular fancy quailed at the words they might have used. Perhaps the fiend was maddened finally by the one tune ringing in his ears; or perhaps the Piper's magic truly forced it from the fastnesses of Hell. The Piper played a song of rage against it; it laughed at that and grew larger, physically more powerful. It towered in the glade, triumphant; and the Piper understood, and turned the lay. He played the songs of contempt, indifference; finally he played the song of laughter, and at that the demon quailed. So he played the songs of *her*, the songs of beauty; her hair and eyes, her legs, the lovely centre of her being. He played his love; and at that the demon cringed, covering its eyes and moaning.

He capered toward it, triumphant in his joy; and it was shrinking, dwindling as he watched, reducing to a black thing smoking on the grass, a thing on which he could set his heel. He smashed his foot down again and again, with all the force left in him; and the piping stopped at last. He stared round the glade, peaceful now and still, and knew that he had won.

His sight flickered. He sat down, passed a shaking hand across his face. In time his vision returned. His breathing steadied, and he looked about him once more. At the unmoving, gentle leaves, the grass, the green shades through which she would soon come walking. The demon's power was broken, after a weariness of time; so

by Keith Roberts

the power of his minions was broken too. This he knew infallibly, without question; all would be as it had been before. He smiled at the flute, the flute he would never need again, set it down gently at his side. Its purpose, at last, had been fulfilled.

He turned his head slowly, listening with all his being. The sound came again; the softest scuffing of a foot, faint snapping of a twig. Joy flooded him at that; the joy he had known before, but had never hoped to feel again. Joy at first sight of her, at her perfection, joy as she scraped his cabin door. For he could not mistake, he could never mistake; her lightest tread, soft whisper of her footfalls. He waited, breath stilled; and for him the birdsong faded, the roarings that had plagued him vanished quite away.

She stepped into the glade, and paused. He rose, slowly, from where he sat. He saw that once more she was perfection; her skin and hair, her dainty hands and feet. He held his arms out; and she came running. "Thank you, Piper," she whispered. "Thank you . . ."

He held her, the warm slightness of her; and there were tears on his cheeks. He said, "It is ended," and she said, "I know, I know . . ." He kissed her, and she returned his love; soft brushings of her lips, childlike as she clung with all her strength. He fondled her hair, smelling its sweetness; and she pushed away, gripped his hands to stare up into his face.

"All the course we ran is in the past," she said. "Now we begin again. It's a new world, Piper." He swung her up at that, no longer able to restrain the happiness, waltzed her round while she laughed and struggled. "Put me down," she said. "Put me down . . ." He set her on her feet; but she had not done. "One more thing," she said. "One more thing, Piper. For me . . ." Her eyes had lighted on the flute, where it lay discarded on the grass. "The Joining," she said. "Play the song of Joining. Then nothing will come between us, it will truly be for ever . . ."

He shook his head. "We don't need it," he said; but she grasped his hand again. "Piper," she said urgently, "if you knew the fear I felt. The pain, the degradation . . . Do it for me," she pleaded. "Then we are safe twice over . . ."

Never had he refused her; he wouldn't begin now. He smiled, took up the flute. She sat at his feet, watching with troubled eyes; he thought he had never seen a thing more divine. He set the flute to his lips and began, softly, to play his final charm. And an ancient charm it was, the oldest in the world; something that reached back beyond the Celts, beyond the Flint Men with their great towns; back to a time before the hills were made, when there were none but Gods. He saw the smile form round her lips, spread to her eyes. It was the greatest spell he cast; and it was for her alone. It joined her to him for ever.

His breath froze on the final note. An icy pang shot through him; for the smile, that had been so innocent and sweet, was broadening, becoming fixed. Turning to a rictus, the preparation for a scream.

The flute fell from his hands. He saw the eyes fixed on his face were dead once more; dead, but themselves lethal. She raised her skirt, leaned back on the grass. She raised her knees, as slowly parted them. He saw the other smile that waited him, and wondered of the two which was the more hideous.

Dimly, he understood. That demons traffic in deceit; that his song had not released her, that nothing would release her. Because she herself had never willed it so. He realized the fiend had played a part; and played it cleverly, to snare him. Now she was his for ever, still in the demon's thrall; he'd forged the bonds himself, bonds no power could break.

He took the knife he carried from his belt, touched the tip to his throat while she still laughed, with lips and loins. He drove deep, one firm and steady thrust; and as the hot gushing began, as his sight began to fade, he realized even death was not an end. She would have followed him through all the world; now she would follow him through every Hell. Because God Himself had permitted him to fall. It was the fruit of arrogance. "Beloved," he whispered; then, for a time, the blackness claimed him.

And that is the tale of the Piper, that is the tale of why he waited; and that is the tale of what came. Ω

A CUP OF HONEYSUCKLE

by Kevin Andrew Murphy

He is dead, and there is no help for it. My husband, dead.

They say it is better like this, an honorable death, a suicide rather than falling into the hands of the enemy. They then shake their heads and say it's a pity that a brave warrior would choose a woman's weapon to take his own life, rather than use his own sword. Some of them look at me, and wonder if it was not suicide at all, but if instead it was I who gave him the poison. I Lywella, who would rather see her beloved husband dead then chained in the dungeons of his castle.

I wonder that, myself, but it was not I who killed Harald. It was not himself either, not really. It was the cup.

I hear them outside my cell, hear them talking. There, let her stay there, let the murderess contemplate her own weapon, let the grieving widow contemplate the cowardly choice her husband used to take his own life, let the babbling madwoman have the cup she swears killed her husband. They do not know which is true, and it doesn't matter to them anyway except as an object of idle speculation. I would fear for my own safety if I did not know better or I were not past caring. They'll hold me for ransom and sell me to my brother's keeping. That is all.

But why won't they understand? It was the cup, the cup that was responsible for it all, the accursed cup. The cup that started this madness, and is here at its end.

I hold it in my hand and it seems such an innocent thing, so pretty, so fine. The bowl of polished gold with flights of bees and the bells of flowers graven around its rim. Below them are twined honeysuckle vines, and bees on the comb, and countless other pretty things. But the bee has a sting, tipped with poison, something I never had cause to notice until now. Poison to drive a man to madness or to shock him into death.

The witch who sold it to us told of its power, and the enchantment had seemed such a pretty thing too. A pretty spell and a pretty cup for Harald and me to hold up and say, "Yes, our castle has magic." For us to show that we were worthy of legend. What a foolish wish, for I know of no legend that does not include death in some part of it.

Harald drank from the cup and dreamt of conquest, of forging an empire, of being King of all the land. I dreamt of that too, and I regret it now, but it was our foolish wish, our foolish desire.

That was the spell. The cup, when asked, would fill with any drink the holder craved. But the cup never listened to the mouth. I knew better. It listened to the heart and fulfilled the desire that was writ there, whatever it might be. Harald wanted glory, and the cup filled him with passion and battle fury. But that was all it could give him, and it wasn't enough.

Afterwards he came home, tired and bloody from the battle, routed and ready to admit defeat. He asked me for the cup, and fool that I was, I gave it to him. Harald wanted honeysuckle wine to quench his thirst. But the cup looked deeper and gave him the draught he truly craved.

I now hold the cup, sitting in the dungeon of my castle, the enemy outside my door, being thought of as murderess, widow, madwoman and worse. I cannot know what I want.

"Honeysuckle," I say softly, and the cup fills, cool and golden. But as I raise it to my lips, I wonder what it truly is. A drink of forgetfulness? A balm for a weary spirit? A draught of healing sleep, bravery to face the coming day, or that bitter wine that was poured for Harald? Ω

Summer 1996

ISSN 0898-5073
Cover by Ian Miller

Worlds of Fantasy & Horror is published 3 times a year by Terminus Publishing Co., Inc., 123 Crooked Lane, King of Prussia PA 19406-2570. Single copies, $4.95 in U.S.A. & possessions; $6.00 by mail elsewhere. Subscriptions: 4 issues $16.00 in U.S.A. & possessions; $22.00 elsewhere, in U.S. funds. Publisher is not responsible for loss of manuscripts in publisher's hands or in transit; please see page 5 for more details. Postmaster: send address changes to *Worlds of Fantasy & Horror*, 123 Crooked Lane, King of Prussia PA 19406-2570. Copyright © 1996 by Terminus Publishing Co., Inc.; all rights reserved; reproduction prohibited without prior permission. Typeset, printed, & bound in the United States of America.

THE OWL'S NEST

So, where have we been?

It has been almost a year since our last issue, a circumstance we are not proud of. The truth of the matter is that since then the magazine has been sitting around looking for the money and opportunity to publish another issue. This problem has been solved, so here we are. We regret that we haven't been able to stay on schedule since 1991, which was the last time we actually published four issues of *Weird Tales®* in a year. But that was five years ago, and here we are. We *are* proud of our ability to survive. Times have been tough for small magazines, with the costs of paper and postage rising astronomically. Many have failed. Many more have become irregular, as *Worlds of Fantasy and Horror* has, but we think that what matters is survival. We're heartened to learn that our colleague Charles Ryan will have a new issue of *Aboriginal SF* out by the time you read this, after a hiatus of nearly two years. *Pulphouse* comes out whenever *Pulphouse* comes out, and we're always glad to see it, but we never know when to expect the next one. All of us are members of the Survivors Club.

We hope to continue publishing the magazine three times a year, with the next issue in the summer of 1996. Remember, in any case, that your subscription is for a number of issues, not a period of time, so you won't miss anything, no matter what happens. Please bear with us.

We continue this editorial with a filing accident: every time we go to write one of these pieces, we reach for the "Eyrie" file — still called that, after the editorial-and-letters section in a Certain Other Magazine with a Large **W** in the Title, which we used to edit — which contains assorted notes and, most especially, letters of comment from you, the readers, which not only count for the Most Popular Story voting each issue, but sometimes spark the editorials themselves.

(Yes! We really do want to hear from you!)

This time we discovered that half the letters had been inadvertently slipped into the "Nut Case" file which had been placed right next to the "Eyrie" file. The "Nut Case" file is something, we assure you, every editor and publisher has. It contains the angry and argumentative replies to rejections, occasional threats, and just plain strangeness which accumulates at any editorial office like so much flotsam. It is *not* a

"blacklist" but merely something we keep for our own reference, in case one of those problematical people writes in *again*. Then, at least, we have the whole "case history" on hand.

No, we're not going to quote anything from that file. It remains strictly private. But, it so happened that in order to separate out the "Eyrie" letters from the less desirable ones, we had to go through and reread them all.

Fortunately the "Nut Case" file is very thin and shows no sign of getting any fatter. But the experience *did* cause us to reflect a bit on what it means to be a writer, particularly a magazine writer, the sort who submits stories to *Worlds of Fantasy and Horror*.

There are three Rules for *being* a writer: First, you must write. Second, you must write well. Third, you must behave like a writer.

The first is obvious enough. There are a lot of people who talk about the great stories they'll write someday, if only they can find the time. When we were in college, it was still fashionable for literary intellectuals to be "working on a novel." We're not sure if that is *still* the fashion — possibly they're "working on a screenplay" these days — but we are certain that we never saw any of those novels in print. As magazine editors, we never see any of the great stories folks will write whenever they finally find the time, because those stories never do get written. So, Rule #1 is self-explanatory and self-correcting.

The second is the crux of the matter. You must write well. At this point you may expect us to give you an objectively verifiable definition of "good writing," which is of course impossible, but we're going to let you in on a little secret. There are certain criteria *all* editors agree upon. After a while, an experienced editorial reader can detect a potentially publishable story as easily as one can tell if the water's warm by dipping a foot in it.

You know immediately if the prose is literate, if the scenes are in focus, if there is dramatic development, and if the dialogue sounds like people talking. Most stories that get rejected are rejected not because they didn't, as the phrase has it, "meet the magazine's present needs." Instead, they are rejected for other reasons than for failing to conform to editorial policy (in the sense that *Analog,* a hardcore, science-fiction magazine, does not publish ghost stories and will therefore turn down a ghost story, no matter how well-written) or even for failing to match the idiosyncratic personal taste of the editor.

Many rejected stories are simply not written well enough to be published anywhere, under any circumstances, unless subsidized by the person who wrote it. This fact should encourage writers: if your story *is* of publishable quality, and it doesn't happen to "fit the needs" of one magazine, it will almost certainly fit the needs of another. We now live in a golden age of small-press, bookstore-distributed magazines. There are more magazine markets for all kinds of short fiction than there have been since the pre-television era of the 1940s, when pulp magazines proliferated. So, hang in there. Persistence pays off for stories of publishable quality.

You must write well. The important thing is that your story be gripping, amusing, emotionally moving, or whatever it sets out to be. The *crucial* thing is to be entertaining enough that someone who is an absolute stranger to the author will want to pay money to read it. If you write well enough, there are no obsolete ideas. Sure, we at *Worlds of Fantasy & Horror* are tired of stories about re-animated roadkill, or desperately romantic/tragic/decadent vampires. We also dislike mock-medieval fantasies which merely rehash parts of old rôle-playing games or even older fantasy novels. But this doesn't mean that we never buy stories about vampires, wizards, or even (should someone happen to surprise us with a sufficiently good one) roadkill.

The key to writing a good story is having something unique and important to say. It's not just a matter of the money. If you think you can just toss together a few clichés and collect a check, *even if you're right,* consider the following: If you're very successful and sell five stories that are 5,000 words long to major markets within your first year, you have made a cool $1500 there. (At 6 cents a word, the common professional rate, that's $300 per story.) Now, suppose you do even better and sell your first novel to a paperback house for a typical first-novel advance of, say, $4000 . . . well, you see where this is heading. Don't quit your day job.

Writing — being a writer — is a way of life. The *being a writer* part is actually quite distinct from putting words on paper. That is what the dozen or so people — out of the thousands and thousands who have submitted stories to us over the years — did so badly that they ended up in the "Nut Case" file.

The worst thing you can possibly do is to open your author-editor dialogue with a threat. It usually goes something like this: "My story is copyrighted. Don't you dare *steal my ideas* or else I'll sue!" Magazine editors don't steal stories from writers, and *especially* not from previously unpublished writers. That would drive away writers (who are much more valuable the second, and third, and . . . time around), and without writers — well, it's another deeply held secret in this business that blank pages don't sell. Ideas, incidentally,

STAFF:

Publisher: George H. Scithers
Editor: Darrell Schweitzer
Managing Editor: Carol Adams
Art Editor: Diane Weinstein
Assistant Editors: Leslie Smith, Dainis Bisenieks, Michael W. Betancourt, Jan B. Berends, Rich Harvey, & Carol Pinchefsky
Computer Consultant: David J. Williams III
Typesetter: Owlswick Press
Printer: News Publishing Co., Inc.

MANUSCRIPT SUBMISSIONS:

Before sending us your material, please ask for our guidelines, which we will send you if you send us a business-sized envelope, with postage affixed, addressed to you.

Yes; we read unsolicited submissions — but *only* if they are in standard manuscript format. To survive, all editors insist on a few Rules: each submission must be in proper format and must include a return envelope, addressed to you, with enough postage affixed to bring the manuscript back to you. If you want us to discard the manuscript if we don't buy it, tell us so, but include a business-letter-sized envelope, addressed to you, with proper postage affixed, so we can send you our comments. No loose stamps, please!

We recommend either of two books on writing (after all, we wrote one of them!): *On Writing Science Fiction: the Editors Strike Back!* by Scithers, Schweitzer, & John M. Ford; $19.50 in hardcovers; and Barry B. Longyear's *Science-Fiction Writer's Workshop,* $9.50 in trade paperback, available from the Owlswick Press, 123 Crooked Lane, King of Prussia PA 19406-2570. These prices include shipping & handling; in Pennsylvania, please include 6% sales tax.

We are not responsible for manuscripts in our hands or in transit. You *must* keep a copy of every manuscript you send out. You *must* put your name and address on the first page of every manuscript. Please: *no* binders, folders, or padded envelopes; and especially: *no* registered or certified mail for which we would have to stand in line at the post office!

are free. No one owns them. Many anthologies are assembled by editors who give the same idea to *all* the writers involved, and those writers then write enough distinctly different stories to fill a book.

The paranoid who threatens to sue before the editor even reads the first page merely guarantees that no prudent editor will ever read the first page.

The next worst thing you can do is argue about a rejection.

Don't.

Ever.

You have everything to lose and nothing to gain. The editor is not going to change his mind and buy the story after all. You may well make yourself a memorable nuisance and bias him against future submissions. If you think the editor is wrong, the only way to prove him so is by selling the story elsewhere. If you try, but fail, do consider the possibility that he may be *right*.

A surprising number of Nut Case letters argue about format, often using decidedly eccentric spelling and grammar to do so. Content is what matters, they say; and they go on to claim that a real editor can see through the red ink on orange paper, the faded, single-spaced, draft-mode, dot-matrix printing, the smeared carbon-copy manuscript (which may be on both sides of onion-skin paper), or even the author's crabbed handwriting to discover a brilliant gem of artistic beauty. . . . Don't bet on it; editors survive only by insisting that stories be submitted in a form that the editors can evaluate and can typeset if bought.

See how easy it is to be a writer? All you have to do is avoid being a Nut Case, follow a few simple rules, and let your writing speak for itself. Go back to Rule 2. Concentrate on that. Rules 1 and 3 tend to take care of themselves.

But *why?* You're not likely to get rich this way, particularly at the start. We (or, one of us, Darrell Schweitzer) have interviewed many writers, in the course of which such writers often make statements about "it beats working" or that they're in it for the money. But when probed a bit, the subject will usually admit that, if he or she were independently wealthy beyond the wildest dreams of avarice, had no responsibilities and all the time in the world, but *would not get paid for writing*, he or she would in fact continue writing. Possibly not the same things, but something. More short fiction. More poetry. Less journalism. But *writers* will keep on writing anyway, because they have something to say, or something to create, which simply would not get said or created otherwise.

Literature then, like virtue, is its own reward. That being said, writers like to get paid, and should get paid, but getting paid isn't the first purpose of writing. It actually *doesn't* beat "working." It's a lot harder than working. But, in several ways, it also "pays" a lot better too!

It is indeed possible to *write* without managing to *be a writer.* Emily Dickinson accomplished this most notably. All her success was posthumous — which is no fun at all. To be *published,* one must also put your work before someone who might buy it, and present it in a form that can be evaluated and used.

Obituaries.

Karl Edward Wagner, innovative editor of *The Year's Best Horror Stories,* celebrated author of the revolutionary "Kane" series of sword-and-sorcery stories, and of some of the finest modern horror fiction (collected in two books, *In a Lonely Place* and *Why Not You and I?*) died last October, shortly after we wrote the previous editorial. The appalling thing was that he was only 48. He should have been with us for many more years to come. He will be sorely missed. We devoted a special issue of *Weird Tales* to Karl's unique talent back in 1989.

Stanley McNail, whose poetry graced our pages as recently as *Worlds of Fantasy & Horror #1,* died in early April 1995. He was 77. Two of our editors (Darrell Schweitzer and Diane Weinstein) remain ever grateful to the redoubtable Don Herron for taking us to meet Mr. McNail when we were in California in 1993.

Stan McNail was a wit, scholar, and gentleman, a performing poet who could recite everything from bawdy limericks to very fine, fantastic verse off the top of his head. His own eerie work is mostly to be found in his 1965, Arkham House book, *Something Breathing,* which was also reprinted in 1987 by another publisher.

Editorial book reviews. Among our recent reading, we particularly recommend:

Lord Dunsany, Master of the Anglo-Irish Imagination by S.T. Joshi. Greenwood Press, 1995. 230 pp., $55.00. For years to come, we suspect, this will be the definitive study of the great Irish fantasist and his work. Dunsany (1878–1957) is often cited merely as an influence on Lovecraft, Leiber, and some others, but he should be appreciated as a great fantasist in his own right. It is unfortunate that most of his work is currently unavailable. Nevertheless, Joshi's book is an illuminating guide to the entire body of the author's work. Joshi's own training in classics and philosophy stands him in good stead, as he convincingly reveals depths and subtleties in Dunsany's work which many readers may not have suspected were there; he shows the continuing and coherent development of Dunsany's thought.

The steep cover price will probably restrict this book to university libraries, but seek it out. The highest compliment one can pay to a work of criticism is that it illuminates its subject. This does.

100 Wild Little Weird Tales edited by Robert Weinberg, Stefan R. Dziemianowicz, & Martin Greenberg. Barnes & Noble Books, 1994, 581 pp., No price listed. Look for this one in the "instant remainder" section of Barnes & Noble bookstores, where it is

by the Editors   7

usually priced at about $10.00. This is a fine collection of the often neglected shorter fiction published in the back of each issue of *Weird Tales*'s original incarnation. Some big names are here: Lovecraft, Wellman, Clark Ashton Smith, and Fritz Leiber, but so are dozens of hitherto unreprinted tales by forgotten writers.

Towing Jehovah by James Morrow. Harcourt, Brace, & Company, 1994. 371 pp., $23.95. For sheer audacity, this satirical fantasy can't be beat. A disgraced oil-tanker captain is offered his old ship back, and a chance at redemption, if only he will fulfill a mysterious mission. . . . It seems God has actually died and been found floating in the Atlantic Ocean. The Corpse must be towed to its final resting place in the Arctic before It starts to rot. Plots and counterplots thicken as atheists, feminists, and even the Vatican attempt to sabotage the mission. And were the angels who commissioned this acting on orders or not?

Morrow, the World Fantasy Award winning author of *Only Begotten Daughter* and other novels, is a wonderful writer whose work everyone should discover. What impresses us the most about *Towing Jehovah* is that, while it is comedy, it *isn't farce*. This is comedy with substance, with real characters who hurt and die, about whom we can care. Morrow shares the gift of T.H. White in his ability to use comedy as an approach to very serious, often very dark material.

The Sixth Dog by Jane Rice. Necronomicon Press, 1995. 28 pp., $4.95. For decades, Jane Rice (no, not the same as *Anne* Rice!) has been one of the enigmas of our field. She published a dozen or so marvelous stories in the celebrated pulp magazine *Unknown Worlds* in the 1940s, and two more in *The Magazine of Fantasy and Science Fiction* in the '50s. Her fiction has never been collected into a book. A few of the stories, particularly "The Idol of the Flies," have been repeatedly anthologized. No reference book in the field seems to contain any data about her. Your editor was once contemplating writing an article entitled "Who Was Jane Rice?" and asked various senior figures this very question, and drew a blank.

So it is something of a surprise that Ms. Rice should re-enter the field after nearly forty years. *The Sixth Dog* is not some old manuscript now unearthed, but a new story — and it's good. It's an intriguing portrait of Southern small-town life, its odd characters and not-quite-ordinary goings-on, which gradually turn more sinister. We now inevitably wonder what Jane Rice has been doing all these years. Certainly her very special talent remains undiminished.

Letters from Our Readers.

Several people wrote in to praise the resplendent Jason Van Hollander cover last issue. Many asked how such realistic effects were achieved. "Wow!" wrote **Lelia Loban Lee**. "Everything he does looks as if it's moving." There are two possible explanations. One is

that Jason Van Hollander is a superbly talented artist who gets such astonishing results from a combination of painting and computer technology (specifically a Macintosh program called Adobe Photoshop). The other is that, like Lovecraft's Richard Upton Pickman, he uses *photographs from life!!!!* (At least four exclamation points required.) That is, he simply got real ghosts to pose. We leave you to figure out which.

Author **Charles de Lint** sent in the following clarification of a point raised in the interview with him last issue: "Because of the long time-lag between when the interview was conducted and its seeing print, the impression is given that I'm unhappy with the Tor cover for Svaha, which is far from the case. I hadn't seen the Tor cover at the time of the interview and was speaking of the original Ace cover. I love the Tor cover."

S.T. Joshi's column drew considerable attention, including commentary in other magazines. In his newsletter *Horror,* John Betancourt devoted an article to advising small-press publishers how to avoid the sort of production errors Joshi berated.

On this point, **Michael Thomas Dillon** injects a cautionary note. ". . . it seemed unfair to assume that [Lucy] Taylor was responsible for the grammatical errors [Joshi] cites, when the editor could just as easily be the culprit. . . . I also disagree with his thumbs-up for Partridge's novel *Slippin' into Darkness*. It's the first novel I've read in a good many years, admittedly, but it's still hard to believe I could be so wrong about it. To me, it was boring, made promises of supernatural goings-on that never came to light, and was easier to put down than a hot piece of coal. The theme of guilt ruining people's lives was far from original, as was the reason for the guilt. A shame, because I generally like his [i.e., Norman Partridge's] short stories and was quite disappointed."

The Most Popular Story.

Once again, the voting is very light. The winner seems to be "When Desert Spirits Crowd the Night" by Charles de Lint. There aren't enough votes to clearly rank the runners-up. (No kidding, folks. We really *do* want to hear from you!) De Lint's "The Forever Trees" and Lord Dunsany's "The Story of Tse Gah" also drew notable praise.

Coming soon in *WoF&H*.

We have recently acquired several exciting stories which will be printed as soon as possible, including a novelet, "Teatro Grottesco," by one of the horror field's true originals, **Thomas Ligotti**, and a triptych of linked stories by **Tanith Lee**, "The Sequence of Swords and Hearts." We are negotiating for more rare, hitherto unknown stories by **Lord Dunsany,** and have on hand a long and grim tale, "The Bible in Blood," and a shorter and surprising one, "My Vampire Cake," both by **Ian Watson.** We also have stories by **Melanie Tem, R. Bretnor, Darrell Schweitzer, R. Chetwynd-Hayes,** and several new talents we've discovered. Ω

SHADOWINGS
by Douglas E. Winter

FINDING MY RELIGION

. . . it is easier to sail many thousand miles through cold and storm and cannibals, in a government ship, with five hundred men and boys to assist one, than it is to explore the private sea, the Atlantic and the Pacific of one's being alone.
— Henry David Thoreau

During a recent interview for a documentary on low-budget filmmaking, I was asked an innocuous and perhaps inevitable question: Do I prefer supernatural horror or psychological horror?

The answer surprised the interviewer, and may surprise some readers:

I don't think there is a difference.

I've devoted the better part of my writing life to knocking down the fences of categorization, and certainly the impulse to reject such broadbrush distinctions as supernatural/psychological (or quiet/loud) informs my thinking. But I find no rational split between "supernatural" and "psychological" for the simple reason that there is no such difference in our daily lives. And since fiction is a mirror, however warped, of our existence, then there is no useful purpose (save for marketing and mind-numbing criticism-by-numbers) for dividing up sides this way.

Consider: The "real" world mimicked by fiction is a supernatural one. Even if written by an atheist, a story must acknowledge that our world is filled with people who believe, principally through religion, in the existence of the supernatural. Our world is also not entirely explicable; it is filled with mysteries that aren't all capable of purely psychological solutions. Thus the "real" world includes, at the very least, the *possibility* of the supernatural, if not the supernatural itself. And any "psychological" fiction set in that world is thus, to my mind, supernatural — just as any effective "supernatural" fiction is undoubtedly psychological, for what is horror but an emotion, a state of mind?

Ironically, a hard look at most "supernatural" horror stories reveals them to be "psychological" fictions that have as much to do with the supernatural as hard science fiction. Contrary to popular belief, the typical vampire is not a supernatural creature, but a logic-bound construct who exists (and desists) by easily explicable — and natural — rules. Burial soil, crucifixes, garlic at the window, the need for blood: all hallmarks of a natural (if not necessarily human) being; Ed Gein, an icon of "psychological" horror, is much more difficult to comprehend. The traditional werewolf is the better example: A hirsute Mr. Hyde, the overtly physical manifestation of the beast within — not at all different from a run-of-the-mill psychotic killer. That you might need silver bullets instead of hollow points to drop him is irrelevant. We may as well argue that an alligator is supernatural; the only difference is that some of us have actually seen live alligators. In other words, vampires and werewolves are imaginary monsters, but not imaginary theosophies, ways of explaining, in direct terms, the dilemma of our existence.

When presented with a creature — whether vampire or gator — the question is not whether the creature does exist or could exist. The question should be: What does the creature represent?

Or better yet, the one so rarely asked: What does the creature believe?

Which, in turn, leads us to the more important question: What do we believe?

We think of "religion" as another box to be checked on the form, right after male or female, single or married, Caucasian or African-American or Native American or Pacific Rim American or Other. What will it be . . . Baptist, Catholic, Adventist, Buddhist, Atheist? In other words, we think of religion in organized terms, as a rigid system of beliefs that can be packaged and marketed as "Lutheran" as neatly as a kind of fiction can be packaged and marketed as "Horror."

Wrong. And that kind of thinking leads to quick denials, and to more dividing lines: pro-this, anti-that, religious right, godless left.

The Bible is the best selling book of the Western world, and whatever we might think of it (or the many lies built around it), there is no doubt that it is a fascinating document — and one that cannot easily be neglected, since its words rule our lives. Whether we like it or not, the Bible is the moral dialectic upon which our culture was founded and bred — and is regulated.

One of the curiosities of fundamentalist creeds — those that purport to read the Bible literally or, at the least, directly — is that their ministers work less often from the Bible than from their own versions of the "truth."

The ever-angry Kenneth Copeland, for example, hawks an "amplified Bible," whose title alone serves notice that it is an embellishment — a fiction.

But then again, the Bible itself is fiction — at least in part. Even if we hold to its truth — the truth of its words, the truth of its God — we must consider its writers, who, after all, were only human. Whether inspired by grace or special wisdom, they saw the world through their own eyes and used their own words to put "truth" to the page — just as, centuries later, translators would use their own words (many of them inaccurate) to convey the message to new readers. More important, the Bible *uses* fiction; and that, you see, is the rub.

My real problem with the fundamentalists — the supposed Biblical literalists — is that Jesus Christ, the hero of the very book in which they find their literal "truths," speaks in parables. He tells stories. He knew the power of fiction, and used fiction to instruct and elevate those who would listen to Him. And the very act of storytelling by the man whom many believe was God incarnate is rather convincing proof that the God of the Bible indeed works in mysterious ways: that He will, when appropriate, offer stories rather than literal truth to explain the human condition — thus, perhaps, a creation story to explain evolution and its responsibilities.

The ministers have hijacked the Bible, and the time is long overdue for the people to take it back. Clive Barker is doing just that.

His first books were titled in blood, and he was knighted "the future of horror," but Clive Barker was not typecast so easily. After *The Damnation Game* (1985), an accomplished first novel that was unmistak-

by Douglas E. Winter

ably the stuff of horror, Barker surprised and confounded many readers by penning a series of books that broke ranks with expectation and genre.

In *Weaveworld* (1986), he gave notice that horror fiction was merely the beachhead in his British invasion of the realm of the *fantastique*. By the time of his monumental *Imajica* (1991), reviewers and copy writers were scrambling for a new label — "dark fantasy" was a favorite — but by then, Clive Barker was a genre unto himself.

Barker's new novel, *Everville* (HarperCollins hc, 697 pp., $25.00; HarperPrism pb,), is the second book of a trilogy-in-progress known as *THE ART*. Although their literary antecedents include Eddison's Zimiamvian novels and Tolkien's *LORD OF THE RINGS*, the books of *THE ART* are written without the affectations of latter day faerie. This is decidedly contemporary fiction that speaks in every critical passage to reality.

The opening novel of *THE ART* was *The Great and Secret Show* (1989), a hallucinatory battle royale between men and demigods centered on the discovery of an unChristian cross and an evolutionary drug known as the Nuncio. Set firmly in, and then subverting, the *Salem's Lot* template of eighties horror fiction — the small town isolated and besieged by evil — *The Great and Secret Show* eschewed the generic ploy of a monster-threatened reality and proposed instead an interpenetration of realities, a setting in which characters might dream with their eyes open. Barker cleverly poised one dream of America — the false dream of Hollywood, played out on ever-flickering screens — against the true dream of self-knowledge, the hope for an existence that transcended flesh.

In *Everville*, Barker deconstructs another American dream — the dream of the West, of pioneers and *lebensraum*. (It is no small irony that Hollywood, at the westward limit of the continent, should become the dream machine of America, the means by which we have sought to conquer the remainder of the globe.) His story does not pick up on the trail of *The Great and Secret Show*, but nearly 150 years before the events of that novel, on the Oregon Trail.

The time is October 1848; the place is Wyoming. A lost and ragged band of pioneers, many of them immigrants, shrugs through a violent snowstorm, the final test of an ill-fated trek that left Independence, Missouri, in search of a promised land but found only spiritual reckoning and death.

One child has survived: Maeve O'Connell, a sickly twelve-year-old whose daft father dares to dream of the glorious, shining city that he will build when their travails are complete — a paradise on the far side of the Rocky Mountains called Everville.

At Independence, Maeve's father had met Owen Buddenbaum, a prissy student of the occult who seeks the parallel reality known as the Metacosm — the home of the eternal dream-sea, Quiddity, which is visited but three times by humans: at birth, at death and upon consummating true love.

Buddenbaum's name — Thomas Mann's Buddenbrooks by way of L. Frank Baum — evokes his transplanted European sensibilities, the decadence and old money of *The Damnation Game*, and a hint of the diabolical. But the stakes of his game are beyond damnation; he plays for redemption and that secret wisdom known as The Art.

Buddenbaum gives Maeve's father a strange cross — twin to the medallion of *The Great of Secret Show* — to be buried at the crossroads of Everville, and tells him: *"Dreams are doorways. . . . If we but have the courage to step over the threshold."*

Fast forward to the Twentieth Century and the Oregon town founded by the handful of surviving pioneers. Everville has become, with enough time and revisionist history, as American as apple pie and assassination. It is a setting that, like Palomo Grove of *The Great and Secret Show*, seems consciously Kinglike: a small town in bucolic retreat, laced with petty intrigue — unsolved crimes, infidelity, oldtime religion. This Norman Rockwell façade is peopled by those who came after the settlers, the builders of suburbs and founders of committees: "men and women who had lost all sense of the tender, terrible holiness of things." The town's secrets are locked securely inside the walls of the Everville Historical Society, which prefers the official history: "It was highly selective of course, but then were so many history lessons.

There was no place in this celebration of the Evervillian spirit for the darker side; for images of destitution, or suicide, or worse. No room, either, for any individual who didn't fit the official version of how things had come to be."

There is no mention of Maeve O'Connell, her father or the true genesis of Everville in this hallowed fabrication. Maeve fulfilled her father's dream, and Buddenbaum's desire, by burying the cross and then singlehandedly creating the town of Everville through feminine wile. She built a whorehouse at the crossroads, filled it with beautiful women, and men — and, in time, the town — followed. But then, for the usual reasons — "too much righteousness and too little passion" — the whorehouse was burned. Maeve was exiled; later, she and her family were hanged, and the ashes of deception were spread.

Each year, Everville celebrates its fable with a festival; but this year, time folds backward and, as truths both physical and spiritual are revealed, a different kind of celebration occurs. What Buddenbaum set in motion those many years ago — a dance of being and becoming — reaches its grand (and occasionally gory) finale.

The dance card features a pair of starcrossed lovers: Phoebe Cobb, an overweight doctor's receptionist, and a black painter, Joe Flicker. Phoebe's marriage, and her life, have reached a dead-end. The faces of terminal patients look back at her as if from a mirror:

There was always such emptiness towards the end; such bitter looks on their faces, as though they'd been cheated of something and they couldn't quite figure out what. Even the church-goers, the ones she'd see in front of the tree in the square at Christmas singing hallelujahs, had that look. God wanted them in his bosom, but they didn't want to go; not until they'd made sense of things here.

But suppose there was no sense to be made? That was what she had come to believe more and more: that things happened, and there was no real reason why. You weren't being tested, you weren't being rewarded, you were just *being*. And so was everybody and everything else, including tumors and bad hearts: all just being.

She'd found the simplicity of this strangely comforting, and she'd made her own little religion of it.

Then Joe Flicker enters her life, offering, as his last name suggests, a flicker of love and hope — the dream of an existence beyond that of simply being. When Phoebe's brutal, vindictive husband interrupts their lovemaking, Phoebe fights back and then accidentally causes his death. Joe, a wounded fugitive, ventures up the mountain overlooking Everville and finds a crack in the world, escaping into the fabled Metacosm, where he explores the wonders of Quiddity. He eats of the dream-sea's fishes, drinks of its water, and finally sets sail on a harrowing voyage with a peculiar Noah and a crew of zombie slaves. His fear brings revelation:

It was a long time since he'd begun a sentence with *Our Father*, but the words came back readily enough, and their familiarity was comforting. Perhaps, he thought, there was even a remote chance that the words were being heard. That notion — which would have seemed naive the day before — did not seem so idiotic now. He'd crossed a threshold into another state of being; a state that was just like another room in a house the size of the cosmos: literally a step away. If there was one such door to be entered, why not many? And why should one not be a door that led into Heaven?

All his adult life, he'd asked why. Why God? Why meaning? Why love? Now he realized his error. The question was not *why*, it was *why not*?

Why not? The question resounds throughout *Everville*. Metaphysical issues have always haunted Clive Barker's fiction, but in *Imajica* (1991) and now *Everville* he confronts them with a courage unprecedented in post-Vietnam horror and fantasy. This is the stuff of C.S. Lewis and Charles Williams — though by no means as orthodox, and exercised without the polemics of William Peter Blatty or Russell Kirk. It is the fruition of Barker's longtime enthusiasm for William Blake: a visionary, illuminated fiction for the Millennium.

Why not? Joe Flicker's perilous voyage is paralleled in the night journeys of the novel's other lead characters, but its imagery is the most explicit. He sails

by Douglas E. Winter

Thoreau's "private sea" — "the Atlantic and the Pacific of one's being alone" — without knowing, but in time learning, that its waters are public, the realm of humanity's relentless wishing, hoping, dreaming.

The unlikely — and unwilling — heroine of the epic is Tesla Bombeck, the failed screenwriter of *The Great and Secret Show* who, touched by the Nuncio, rose like any good messiah from the dead but who does not know, or care, why. Her allies are Nathan Grillo, the putative lead of *The Great and Secret Show,* who now slumps, withered and dying, before a computer database devoted to the weird; and demon-haunted New York private eye Harry D'Amour.

Tesla is cynical, hardbitten and tenacious — a pistolpacking skeptic with a taste for lost causes. The personality of Raul, the ape evolved to a man through the workings of the Nuncio, still lives inside her, wondering: "*Would it be so bad . . . To have a messiah . . .*" "You know," Tesla says. "I have a very good soul in my head. . . . The pity of it is, it isn't mine." She refuses to believe in saviours or love or hope or inevitability, and resolutely denies the power that has found her. Her definition of life? "One big fucking joke." Over the past five years she has traveled by motorcycle across the mainland states, finding nothing but a bitter truth: "All I know is, you're alone in the end. Always." Now the onetime screenwriter finds herself with nothing but beginnings — "always setting off on an unknown highway or opening a conversation with a stranger — and never getting to the second act. If the painful farce of her life to date was going to have any resolution, then she was going to have to move the story on."

Nathan Grillo has encamped in Omaha, the Crossroads of America, to become a clearinghouse for information about the events in Palomo Grove and, soon enough, baffling events of all kinds — "putting the pieces together, one by one, until he had the whole story." Like Tesla, he searches for connections, explanations, somewhere in the chaotic rumourmill of modern America. His ever-expanding database, an electronic bulletin board called the Reef, fills a network of computers.

Faced with nationwide sightings of martyred John Wesley Fletcher — a nascent Elvis or Bigfoot — Grillo muses: "I used to think it mattered whether or not things were real. I'm not so sure anymore. . . . Maybe the messiahs we *imagine* are more important than the real thing." In his forty-third year, he has succumbed to multiple sclerosis: "a mystery as profound as anything in the Reef, and a good deal more palpable." Death is coming for him, and soon.

Harry D'Amour, a cameo player in *The Great and Secret Show,* moves to center stage in *Everville.* (He also features in the Barker short stories "The Last Illusion" and "Lost Souls," and the forthcoming motion picture *Lord of Illusions.*) As always, the Devil is on D'Amour's mind. The devout detective is Barker's Jacob, wrestling not with flesh and blood, but with

spiritual wickedness in high places — demons, within and without. "The demons find you, because you need them," a psychic tells D'Amour. "You need them for the world to make sense to you."

Through D'Amour, Barker dispenses with the essential argument of Blatty's *The Exorcist* (1971): that the existence of demons confirms the existence of angels — that, if there is a Devil, there must be a God: "It's one of those useless subjects." But D'Amour embraces Blatty's view of the singleminded purpose of spiritual evil: his demons, like those that torment Father Damien Karras, are relentlessly excremental "because that's what they want the world to be: Shit." They would make us despair of our humanity, of the possibility that the human condition is joyful — and possibly divine. Sadly, no one is willing to listen to such thoughts — just as many are unwilling to listen to the likes of Clive Barker:

At the beginning of his career — when his investigations as a private detective had first led him into the company of the inhuman — he had entertained the delusion that he might with time help turn the tide against these forces by alerting the populace to their presence. He soon learned his error. People didn't want to know. They had drawn the parameters of belief so as to exclude such horrors, and would not, *could* not, tolerate or comprehend anybody who sought to move the fences.

Death, demons, dismay: Barker's haunted investigators move through a world of sorrows — not the cotton candy realm of generic horror fiction, where order can and will be restored, but the shrouded uncertainty that we know as life. We should know by now that answers to the real questions are never easy, but we choose too often to embrace the bright light of escape — sunshine and television and the fiction of happy endings. As a mysterious wise man (who looks suspiciously like Jesus) tells Tesla: "You wanted connections, and they're there to be found. But you have to look in the terrible places, Tesla. The places where death comes to take love away, where we lose each other and lose ourselves; that's where the connections begin. It takes a brave soul to look there and not despair."

As Tesla, Grillo, and D'Amour search out those terrible places, Phoebe Cobb pursues her lost love, Joe Flicker, through the phantasmagoria of the Metacosm, experiencing its wild wonders: the ceaseless gaze of the golden-eyed fish known as the Zehrapushu; a man of dust and rock called King Texas; the miraculous b'Kether Sabbat, an inverted, populated pyramid that would dwarf Manhattan; and the curious city of Liverpool, constructed by the dreaming of an ancient crone named Maeve O'Connell. For Maeve, the eternal orphan and outcast, lives on; and inevitably, she must return to Everville — for something is summoning her home.

The end times are approaching. "The fact was,

14   **SHADOWINGS**

something would happen. If not tonight, tomorrow night. If not tomorrow night, the night after. The world was losing its wits."

There is danger at large, and it is not mere demons: "Demons were simple. They believed in prayer and the potency of holy water. Thus they fled from both. But men — what did men believe?" Like Phoebe before she found love, most men believe only in being — a polite way of saying that they believe only in self, and thus, in time, in nothing. And to believe in nothing is to give that most horrible of things — nothing — life.

From beyond Quiddity comes the living nothing called the Iad Uroboros — a tsunami of fleas and mountains, mountains and fleas — "Not *it*. Them. It's a nation. A people. Not remotely like us, but a people nevertheless, who've always harbored a hunger to be in your world." When Flicker asks why, the reply is simple: "Does appetite need reasons?"

The Iad swarms over the Metacosm and into our world, undoing everything in its path. For D'Amour, the Iad and the Anti-Christ are the same thing: "It's all the Devil by another name." But the Iad defies such simplistic notions as good and evil. Perhaps we dreamed it into being; perhaps it is the darkness in the collective soul of our species: "Uroboros, the self-devouring serpent, encircling the earth while it ate its own tail. An image of power as a self-sufficient engine: implacable, incomprehensible, inviolate." The Iad is the ultimate cancer, the AIDS of the human spirit: "What she saw put her in mind of a disease — a terrible, implacable, devouring disease. It had no face. It had no malice. It had no guilt. Perhaps it didn't even have a mind. It came because it could; because nothing stopped it."

While a traditional horror or fantasy novel would concern itself with the answer to this juggernaut — how it might be stopped, put back in the box — *Everville* is concerned with a much greater, more vital mystery: The mystery of life in its shadow.

The annual festival begins with a pageant, telling the story — that shameless fable — of the founding of Everville. It ends in chaos — but a gloriously inventive, life-affirming chaos — as countless other stories, the secret histories and the secret fantasies, are told. Buddenbaum's patient puppetry has engineered a gateway to The Art. The long-buried medallion shining bright at the crossroads has accrued the power to change the world; but The Art is not his to possess. It is Tesla who falls into its everlasting embrace and who, at the moment of death, sees the simple truth, buried for so long in our consciousness:

And there it was, shining in the dirt: the cross of crosses, the sign of signs. In the long, slow moments of her dying fall, she remembered with a kind of yearning how she'd solved the puzzles of that cross; seen the

four journeys that were etched upon it. One to the dream world, one to the real; one to the bestial, one to the divine. And there at the heart of these journeys — where they crossed, where they divided, where they finished and began — the human mystery. It was not about flesh, that mystery: It was not about hanging broken from a cross or the triumph of the spirit over suffering. It was about the living dream of mind, that made body and spirit and all they took joy in.

Buddenbaum's invocation: "*Dreams are doorways. . . . If we but have the courage to step over the threshold,*" proves true. "Maybe the door's *supposed* to be open," D'Amour is told. "Maybe we have to start looking at what's in our dreams, only with our eyes open."

Dreams are the signs that the promise of The Art — the promise of that higher being, or higher state of being — was not a hollow promise; that the human mind could know the past, present, and future as one eternal moment.

"Every art but one was a game of delusions." That art — The Art — is the living dream of mind: the imagination, always creating, showing, telling. For there is indeed one True Religion: "It's the stories that matter, however they're told. . . . And every life, however short, however meaningless it seems, is a leaf . . . on the story tree."

Everville is a celebration of story — and of life in the constant shadow of death (and the darker shadow beyond). It speaks to the only kind of fantasy that matters: the fantasies of reality, the stories whose telling informs and uplifts the human condition.

It is also a book of beginnings, from a writer who, like his own Tesla Bombeck, is a connoisseur of stories and journeys, always beginning and rarely ending. (Tesla's need to "move the story on" is wryly self-conscious.) While *The Great and Secret Show* walked paths familiar to readers of horror and fantasy, *Everville* wanders deeper into the dark forest. It may be read on its own, though clearly the books are best read in sequence.

Working with unbridled enthusiasm and ambition, Barker has created a unique middle book that is much more than a bridge to some grand finale, spinning out new, and sometimes supervening, stories while embellishing not so much the action but the ideas of the first book. The narrative veers, circles, collapses, moving forward less through plot than the insistence of its imagery.

The casual reader may find the sheer profusion of characters, plots and images overwhelming — or hypnotic, as Barker's psychotropic prose engages and eludes, focuses and blurs, offers illusions and delusions, truths and lies. With its epic sprawl and constant spiraling, *Everville* is not for the lazy, but it is profoundly rewarding — and, in its closing pages, deeply moving.

BRIEFLY NOTED

The Informers by Bret Easton Ellis (Knopf, 226 pp., $22.00).

The master of the mock savage follows his controversial *American Psycho* with a deceptively powerful — and horrific — excursion into the Los Angeles of the eighties. This "novel" — actually a series of disjointed story/chapters that progress with the nightmarish insistence of J.G. Ballard's *The Atrocity Exhi-*bition (1969) — evolves (a bit too slowly) from shallow sociodrama into a disturbing glimpse into the darkness that hides in bright sunshine.

Red London by Stewart Home (AK Press, 158 pp., £5.95, $12.95); *No Pity* by Stewart Home (AK Press, 143 pp., £5.95, $12.95).

Stewart Home is the kind of writer whose fiction invariably is labelled "cult," if not "trash" — in part because most reviewers lack the interest or courage to accept that this kind of writing exists, and in part because it is impossible to imagine these words being read by a mass audience. Home tosses off effusively anarchic stories that crawl out of a splatter/sperm/shit-soaked squalor into bright moments of genuine wit. At his best, he reads like a pulp fiction version of Dennis Cooper, mingling violence with rampant (and, for the most part, homoerotic) sexuality — all told with the mantralike obsessiveness of pornography ("liquid genetics" and "rim of dark pleasures" being two of Home's favored phrases). *Red London*, a novel of skinhead sadism, is the better of the two books; *No Pity*, which collects stories written from 1986 to 1993, includes both outright embarrassments and strident successes.

American Tabloid by James Ellroy (Knopf, 576 pp., $25.00).

Ellroy's take on the macho hijinks preceding the assassination of John F. Kennedy re-enacts some seedy moments of the late fifties/early sixties Americana through the eyes of three law-enforcement lowlifes.

Although exceptional at times — particularly in its damn-the-torpedoes action sequences — *American Tabloid* is overdone and overlong. Like most Kennedy conspiracy whodunits (whether published as fiction or "fact"), the novel requires a suspension of disbelief that is not justified by the facts, and a conviction that the Kennedy brothers were naive and incapable men. Camelot was a myth, but in hammering this truth home, *American Tabloid* loses its own sense of reality. An entertaining but ultimately disappointing novel from a great writer. Ω

THE WEREWOLF
by Tanith Lee

illustrated by Stephen E. Fabian

The house overhung a corner of the heath, where the columns of the trees climbed up into the lanes and streets above. The building was like an outpost, for no other houses were on the road for half a mile, and the streetlights were few. An occasional car passed by on its speeding way to somewhere else. The house was sometimes noted, for it was Gothic in design and had a high tower, turrets, and tall windows fruited with coloured glass. No one approached, and certainly no one was near enough, on nights of the full moon, to catch the screams within the house of the werewolf, as he was translated into his bestial shape.

It was a hot summer, and at night a low mist lay along the earth. The tree tops were clear, and high above the house stood the smudged white plate of the moon. About eleven, something dark might be seen slinking grotesquely down the outer stairway of the house, between the shrubs.

This was the manner in which the werewolf descended to the heath. The heath was his hunting ground. But not always did he locate prey there, and then not always human — the kind for which he lusted. It was the moonlight night between the trees which drew him primarily, perhaps more than the severe hunger for blood. In the form of such a thing as he became, he could not stay inside the walls of a house, even the Gothic house on the slope.

The heath by night was like a frame of the past. The werewolf's beast eyes did not see the litter of chocolate wrappers, cans, cigarettes and condoms. The beast existed in a world of primal timelessness. The beast did not think, or have a need to.

Now and then, the remains of the werewolf's feasts had been uncovered, and had given rise to an on-going legend of unsolved murder cases, loosely known by the title of The Heath Hacker.

Though unnatural they were not rated as *super*natural, and though once or twice over the years police had called at the isolated house, its occupant had never been under suspicion.

He was a small, mild, fussy man of late middle age, the antithesis of anything dramatic, and obviously without the physical strength the murders had required.

Generally bodies were not found, the very little that had been left of them trampled or buried in leaf mould, under boulders, or rolled into deep bushes. Dogs too were inclined to avoid these kills. They ran to their owners with their tails down and their eyes full of green horror.

The dogs knew what the travellers and the questing police did not.

"There is a werewolf on the heath," said Constant to Vivienne.

"What rubbish," said Vivienne, a slender white girl of twenty with maroon hair. And, after a pause, "Why do you say such things?"

"Because of the bones. Look," and bending gracefully he picked up a long stick of creamy grey. "A tibia. And over there another. The third evidence I've seen this afternoon."

"Even if it is a bone," said Vivienne, swinging her heavy rufous hair, "it's animal. Picked clean. A fox, maybe."

"Not of a fox or by a fox. I've noticed, none of these bones, therefore none of the carcasses, were dragged into a lair. Normally you'd expect animals to polish off the left-overs whoever caused them, but these they've left strictly alone."

"Terrified by the taint of wolf."

"Not wolf. *Were*wolf. You mustn't confuse the two."

"But I thought," said Vivienne, "that a werewolf was someone who turned into a wolf."

"In a way," said Constant, elusively. He infuriated her subtly, which was the other reason, aside from his handsome foreignness, which attracted Vivienne to him.

"Well," she said, "we're quite safe by daylight, aren't we? It's only at night that werewolves walk, or stalk, or whatever they do."

"The three nights of the full moon. The full moon affects all of us to some extent. It moves the tides of the sea, and the tides of the water which makes up so much of the human composition. How could we not be affected? But to a werewolf the tidal urge draws up its inner nature."

They crossed one of the many tracks of the woodland, and came out in a great meadow lit by flowers and sun.

"What a lovely summer," said Vivienne. "And no people."

"This is the advantage of a week day," said Constant. "At night, of course, people do come here."

"For illicit sex," said Vivienne, primly, having made love with Constant not two hours before.

"And other darker things," said Constant, looking about.

"Murder and evil," said Vivienne.

"You're right," said Constant, "to separate the two concepts. Evil is by itself."

"And the werewolf hunts here," said Vivienne, "over the moonlit grass, chasing the sly rapists and skulking muggers."

"Of course."

"You really believe what you say," accused Vivienne.

They left the meadow and were under the trees again. "This is a fearful place," said Constant, "a sink of ancient crimes. You can only see the yellow flowers and hear the birds singing. At night everything is black and white. The birds hide, the flowers close fast."

"And the werewolf bounds between the trees."

Constant stopped.

Vivienne stopped also and turned to see.

Above the wood the ground ran upwards.

"That's the way on to South Heath Road."

"That house," said Constant.

"Oh that — it's marvellous, isn't it," said Vivienne. "You can see it further up on the heath too, by Walworth Lane. But here's best. I used to come and draw it years ago."

"You were most unwise," said Constant.

"Nonsense," said Vivienne, "there were six or seven of us used to come here in a group. Once we saw the funny man who lived there. He came out and sort of hippity-hopped down that stair to put something out over the garden wall."

"I hope you didn't go to see what it was."

"Joanie did. It was a great mound of awful old curtains. There was a place where things were burnt. He was obviously going to burn them sometime."

"And this man with the curtains," said Constant, "what was he like?"

"About five feet five, slim in a plump, weak sort of way, with a round pudding of a face. He had thin hair and baggy trousers and a cardigan, and he wore slippers."

"What a good memory you have," said Constant slowly.

"I wonder if he still lives there?" pondered Vivienne.

"I should think so."

They were walking up through the wood towards the house. Its wall and flight of steps hung over them through the poles of the trees and the garlands of thick green leaves.

"There's the burning place," said Vivienne. "And look, something's smouldering there now. Naughty, in this heat."

"He would find fire attractive," said Constant, "in his human form. Things that sparkle. Fire, water, jewels."

"Oh yes?"

"One of the oldest ways to hypnotise his kind," said Constant, "a diamond in a bowl of water. Or a ruby under a candle. In the human form only. Once transmogrified, nothing can reach him. He is all beast."

"You think the funny pudding man in slippers is your werewolf?"

"Look at the house," said Constant. "The coloured bright windows, the dark tower."

"Isn't it just too apt?"

"Your reasoning is overly sophisticated," said Constant. "You're dealing here with something very simple, and utterly terrible."

"Brr," said Vivienne. "Can we come back at full moon and see?"

"Tonight is full moon."

"Is it? Well, then. We can lie in wait. Catch him out."

"You don't understand, Vivienne. It's he who would catch you. He would tear you in pieces and devour you."

"Nasty. Then I'd need a silver bullet."

"A silver bullet isn't necessary. Is useless."

"Now you should know," said Vivienne, "you can't kill a werewolf without one."

"It's just a misunderstanding," said Constant. "Usually such executions were carried out by villages in remote places where ammunition was scarce or obsolete. The bullet was made from some holy object melted down, a cross from the church, say, or the replica of a saint. It's the faith of the hunter which assures the shot. Otherwise a werewolf is impossible to kill."

"You mean you must have faith in God."

"Yes, I mean exactly that. Faith in something other than the power of evil."

"I wouldn't be any good then," Vivienne said seriously, after a silence.

"I know. You're too young, Vivienne, and your culture is too young."

"Oh really? Well you're no better."

"My country to yours," he said, "is an old bowed man. And I'm far older, Vivienne, although not in years."

"Then you can kill the werewolf?" she asked, mockingly, as they stood among the trees below the Gothic house, and the birds sang in the sunlight.

"I believe in God," said Constant. "Perhaps I could kill the werewolf. But who said I was going to try?"

By the late afternoon a golden glow filled the heath, and the dark amber of the shadows lay thickly twisted on the ground between the trees. The things of the day fed and played and darted in the last spaces of sunlight. Everything busied itself, for now time was running out.

The westering sun worked tricks too with the windows of the house, finding in them long daggers of rose red and Egyptian green.

The door was of oak, with a black iron knocker of an imp's head. Constant, standing alone in the porch, considered the knocker, and then used it decisively.

There was an extended interval between the knock and any sound inside the house, but Constant did not knock again. He knew the house's inhabitant was obedient and law-abiding, and would come to answer the summons. Presently there was a faint shuffling from beyond the door. It opened.

"Good afternoon," said Constant.

by Tanith Lee

"Yes?" asked the inhabitant of the house. He was the height Vivienne had described and had to look up half a foot into Constant's face. Though slim, his body was composed of curves, and a little round tummy pushed at his poplin shirt and fawn trousers. His head was also round, and in the round countenance two fish-pale eyes gazed, not unfriendly, into Constant's own. It was a mild creature, shy but trusting. "How can I help you?"

"It was your wonderful house," said Constant.

"My house."

"I was wondering if you would object if I took some photographs? Only for my own personal record. I am intrigued by architecture."

Constant put out his left hand and readjusted the camera case he was holding. Something glittered. The man's eyes shifted and came to rest there. As Constant put down his hand again, the man's eyes followed it avidly.

"No, no objection, of course. Please feel free."

Constant thanked the obliging householder, who stood and watched him as he went back down the steps, and retreated a little way along the slope. Here he removed from the camera case an impressive looking Nikon, set it up on a monopod, and began apparently to frame a shot.

After Constant had taken two or three photographs of the façade of the house, the man went back inside. Maybe he would watch from windows, between the screens of coloured glass.

Constant went about the building slowly, sometimes ascending the slope, now and then kneeling in the grass.

On the smallest finger of his left hand the diamond flashed in his father's ring, a piece of jewelry which Constant did not normally wear.

After perhaps fifteen minutes, the front door of the house reopened. The man came out and stood watching Constant take a long angled shot of the tower.

"Have you finished? I didn't want to disturb you. I wondered if you'd care for a cup of tea."

English tea, probably from tea-bags, and with milk, had never appealed to Constant, but now he nodded enthusiastically. He returned to the house, having closed up the camera in its case and telescoped the monopod.

"That's very kind of you."

"I thought you might like to see something of the inside as well."

"I would," Constant said.

From a black and white checkerboard floor a stair curved up, a carved indulgence, and highly polished — someone must come in, presumably in the mornings or early afternoons, leaving, in winter, long before it got dark. Above the stair a huge window of crimson lilies and Nile water showered the hall, and their skins, with tinted lights like some beautiful disease.

His host led Constant into a drawing-room. There were two more windows, each with an ornate fe-male figure, perhaps Muses, for they were classically adorned, and with Burne-Jones hair, rather like Vivienne's in colour. Otherwise the room was stuffed full of elderly furniture, bulging couches and chairs and a plethora of small tables. The ceiling was a carousel of plaster shapes, fruits and vines, echoed in a gilt mirror above the fireplace. Despite the attentions of the help, there was an aura of dust, weightless as the deepening sunlight.

They sat down, and the man poured out the tea in a careful, feminine way. Constant took his without milk, and was pleased to note the werewolf had used leaves.

"I hope you got the pictures you wanted."

"I hope so too; the light's a little undependable at this time."

"Yes, the evening draws on. I like this hour of day. I find it restful." Constant smiled politely and raised his cup. "Forgive my saying so, but I'm quite fascinated by your ring."

"A family heirloom," said Constant, "it belonged to my father. Would you like to see it more closely?" He slipped off the ring and handed it to the little man in the poplin shirt. Who grasped it, *absorbed* it, and taking it over to the light, *played* with it, turning it this way and that, over and over, to make it glitter.

Constant surreptitiously timed him. It was a full six minutes before the werewolf turned and said, regretfully, "An excellent stone. I confess I'm drawn to such things — as you are to houses. I have a small collection, some rubies, a diamond."

Constant retrieved the ring from reluctant fingers, and got up. "Thank you for the tea."

"But stay a little longer," said the werewolf, looking at him with luminous lonely eyes. "I can show you over the house."

"That's remarkably kind of you, but unfortunately I have to be in Walworth by seven."

"Meeting a young lady perhaps," said the werewolf, playfully.

"No, actually. Then again I sometimes walk the heath at dusk, the quietest time, I find. Perhaps I could call on you again."

The eyes of the werewolf gave off a peculiar stony flash. Had no one ever noticed this before, police questioning after murders, shopkeepers, the weekly help? It was the beast part of the subconscious brain incoherently communicating. For there were nights like tonight when the full moon rose at dusk. Perhaps it would be possible to add this diamond to the collection? Off what bitten and ravaged fingers, ears and throats had the other trophies come?

"Of course, feel free to knock. I may not answer unless I can be sure it's you. I'm sensibly rather nervous of callers after dark."

He took Constant back across the checkered floor where the colours of the window had deepened to blood and chartreuse.

They parted at the door with expressions of mutual friendliness, having not exchanged their names.

Outside on the mellow heath, Constant studied his watch. Two hours before dark.

The light perished in stages. Birds quartered the sky, sank and vanished into the high coronas of the trees. A deft rustling in the undergrowth signalled the passaging of other daylight entities to their holes and burrows. A few people came walking along Walworth Lane, heading out of the woodland towards the traffic lights and busy high street of Walworth one mile off along the road.

Constant sat on a fallen tree beside the Lane. Behind him, still partly concealed in bushes, was his motorbike. As the flame began to leave the sky, he drew the bike out and walked it up the steep incline. He stood among the tree trunks, looking down across the umbra of the heath.

To the naked eye, the towered house a quarter of a mile away was quite visible, small and perfect as a model above the trees. It stood in a bowl of gold, the last traces of the sunset. A pale ghost, caught on the rim of the light, the moon had already risen.

The heat of the sky went to ashes.

Constant set the camera on the monopod, and attached the powerful zoom lens. He set his sights for the outer stairway of the house.

The image leapt towards him. He could see the brickwork on the wall, flower heads on the shrubs. As the afterglow faded the sullen marble stare of the moon took over, a cold blind eye.

He saw now in black and white.

Constant waited.

After ten minutes something dark appeared on the stairway. It might have been anything, perhaps a large dog let out. It passed between the shrubs, and paused, and the moon came over the house, so everything was lit up in a cool white searchlight. The thing on the stairway raised its head. Constant saw it through the lens.

It was black like a ball of shadow. The skull was a little too large for the body so that in form it was like a boar, heavy-headed, powerful in the shoulder. The black head was something like a wolf's, with a great ruff of black hair. The mouth came open and all the teeth appeared in the muzzle, not the teeth of a wolf but each pointed, the canines enormous, and between them the movement of a thick black tongue.

Constant touched the button of the camera, and the head swung. Across a quarter mile of dusk and sudden silence, the eyes of the thing on the stair met Constant's eye within the lens. The eyes were red even in moonlight, with a sheen like oil. They held a thousand years of awareness but not a single thought. They were not the eyes of a wolf, but of some creature older and unremittingly terrible, inimical to yet entirely belonging with man. The eyes of a monster not a beast.

Constant depressed the button of the camera.

The tiny click echoed sheer and sharp across the sloping valley. It was the only sound.

The werewolf heard.

Its muzzle wrinkled and its soulless eyes became two pits of blood. Constant heaved the camera free and thrust it and the lens into their case, folded up the monopod, and slung them on the bike.

Mounting the bike, he gunned the engine into life.

In his vision was the image of the werewolf pouring suddenly over down the stair like a bolt of black liquid.

The motorbike cannoned into motion. It swerved down the hill between the trees and skated out on to the road. Bearing left, it burst forward and the pillars of the trees became a blur. Ground erupted beneath the wheels and was gone.

The bike could outrace death. As he rode between the shadows, Constant murmured a few words of thanks, in Latin.

He was almost off the Lane when he made out the two figures walking towards him along the edge of the road.

Constant jammed the bike to a standstill.

He waved at them, the two young men in denims and T shirts, walking hand in hand until they saw him coming, not pleased to encounter him.

"Don't go on to the heath."

"What's he say?" one of them asked the other.

"A member of the moral majority," said this other, and grinned.

"There is a wild animal loose," said Constant, "there is danger."

"He's nuts," said the first boy.

"Piss off," said the second boy to Constant.

They shrugged him away and strolled on along the Lane, the black shade of the trees coming down to smother them. The low mist was forming in veils.

Constant shouted after them once. It was useless. What could he tell them they would believe? They would have to take their chances along with the other creatures of the night. Perhaps something might distract the werewolf, it might take a different path. It could not have seen the camera, though it had looked straight at it, and the sound of the button might have been anything. To the thing it was, a camera anyway was senseless.

Constant raced the motorbike on and came to the lights, the intersection, the brink of the high street, its shops, and cars in flight. Only there, hesitating a moment, did he seem to hear a distant noise, far back among the trees. It might have been a squeal of brakes, the call of a night bird, or a human cry, stripped of all meaning but fear.

"What have you been doing all afternoon?" asked Vivienne.

"Developing some film."

"Let me see."

"No, there's nothing that would interest you," said Constant.

"You've been back to that house," said Vivienne, shaking her sea green beads. "What did you find?"

"Which house?" said Constant.

"Did you know, there's been another murder on the heath. Not The Hacker. Did you read about it?"

"I never read newspapers," said Constant.

"It was very gory," said Vivienne. "But a jealous lover, they think. The man was gay. Torn in pieces."

"Just one," said Constant.

The other must have run, perhaps been felled in another place, more thoroughly devoured, or hidden.

"The heath is horrible," said Vivienne petulantly.

"I would advise you then to avoid it," said Constant. "For now."

The black iron imp knocked against the oak door with especial force, and birds in the neighbouring trees took fright.

Constant attended on the knock as he had done before. And after some while, as before, the door was dutifully opened.

Late afternoon light fell slanting on the curves of the gentle face, the innocent belly. This time the shirt was of grey rayon.

"Good afternoon," said Constant. "Do you remember? I took some photographs of your house and you were kind enough to give me tea."

"Ah, yes," the man said. "I do indeed remember."

"I thought," said Constant, "you might care to see the pictures." With his diamonded left hand he tapped a folder.

"Oh yes, oh yes indeed."

The door was opened wide, and Constant admitted.

Familiar, rose and green fell from the window. In the drawing-room the two Muses were at their stations. A faint cobweb floated high up in the plaster carousel of the ceiling. Peach-coloured, the light leaned on the mirror above the fireplace.

The sat down. One by one, Constant handed the householder his views of the house. Of the tall facade, the windows and the steps, the angled tower.

"These are really quite splendid," said the man, admiringly. "A true professional job. The hour is rather later today; can I offer you a sherry?"

Constant, who did not like sherry, professed pleasure.

The man brought two small glasses of gold and set them on the table where the pictures lay.

"There's one more I should like to show you," Constant said. "It was taken from across the heath, and the sun had gone down. Infra-red film. The quality is rather grainy, I'm afraid."

The little man took the photograph and stared at it. He stared a long time.

"But what is this?"

"A view of the outer stairway."

"Yes, I see — but —"

"You notice something on the steps," said Constant.

"Surely," said the werewolf, "only a strange shadow."

"Do shadows have eyes?"

The man laughed uneasily. He took a sip of his sherry. "What can it be, I wonder?"

"Perhaps you own a dog?" said Constant, helpfully.

The man blinked. "No. No dog. I've never been able to get on with animals."

"I wonder what it is, then," said Constant. "It looks like an animal, doesn't it?"

"Yes . . . very like one. How odd." The windows were clouding, the peach ray was gone from the mirror. "Possibly, some light . . ." The man went to a series of lamps and switched them on one by one. The room lit up and the windows turned blue. "Once the sun goes down," said the werewolf, "this house grows very dark."

"The moon was shining when I took the photograph," said Constant. "A full moon, very bright."

The werewolf lifted up the photograph a second time and peered at it shortsightedly. "Probably I should fetch my glasses. I can't make it out at all. What do *you* think it is?"

"Oh," said Constant, "*I* think it's a photograph of you."

"Of me?" The werewolf raised his head.

All at once there was a suggestion of heaviness to his skull and shoulders, something ape-like, and the eyes were flat and thoughtless, some instinct struggling to pierce to their surface. Failing.

"If I had come back last week," said Constant, "there would have been no doubt. But of course the nights of the full moon are over until next month, aren't they?"

"But this isn't human," said the man resentfully.

"Not human? Would you say it was a wolf?"

"Maybe," said the man, cautiously, almost bashfully.

"No, it isn't a wolf," said Constant. "That is a misnomer. The wolf is a clean animal whose eyes are like a man's. What eyes does this thing have? Like the Devil. Perhaps the superstitions of wolves, the lies, what men fear when they hear the cry of a wolf: That. But this is a beast from the swamp at the bottom of man's soul. A beast from the id. Solely man's. Completely *human.*"

Constant got up and drew something else out of the folder. He unwrapped it quickly. It was a steak knife from Selfridges.

"No," said the man, moving backwards, judging his route, through long proximity, between the bulky furniture.

"There is another way, of course, to see the change," said Constant. He ran forward and stuck the knife into the werewolf's round belly, until only the handle protruded.

The werewolf gave a scream and fell on to the floor. His blood splashed round him. He tried to pull out the knife and did not have the strength.

Constant watched.

Outside was the shadow of a moonless dusk, but in the room the lamps fully illuminated the death-throes. Then they illuminated the long after-spasms as the body altered, the clothes splitting and the skin heaving, the great muscles pumping up and the hair swarming out like a dark forest. Halfway through, the transmogrification ceased, unable to sustain itself without life. What was left on the carpet was a thing one third a man and two thirds some sort of beast, unlike anything yet reminiscent of a wolf. From the guts of this Constant plucked his knife, wrapped it, and replaced it with the photographs in his folder. What the police would say when they were called by the help was a matter for conjecture.

Constant left the lights burning, and went out through the hall. The window cast on him a last meteor shower. The rest of the house hung dark and silent in a void. He closed the door with care, and walked away over the heath in the night. Ω

BAD WHEELS
by John Accursi
illustrated by George Barr

One minute till midnight.

The only sound in the garage was the low buzzing of a digital clock; the only light came from the glowing red 11:59 that shone on its display. A thin wire connected the alarm clock to a small dust-covered cassette player, and both of the devices sat on an ancient black paint-spotted sawhorse that had been moved to the center of the garage. Next to the car.

The temperature outside had climbed to a hundred and five degrees before night had mercifully fallen and pressed all that heat into the ground. Now a dry wind was pulling the warmth back up again, stirring it up and letting it just hover over the empty streets. The black-as-night 1955 Corvette sat in the sweltering darkness of the garage, shining and untouched by dust, though every bench, chair, and discarded tool in the garage was blanketed with it. When the time on the clock changed, the Corvette's black-tinted windshield reflected the digits as clearly and sharply as a mirror.

Midnight.

The instant the display showed 12:00 there was a high-pitched, strained whining from the old cassette deck as its dust-clogged motor slowly came to life. The message on the tape began to sputter through the player's single speaker.

Aglon . . . Tetragram . . . Vaycheon . . . Stimulamathon . . . Erohares . . . Retragsammathon . . . Clyoran . . . Icion . . .

The wind outside began to blow dead leaves and bits of tree branches against the door of the garage. The heat grew worse. The garage door began to rock back and forth within its frame, as though something was trying to pry it open. The darkness in the garage seemed to constrict around the Corvette.

Esition . . . Existien . . . Eryona . . . Onera . . .

The Corvette began to shake. Its wheels squeaked faintly as they vibrated against the cement floor. The garage filled with an odor as though the very air were burning, and the layers of dust that covered everything suddenly turned to dark, thick ash.

‡ ‡ ‡

Erasyn . . . Moyn . . . Meffias . . . Soter . . . Sabaoth!

The tape recorder clicked itself off just as an explosion of orange light flooded the garage, and there was a flicker of movement behind the Corvette's tinted windshield.

The demon's name was Adrammelech, and it had materialized in the driver's seat, with four spider-like arms already wrapped around the steering wheel. This time it had managed not to scorch the leather seat, and it was very pleased about that. It changed one of its arms into something nearly human in order to turn the key in the ignition.

Adrammelech looked over at the clock on the sawhorse and saw that it was not yet even a minute past midnight. The Corvette started as always on the first turn of the key, and the demon opened the garage door and backed the black machine out onto the empty street, pointing it toward the familiar glitter of the Los Angeles skyline, several miles away. The Corvette's gold-framed license plate read: **DEMON 1**.

The demon made 0 to 60 in just over three seconds.

The driver of the beige Volkswagen SuperBeetle glanced up into the rear-view mirror and saw the headlights wink on about a mile behind him. It had been ten minutes since the last car had passed him, and he had been enjoying having the dark swath of highway all to himself. The steady humming of the Beetle's engine and the sensation of the freeway rushing by underneath the car were almost hypnotically soothing. And now this bastard behind him with his brights on was going to ruin everything.

The driver slowed down to let the other car pass him more quickly, so that he'd have the road to himself again. As he decelerated, the headlights began to gain on him rapidly.

Too rapidly.

The headlights had been in the fast lane, to the left of the Beetle, but now they weaved into the number two lane, only a hundred yards away and still picking up speed.

"What the Hell?" the driver asked the rearview mirror. He swung the Beetle into the number three lane, hoping the driver of the other car would leave him alone and just pass him. Fifty yards behind him, the headlights swung into the lane with him. The glow of headlights in the rearview mirror was blinding.

The driver of the Beetle panicked and began to accelerate, but the headlights did not fall any farther behind. He became aware of the roar of the other car's motor as it barreled down on him.

When the black machine was five yards behind it the Beetle skidded onto the shoulder at seventy miles an hour. The car ran off the far side of the shoulder and onto rough dirt, just as the side of the highway gave way to an underpass for one of the surface streets. He lost control of the steering as one of the front wheels lurched over a large rock and the car tore through a chain-link fence. The Beetle left the road entirely and was in free fall for about thirty feet before its front end flattened against the ground in an explosion of tearing metal and shattering glass. Flames and smoke erupted out of the engine and gas tank in waves.

The demon laughed so uncontrollably that it turned into a glob of translucent jelly and had to ooze back up to the seat to see through the windshield. It accelerated to ninety miles an hour, still laughing horribly, and headed for the off ramp just over a mile ahead.

Adrammelech took the sharp turn onto Wilshire Boulevard much too quickly and had to touch the brakes to keep from losing control. Having to touch the brakes always made the demon fume.

Too angry to drive, it dissolved the insect body and simply *possessed* the Corvette. For some reason the car always performed better under simple demonic possession; but, for the demon, there was no longer any real challenge involved. So, after about three blocks, Adrammelech re-materialized as a gigantic, brown, thorn-covered squid and took manual control of the Corvette once again.

He roared up and down rows of narrow residential streets at close to fifty miles an hour, just *waiting* for someone to step out from behind a bush and off the curb. In a series of beautiful, quick, sharp turns the demon rolled up onto the sidewalk in an attempt to catch a cat asleep on one of the freshly-cut lawns. At the last minute the cat shot off into the bushes and avoided destruction, and the demon swung the Corvette off the curb and back onto the asphalt. Just in time to see a wrong-way driver turn onto the narrow one-way street.

Because of his rapid residential zig-zagging, the demon happened to be going the right way up the street, so the driver of the oncoming car was obviously very drunk or very lost. Adrammelech accelerated.

The gap between the two cars narrowed quickly — it was as though the other car was accelerating as well. The Corvette raced through an intersection and was out of the residential area — the street widened but remained one-way, and the speedometer needle in the Corvette climbed to sixty-five miles an hour. The other car was now definitely accelerating.

by John Accursi

Adrammelech laughed his horrible laugh. In just a few seconds the driver of the approaching car would be dead, pressed into nothingness in the interior of his own machine.

The Corvette was twenty yards from the wrong-way driver when the demon could distinguish the make of the car — a blood-red '32 Ford three-window coupe, with a brightly polished full-race engine exposed. The windows were heavily tinted so the car's driver could not be seen. The Ford's front license plate frame said **DAMNATION IS THE ONLY WAY** in two-inch-high sparkling red letters, punctuated with an inverted pitchfork instead of an exclamation point. The plate itself read: **THE WORM**.

Both cars swerved to opposite sides of the road, tires shrieking across the asphalt, spraying street-gravel and sending up clouds of white smoke. The black Corvette and the red Ford slid to a stop at exactly the same moment.

Adrammelech elongated his neck and craned it over the back of the seat, watching the Ford and waiting to see if it was going to take off again. The Corvette's engine was humming almost inaudibly, so the demon could hear the loud, thunder-like revving of the other car. Exhaust fumes were jetting out of the Ford's tail pipe, dissipating the last traces of tire-smoke from around the car's wheels. The front wheels turned and the car began to pull around slowly, behind the Corvette.

A fat man on a Harley-Davidson drove through the intersection, slowing down to look at the two stopped cars, then speeding up again, uninterested. The motorcycle disappeared as it took a turn back toward the residential area, and once again the demons were alone on the street.

Now the Ford had pulled up right beside the Corvette. Its immense engine roared. The tinted window on the Ford's passenger side rolled down just a crack and Mötley Crüe's *Shout at the Devil* exploded out of high-powered speakers, pouring out into the empty street.

The pilot of the red coupe revved the engine in a slow succession of long powerful counts — ooooone. . . . twoooooo. . . .

On the third rev the rear tires on both cars began to smoke against the street as the vehicles rushed forward. The street was barely wide enough to accommodate both of them, and an accidental swerve of mere inches would send one of them into the line of cars parked along the curb.

The Ford began to edge ahead of the Corvette, its engine moaning like a burning soul. Adrammelech could still hear the music coming from the Ford's speakers. The speedometer needle vibrated frantically at seventy miles an hour.

Something small and furry darted out from behind a parked car and the Corvette pressed it into the asphalt before it could make a sound. That put the demon in a better mood and he squeezed a little more

speed out of the car. Now he was even with the Ford.

The two cars came up on Hollywood Boulevard like rockets, and Adrammelech swung right, onto the wider street. The Ford swerved with it, keeping perfect pace. The cars raced side by side, less than a foot apart.

There were still a few other cars on the street, most of them cruising at fifteen miles an hour or less. The silhouettes driving the cars were slumped down low in their seats — arms dangled out of the car windows, trailing lines of thin gray smoke from smoldering cigarette tips.

Mann's Chinese Theater loomed up on the left side of the street, flashing neon reds, yellows, and greens. The Ford drove its immense front bumper into the back of a slow-moving sedan and forced it onto the sidewalk and into the theater ticket booth. Glass shattered everywhere and neon sparked and smoked.

Adrammelech had driven the Corvette onto the sidewalk on his side of the street, destroying two bus stops and sending people diving through the glass of shop windows.

Both cars came back onto the street at Vine, resuming the race, their front ends now utter wrecks.

Adrammelech could feel the Ford beginning to pull away again and realized that if he was going to win the race, he was going to have to do it quickly. The Corvette would not be able to hold its own against the Ford for a long stretch.

The shriek of police sirens filled the night, coming from every direction, and a twisting line of squad cars pulled onto the street less than a mile behind them. The Ford's engine roared. In a moment it would be ahead of him, and he would not be able to find the speed to pull up to it again.

The Corvette turned hard right down a narrow, palm-tree-lined street. It was his only chance — he wasn't fast enough for the Ford, so he was going to have to try to out-drive it. But there could be no mistakes, because if either car had to slow down or stop here, there would be no getting back home.

The Ford followed the Corvette hesitantly, into the series of dark, narrow streets known as the Church District. Over a dozen churches — Lutheran, Presbyterian, Methodist, and *Catholic* — lurked at every corner and around every turn. Driving off the street here, for any reason, was simple suicide.

Gigantic, spired silhouettes loomed up from behind even the tallest trees, some of them like red-brick ghosts from the Middle Ages. Immense stained-glass cathedral windows cast their faint glow through the bare tree branches.

Adrammelech slowed to fifty miles an hour and untinted his windows. He was currently in the shape of a skinless, six-foot-tall sewer rat. He took a turn too sharply and had to touch the brakes, and he grew weak with terror at even the slight slowing of the Corvette. The churches seemed to be leaning toward each other across the street, closing in on him and trying to trap him. He came out of the turn and accelerated again.

The Ford was right by his side, its engine purring almost effortlessly at the low speed. The Ford's windows slowly untinted and an immense glistening cockroach pressed its face against the clear glass for an instant before turning away. Even Adrammelech found the demon gruesome. The cockroach held up a twisted five-fingered hand with one finger turned up. It shook the hand violently at the Corvette, as though to make its point more strongly. Then, to Adrammelech's horror, the Ford began to pull ahead again.

Adrammelech smashed out the side window and leaned a rapidly bloating purple-jelly head out of it. He edged the Corvette over until it was only a few inches away from the Ford. Then the demon leaned out of the car just a little farther and exploded the immense dripping, swelling mass of purple jelly.

Putrescence covered the speeding Ford like a bubbling blanket — foaming over the back window and roof, then dripping down in a thick ooze over the front windshield and side windows. There was no way that the cockroach would be able to see through that mess.

Adrammelech spun the steering wheel hard left and bumped the back of the Ford violently. The red car weaved out of control in front of the Corvette and off to the far side of the street.

The blood-red Ford coupe, covered with purple muck, rumbled to a stop on the front lawn of the largest church in the entire district.

Adrammelech watched the horrible scene in his rearview mirror as he sped off down the street — the Ford imploded like a slowly crushing tin can as the immense church sucked the car in toward it. The cockroach-demon shrieked as it was crushed, and Adrammelech could see its long insect arms reaching out through flattening window frames, scratching at the church lawn and sending up clumps of grass and mud.

Then the lawn opened like a gigantic dark mouth and swallowed the Ford up entirely. The ground closed up again and the only sounds from behind the Corvette were the brushing of dead leaves against the sidewalks and the rattling fronds of the palm trees along the sides of the street.

Adrammelech got out of the Church District quickly and headed for the highway, staying clear of the wailing sirens of searching police cars.

A quarter mile before the on ramp the Corvette passed a fast-moving Harley-Davidson chopper being driven by absolutely nothing. The seat was empty and the handlebars seemed to move at the whim of the air.

Adrammelech leaned out his broken window with the nearest thing to a human face he could come up with in his fatigue, and shouted at the demon on the Harley.

"That's brilliant, you irresponsible idiot! Go ahead and call attention to yourself! Ruin it for all of us, why don't you!"

Adrammelech fumed. He was so upset that he missed his turn and mistakenly drove up the highway off ramp. A lone Mack truck was barreling along in the number two lane.

The demolished Corvette was no longer of any use to the demon — its wheels rattled from striking too many curbs, the engine rasped, the gears clattered and clicked when they were shifted. He would have to find a new vehicle.

He drove the Corvette into the number two lane and accelerated toward the truck. He'd get rid of the car and have some fun at the same time. But then he'd have to be getting back to the garage, to reset the alarm clock and rewind the invocation tape for next time.

The Corvette rammed the truck head on, and the demon sat back in the seat to enjoy the collision. The Corvette flattened under the Mack's first set of wheels and the demon laughed hysterically as he felt the truck tipping over into the beginning of what was sure to be a wonderful flaming crash.

Without warning the demon began to grow cold. It stiffened and shrieked in terror, not knowing what was happening and trying to dissolve itself and get out of the wreckage of the Corvette. It was powerless. The demon felt itself beginning to crystallize. By the time it realized what was destroying it, time had run out.

The truck rolled over and smashed down against the highway, and the demon Adrammelech shattered into a million shards of sparkling black glass.

The truck burned like a furnace because of its cargo. It had rolled twice, finally lying over on its side and blocking all four lanes. The logo on the truck's cargo shell was facing upward, and the tall calligraphy lettering sparkled under the glow of the highway lamps.

SAVE YOUR SOUL . . .
READ THE WORD

By the time the fire department got there, half the Bibles had already burned. The rest were ruined by the water used to put the fire out.

The crushed wreckage of the black Corvette, full of sparkling, almost powdered black glass, was hauled to the nearest junk yard and left there to rust.   Ω

HANGMAN'S HAIKU

A taut rope, creaking
Like the rigging of a ship:
A soul sails Hellward.

— J. D. Hunt

THE NARROW HOUSE

by Robert Sampson

illustration by Jason Van Hollander

Empty, clean, silent, the narrow house sat within a row of similar houses, a book on a shelf of books, a shell in a row of shells, a single grave in a row of graves, lifted up on end, faced in brownish-red brick, waiting for occupancy, silent, clean, empty.

Inside the house, the late afternoon sunshine glowed across a floor of old wide boards. The Emorys sat together on the landing of the second floor, dabbling their feet in the pool of light.

"We won't be in this place all that long," Sam said. He leaned back, as thin and long-legged as a sea-marsh bird. "We'll be out of Charlottesville in three months. Tops, three months."

"You're sure? You're positive?" Janet said, faintly mocking.

"Sure I'm sure. It'll only take three months to coax our Lancaster branch into the world of computers. By the time I get that done, Mr. Hinton will have retired. He's already signed his papers for the first of September. So then, we'll move to Harrisburg and I finally get promoted and you can have the best house in Camp Hill. Or wherever the mansions are."

All this she had heard before. Listening to his confident voice narrate their future, she felt the familiar tensions clamping her mouth and eyes. One day, she thought, the marks would become visible, engraved by his optimism upon her face.

In her small, tight voice, she said: "We won't need to unpack everything."

"Just the coffee pot and some pillows."

"I guess we can make do. It's such a little house, isn't it? So up and down, and narrow."

"The grave," he said in a voice of hollow menace, "is narrower still."

Grinning, he slipped an arm around her shoulders. She rose, allowing his arm to slip away, and crossed the landing into the bright emptiness of their future bedroom. Three tall windows in the rear wall let in a cascade of sunlight. The room smelled strongly of new wallpaper and fresh paint. Janet's shoes clattered on the shining floor.

Sam came to stand beside her. From the windows, they looked down into the narrow back yard, defined by a tall wooden fence. Directly beneath them sprawled fat rose bushes flecked with pink bloom.

"Your uncle must have spent a lot of money fixing this place up," she said. "Why doesn't he rent it?"

"Can't rent it," Sam said. "An old row house practically in the middle of a business district? Who'd want it? I'm surprised Uncle Bill spent a nickel on it. He didn't want the place when great-grandmother willed it to him. Said nobody who lived in it ever had any luck. 'Course that was after Aunt Della died."

"That makes it a great place for us to live in," she said, more sharply than intended.

"Well, it's rent free," he said, using that carefully soothing voice she hated. "Besides, we're not really living here. We're just visiting a couple of months. You have to live in the place before the jinx bites you."

"The people who lived here — did they have bad luck?"

"Oh, Lordy, yes!" he cried dramatically. "Terrible luck. They had to live here in Charlottesville and commute to Lancaster."

She almost smiled but not quite. "Oh, it's all right," she said dispiritedly. "It's a pretty house. I like it."

Sam looked down on her, his mouth hardening at the undisguised regret in her voice. His arm tightened around her shoulders, just briefly, just barely enough to notice. But he said cheerfully enough: "Welcome to Pennsylvania, Land of Free Housing."

She turned away, her mouth a cold thin thread. He was forever joking, forever facetious, forever inconsequential. His humor, so amusing only two years before, now seemed a device to avoid any serious emotion. Marrying him had been an inexplicable blunder. She had been self-deluded, tricked by hope, too much afraid of time as thirty passed and she remained alone. And now this. Humor that did not please her. Affection she could not return. It grew ever harder to return even civility. Whatever the future held, it probably would not include a mansion in Camp Hill.

They moved in five days later. The movers thumped through the house like uncontrollable mechanisms, sweating and loud. Their contemptuous eyes challenged her to ask that bed, bureau, boxes be carried to the second floor.

"Lady wants this upstairs, Donnie."

Donnie, bitterly eying the stairs: "Awwww, crap."

Their feet hammered the shining floors. They jabbered a continual stream of inanities:

"You ever been in a crazy place like this one?"

"It's a tall one."

"Built like a mine shaft."

"Straight up and down."

by Robert Sampson

"It's a wonder."

Finally they were gone. Then for the next two days, it was chaos, a jungle of boxes, clothing, packing paper in crumpled hills, all heaped in rooms too small, lighted by bulbs the size of pigeon eggs in remote ceiling fixtures. The leg of her best table had been savagely scarred. Their two small rugs, enormously large for these minute rooms, lapped eighteen inches up the walls. The only closet upstairs was not in the bedroom but in the hall, and so shallow that coat hangers would not fit.

Janet banged the closet door viciously and stamped across the hall to wash her hands. She felt itchy and soiled, as if the dust had melted into her skin, encasing her in a delicate gray crust like a seed.

She regarded herself despairingly in the mirror. In three months, all this mess to go through again. More surly movers. More damaged furniture. The future rose up at her like an angry dog.

Downstairs, Sam whistled destructively through "Pretty Baby." His blond hair sticking straight up, no doubt. His long face concentrated as he crashed a hammer repeatedly against something undoubtedly fragile.

But there was no use telling him, he was that stubborn; let him smash it apart, then come to her with that feeble grin explaining how it happened, till her face burnt and pressure beat inside her head.

Seeking coolness and silence, she entered the bedroom and pushed up a window. Leaning out, she critically surveyed the yard below. Only a week and the grass already needed cutting. It looked knee deep. They had no mower, of course. Maybe Sam could rent one. Another unexpected expense, capping all the other unexpected expenses.

From some distant place, a baby howled thinly. It was a cruel, persistent sound like the whine of a chainsaw. She wondered how the mother could endure that abrasion of noise?

Well, she had to. Have a baby and there you are — stuck.

She gazed glumly down into the yard. There you are, alone in Pennsylvania in a town the size of a wart. The back of her head throbbed. She felt half sick. Why hadn't they stayed in Fort Wayne? Bill had a good job in Fort Wayne, but no, he wanted a better one. So here they were, in Wartsville, Pennsylvania. Not knowing a soul. She'd known everybody in Fort Wayne for twenty-two years.

No, twenty-three years, remember your birthday. Twenty-three my God years old, alone in Wartsville. Stuck with the baby.

Self-pity burnt her eyes. The back yard looked like an uncombed head. Great flakes of paint peeled from the wooden fence. Over by the tree, a board had simply rotted off. Rotted and fallen clear off.

She felt rotten, too, and ready to fall.

Sam was calling from downstairs.

"What?" she cried. "What is it? What, what, what?"

And rushed from the room. And clattered furiously down the stairs.

The following afternoon, Janet walked half a block to downtown Charlottesville. At the Blue Pigeon Supermarket, she bought half a pound of coffee and a packet of Lebanon bologna. When she requested a check-cashing card, the clerk eyed her with sharp suspicion. She left the supermarket feeling obscurely guilty. It was as if a shameful memory had stirred at the bottom of her mind.

She moved hesitantly along the sidewalk. Sunlight bit at her eyes. Near the corner, a deeply-recessed glass door displayed the name "Archimedes Soft Pretzel Company" in worn gold paint and archaic lettering. Amused, she entered a large room filled with empty shining display cases and the smell of warm bread. A dispirited young woman, drooping by the cash register, slowly filled Janet's order for four of the big pretzels, glinting with salt.

As she squeezed the final pretzel into a sack, the young woman muttered, with a kind of frightened curiosity, "Isn't that a creepy place where you're living? Have you seen anything yet?"

Janet firmly laid down two dollar bills. "Anything what?" The young woman was a complete stranger.

"You know. Anything."

A fierce gray woman strode from the back room, saying sharply: "Charlie needs help with the pans." She seized Janet's dollars and offered change.

"I wonder what she was talking about?" Janet remarked, as the girl slouched glumly away. "It sounded interesting."

The gray woman's eyes flickered remotely over Janet's face. "I wasn't listening."

Like fun you weren't, Janet thought, banging the door. She walked slowly past a small drugstore whose windows were entirely covered by advertisements for baby products. So I'm living in a haunted house, am I? Everybody knows it but me. Reflectively she pulled one of the pretzels apart and bit into its soft saltiness.

I wonder what kind of a ghost we got, she thought. I hope it's cute.

She felt vaguely depressed, as if tomorrow she would have the flu.

That evening, Sam returned late from the office to find her stretched silent and grim across the bed. As he entered the room, her eyes lifted in a stab of cold desperation. She turned away her head.

He knelt by her side: "What is it, honey?"

"Nothing."

"You aren't feeling well?"

"I'm all right."

"No," he said. "Come on now. Tell me."

"I'm all right."

His fingers slipped gently across her unresponsive shoulders. "You've been overdoing it," he said. "You're trying to do two weeks' work in two days."

Silence, across which intruded the harsh sound of her breathing.

"Why don't we go out and get a salad bar tonight? It's too hot to cook."

"I hate it," she said. Her voice was remote, as if she spoke of uninteresting things. "I hate it here."

"It's hard to move away from home. I know. I feel like that too, sometimes."

"We should never have moved," she said. "We should have stayed in Fort Wayne."

"Fort Wayne?" He stared blankly down at her. "Why Fort Wayne?"

"Why," she said, "that's where . . ."

Confusion clouded her face, making her nose seem longer, sharper than ever.

He said: "You mean Dayton?"

Her hand crept slowly across her lips. "Yes," she whispered. "Dayton."

He bent over her, apprehension like a hot cloud in his eyes. "Where'd you get Fort Wayne from? That's Aunt Della's home town. Before she married Bill and moved here."

Janet, unmoving, eyes closed, whispered: "I hate it here. Nothing's like the way it was."

Late that night, she slipped from bed and roamed the halls and stairways of the narrow house. Downstairs was dark as blindness. She moved silently through it, barefooted and listening, fingers slipping along the walls. Far off she heard the baby wail.

On the second floor, the cry seemed louder, calling her in its misery. Moonlight pooled on the landing. Twenty feet down the hall, a slash of shadow concealed the door to the front bedroom. Her heart felt tiny and cold, a stone in a glacier. She crept carefully toward that door, listening. She could no longer hear the baby.

Tentatively, she pushed at the bedroom door. It swung partially open. She pushed it again with a firmness that was part fear. The door swung silently back, and sudden moonlight washed across her face.

She stood listening. She could hear only the delicate whisper of her own breath. Nothing more.

The room was piled with unopened cartons of their possessions. Against the silver-blue glass of the moonlit window, box edges were sharply outlined. Moonlight angled across the room, spilling past her into the hall.

Finally she turned to go. As she did so, she looked down. Felt a single cold pulse strike from the center of her body. For some brief fraction of time, it had seemed that she cast two shadows across the moonlit floor.

In the morning after Sam left for work, she stood irresolutely on the second-floor landing. Boxes in the front bedroom to be opened and searched. The kitchen to be thoroughly scrubbed and waxed. And more wax needed up here. The movers, she noticed grimly, had completely messed up the polish on the stairs and landing.

Too much to do. Too much. Her eyes half closed.

Without warning, the bright world rushed away and despair flooded into her. When she was a small child on Florida's East Coast, a storm wave had rushed over her. Trapped and strangling, she had been whirled tumbling through a boil of sand and water, helpless within the rush. Like that terrible wave, emotion gripped her now — a weight of hopelessness and regret, rage and loss, pouring through her like burning fluid. Unendurable.

The baby was crying.

She felt stupefied. Her body felt inert as death. In a rage of misery, she forced her thick legs to movement. Dragged herself away from the stairs. Lumbered slowly into the hall, one heavy step at a time. Plodded up the hall, past the master bedroom, past the bathroom, dragging her shoulder and arm along the wall. Liquid fire flooded her eyes. She could not see. She did not want to see. Grief stunned her.

Far away in Fort Wayne, familiar faces laughed and familiar voices called out, warm and well-remembered. The air like candy. Color and joy. Friendship and delight.

In this narrow prison house, the baby shrieked again. Its voice was the sound of a bleeding wound. She changed the foul diaper, her fingers clumsy. Single tears burnt her cheeks. Her mind was black, all black and terrible, like a hole in the earth.

The baby shrieked.

Fury lifted her. The room went unreal. She forced both hands against that howling mouth, damming back the sound. The baby's face flushed scarlet. Its minute arms flailed. Then they did not. In a convulsion of guilt, she jerked her hands away. Bending forward over the little bed, fingers against her mouth, she stared, nauseated.

Strength drained out of her. Her gross limbs shook. She sprawled heavily back against the wall.

Downstairs the front door slammed. From the foot of the stairs, Sam's voice:

"Hello, angel, I'm back."

Deep movement in her mind, as if a great door slowly closed. As if heavy rain slowly stopped.

She stood in the front bedroom amid cardboard cartons of their possessions. One box she had torn open. Bright sweaters scattered the floor.

She moved unsteadily into the hall, not understanding the lightness of her body.

From the foot of the steps, Sam grinned up at her.

"How was your day?" he called.

"You're home early."

"It's after five," he said.

Late afternoon sunlight slanted through the bedroom windows. She still wore her nightgown and her hair had not been combed.

After dinner that night, they sat together in the little downstairs living room. All four floor lamps had been turned on. Hard white light poured mercilessly across the gold carpet. Janet sat stiffly upright in a straight chair, holding a green mug of coffee. She wore a yellow blouse and a cocoa-colored skirt, with large wooden beads around her neck and a belt with a massive wooden buckle. She looked carefully arranged, as if prepared for a television interview.

Sam flopped down in a chair and tugged it around to face her. "Listen," he said, seeming bitterly uncomfortable. "Listen, I've been thinking. Why don't you take a couple of weeks vacation and go back to Dayton? Take a rest. Visit with your mother. Couple of weeks and I'll have this place pretty well fixed up — or maybe I can hunt us up a nicer place in Lancaster. They should have lots of nice places in Lancaster. We just didn't have time to find them. Just let me look around for a while and see what I'm able to find."

Janet finished her coffee and placed the empty mug on a small table and folded her long hands gracefully. The rigid sweetness of her smile persisted.

She said: "Your Aunt Della and Uncle Bill, they had a baby, didn't they?"

Sam widened his eyes and rubbed his nose. "Did they?"

"The baby died," she said.

"I just don't know about that."

"It wouldn't stop crying. She tried to hush it up and accidentally smothered it. Probably accidentally."

"Where in the world did you hear something like that?"

She sat erect in the straight, polished chair, a straight, polished smile on her lips. "I was there," she said.

While she explained, Sam sat grinning rigidly at her, his face without color, harshly lined.

Long after Sam fell asleep, she lay wide-eyed in the darkness. He had thrown one arm protectively across her, but she did not feel protected. She felt in danger. She felt a cold, light falling sensation through her middle, and tight temples, and cold patches across her skin. She was afraid. She was a ringing hollow containing nothing but fear.

In books and movies, people always knew what to do. Get a priest; throw Holy water; pray. Hold up a sprig of something. Be gone, reciting a formula of exorcism.

Be gone what? There was nothing here. A mood, a sound, a feeling. A confusion in her own mind. A blurring of who she was, as if another personality had partly dissolved into her like instant coffee dissolving in water.

Her fingers dug against the sheets.

That's what was horrible and nasty. That's what was disgusting. Not being torn to pieces by something with scales and teeth. What was horrible was to fade from your own mind. To know you're fading, memory by memory, canceled, at last, the way a computer cancels a line. Flick. Gone.

Her fingers gripped the sheets. Her mind circled in

fear. She lay under the shelter of his arm and it was not enough.

Toward dawn she slept.

The kitchen clock said nearly seven. Sam ate toast and said in a guilty voice: "I got a meeting first thing this morning. But I'll be back in a couple of hours. OK?"

Janet nodded wordlessly. She felt as if she drifted downward from a high place through a glare of light. Her eyes ached.

"You'll be all right?" Sam asked.

She nodded.

"God knows," he said, "I don't suppose haunts come around in the morning, do they?"

"I hope not," she said.

After the door closed behind Sam, the exhilaration of decision poured through her like cold wind. She would leave for Dayton now. At once. Her mind leaped across the future, as she methodically washed the breakfast dishes and put the kitchen to order. She felt rushed and excited; her lungs could not seem to take in enough air. She moved slowly through the narrow house, looking at it for the last time. Her mind glowed with tightly restrained emotion that felt vaguely unpleasant, as if she were behaving in a way she would later recall with humiliation.

She pulled open the front door. Thin morning sunlight streamed across the floor, worn by years of passage. She stared down at it. Only a few days ago, it had glowed so brightly under its coating of polish.

Her eyes narrowed. Crossing to the stairway she peered up at the wall. Sunlight fell across faded beige paint beneath which showed a vague wallpaper pattern, like the outlines of a drowned city. The wood of the stairs and banisters, clean but lusterless, had obviously not been polished for years.

Yesterday she had seen it all newly painted and polished, the wallpaper crisp and bright, smelling freshly clean.

She darted halfway up the stairs and thrust her face close to the sunlit wall. She strained to detect any trace of redecoration.

Nothing. Paint and paper, chipped, faded, soiled. Wood worn, begrimed, scarred, gouged, scraped. Exactly as a house this age would look, given no refurbishment.

"I can't understand," Sam had said, "why Uncle Bill would spend a nickel on it."

But he hadn't.

Nothing had been done. Nothing at all.

Some part of her mind slewed into slow revolving motion, as if a fundamental restraint had broken.

She ran upstairs, touching the walls. In their bedroom, her cold fingers slipped along the window sills, lifting up chips of paint, old paint, old broken paint. The floor had no more gloss than a worn-out carpet. The continued slow spiraling in her head nauseated her.

Returning to the hall, she wrenched open the hall closet, began pulling blouses and skirts from hangers. Her cold hands gripped inaccurately. Back in the bedroom, she layered garments into her blue bag. As she packed, her mind wove fantastic ribbons of words. One bag would not hold much, but the rest could be shipped to Dayton later. Sam (Bill, cried her mind) could do that. Just put them on the bus. He could do that.

He would do that even for a wife who ran away home to Fort Wayne (Dayton). Unless he forgot all about her. Forgot they had ever been married. Forgot what she looked like. Whose clothes are these? Aunt Della's (Janet's)? Who was this fugitive woman. I don't remember. Tall. She was tall (heavy). She killed our baby, you know.

No, I did not. I killed nothing. Only this bitter marriage begun with such promise, ended far from home, alone in this narrow house.

From down the hall drifted the thin whining of a baby.

"Dear God!" Janet gasped. She snatched at a pair of shoes, slapped the bag shut, heaved it from the bed. The weight hurt her fingers.

She stumbled into the hallway. Sunlight spilled across fresh wallpaper and wood gleaming warmly with polish.

The bag thudded to the floor. Her body drew into itself like a collapsing sun.

The baby began to scream.

She stood staring down the staircase. Sunlight lighted the top steps. The lower stairs lay in an ambiguous gray light, confused and inexact. Immensely long, the staircase. Sixty years long. Today's sunlight at the top; below that, the past. The dreadful past. She could not think about the past.

The baby shrieked.

Fear chilled her throat and stomach.

She swung about to face the bedroom. She knew with great clarity that she should snatch up her bag and race from the house. Outside, the bus would come through the bright air. At the end of the highway was Fort Wayne and the joyous life she had abandoned so many months ago.

Instead she ignored the bag. She began to inch down the hallway toward the front bedroom. Small teeth showed behind her grinning lips. The crying grew intense, waves of searing sound. She moved unsteadily, touching the wall with her palm.

At the door to the bedroom, she stopped. The infant's desperate screaming surged all around her. She felt one eyelid shivering, as she pushed open the door.

Inside, a pink-walled room, filled with heavy brown furniture. Neatly hand-stitched cloth pictures circled the walls. By the door stood a huge, old-fashioned crib, broad and high and frothing with covers. Over one end arched a small canopy, merry with pink ribbons. Beneath the canopy shrieked an elaborately gowned baby, its body rigid with fury.

Outside the window, traffic droned in the street.

She moved toward the crib, smiling the hard white smile of fear.

The baby's face, scarlet against the white bedding, jerked toward her. Its eyelids flickered open, exposing eyes like bits of black glacier. She had the startled impression that something quite self-controlled was examining her. That it was contemptuous of her distress and amused by her pity. Before she could express those impressions as words, its eyes clamped tight. The mouth gaped. The baby screamed.

She found herself in the hallway. She had slammed the door and jerked away as if the wood had bitten her. Behind the door, the baby's voice rose in a shriek of rage.

Janet began to edge back down the hall, eyes fixed on the door. Heart beat shook her body as a freight train shakes the crossing. She knew with sick certainty that the baby could hear the violence of her heart.

She retreated down the hall, until her back pressed painfully against the protecting wall. The bedroom windows spilled pale sunshine across the blue bag on the landing. The bag cast a firm rectangle of shadow. Bright bits of dust, like tiny suns, glinted in the sunlight. The air smelled warm, a little stuffy. In the bedroom, a crumpled white sack projected from the wastebasket by the dresser.

She looked eagerly at these details. They were firm and clear and unchanging, a reality of exact detail and specific surfaces. Comforting, concrete reality. But her body continued to shake and her sweating hands smeared the wall. She peered past the bag down the terrible chasm of the stairs, wondering how she could get down them without falling.

And found herself staring directly into a man's eyes.

She could not quite make out his face. It was either Sam or Bill. The thickened air of the stairwell blurred his features. He called out, his voice high and strange. Even sixty years away, she could hear the misery in his voice.

Sick instability ran through her. She felt something at the underside of her mind loosen. She felt a rush of long-restrained emotion, fetid and dangerous, like contaminated water.

It was familiar emotion. She knew it well. Like the face of the man in the stairwell, it was slightly out of focus. As if two images or two emotions had almost, not quite, been superimposed, so that from behind the first protruded the outline of the second.

She recognized despair, so like her own. Similar resentment and sense of dislocation. The same corroding unhappiness and regret.

The man below called and his feet thudded on the stairs. Those sounds seemed far off and of no importance.

Two sets of emotions, so much alike.

Common feelings that should merge to one.

For shared unhappiness was better than unhappiness endured alone.

"Surely," she thought, "this isn't true."

Down the hall, the front bedroom pulsed like a great heart. She had only to take a few steps and open the door and step inside. To join, to merge, to share.

A feeling of airlessness closed over her. She might have been strangling in white foam. She heard her voice lift in a ridiculous squeak:

"For God's sake, no."

She twisted blindly away from the wall, and plunged heavily against Sam as he ran up out the stairwell.

"What is it?" he cried.

Ignoring him, she bent over her bag, fumbled with the catches. Her fingers, nerveless as icicles, felt thin and easily snapped.

The bag fell open. She dumped its bright contents across the floor. Jerking the bag wide open, she lifted it high between outstretched arms, shook it defiantly at the bedroom door.

"I'm staying with Sam," she shouted. "We're going to Harrisburg."

She slammed the bag down on the landing.

"Janet," Sam whispered. "Janet." She was shocked by his anguished voice. He said gently: "Let's get a cup of coffee. Let's sit down. You'll feel better if you sit down."

"I feel wonderful," she said.

He took her arm, lightly, lightly, his fingers floating across her skin. A white look distorted his face. When she reached up to smooth his grooved cheek, he stepped suddenly back, staring at her. His foot plunged into the open bag.

The bag grated as it slipped from the landing.

For an instant, his lanky figure poised over the hollow of the stairs. It seemed a playful position, as if he could recover his balance whenever he wished. He shouted urgently. Teeth shone in his blanched face. Then he was gone.

The stairway filled with sound.

The stairway filled with silence.

At the bottom, Janet flung herself down beside him. Something was wrong with the shape of his head. His fingers jerked against the floor before they became still.

She strained herself against him. Love dissolved her. She was stunned by love, as if a star had exploded at the center of her body. Behind that flaring blaze, grief extended its rending hooks. That, she knew, would be very terrible, more agonizing even than love.

The sound of a baby crying roused her.

She looked up blinking, her crusted face loose. Her legs had gone numb and she had to clutch the banister and pull erect, hand over hand.

The dead man lay at her feet, his eyes enigmatic. Clinging to the banister, she looked down on the unreality of his face.

Someone distinctly said: "Now you're free."

The baby's crying became a continuous shriek.

She stood in the twilight of the narrow house, listening to the baby scream, feeling the weight of her body, feeling the edges of her mind flare to scarlet, as fire in the fields flares before the wind. Ω

hell book

OUR LADY OF THE THORNS

The Grand Duchess of
Hades, consort of Belphegor,
eminent demon. Sorcerers
summon her to enhance the
agony of imprisoned foes.

A FLY CALLED JESUS
by Chet Williamson

illustrated by Philip H. Williams

At first Albie Byrne didn't believe the fly when it said that it was Jesus come for the second time.

Of course it didn't really *say* it was Jesus, since flies have no capacity for speech. It spelled out the message by walking in the sand. It had been a pretty normal day up to that point, full of sun, warm breezes, and loneliness for Albie Byrne, like most Sundays in the summer. Around ten he would wake up; around noon he would get bored; and around 1:30 he would leave his tight, steaming apartment and drive his '79 Chevy Nova twenty miles north to the state park, where he would swim in the lake, lie on the sand, eat several dollars worth of concession-stand hot-dogs and Nutty Buddys, and ogle the women old and young, one piece and two.

He was lying on his back, admiring a young woman with Latin eyes, Mediterranean skin, and a strategically cut, two piece suit held together by the most fragile strips of fabric imaginable, when the fly landed on his nose. At first he thought the black blotch intruding on his vision was the result of a fortunately snapped lower strap that exposed the beach nymph's hirsute and forbidden cleft to his wanton gaze. But when the supposed tuft started to rove over the girl's magnificently tanned abdomen, he tightened his focus.

His eyes crossed upon the fly at the end of his nose, the largest specimen of the species he had ever seen, more like a small hawk than a fly. He let out a whoop, swung both hands toward his nose, and rolled off his blanket into the sand, his hands flailing.

"Mommy?" said a tiny voice that nonetheless managed to carry a good twenty yards outward on all sides from its owner, "what's that fat man doing?" Faces turned, dozens of them.

"Shh, dear. It's not nice to call someone fat," said the child's mother.

"But he is, Mommy . . ."

"Spade a spade," said the child's father approvingly, not looking up from his *Sporting News*. If he had, he would have seen Albie Byrne turn crimson with embarrassment, the beach nymph turn away with disgust, and the fly turn a few barrel rolls over Albie's head.

Slowly Albie crawled back onto his brown army blanket, and slowly the crowd within the twenty foot radius of Albie's frenzied contortions and the little girl's piercing voice turned back to their own business. Albie lay on (or over) his distended stomach, eyes cast down to the soft gray sand just off the protective island of his blanket. The fly landed a foot and a half in front of his nose.

Shit! thought Albie. *Shit shit shit I'm gonna smash your ass, you little bastard!* And very carefully Albie picked up a section of the local Sunday paper. Noticing that it was the comics, he set it back on the blanket and picked up real estate instead, rolling it into a tight cylinder and raising it stealthily above his head for the kill.

The fly was still on the sand, but so was something else. There, spelled out in a graceful script, were the letters, *S O R R*, and the fly was just finishing the tail of the *Y*. Then it leaped into the air and came down hard to make one final spot.

SORRY., it read, complete with a period.

Sorry. Written by a fly crawling through the sand, a fly that now stared up at him with complex eyes that he swore registered apology.

Sorry?

Albie looked up nervously, then to the left and right to see if anybody had noticed the little exercise in insectoid penmanship. He almost expected to hear a little voice pipe up, "Look, Mommy, that fat man's hallucinating."

But no, everyone was doing something worthwhile. No one was forced from boredom to watch Albie Byrne. The little girl was making sand castles by the shore, and the nymph was sucking on a Fudgsicle. Albie considered the symbolism for a moment, then turned back to the fly, who, to his amazement, had written more:

— DIDN'T MEAN TO STARTLE YOU.

Albie could only lie there, his lower jaw hanging slack, eyes bugging out of his skull. "*SORRY*" he could have accepted, charging it off to the old infinite number of monkeys and typewriters theory. But "*SORRY. DIDN'T MEAN TO STARTLE YOU,*" with the apostrophe in the right place could not be attributed to random fly trails.

Now the fly flew off the sand, diving and gliding over this handiwork and brushing it with wings and legs until it was expunged. Then he wrote:

— PLEASE WIPE THE SAND CLEAN AFTER YOU READ IT. SAVES ME TIME.

After a moment's hesitation, Albie reached out with a pudgy, trembling hand and smoothed the sand until the tiny grooves of script disappeared. The fly wrote:

— THANK YOU, ALBIE. MY NAME IS JESUS.

"Holy shit," muttered Albie Byrne.

The fly waited by the word, "*JESUS,*" for a few seconds, then began to laboriously clear the sand. Albie reached out and helped it. It wrote:

— LET'S GO DOWN TO THE END WHERE THERE'S MORE ROOM.

It rose into the air and began to buzz down the beach toward the area posted with **No Swimming** signs. Albie watched the little speck get smaller and smaller. When it was lost to sight he sprang up and ran after it, ignoring the cries of sunbathers whose bodies and blankets his plunging feet sprayed with sand.

In another minute he found himself at the end of the beach. The only people nearby were a teenage couple who had apparently sought the imperfect privacy of the no swimming area for some amorous dalliance.

Albie tried to avoid looking at their annoyed scowls as he sought the large and literate fly. Finally he saw a patch of sand on which had been written:

— HERE, ALBIE.

He walked over to it, and there was the fly sitting by the final *e*, making a large, black period. Unencumbered now by restrictions of space and the need to wipe the sand clean after every few words, the fly wrote rapidly:

— ARE YOU SURPRISED I KNEW YOUR NAME?

Albie started to answer, then turned and looked at the embracing couple fifteen yards away, who seemed to have forgotten his presence and were again attempting to suck out each others' tongues by the roots. Albie looked at the fly.

"Uh . . . yeah. Yeah. How'd you know my name?"

Holy shit, he thought, *I'm talking to a fly. I'm loony. I'm really loony. Mom said this would happen if I kept beating off.*

The fly replied:

— I KNOW EVERYTHING. AND DON'T WORRY, ALBIE. YOU'RE NOT LOONY.

And it's a telepathic fly! thought Albie in panic. "How . . . wha— . . . how'd you *do* that?"

— I TOLD YOU. I KNOW EVERYTHING. I AM JESUS, ALBIE, COME BACK TO THE WORLD ONCE MORE, AND I AM REVEALING MYSELF UNTO YOU. YOU ARE THE FIRST TO KNOW OF MY COMING.

"Oh, come *on!*" cried Albie Byrne in frustration, so loudly that the coupling couple gave him a withering glare and stalked into the more private confines of the woods. "Come *on!*" repeated Albie. "This isn't real — this is a trick!"

— IT IS NOT A TRICK.

"A fly can't be Jesus! A fly can't know everything!"

— I KNOW THAT YOU HAD THREE EGGS FOR BREAKFAST THIS MORNING, AND FOUR SLICES OF TOAST WITH WELCH'S GRAPE-ADE.

Albie's jaw hurtled dropped again. After a moment's thought he replied, "I know now. This is a dream. You know this stuff because *I* know it."

— IF IT IS A DREAM, COULD I KNOW THINGS YOU DON'T?

"Heck, no."

— DO YOU KNOW HOW MANY POPULAR VOTES THE PROHIBITION PARTY'S CANDIDATE FOR THE PRESIDENCY GOT IN 1904?

A FLY CALLED JESUS

Albie frowned. "I didn't even know there *was* a Prohibition Party."

— *THERE WAS, AND ITS CANDIDATE, SILAS C. SWALLOW, RECEIVED 258,535 POPULAR VOTES.*

Albie's eyes narrowed. "How do I know you're telling the truth?"

— *LOOK IT UP. THE RECORDS SAY 258,536, BUT OTIS P. BIRD OF DETROIT VOTED TWICE. OF COURSE NO ONE KNOWS BUT ME. AND MY FATHER, NATURALLY. NOW DO YOU BELIEVE ME?*

"No. No! Maybe I just made this all up in my dream!"

— *I HATE TO TELL YOU THIS, ALBIE, BUT YOU DON'T HAVE THAT VIVID AN IMAGINATION, AND CERTAINLY NOT ONE VIVID ENOUGH TO IMAGINE ME COMING BACK AS A FLY.*

Albie sighed. "You got a point," he told the fly. "But . . . but Jesus? A fly? Why a fly?"

— *BECAUSE IT TAKES LITTLE FAITH TO FOLLOW A MAN, ESPECIALLY ONE AS SERENE, SELF-CONFIDENT, AND GOOD-LOOKING AS I WAS IN MY FIRST COMING. BUT TO FOLLOW A FLY? THAT TAKES <u>GREAT</u> FAITH.*

"But why me? I don't have much faith, I never go to church or Sunday School —"

The fly interrupted with a loud buzz, and wrote:

— *YOU HAVE BEEN CHOSEN. IT IS THAT SIMPLE. YOUR SOUL IS PURE, YOU ARE A VIRGIN,*

Not for want of trying, thought Albie Byrne.

— *AND YOU WILL FOLLOW MY GUIDANCE FAITHFULLY AND HONESTLY. YOU WILL BE MY DISCIPLE.*

"Disciple." Albie read the word aloud. It had a nice ring to it.

— *WILL YOU FOLLOW ME, ALBIE BYRNE? OF YOUR OWN FREE WILL?*

Albie shivered a little. It was now or never. He could follow Jesus, be his chief disciple, or spend the rest of his life as a putz who blew the biggest chance of all.

But a *fly?* Oh well . . . "Yeah, okay, you got a deal."

— *YOU MAY CALL ME JESUS.*

Albie swallowed heavily, looking at the big black insect sitting on the sand. "Okay. you got a deal. . . . Jesus."

In his two-room apartment with bath, Albie Byrne sat at the kitchen table watching the fly as it hopped from letter to letter of the old Ouija board Albie used as a tray when he ate supper in front of the TV (which was almost every night). At first he had given the fly an old Smith-Corona typewriter, but its weight had not been enough to depress the keys. The fly had then spotted the Ouija board, landed on it, and Albie had gotten the idea pretty quickly, for Albie.

The Ouija board proved to be an excellent method of communication between the two, even though the fly had to respell some of the longer words. The fly devised a punctuation system of hopping once for a comma, twice for a period, and three times for a question mark. Any further vagaries of style would have been wasted on Albie.

Now Albie watched and responded to what the fly spelled:

— *THE TIME HAS COME FOR A NEW HEAVEN AND A NEW EARTH. THE FINAL DAYS ARE AT HAND.*

"A thand? What's that?" asked Albie.

— *AT* [the fly paused] *HAND.*

"Oh, at *hand.* Wait a minute . . . Jesus." He still had trouble with the name. "You mean like the end of the *world?*" Albie felt a nervous burble in his stomach.

— *THE END OF EVIL IN THE WORLD, YES.*

"Like . . . like, Amma . . . Arma . . . "

— *ARMAGEDDON.*

"Yeah! Like a final battle between good'n bad? And the whole earth gets blown up"

— *RELAX, ALBIE. A BIT OF PROPAGANDA DEVISED BY MY EARLIER DISCIPLES TO TAKE THE FOCUS OFF THE WORLDLY AND PLACE IT ON THE ETERNAL.*

"Hoo boy, *that's* a relief. But how's all this evil gonna be got rid of?"

— *BECAUSE OF WHAT YOU SHALL DO FOR ME.*

"*Me?*"

— *YES. I WISH FOR YOU TO BUILD ME AN ARC.*

"Oh, come *on,*" Albie said. "That's been done already. Besides, you spelled it wrong. How can you be Jesus and not know how to spell?"

— *NOT AN ARK. AN ARC. AS IN ARC LIGHT.*

"Like electrical? I'm no good at electrical stuff. I hate changing fuses."

— *HAVE NO FEAR, FOR I AM WITH YOU. MY WORDS SHALL GUIDE YOU, AND I SHALL BE A LAMP UNTO YOUR FEET. NOW, HAVE YOU EVER DONE ANY SPOT WELDING?*

"No."

— *YOU CAN LEARN. HERE IS A LIST OF THINGS YOU SHALL NEED TO BUILD MY ARC.*

The list was long and, for Albie, very confusing. "Where'll I get all this stuff?"

— *AROUND. ELECTRICAL SUPPLY STORES, CHEMICAL HOUSES, HARDWARE STORES.*

"Uh, what about money?"

— *HOW MUCH DO YOU HAVE?*

"Three hundred in savings. In Checking . . ." He took a seldom used checkbook from a kitchen drawer and turned to the last stub. "Thirty-seven dollars and twenty-eight cents."

— *CASH?*

"About ten bucks."

— *IT WILL SUFFICE. LOAVES AND FISHES.*

"Huh?"

— *THE RICH MAN, THE CAMEL, THE EYE OF THE NEEDLE.*

Albie shook his head in confusion.

— *I SHALL PAY YOU BACK, ALBIE. BUY THE THINGS TOMORROW.*

When Albie went back to his apartment the following day, his car was packed with jars of chemicals, electrical instruments, plugs, wires, condensers, and batteries, none of which Albie knew a thing about. As he hauled the last box into the apartment, he said,

by Chet Williamson

"Y'know, you've never told me what this stuff is for. I mean, what's this supposed to do anyway?"

— *IT WILL BRING MY KINGDOM UNTO THE WORLD, ALBIE. IT WILL POUR OUT ITS LIGHT TO SHINE UPON ALL MEN, GOOD AND EVIL ALIKE.*

"Oh. But what'll it *do?*"

— *YOURS IS NOT TO REASON WHY.*

Fortunately, Albie did not know the second line of the couplet. Instead he sighed and accepted and did what the fly told him.

It took weeks.

The problem seemed to stem from the inferior nature of the gray stuff that sat like half cooked bread dough in Albie's brain pan. A skilled electrician would have finished the job in two days. A typical layman with no prior electrical knowledge might have taken six at the outside.

Albie took weeks.

When the fly told him to get a condenser, Albie had no idea of what a condenser looked like. Then the fly had to spell out a description, which took time, or fly to the specific part and land on it. This posed a problem because of the vast amount of puzzle pieces in the apartment. Often Albie would lose the fly in the electrical labyrinth, and it would come buzzing out of some pile to pick him up again.

The results of the welding and soldering were abominable, not only for the device but also for Albie's hands, which very quickly became a red mass of burn tissue. Asbestos gloves proved necessary, but what was gained in protection was lost in dexterity.

The first few days Albie called in sick at the floor covering store where he worked in the warehouse. The fourth day, however, the owner asked him what exactly was wrong with him.

"Uh, they don't know exactly." Albie raised his eyebrows as the fly started hopping on the Ouija board. "Just a sec . . ."

— *SOMETHING FATAL.*

Albie slammed his meaty hand over the mouthpiece. "Hey, I need my job!"

— *I AM ENOUGH FOR ALL YOUR NEEDS.*

Albie looked panicked.

— *PUT YOUR TRUST IN ME. HAVE FAITH.*

Albie took his hand away. "Cancer," he barked into the phone. "I got cancer. . . . Yeah, I'm sure. . . . Anytime, I guess. . . . I gotta go now . . . That's okay. Bye." He hung up and looked with a hangdog expression at the fly. "Aw jeez . . . " The fly started to hop.

— *BACK TO WORK. GET A THREE INCH PIECE OF COPPER WIRE.*

"Copper . . . is that the silver stuff?"

But one day the machine was finally completed. It sat there in the living room like a whiskey still insanely crossbred with an espresso machine. Two huge metallic cones jutted upward form the mass of metal, wires, glass, and Bakelite. They made Albie think of the girls with the big, metal-brassiered bazooms in the old science-fiction magazines.

He smiled, both at the image and in pride at his accomplishment. It was bizarre, it was erratic, it was downright sloppy, but it was the only thing he could ever remember building all by himself, except for some popsicle-stick baskets in the fourth grade.

"It's beautiful," he sighed, slopping onto the only empty chair that remained in the gadget-crowded room. "It's really beautiful." He turned to the fly. "When do we turn it on?"

— *AT DAWN. TOMORROW THE SUN WILL RISE ON A NEW HEAVEN AND A NEW EARTH, ALBIE. AND YOU SHALL SIT AT MY RIGHT HAND.*

Albie smiled and sighed again. Then his stomach rumbled, and he realized how hungry he was. He walked to the refrigerator, but it was empty.

"Hey, look," he said to the fly, "I'm really hungry, but I've spent every penny on this thingamajig of yours. Could you like produce some food? Like a miracle, you know?"

The fly started hopping.

— *REMAIN WITH ME THIS NIGHT WITHOUT BODILY SUSTENANCE. LET US FAST TOGETHER AND WAIT FOR THE MORN OF GLORY WHEN YOU SHALL BE FILLED WITH FAR MORE THAN FOOD.*

"Oh, all right," said Albie grumpily as he started to fast. Sometime after midnight he fell asleep and was able to forget the dull ache in his gut.

He came out of the dreamless sleep with a start. The fly, to awaken him, had crawled inside his nose. Albie snorted and gasped, but soon came to himself enough to see the fly doing graceful turns and parabolas in the humid, sticky air of his apartment.

"Is it time?" He rubbed his eyes sleepily.

— *THE HOUR IS AT HAND. OPEN THE WINDOW.*

Albie did. The eastern sky was dimly glowing with a diffused pink light. Not having seen a sunrise in years, Albie was duly impressed.

— *WHEN THE SUN RISES OVER THE HILLS, THROW THE SWITCH.*

The fly rose and began to buzz toward the open window.

"Wait! Where are you going?" Albie yelled. The fly settled once more on the board.

— *I GO TO MAKE STRAIGHT THE WAY.*

And then he flew off, Albie hoped, to make straight the way.

Albie sat and waited for the sun, scared and nervous. He thought about forgetting the whole thing, but finally decided that since he had come this far, he might as well do it. He was neither talented nor bright, but he was tenacious. And gullible.

As the sun peered over the hills, Albie took a deep breath and threw the switch, as the fly had ordered. Instantly there was a hiss which became a buzz that grew to a throbbing that developed into a monstrous roar that filled the little room with the sound of a dozen dams breaking at once.

Albie went deaf.

Then between the two huge cones a light started to

glow, getting brighter and brighter until the ribbon of incandescence flared like the combined glow of a thousand acetylene torches.

Albie went blind.

Suddenly the machine's noises softened, its light dimmed, and was replaced by a dull red glow that grew outward on all sides, an ever expanding circle that in a few seconds held Albie inside its perimeter.

Albie died.

The circle kept growing, passing through the walls of Albie's apartment, through the streets of Albie's town, out into the countryside, picking up speed at a tremendous rate, leaving death behind as it passed.

Chicago was the first major city that it hit, only two minutes after it had begun.

Everyone in Chicago died.

Outward it grew, ten miles a second, then twenty, then thirty. It was as if a giant pen point had been touched to a giant paper towel, and all the ink had come out at once. Over the United States, up over the arctic, down to South America, out across the oceans to Europe, to Asia, to cover the whole world with a crimson glow.

That evening, if anyone had been alive to see it, the moon would have appeared as a celestial clot of blood.

At dawn the next day, the fly arrived at the top of the world's highest mountain.

There it alighted on the shoulder of its master, and changed into its true form, that of a small, batwinged demon.

"You've done well," said the demon's master. "And all of his own free will. That was the tricky part."

The demon bowed his head humbly, happy to have served, and his master smiled at the unspoken obeisance.

"And now that the battlefield is cleared of vermin, we shall begin. The gauntlet is thrown. The pets are dead."

And Satan, the lord of the flies, gathered his host and looked for one last time upon the world below before he advanced to meet the Foe, the trumpets of Armageddon blaring in his ears.   Ω

THE MASHGEAKH REJECTS
THE DRAGON-SLAYER

They're not kosher, these wonder-beasts.
All those wizard recipes calling for dragon's blood —
Now, a dragon's blood is a dragon's life,
And life's blood's not kosher.
Dragons are out.
Anyhow, reptiles, even fire-breathing,
Are unclean.

    The eagle's an unclean bird, and the lion's got no hoofs.
    Griffins are out.
    Horses have hoofs, but not cloven.
    No hippogriffs.

Leviathan's a Biblical beast,
And officially to be, one day, the feast of the righteous,
So it's got to be kosher,
But the general opinion that it's some kind of wonder-whale
Has the ultra-frum worried.
They'll want to see scales before they dive in.

    A unicorn, though —
    Listen, you bring me some proof that it chews a proper cud
    And isn't just some thin white funnyfaced pig
    Been prettied up with a golden horn
    To go with those dainty cloven hoofs,
    There'll be a gourmet market
    You wouldn't belive.

— **Ruth Berman**

For an instant an unpleasant picture formed in his mind--that of an inky, humped creature crouched behind the parapet, waiting.....

"SMOKE GHOST" by FRITZ LEIBER

A WITCH IN THE BALKANS
by Lord Dunsany

illustrated by Keith Minnion

It was a Christmas Eve at a country house, in which the house-party were gathered in arm-chairs before a fireplace that had never been modernized, and which still had room for big logs, which were now quietly burning. Ghost stories had been told, while one of the guests, one named Frederick Parnet, who in his time had wandered about the world a good deal, sat silent. As a tale ended, his hostess turned to him and said, "Won't you tell us a ghost story now, Mr. Parnet?"

"I have never seen a ghost," said Parnet.

"It needn't be a true one," said his hostess.

"I shouldn't tell it if it were not," said he.

"Don't you know any tale of banshees, goblins, or witches?" she asked.

"Oh, witches," he said. "That is a different matter."

"Then tell us a tale of a witch," she entreated.

"Well," he said, "in the Balkans they all believe in witches. At any rate in the parts of the Balkans I know. And it's very hard on the people they think are witches. They don't give them a chance."

"What country are you speaking of," he was asked.

"I was among the Vlachs," said Parnet. "They don't quite belong to any particular country in the way that we do. They come south out of Macedonia to the hills of Greece in the winter, and when it gets warm they go back to their mountains in Macedonia and Bulgaria. They bring their flocks with them and build reed-huts and go north again when the violets are over.

"There was an old woman who lived in a cottage near their huts, and they said she was working witch-craft against them. She had frightened their children somehow, and they had run with some story to their parents, and they had got as frightened as the children and wanted to kill the witch.

"That is how things were when I happened to come along and, seeing a crowd and hearing a noise, I asked what was the matter. And the Vlachs told me that the old woman was a witch and that they were going to kill her.

"Well, I was young and had no experience with such things, and I told them that it was all nonsense. I told them I was English and didn't mind witchcraft, and that I would go into her cottage and she could practice her witchcraft on me, and then she wouldn't want to be bothered with them and they would be all right.

"Their children gazed at me all the time with big round eyes, and their elders talked with each other for a little while; and then they said, if I would do that,

they would leave the witch alone. And so I saved her life.

"Well, I walked into her cottage then and found her seated in front of her fire, and I said, 'Look here, those silly devils think you're a witch. But I told them that is all nonsense.'

"And she looked at me and did not say thank you.

" 'All nonsense,' I said again.

" 'I make spells,' she said then.

" 'Yes, I know,' I said. 'All nonsense.'

" 'I make them out of this book,' she said. There was a great book beside her bound in black leather.

" 'Well, you can make them at me if you like,' I said.

"And then she opened the book. I really don't think she understood what was going on. She had heard the Vlachs shouting all round her cottage, and probably thought I was in with them. My Greek wasn't her kind, and she can't have understood me very well. Anyway, she opened her book and began to read aloud out of it.

" 'Look here,' I said. 'I'm English. You needn't read at me. Spells don't impress me. I'm not a Vlach.'

"And she smiled a very curious smile, and as I looked at her the spell worked. I never dreamt it was possible. She made me into a cat.

"It was so utterly astonishing, I did not know what to do. And gradually the instincts of a cat went surging through me, and I walked to the fire and lay down. It was a fine big fireplace, as big as this one, and I lay looking into the fire and began to think. And the more I thought, the more awful my predicament seemed to be. I couldn't speak, I couldn't explain, and the Vlachs had gone away. They couldn't have helped me even if they had stayed. There I was in the old woman's cottage, and she evidently thought I was in with the Vlachs. I thought and thought, and the only thing I could think of was that I had better be a good cat.

"But even that didn't promise any chance of escape, since the better the cat I was, the more she would want to keep me. It was an awful predicament. She gave me one look, as much as to say, 'That is what comes of meddling with witches,' and then went on with her work, which seemed to be chiefly muttering into the fire, whether spells or old memories I can't say. I was never in a situation I liked less. Never."

"And do you mean that you were actually a cat?" said our hostess.

"I was actually a cat," said Parnet. "There was no doubt about it. A black cat covered with fur. And I was gazing into the fire. That would have been pleasant if I could have thought of any way of escaping, but not doing it for the rest of my life. I had other things to do. But for the moment it was pleasant. You have no idea how pleasant. It seemed to supply all that we get from a whisky and soda, and a good book to read, and a comfortable chair. However, I didn't want to go on doing it all my life; and I could see no way of avoiding it.

"The witch sat there perfectly content. She wasn't going to do any more. I heard the Vlachs call to their children a long way off. They weren't going to do any more either. What on earth was I to do? After a while she gave me a saucer of milk, which I accepted gratefully. The milk tasted extremely good. Better, in fact, than anything I had ever tasted before. I don't like milk as a rule. But I did then. The windows of the room began to grow blue and dim.

"Then it got quite dark, and not till then did the old woman light a candle. Time went by more pleasantly than when it does here, in spite of my awful predicament; it went by more cosily and without impatience, and somehow there seemed more in the fire than there is in our newspapers and our talk, and all the things with which we concern ourselves. It seemed to have more interest in it and to be more full of change.

"It's difficult quite to explain, especially as none of you have studied it as I had to do. I had nothing else to occupy me for weeks, except plans for escape; and none of them turned out to be any good.

"Soon after the old witch lit the candle she picked it up, and without a word to me went out of her kitchen and into her other room, and I heard the creak of her bed as she lay down for the night. I was up on the table, where lay her old black book, in a moment. I realised that was the key, but could I turn it? I opened it with a paw, and it was all full of black spells. But they were in Chinese. That was no use to me. So I closed the book and went back to the fire and looked into its red and golden and orange depths; a very pleasant occupation, if you had nothing more serious to worry about."

"I shouldn't have thought . . ." began one of us.

"No," said Parnet, "nor would I. It wasn't until this unfortunate thing occurred to me that I realised how much interest there can be in the glow of a fire. I can't get it now. But at the time it supplied nearly everything. Everything except what I wanted most, a plan of escape. I had no hope from the Vlachs. What they ought to have done was to go in and rescue me, and when they saw what had happened, demanded my release. But they were evidently content with things as they were. The witch was working her witchcraft on me, and that suited them, and they felt their children were safe.

"Soon they would go back to their mountains, for the great carpets of violets that grew in those lands were nearly over. Then I should be all alone with the witch, and no one would know what had happened to me, for the Vlachs wouldn't bother to tell anyone.

What was to be done? I pondered for some time. And then I turned to watch the glow of the witch's fire and the little flames that jumped up every now and then, and the grey ash that covered more and more of the glow. And watching the embers I must have fallen asleep. And the morning came, and I was still a cat. First the dim light came into the room through the windows. And then came the witch. She took no notice of me at first, but boiled an egg in a great pot over her fire. Then she went to the cupboard and took out a piece of meat and threw it down beside me.

"I looked at her gratefully and purred, which was all I could do. It was no use resenting her offhand way, as my only chance seemed to be that she might disenchant me, though it didn't seem very likely. As soon as I began to eat the meat, another black cat walked in from the other room and came up and looked at me. I looked back at it, and it lay down and went on looking with pale-yellow eyes with dark slits down the centre. I suppose my eyes looked the same. I wondered what it would do.

"Then it shut its eyes, and opened them no more for an hour. I never knew whether it had been a cat always, or whether it had been enchanted like myself. I thought for a long while of how to communicate with it, in the hope of planning some sort of escape; but then I gave it up, because I didn't trust that black cat. It did not do anything that I could complain of; I only went by its looks, which is often a good thing to go by.

"Somehow I felt I would sooner have trusted the witch. There was no sound now from the Vlachs, and I fancied they must have gone. I was quite alone with this witch and her other cat. That black book on her table was the only hope that I had. But what good I could get out of it I did not know. I could tell you a great deal of those days in the witch's cottage, if I thought that you would be interested; but I spent so much of the time looking into the fire, and in spite of its mystery and wonderful beauty, I am afraid that that is a thing to which you would scarcely care to listen to me, were I to describe to you all those caves of colour and golden valleys and mountains that I saw for many weeks in that witch's fire. Yes, I was there for weeks.

"And all that time the old witch never allowed her fire to go out. She used to drag in large logs and throw them down on her fire and then sit in front of it muttering; spells or old memories, I never knew what she muttered. Sometimes she boiled meat in her cauldron, sometimes tea, and that was about all the housekeeping that she did. Where she got her meat or her tea I never found out. Easily enough, I should say, considering what she could do. All day I sat and looked at the fire, and the other cat did the same. It was a lovely thing to look at.

"As the evening came on and the light of the witch's window grew less and less, the dark part of the eyes of the other cat grew rounder and rounder, and I suppose mine did too. Then we were each of us given a saucer of milk, and the old witch went to bed. Many days passed like that, and then one day it struck me that, pleasant although it was to look in the fire, I should think of no plan of escape if I did that, but would just grow like the other cat and stay all my life, as he appeared to be going to do, whatever he may have been before.

"Perhaps he had been a cat all his life, but never by the slightest hint did he let me see whether he had been or not. And the spring was coming on well, which is like summer here, so I lay outside the door in the sun. The old witch didn't mind. There was a path that went by close to the door, and sometimes as many as ten people would go by in a day. Sometimes nobody went by at all. I watched them all, even though I knew that none of them could help me. And I thought. But I could never think of a plan that would disenchant me.

"One thing I knew at once: and that was who was friendly and who was hostile. All cats know that. But it was no use going away with a friendly old woman. She couldn't disenchant me. The other cat knew that I was up to some game, though that was more than I knew myself, for the problem beat me. What depressed me more than anything was that that black tom-cat did nothing to interfere with me, but merely sat there with a supercilious look that seemed to show it was hopeless.

"People of every race in the Balkans went by in a fortnight, as well as some that looked like Arabs, and all kinds of Turks, not only Balkan Turks but some that looked almost Mongol. I watched them all going by, and the other black cat looked at me every now and then with the look that seemed to show I was doing no good, and never would do any, either. And then one day a Chinaman came by. I wasn't surprised: I had seen so many different kinds of men and women go by as I lay there in the sun. The old witch had gone away to milk her cow, and the other black cat had followed her, and I was quite alone.

"And all of a sudden I remembered the old black book. I ran up to the Chinaman. He would be able to read the book whose spells were all in Chinese. You know how appealing a cat can be. I was all appeal. I had to be. I knew this was my only chance. I rubbed against his legs; I stretched out a paw; I miaowed; I did everything I had ever seen a cat do to attract attention; and when I had got it, I ran a little way and looked round till at last he followed, and I led him right into the old witch's kitchen. If I could get him to read from that book, he might hit on the right spell.

"It was pure chance, but the only chance. I jumped upon the table and opened the book with my paw. He was a very intelligent Chinaman. He saw at once that I wasn't an ordinary cat. I think a European would have been surprised, but he was evidently not that. That saved a lot of time. I pointed to the book and looked up. Then I put my paw to my ear, the ear that was turned towards him, and sat in a listening attitude.

"The Chinaman understood at once, and began to

read aloud. Queer things happened in the room as he read, for — of course — the spells that he read were chosen purely at random. A pair of tongs, for instance, got up and walked out of the room. That, too, would have surprised a European; but the Chinaman read on. Then for a long time came nothing but little spells: flies, for instance, fell dead; and mice ran out of the room backwards; and dust got up in little eddies and whirled away out of the door like dust-devils in Africa.

"It was evident that it was by spells that the old woman did most of her housekeeping, though I had not seen her using them. These little spells soothed me, for I had been rather afraid of some big spell, and did not know what might come into the room, though I comforted myself with the thought that a cat can generally look after itself, whatever comes. I looked up to the low rafters, and saw that I could easily get up there and hide between them and the thatch.

"But nothing bad came. Still nothing useful appeared among the spells, and I remained a cat. I watched the Chinaman continually, fearing that he might grow tired of reading. But he seemed to understand, and read on. Of course, I did not know a word of his language, but I could tell what he was reading by what happened. There were, for instance, several cockroaches running about the floor; and, as the Chinaman read one of the spells, they all fell dead at once; and another spell swept them out the door like a broom.

"Then the other cat walked into the room. It seemed to know what was going on and looked unpleasantly at the Chinaman and at me; but then, it always looked unpleasant. For a moment I thought it would attack the Chinaman, but then it lost interest and sat down and looked at the fire. The Chinaman read on. I feared now that the witch might return.

"Her cat was never very far away from her. If she came in, she would snatch her book and drive the Chinaman out, either with her old broomstick or with some spell; and my only chance would be gone. Still she did not come. A small imp ran into the doorway, called from a wood by one of the spells, and looked inquiringly at us and saw that he was not wanted and ran away. An owl flew by and swept two or three times round the room on his great white wings, and hooted something that witches would have understood, and sailed out again.

"Then a great number of bats appeared, and they fluttered away too, when they found that they were not wanted. And I saw a great many lizards. Of course I never knew what was coming next. And all of a sudden the Chinaman, who had just turned a page, stopped reading straight on, and seemed to pick out a spell, and looked at me with what almost seemed like a smile, but you couldn't tell. And then he read it. It was the right spell, a spell to turn cats back into men.

"When I say back, I do not know if it only turned back cats that had once been men, or whether it would turn any cat into a man. I felt a very odd change at once and the room swam in a mist, and when it cleared the first thing that I saw was that other cat getting up from the fire and hurrying out of the room, no longer a cat, but a man, the kind of man I don't greatly like, a sharp, slick sort of fellow; but not sharp enough for the witch, for he had not escaped being turned into a cat, unless, of course, he had been a cat all the time. Anyway, I was glad to see the last of him. And the next thing I noticed was that I was a man again.

"Well, I thanked the Chinaman in English, and such Greek as I knew. But he didn't know any English and could make nothing of my Greek, and I tried a little French with the same result. But he understood I was grateful. Then he smiled and he went away. What he was doing in the Balkans I never found out, and I never saw him again.

"Then I thought the best thing to do was to follow the example of the other cat and clear out as fast as I could before the witch should return. So I cleared out. And I was only just in time, for I got a glimpse of her coming back with a pail of milk; but, fortunately, she did not see me. It was a lovely summer's day, and the Vlachs were all gone with their straw huts from that part of the country, and I thought I had better go, too."

I wondered what our hostess and the rest of the party would say of that story. So I said nothing, and listened. But the story had been long, and it was late in front of that lovely hot fireplace, and all but I and the man who told that strange tale were asleep.   Ω

THE RESURRECTIONIST AT BOARDING SCHOOL

My roommate, young Burke, I'm afraid,
pursued an unsavory trade,
    which caused him some strain
    to entirely explain
why he slipped out each night with a spade.
                            — Darrell Schweitzer

DEAR DADDY
by Kiel Stuart

illustrated by Rodger Gerberding

It lay between the stark beauty of Big Bend National Park and Alpine, Texas, along Highway 170.

It was as if The Frontier Palace Megamall had magically appeared atop scrubby caliche ground, reminding Rory MacLaren of those crystal-growing sets a baby has for Christmas. As big as 100 football fields, the mall was crammed with facilities: over 800 stores, an arena, zoos, beaches, fortune-tellers, doctors, lawyers, Indian Chiefs.

And now, wrestlers, Rory thought.

Dear Daddy: Greetings from the other side of the world. You'll never guess where I am now. And we're going to be the headliners: The Ripper and The Savannah Beach Boy.

From the instant he and Trent Hoffstead nosed into the mall's vast parking lot, Rory sensed a unique symmetry: this fortress of solitude, governed by its own rules, springing from the flatlands. Alone. But complete.

Well, a job's a job, he thought, *whether you're working for some slimy little promoter in upstate New York or a crazy, bigbucks Texas businessman.* Just one more gig in the endless series of his gypsy life.

Trent guided the Chevy Suburban into a parking space, and Rory took in the mall's white-stucco façade, the people flowing in and out of its entrances. "Look at this place. In the middle of nowhere! How can it survive?"

Trent shut the motor off. "Hell, this is the wave of the future. You don't *need* anything else with a mall like this. It's got gyms, hotels, a post office, medical facilities, even a newspaper. At least that's what the promoter told me on the phone."

They climbed down from the car into hard dry heat, the sky an aching turquoise.

Could something this new, this good, withstand him? Rory hesitated to step forward.

"What?" said Trent.

"Nothing," he murmured, and set his legs into motion. He had to be somewhere. Might as well be here.

Inside, Trent leaned against a pillar, gazing at a map to figure out where the promoter's office was. Rory sat on a nearby bench. Its icy touch seeped into his legs. He gripped the stone rim tight enough to cramp his hands.

Dear Daddy: I see this scene. It's in one of those gin dives we used to go to, when I was a kid. There's this red-haired torcher, and she's singing an old song, "My Heart Belongs To Daddy."

Now why would she do a thing like that?

There was no sense of time or season in the modern feudal state of The Palace — only a glittering, endless array of modern fancies. Things you never knew existed, but could not live without.

Posters and signs grew like leaves, hawking every sort of information from sales to soap opera star appearances through one or two signs about the wrestling-to-come. See it here, see it now, the grudge match of the century.

Rory thought this a particularly appropriate place to have "rassles": In its own way the mall was as phony, and as real. Maybe this yahoo promoter wasn't nuts after all.

Walking through the mall, Rory sensed air held at a constant temperature, devoid of any scents pleasant or unpleasant, any sense of humidity or dryness, anything at all except a faint throb of jangled shopping nerves. They might have been underground, in some post-nuke Brave New World. Only he was the bomb.

Were people staring at him? Did they know?

Skin shrank. Defensive shell grew. He put his head down.

They reached the office and signed their contracts. Handshaking all around. As quickly as it had begun, it was over and they were spat back into the mall.

By the time they got to the hotel Rory could feel the cumulative effects of how he'd spent the last few years. The long drive there hadn't helped either. His tongue dragged a bit.

So he gaped at the hotel lobby, to cover his shortness of breath. It looked either like the ceiling of Madison Square Garden, or the latest Steven Spielberg spaceship, he couldn't decide which.

Trent said, "I'll park the car. Don't forget you owe half on the room."

"Don't you trust me for it? Besides, where the Hell am I going to run to?" Rory scratched his name on the register.

"Take a look around. There are a million places to hide."

Dear Daddy: Hear that?

Upstairs, Rory slid the key into the lock and clicked it open. He took a step inside, and held his breath.

A dungeon. How appropriate for him.

The room was decorated in varying shades of gray and black, with macramé spiderwebs, fake iron bars, and shackles on the imitation stone walls. It shared a timeline with modern, gleaming bath fixtures and refrigerator.

He let his breath out. Two black four-poster beds were divided by what seemed to be a huge floor-to-ceiling window. He went to it, touching its gray burlap curtain aside.

It wasn't a real window. It was some kind of light fixture. The light emanated from a glassed-in fake moon soaring high in a phthalo-blue sky, too much detail for a real moon to have. It was painted so there appeared to be a forest down below, with another castle far in the distance.

It wasn't real, but it was something to look at. He leaned on the "parapet" and gazed at the moon.

Dear Daddy: Something about this place almost smacks of home. Clarendon, New York. The beautiful Catskills, just minutes away from major metropolitan areas. I'm glad you aren't here to share this. But then that's me all over.

"Jesus! Where are the lava lamps?"

He turned to see Trent framed in the doorway, bags dripping from both hands. "Don't get up on my account," he grumbled.

Of course not. Why would he? That would show courtesy. That would make him human. The room was suddenly very quiet.

Trent looked down at his hands. He shifted, clearly uncomfortable. "Well," he said at last. "What have you been up to?"

Why ask? Rory thought. *The usual. Getting loaded, going to jail, beating up innocent folk.* "Oh, hardly anything." And then, because Trent was the closest thing to a friend as he'd ever had, added, "What about you?"

Trent blinked at the ceiling. "Well, now that you mention it . . . I seem to have landed this very lucrative gig in a big old mall."

Rory tried to think of something to say.

At last, Trent moved. "Well, I gotta shave. Wonder if they have little elf-shaped soaps in that bathroom there."

Rory rolled over. He couldn't breathe. Something was sitting on his chest and it wasn't going to move.

Much to his surprise, he closed his eyes, and went out between one breath and the next.

That night he wakened.

Why? What had awakened him this time?

He felt wet. Wet and hot and sticky. He touched the sheets. They felt as if they were covered in warm jelly. He reached over and batted the light on.

In the soft yellowish lamplight his eyes focused on sheets pooled with blood.

He opened his mouth, but it was the slow creaking of a machine, long rusted dead. His throat closed down, the individual cells swelling and growing together. No sound emerged.

He looked down again. The blood didn't want to let him go, clung to him with a hundred tiny clutching arms. He peeled away from those red grasping hands, staggered to a mirror.

Standing behind him was his father. *Did I kill someone this time?* Rory asked, soundless.

Daddy shook his head. In his eyes a pool of infinite sadness shimmered. "Poor little sinner," he said, then was gone.

Rory looked down at his chest. Normal, no wounds. But the pain lingered. As he listened hard for signs of Trent awakening, he rubbed nervous fingers through the chest hair. Nothing. Just a dreaming manifestation of his own rotten insides. The blood of lambs. Slaughtered lambs.

Dear Daddy: It's showtime. I'm changing.

He heard the ring announcer. "In our main event, a special heavyweight grudge bout! Making his way to the ring now . . ."

Trent gave him a little push. He took a step into the aisle.

". . . from the fabulous state of New York, weighing in at 240 pounds . . . The Ripper!"

The crowd heat built. He tensed his arms and shoulders, set his face in a sneer, and felt the Ripper persona slide easily into him.

He swaggered down the aisle, pausing to hurl a wolf's snarl at some of the front-row marks. They returned the favor. He stopped, a hand on the ring ropes, ready to climb in, and swiveled his head around.

The crowd shifted toward him, a low murmur underneath the louder roars. They knew him. Knew his perverted nature, were already responding to it. He ducked inside the ring, prowling its perimeter, ignoring the announcer and referee, raking his gaze from head to head in the stands. He picked out the promoter, up and away near the nosebleed seats, the king checking his subjects.

". . . and his opponent . . . weighing in at 251 pounds, The Savannah Beach Boy —"

A ripple of delight fluttered through the crowd even before the announcer could get out the full name.

"— Trent Hoffstead!"

Pandemonium. Trent burst from the wings, racing straight for The Ripper. The Ripper felt his lip curl.

Trent charged, vaulting into the ring, looking every inch the worldclass athlete. Women and children, teens, even grown men stood to cheer him on.

Dear Daddy: What's it like to be the hero? How does fighting evil feel?

Trent skipped backwards, as lightly as a bullfighter evading his vicious nemesis.

The Ripper clenched his teeth, and lowered his head. *Damn you,* he thought. *Who died and made you Pope?*

He leaped for Trent, locking up, then taking him over in a hip toss.

"Pretty good," Trent whispered, remembering to keep it down.

Good? How dare he? The Ripper fed on rage, used it, forcing the reaction from his own tired frame, sizzling the crowds and astonishing himself with his own intensity.

Trent took his momentum and flew with it, springing off the ropes like a rocket made of flesh, soaring over and under him, the screams of the crowd echoing around The Ripper's head until Trent put him in the finish hold, and he sneaked out his "illegal weapon."

Of course, the ref didn't see it, but the crowds did. The Ripper made his gesture, whistling the loaded fist for Trent's temple, stopping, just barely stopping, short of actual contact.

Trent went down with a crash, The Ripper covered him, and the ref counted to three. Instantly the crowd leapt up, shouting protests.

The Ripper slammed his triumphant arms skyward, and fled for the locker room, leaving the groggy Trent to be "wakened" by the ref, find out about the finish, and boil the crowd to a frenzy.

The Ripper sailed straight past a startled tag team, straight into one of the toilets, and crashed his fist against its steel wall.

Rory woke before dawn and could not get back to sleep.

As quietly and quickly as possible, he dressed and crept out the door. In minutes he was at mall level ready to run.

At this hour, it was a softly deserted ghost town. Down one end of the long arm which housed the hotel, Rory could see only the clean-up crew at work. He stretched out, paying close attention to his tight hamstrings, and started off at a lope, toward the New Age addition.

It was the second mile and he was just beginning to warm up. His breathing was steady, even, strong. He felt light, free.

He ran down the corridor past the clothing stores and candy shops and record stores, now closed.

He smiled. This wasn't a bad place for an early jog. No traffic, no smog, no hot sun or biting insects or barking dogs.

Picking up the pace a little, he neared the area still under construction and nosed down its half-built corridor. Fewer obstacles to run around, since the mall architects hadn't yet carted in those everpresent palm trees and fountains. His legs were warm and fluid in their motion. The Brave New Construction site made it easier, almost like running a track.

Dear Daddy: They noticed me last night. How could they not? You always notice the one who's different.

Now even the cleaning crew was out of sight. The ghost town closed its arms around him. *I think we're alone now,* he sang to himself. *There doesn't seem to be anyone around.*

Instantly, he sensed that was a lie.

A sound followed him. He swallowed, picked up his stride again. Echoes of his own footsteps, or another runner, pacing him from behind? Maybe it was Trent, playing with him. Maybe it was another wrestler who also ran. He glanced over his shoulder. All he saw was a long dark tunnel. Not another human soul.

by Kiel Stuart

Human . . . He lengthened his stride, blowing rhythmically in and out, pumping his arms to speed along. The footsteps slapped loud and close. Their cadence was different from his own. He set his jaw and dodged, but the noise dodged with him.

It was then that he felt hot breath whistling in his ear, steely fingers plucking at his clothes. He stretched his stride further, body slanting low, arms flying. Something that felt like a hand dealt him a blow.

Who was it? An angry mob, torches aloft, closing in on him at last? He felt another blow, twisted his head to look over his shoulder again, running blind.

He ran smack into a wall.

And something swarmed all over him. Rory went down hard, tumbling sideways, scrambling to avoid the hands that now tore at his clothes. He tried to gain his feet. The hands smacked him down. He tried to roll away. They dragged him up, then slammed him against the wall. He heard breathing, grunting, from the unseen thing.

There was nothing to fight, but he fought, bared his teeth, flailed silently. The hands punched him in the solar plexus, doubling him up. They yanked him by the hair, forcing him straight. They poked, clawed, tore, striping his body with pain.

He stumbled along the wall, trying to grab for one of the unseen hands. A step here, another. The grunts rhythmic now, punctuated by low garbled noises, like a voice bubbling up through the mud.

Splat! — he felt something, bigger, harder than a hand, whip him, and the eye-gouging pain of a broken cheekbone burst across his face. Three of his teeth went flying. He reached a corner. The juncture pressed against his back, holding him as neatly as a trap.

Nowhere else to go.

An invisible two-by-four whistled through the air toward his head. He jerked his body backward, clawed at the wall behind him, flung his hands out to seek escape, any escape.

The sound of breaking glass.

The shards were a thousand razor blades digging into his left hand and arm, shredding it to strips of bloody meat. The villagers had their monster cornered.

He tried to pull away. His body ignored the directive. The floor began to sway. He felt his eyes closing, shuddered once, slumped sideways, and hit the floor.

The noise of a vacuum cleaner made him open his eyes.

He was lying in a corner of the partially-constructed corridor. Breath hissed out of him. He scrambled to his feet. At one end of the corridor, the cleanup crew polished the mall floor.

He grabbed for his face. No pain, nothing broken.

He turned to an empty store window for his reflection. No blood, no bruises. His tongue slid along his teeth, searching for damage. No. He had all the teeth he came in there with. He let out a thin breath, slid to the floor, like a sleepy child, and sat there, head in hands. *They almost got me, he thought. But I was one step ahead of them. Evil is clever.*

By the time the cleanup crew drew near him, Rory had recovered enough to get up and slump along toward the hotel, ignoring the curious stares of the mall workers.

Dear Daddy: Here we go again. Time to feed the crowds. But don't look at me. Not tonight.

Rory leaned his back against the locker room's cold hard tiles and closed his eyes. He tried to imagine his mind a large windshield, the wiper arm busily washing it clean with each stroke.

By the time they announced The Savannah Beach Boy versus The Ripper, he was ready.

And so was the crowd. They wanted revenge against him, wanted it so bad they could taste it, judging from the screams.

The Ripper swaggered down the aisle, engaged in some fan-baiting, when Trent charged him from behind and he tumbled forward.

A roar of approval. They liked that. They were one with Trent. Their righteousness his.

The Ripper felt a faint stirring, an angry churning in his gut. *Oh, yeah? Well fuck you too.*

Trent rolled him into a pin and the little ref counted two.

The Ripper kicked out, jumping to his feet. He backed up, showing fear and anger. *Coward that you are,* he taunted himself.

His opponent took advantage of his hesitation, locking up with him. Trent's belly pressed against his, corded arms snaking around his waist.

The crowd applauded. From Trent's bulging muscles, it appeared that The Ripper would be squeezed in two. But Trent had a touch as light and soft as a baby's, and it felt like a dance embrace.

The Ripper caught a joyful gleam in Trent's eyes; he loved this, the fast hard work, the split-second timing of aerial and mat moves, and he was working right up to his potential.

Trent tapped him to signal their next move, popped him up and over in a belly-to-belly suplex. The Ripper landed, twisting, and arched away from a certain pinfall into a bridge as the ref counted to two. Trent grasped him tighter, reversed the bridge. Another two-count. The crowd was on their feet and screaming.

So they locked up again. The Ripper closed his eyes, turning his head away.

The crowd had no faces. The crowd was a mist, swirling around his throat and into his lungs, choking the badness from him.

His eyes flew open to see Trent and the angry-faced crowd. He jerked free, caught Trent in a single-leg takedown and they went a hard twenty minutes to broadway.

Tumbling down the aisle after Trent, The Ripper split off on his own the minute they were out of the crowd's sight.

He took his time coming back down, in the locker room.

Their finish had worked like a charm; the crowd, many repeats among them, willingly suspending their disbelief, outraged at this latest turn of events. They wanted no double disqualification. They wanted Trent to thrash the Ripper, to beat his sniveling cowardly brains out.

Dear Daddy: That's the way it goes, ain't it?

Rory opened his eyes to find himself jogging through the mall, far away from the hotel, away from the construction site, down toward the wing that housed The Animal Farm, with its fake barns and real hay.

No one there. No one but him. He looked down at his black-clad legs, at the black running shoes, moving rhythmically and easily.

And then.

He took a step and the little zoo melted, smearing into a field under a bright Catskills sun. A real barn stood some distance off, and he was running toward it.

Home!

No — his fat little legs pumped hard. He looked over his shoulder. Didn't matter that the barn was all old and jumbly or the fields overgrown. He panted, running closer and closer to the barn.

But then.

Something stepped out of the barn, and came running to meet him. He looked around wildly.

Panic. A gleaming, a shimmer before his eyes. Scalp tightened. His guts melted to liquid. Hands reached for him. In another minute they would have him.

No . . . just another step more . . . He stumbled. Put out his hand to steady himself.

Touched the farm's wooden rail.

He was back in the mall. He shut his eyes in relief, sagged against the railing, breathing deeply.

"Welcome to the Gouge Palace," Daddy said.

His eyes shot open. His father stood to bar his way.

"Wait," said Daddy. "Wait, boy! Look over there."

Rory, teeth chattering, looked down, where Daddy's avenging finger pointed.

The floor was littered with bodies. "Your fans," Daddy said.

Rory turned soundlessly to run. But Daddy stepped out and blocked him, pointed sadly. Another body on the ground. "More of your handiwork?" Daddy asked.

It was a large body, a very large body, lying twisted away from him. Rory put out a shaking hand to touch it. It rolled toward him, blank-eyed and stiff.

Trent. He buckled, folded, and went out.

Trent woke him up in time for work. He didn't ask why Rory had slept all day, or why he now stared at Trent's living form. Rory didn't volunteer the information. Neither said much of anything on the way to the arena.

Jesus, Rory thought, *I'm tired, so tired.* He trudged

to the lockers, leaned against the cold metal as if the temperature would shock him to life.

Dear Daddy: I'm back at work now. And how are things where you live?

Wrestlers and groupies and go-fers were coming and going in a dizzying buzz, but Rory noticed almost none of it. He sat alone on a bench waiting for his persona to arrive.

The Ripper finally took hold. A go-fer came over to say that it was time. He could feel his lip curling already. He got up slow, moving to the runway as if stalking.

They announced him. He held back, hesitating, putting off the walk to the ring, like the reptilian belly-crawler that he was. He peered out from the head of the aisle. Trent was already inside the ring, strutting, walking tall. The crowd showed its approval of him.

Trent "noticed" him holding back. "What's the matter?" His throaty roar carried down the aisle. "Did your mommy say you couldn't come out and play with the big boys?"

The Ripper hesitated, cursing softly. Trent turned his back, playing the crowd.

The Ripper timed his move. Then he charged, bowling Trent over.

But Trent reversed it easily, and flung The Ripper across the ring. They whipped past one another, a sonic cruciform.

"Get him!" Screams from the crowd. "Get the bastard!"

They collided. He had his hands around Trent's thick neck, trying to choke the life out of him.

Trent knocked his hands away, slapped the Ripper flat on his back, then hauled him up again easily, taunting with his fists, polling the crowd for reactions.

Should he? Should he?

The crowd said he should. He pulled the rubber-legged Ripper around, giving everyone in the arena a great view. Helpless in Trent's iron grip, The Ripper staggered this way and that, as pliant as a puppet.

Trent wound up for the big blow, gave it to him good, and was on The Ripper in a flash as soon as he went down.

More screams, gut-level killing joy.

Trent pinned him clean.

Damn you, he thought, *damn you to the grave and back!*

The Ripper shook away after the count, and rolled onto the ring apron. He staggered outside the ring, grabbed a chair. While Trent still had his hand raised by the ref in victory, The Ripper leapt back inside and brought the chair whistling down on his head. Trent dropped like a sack of feed.

Who's the puppet now? thought The Ripper. *Who?*

He beat Trent up afterwards — very, very thoroughly, kicking him when down, using the chair, choking him with a loose tag rope. The crowd screamed for The Ripper's blood. It was music to his ears. Let then scream, let them raise their torches against him. Try and stop me now, he thought.

He gave the prone Trent one final kick, then fled to the locker room and sealed himself off in one of the showers until the hot water had scalded The Ripper out of him.

Then he ducked out the back way. If he said so much as one word to anyone, he would never find the strength to make it to his room.

He was seven years old, in bed at night.

Moonlight splashed across his face, making him twist his head away and scrunch his eyes shut. It hurt.

His nose itched! He wanted to scratch it. He tried to raise a hand to scratch it, but it was no good.

His wrists were tied to the bedposts, and even if he could have managed to roll up his body to scratch with his feet, that wouldn't be any darn good either because his feet were tied too.

Daddy came in and stood there. He heard heavy breathing through the dark and closed his eyes, praying Daddy wouldn't come in.

But he did. He always did.

Without any words, Daddy hovered over him. Then he said, "Poor Rory, all alone. No one to touch him or hold him."

"It's okay, Daddy." His voice was tiny.

"Aren't you scared? Scared of the dark?"

It wasn't the dark that frightened him. "It's okay, Daddy," he repeated. "Really."

"Poor sweet Rory. I'll hold you."

Rory woke with a sharp hiss of breath.

Where's Daddy?

Out of bed, he staggered for the fake Castle window. He opened his mouth, breath shuddering back into his lungs. His hand went to his chest.

The dream took on acid clarity. Long-suppressed memory flooded back.

He closed his eyes against it. But the memory came anyway. Blood on the sheets: his small smooth hairless chest, the skin scraped away by vengeful scrubbings with steel wool. That crowd-turned-mist: the near-drownings. The attack in the mall: the night Daddy had knocked three teeth out of his head. The blood of the lamb. The things Daddy had done, back on the farm.

The farm . . .

(*Rory sensed a unique symmetry: this fortress of solitude, governed by its own rules, springing from the flatlands. Alone. But complete.*)

Of course. Just like back home.

Quietly, he opened the curtains and stared out at the Castle's fake, shiny moon, feeling its unreal light pierce his eyes all the way back to his skull.

He tried to stand in silence, tried not to breathe or make a sound.

But he must have made enough noise to wake Trent. He heard Trent stir, then sleepily call over, "What's up? Why are you starin' at the moon?"

It was a long time before he answered. "Because I can," said Rory.

Trent grunted, then rolled over, and the sound of his steady breathing filled the room. Rory gazed at the phony moon. It was quiet and still.

In the lingering clarity of recall, he thought:

So it wasn't me. It was him. I wasn't the one who took us to bars when I was six. I wasn't the one who sold me to men when I was eight. I wasn't the one who asked my father to come to my room when I was tied down and —

— And then he blew himself away the day I turned fourteen.

He swallowed the lump in his throat. *They're not really staring at me, all those people.*

But a tiny sound snaked around his ears. Soft whispers danced in the room.

He tried to close his ears to it.

The sounds welled up. He shifted from one foot to another, put his hands over his ears, and still he heard it.

Thrumming in his ears now.

No.

He closed his eyes, cutting off the light from the artificial moon. A tear squeezed out and made its way down his face.

The words hovered close for another heartbeat. Finally took shape.

"Daddy's here. Daddy will always be here."

He tensed.

Okay. I'm ready. No more running.

He prepared for the wrestling match of his life.

And felt his father's large bony hand, laid on his shoulder. Ω

A TALK WITH JOE LANSDALE
by Darrell Schweitzer

Worlds of Fantasy & Horror: In the introduction to *By Bizarre Hands,* Lewis Shiner goes to some length to define your place in the horror field. I have my own theory that you're the Warren Zevon of horror. I'm thinking of the song "Excitable Boy," which, if it had a Texas accent, would be a Joe Lansdale story. Where do you see yourself in the context of the field?

Lansdale: I don't give any thought to where I see myself. I just do what I do. Whatever interests me at the time, that's what I pursue. But I don't have much conscious attitude about it, other than I try to write about the people I know, the characters I know — which is not to say that all the people I know are bad people, but those are the ones that interest me.

WofF&H: Is it because there aren't enough plot conflicts in the lives of good people? What's the fascination with the bad ones?

Lansdale: I think we all know bad ones from afar. I think it's that they're so different. I think too that anytime you see something that's bad, you recognize something of yourself in it, whether you admit it or not. I think that the worst things that people do are in all of us — not that all of us do those things — and also the best things people do are in all of us. So I think it — the evil side — is an interesting side to explore, because it's a side that you don't think about too much. Publicly you have to pursue something else. So it's kind of nice, in fiction, to be a human monster for a while, or at least try and understand what makes 'em tick. It's just one of the mysteries of life that this kind of stuff exists. It doesn't mean that I want to be these people or that I'm impressed with them. But I'm amazed by them.

WofF&H: How much of your material is based on fact? Have you ever found yourself confronted by such people? A lot of your stories seem to be about secret, murder rituals in back-country towns.

Lansdale: Yeah. A lot of them are based on the truth. One story, "The Night They Missed the Horror Show," most of the things in that story either happened, or they were apocryphal stories that I'd heard when I was growing up, and I put them all together. They didn't all happen to those people in one night, but a friend of mine is actually the guy that dragged the dead dog around. He wasn't a bad guy like in the story. He was just drunk and a little stupid that night. But the events that happen to these characters supposedly did happen to some people and I just took them and consolidated them. The two guys who were the villains, Vinnie and Pork, I knew those guys. They weren't

called that. But they were real and they did things very similar to that. So, that's realistic, yeah.

I write about things which I generally think are despicable, but I often write about them straight-on to the point where people sometimes think I have sympathy for them, which always surprises me.

WofF&H: You always write about rural degenerates, which seems to give rural people a bad name.

Lansdale: I think about that sometimes, but I think what it is, is that I'm so drawn to the horrific, and to crime in general, that I'm not going to be writing about the good people. I'm not trying to say this is the way *all* the people I know are, or this is the way all the people are in East Texas, but these are the sort of people I'm writing about — at least now. If I lived in Maine or California or New York, I'd still write about those people. They may not drive the pickup trucks, but they're there. Stephen King has certainly written about rednecks in Maine. They're everywhere. I don't think ignorance is a Southern thing by any means. I think we Texans know ignorance when we see it though, and I am not sure that some others do.

WofF&H: For a long time, everyone seemed to assume that that sort of behavior was a Southern thing, but then I come from Philadelphia where we had Gary Heidnick's famous body shop.

Lansdale: I think it's just that the Southerners are fascinated by that. We have the term Southern Gothic because for some reason it has always been part of our culture to observe weirdness. We look at it straight on. I think Flannery O'Connor said, "We still know weird when we see it."

WofF&H: Some of your stories strike me as being like more straightforward Faulkner. I'm thinking of Faulkner stories like "The Hound," for example.

Lansdale: I like Faulkner. I tend to lean more toward the humorous grotesque stuff he did, stuff like "Mule in the Yard." I thought that was good. Or one that was very creepy, was "Barn Burning." To me, that's the way I tend to think of horror. I don't think so much of ghosts and rattlings in the attic. Stuff like that doesn't do much for me. I'm not saying that I haven't read stories like that that don't work for me, but as a writer, if I'm going to spend any time on something, it's hard for me to believe in something like that. I'm more interested in what people do to one another, because that scares me more. Therefore I'm able to make that more real, because those things happen. I don't mean that I feel *obligated* to write about that, or that I only write about that, but the older

I get and the more I write, the less interested I am in things that go "Boo!" in the night, unless it's some*body* doing it.

WofF&H: You'd say, then, that you're not all that much interested in supernaturalism?

Lansdale: I am as a reader, but not so much as a writer, because I don't have the patience for it. As I reader, I have to be in the mood. I grew up on supernatural fiction, and I loved it, and I still love it in a certain compartment of my mind, but I don't read as much of it, and I certainly am not drawn to write it as much. Once in a while a story will occur to me. I have written some supernatural things, but it doesn't seem to be what I'm designed to do as a writer. I often like a lot of things as a reader that I'm not interested in writing.

WofF&H: How about using supernatural lore from Texas? Robert E. Howard made a couple of attempts, but otherwise I don't know that very much of it has ever been done. It's probably a very rich subject.

Lansdale: Most of the stuff that's been done has been non-fiction books, Texas ghost books, and such, most of them not too good. But, as a writer, that doesn't interest me too much. I won't box myself in and say I won't do that. If something interests me enough and excites me enough, I just might; but it seems that my mood is more toward the more realistic horrors. It's what really scares me. It seems to be what I am able to put down in a convincing manner, and that's why I pursue it.

WofF&H: At what point does this sort of "horror" become what we at least used to call crime fiction? Is there a meaningful difference between horror fiction and crime fiction?

Lansdale: I don't know that there always is a difference. I thought a lot of the stories I wrote were crime and that's where I tried to publish them, but the horror editors bought them. I thought "The Night They Missed The Horror Show" was a crime story. I had written part of it and had it lying around for a long time, and then David Schow was doing the anthology, *The Silver Scream,* and asked me to write a story for him. I said, "Well, I've got one, but it's not spooks. It's the stuff that really scares me. It's the attitudes that really scare me." And he said, "Hey, write it." So I did. And when I wrote *The Nightrunners,* I thought it was a suspense novel, and that's the way I tried to market it for five years. Nobody would buy it. A lot of the stuff that I wrote that was later published as horror, I wrote as crime or mainstream. I didn't have any idea it was horror. I have nothing against horror. It just never occurred to me. When people started buying it and wanting to call it horror, they didn't hurt my feelings any.

WofF&H: Since you're so much of a regional writer, your background must be important to what you write. So, could you describe where you grew up, traumatic childhood encounters with hatchet murderers, that sort of thing?

Lansdale: I had a real happy childhood. I did grow up very rural, small towns, in the country much of the time. My father couldn't read or write, but he was an extremely good man, a powerful man. I had sort of a Huck Finn existence growing up because of where I grew up, in East Texas. Most people when they think of Texas think of sand and cactus and stuff like that. Texas is very varied. Where I come from is more like Arkansas or Louisiana, a lot of woods and a lot of rivers and creeks.

I did grow up with a lot of old ghost stories, though. But as far as things that happened in my life, it mostly happened to others that I observed. And there were stories I heard my father tell. My father was in his forties when I was born, so it was sort of like being raised by grandparents, to some extent. My people date back through the Civil War. My grandmother, who died in her nineties, remembered travelling in a covered wagon and saw one of the last Buffalo Bill Wild West Shows.

So I grew up with a storyteller tradition, too, which a lot of East Texans have. I think that, in the past, a lot of it may have come out of the fact that they couldn't read or write. So they passed on what they wanted to tell through stories, which of course were embellished as they went. I heard stories from my father which were obviously stories handed down from the middle 1800s and still going. I've used variations of them. I don't think I've ever told any of them literally. I probably should, to preserve them. I'll probably tell my children those stories. But my background was rural, country. Among the people I grew up with, there was no college education at all. They were mostly blue collar, a lot of farm stock. My generation was the first where anyone went to college. I had a couple of years. My brother had a couple of years. I think his son, my nephew, is the first one to have a college education among the Lansdales that I know of, at least on my side of the group.

WofF&H: Coming as you did from such a background, what made you become a writer?

Lansdale: My mother was a reader, of non-fiction especially. But she always encouraged me to read, and by the time I was nine years old, I never wanted to be anything else. I really don't know how to explain it to you. I think a lot of writers find that. I don't know about you, but as a writer I seem to have a knack for remembering things from my childhood real well. I *distort* them a lot, for stories, which I'm sure every writer does, but I can't remember anyone coming to me and saying, "You ought to be a writer." I do remember wanting to be one since I was nine. I do remember, when I was about twelve or thirteen, discovering Edgar Rice Burroughs, and then I knew that was what I wanted to do. I read the *Iliad* and the *Odyssey* as a kid. I used to keep the *Iliad* under my pillow because I read that Alexander the Great did that. I've just always been fascinated with stories.

WofF&H: Did your family encourage you?

Lansdale: Yeah, they did. My father, he always said, "Whatever you want to do, you'll do it." I never lacked for confidence. I don't want this to sound like plain ego. I certainly know how to fail, and I think learning how to fail is important too. But if you have confidence in yourself, failure doesn't scare you any. That's one thing that my parents instilled in me, confidence. They were very straight-ahead people, who always felt, "Eyes forward, ears back, go get it done."

WofF&H: A lot of writers from blue-collar backgrounds encounter parental pressure to "get a real job."

Lansdale: My mother always used to say I should have something to fall back on. I think a lot of parents did that. I never really had anything to fall back on. I did all the blue collar jobs. I went to college for a little while, and I was going to be an archaeologist, but at some point I said, "Hey, I want to write." So I dropped out, I didn't drop out because of a lack of interest in archaeology but because I had a greater interest in writing and felt like what I was being taught in school wasn't helping me any. Even in the English courses I didn't think they knew what they were talking about, and for the most part, I still don't. I don't think a course in writing will do you any good unless it's taught by a writer who's published; somebody who's writing now, not someone who wrote thirty years ago.

WofF&H: So you wouldn't want to take a course from a brain surgeon who had never taken a brain out . . .

Lansdale: Exactly.

WofF&H: What sort of things did you do while you were learning to write?

Lansdale: Actually, I dug ditches. I was a bodyguard very briefly. I was a bouncer. I tried farm work. I was a janitor. I worked in public relations for Goodwill Industries, and as a transportation manager for Goodwill Industries as well. And, I worked in a rose field as a farm laborer for other people. Just every damn, dirty job you can think of. When I was in high school I worked on garbage trucks in the summer. Whatever there was to make a buck, to survive, I've done it.

WofF&H: Presumably all this really paid off by adding to the background of your fiction.

Lansdale: Oh, yeah. That's where I get a lot of the assholes I write about, and all of the good people I write about too. Some of the best people I ever met, I met them on those jobs. And still, while a lot of the people I hang out with are writers, a lot of my friends are carpenters and people who do blue collar work. I generally prefer their company.

WofF&H: Because they're more straightforward and less pretentious?

Lansdale: Yeah. Less bullshit. Also, too, I think it's because their backgrounds are similar to mine, so I know where they're coming from and what they're talking about, and I have a lot of respect for people who

make their living with their hands. I certainly couldn't do it, other than I was the guy who could lift the big rock. That's as good as I got. I didn't have any real skills. I wasn't a carpenter or a painter or anything. Everything I did like that, I screwed it up. [Laughs]

WofF&H: How long were you trying to write before you started to sell?

Lansdale: It depends on how you look at it. I had been writing, as I said, since I was nine. It took me about two years from the time I decided I was going to start writing to when I started to sell. Actually, the first thing I sent out was an article I did when I was twenty-one. It sold. I did four more articles, and they all sold. Then I decided to switch to fiction, and I didn't sell anything for two years, I think. Then I started selling, and gradually it picked up, more and more. *Mike Shayne's Mystery Magazine* bought my first fiction, a thing called "The Full Count." It was a novella. I went on from there.

WofF&H: The earliest thing of yours I can remember is *Dead in the West* as a serial in *Eldritch Tales*.

Lansdale: Which is very different from the book. The serialization is pretty sloppy. That's my fault. But, actually I had a novel before *Dead in the West*, which was *Act of Love*. And then I wrote one under a pen-name — Ray Slater — called *Texas Night Riders*. I wrote it in eleven days, and it shows. That was actually my first novel sale, but it came out three years after *Act of Love*. I was writing short stories well before that. In the middle to late '70s I was writing short stories for different magazines, and non-fiction for *True West* and *Frontier Times*.

WofF&H: Have you thought to write more on the order of horrific westerns? You might be uniquely suited to do this.

Lansdale: It's occurred to me. I don't know that I will. I really would like to write westerns. I don't know that I'd want to do that and nothing else. I'm happy with what I'm doing now. I'm writing two crime novels for Mysterious Press right now. But I feel that the western aspect of my work is far from finished. At least I like to think so. As for there being more horrific westerns, I don't know.

WofF&H: Does the western today have very specific, generic expectations which restrict the writer?

Lansdale: About like horror. About like science fiction. The same ones. It's there for every genre if you let it take you over. I don't think it's any more restrictive than any of the others. I think if you want to do interesting work, you can. When I wrote *The Magic Wagon*, I thought it was a western. It just had some potential fantasy elements in it. It depends on how you look at it. If you read it one way, there are no fantasy elements at all. But the characters perceive them as fantasy elements. So, I don't know. I don't think the restrictions in westerns are any worse than anywhere else. I think it's what you do with it. It's what you bring to it. If you can't find your own voice, if you can't find something about the subject that interests you, you're going to write the same dull, old stuff.

WofF&H: How does the creation of a story occur for you? Do you write it out in a burst, or take notes, or what?

Lansdale: Very seldom do I ever take notes. Once in a while something will come to mind and I'll write it down on a sheet of paper and promptly lose it. But usually if I do write it down, it'll stick with me. But more likely, a couple of ideas will hit, and I'll think about them and I'll sit down — I work a regular schedule. I try to work in the mornings until noon, then take off for lunch and go back and work in the early afternoon. I used to do that seven days a week. I don't work seven days a week now. It's about five and a half.

But the stories vary. Usually it's some particular scene or a character will come to mind and a story will grow out of it, or an incident. But there's no set pattern to the way I work. I don't outline, if that's what you mean. I don't take a lot of notes. If I feel like a story needs research to make it believable, I'll research.

WofF&H: Have you had much feedback from the sort of people you write about? I don't particularly mean the crazed murderers, but the farmers and blue-collar-people. Do they read your stuff? How do they feel about it?

Lansdale: I haven't heard much from them. I've had a couple of people who wrote and said, "I hate niggers too," and I had to write back and say, "I think you missed the whole point of the story." They didn't catch the satire. A lot of my stories certainly have that interest or edge in them. I got that from Mark Twain. He's one of my favorite writers. But, other than that, no, not really.

WofF&H: A friend of mine once described the typical Joe Lansdale story as one in which, "You don't know whether to laugh or throw up."

Lansdale: [Laughs]

WofF&H: In order to prove the point, she then proceeded to read to those assembled, "My Dead Dog Bobby," from your Pulphouse collection.

Lansdale: I don't know what to say to that. Yeah, that's true. That story is certainly a sick puppy, if you'll pardon the expression.

WofF&H: You can read that story as horror or as humor. You've got both sides of the coin there.

Lansdale: I learned that from Robert Bloch. I doubt Robert Bloch would claim any connection to my stories. [Laughs] I love his work. I grew up on it. I think he showed me that horror and humor are very similar. You can walk an edge there. You can also fall off and the story can be destroyed. It can be too horrific, just plain ugly, nasty, or it can be just too damn funny to get your point across. So it's a hard line to walk, but that's what has always interested me, walking that line between the outrageous and the horrific. Actually I find that the outrageous stuff is what has actually *happened*. And that's what you'll think I made up. The stuff that seems not so outrageous, I made up.

WofF&H: You must indeed get some interesting fan mail.

Lansdale: Yeah, like I said, I get a note every now and then that says, "Yeah, I hate niggers too," and that upsets me, but I can't be the Cliff Notes for everybody. Most of the stuff I get is pretty intelligent. I was talking to a lot of other writers who have some real weird fans, and I've had a couple of odd things, but for the most part it's been real intelligent and interesting because they seem to run the gamut from your blue-collar to your academics who read it. A lot of the stuff that I've written has appeared in literary magazines, so it's an odd audience.

WofF&H: I'm surprised they'll let you be that violent in literary magazines.

Lansdale: Well, I don't know that they would publish "The Night They Missed the Horror Show." Some of the things that were done in literary mags were things like "Trains Not Taken," which is just strange. It's an alternate universe western sort of thing. There's that western influence again. And there was another one I did for a literary magazine, called "A Car Drives By," which was redone as "Not from Detroit." But I've also done some other oddball things of that nature that I wouldn't have expected to appear in those kind of magazines, but did.

WofF&H: No writer can remain creatively healthy and do the same thing over and over. Presumably there must be a limit to the number of stories of strange, secret rituals in back-country towns and to the number of crime-suspense novels you can write. What next? Where would you like to evolve as a writer?

Lansdale: I think you've got to change. If you look at the collection, *Stories by Mama Lansdale's Youngest Boy*, which contains primarily my earliest work, you'll see that most of it isn't about that at all. It's about weird false teeth and creatures out of the dump — more traditional horror subjects — and then you have the stuff in *By Bizarre Hands*, and then the stories I'm doing now are a bit different. They're much more crime-oriented. They're a little more traditional in structure, but I don't think of them as traditional stories. I think you have to change or else you die. I don't want to be known as the guy who writes the same type of story over and over. You can write one redneck story after another, but after a while, what's the point? I'm doing something new now, and I hope ten years from now to be doing something new again. I hope it doesn't take that long.

WofF&H: You also have to watch out for repetition of details or devices. I noticed recently when I put together a collection of my own stories that I had three stories in a row in which people came back from the dead and manifested themselves by rustling around in the kitchen. You had two stories in a row in *By Bizarre Hands* in which cars break down.

Lansdale: No matter what you do you're going to repeat some themes, but if you're careful you can try and not repeat them as often. But you have certain themes and certain obsessions and you can't get away from them, but if you find new approaches and new ways to express yourself, you can do better work. I find that I'll think, "God damn, I used that element in some other story." So you're going to repeat yourself to some extent. But the idea is to tell a different story in a different way, and that's the best you can do. What makes your stories work if they work at all is the fact that you do have certain obsessions.

WofF&H: Most writers have a limited cast of characters. There are usually about five, and they're based on yourself, a few people you've known, and so on. But sometimes you deliberately try to vary this —

Lansdale: I think you can try so hard that you develop artificial material. Some people just have a very limited approach and there's not anything they can do about it, no matter how hard they try. I think to some extent, I have forced myself to relax and say, "Okay, just back off and let's just see what else is inside your head, and what new themes you can put into your work." The best thing to do is to be observant, to read a wider spectrum, to observe people, to run in different circles. That's what's happened to me in the last couple of years: my work is usually changing before I'm able to change it. By the time I'm writing certain stories, I already have a new attitude, new emotions, new stories in mind, and it'll take me two years to get to them. Recently Ellen Datlow said of one of my stories that this sort of thing — redneck horror — is getting tired. And if you really look, only seven or eight of my stories are like that. The rest of them are totally different. Those are the ones that people remember, see. I didn't think of it as a criticism. I thought superficially she was right. Technically she was wrong, because there's only a handful of stories of that nature. (I don't want people to remember just those.)

WofF&H: But if you wrote New England yuppie horror no one would believe you.

Lansdale: Well, I have to write what interests me. I don't write for other people so much as I write for myself. I think that's the best thing I can do, because I'm the one who's going to get bored quicker than anybody else over a certain type of story. I'm the guy who has to labor over a story that somebody might read in an hour or less. A story that may take me a week or a month to write. Or a novel might take six months or a year to write.

WofF&H: The public perception of your work is obviously based on what has been published. What about the material that hasn't yet appeared, which will surprise them?

Lansdale: I hope it'll surprise them. You never can tell. I don't want to say that the fiction I'm writing now is more upbeat — that implies something I don't mean to say — but it has a totally different attitude, even though the voice remains the same. I have no way to describe it until people see it and they can tell me. I seem to be working more directly into the crime field than horror. I am still using some of the off-the-wall

things that interest me, as for what kind of stew I put together, I guess the readers will have to tell me.

WofF&H: Do you think that you'll ever face a publisher-typecasting problem? I've always wondered what would happen if Stephen King wrote a romantic comedy. Would they bring it out with a black cover and something menacing on it?

Lansdale: Probably. Obviously I don't have the great popularity that Mr. King has, which makes him more of a brand name in the eyes of the publishers, but if you look at my books, for *Act of Love* I think it said "Novel" on the spine. *Dead in the West* was obviously published as horror. *The Nightrunners* was published as horror. The two *Drive-In* books were published as science fiction. *The Magic Wagon* was published as a western. *Cold in July* was published as a novel. *Savage Season* was suspense, although they're both akin to each other. *By Bizarre Hands,* horror. *Stories from Mama Lansdale's Youngest Boy,* horror. Now I'm doing two novels that are being published as crime-suspense from Mysterious Press. But I think everybody wants me to buy a label and say, "This is what I do." Probably the closest I've come to doing that is what I'm doing for Mysterious Press, because they're giving me an opportunity to reach out to a bigger audience. As for whether I will continue to say, "Yes, I'm a crime-suspense writer," that remains to be seen. As long as I am interested in those types of stories, I will write them. When I get interested in something else, I won't write them. Even though I'm doing these two for Mysterious Press, I'm also doing one small *Drive-In* book, the last one, and I am also doing a novel that takes place in East Texas in the 1930s and has some possible supernatural elements. So I am keeping the subjects mixed.

WofF&H: If you get popular enough in a certain way, some publisher may say, "Here's five million dollars. I want another book just like the last one."

Lansdale: I'm not that popular, and I've already had that. I've had publishers tell me "You're never going to make a career until you settle down to do one thing or another." And to some extent, Mysterious Press is saying, "Okay, we'll call these suspense novels, but what we want is Joe Lansdale." Obviously I'm not going to write a romance for them. It has to have a crime element. So much of my work has that anyway and I seem to naturally lean in that direction. I find suspense such an open and varying field. I think you could write a horror novel and it could be suspense, of a sort. I think it's true of science fiction, whatever. It excites me right now. It's a wide-open field. It's a different approach. Hey, they're paying me money too. I'm not in this just for the art. But I'm going to do what I think is both artistically-correct and Lansdale-correct. That's really all I can do.

WofF&H: Has there been any movie interest in your work?

Lansdale: I've sold a lot of it to the movies. *Cold in July* to John Irvin, who did *Ghost Story*; *Hamburger*

Hill; and *Tinker, Tailor, Soldier, Spy*. He's had a real varied career. He did the *Robin Hood* made for Fox. He's had *Cold In July* for about four years now. I did a screenplay for it. *Savage Season*, John Badham has that one. *The Drive-In* has been optioned. *Dead in the West* has been optioned four years in a row. There's interest in it again right now. "The Far Side of the Cadillac Desert" was optioned a couple years in a row. I don't know if it's going to be renewed or not. "The Pit" is supposed to be filmed soon. Whether it'll actually happen, or not, I don't know. I read the screenplay. It didn't owe a lot to my story that I could see. They used dialogue out of it, but they didn't understand the essence of it at all. And there's been some interest in a couple of others that I think will be nailed down before long.

And a lot of comic-book interest. There will be a lot of things adapted into comics, and I will be doing some original comics inspired from some of my stories. There will be a *By Bizarre Hands* comic book soon from Dark Horse Comics.

WofF&H: Well, to wrap this up, any thoughts on where you'll be twenty years from now?

Lansdale: I hope I'll still be writing novels and short stories. I hope I'll still be writing films and comics. Primarily it's the prose that I'm interested in. Short stories are what I love, but right now I feel that I'm temporarily burned out in short stories. That's one reason I've put a lot more effort into the novels. But, who knows? I go where the wind blows, at least where the Lansdale wind blows.

WofF&H: Thanks, Joe.   Ω

BAD MEAT

Not watching nor waiting
But casually sitting,
Aware that awareness
Is rarely quite fitting,

It snorts once for nothing
And rubs its fat belly,
And laughs that it's living
And stuck in a deli.

The chilly display case,
With pickled boned herring,
And olive bologna,
And customers leering,

It only need thump once
To dissuade all from buying,
But instead it sits pretty —
An enticement to trying.

— **Frederick Stansfield**

SOMEWHERE, UNDER THE RAINBOW

The ghost of Judy Garland
   Is visible at night:
Amphetemine-white phantom
   Floats through moon-mist light.

The Emerald City's toppled,
   The yellow bricks are dust,
And Dorothy's dead in Kansas;
   Tin Woodman's gone to rust.

The ghost of Judy Garland
   Is audible as well —
New York, New York's her kind of town —
   Manhattan-angel's Hell.

— **Steve Eng**

THE WANDERER

Sunrise blazed and woke the sand,
Shimmered light across the land.
A lonely figure draped in black,
Cowl loosely shrouding head and back.
No feature shown through open slit,
The eternal wanderer, backlit.

Winds of time bleating, blowing,
Robes forever flapping, flowing.
Pleated layers intertwining,
Ropes around the waist unwinding.

Not a whispered word is spoken,
All is said; the peace unbroken.
Horizon bound the vision sailed,
He fell from earth as twilight paled,
And disappeared without a trace,
Emerged at dawn in a distant place.

— by and illustrated by Jill Bauman

THE WANDERER by Jill Bauman

FATHER VADIM'S ANGEL

by Donna Farley

illustrated by Keith Minnion

March's unkind wind shrieked at the doors of Saint Philoskotia's Orthodox Church. Inside, Father Vadim's guardian angel felt a nervous flickering run through his luminescence as he watched the congregation preparing for the first service of Lent, vespers with the rite of mutual forgiveness. This ceremony consisted in each member of the parish prostrating himself before each of the others in turn, saying, "Forgive me, my brother," or "Forgive me, my sister."

The first year of Father Vadim's appointment, many of his parishioners had avoided the vesper service altogether, but they were cured of their truancy thereafter when Father spent the entire next day seeking them out at their homes and workplaces to fall on his face before them, begging forgiveness and then taking them into an enthusiastic bear hug. They had little choice but to respond, but some of them never did learn to look their priest in the eye during the now-annual rite.

Father Vadim's guardian angel was named Ariel — no relation to the Shakespearian sprite, his name meant "lion of God." It was appropriate, for he had been fiercely devoted to his charge for fifty-seven years now.

"The man is a living saint," the angel remarked to his partner as they watched the mortals exchanging forgiveness. If the observed could have become observers, the angels would have appeared as man-sized balls of light, their intensity varying from moment to moment with the spiritual states of their charges.

Shelumiel, Ariel's partner of over thirty years (being in charge of Father's *matushka*) responded to Ariel's remark by allowing his globular luminescence to throb slowly, the angelic equivalent of a nod.

Ariel had made the same remark many times before. It was usually occasioned by the priest's patient response to the slings and arrows of the outrageous president of the parish, Andrei Skolopsky, who regularly denounced such damnable offenses as Father's insistence on the use of English as opposed to Slavonic, or his rather pointed sermons about drunkenness or tithing. Poor Shelumiel's protégée, *Matushka* Tamara, would weep bitterly, railing at this continual nastiness. Her husband took it all in stride; yet nowhere was his holiness more apparent than at this first service of Lent each year.

Ariel could not help casting a slightly worried glance at his partner. On Forgiveness Sunday in previous years, Ariel knew, *Matushka* Tamara's soul had been like the moon: clouded with bitterness and anger, it had taken an immense amount of energy from Shelumiel to clear the darkness so his ward could once again shine, reflecting the Light of all. But this year, she was like a damnable black hole, draining her guardian's light into a pit of sinful despair.

There were unfortunately many church members at Forgiveness Vespers that evening whose shameless hypocrisy had long ago caused their guardians to desert them, and some even had demons tagging at their heels. One purpose of the forgiveness rite, though the participants little suspected it, was to drive away devils and re-attract estranged guardian angels to newly-cleansed souls.

Shelumiel's luminescence suddenly ebbed alarmingly as Andrei, having escaped the beaming and forgiving Father Vadim, made his reluctant prostration before the priest's wife.

Matushka stood mute and trembling, clutching her skirt with white knuckles. When Andrei stood up and muttered, "Forgive me, my sister," she turned slowly on her heel and walked down the nave and out the doors of the church.

"Tamara!" cried Shelumiel, though of course only the other angels could hear him, and they were too busy with their own charges to spare more than a glance for the spiritually repulsive woman.

"Shelumiel!" Ariel said, for his partner was hovering motionless beside him. "For Heaven's sake, get after her. You can't leave her alone in that state!"

"I . . . I can't do it," moaned Shelumiel, his celestial voice all stretched thin and scratchy. Ariel realized his partner's powers were even more shockingly depleted than he had imagined.

"Shelumiel, your luminescence wouldn't light a birthday candle! Why did you let it get so low — you should have left her long ago!" Ariel chided him.

When Shelumiel did not reply, Ariel sent a call for aid Heavenward. To his surprise, an immediate response came in the form of a very highly placed archangel, a flaming presence who made the crowd of simple guardian angels look like so many faint stars beside a brilliant sun. The archangel gathered up Shelumiel's essence and prepared to rapture him back to Heaven.

"Shelumiel is on furlough as of now," the archangel informed Ariel. "You are assigned to watch your partner's ward until we can find another worker strong enough to take her on."

"Me?" Ariel's own luminescence suddenly paled.

"You needn't leave your own work. Just do what you can for her whenever she's with your man."

"Please, Ariel," Shelumiel said faintly, "for the sake of our partnership, keep watch on her for me!"

Ariel observed Father Vadim for a few moments as he wound up the service, then turned back to the impatiently flickering essence of the archangel. "I'll do my best, but Father has so many trials himself —"

"So have we all," the archangel remarked unsympathetically. "What with the population explosion and all, the guardian angel shortage is getting desperate. Don't expect any help for a while." And with that the double luminescence vanished back to the celestial plane, leaving Ariel to trail Father Vadim out of the church to the car, where *Matushka* sat weeping behind the wheel.

"Ah, my dear, don't cry," said Father as he slipped into the car and put one arm around her.

"I have plenty to cry about!" she shrieked. "I hate Andrei Skolopsky! I hate this wicked parish! I hate the whole Church and I hate God too!"

Father stroked his beard sadly and thoughtfully. Ariel shuddered at the blasphemy and huddled in the far corner of the car, as far as possible from the putrefying spiritual bog the woman had become.

Tamara jammed the key savagely into the ignition and started the engine. Ariel's essence tingled with apprehension, and he hovered closer to Father.

"Tamara dear, let me drive," Father said gently.

"I want to drive!" said Father's wife, and put the vehicle into reverse. It lurched out of the rector's parking space, and she shifted to drive and shot out of the parking lot, narrowly missing several parishioners whose guardian angels glared redly at the hapless Ariel.

The car blasted down the road like the proverbial infernal bat.

"Tamara, stop!" cried Father. "You will kill us!"

"Good!" she screamed back. "No more Andrei, no more nasty gossip, no more Forgiveness Vespers!"

Ariel saw the impact coming, and slipped into telescopic time. While he hovered, time slowed to a near-stop, and he eased out of the car to examine the site of the accident-to-be.

Father's wife had been doing thirty miles over the limit, and a bump in the road had forced the steering wheel out of her control, placing the car's trajectory on a collision course with an eighteen-wheel truck.

Ariel picked over the scenario as if he had all the time in the world — which he did, but the longer he remained in telescopic time, the more of his resources he used. Furthermore, to create any physical effect that would alter the course of the impending crash, Ariel would be forced to assume a material form. Such an energy-draining metamorphosis might leave him unable to phase back to his natural pure energy form

by Donna Farley

for a while. Worse, he could be caught in the impact himself. That wouldn't mean death, as it would for a mortal, but it would mean a lengthy convalescence in Heaven, longer than Shelumiel's furlough. He would almost certainly be unable to return to work in Father Vadim's lifetime.

That thought made him desperate, for he was fonder and prouder of his current assignment than he had ever been of any other protégé. He floated over to where the truck driver sat frozen behind his wheel, not yet aware of the car that was poised to hurtle into his front end like a meteor. Ariel did not like what he saw. Even with help from an angel, there was just too much truck there for the driver to turn it out of the way fast enough.

Ariel flashed back to Father's car. He could see no way to fix the problem but to jerk the wheel out of *Matushka*'s hands and replace it on the right path.

Ah, but would such a close call do anything to alter her dangerous hysteria? She could just as easily cause another accident a few moments from now — *now* being the moment when Ariel had stepped out of realtime. And he had no illusions that he would have any resources left to cope with a second crash.

There was one other possibility. Though the thought of such a failure made Ariel's luminescence whirl dizzily, like snowflakes in a blizzard, he did not see how the archangel could fault him, under the circumstances. His primary duty, after all, was to his own charge. What he would do would be to haul Father Vadim free of the car here in telescoped time, then allow the impact to occur as projected.

And so, outside the car again now, Ariel steeled himself for the miraculous effort and coalesced his luminescence into a pseudo-corporeal form. In telescoped time, no one would see him even if he took the appearance of a businessman in a three-piece suit; but even in realtime, this present form would be invisible to any but prophets and saints, of whom there were precious few in this twentieth-century midwestern city. This was the form the celestial hosts had been using when Elisha prayed for his servant's eyes to be opened; Elisha, of course, being a prophet, had been able to see them all along.

It was a very powerful form, able to accomplish physical feats far beyond human capacity, but it used an accordingly large amount of energy, and Ariel gave up any hope of an immediate return to his pure energy form. Perhaps most worrisome, his spiritual powers were rendered almost inert; but the first thing was to get Father out of this alive.

A sword of light swung at Ariel's side, but he had no need of it for this task. He tentatively flexed the wings attached to his ox-like shoulders, which would tower above the average man's head, then reached for the car door.

Here in telescopic time, it took a monumental effort simply to lift a handle and swing open a door. Father, frozen with a worry-puckered brow and one hand reaching for his wife's shoulder, might as well have been a statue of solid bronze. Straining every angelic muscle, Ariel lifted the priest out of the car and staggered backward to the roadside, dropping him just as he slid back into realtime.

Behind him, Ariel barely heard the sickening squeal and smash of the impact, for to his horror he found that Father Vadim had hit his head on the pavement, knocking his glasses askew, and now seemed to be unconscious.

"Oh, Heaven!" cried the angel, bending over his charge. "Father!"

A cluster of onlookers gathered, and Ariel stood up, searching the road impatiently for any sign of an ambulance. When it finally came, the paramedics gave Father a cursory examination, then went to extract the truck driver from his cab, which was crumpled up like a discarded paper cup. Ariel hung about the paramedics, trying to implant suggestions that they should give the man at the curb a second look.

But then the angel remembered that such powers of suggestion were beyond the capacity of his present form. Helpless and frustrated, he paced around the site, barely remembering to side-step people and broken glass. Once the trucker was on the stretcher, one of the paramedics turned to the broken remains of Father's poor wife, who had been thrown clear through the window of the car, bounced off the front end of the truck, and hit the pavement with bloody finality.

Ariel shook his head. Shelumiel was going to feel badly, but perhaps it was best for him — he deserved a somewhat easier case next time.

At last one of the paramedics began to tend the angry-looking lump on Father's left temple. When a second ambulance arrived, and they had gotten him onto the stretcher, Father's wise eyes fluttered open. Ariel nearly clapped his wings for relief.

"Tamara?" the priest asked.

"Just rest, sir, we'll be at the hospital soon," said the paramedic, and closed the ambulance doors. Ariel spread his wings and lifted to the top of the ambulance, where he clung until they reached the hospital. Once there the examination and x-rays turned up nothing serious, but the bad news about *Matushka* had to be broken.

"My Tamara? Dead?" Father suddenly looked older than fifty-seven, and his eyes spilled over.

"I'm very sorry, sir," the doctor said, professionally sympathetic. "Now, I suggest you stay overnight — it's best to be careful with head injuries. It's a miracle you weren't hurt worse."

Ariel trailed the gurney into the room, which happily had no other occupant, and settled his Goliath frame into a chair to pass the night on watch.

But Father Vadim did not go to sleep, and went on quietly weeping in the dark until Ariel almost thought his own eyes would overflow, had angels been capable of tears. At last he reached out to touch Father's arm.

"Oh, dear Father, console yourself!" he said.

The priest stiffened suddenly, and there was silence. Then his familiar, Slavic-accented voice in the dark: "Who is there?"

Had Ariel had any blood, it would have drained abruptly from his face. As it was, he perceived in his material form a horrifying numbness which intensified as Father sat up and snapped on the light.

Ariel telegraphed an immediate S O S to Heaven. Shocked at first to find there was no reply, he soon realized that this was another drawback of his present, unspiritual form. Unlike members of the Adamic race, who were forced to rely on faith, Ariel had the advantage of *knowing* that his prayers were heard; but to be left in suspense as to the reply gave him an unexpected taste of what faith must be like.

"Who are you?" Father asked again, scrabbling for his glasses on the night table. Ariel stood up, watching the now-bespectacled human eyes grow rounder and rounder.

Not knowing what else to do, he said, "I am Ariel!"

"Lord have mercy!" said the priest, crossing himself. He set aside the blankets and began to ease off the high hospital bed, reaching toward the floor for a *poklon*.

"No, no, Father! Please, get back in bed!" said Ariel, taking him by the arm. "I am only your guardian angel, you know!" Ariel was hotly embarrassed at Father's offering of the reverential gesture; the very fact that Father could see his guardian angel was tangible proof of what Ariel had always said, that Father Vadim Karizomenoff was a *bona fide* saint and so destined for a celestial exaltation far above anything the humble guardian angel would ever desire for himself.

"You have come to tell me about Tamara?" Father asked hopefully.

"I — I haven't really *come,* as you put it, Father. I have been with you all along. It is only that — that a change in my form has made it possible for you to see me."

The priest looked puzzled. "But — O blessed guardian angel, can you not comfort me with the knowledge that my dear wife is in the heavenly mansions?"

The blunt question staggered Ariel, for it was not possible for the angel to lie. *Matushka*'s soul had been encrusted with the foulest growth of sinful bitterness at the moment when Ariel stepped back into realtime. He had not observed the moment of her death, to see whether her soul had been taken by his co-workers — or by the enemy.

"Perhaps I can find out," he stammered. He could not look at those sad, saintly eyes and say nothing.

"Ah! then you have made this appearance out of your kindness solely to console me! O holy angel, I thank you from the bottom of my heart!" Father's gratitude beamed through his grief.

Ariel was feeling the agony of his angelic honesty. "Oh, Father, it was not my design at all that you should see me!" he said, and explained that he had taken his pseudo-corporeal form only to rescue Father.

Father Vadim nodded, stroking his beard thought-fully. "O my angel, how I thank you for your devotion! To trap yourself in this inconvenient form to help me." He sighed. "Ah, tell me, had my Tamara no such good protector as yourself, that I live and she is dead?"

Ariel shook his head. "Ah, no, Father, at the time her angel had been driven off by her terrible state of mind . . ."

Father looked hurt. "But surely he left her when she needed him most!"

"Shelumiel couldn't help it," Ariel said. "Why, the state of her soul would have tried the very cherubim and seraphim!"

Father Vadim tearfully made the sign of the cross. "Ah, may God forgive me that I did not take her away from this terrible parish long ago!"

"Now, Father," said Ariel. "You are in no way to blame."

"O my angel!" the priest lamented. "Could you not have saved my Tamara?"

Compelled to answer truthfully, Ariel said, "Well, I could have, but I was more worried about you."

"About me? Come, come! I am a sinful man, but I am fresh from Forgiveness Vespers, resting in the mercy of the Lord! Do you mean you might have spared my Tamara, so she might have time for repentance, and yet you did not?" Father Vadim was looking at Ariel as if he had made some unthinkable assertion, such as that the creed was untrue, or that Father was not a priest. As if Ariel were anything but a holy angel. "How much better that I should have died than her!"

"Father, don't talk like that," Ariel said firmly. "She *did* bring it on herself, you know —"

Maybe if Ariel had had his spiritual faculties he would have seen that it was the wrong thing to say, *before* the words were out, instead of after.

"Tell me again," the priest said gruffly. "Tell me, I cannot believe it. You could have saved her, but did not?"

"Yes. But —"

"Then I do not want you for my guardian angel!" he shouted. "Go back to Heaven!"

Ariel stared in dismay. "I can't do that. I have to stay by you —"

"Go, I tell you!" Father's voice rose to a shriek. "Get out of my sight for good, to Hell if not to Heaven!"

The clamor brought hospital staff, who soon tranquilized the poor hallucinating old widower, and left Ariel once more in the dark with his charge.

In the morning, when Father was pronounced fit to go home, Ariel paced worriedly after his protégé as he checked out of the hospital. Father pulled the cab door shut behind him in Ariel's face, and Ariel was forced to use some of his precious energy to pass through it, slipping between the molecules.

At Father's apartment, Ariel skulked about the kitchen, almost feeling the chill of the priest's cold shoulder.

Father stuck his nose into his favorite book, *The Way*

of a Pilgrim, drank tea and ate toast, and Ariel realized that he too was hungry. In his natural form he fed on sunlight, but his present body was that of a celestial soldier, and he needed his C-rations. Unfortunately, not having set out from headquarters in this form, he had brought no manna to sustain him.

His gaze went to the icon above the kitchen table where Father sat. It was Rubljev's famous "Old Testament Trinity," the depiction of the three angels receiving Abraham's hospitality.

"Pardon me, Father, but could I ask you for a little bread?"

Father scowled at him, then turned back to his book and lifted his teacup again.

Ariel cleared his throat. When he got no response, he lifted the icon off the wall and placed it on the table by Father's plate.

Father put down his book and stared at the icon. He took off his glasses, peering at the picture, then replaced them. He stood up, and lifting the icon carefully in both hands, he kissed it and replaced it on the wall. Then he sat down and took another bite of toast as he found his place on the page again.

Ariel was alarmed. Since Father had refused him hospitality, it would be theft to use anything available in the apartment. Without any kind of food at all, it could take forever to build his reserves in preparation for the metamorphosis back to his normal form. But overshadowing his personal hunger was his worry over the spiritual danger in Father's attitude.

The food problem was temporarily solved that afternoon, when Father's sister arrived with a vast array of pickles, piroshki, cakes, bread and fish for the use of funeral guests, who streamed in and out of the apartment for several days. Ariel reasoned that he was enough like one of the family that it would be permissible to sneak a honey cake or two as long as everyone else was eating too.

The funeral itself was uneventful. After the third day *panikhida* service Father's sister packed up and went home; after the seventh, her food was all gone too. Lent settled in, in earnest; and Father, ascetic that he was, fared on nothing but beans and bread the whole time, of which he never left a crumb that Ariel might glean in good conscience. Instead, the angel subsisted on the bits of *antidoron* left after the liturgies each Sunday. Since that bread was merely blessed and not part of the sacramental Body and Blood in the chalice, Ariel thought it good enough for angels as well as mortals.

On the fortieth day, Father again held a *panikhida*, which was customary. How often he had done this memorial service for departed parishioners, compassionately ushering the bereaved into the new reality of life without their loved one. *Matushka*'s panikhida, however, was attended only by a half-dozen old *babas* who frequented any and all church services, like birds at a winter feeder. To Ariel's surprise, they were joined at the last moment by Andrei Skolopsky.

It was Palm Sunday, for in the Eastern church the forty days of Lent are counted separately from Holy Week. Andrei and the *babas* followed Father to *Matushka*'s grave in the churchyard, still clutching the pussy-willows that replace palms in the Slavic tradition, and muttered "*hospodi pomiloi*" in response to the priest's English petitions. When the old ladies had held out their cupped hands for a blessing and kissed Father's hand and left, Andrei (hands in pockets — no blessing for him, *spaceeba*) said gruffly, "You come our house tonight, Father. Palm Sunday fish dinner, like in old country."

He walked off without waiting for an acceptance of the invitation, and Father smiled.

Ariel smiled, too, broadly. Then Father's eyes met the angel's and the priest, sobering, went to remove his vestments, all business and ritual.

At Andrei's house, Father slammed the door in the face of his long-suffering angel, as he had done repeatedly all throughout Lent. Ariel worried that sooner or later his resources would be so low that he would no longer be able to walk through doors. This time however, he squeezed through, and breathed in the smell of baked fish as if it were the very incense of Heaven.

Ariel leaned against the door as the humans sat down to dinner. The Skolopskys' black and white cat rubbed up against the angel's legs, purring, and Ariel couldn't help feeling grateful to the creature. (Cats of course can see pseudo-materialized angels, but they don't seem to distinguish them from humans.)

Now the smell of the fish was making his mouth water, though he cringed at the very idea of eating the flesh of a creature that had once had breath in it. He spent the whole dinner hour in torture, but by the time Father and Andrei had retreated to the living room, Ariel had made up his mind to break his fast.

Mrs. Skolopsky began to pick scraps off the fish bones and put them in the cat's dish, dropping the bones in the garbage. She put all the other leftovers in the refrigerator and took the laden tea-tray out to the living room.

The cat attacked its bowl, purring joyously, and Ariel's heart sank. With a sigh he pried the lid off the trash can and pulled out the bones. He sat down beside the cat, and began to munch, feeling his angelic metabolism responding favorably to the fresh fuel, skeletal though it was. He relaxed a little, and stroked the cat's fur as he ate.

Suddenly the telephone on the counter jangled, and in the living room Father Vadim leapt from his seat saying, "Ah, I nearly forgot, Vanya was to call me here at seven o'clock. Excuse me please!"

Ariel felt as if he were a frozen being in telescoped time. Father Vadim burst into the kitchen and stopped, staring at the spectacle of his guardian angel, reduced to eating garbage.

The telephone rang several more times.

Father Vadim tore his eyes from the angel and picked up the receiver.

Ariel scarcely heard the inconsequential conversation. The remainder of the bones slipped from his fingers. With a mounting horror, he realized that he had let hunger drive him to the unthinkable, to voluntarily remaining in a separate room from his charge. Thank Heaven no evil had come of it! When Father hung up the phone (now pretending that he did not see the angel), Ariel tagged meekly behind him, and stood in a corner of the living room for the rest of the evening.

The following Sunday was of course Easter, the Feast of Feasts. The abundance of the midnight Paschal feast left plenty even for a famished angel.

But when Easter was over, pickings were slim again. The summer passed, then Advent and Christmas, and the new year came in with Epiphany house blessings. Ariel had not spoken to Father since the day they came home from the hospital, but on the final Saturday before the beginning of Lent — one year since *Matushka*'s death — Ariel decided it was time for radical action.

He stood by Father's place at the breakfast table, respectfully waiting until grace was said and Father had seated himself before his tea, toast, and jam.

"Father Vadim, may I have some bread?" asked Ariel. But the priest only twitched one eyelash, imperceptibly to any eyes but an angel's, at this sudden shattering of the year-long silence.

Ariel wished that he could weep. If he had had access to his spiritual faculties, what changes would Ariel perceive in his protégé's spiritual state since the first time Father had refused the holy duty of hospitality? What Ariel *could* perceive was the dangerous deterioration of his own health. In such desperate straits, would it be permissible for him to duck out for a half hour to scrounge a meal in the garbage bins of a nearby restaurant?

He at once answered himself with a resounding NO. The demons were only too delighted to exploit the briefest of moments when the guardian was repelled by some sin committed by his charge. Ariel was suddenly puzzled by his own tenacity. He would have thought that a sinful episode like this would reduce any soul to a state much like *Matushka* Tamara's, and yet Ariel did not feel repulsed by Father at all, but only very fearful indeed for the priest's soul. Perhaps, Ariel thought, without any spiritual senses I am not reading the situation correctly, and . . . Suddenly he was overwhelmed with horror. What if Ariel had indeed chosen wrongly at the accident? He had done the best he knew how to do — but Father Vadim was a saint, and Ariel only a lowly guardian angel.

What if Father's anger were only righteous indignation?

Ariel stared at the priest, who was placidly pouring himself another cup of tea and reading *The Way of a Pilgrim* as piously as ever. Supposing Ariel was guilty of presumptive pride — was that the reason no help came from Heaven when he cried for it?

His wings were trembling. If any charge of his had ever had fears about having committed sin without knowing it, Ariel would have been swift to redirect the mortal's thoughts to the practicality of known sin. But Ariel was not of Adam's race, so sin was something he only knew second-hand.

Ariel followed Father Vadim on his pastoral rounds that day in a daze. When Father said his bedtime prayers, Ariel forgot himself and chimed in with a heartfelt "Lord have mercy!" which the priest managed to ignore completely. The angel took up his sentry position by Father's bed, praying to the still silent Heaven with such absorption that he didn't notice quite when the priest fell asleep. He noticed immediately, however, when the devil appeared on the other side of Father's bed.

The intruder was not The Devil, of course, but one of his minions. The fallen angel looked much like Ariel himself, a tall, man-like figure with wings, but with the tell-tale light of infernal fire in his eyes.

Ariel drew his light sword to warn off the daring spirit, but to his horror found he was brandishing an impotent, bladeless hilt; the vanished sword, an extension of his own angelic power, proved that he was even more debilitated than he had realized.

The demon laughed, but Ariel launched himself protectively across Father Vadim's sleeping form. "Go back to Hell, traitor! You have no right to be here!"

The devil stepped back, carefully avoiding actual contact with the guardian angel, but he still grinned smugly. "I've been here for months. You just didn't happen to see me."

Ariel felt weak as never before. He couldn't hope to handle this alone in his present state!

"No answer, eh?" the Satanic angel gloated.

"No," said Ariel. "I won't talk to you."

The devil's eyes gleamed. "You can't keep from listening though. And at least I *will* talk to you, which is more than I can say for your heavenly compatriots."

When Ariel said nothing, the devil went on, "See, I used to be a guardian angel too. I made a mistake and ended up being shunned, like you. It's bad publicity for Him you see, if His servants are less than perfect. But He's supposed to be so damned merciful and all, so they shun you like this, and pretend it's like a test, so when you cave in and take up with us rebels, they can say you chose it yourself. And don't be fooled — if it doesn't work the first time, they'll put you in a tougher spot next time. Sooner or later you'll be damned to Hell, because Heaven wants rid of you."

Lies, lies, lies. At least it appeared Father Vadim was not yet reprobate enough for a soul-reaping hellion to be sent for him, for this angel of darkness was an ordinary tempter, doubtless no higher in Hell's hierarchy than Ariel was in Heaven's.

"God, look at you," the devil shook his head. "Not much left of you. The pity is it's all for nothing. After

by Donna Farley

all, this bugger's already damned you himself. You remember at the hospital?"

Heaven's mercy! Had the demon been with them that long?

"He told you to go to Hell, pal. The guy is a priest, a saint. Remember all that stuff about binding and loosing? He's got the authority to send you to Hell, he really does. And what do you expect? You botched the accident, you let his wife die in a state of mortal sin."

"She did?" Suddenly it no longer seemed as if he really had done his best at the accident.

"Hell, yes," the evil angel laughed, and Ariel felt himself shrivelling inwardly. If he listened to much more of this devilish talk, he was going to be mired in the certainty of his own guilt. Instantly he made an action decision, and began to shake Father Vadim. "Father! Wake up! Pray your *chotki,* Father!"

"Cheez!" The devil suddenly winked out of sight, just as the groggy priest sat up in bed, mumbling the Jesus prayer. He continued muttering and telling knots, gradually slowing down until he came awake. Then he fixed a furious eye on the anxious guardian angel.

"Father, there was a demon here!"

Father Vadim crossed himself. "I think there still is."

"Yes, I think so, he's just dematerialized to avoid being seen by you —" Suddenly Ariel realized the priest was referring to *him.* "Father," Ariel whispered, "take care not to blaspheme the Holy Spirit!"

"Holy Spirit? Will you call yourself the Holy Spirit?"

Ariel wished he could sink into the ground. "You know I am a guardian angel. Angels *are* holy —"

"You killed my wife! This is a guardian? This is the work of a holy angel? You are more like the angel of death that was sent for Pharaoh's firstborn!"

When Ariel merely stood there in silent misery, the priest said, "Hmmph!" and crawled under the blankets again.

In the morning, Ariel trailed after Father to the church, swaying dizzily for lack of food until he could gather some crumbs from the *antidoron* tray when Liturgy was over. It kept him in one piece for the rest of the day, but when it was time for the Forgiveness Vespers service again, he felt hungrier than ever.

He phased out through the door of the car with great difficulty into the March wind and rain, and found himself many paces behind Father on his way up to the church. Alarmed, he quickened his pace, but the church door slammed shut in his face. Parishioners were arriving, and he had to stand aside for them. To his dismay he was unable to sneak in behind anyone, for they all pulled the door quickly shut behind them against the rain, until he was alone in the downpour with the vesper bells ringing.

Grasping the latch handle, he pulled the door open a crack and peered in. Half a dozen heads turned toward the creaking door, Andrei Skolopsky's among them, and Ariel let it go again. If he wanted to avoid

attention, the energy-draining walk through the door was his only choice.

His drenched wings felt like a hundred-pound hiking pack on the shoulders of an old man. Sending one more prayer Heavenward, he summoned all of his fading strength to vibrate his molecules and slip them between those of the door. But as he stepped forward the molecular vibration died, and his body met solid oak. Ariel stared wide-eyed at the cross-inscribed obstacle.

"Having some trouble?" a voice behind him asked, and Ariel whirled to see the demon's hateful grin. "I'd like chat," the enemy went on, "but I don't want to get my wings wet." Carefully avoiding the cross on the door, he stepped through the wall and into the church.

"No!" Ariel cried in terror. "Father Vadim!" Abandoning stealth, he flung open the door, ducking into the building.

"*Bozhe moi,* what a wind!" said Andrei, and pulled the door closed again. Ariel sloshed past him into the nave, trying not to jostle the assembled faithful, his sodden wings trailing behind him.

"Where's that water come from? The roof must be leaking!" Ariel hardly heard the comments, his attention glued to Father Vadim. The demon evidently had only materialized in order to needle Ariel, and had now vanished again.

Without the spiritual perceptions he had had last year, Ariel felt blind. All over the church, he knew, demons were being pried loose from the coattails of people they had been afflicting, and formerly estranged guardian angels were hovering about their charges like joyous, affectionate globes of light. But all Ariel could see was mortals prostrating themselves, embracing, murmuring, "Forgive me, my brother; forgive me, my sister."

Ariel seated himself out of the way on the chancel step behind the great Golgotha cross which had been stationed in the center of the nave for the occasion. At last it was Andrei who stood in front of Father. Was Ariel imagining it, or did Andrei appear more sincere than he had ever done on one of these occasions?

Suddenly Ariel leapt to his feet, thinking that not only his energy but also his intelligence must have been dulled by his starvation. Mortals needed not only to *be* forgiven — they also needed to forgive! He came around to stand on the Saint John side of the Golgotha, until the last of the parishioners had made their prostrations, first to the crucified Christ, then to Father Vadim and their fellow parishioners on the Mother of God's side of the cross. Then Ariel himself took a step towards the crucifix; but suddenly, there before him, was his demonic rival.

"Give it up," said the devil. "You can't beat Hell. Join it instead."

Ariel made to step around the demon, but his enemy swiftly countered his move. Ariel tried again, only to find a sword of black flame barring his way.

"Join us," said the tempter, "or I cut you down, and

your man will be without a guardian anyway until he repents, if ever."

Ariel was shamed now, at a whole year's failure to draw his charge out of the spiritual quagmire he'd fallen into. But Father Vadim without a guardian — that was the part that hurt.

The devil still blocked the way to Father Vadim. Ariel turned and prostrated himself before the cross.

"Fool," the demon sneered. "That was never for angels. Only for sons of Adam, He's one of them Himself, for crying out loud. Why should an angel want to run with His pack?"

Ariel forced himself up onto his knees, groaning under the weight of his soaking wings. He wished desperately that his angelic body were equipped with the adrenaline that could galvanize a human into profitable action under such pressure, but everything here depended solely on the strength of Ariel's will — and whatever it was that Heaven willed.

"I will not be separated from my charge," he said through clenched teeth, and slowly raised himself to his feet. The demon was cockily swinging his sword.

Ariel caught Father Vadim's eye for the first time, but found he could not tell: was there any more forgiveness there than there had been on the day of the accident?

The demon glanced over his shoulder at the priest, who had turned his attention away and was now reciting some concluding prayers. The tempter grinned triumphantly, dropping the sword languidly to his side again.

"Game over," he said. "Next time, maybe you'll be smart enough to play on the winning team."

But Ariel gathered up his few remaining tatters of strength and catapulted himself past the devil. At the last moment, the surprised demon's sword came up to slice through Ariel's middle. The angel screamed; the demonic blade, intangible, did not physically cut him, but it severed the flow of energy in his inner being, siphoning it off. He toppled forward, one arm outstretched toward Father Vadim, and crashed at the priest's feet.

A bare spark of energy remained, the essence of Ariel's immortal angelic self, which could not be taken from him even by a Hell-forged sword. With all of that atom of power he strained to touch the hem of Father Vadim's stole and to speak two words. "Forgive . . . me."

Incapable of losing consciousness, he lay utterly still on the church floor, powerless even to seek Father Vadim's face. He could hear the devil muttering profanities, and then everything was so still that Ariel almost thought he was in telescoped time again.

Then there was a rustling of vestments above his head, and he saw Father Vadim's head lowered to the floor, level with his own. The priest slipped his hands under the angel's inert arms, lifting him to his knees and supporting him as he kissed him, in the Russian manner, three times.

by Donna Farley

"Forgive me, O my angel," said Father Vadim, "Forgive me!"

The demon howled like a sick dog, and immediately new, powerful arms took Ariel from Father Vadim.

"Well done, Ariel," said the rescuing angel. Ariel caught a rather fuzzy glimpse of the burnished wings and the fiery eyes that were the trademark of archangels. "Just rest now. I'm afraid what the enemy told you is half-true — your next assignment will be even more difficult. But it won't be for a long time, believe me."

"Don't leave . . . my charge . . . unguarded," Ariel murmured.

"It's already arranged, Ariel," another angelic voice said, and Ariel found himself looking into a face framed by the simple white wings of a fellow guardian angel. "It's me, Shelumiel. I've had a year off, and can't wait to work again!"

"Shelumiel . . . sorry . . . about Tamara," Ariel whispered.

"But she's safe, Ariel, safe. It's been a rather purgatorial year for her, but Hell had less of her than they thought. Rest well now!"

Ariel was beyond further speech, but it made no difference, as long as he knew Father Vadim was well guarded. He closed his eyes, letting himself be held by the archangel, whose wings buzzed like golden fans in preparation for departure to the celestial sphere.

Through the heavenly whirr, Ariel heard Andrei Skolopsky remark to his wife, "Poor Father, he is not right since his *Matushka* died."

"*Da,*" Mrs. Skolopsky agreed. "Perhaps it was her he was forgiving, there."

"*Nyet, nyet,*" said Andrei. "He was never angry with her in his life. But whoever it was, they are forgiven now." Ω

OUR HERO BECOMES ENTANGLED WITH A BLOODSUCKER

'Twas her exotic eyes made him suspect.
He looked for fangs, but that was a mistake,
They turned to kissing; all night long they necked.
So to protect (and keep her from infect-
Ing) him, he purchased garlic, cross and stake.

He added garlic to their evening stew.
It didn't bother her, she stayed alive.
Where he ate one huge bowl, she stuffed down two!
When she was through she reached for him anew.
He had to plead a headache to survive.

Next day Our Hero wore his cross of gold.
It should have served to frighten her away,
As he'd heard in the stories he'd been told.
She grew more bold, kept trying for a hold;
He squirmed in desperation all that day.

'Til finally he took his stake and cried,
"Foul Vampire Beast, this is your final day!
For I have lost much blood and should have died."
Then deep inside her with his stake he tried
To pierce her heart. She smiled, he heard her say,

"My kiss will only make you slightly sick,
With the full moon, I'm Were — not Wolf, but Tick."

— **John S. Davis**

ISSN 0898-5073

Winter 1996-7

Cover by Douglas Beekman

Worlds of Fantasy & Horror is published 4 times a year by Terminus Publishing Co., Inc., 123 Crooked
Lane, King of Prussia PA 19406-2570. Single copies, $4.95 in U.S.A. & possessions; $6.00 by mail
elsewhere. Subscriptions: 4 issues (one year) $16.00 in U.S.A. & possessions; $22.00 elsewhere, in U.S.
funds. Publisher is not responsible for loss of manuscripts in publisher's hands or in transit; please
see page 5 for more details. Postmaster: send address changes to *Worlds of Fantasy & Horror,* 123
Crooked Lane, King of Prussia PA 19406-2570. Copyright © 1996 by Terminus Publishing Co., Inc.; all
rights reserved; reproduction prohibited without prior permission. Typeset, printed, & bound in the
United States of America.

THE OWL'S NEST

On Having Read

Just about any writer (if he's being a tad indiscreet) can tell you a story about a lurching moment of unreality that happens when a supposedly knowledgeable editor (or other writer, or critic) in the field (whatever field they're all working in) is discussing matters learnedly for some time, then displays a flash of ignorance so astonishing it's like a suddenly yawning chasm. Imagine a scholar in Elizabethan drama, discoursing about the use of the supernatural on the 16th century English stage, without (as one's curiosity is raised after a while) mentioning Christopher Marlowe. There doesn't seem to be any point to this. When asked, finally, why *The Tragical History of Dr. Faustus* doesn't seem germane to the topic, the scholar replies, "Christopher Marlowe? *Dr. Faustus*? Should I recognize these?"

And suddenly we seem to be on another planet, with severe doubts about the competence of the people who put us there.

Or, more realistically, we're listening to what seems to be a perfectly intelligent panel discussion and all of the sudden somebody pipes up about that "new writer" Robert Bloch because the panelist had just discovered Bloch in a modern paperback, not looked at the copyright date, and assumed this was a brand new writer.

These things happen more often than you might think.

I used to have arguments with fellow students at the Clarion Workshop, lo these many years ago, back some time between the Jurassic and the end of the Typewriter Era (I will not be more specific, but it brings responses of "Oh, you're one of the early ones," which make me feel old) on the virtue of *having read*. At Clarion, which is a pressure-cooker environment for neophyte science-fiction writers (with some grudging allowance for fantasy) run for six weeks at Michigan State University and elsewhere by top professionals, no one wanted to hear the suggestion that so-and-so may have handled this particular motif better twenty years ago, or (this specifically came up) that Fredric Brown had so mastered the form of the short-short story that his work repaid study for anyone who wanted to write that sort of thing.

No, the other side insisted, a writer must be original and fresh and free of tradition.

But you don't want to reinvent the wheel, I replied, particularly when you plan to put corners on it. Ignorance, in any case, is never a creative virtue. Since we live and work (and read) in a culture which has many traditions (artistic and commercial) and any art form becomes part of a continuing dialogue with what has gone before, *having* read is virtually as important as being *able* to read, particularly for the writer (so he won't attempt to sell the re-invented wheel, with corners) and for the editor (so she won't buy it).

I couldn't help but notice that the students who argued the most strongly against knowing anything about (in this case) science fiction tended not to be the ones who actually went on to have professional writing careers.

I think that *having read* is important for the reader too.

It's more a matter of sensibility than recognizing specific allusions. Certain writers liberate our outlooks. If you've come to appreciate Poe or Lovecraft or Dunsany (or Tolkien or Ellison or Stephen King), then you're more likely to appreciate *Worlds of Fantasy & Horror* than not. You've been to some of the places we have. You're picking up the common language.

This is not to say that the magazine is or should be incomprehensible to someone who is absolutely new to fantastic literature, but we think that a little recommended reading is still in order.

The best anthologies we know of which trace the development of the horror story are these: *Great Tales of Terror and the Supernatural* (1944), edited by Herbert Wise and Phyllis Fraser; this is still the standard work, available in many editions and kept constantly in print. It is ably supplemented by several anthologies edited by David G. Hartwell and Kathryn Kramer, most notably *The Dark Descent*, which we cannot recommend too highly. Hartwell's name is one to watch. He has edited or co-edited quite a few fine horror and fantasy anthologies. If you've read them, then you already have the beginnings of a very good grounding in fantastic literature.

But, beyond that, here are a few writers we think central to the *Worlds of Fantasy & Horror* aesthetic:

Edgar Allan Poe, the master of madness, and of

deranged, unreliable narrators who reveal more than they intend to. "The Masque of the Red Death" is a masterpiece of symbolic fantasy which has seldom been equalled, although it points the way to such early 20th century masters as Clark Ashton Smith and Lord Dunsany. Smith's work is presently being reissued by Necronomicon Press. Look for the volumes *Zothique* and *Hyperborea*. Dunsany is the author of more than sixty books, the most important of which are a series of short story collections issued in the first decades of the 20th century, *The Gods of Pegana, Time and the Gods, A Dreamer's Tales, The Book of Wonder,* and the like. Most of these are still catch-as-catch can, although we have hopes of seeing them all reissued soon. (We hint at something, but do not feel free to give specifics.)

Do not overlook *Arthur Machen,* whose works have seen many editions over the years, some of which are still in print. The body of important Machen fiction is quite small. Key collections are *The Three Impostors* and *House of Souls.* Machen, who did his best work around 1895, was a master of subtle suggestion, and one of the finest prose stylists ever to work in English literature. *H.P. Lovecraft* admired him extravagantly, learned much from him, but never could write half as poetically, for all that Lovecraft's towering imagination and surprisingly modern philosophical outlook have dominated much of what came after. Lovecraft, too, is essential reading, best encountered in the revised Arkham House versions (*The Dunwich Horror, At the Mountains of Madness,* and *Dagon and Other Macabre Tales,*) as edited by S.T. Joshi, who has cleared up literally thousands of errors which have crept into the standard editions over the years. (Regrettably, for all that there are many, *no* paperback edition of Lovecraft is textually reliable.)

After Lovecraft . . . and Lovecraft is such a watershed writer that we can divide up the field into "Before Lovecraft" and "After Lovecraft" . . . we come to the moderns. Do not miss Ray Bradbury's *The October Country,* a truly classic and ground-breaking volume of modern-scene horror fiction, which moved the whole field into new territory, emotionally and imaginatively. Other important contemporaries of the early Bradbury and immediate followers include Fritz Leiber, whose twice-filmed *Conjure Wife* is a classic of the first order and whose short stories contain many small masterpieces; Richard Matheson, the author of *I Am Legend,* who showed the way (by King's own admission) to Stephen King; Shirley Jackson, whose *The Haunting of Hill House* and "The Lottery" remain enduring landmarks in our dark dreams; and Harlan Ellison, whose work has a way of jumping off the page and screaming at you, albeit in a surprisingly poetic voice sometimes. His *Deathbird Stories* contains most of his truly essential supernatural fictions, although many more are scattered throughout his many collections.

There are many directions you can go into mainstream literature, where, for instance, you'll find the Argentine writer, Jorge Luis Borges, who could make

STAFF:

Publisher: George H. Scithers
Editor: Darrell Schweitzer
Managing Editor: Carol Adams
Art Editor: Diane Weinstein
Assistant Editors: Leslie Smith, Michael W. Betancourt, Kyle Phillips, Jan B. Berends, & Tasha Kelly
Computer Consultant: David J. Williams III
Typesetter: Owlswick Press
Printer: News Publishing Co., Inc.

MANUSCRIPT SUBMISSIONS:

Before sending us your material, please ask for our guidelines, which we will send you if you send us a business-sized envelope, with postage affixed, addressed to you.

Yes; we read unsolicited submissions — but *only* if they are in standard manuscript format. To survive, all editors insist on a few Rules: each submission must be in proper format and must include a return envelope, addressed to you, with enough postage affixed to bring the manuscript back to you. If you want us to discard the manuscript if we don't buy it, tell us so, but include a business-letter-sized envelope, addressed to you, with proper postage affixed, so we can send you our comments. No loose stamps, please!

We recommend either of two books on writing (after all, we wrote one of them!): *On Writing Science Fiction: the Editors Strike Back!* by Scithers, Schweitzer, & John M. Ford; $19.50 in hardcover; and Barry B. Longyear's *Science-Fiction Writer's Workshop,* $9.50 in trade paperback, available from the Owlswick Press, 123 Crooked Lane, King of Prussia PA 19406-2570. These prices include shipping & handling; in Pennsylvania, please include 6% sales tax.

We are not responsible for manuscripts in our hands or in transit. You *must* keep a copy of every manuscript you send out. You *must* put your name and address on the first page of every manuscript. And please: *no* binders, folders, or padded envelopes; and especially: *no* registered or certified mail for which we would have to stand in line at the post office!

the universe into a puzzle and pack more wonder into a couple thousand words than most writers could into a novel. (Try *Labyrinths*, *Ficciones*, and *The Book of Sand*.) There are many more such writers, from Franz Kafka to Angela Carter, whose works will be in the Literature section of the bookstore. Explore them.

Also, do not shun best-sellers merely because they are best-sellers. Books sell, not because they are good, but because their content is what the public wants to read about at the moment. Tom Clancy's *The Hunt for Red October* became a runaway success because the public wanted a high-tech thriller with a Cold War background just then; the quality of his prose is irrelevant. But that irrelevance is the key. Bestsellerdom does not preclude quality. Some of Stephen King's works, particularly such early novels as *The Shining*, *Salem's Lot*, and *The Dead Zone* are actually quite good. Explore there too. Look into the work of Robert McCammon and Peter Straub.

But it's always better to *have read* than to have not read. We can't all read precisely the same books, because there are too many of them, but there is a common country of dreams, which we all can enter. There, riches abound. Not to avail oneself of them is to be deliberately impoverished.

We are heartened to note an increase in reader correspondence, as the magazine re-establishes itself on something which (at least vaguely) resembles a regular schedule. The letters weren't very lengthy, but we can summarize what's in some of them:

Conrad Rostan asked to see more stories by Thomas Ligotti, John Brunner, Ian Watson, and Darrell Schweitzer. While this last may be flattery, and, we regret to mention, John Brunner died in 1995, Mr. Rostan otherwise seems to be getting his wish, although we do not think we'll be able to fulfill his desire for classic reprints in every issue of *WoF&H*. He asks for Bierce, Blackwood, Machen, Fitz-James O'Brien, and Ernest Bramah, all of whose works are available in books, elsewhere. We hasten to point out (again) that the Lord Dunsany stories we have been running are not really "reprints," since they are all stories from old British magazines, stories which have never appeared in North America before in any form, and are not collected in any of Dunsany's books. Thus our printings are First North American Serial publications.

Lelia Loban Lee indelicately describes Ian Miller's cover painting last time as a "snot monster," remarking that she can't recall ever having seen one on the cover of a magazine before, and while we don't necessarily endorse this interpretation (as many of the little critters seem to be coming out of the big critter's mouth as, ah, elsewhere), we're glad to see that at least she likes the painting, and the magazine. She also ex-

presses admiration for Jason Van Hollander's "Our Lady of the Thorns" drawing.

Gene Stewart comments, *Having read much of Clive Barker's work, including* The Great and Secret Show *and* Imajica, *to both of which I had a fairly neutral-to-positive reaction; and rented a tape of* Lord of Illusions, *to which I had a distinctly negative reaction, having found it necrophiliac, dull-witted, & ultimately despairing in the way of most such crapflings; I report with surprise that Douglas Winter's lengthy explication/analysis of Barker woke me up to some interpretations I'd not considered and generally illuminated darker corners in the work, perhaps because he considers it as an* oeuvre *rather than as sequential works.* Shadowings *was certainly top-notch this issue. Please keep it as a regular feature.*

C.R. Dunn wonders if the preponderance of stories with Christian backgrounds last issue is a trend, or something that just fell that way. Actually, it is something that just fell that way, since, but for the Dunsany story (which had a contractual time-limit) and the Tanith Lee (chosen to be the lead item), the last issue was sort of a clear-out-the-drawer one, consisting of perfectly good stories which we had somehow not gotten around to publishing for a long time. We felt we owed it to the authors to get the oldest stories into print first. Maybe it was their faith which made them hang in there.

Elaine Weaver enjoyed Reginald Bretnor's story "Rokuro-Kubi" in *WoF&H* #1 and asks where she can find more by the author. The answer is, alas, mostly in used-book stores. Bretnor (1912-1992) was a master of slyly humorous erudition. His science fiction and fantasy stories appeared from the late '40s until his death. He was a regular contributor to *The Magazine of Fantasy & Science Fiction* from the very first issue. Some of his books include *The Schimmelhorn File* (1979), *Schimmelhorn's Gold* (1986), and *Gilpin's Space* (1983). Under the byline of Grendel Briarton, he popularized the short-short, shaggy pun story, commonly known as a "Feghoot" after his continuing series about the space-time adventurer, Ferdinand Feghoot. We do have one more Bretnor story in inventory, which will appear here soon.

The Most Popular Story

We're gratified that reader voting is up this time. #3 drew an interesting spread. First place is tied between "Werewolf" by Tanith Lee and "The Narrow House" by the late Robert Sampson. Second place is a tie between Lord Dunsany's "A Witch in the Balkans" and Donna Farley's "Father Vadim's Angel." Third place goes to "Bad Wheels" by John Accursi.

Thanks for voting. Let us hear from you! Ω

CHE DEN

by S.T. Joshi

Child prodigies are tolerably common in horror fiction. Matthew Gregory Lewis was twenty-one when *The Monk* (1796) was published, as was Mary Shelley upon the publication of *Frankenstein* (1818). Edgar Allan Poe was twenty-two when he wrote his first significant weird tale, "Metzengerstein" (1831). All this might lend further fuel to hostile critics' claims that horror fiction is fundamentally juvenile; but it could as easily be maintained that the imaginative fire that leads to vivid, dynamic work in this field requires the stimulus of flaming youth.

In recent decades two writers in our field have been deemed (or have deemed themselves) prodigies, and it is worth studying the actual merits of their work to see whether such a designation is in fact justified.

Poppy Z. Brite (b. 1967) has to her credit a short story collection, two novels, and an anthology of erotic vampire stories, *Love in Vein* (1994). As the latter contains no work by her, I shall not discuss it here but rather turn to her own creative work.

It is perhaps best to start one's reading of Brite with her most recent book, the short story collection *Swamp Foetus* (Borderlands Press, 1994; reprinted in 1996 by Dell as *Wormwood*), since this volume collects tales written prior to her novels. They are, certainly, a mixed bag. Brite can write, but in many cases she has nothing to write about. She can craft a fine descriptive passage like this vignette of New York City's red-light district:

The light of the setting sun was as red as desire. X's paraded across every marquee. The poster girls' nipples and lipstick had long since faded to a dusty orange. The signs and lampposts and even the square of sidewalk we stood on seemed to vibrate silently in the hellish glow, as if some enormous city-machine thrummed far below the pavement. "You've gotten us lost," said Robert, licking his lips nervously, and then we rounded a corner and saw the pinnacle of Chinatown's first gaudy pagoda rising above the city.

Let it pass that one does not get to Chinatown from the red light district by rounding a corner. But it should be pointed out that, evocative as this passage is, it is entirely a description of a physical object or series of objects. There are many such word-pictures in Brite's work, but they never go beyond the level of physicality. She has much more difficulty describing mental states or things beyond the realm of the senses.

Most of Brite's stories are not so much stories as vignettes. Very few actually go anywhere, narratively speaking. The story — "Xenophobia" — from which the above passage was taken is a case in point: it is really nothing more than a series of impressions about New York City and, to this Manhattan resident, seems to be a rather naïve and hyperventilated rant about the dangers of the city. "How to Get Ahead in New York" is similar. "Calcutta, Lord of Nerves" is better in that it does not pretend to be anything more than a prose poem (and a very fine one) about the city of Calcutta. But the best tale in *Swamp Foetus* is "The Sixth Sentinel." Narrated by a ghost, this tale very skillfully uses the supernatural as a vehicle for the exploration of character, as the ghost has the ability to enter the mind of a haggard stripper who lives in his flat. This is what weird fiction is all about.

Brite has resurrected two characters who appear in several of her stories, Steve and Ghost, in her first novel, *Lost Souls* (Delacorte Press, 1992); but the result is confusion, verbosity, and lack of focus. Here even Brite's usual virtues as a prose stylist are not on very good display: the language fluctuates wildly and jarringly between high-flown prose-poetry and grating colloquialism and slang, and the work shows how far Brite has to go to master that critical element in a fiction writer's arsenal called narrative drive.

We are here concerned with two intersecting tales. One involves the efforts of a trio of vampires, Zillah, Molochai, and Twig, to carry out their bloodthirsty activities as they drive somewhat aimlessly in a van across the southern United States. The other is the story of Steve and Ghost, two-bit rock stars who lead equally aimless lives until they finally become enmeshed with the vampires. The connecting link is a boy named Nothing, who turns out to be the son of Zillah and a sixteen-year-old New Orleans girl and who is fascinated with the music of Steve and Ghost's band, called Lost Souls.

This is an acceptable premise for a novel (at least, no less acceptable than that of many other novels in this field), but Brite's execution of it leaves much to be desired. The flaws in *Lost Souls* can be specified as follows: 1) implausibility of the supernatural phenomenon; 2) structural problems, especially the excessive use of coincidence; 3) lack of interesting or sympathetic characters; 4) lack of overall thrust or purpose.

Brite has chosen to utilize the vampire myth but to dispense with most of its features and "rules." This is her prerogative — certainly the standard vampire legend must be utterly played out by now, although one would never know it from the continual proliferation of books and stories about these wearisome entities — but what she has put in its place is confused and paradoxical. In Brite's metaphysics, vampires are a separate race or species from human beings altogether; they are also not "undead," but are born from the union of a male vampire with a human woman, and each vampire kills its mother by eating its way out of the womb. This is rather picturesque, and it allows Brite to dispense with the vampire's fear of crosses or of daylight and much other rubbish; but it causes significant conceptual dilemmas. If vampires are a different race, how did they become so uncannily similar to human beings? Where did they come from? Brite presents no "origin of species" for vampires here, as Anne Rice does in *The Vampire Lestat*. Also, Brite's vampires can live for hundreds of years unless they die by violence; but when do they stop "growing" outwardly? All the vampires in the novel seem to be of different (outward) ages, from Nothing (who is both fifteen and looks it) to Molochai and Twig (who seem in their early twenties, although clearly they are much older) to Christian, a 368-year-old vampire who looks middle-aged. Brite has one character say that "after a point they do not age" — but at what point? Writing a supernatural tale does not absolve an author of the duty of making the supernatural plausible — aesthetically if not scientifically.

Then there is the matter of the very frequent coincidences Brite uses to keep her plot moving. Nothing, feeling dissatisfaction with his sterile middle-class existence (Christian had left him as a baby on the doorstep of a family in the suburbs), runs away, and as a hitchhiker runs right into Zillah's van! A short time later they pick up another hitchhiker, who proves to be none other than a young friend from Nothing's town. Nothing persuades Zillah to go to Missing Mile, North Carolina (the home of Steve and Ghost), so that he can see his rock idols. Somehow or other Christian winds up there also. While in Missing Mile, Zillah bewitches

and impregnates Steve's estranged girlfriend Ann. All the characters then uncannily find themselves back in New Orleans, where Steve and Ghost just happen to run into a man whose brother had been a vampire victim and who knows of a potion that might abort Ann's fetus before it kills her. This proves to be a vain hope, and Steve, enraged at Ann's death, wants to kill Zillah. Steve and Ghost track down the vampires, who just happen to be somewhat incapacitated because they drank the blood of a cancer victim and are suffering a type of blood poisoning; this allows Steve to kill Zillah with remarkable ease. They walk away and the book is over.

Brite makes efforts now and again to portray these coincidences as some sort of overarching destiny (of Nothing's hitchhiking encounter with Zillah and his crew it is said, "this had all been meant to happen"); but this is an evasion. Coincidences and conveniences of this sort are the author's way of cheating; it is like someone painting himself into a corner and then painting a door to walk out of it. It makes writing too easy; it allows the author to skirt the issues of how things actually happen in the world and how people actually behave.

Perhaps these things would not make a difference if the characters in *Lost Souls* were at all compelling; but they are not. We are presumably meant to sympathise with Steve and Ghost, but the former is a jerk who brutalizes his girlfriend and then feels sorry for it afterward, while Ghost — who, to the convenience of several plot twists, is a "sensitive" who can read minds — seems merely colorless. Incredibly, we are also meant to sympathise with Nothing, even though he brutally sucks the blood of his best friend. As for the vampires — they give the term "banality of evil" a whole new meaning, although toward the end Brite coyly denies the possibility of passing a clear moral judgment on them ("Maybe they did what they had to do to live").

But the greatest problem with *Lost Souls* is simply a lack of focus. What is this novel about? Where is it going? What is it trying to say? Brite seems so intent on shaping individual scenes that she has given no thought to the effect of the whole. In the middle of the book we are told: "when you have too much faith in something, it is bound to hurt you. Too much faith in anything will suck you dry. In this way, all the world is a vampire." I hope to heaven that this supreme epitome of high-school philosophy is not the message we are to derive from this work; but in the absence of any other, I fear it will have to do.

It is debatable whether Brite's second novel, *Drawing Blood* (1993), is or is not an improvement over her first; my general feeling is that it is not quite as bad — or is bad in less pronounced ways — but it still reveals significant flaws in conception and execution and has even fewer countervailing virtues than its predecessor. We here return to Missing Mile, where in 1972 a troubled comic-book artist, Robert McGee, kills his wife, one infant son, and himself one night; his five-year-old son Trevor survives, and twenty years later returns to his hometown to see if by some means he can ascertain why his father left him alive when by all rights he should be dead. Trevor has himself evolved into an accomplished comic artist, and he seems to use his art both as self-expression and as a means for investigating his own psyche.

What begins, however, as a promising rumination on the nature and purpose of art quickly loses focus when Brite introduces a whole new set of characters centering around one Zachary Bosch, a nineteen-year-old computer hacker, and his various friends. Zach finds himself compelled to flee New Orleans when he learns that he is about to be arrested by government agents for some entirely unspecified criminal activity related to his hacking. He heads northeast and just happens to end up in Missing Mile! He encounters Trevor brooding in his now abandoned house, and the two fall in love with a haste and intensity that is entirely unconvincing given how little we still know about either of them and how little they know about each other. But it allows Brite to engage in lavish descriptions of homosexual sex, even if it bogs her plot down woefully.

On top of this, a supernatural element is suddenly and incompetently introduced about halfway through the book. The house at which Trevor and Zach are staying begins inducing wild hallucinations in them; but instead of fleeing, they stay and take drugs (mushrooms, to be exact) to induce *more* hallucinations. As a result, they enter some nebulous fantasy realm which may or may not be the cartoon universe (Birdland) created by Robert McGee. Coming out of it more or less intact, although with sundry injuries, they are abruptly forced to leave Missing Mile when they find the government agents on Zach's trail again; they end up — happily ever after, one imagines — in Jamaica.

In *Drawing Blood* Brite has at least pruned her overly lush prose so as actually to carry the narrative forward a little more briskly than in *Lost Souls*; but in some ways she has gone to the opposite extreme by writing in a commonplace, slang-ridden idiom that repeatedly deflates any atmosphere of horror she has managed to create. At one critical juncture toward the end, when Zach and Trevor are in Birdland, Brite comes out with: *"We're so fucked up, Zach thought. We could be the Dysfunctional Families poster kids if either of us lives long enough."* Buffoonery of this sort is exactly what is *not* needed at this point.

Brite has, in fact, erred seriously in the very introduction of the subplot about Zach's hacking and his pursuit by the government, which is really not very interesting and takes up valuable time away from the potentially compelling supernatural phenomena at the McGee house. It is, in fact, never made clear *how* the house suddenly gained its supernaturalism: Did it have it beforehand, so that it induced McGee to kill his family? or did the killing itself engender it? Trevor

by S.T. Joshi

remarks toward the end, "This place preserves its dead" — but there is no telling how this could possibly have come about. Indeed, it does not even seem as if Trevor even finally learns what he came to the house to learn — why he remained alive when the rest of his family was killed. We are only told at the end:

> Sometimes Trevor thought about the house. Sometimes he dreamed about it, but remembered only frozen images from these dreams: the shape suspended from the shower curtain rod, slowly turning; the terrible dawning recognition in Bobby's eyes as he looked up from the bed of the sleeping son he had meant to kill after all, but could not.
>
> Had Bobby meant to die already, or had the sight of his elder son grown, in Birdland, driven him to his death? Trevor would never know. He no longer worried much about it.

Didn't worry much about it? The whole novel has been leading up to the resolution of this point — but now Brite is saying it doesn't much matter!

There are other problems in *Drawing Blood*: a lot of excess verbiage, both on the level of words and of entire scenes (including one long passage about Zach becoming a rock star for one evening, which has absolutely nothing to do with the thrust of the book); gaucheries such as the inclusion of an actual individual (the comic book publisher Steve Bissette) as a character and the caricature of Stefan Dziemianowicz (who had given Brite's first novel a poor review) under the transparent guise of a young hacker, Stefan Duplessis; absurdities in the conception of Birdland, including a talking saxophone ("Hey, cat — you in a cartoon, dig? Cartoons is s'posed to be silly"); and more owlish schoolgirl philosophy, this time placed in self-important italics: *"This isn't just about having someone to wake up next to,* Trevor realized. *It's about trusting someone else not to hurt you, even if you're sure they will. It's about being trustworthy, and not leaving when it gets weird."*

I have already remarked that *Drawing Blood* is chock full of sex, mostly of the homosexual variety. This is itself an interesting phenomenon, indicating that straight women find homosexuality as fascinating as straight men find lesbianism; and I actually praise Brite for her loving and honest descriptions. We live in an age when too many self-appointed guardians of morality want to tell us what we can or cannot do. I think Brite does go on a little too long and a little too sentimentally about it, so that parts of her work begin to read like souped-up Harlequin romances; but only a hypocrite or a Republican (much the same thing, actually) could find such passages offensive.

I repeat that Poppy Z. Brite can write — she is probably a better prose stylist than many of the more commercially successful writers in our field, although this is not much of a compliment — but at the moment she has nothing to write about. I have been led to wonder whether this is simply a generational thing:

maybe I simply cannot sympathise with all the young characters (almost no one in Brite's work is over the age of thirty) she so lovingly puts on stage. But maybe it is the case that Brite has not really figured out what she wants to say, or — worse — thinks she doesn't really have to say anything in particular so long as she keeps writing pretty sentences. Even Thomas Ligotti, a far superior writer, suffers occasionally from this problem.

What Brite lacks is discipline. If she is going to write supernatural fiction, she had better make sure that the supernatural is made to seem both real and plausible. Her work is also seriously marred by treacly sentimentalism, verbosity, and lack of direction. She takes herself too seriously. She thinks she is a better writer than she is. One does not wish to harp on her youth, but her general attitude to the world seems even younger than her years — teenage rather than twenty-something. It is conceivable that she may amount to something in the coming years, but she has a long way to go.

It seems hardly appropriate to refer to Ramsey Campbell (b. 1946) as a prodigy: for more than twenty years he has been one of the most distinguished writers in our realm. But when *The Inhabitant of the Lake and Less Welcome Tenants* appeared from Arkham House in 1964, readers were quick to notice that the volume's gawky-looking author was just eighteen. (In fact, he had written most of the stories in the collection between the ages of fourteen and sixteen.) It is certainly the mark of a prodigy to have published a book at so tender an age, even if its actual merits leave something to be desired. *Inhabitant* contains, of course, Campbell's enthusiastic but derivative pastiches of Lovecraft's Cthulhu Mythos, the only novelty being that the stories are set in England.

After a nine-year apparent silence, Campbell issued *Demons by Daylight* (1973) — a volume that, to my mind, almost single-handedly ushered in the modern age of horror fiction. Here is a Campbell who has found his own voice: the tales are compact, subtle, allusive, laced with sexual tension (very rare in the chaste horror fiction up to that time), and potently horrific in a manner difficult to define but easy to feel. Campbell in fact wrote most of these stories in the four or five years after the publication of *Inhabitant*, which makes his radical change from imitator to innovator all the more remarkable. Since then, of course, he has gone on to publish as impressive an array of short stories and novels as any writer in the history of weird fiction.

Campbell's latest novel, *The Long Lost* (Tor, 1994), can only confirm his stature in the field. His recent works have wavered between visionary horror reminiscent of Algernon Blackwood (*Midnight Sun* [Tor, 1991]) to surrealist fantasy (the novella *Needing Ghosts* [Legend/Century, 1990]; reprinted in *Strange Things and Stranger Places* [Tor, 1993]) to unnerving non-supernaturalism (the comic serial killer novel *The*

Count of Eleven [Tor, 1992]). It has come to seem as if no one — even Campbell himself, perhaps — can predict what his next novel or tale will be. *The Long Lost* continues this tendency, and does so magnificently.

Overt supernaturalism is reduced almost to the vanishing point in *The Long Lost,* which could easily pass for a poignant mainstream novel of domestic life. This novel shows how keenly Campbell has learned to depict — again in prose of exquisite fluidity that unites the subdued vitality of *Midnight Sun* with the intermittent comedy of *The Count of Eleven* — the manifold ironies and absurdities of everyday existence. He displays an uncanny knack for showing how ordinary people can fall haplessly into the most grotesque situations, and the deft strokes of character portrayal put to shame the plodding verbosity of Stephen King and instead bring John Fowles or Evelyn Waugh to mind.

The Long Lost is based on the theme of the sin-eater — a stranger who, according to ancient Celtic legend, must come to the home where a wake is being held and eat the food (usually a small cake) symbolising the sins of the deceased; the stranger is then given money and hounded away lest he spread the sins he has absorbed. In fact, the sin-eater motif is not immediately evident in this tale of modern England, although anyone who has read Fiona Macleod's superb story, "The Sin-Eater" (1895) — or its skillful adaptation on Rod Serling's *Night Gallery* — will develop an awareness of it from the obscure hints Campbell supplies. In this case, the sin-eater is an old woman, Gwendolen, who is found lying in a catatonic state in a cottage on a small island off the coast of Wales by David and Joelle Owain, who are vacationing there; Gwendolen claims that her last name is Owain, so that David takes her for a long-lost relative. Bringing her back to Chester, the Owains invite her to a barbecue with some of their friends, at which time she distributes certain odd-tasting cakes she has made.

Gwendolen is a sin-eater, and has been for years, decades, and perhaps centuries: David only realises toward the end that the old photograph showing his grandfather as a small boy also showed Gwendolen *as*

an old woman. And yet, Gwendolen is far from being an "evil" figure; indeed, her portrayal as an ineffably sad person who seems to bear very heavily the ills of a long life (" 'I doubt you'll meet anyone who believes in sin more than I do' ") is a masterstroke of characterization. In effect, Gwendolen distributes the cakes — the sins she has accumulated from her anomalous occupation — lest she herself die with them. David asks her at the end: " 'Did being frightened keep you alive somehow, Gwen? . . . What could make you so scared?' "

The effect of the eating of the cakes by the guests at the barbecue is nothing more than an emphasis of the "sins" or flaws of character each of them possesses. David himself, although otherwise a loving husband, begins to develop an unhealthy sexual attraction to Angela, the fourteen-year-old daughter of a friend; Angela herself seems to be trying to seduce David with her young, healthy body; Herb Crantry, whose wife has left him for another man, kills himself and the man in a fit of jealousy; Doug Singleton, a lawyer, adopts a coldly legalistic attitude toward even his friends; and so on. In one of the most harrowing tableaux in all Campbell's work, Richard Vale, owner of an unsuccessful computer store, falls into despair over his economic troubles and seeks to kill himself, his wife, and his two teenage children. The long chapter in which this scene is narrated — beginning with the family's wholesome day at the seaside but with the reader's slowly dawning realization that Richard's harried remark, "We're together," signifies both his earnest and genuine love for his family and his belief that killing them is the only solution to his problems — is one long *conte cruel* unrivalled by anything even in Campbell's earlier serial killer novel, *The Face That Must Die* (1979).

Poppy Z. Brite and Ramsey Campbell are only two of the prodigies, past and present, in our field. Whether Brite ends up having as distinguished a career as Campbell is, frankly, much to be doubted; meanwhile, Campbell himself is by no means finished as a creative artist, and at the age of fifty he is still exploring new visions and new ways of saying the many things he has to say. The careers of both are worth watching.   Ω

THE SEQUENCE OF SWORDS AND HEARTS
by Tanith Lee

Illustrated by George Barr

To my husband, John Kaiine, who told me the souls of these three.

MORRA

In those days the rain fell very much, down from a sky the colour of a dove's breast. The distant hills were purple as the thunder, but the land was green, like a cushion of moss, and in the midst of it the bog, old as the world, green and black-green and black. And here it was, in the heart of the bog, the Lord Skarl had his great broch tower.

The tower too was old, though to the bog it was but a child. A gloomy child to be sure, dark and leaning, and something shaped like a thin old head that had partly fallen away. By day the birds went round the top of it, and by night the rainy moon stood blue behind it, and from its high and narrow windows, shone out the dimmest of faint lights.

Lord Skarl had his servants to wait on him, and they were all ancient men with their skulls showing through their faces. Some were half blind, and some bent almost double, but they served him as well as they could, for he was a cruel exacting master. In his broch tower, Lord Skarl kept all his treasure, some rooms of it, piled by great plates of hammered gold and goblets of gold with jewels set in them, swords with silver hilts and helms with crests of silver and gold, and ropes of pearls, pink and grey and white, that must be wound four times about a slender throat, and still fell down upon the wearer to her waist. But no one wore them, and no one had use of the weapons or the plate. Elsewhere in the tower was furniture of heavy dark wood, vessels of iron, and some knives and swords of steel. Lord Skarl dressed in plain cloth. He had one fancy, and that was for his masks. He had, too, one daughter.

Her name was Morra. She was pale as a swan, but her hair was black, and her eyes like the wild blue lavender that blows on the hills.

From the beginning, or that is to say, from the moment Lord Skarl noticed his daughter, which was when she was some seven or nine years of age, he had realized that here was another treasure. Who her mother had been it cannot be said, perhaps only some girl he had had brought to him out of the land, one night when he wore the mask of festivity and appetite. And later then the child was brought to him as well, to be rid of it. Or else some woman of the tower had borne

her, when there were women there, if ever there had been.

Once he saw her, and saw she was a treasure, he thought he might lock her too into a room. But then he thought the tower itself would do. For who could ever get to it, over the treacherous paths of the bog, where one misstep, and there were many, would plunge the venturer down into the basement of the world, where bones lay of great beasts with horns, and huge tigers and dragons?

So, he let her be. He let her go about the tower, from room to room, even into the rooms of treasure — indeed, these he showed to her, not as something of use, but as another thing like herself, for what use to him was she?

She wore old dresses that had been in the tower from the days when women were there, or expected. Some of the dresses had once been fine, but now were tarnished. Some were the garments of scullions. Morra paid no heed to this, whether what she wore was fine or fair or ruined or coarse. She would rise and wash herself and comb her hair, which hung down nearly to her ankles, and put on whatever came to hand. In the grim hall with its beams like stone, she would break her fast on sombre bread and vinegar ale. All day she would go up and down and round and about the tower. And sometimes she would meet her father, wearing his smiling mask of wood that was painted, and then she would stand and he would observe her, and he would sometimes show her something — a place where a piece had fallen from a wall, or how a spider spun, or the rooms of treasure, or an old book where damp had eaten off the words. But if she met him in his angry frowning mask of brass, Morra would draw aside and hide herself till he had gone by.

At dusk, when the purple hills grew up into the sky, and became the sky, they would dine, the Lord Skarl and his daughter Morra, in the hall. Then would come trenchers of burned meat and dishes of withered apples and soft plums from the traps and the wild garden plot the old men kept below. The wine was bitter and the water sour. But they knew nothing else.

"Draw the candles near to your face, and let me look at you," said Lord Skarl. And so she did. Then he would stare through the eye-holes of his meditating mask of

12

THE SEQUENCE OF SWORDS AND HEARTS

white plaster. He would see her skin and her hair and the candle-flames blue in her eyes. He would say: "My treasure. What use are you to me? You are my daughter. I may not touch you. I may not sell you, for I lack nothing. Useless you are to me, my treasure."

And Morra would say nothing. She seldom spoke, for though she had somehow learned language in that place, she was not much required to use it.

Once, when she was fifteen, he took the notion, her father, to have her dress herself in a gown of gold thread from the treasure rooms, and round her neck four times he wound a string of large ruddy pearls, then let them fall across her breast to her waist. Into her hair he made her fix little bees of gold and silver, and in her ears two blue jewels. And then he did shut her in the room three days, and when he came back she lay asleep on the floor in her old dress of tarnished silk, and she had put all the jewels away, so he let her out again, into the tower.

Sometimes, Lord Skarl would put on his magician's mask of copper and shell, and study antique volumes. Although much of them was wiped away, fragments of things remained, which interested him more. Or again, he would set a mirror before him, stood sidelong so nothing reflected in it but for a dark curtain. And he would stare in the mirror, and now and then a shape would come into it, some ghostly thing of the tower, or dead creature of the bog, or energies that danced and faded.

So then, in this mirror he was gazing, and beyond the narrow window of that chamber the rain fell as always the rain fell. Till in the mirror it began to fall too, the long bright rain from the sky that was a dove's breast. Riding through the rain came a massive figure, into the mirror's central part.

And there it paused, and looked about itself, and he knew, Lord Skarl, that it would be, or that it would come to be, the broch tower at which the figure looked.

In every detail there it was to be seen. A man in armour, huge plates of metal upon a mighty frame of flesh. Of steel the armour was, chased by gold and bronze, and the flesh beneath was visible only at one point, the eyes. Out of the mask of the vizor they glared, and they were cold and bright and grey as the falling rain. He sat, this knight, upon a colossal horse, big enough to bear him. And it too was armoured over like some vast insect from a dream, and from its steel forehead pierced two horns of silver. In the mailed hand of the knight rested a mace with a head of spikes. One blow of it upon the door of the tower might bring the door down.

Yet surely through the mire of the bog he could not get, so massy and heavy, so weighted with metal, on the monstrous horse.

Yet and yet again, in the cold clear eyes, which were all that was to be seen of what he was, beyond his size, in them was a light which might lead him safely wherever he willed to go. Was he death? Was he life?

© G. Barr - 1996

Lord Skarl sat still and presently only the rain fell in the mirror, and then only the rain fell outside the broch.

He drew off the mask of magic, and put on his angry mask. And then he went to find his daughter Morra, and took hold of her before she could hide.

"My treasure, you are useless to me, but no one else shall have you."

Lord Skarl called one of the old men up from the bottom of the tower, the old servant who had made the masks.

"Make one for her."

"My hands are no longer of the best," said the old man slowly. He held up his fingers and they were twisted.

Lord Skarl viewed them. He said: "Then the mask will be grotesque and out of joint. All to the good."

So the old man glanced once in Morra's fair face, and then he went away below to make for her a mask that should be terrible.

In two days and nights it was done, that deed, and he brought the mask to Lord Skarl and Lord Skarl fastened it over his daughter's face. From it, her black hair flowed away, and out of it, through two small slats, shone her eyes like the blue lavender, but they were barely to be seen. She had now the wooden face of some crooked, awful creature, some smothered, drowned thing from the bog, and from a little distance, so dreadful it was, it seemed quite real.

"Go now," said Lord Skarl to Morra, "gaze from all the windows. Look in every direction often."

The months passed like the birds wheeling over the broch tower of Lord Skarl, and every day Morra rose and washed herself and put on some gown, and on her face, every hour, was the crooked mask of the beast. When she went to break her fast, she fed in, through a tiny hole, tiny pieces of rough bread, and she drank her ale from the cup through an iron straw.

Day in and out she would go about the tower, and she would look from the windows of it, in all directions. To the east, where the rainy sun had come up and where the rainy moon would appear, to the west where they would go down. To the north, the hollow of winds, and to the south, where all flowers turn. But no longer was Morra like a flower. She was a nightmare on a flower's stalk.

One afternoon the rain eased and the sun shone, kindling a thousand crystal lights upon the bog and the stones of the broch. A veil of sparkling mist hung low upon the green isles and the black sludges of the mire, and through this mist came a figure riding.

It seemed to Morra then, who seldom had thoughts as she seldom used speech, that she was looking in a mirror. For there, riding through the passes of the bog, came her own self. But it was not Morra in a gown nor Morra in the mask of a beast. It was Morra in the thinnest of silver mail, and on her head a silver helm, from which her black hair streamed out like a banner.

And her face was a pale shape marked with lavender eyes.

The mirror-Morra wended safely through the mire, and up to the door of the tower. This she struck with a little dagger of gold drawn from her belt.

For some while no one answered, and masked Morra looked down upon her mirror, on mailed mirror-Morra on her horse, minute by minute, until at length one of the slow old men arrived to undo the door.

Then into the yard of the tower mirror-Morra rode on her silken swan-white horse.

Lord Skarl came instantly to inspect his guest, and stood in the grim hall, in his clay mask of impatience.

"Who are you?" said Lord Skarl.

"I am a knight," replied the mirror-Morra, removing her helm and tossing her long hair blackly.

"You are not as I was forewarned."

"A question for a question," replied the mirror-Morra. "Why is your daughter so ugly? She has the face of a twisted, smothered beast."

"I have made her so," said Lord Skarl.

"Oh, is it you?" asked the mirror-Morra.

They sat at the table. Trenchers came of black meat, charred bread, unripe berries. Bitter wine was served, in the iron cups.

"And her mouth," said the mirror-Morra, "is so small she can only drink at all, I perceive, through a straw." The mirror-Morra ate and drank freely. "Never have I tasted such food and wine. Come, why do you want an ugly daughter? I will be yours in her place."

Lord Skarl stared long at his guest. She was beautiful. Her eyes bloomed. She spoke. She was not his daughter and therefore he might use her.

He thumped his fist upon the board and called for his mask of festivity and appetite, which was the only mask he had that was made of gold, and set with red jewels. The old men brought it, three of them, for it was heavy. Lord Skarl slipped off the clay mask, and for a moment there was a glimpse of his face, leaden and sunken and swollen together, with small shut eyes. Then he was all gold, smiling, with a tongue studded by rubies.

"I foresaw a knight would come to my tower," said Lord Skarl, drinking deep of the bitter wine. "But not one like you. I will take you to see my treasure rooms, and to my chamber."

"Take me where you please," said the mirror-Morra, "into your very bed that is lined with thorns and groans. But send this other one away. This ugly one. I cannot rest while she is near."

"She is my daughter," said Lord Skarl. "She is useless. And how ugly she has become. She is not a treasure. She shall go out where I throw the bones. Let them cast her from a window."

"Let them cast her from the door," said the mirror-Morra, "otherwise she will break and lie there howling, to disturb us."

The Lord Skarl got to his feet and motioned his

THE SEQUENCE OF SWORDS AND HEARTS

daughter in her mask to leave the table and the hall and the tower. "Go," he said, "far away."

She did at once what he said, for she had always, as the rain fell, obeyed him. And outside indeed, again the rain was falling, and into the falling rain of the bog she went.

But the mirror-Morra danced gaily up through the tower on the arm of Lord Skarl. And into the treasure rooms he took her and she laughed, and then into his chamber. There she stripped from her, her shining mail and stood in her whiteness and nothing else. And the door to the chamber was barred inside.

Lord Skarl's daughter, Morra, moved from the bog by an easy way, without knowing what she did. For the hoof-prints of the white horse of the mirror-Morra had left clear traces in the mud of the mire and on the moss-green islets, and these Morra followed without thinking. So she came safely from the region, and up into the hills that were old as the bog but did not remember it, the hills green-haired with grass.

In her mask of a beast Morra travelled, for no one had told her that she must take it off. At night, she lay to sleep on the ground. The sun woke her and she journeyed on. Go far away, he had said.

Among the hills was a sprawling village. The people there were wild and ignorant, short-legged and hairy, and they lived by hunting and snaring. To this village, Morra presently came, and paused because she had never seen such a huddle of buildings so squat and uncomely, and so many dark and matted beings, both men and women, for beside herself she had seen no woman at all.

In their turn the villagers saw her, and they saw her wooden face, the hideous mask. They found it ugly too, in the way ugly things find ugly things. They ran from their hearths and their traps, and took up stones, which they hurled at Morra. Just then, aroused from sleep by the commotion, the head-man of the village shambled out to see. Though he was like the rest, his sight was better. He said: "Leave off, you fools. That is only a mask she wears." And then he said: "Bring her to my hut. I will take off the mask and see what she really is."

So then they dragged Morra, who had been dazed by their stones, into the smoky unclean hut of their lord, and here they left her. And he, pulling the mask of the beast from Morra's face, beheld her as she really was.

"Now," he said, "you will be of use to me."

And then he pushed her down upon his bed, which was of rushes and leaves, where rats nested.

By morning, Morra was the wife of the head-man, the village's lord, and he led her out, in her shabby torn dress, and showed her to them all. After that she lived with him ten years, as his lady. And every year, around the same time, she bore him a child. But all the children died after a few days, and he cursed her. He told her to clean the hut, to sweep and fetch water and make the fire. She did as she was told. One sweet thing, she seldom spoke.

At last Morra died on the bed of leaves and rats, died giving birth to the final child which died.

Then the head-man had her carried out into the hills and thrown into a pit. The men who did this muttered that they did not know what he had found in her, for she was ugly as a broken beast, her hair grey and thin, her skin yellow and wrinkled, her eyes faded like ill milk.

But in the broch tower over the hills, the other Morra rose and washed herself, and combed her hair, and putting on only her whiteness, she went to the bed of Lord Skarl, and in his throat she stuck her little golden dagger so that he too died. But what became of her — as how she was begun — is veiled like the hills through mist and rain.

There fell a day, a century after, when the rain had stopped, and the dark tower had crumbled down into the bog, leaving there just a stump, with the birds circling it. And to this spot there rode a knight. He was a mighty man, tall and broad and clad in armour of steel, bronze, and gold. From his helm ran a plume of scarlet and black, and through his vizor looked his eyes, bright like the rain had been.

He stared upon the wreck of the Lord Skarl's tower, as if perhaps he had once seen it in a dream, but in the hand of the knight the heavy mace lay still. And soon enough he touched the great metal horse, and it, turning its head of silver horns, bore him away from that place.

AIN

He was a warrior knight from a far land, a land across lands, and over the brimming sea. But he had forgotten that almost quite.

He had had another name too, but as he travelled they altered his name to suit their mouths, those people of those lands he came to. Now, he was called Ain. He was mighty, taller than most, broad in chest and arms and legs, his central body the pivot of the pillars of him. His armour had been made for him, for Ain, by a king he had championed. With sword and mace Ain had killed a hundred men that day in that armour, then sheered off the hundred heads with his axe, and brought them, in a net of bronze, to scatter like yellow fruits at the king's feet.

But Ain's father had been also a king. And though Ain was unlawfully got, a bastard, yet he remembered he had in him, with his strength, the flaming blood of that royalty. His hair was like that flame, red as the plume of his helm, sometimes, it seemed, the redder.

Ain lived by war, and by battle, going from place to place, and often his name — the name they had given him — went before him. In beleaguered towns they would say, We shall be free now. We have nothing to fear, now Ain will come to us.

So, as he journeyed, he gained riches. Here, where he fought before a castle and slew its enemies, or there, where he rescued some maiden from a tower in which cruelty had shut her, and brought her where she might be loved. Yet the riches melted away. Sometimes he rested a little, but never for very long. Before him always he saw a road that ran on and on, and by the road the towers and castles and towns, the maidens and the warriors, like a game-board.

But as he went, the years too went by him, going back from him as he rode forward, and he left his youth upon the road, at some well where he had killed ten knights, or under some chapel roof where he had slept one hour too long.

Then there came an evening of low sun, and he turned in his hand, from which he had drawn off the glove of mail, a single golden star set with a perfect emerald, the very last of his rewards. And glancing up, across the valleys of the land, he saw a golden place, darker than the gold of the star, green like the emerald.

Ain looked to the priest who had given him wine at that stop, which was a shrine to a saint. "What lies there?"

"That is the Great Forest. Men go there to be lost."

"Has no one then," asked Ain, with a grim smile, "come out of it, having gone in?"

"If it is their will, they have. But there are clearings in the trees, and the people there are kind and gentle."

"An area of danger then," said Ain. "For evil strength preys on such gentle folk."

And through the sunset, Ain beheld his road run on into the forest. Thanking the priest, he left the golden star to assist the shrine, and mounting the big horse in its armour, he put on again his mail glove and the helm that showed only his eyes.

Ain rode towards the forest as he had always ridden, sure and silent. He rode for two days and half a night. Then as the moon was gliding up the sky, white as a girl's face at a turret window, the trees began, and Ain rode in among them.

The trees of the forest were vast pines that strove towards the sky, and soon there were ancient hemlocks, black and clad in rags, and balconied cedars, and all these went up and finally the sky was gone and only here and there came the glitter of a star or a glimpse of the moon.

Ain rode wondering, for the forest was a place of silence larger even than his, and this silence sometimes hummed with insects or whispered to the wind, but that was very nearly all. Now and then a stream flickered through among the roots of the trees, and mosses dripped and strange bell-shaped flowers. Once an owl, like a stone gargoyle, stirred on a branch above, and he saw its eyes like jewels from a crown. Once a hare ran across the path. The forest smelled aromatic and sweet, like a church.

Ain rode all night, silent through the silences, and in the dawn the sun touched rose and gold along the columns of the vast trunks, and as the land went down, he came to a valley, open like a bowl in the morning.

Here in this valley, ringed by the ocean of the forest, a village lay. And Ain sat his horse some while, looking at it, for this was a village of those kind and gentle people the priest had told him of.

He thought. And then he put back the vizor of the helm that masked him. He did not want to frighten them, since he had come to be their champion against others.

Ain rode down on to the earthen track that ran between the houses. They were built of the forest, logs rolled together, and their roofs were of golden thatch. It was early, and the men sat before the doors, sharpening axes but only for wood, or cleaning metal things but they were only tools for making and mending. The women came and went from the wells with brown jars on their shoulders, and the children played between. The scent of baking bread lifted on the balsam air of the trees, and in an open yard a girl milked three white goats.

At the armoured knight they looked up, not in fear but in amazement, in a sort of wonder — perhaps as he had wondered at the majesty of the forest.

Presently they followed him, and so he came into a place where some houses stood that were a little larger, and out from one of these a man stepped, and he wore a wooden circlet like a diadem.

"You are welcome," said this man to Ain.

Ain replied: "Doubly so, I hope. I have come to defend you against wrong. I have fought in many lands, and never once been beaten. I will be your champion."

The forest people murmured, softly. Ain saw that they smiled on him, and presently a child came and put a flower into Ain's mailed hand.

The head-man, their king, said: "Then be doubly welcome, our champion knight."

So Ain became the champion of the village in the Great Forest. And they showed him at once to fullness, that they valued him.

To his use was given a mansion that they built. It was constructed of the logs of trees, but hammered in were nails with heads of gold, for gold they had, though they seldom employed it. And in the golden thatch of this largest of all the houses, they plaited coloured ribbons and medallions of bronze, and planted there roses, red for war. Boys of the village served Ain, oiling his armour, shining his sword and axe and the spiked mace. They made much of his horse, and gave it a stable like the

THE SEQUENCE OF SWORDS AND HEARTS

house with golden nails, and every day the horse was groomed and its mane and tail plaited like the roof with ribbons and flowers. They fed it corn and oats and apples from their fields and orchards, and to Ain they brought too the best of all they had, and though they did not eat any meat, when he had hunted they would dress the kill, and the women cook it for him with herbs and sauces, so it was a dish better than he had tasted even in the halls of mighty kings.

In his mansion of logs stood a wooden chest, marvelously carved, and into this they heaped riches, as if to pay his reward, his wage, in advance. Beautiful things they were too, slender cups of silver, strings of honey amber, curious statues of forest creatures, owls and hares and foxes and bears, fashioned of gold with green stones for eyes. A fortune they gave him, and he need spend none of it, for every thing else they gave him also.

He said to them that when danger came, he must be ready. Their peace had been so long that the final threatening would be terrible, a darkness and a power. The smiths of the village made for Ain then many new weapons. And these he hung on the walls of his house. maces and lances, spears and daggers, swords of foreign design which he described to them, bows of wood and arrows tipped by bronze and iron. Another helm they made for him, if he should need it. It had a dragon's crest. And they made too a chariot, tall and big to hold his warrior's girth. It was of iron with furnishings of gold, and when he stood in it he seemed to ride above the world.

The women wove for him cloaks of scarlet and purple and black. They embroidered scabbards for the awful swords with roses on them.

Every day, the king of the village would come and speak to Ain. He taught Ain a game with figures of bone and silver. The game was like a battle, and reminded Ain too a little of his childhood, for in his father's house such games had been played for sport. But Ain worked out battle-plans from the game.

Sometimes the village king spoke of the people's tranquil life, and Ain in turn would recount the adventures of his travels, the wars and combats. All the village would seem to come then, and they would listen. Their interest was very great. But once a memory disturbed Ain, of a child in the house of his father, a small girl, and how he had held her high up and she had laughed.

When he told this story, the king of the village said to him: "You are our champion. Will you take a woman to be your wife here?"

Ain had known many women, even sometimes those maidens he had claimed back from towers and savage beasts. His blood stirred, and he looked about. But all the women of the village were alike, lovely, and slender, with long yellow hair. He said that the king should choose for him a wife.

So, that dusk, when the sun had gone rose-red into the trees, a lovely woman with long yellow hair came to Ain's mansion. Her name was Suva and she was the daughter of the king.

She touched Ain's cheek with her lips, and then cooked for him a dish of meat so sumptuous that he lingered over it. And next she poured his wine into the golden beaker they had given him.

All the while he could not take his eyes from her. And at last she drew his hand into hers, and they went in to the sleeping-place, to which long since the village had brought a huge carven bed. And here Suva lay down with Ain and became his.

The summer season waned, and the winter came, but the winter was mild among the enormous walls of the trees. Ice glittered and gave way. Frost lay silver and vanished. Birds and hares fed from the hands of village girls.

Before long, the spring folded over the forest, and bright green grass broke through the ground, and flowers like beads.

Ain rode out on his horse. It had grown fat and leisurely. It stepped carefully in the aisles of the forest, not to trample things. When Ain drove it to exercise, it was unwilling. But then, the horse had earned its rest. He would not need the horse.

In his house, Ain sat long hours polishing the weapons and the armour, while Suva wove at her loom or made bread, her fair arms whiter with the flour.

Ain exercised himself with lance and mace, axe and sword. The enemy, so long delayed, would be duly tremendous for sure, when once he arrived.

Suva brought Ain wine. She said: "Dear husband, in the summer I shall bear you a child."

Ain stared at her, for though he had known many women, not one of them had ever said this to him, for not one of them had ever had the space to say it.

Suva grew round like a loaf. She did not seem to

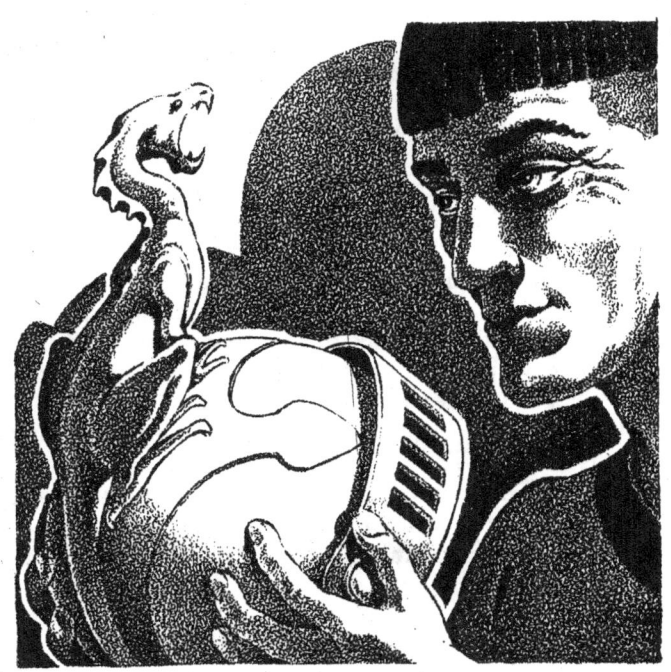

by Tanith Lee

mind it. When the summer dawned, she would sit at the house door spinning, and sometimes she would look up at the nighttime stars, as if she shared with them a secret.

One night, there in the web of the forest clearing, Suva gave birth. And Ain, standing by the door, listened to her cries of pain.

That filled him with rage. He wished he might defend her from it. At length he went into the room and the women touched him gently, as if he were a child himself who must not be made afraid. He said to Suva: "If I could rescue you from this —"

Suva said: "It is only the pain of life." So he left her then, and as he waited in the dark beyond the house, he heard her scream. And soon after a woman came and told him he might return and see his daughter.

Ain was astonished when he saw, astonished when he held this baby. That he should make, he of all men, a warrior knight, this girl. Yet it seemed to him she was her mother's making, woven on the womb-loom of her body, fair as morning, with golden hair.

Every day, Ain would walk the edges of the forest, his mace in one hand, sword in the other, the axe slung on his back, helmed and in armour. He would walk there, and test the depths of the trees, calling a challenge. Birds lifted like leaves, and flew away. A distant woodpecker hammered uncaring at the wood.

None answered Ain but these. Yet every day he walked there, and he shouted.

By night he did not rest. He kissed Suva and left her in the carven bed, with the girl child sleeping in the carven cradle. Ain went up to the roof of the mansion, and stood on the thatch and stared this way and that to see if any light moved in the forest, the torches of some army.

Dimly and far off, he noticed that his child grew taller. She was like a smaller image of her mother. He was kind to her and she was kind to him, and sometimes she would bring him flowers, as the first child of the village had. And he would take the flowers, but later they would fall to the ground and wither.

Each day, when he played the board-game with the king of the village, Ain would tell him of the terror that must come. Ain would describe his methods of slaughter, and the old man, he was old now, would nod. But seldom did the villagers come any more to listen. In the distance, like the distance of the woodpecker, and his child, Ain heard them singing as they tilled the ground and plucked apples and the grapes.

One noon Ain went to the building where they had set his chariot. There it was, and it had been overwhelmed. Down through the roof, between the logs, wild flowers and vines had grown. The chariot was roped and twined and roses bloomed in the iron wheels. Sparrows nested where he had stood up, a warrior.

Ain smote the chariot with hand and food, and the sparrows flew out. But then they came back and perched along the flowery chariot rail and scolded him.

Ain went from the chariot house and saw a girl of fourteen walking from the well with a brown jar on her shoulder, singing. And it was his daughter.

Ain dreamed at Suva's side, but he had forgotten her. He dreamed that the sun woke, and down from the forest came the noise of metal and anger.

In the dream Ain rose and put on his armour, and took his mace and sword, his axe and lance and spear and bow. The horse had long since gently died, so up from the village Ain walked, and behind him ran the plumes of the helm, and through its mask his eyes burned cold and bright.

There at the trees' edge the enemy loomed. Big as a mountain he looked, in armour blacker than night.

They came together with the shock of war, and the forest rang with it, so the sounds of the endless silence ceased. In the hollow of that emptiness the two knights battled. Axe struck upon steel, mace clove iron, swords blazed, and the world spun.

All the morning here they fought, and the stricken village watched in awe. All morning, blow on blow. When the sun was high they fell back and breathed, and the armour of both now was red with blood.

Once the sun moved they met again. The sound of their fight was like primordial engines. The green trees held away.

As the sun westered Ain heaved up the double-headed axe and crushed in the skull of the enemy. When he had fallen, Ain cut off his black-helmed head.

Ain woke from his dream with a roar of victory, and after this his body turned cold. He left the bed where Suva lay watching him with her quiet cool eyes. He donned his armour and took up his weapons, and went out.

The dew gleamed like a mirror on the earth, and above the green forest waited, and no one was there. But Ain ran heavily, up into the forest, up among the great and ancient trees, and there he saw a darkness, tall as he, armed and armoured as he was, and when he bellowed and raised the axe, this too raised an axe against him.

All morning Ain fought his shadow in the forest. Below, the village went on about its peaceful day.

At noon, Ain fell, and the clash of his armour broke the sounding silence of the trees. He lay unmoving in the grass that bled with flowers. His heart had burst as if cloven by an axe. He thought, as the darkness fell away into pale light, At last, at last, I have beaten you, my foe.

RHOMENE

Within the courts of the king, there was coolness. Water trickled from the mouths of stone lions into bowls of marble. In the garden of the king, shade trees had been planted close together. Under blue awnings they sat, the royal kindred, and drank wine chilled at making by the snow of far-off mountains. But beyond that palace the desert stretched away, tawny red like a lion, and with lions in it. For miles then the desert ran, until at last it met with an indigo sky that might have been, perhaps, world's end.

Among the many sons of the king, he had one daughter, and her name was Rhomene. Her eyes were dark like all their eyes, but her hair was the colour of malt and fell down her to the very ground, to the mosaic floors of the king's house. And it had a glint on it, her hair, like gilt.

When she was a child, Rhomene, two or three years old, had been standing on the dun earth of the garden under the dark shade trees, and she had lost her golden ball. She was weeping, not for herself, but for the ball, for she thought it would be afraid, caught up among the shadows of the garden and no one to help it. A boy came then with red hair, and he found the ball for her behind the fountain. Then he lifted her high up, and she saw it seemed a hundred miles, over the fountain, over the garden's top, away and away. Rhomene laughed. But presently the red-haired boy put down Rhomene, and went into the palace, and she never saw him again.

For a long while she would ask for him. At first her nurses would tell her nothing. At last, when she was five, her father came into her mother's rooms and looked at Rhomene. He seemed pleased with her, and Rhomene's mother seemed in her turn glad. And so Rhomene felt she was able to ask again her question. She asked her father, the king, where he had gone to, the lion-haired boy, so tall and strong.

The king frowned. Then he smoothed the frown. He took Rhomene on his knee and clasped on her narrow wrist a little snake of gold.

"He was your brother. He is far off."

"But where?" she asked, her thoughts already wandering to the beautiful snake.

"There was nothing to be had here. He went across the lands and over the sea."

Rhomene looked up, her dark eyes passing into the dark eyes of the king, her lawful father.

"The sea — what is the sea?"

The king smiled. He said: "The sea is a great water."

"Like the pool in the garden," said Rhomene.

"No. Oh no. The sea is a million pools and more, little child."

Then the king put Rhomene into her mother's arms and he too went away. He was a man who asked questions, did not answer them.

Rhomene toyed with the golden snake. She questioned her mother not at all, for her mother generally thought only of herself, was constantly enwrapped by herself. She set Rhomene aside soon enough, and crossed to her cosmetics table. In the oval mirror, Rhomene's mother examined her own fair face. She darkened her eyelids, and drawing to her her long-haired cat, Rhomene's mother dipped the cat's obedient tail into the pink powder, and rouged her cheeks.

Rhomene was next taken off, and in her room of play she turned to her nurses.

"Regard my bracelet," she said, and the nurses beamed and told her the king had favoured her. Rhomene said: "Then tell me about the sea."

But the nurses were baffled. Though they had heard of the sea to be sure, they had never seen it, only the red deserts, and one, the far off mountains that were the same tint as the sky.

Rhomene went into the garden of the palace and looked long at the pool. She tried to imagine a million of these pools all joined, but she could not do it.

Her first question had been answered — the boy, her brother, was gone — and now her second question went unanswered. She asked them all, all save the king and his warriors, who were remote from her, like golden statues in their armour.

Even the slaves of the house Rhomene asked, carefully, for she did not mean to distress them. And one day, when she was six years of age, a new slave girl entered the palace. Her hair was brown as a bird's breast, and as she kneeled to wash the painted floor, Rhomene came to her quietly and said: "What is the sea? Do you know?"

The slave lifted her head and tears fell from her eyes. Then she touched one of the tears from her face, and offered it to Rhomene. "Taste, princess. This is how the sea tastes."

Rhomene put the tip of her tongue to the tear, and tasted. It was salt. "Is that how?"

"Yes, princess. Salt is the taste of the sea."

"And is it blue?" asked Rhomene, for evidently this slave knew everything.

"Sometimes it is blue. But like no blue you have ever beheld."

"Blue like the sky?" hazarded Rhomene.

"Not like this sky. This sky is too dark."

"Like mountains," said Rhomene.

"No, not like mountains, they are too hard. The sea is blue only like itself. And when the sea is angry the sea is black. But then it is calm, and in the cold time the sea is green."

"Green like the trees of my father's garden," said Rhomene.

"Not like those trees. Those trees are too dry. It is green like a kiss. And then, when the sun rises there, the sea is redder than the desert."

mortar. And in the heat a sweet smell came from them, and bees flew in and out the palace, gathering from the stones, and in season stony honey was brought to the king's table. These too Rhomene studied with her nose. And even the meat the butchers prepared, or the stink of dead flowers.

How can I know? Rhomene asked now of herself. I cannot be certain.

She learned meanwhile the royal woman's arts in the palace. How to weave silk and how to sew with golden thread, to make herbal medicines, to paint on clay and paper, to read from the women's books in the king's library, how to adorn her face with tinctures for the eyes and lips, though she used for the application of her rouge a feather, and not the tail of a cat.

Rhomene was docile. She did as she was told. However, in books she hoped to find mention of the sea and did not find it. On clay she painted images that were meant to be the sea, but observing them the women only said: "How well the princess paints the desert, blue with evening and distance."

Rhomene dreamed of the sea. But in her dreams she never saw it, only knew that it lay near. By night she would steal into the ante-room where her nurses slept. She would listen to them breathe. A soft ascent, a mild hushing fall. She would think, Do I hear the sea? But she knew she did not.

When she was eleven, Rhomene was allowed to sit with the women in her father's hall, at the morning meal and at the night's dinner. For this she was dressed in silk and put on her jewels. She had two slaves now of her own. She was kind to them and gave them presents, but never the golden snake, for that had been buried with the slave who had brown hair.

From time to time, travellers arrived at the king's hall. They brought merchandise and sometimes animals, velvet and panthers, steel swords and ostriches, fruits that were unknown, wines from far off.

When they were permitted to show these things to the king's women, Rhomene would send one of her slaves — for she must not, now, ask anything directly — to inquire if the travellers had seen the sea. Again and again they answered that they had not.

And then one sunset a man came into the hall who produced pigeons from his sleeves and ate fire from a lamp. And when he visited the women's corner, to show them rare jewels, purple as the dusk had been, Rhomene sent her slave to ask the question.

"The sea, princess? Yes, I know the sea."

Rhomene spoke to the man directly, although later her mother would reprove her and strike her once across her left hand with a correcting rod. "Tell me what the sea is like."

"Like a woman," said the conjurer. "For it is fair yet changeable, strong yet cruel, gentle and soft, and it sings."

"Can you show me the sea?" asked Rhomene.

"Alas, I cannot. It is beyond my powers. There is too

Rhomene took off her snake bracelet and put it on the wrist of the slave, who was so thin that the snake fitted her.

"How big is the sea?" asked Rhomene.

The slave said: "If this desert were turned all to water, it would not be half so big. And it moves."

Rhomene considered this. Then she said: "Of what does the sea smell?"

"I cannot tell you," said the slave. "Of everything. Of a vastness. Of another world."

Rhomene said: "And does it make a sound?"

"Yes," said the slave. "It is just like breathing."

Rhomene thought of the sea. She went about to compare things to it. She was not able again to ask the slave, for one day the slave lay sick and then she died. Rhomene wept for the slave. Plainly she had missed the sea so much it had caused her death.

Rhomene begged her mother to show her jewels, and Rhomene's mother did and hung them on herself, haughtily. And Rhomene looked at the blue gems and the green jade and wondered.

And Rhomene would take a little salt from the silver cellar in the king's hall, and sprinkle it on her palm, and taste it. But it did not taste quite as the tears of the slave had done. Rhomene did not think to test her own tears — she had never seen the sea, how could her tears taste of salt?

She stood, once she was tall enough, about her ninth year, and looked out from her latticed window, over the desert at sunfall. She partly closed her eyes, Rhomene, and pictured to herself the desert, and half believed it moved.

Rhomene sniffed at essences and perfumes, and at the baked ground, and at the water in the pools, and at her own pure flesh. The stones of the king's house had had, when they were laid, musk mixed in with the much of it. At one place it growls and breaks upon the rock like crystal. But then it is whole again. At another spot it lies clear as glass, and at another it is deep and still and dark as wine, so you know it reaches to the bottom of the earth. But I will tell you this, things live in the sea. Also things we have never beheld. There are fish like pearls and other fish like black ebony. And great fish that leap. And if you are in the sea, for it is possible to float there, these fish will come and bear you up. They are called dolphin, and they are fond of men. Then too there are fabulous creatures, sirens who call from the waters and have green hair and the tails of fish or serpents. And monsters live in the depths, bigger than cities, that could lift the lid of the sky off on their backs, but they fear the sun and never surface."

Rhomene closed her eyes. "Have you been then often at the sea?"

"No, never. But I have met men who have. Men who have swum there, or ridden there in chariots that have wings called sails."

"Come," said the king. "Enough." And he summoned the conjuror back to him so he might look again at the purple jewels.

Later, after she had been struck by her mother, Rhomene sent one of her slaves to the man. The slave asked him if he had anything in his possession that came from the sea. The princess would buy it with his two hands' weight of gold. But the man was honest and said what was true. He had nothing. In the morning, he had gone away.

Rhomene was fourteen years old, and the king called her before him into his own chamber. He sat some while looking at her, and she waited meekly, her darkened eyes cast down so she saw only her rouged toes and the pictures on the floor.

"You are lovely, my daughter," said the king at last, "and accomplished, I am told, in all the womanly arts, but one — you have never learned to play the lute."

Rhomene said that she was sorry. The king said that this did not matter.

"You are now," he said, "of marriageable age. It is time that a husband was found for you."

Rhomene sighed. She had known all her life this moment would come. She made no other protest.

The king her father said, "There is a royal man from the desert land beyond this. His father and I are allies and firm friends, although we have not met for three decades. This prince, Siender, is bold and brave, a warrior, and noble. In fourteen days, the number of your years, you will go to him with my blessing."

Rhomene thanked her father and sought her chamber. Her two slaves crept away. Rhomene wept. She wept for the lute she had never learned to play, for fear it would feel she did not love it. She nursed it in her arms. She told the lute she would take it with her to the new lands, and try there to master it.

The journey took a month or more. Through the lion-land the caravan wended. The plains of earth and sand flowed away. Here and there was a small place of trees and water. Sometimes great stones rose into the sky. By night the moon was gigantic, blue and old. By day the heavens were no longer blue but pulsing and blond and merciless.

They reached a wide road lined by columns of marble, and here they entered the country of the neighbouring king. The second day upon this road, as dawn was breaking and the caravan making ready to go on, messengers rode in upon tall camels, and they said the king's son, Siender, was close behind them. He had come out to meet his bride.

Rhomene's slaves bathed her in essences of asphodel, and combed her malt hair with sandalwood. They clad her in a green gown and round her throat and arms wound gold and silver, and put a cap of silver coins upon her head. She was painted like the dawn too, and on her feet were tied little bells.

Rhomene stood under a fringed awning and looked away along the road, and soon she saw a cloud of red dust as the prince approached her with his retinue.

At last they drew near, and from among them all Siender rode to meet his bride. He sat upon a horse that jingled with gold. And Rhomene in her bells and asphodel looked up at him.

He shone as if burnished, but he was only a man, like other royal men, and she did not know him. Leaving the horse, he came towards her, and Rhomene bowed low. He raised her and kissed her forehead. He was a stranger with a stranger's face.

Then they sat under the awning, the bride and groom, and slaves brought to Rhomene the gifts of Siender. Scents and unguents in alabaster pots, silks sewn with rubies, caskets of gems, hair-ornaments of golden leaves, hunting dogs aloof and proud, singing birds in silver cages.

Rhomene thanked Siender over and over. Her eyes grew blurred and all the splendour was glowing mist. And from this mist there walked one last slave, who held before him very high a golden-stoppered vase.

"I have heard, Rhomene," said the prince, "how you are fascinated by one thing. It is a fact, I have never looked upon the sea. But knowing I was to wed you, I sent ten men to travel there, miles beyond miles, almost it seemed up to the moon."

"To the sea?" asked Rhomene.

"To the brink of it," he said. "And of the ten men, only one returned to me. But return at last he did. And in this golden vase, as I instructed him, he had captured three cupfulls of sea water."

Rhomene stood up. Her eyes were clear as stars. She stretched out her hands.

"Oh, give it to me!"

The vase was placed in her grip. She held it close. And then, breaking the seal of wax, as Siender gazed smiling on, she prized out the stopper.

Rhomene looked into the vase that had in it the sea. Great sadness sank into her countenance, so for a moment Siender glimpsed how she would be, when very old and at the threshold of her death.

"Why, what is wrong, Rhomene?"

"The desert heat," she said, "has dried it up. Despite all your care. There is only dust in the vase."

But then she remembered the salt tears of the slave. Perhaps the dust at least was salt.

And Rhomene reached in her hand, to the bottom of the vase. At first it seemed nothing was there. But then her fingers felt against them something curious and odd and smooth like glass. Amazed, she drew it out. White and pleated like a flower, the shell lay in her hand.

Rhomene raised the shell and put it to her lips, but it had no taste, to her nose — it had no odour. But then, then to her ear she put it. And there she held it close. And Siender, who was to be her husband, saw her face light young as that of a child. And her dark eyes came to him and now they filled with utter lasting love. "I hear it," said Rhomene. "I hear the sea." Ω

FROM THE SHORES OF TRIPOLI
by Jonathan Shipley

Illustrated by Keith Minnion

Somewhere — in all those divorce proceedings — things got jumbled. Emotions got jumbled. Names, too. Alicia . . . the Wicked Witch of the West — they both sounded the same after a while. I remembered having loved her, but nothing of the feeling remained.

She got everything. The court called it a fair settlement. By that point, I was beyond caring. Let her have the apartment, let her have the condo on the coast. I just wanted out.

I packed up what was left in two suitcases and went in search of a new life. A life, period. What I found was a small town where the pace was slow and real estate cheap. That's where I unpacked.

The house itself was exactly what I needed. It was big; it was old; it was structurally sound but needed lots of attention. The type of house Alicia would never set foot in, let alone live in. A little garlic around the windows and I might never have to face her again.

It was turn-of-the-century something revival — four rooms up, four rooms down with big center halls and a grand staircase. The realtor said it had lots of potential and a colorful history. Translation: Needed lots of work to be fit for human habitation. I moved in and started fixing cracked plaster.

I lived the life of a hermit, ignoring the rest of the town. That was all I asked of this new life — to be left alone.

Then, I had company. No, that's too normal sounding. Company *befell* me one night in the back bedroom.

I was still up reading when the creaks and thumps began. I'd already overreacted to old house noises so many times that I wasn't even thinking burglar. Raccoon, maybe. I grabbed a broom and headed down the hall.

I barged in on a college-aged kid changing clothes. He looked up, grinned, and continued dressing. He was so casual about it all that my first inclination was to apologize and back out. I squelched it. What was he doing there at two in the morning? And it evidently wasn't a random visit. He was working out of the closet that I hadn't gotten around to prying open yet. Stuck was what I'd assumed. Locked seemed to fit better now.

"Sorry, didn't mean to disturb you," he said while I was still putting these pieces together. "Guess you're the new owner — Andrew Peale, right? Heard the Jacksons moved back East to be near their grandkids."

So calm, so civilized. Like old friends. "Who the hell *are* you?" I finally blurted out.

"Oh, yeah. Kirk." He grabbed my hand and pumped it. "Glad to meet you."

Somehow "Get out of here before I call the police" didn't feel like the right follow-up. "Are you related to the Jacksons?" I asked instead.

"Me?" He laughed. "Now *that* really would have shocked their friends in the NAACP."

I hadn't met the Jacksons. Obviously.

"Look," he said before I could try another question. "What about we talk tomorrow? I just flew Tripoli to Chicago in a cargo bay, and feel a little dead. OK?"

He eased me gently out of the room — "G'night" — and closed the door.

I stood there, leaning on the broom, trying to decide how a sane person ought to react to a not-so-sane situation. After a couple more minutes, the light went out under the door.

I went downstairs and made some coffee. Sleeping was out of the question with a stranger of unknown origin and intent down the hall. Tripoli? That was in Libya, wasn't it? And what was he doing in a cargo bay? I didn't think those were even pressurized.

After my second cup, I decided to work a while. I wandered into the parlor and mixed up some more patching compound. If I wasn't going to sleep, I might as well do something productive.

I was still working when the sun came up. Someone pounded on the back door. I set the trowel down and headed for the kitchen.

There was Kirk again, standing on the stoop, a grocery bag in either arm, kicking at the screen door. I glanced back at the stairs, wondering for one strange moment if he had a twin.

I opened the door and caught the white pastry sack hanging from his mouth.

"Thanks," he said, setting the groceries down on the table. "Noticed the 'fridge was a little low — hope you don't mind. Croissants," he added, nodding at the sack in my hand. "From that little bakery on Hill Street. Really great stuff. You oughta get to know the place."

"Looks like you're moving in," I muttered dubiously.

Kirk shook his head. "Just passing through. Always just passing through. Too much world to see." He moved over to the counter. "Can I toss this?"

He was holding the remnants of last night's coffee, getting ready to make fresh.

I nodded, nonplused by the sudden domesticity. I wasn't used to strangers acting like family. Lately I'd had just the opposite.

I half-heartedly began unloading the grocery bags,

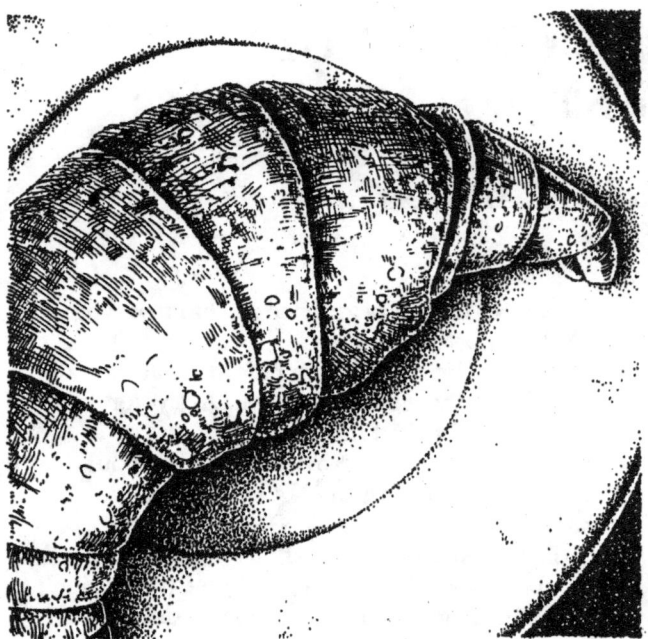

hoping the act didn't commit me to anything. This thing with Kirk was already way past the "I'm calling the police" point, and I didn't want the "this is my house — please leave" option to slip away.

"Now, about you —" I began.

"Hang on." He shoveled the croissants onto a plate, handed it to me, and grabbed the coffee pot and mugs. "This way."

He led me out onto the veranda and perched on the railing. "This is the greatest place for breakfast," he said, handing me a filled mug. "It's worth getting up early just to sit here and enjoy."

It was great. The street was quiet. A bit of morning haze still hung in the air. Cool, relaxing. I hadn't used the veranda much. The thought of having breakfast out there had never occurred to me.

"I sort of come with the house," Kirk said before I could launch into my questions. "Yeah, it's weird, but so's life. If it bothers you, I can work it so you don't even notice. You know, come and go in the night without a trace."

That idea bothered me even more. I preferred knowing if I was alone or not. I noticed he didn't offer finding totally new quarters as an option.

"I don't understand any of this," I said. "Suppose you explain from the beginning. Pretend we just met."

He caught the irony and laughed. "What do you want to know?"

"Everything. Did you live here?"

"Not really. Even as kid, it was always come and go. My mom never stayed put. What about you? Married?"

"This isn't about me," I snapped. It came out more harshly than I intended. That nerve was still plenty sensitive. But it annoyed me that the conversation was slipping out of control. Plus, it was getting harder not to like the kid, which also annoyed me. It was going to make throwing him out even messier, and I really

didn't see any other resolution. It was *my* house, dammit.

"OK, sorry," Kirk backpedaled. "So we talk about me, right?" He frowned, as though unsure what to say after that. "Want to hear about Tripoli?"

I did, but I didn't. "Will it explain why you're in my house?"

He shrugged. "No, but it's a hell of a story. Even for me. And they say piracy on the high seas is dead. It isn't, believe me. I found out the hard way. If it hadn't been for that clock maker in the Old Town, I would have been twice dead. But his services didn't come cheap. He wanted everything down to my Reeboks to get me out of the country. Made it real awkward at the other end, I tell you. But not as bad as Bangkok, though. Now there's a place you don't want to get caught short. They feed you to the pimps."

I caught myself being drawn right in. "You're not telling me anything, Kirk."

"I know. I ramble. My brain's just like the rest of me — always on the move. More coffee?"

I tried again. "You're a friend of the Jacksons?"

"Yeah, great people. The grandkids are jerks, though. Tried to convince their parents I was just a hallucination, a sign of senility. I hated that. Real lose-lose situation. If I'd shown up to prove them wrong, they probably would have had me busted for breaking and entering my own room."

"*Your* own room?" I didn't like the sound of that.

"You know what I mean . . ."

I did?

". . . I have to have someplace to roost every now and then. And it's not like I want purple walls and rock posters on the ceiling, or anything. Just a bed and a closet for my stuff." He sighed and offered me a tentative smile. "What can I say — it's home. And you're probably going to have to claim the body someday anyway."

I gave a start. "What body?"

"*My* body," he said. "Sure, they might dump it with the trash, depending, but if it goes anywhere, it's coming here."

He unbuttoned his shirt and pulled it down off his left shoulder. There was a tattoo — an address. *My* address.

"Not me," he said, grinning at my shocked expression. "My mom. I couldn't stay put as a little kid, either. Scared her to death. The second time I went AWOL and ended up across the border, she had me stamped with a permanent return address. It worked. I still got lost all the time, but somebody always shipped me back."

Suddenly I could see it all. I'd open the front door one day and find a coffin covered with airmail postage from Bangkok. And I'd spend the next six months trying to explain to police why the body of a complete stranger had been shipped to my address following some bizarre and violent incident halfway around the world.

The phone rang. I was relieved. What do you say to someone who's just attached his corpse to your house? I picked up quickly. "Hello?"

"Andrew?" From the Twilight Zone to Transylvania. It was the Wicked Witch herself.

"Hello, Alicia." It could have been worse. She could have shown up in person.

"We need to talk, Andrew. I've always tried to be honest with you, even through the difficult times. I wanted you to know I've started seeing someone . . ."

My wife had a boyfriend. Wouldn't you know it. Yes, of course she'd want me to know that. Insert knife and twist.

". . . and in the interest of honesty, I want you to meet him. It'll be easier in the long run."

Easier than what — slow dismemberment? Friends had warned me about the show-and-tell phase with your ex, but I hadn't really believed them. "I don't know, Alicia. I'm pretty busy with the house right now. Maybe later on when I can get away."

"I wouldn't dream of inconveniencing you, but Roger and I are driving to the coast and you're right on our way. We won't stay long. This afternoon, then?" She hung up before I could answer.

I collapsed into a chair by the kitchen table and stared at the cracked floor tiles. Alicia was going to love this.

"Trouble?"

I blinked at the young man in the doorway, surprised somehow that he was still there. "Ex-wife," I muttered. "Coming over to show off her new boyfriend."

"Do you want me to leave?" he asked hesitantly.

The words I'd been waiting for all morning. "I don't care." And I didn't anymore. I didn't want to fool with him right now, one way or the other.

He took the hint and disappeared. But he was still around. I'd come into the kitchen and find the dishes washed and put away. Or the trash emptied. Or the bathroom scrubbed. That one really stopped me.

He didn't strike me as the type that went around cleaning toilet bowls. Then I realized he understood. Understood that the state of the house would be ammunition for Alicia's arsenal. It might be a wreck, but it didn't have to be a mess.

I stopped brooding and started pulling buckets and drop cloths down to the basement. The plaster might be cracked, but the woodwork in both the hall and the parlor was wonderful. *Could be wonderful*, I amended, noticing the layers of white dust over everything.

"Kirk?" I yelled. No answer, so I yelled again.

He appeared at the front door in ragged workclothes, hedge clippers dangling from one hand. "Need me?"

Several of you, I thought. "You know the house. What do I do about this woodwork?"

He looked at the oak wainscoting. "Murphy's Soap. You can sponge it on all the carving, the floor, everything. Shine doesn't last, but it'll be clean."

I assembled my attack force and started scrubbing.

He didn't warn me how long it would take. Of course, there was a lot of woodwork and it was all pretty dirty. There probably wasn't a quick fix.

I was still dabbing at some of the deeper carving late that afternoon when the Lexus pulled up to the curb.

Great. A Lexus. I stuffed the scrub pail in the closet and pulled on a jacket that almost matched my slacks. I'd already been practicing the smile all day. I opened the door before they had a chance to test the out-of-order doorbell.

"My," said Alicia, glancing around the bare hall. "It's so interesting, this renovation project of yours. So different."

My attention was focused on the middle-aged gigolo beside her. Too tan. Too well-dressed. Teeth too white and too straight. What did she see in him?

"Come sit down," I said, ushering them into the parlor. I'd had to scrounge the whole house for three presentable chairs and a small table. "The coffee's still perking."

I made sure they took the seats facing the fireplace, the seats with the best view. Through the hall doorway, a flicker of movement caught my eye. Kirk was on the stair landing, sinking down behind the balusters where he could see without being easily seen.

I frowned. I didn't need an audience — not even a sympathetic audience. "Let me check on that coffee," I told my guests.

As I passed the staircase, I made silent, shooing motions to tell him to get lost. He nodded but didn't budge.

"So," said Alicia when I was back — the coffee wasn't quite ready. "I want to hear all about you and your little projects. But I also want to tell you about Roger. He's made me so happy." Her hand reached over to close on his. Sickening. "He's a genetics researcher, you know."

Oh, he had a brain. Even worse.

Roger cleared his throat. "I know this is a little awkward for all of us, but we *are* mature adults."

Speak for yourself, lab boy.

"Hi, am I late?"

I turned to find Kirk standing right behind me.

"Who's this, Andrew?" Alicia asked, frowning.

"This is . . ." How could he do this to me? He was making a bad situation impossible.

"Kirk," he supplied when I wouldn't. He shook hands with both of them.

"Are you helping Andrew with the house?" Alicia asked, eyeing his workclothes suspiciously.

"Sure," Kirk answered cheerfully. "After all, it's my home, too."

I could have killed him right there with my bare hands.

Alicia's frown swung my direction. "Andrew, why is this young man living with you?"

How could I say, "I don't know," without sounding like a moron?

"Long story," Kirk answered, perching on the arm

of my chair. "So, Roger, you're a geneticist. Know Dr. Örlentrager?"

Roger gave a start. "Dr. Örlentrager, the biophysicist? Yes, of course. How do *you* know him?"

"Part of his experimental group last year in Geneva. You know, the cell regeneration tests."

Roger nodded. "If those test results are half as conclusive as Dr. Örlentrager claims —"

"There are claims and claims," Kirk interrupted. "I know he ran into a couple of procedural snags with the control group. Especially when one of the primary subjects turned out to be a criminal-at-large using a false identity."

"So all the preliminary data were wrong."

"Data nothing," Kirk snorted. "You should have seen what this guy did to the lab when we finally cornered him."

"You mean that rumor about the lab being violently dismantled is actually true?" said Roger, leaning forward. "I'd heard the story, but naturally didn't believe it."

Kirk warmed to his tale. Roger was transfixed. I remembered the feeling, that mix of fascination and utter incredulity. No denying that the kid had a gift. Alicia just stared. When I retreated to the kitchen, she followed me.

"Who is he?" she demanded. "You really expect me to believe this Dr. So-and-So thing is all a coincidence? Why is he living with you?"

I shrugged because I couldn't think of a better answer.

Her expression became grimmer. "Andrew, answer me. Is there something . . . going on between you two?"

My cheeks flamed. She of all people knew better than that. But just for a second I considered saying yes. "No," I said. "I hardly know him. He came with the house."

She opened her mouth several times as she tried to decipher that, but no question emerged.

Kirk pushed through the swinging door and smiled. "How's the coffee coming? Rog needs a little caffeine boost."

I could imagine. Post-Kirk jitters.

"Rog?" Alicia frowned. "Roger hates nicknames."

Kirk just shrugged as he organized cups and saucers on a tray. "Not necessarily. It's all in the delivery."

I sucked air. I'd been through enough arguments to sense imminent danger, even without watching Alicia's color rise. But I wouldn't have intervened for the world.

Kirk glanced at me, oblivious to the storm brewing. "Grab the half-and-half from the 'fridge, would you? Rog says he hates regular milk in his coffee."

"That's ridiculous," she snapped. "I serve him milk in coffee all the time."

"And he hates it. Just goes to show how little you can know about a person. Just like Felicia used to say." He smiled, suddenly the picture of boyish innocence. "Care for a cup as long as I'm pouring?"

Alicia was still reeling from the forbidden name. "No — yes — oh, go to hell."

Kirk turned into a kicked puppy — surprised, hurt, and sad all rolled into one. He did it extremely well, I noticed. Alicia just scowled as she fumed out of the kitchen.

I'd never seen her game off like this, but then again, I was never the player that Kirk was. Through all our years of marriage, Alicia's twin sister Felicia had always been *persona non grata* from some childhood feud. How he came up with that ammunition was one more question for the list. For now, I just chalked it up as a skill that only came with flying cargo from distant parts of the world.

"Shall we join the happy couple?" Kirk suggested, picking up the tray.

"You're enjoying every minute of this," I told him.

He flashed his innocent smile. "I always enjoy meeting new and interesting people." His expression turned more knowing. "But I'm not the only one enjoying the floor show." He backed through the swinging door and was gone.

I paused. I *did* enjoy seeing him bring Alicia down a peg, probably because I'd never been able to in all our years of arguing. But was I really that transparent?

I walked into the parlor to find the three of them sitting in silence. It took me about two seconds to see it wasn't a comfortable silence. Kirk was calmly sipping coffee, but Alicia looked on the verge of exploding, and Roger looked completely flustered. What had I missed?

"No really, Rog," Kirk said, setting his cup down. "I'd love to get together some time. We could talk Switzerland." His grin turned impish. "Or not. More coffee?"

Alicia snatched Roger's cup and sent it hurtling across the room. "That is the absolute limit," she said, prying her boyfriend away from my housemate. "We're leaving, Roger. I don't know why you've resorted to this production, Andrew, but I will not remain in this run-down excuse for a house and listen to . . . *propositions!*"

As she whirled past me toward the front door, she looked back once at Kirk. "Pervert!" she spat.

He just smiled like an angel.

Roger followed, looking a little dazed. Weren't they going to have a fun ride home?

None of this felt real — or maybe it felt too real. Reality seemed to have taken a sharp right in a whole new direction. But I found I really didn't mind, even though I couldn't begin to explain it. Maybe I was getting used to the Twilight Zone. Or maybe I was just seeing things a little differently.

For the first time, it struck me that was the only reason I'd bought the house was because Alicia would hate everything about it. Part of my brain had known all along that she'd come snooping, had known that I couldn't stop her from showing up on my doorstep.

It didn't say much for my newly acquired emancipation.

Kirk came to stand beside me at the window. "How'd I do?" he asked, as the Lexus drove off.

I couldn't begin to answer that. "Which — the housecleaning or the yardwork?"

He found that very funny. As he headed upstairs, I realized he hadn't answered a single question about himself. He just kept raising new ones. But so be it.

"Kirk," I called, catching him on the landing. "You're either truly amazing or the best liar I ever met."

"Maybe," he shrugged. "But I was just doing what you wanted done."

I wanted to deny it, but how could I? Running Alicia out of the house, undercutting her relationship with her gigolo-geneticist. These were good things. There was even a fighting chance that she wouldn't come back. Or maybe I wouldn't let her.

"What about the house?" Kirk asked quietly from above. "You keeping it?"

Suddenly that was a very interesting question. I'd never been that much of a house person. Why put myself through the agony of fixing up an old derelict? Still, it was mine.

And Kirk's, I amended mentally, not knowing if that was a plus or a minus.

"What do you think I should do?" I asked him.

He gave an elaborate shrug. "Hey, I'm the last person to give advice. My life is so screwed up I could sell movie rights. Your life, your call."

He was right, it *was* my call. Whether I kept the house or sold it was less important than finally making a decision without Alicia's ghost hanging over me.

"I'm keeping it," I said after a long moment.

Kirk grinned. "Great. New owners are always Russian roulette."

"But this new owner still wants some answers out of you," I reminded him.

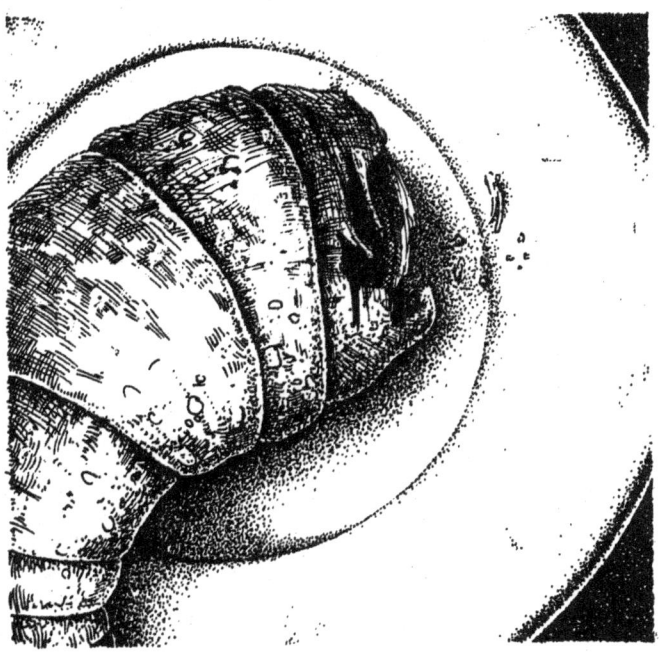

He shrugged. "It'll all come out in the long haul." His glance wandered to the front door. "Poor Rog."

The next morning Kirk was gone. His room was empty and the closet was securely locked. If the house hadn't been so clean, I might have doubted he was ever there at all.

Downstairs in the kitchen was a white pastry sack with fresh croissants. On the outside was penciled a note: *"To* the halls of Montezuma *from* the shores of Tripoli. Off to Mexico and Peru, Machu Picchu calls. Back next fall — or thereabouts. (Please don't forget the bakery on Hill Street. The old man can really use the business.)"

I made a half pot of coffee to go with the croissants, and went out on the veranda for breakfast.   Ω

. . . and while we're on the subject of moving . . . :

Unless you have a mailing address so permanent that, like Kirk, in the story above, you have it tattooed on your shoulder, please tell us whenever you move. We need your old and your new address, both with ZIP or postal code, so we can keep sending you *Worlds of Fantasy & Horror.*

Our address:

Terminus Publishing Co., Inc.

123 Crooked Lane,

King of Prussia PA 19406-2570.

by Jonathan Shipley

TEATRO GROTTESCO
by Thomas Ligotti

Illustrated by Thomas S. Brown

The first thing I learned was that no one *anticipates* the arrival of the Teatro. One would not say, or even think, "The Teatro has never come to this city — it seems we're due for a visit," or perhaps, "Don't be surprised when you-know-what turns up, it's been years since the last time." Even if the city in which one lives is exactly the kind of place favored by the Teatro, there can be no basis for predicting its appearance. No warnings are given, no fanfare to announce that a Teatro season is about to begin, or that *another* season of that sort will soon be upon us. But if a particular city possesses what is sometimes called an "artistic under-world," and if one is in close touch with this society of artists, the chances are optimal for being among those who discover that things have already started. This is the most one can expect.

For a time it was all rumors and lore, hearsay and dreams. Anyone who failed to show up for a few days at the usual club or bookstore or special artistic event was the subject of speculation. But most of the crowd I am referring to lead highly unstable, even precarious lives. Any of them might pack up and disappear without notifying a single soul. And almost all of the supposedly "missing ones" were, at some point, seen again. One such person was a filmmaker whose short movie *Private Hell* served as the featured subject of a local one-night festival. But he was nowhere to be seen either during the exhibition or at the party afterwards. "Gone with the Teatro," someone said with a blasé knowingness, while others smiled and clinked glasses in a sardonic farewell toast.

But only a week later the filmmaker was spotted in one of the back rows of a pornographic theater. He later explained his absence by insisting he had been in the hospital following a thorough beating at the hands of some people he had been filming but who did not consent or desire to be filmed. This sounded plausible, given the subject matter of the man's work. Yet for some reason no one believed his hospital story, despite the evidence of bandages he was still required to wear. "It has to be the Teatro," argued a woman who always dressed in shades of purple and who was a good friend of the filmmaker. "*His* stuff and *Teatro* stuff," she said, holding up two crossed fingers for everyone to see.

But what was meant by "Teatro stuff?" This was a phrase I heard spoken by a number of persons, not all of them artists of a pretentious or self-dramatizing type. Certainly there is no shortage of anecdotes that have been passed around which purport to illuminate the nature and workings of this "cruel troupe," an epithet used by those who are too superstitious to invoke the Teatro Grottesco by name. But sorting out these accounts into a coherent *profile*, never mind their truth value, is another thing altogether.

For instance, the purple woman I mentioned earlier held us all spellbound one evening with a story about her cousin's roommate, a self-styled "visceral artist" who worked the night shift as a stock clerk for a supermarket chain in the suburbs. On a December morning, about an hour before sun-up, the artist was released from work and began his walk home through a narrow alley that ran behind several blocks of various stores and businesses along the suburb's main avenue. A light snow had fallen during the night, settling evenly upon the pavement of the alley and glowing in the light of a full moon which seemed to hover just at the alley's end. The artist saw a figure in the distance, and something about this figure, this winter-morning vision, made him pause for a moment and stare. Although he had a trained eye for sizing and perspective, the artist found this silhouette of a person in the distance of the alley intensely problematic. He could not tell if it was short or tall, or even if it was moving — either toward him or away from him — or was standing still. Then, in a moment of hallucinated wonder, the figure stood before him in the middle of the alley.

The moonlight illuminated a little man who was entirely unclothed and who held out both of his hands as if he were grasping at a desired object just out of his reach. But the artist saw that something was wrong with these hands. While the little man's body was pale, his hands were dark and were too large for the tiny arms on which they hung. At first the artist believed the little man to be wearing oversized mittens. His hands seemed to be covered by some kind of fuzz, just as the alley in which he stood was layered with the fuzziness of the snow that had fallen during the night. His hands looked soft and fuzzy like the snow, except that the snow was white and his hands were black.

In the moonlight the artist came to see that the mittens worn by this little man were actually something like the paws of an animal. It almost made sense to the artist to have thought that the little man's hands were actually paws which had only appeared to be two black mittens. Then each of the paws separated into long thin fingers that wriggled wildly in the moonlight. But they could not have been the fingers of a hand, because there were too many of them. And the hands were not paws, nor were the paws really mittens. And all of this time the little man was becoming smaller and smaller in the moonlight of that alley, as if he were moving into the distance far away from the artist who was hypnotized by this vision. Finally a little voice spoke which the artist could barely hear, and it said to him: "I cannot keep them away from me anymore, I am becoming so small and weak." These words suddenly made this whole winter-morning scenario into something that was too much even for the self-styled "visceral artist."

In the pocket of his coat the artist had a tool which he used for cutting open boxes at the supermarket. He had cut into flesh in the past, and, with the moonlight glaring upon the snow of that alley, the artist made a few strokes which turned that white world red. Under the circumstances what he had done seemed perfectly justified to the artist, even an act of mercy. The man was becoming so small.

Afterward the artist ran through the alley without stopping until he reached the rented house where he lived with his roommate. It was she who telephoned the police, saying there was a body lying in the snow at such and such a place and then hanging up without giving her name. For days, weeks, the artist and his roommate searched the local newspapers for some word of the extraordinary thing the police must have found in that alley. But nothing ever appeared.

"You see how these incidents are hushed up," the purple woman whispered to us. "The police know what is going on. There are even *special police* for dealing with such matters. But nothing is made public, no one is questioned. And yet, after that morning in the alley, my cousin and her roommate came under surveillance and were followed everywhere by unmarked cars. Because these special policemen know that it is artists, or highly artistic persons, who are *approached* by the Teatro. And they know whom to watch after something has happened. It is said that these police may be party to the deeds of that 'company of nightmares'."

But none of us believed a word of this Teatro anecdote told by the purple woman, just as none of us believed the purple woman's friend, the filmmaker, when he denied all innuendos that connected him to the Teatro. On the one hand our imaginations had sided with this woman when she asserted that her friend, the creator of the short movie *Private Hell*, was somehow in league with the Teatro; on the other hand, we were mockingly dubious of the story about her cousin's roommate, the self-styled visceral artist, and his encounter in the snow-covered alley.

This divided reaction was not as natural as it seemed. Never mind that the case of the filmmaker was more credible than that of the visceral artist, if only because the first story was lacking the extravagant details which burdened the second. Until then we had uncritically relished all we had heard about the Teatro, no matter how bizarre these accounts may have been and no matter how much they opposed a verifiable truth or even a coherent portrayal of this phenomenon.

As artists we suspected that it was in our interest to have our heads filled with all kinds of Teatro craziness. Even I, a writer of nihilistic prose works, savored the inconsistency and the flamboyant absurdity of what was told to me across a table in a quiet library or a noisy club. In a word, I delighted in the *unreality* of the Teatro stories. The truth they carried, if any, was immaterial. And we never questioned any of them until the purple woman related the episode of the visceral artist and the small man in the alley.

But this new disbelief was not in the least inspired by our sense of reason or reality. It was in fact based solely on fear; it was driven by the will to negate what one fears. No one gives up on something until it turns on them, whether or not that thing is real or unreal. In some way all of this Teatro business had finally worn upon our nerves; the balance had been tipped between a madness that intoxicated us and one that began to menace our minds. As for the woman who always dressed herself in shades of purple . . . we avoided her. It would have been typical of the Teatro, someone said, to use a person like that for their purposes.

Perhaps our judgement of the purple woman was unfair. No doubt her theories concerning the "approach of the Teatro" made us all uneasy. But was this reason enough to cast her out from that artistic underworld which was the only society available to her? Like many societies, of course, ours was founded on fearful superstition, and this is always reason enough for any kind of behavior. She had been permanently stigmatized by too closely associating herself with something unclean in its essence. Because even after her theories were discredited by a newly circulated Teatro tale, her status did not improve.

I am now referring to a story that was going around in which an artist was not approached by the Teatro but rather took the first step *toward* the Teatro, as if acting under the impulse of a sovereign will.

The artist in this case was a photographer of the I-am-a-camera type. He was a studiedly bloodless specimen who quite often, and for no apparent reason, would begin to stare at someone and to continue staring until that person reacted in some manner, usually by fleeing the scene but on occasion by assaulting the photographer, who invariably pressed charges. It was therefore not entirely surprising to learn that he tried to engage the services of the Teatro in the way he did, for it was his belief that this cruel troupe could be hired to, in the photographer's words, "utterly destroy someone." And the person he wished to destroy was his landlord, a small balding man with a moustache who, after the photographer had moved out of his apartment, refused to remit his security deposit, perhaps with good reason but perhaps not.

In any case, the photographer, whose name incidentally was Spence, made inquiries about the Teatro over a period of some months. Following up every scrap of information, no matter how obscure or suspect, the tenacious Spence ultimately arrived in the shopping district of an old suburb where there was a two-story building that rented space to various persons and businesses, including a small video store, a dentist, and, as it was spelled out on the building's directory, the Theatre Grottesco. At the back of the first floor, directly below a studio for dancing instruction, was a small suite of offices whose glass door displayed some stencilled lettering that read: T G Ventures. Seated at a desk in the reception area behind the glass door was a young woman with long black hair and black-rimmed eyeglasses. She was thoroughly engrossed in writing something on a small blank card, several more of which were spread across her desk. The way Spence told it, he was undeterred by all appearances that seemed to suggest the Teatro, or Theatre, was not what he assumed it was. He entered the reception area of the office, stood before the desk of the young woman, and introduced himself by name and occupation, believing it important to communicate as soon as possible his identity as an artist, or at least imply as best he could that he was a highly artistic photographer, which undoubtedly he was. When the young woman adjusted her eyeglasses and asked, "How can I help you?" the photographer Spence leaned toward her and whispered, "I would like to enlist the services of the Teatro, or Theatre if you like." When the receptionist asked what he was planning, the photographer answered, "To utterly destroy someone." The young woman was absolutely unflustered, according to Spence, by this declaration. She began calmly gathering the small blank cards that were spread across her desk and, while doing this, explained that T G Ventures was, in her words, an "entertainment service." After placing the small blank cards to one side, she removed from her desk a folded brochure which outlined the nature of the business, which provided clowns, magicians, and novelty performances for a variety of occasions, their specialty being children's parties.

As Spence studied the brochure, the receptionist placidly sat with her hands folded and gazed at him from within the black frames of her eyeglasses. The light in that suburban office suite was bright but not harsh; the pale walls were incredibly clean and the carpeting, in Spence's description, was the color of fresh liver. The photographer said that he felt as if he were standing in a mirage. "This is all a front," Spence finally said, throwing the brochure on the receptionist's desk. But the young woman only picked up the brochure and placed it back in the same drawer from which it had come. "What's behind that door?" Spence demanded, pointing across the room. And just as he pointed at that door there was a sound on the other side of it, a brief rumbling as if something heavy had just fallen to the floor. "The dancing classes," said the receptionist, her right index finger pointing up at the floor above. "Perhaps," Spence allowed, but he claimed that this sound that he heard, which he described as having an "abysmal resonance," caused

a sudden rise of panic within him. He tried not to move from the place he was standing, but his body was overwhelmed by the impulse to leave that suite of offices. The photographer turned away from the receptionist and saw his reflection in the glass door. She was watching him from behind the lenses of black-framed eyeglasses, and the stencilled lettering on the glass door read backwards, as if in a mirror. A few seconds later Spence was outside the building in the old suburb. All the way home, he asserted, his heart was pounding.

The following day Spence paid a visit to his landlord's place of business, which was a tiny office in a seedy downtown building. Having given up on the Teatro, he would have to deal in his own way with this man who would not return his security deposit. Spence's strategy was to plant himself in his landlord's office and stare him into submission with a photographer's unnerving gaze. After he arrived at his landlord's rented office on the sixth floor of what was a thoroughly depressing downtown building, Spence seated himself in a chair looking across a filthy desk at a small balding man with a moustache. But the man merely looked back at the photographer. To make things worse, the landlord (whose name was Herman Zick), would lean towards Spence every so often and in a quiet voice say, "It's all perfectly legal, you know." Then Spence would continue his staring, which he was frustrated to find ineffective against this man Zick, who of course was not an artist, or even a highly artistic person, as were the usual victims of the photographer. Thus the battle kept up for almost an hour, the landlord saying, "It's all perfectly legal," and Spence trying to hold a fixed gaze upon the man he wished to utterly destroy.

Ultimately Spence was the first to lose control. He jumped out of the chair in which he was sitting and began to shout incoherently at the landlord. Once Spence was on his feet, Zick swiftly maneuvered around the desk and physically evicted the photographer from the tiny office, locking him out in the hallway. Spence said that he was in the hallway for only a second or two when the doors opened to the elevator that was directly across from Zick's sixth-floor office. Out of the elevator compartment stepped a middle-aged man in a dark suit and black-framed eyeglasses. He wore a full, well-groomed beard which, Spence observed, was slightly streaked with gray. In his left hand the gentleman was clutching a crumpled brown bag, holding it a few inches in front of him. He walked up to the door of the landlord's office and with his right hand grasped the round black doorknob, jiggling it back and forth several times. There was a loud click that echoed down the hallway of that old downtown building. The gentleman turned his head and looked at Spence for the first time, smiling briefly before admitting himself to the office of Herman Zick.

Again the photographer experienced that surge of panic he had felt the day before when he visited the suburban offices of T G Ventures. He pushed the down

button for the elevator, and while waiting he listened at the door of the landlord's office. What he heard, Spence claimed, was that terrible sound that had sent him running out in the street from T G Ventures, that "abysmal resonance," as he defined it. Suddenly the gentleman with the well-groomed beard and black-rimmed glasses emerged from the tiny office. The door to the elevator had just opened, and the man walked straight past Spence to board the empty compartment. Spence himself did not get on the elevator but stood outside, helplessly staring at the bearded gentleman, who was still holding that small crumpled bag. A split second before the elevator doors slid closed, the gentleman looked directly at Spence and winked at him. It was the assertion of the photographer that this wink, executed from behind a pair of black-framed eyeglasses, made a mechanical clicking sound which echoed down the dim hallway.

Prior to his exit from the old downtown building, leaving by way of the stairs rather than the elevator, Spence tried the door to his landlord's office. He found it unlocked and cautiously stepped inside. But there was no one on the other side of the door.

The conclusion to the photographer's adventure took place a full week later. Delivered by regular post to his mail box was a small square envelope with no return address. Inside was a photograph. He brought this item to Des Esseintes' Library, a bookstore where several of us were giving a late-night reading of our latest literary efforts. A number of persons belonging to the local artistic underworld, including myself, saw the photograph and heard Spence's rather frantic account of the events surrounding it. The photo was of Spence himself staring stark-eyed into the camera, which apparently had taken the shot from inside an elevator, a panel of numbered buttons being partially visible along the right-hand border of the picture. "I could see no camera," Spence kept repeating. "But that wink he gave me . . . and what's written on the reverse side of this thing." Turning over the photo Spence read aloud the following handwritten inscription: "The little man is so much littler these days. Soon he will know about the soft black stars. And your payment is past due." Someone then asked Spence what they had to say about all this at the offices of T G Ventures. The photographer's head swivelled slowly in exasperated negation. "Not there anymore," he said over and over. With the single exception of myself, that night at Des Esseintes' Library was the last time anyone saw Mr. Spence.

After the photographer ceased to show up at the usual meeting places and special artistic events, there were no cute remarks about his having "gone with the Teatro." We were all of us beyond that stage. I was perversely proud to note that a degree of philosophical maturity had now developed among those in the artistic underworld of which I was a part. There is nothing like fear to complicate one's consciousness, inducing previously unknown levels of reflection.

Under such mental stress I began to organize my own thoughts and observations about the Teatro, specifically as this phenomenon related to the artists who seemed to be its sole objects of attention.

Whether or not an artist was approached by the Teatro or took the initiative to approach the Teatro himself, it seemed the effect was the same: the end of an artist's work. I myself verified this fact as thoroughly as I could. The filmmaker whose short movie *Private Hell* so many of us admired had, by all accounts, become a full-time dealer in pornographic videos, none of them his own productions. The self-named visceral artist had publicly called an end to those stunts of his which had gained him a modest underground reputation. According to his roommate, the purple woman's cousin, he was now managing the supermarket where he had formerly labored as a stock clerk. As for the purple woman herself, who was never much praised as an artist and whose renown effectively began and ended with the "cigar box assemblage" phase of her career, she had gone into selling real estate, an occupation in which she became quite a success. This roster of ex-artists could be extended considerably, I am sure of that. But for the purposes of this report or confession (or whatever else you would like to call it) I must end my list of no-longer-artistic persons with myself, while attempting to offer some insights into the manner in which the Teatro Grottesco could transform a writer of nihilistic prose works into a non-artistic, more specifically a *post-artistic* being.

It was after the disappearance of the photographer Spence that my intuitions concerning the Teatro began to crystalize and become explicit thoughts, a dubious process but one to which I am inescapably subject as a prose writer. Until that point in time, everyone tacitly assumed that there was an intimacy of *kind* between the Teatro and the artists who were either approached by the Teatro or who themselves approached this cruel troupe by means of some overture, as in the case of Spence, or perhaps by gestures more subtle, even purely noetic (I retreat from writing *unconscious,* although others might argue with my intellectual reserve). Many of us even spoke of the Teatro as a manifestation of super-art, a term which we always left conveniently nebulous. However, following the disappearance of the photographer, all knowledge I had acquired about the Teatro, fragmentary as it was, became configured in a completely new pattern. I mean to say that I no longer considered it possible that the Teatro was in any way related to a super-art, or to an art of any kind, quite the opposite in fact. To my mind the Teatro was, and is, a phenomenon intensely destructive of everything that I conceived of as art. Therefore, the Teatro was, and is, intensely destructive of all artists and even of highly artistic persons. Whether this destructive force is a matter of intention or is an epiphenomenon of some unrelated, perhaps greater design, or even if there exists anything like an intention or design on the part of the Teatro, I have no idea (at least none I can elaborate in comprehensible terms). Nonetheless, I feel certain that for an artist to encounter the Teatro there can be only one consequence: the end of that artist's work. Strange, then, that knowing this fact I still acted as I did.

I cannot say if it was I who approached the Teatro or vice versa, as if any of that stupidness made a difference. The important thing is that from the moment I perceived the Teatro to be a profoundly anti-artistic phenomenon I conceived the ambition to make my form of art, by which I mean my nihilistic prose writings, into an anti-*Teatro* phenomenon. In order to do this, of course, I required a penetrating knowledge of the Teatro Grottesco, or of some significant aspect of that cruel troupe, an insight of a deeply subtle, even dreamlike variety into its nature and workings.

The photographer Spence had made a great visionary advance when he intuited that it was in the nature of the Teatro to act on his request to utterly destroy someone (although the exact meaning of the statement "he will know about the soft black stars," in reference to Spence's landlord, became known to both of us only sometime later). I realized that I would need to make a similar leap of insight in my own mind. While I had already perceived the Teatro to be a profoundly anti-artistic phenomenon, I was not yet sure what in the world would constitute an anti-*Teatro* phenomenon, as well as how in the world I could turn my own prose writings to such a purpose.

Thus, for several days I meditated on these questions. As usual, the psychic demands of this meditation severely taxed my bodily processes, and in my weakened state I contracted a virus, specifically an *intestinal virus,* which confined me to my small apartment for a period of one week. Nonetheless, it was during this time that things fell into place regarding the Teatro and the insights I required to oppose this company of nightmares in a more or less efficacious manner.

Suffering through the days and night of an illness, especially an intestinal virus, one becomes highly conscious of certain realities, as well as highly sensitive to the *functions* of these realities, which otherwise are not subject to prolonged attention or meditation. Upon recovery from such a virus, the consciousness of these realities and their functions necessarily fades, so that the once-stricken person may resume his life's activities and not be driven to insanity or suicide by the acute awareness of these most unpleasant facts of existence. Through the illumination of analogy, I came to understand that the Teatro operated in much the same manner as the illness from which I recently suffered, with the consequence that the person exposed to the Teatro-disease becomes highly conscious of certain realities and their functions, ones quite different of course from the realities and functions of an intestinal

virus. However, an intestinal virus ultimately succumbs, in a reasonably healthy individual, to the formation of antibodies (or something of that sort). But the disease of the Teatro, I now understood, was a disease for which no counteracting agents, or antibodies, had ever been created by the systems of the individuals — that is, the *artists* — it attacked. An encounter with any disease, including an intestinal virus, serves to alter a person's mind, making it intensely aware of certain realities, but this mind cannot remain altered once this encounter has ended or else that person will never be able to go on living in the same way as before. In contrast, an encounter with the Teatro appears to remain within one's system and to alter a person's mind permanently. For the artist the result is *not* to be driven into insanity or suicide (as might be the case if one assumed a permanent mindfulness of an intestinal virus) but the absolute termination of that artist's work. The simple reason for this effect is that there are no antibodies for the disease of the Teatro, and therefore no relief from the consciousness of the realities which an encounter with the Teatro has forced upon an artist.

Having progressed this far in my contemplation of the Teatro — so that I might discover its nature or essence and thereby make my prose writings into an anti-Teatro phenomenon — I found that I could go no further. No matter how much thought and meditation I devoted to the subject I did not gain a definite sense of having revealed to myself the true realities and functions that the Teatro communicated to an artist and how this communication put an end to that artist's work. Of course I could vaguely imagine the species of awareness that might render an artist thenceforth incapable of producing any type of artistic efforts. I actually arrived at a fairly detailed and disturbing idea of such an awareness — a *world-awareness,* as I conceived it. Yet I did not feel I had penetrated the mystery of "Teatro-stuff." And the only way to know about the Teatro, it seemed, was to have an encounter with it. Such an encounter between myself and the Teatro would have occurred in any event as a result of the discovery that my prose writings had been turned into an anti-Teatro phenomenon: this would constitute an *approach* of the most outrageous sort to that company of nightmares, forcing an encounter with all its realities and functions.

Thus it was not necessary, at this point in my plan, to have actually succeeded in making my prose writings into an anti-Teatro phenomenon. I simply had to make it known, falsely, that I had done so.

As soon as I had sufficiently recovered from my intestinal virus I began to spread the word. Every time I found myself among others who belonged to the so-called artistic underworld of this city I bragged that I had gained the most intense awareness of the Teatro's realities and functions, and that, far from finishing me off as an artist, I had actually used this awareness as inspiration for a series of short prose works. I explained to my colleagues that merely to exist — let alone create artistic works — we had to keep certain things from overwhelming our minds. However, I continued, in order to keep these things, such as the realities of an intestinal virus, from overwhelming our minds we attempted to deny them any voice whatever, neither a voice in our minds and certainly not a precise and clear voice in works of art. The voice of madness, for instance, is barely a whisper in the babbling history of art because its realities are themselves too maddening to speak of for very long . . . and those of the Teatro have no voice at all, given their imponderably grotesque nature. Furthermore, I said, the Teatro not only propagated an intense awareness of these things, these realities and functionings of realities, it was identical with them. And I, I boasted, had allowed my mind to be overwhelmed by all manner of Teatro stuff, while also managing to use this experience as material for my prose writings. "This," I practically shouted one day at Des Esseintes' Library, "is the super-art." Then I promised that in two days time I would give a reading of my series of short prose pieces.

Nevertheless, as we sat around on some old furniture in a corner of Des Esseintes' Library, several of the others challenged my statements and assertions regarding the Teatro. One fellow writer, a poet, spoke hoarsely through a cloud of cigarette smoke, saying to me: "No one knows what this Teatro stuff is all about. I'm not sure I believe it myself." But I answered that Spence knew what it was all about, thinking that very soon I too would know what he knew. "Spence," said a woman in a tone of exaggerated disgust (she once lived with the photographer and was a photographer herself). "He's not telling us about anything these days, never mind the Teatro." But I answered that, like the purple woman and the others, Spence had been overwhelmed by his encounter with the Teatro, and his artistic impulse had been thereby utterly destroyed. "And your artistic impulse is still intact," she said snidely. I answered that, yes, it was, and in two days I would prove it by reading a series of prose works that exhibited an intimacy with the most overwhelmingly grotesque experiences and gave voice to them. "That's because you have no idea what you're talking about," said someone else, and almost everyone supported this remark. I told them to be patient, wait and see what my prose writings revealed to them. "Reveal?" asked the poet. "Hell, no one even knows why it's called the Teatro Grottesco." I did not have an answer for that, but I repeated that they would understand much more about the Teatro in a few days, thinking to myself that within this period of time I would have either succeeded or failed in my attempt to provoke an encounter with the Teatro and the matter of my nonexistent anti-Teatro prose writing would be immaterial.

On the very next day, however, I collapsed in Des Esseintes' Library during a conversation with a different congregation of artists and highly artistic persons.

Although the symptoms of my intestinal virus had never entirely disappeared I had not expected to collapse the way I did and ultimately to discover that what I thought was an intestinal virus was in fact something far more serious. As a consequence of my collapse, my unconscious body ended up in the emergency room of a nearby hospital, the kind of place where borderline indigents like myself always end up — a backstreet hospital with dated fixtures and a staff of sleepwalkers.

When I next opened my eyes it was night. The bed in which they had put my body was beside a tall paned window that reflected the dim florescent light overhead, creating a black glare in the windowpanes that allowed no view of anything beyond them but only a broken image of myself and the room around me. There was a long row of these tall paned windows and several other beds in the ward, each of them supporting a sleeping body that, like mine, was damaged in some way and therefore had been committed to that backstreet hospital.

I felt none of the extraordinary pain that had caused me to collapse in Des Esseintes' Library. At that moment, in fact, I could feel nothing of the experiences of my past life: it seemed I had always been an occupant of that dark hospital ward and always would be. This sense of estrangement from both myself and everything else made it terribly difficult to remain in the hospital bed where I had been placed. At the same time I felt uneasy about any movement away from that bed, especially any movement that would cause me to approach the open doorway which led into a half-lighted backstreet hospital corridor. Compromising between my impulse to get out of my bed and my fear of moving away from the bed and approaching that corridor, I positioned myself so that I was sitting on the edge of the mattress with my bare feet grazing the cold linoleum floor. I had been sitting on the edge of that mattress for quite a while before I heard the voice out in the corridor.

The voice came over the public address system, but it was not a particularly loud voice. In fact I had to strain my attention for several minutes simply to discern the peculiar qualities of the voice and to decipher what it said. It sounded like a child's voice, a sing-songy voice full of taunts and mischief. Over and over it repeated the same phrase — Paging Dr. Groddeck, paging Dr. Groddeck. The voice sounded incredibly hollow and distant, garbled by all kinds of interference. Paging Dr. Groddeck, it giggled from the other side of the world.

I stood up and slowly approached the doorway leading out into the corridor. But even after I had crossed the room in my bare feet and was standing in the open doorway, that child's voice did not become any louder or any clearer. Even when I actually moved out into that long dim corridor with its dated lighting fixtures, the voice that was calling Dr. Groddeck sounded just as hollow and distant. And now it was as if I were in a dream in which I was walking in my bare feet down a backstreet hospital corridor, hearing a crazy voice that seemed to be eluding me as I moved past the open doorways of innumerable wards full of damaged bodies. But then the voice died away, calling to Dr. Groddeck one last time before fading like the final echo in a deep well. At the same moment that the voice ended its hollow outcrying I paused somewhere toward the end of that shadowy corridor. In the absence of the mischievous voice I was able to hear something else, a sound like quiet, wheezing laughter. It was coming from the room just ahead of me along the right-hand side of the corridor. As I approached this room I saw a metal plaque mounted at eye-level on the wall, and the words displayed on this plaque were these: Dr. T. Groddeck.

A strangely glowing light emanated from the room where I heard that quiet and continuous wheezing laughter. I peered around the edge of the doorway and saw that the laughter was coming from an old gentleman seated behind a desk, while the strangely glowing light was coming from a large globular object positioned on top of the desk directly in front of him. The light from this object — a globe of solid glass, it seemed — shone on the old gentleman's face, which was a crazy-looking face with a neatly clipped beard that was pure white and a pair of spectacles with slim rectangular lenses resting on the bridge of a slender nose. When I stood in the doorway of that office, the eyes of Dr. Groddeck did not gaze up at me but continued to stare into the strange, shining globe and at the things that were inside it.

What were these things inside the globe that Dr. Groddeck was looking at? To me they appeared to be tiny star-shaped flowers evenly scattered throughout the glass, just the thing to lend a mock-artistic appearance to a common paperweight. Except that these flowers, these spidery chrysanthemums, were pure black. And they did not seem to be firmly fixed within the shining sphere, as one would expect, but looked as if they were floating in position, their starburst of petals wavering slightly like tentacles. Dr. Groddeck appeared to delight in the subtle movements of those black appendages. Behind rectangular spectacles his eyes rolled about as they tried to take in each of the hovering shapes inside the radiant globe on the desk before him.

Then the doctor slowly reached down into one of the deep pockets of the lab coat he was wearing, and his wheezing laughter grew more intense. From the open doorway I watched as he carefully removed a small paper bag from his pocket, but he never even glanced at me. With one hand he was now holding the crumpled bag directly over the globe. When he gave the bag a little shake, the things inside the globe responded with an increased agitation of their thin black arms. He used both hands to open the top of the bag and quickly turned it upside down.

From out of the bag something tumbled onto the globe, where it seemed to stick to the surface. It was not actually adhering to the surface of the globe, however, but was sinking into the interior of the glass. It squirmed as those soft black stars inside the globe gathered to pull it down to themselves. Before I could see what it was that they had captured and surrounded, the show was over. Afterward they returned to their places, and once again were floating gently within the glowing sphere.

I looked at Dr. Groddeck and saw that he was finally looking back at me. He had stopped his asthmatic laughter, and his eyes were staring frigidly into mine, completely devoid of any readable meaning. Yet somehow these eyes provoked me. Even as I stood in the open doorway of that hideous office in a backstreet hospital, Dr. Groddeck's eyes provoked in me an intense outrage, an astronomical resentment of the position I had been placed in. Even as I had consummated my plan to encounter the Teatro and experience its most devastating realities and functions (in order to turn my prose works into an anti-Teatro phenomenon) I was outraged to be standing where I was standing and resentful of the staring eyes of Dr. Groddeck. No matter if I had approached the Teatro, the Teatro had approached me, or we both approached each other. I realized that there is such a thing as being approached in order to force one's hand into making what only appears to be an approach, which is actually a non-approach that negates the whole concept of approaching. It was all a fix from the start, because I belonged to an artistic underworld, because I was an artist whose work would be brought to an end by an encounter with the Teatro Grottesco. And so I was outraged by the eyes of Dr. Groddeck, which were the eyes of the Teatro, and I was resentful of all insane realities and the excruciating functions of the Teatro. Although I knew that the persecutions of the Teatro were not exclusively focused on the artists and highly artistic persons of the world, I was nevertheless outraged and resentful to be singled out for *special treatment*. I wanted to punish those persons in this world who are not the object of such special treatment. Thus, at the top of my voice, I called out in the dim corridor, I cried out the summons for others to join me before the stage of the Teatro. Strange that I should think it necessary to compound the nightmare of all those damaged bodies in that backstreet hospital, as well as its staff of sleepwalkers who moved within a world of outdated fixtures. But by the time anyone arrived Dr. Groddeck was gone, and his office became nothing more than a room full of dirty laundry.

My escapade that night notwithstanding, I was soon released from the hospital pending the results of several tests I had been administered. I was feeling as well as ever, and the hospital, like any hospital, always needed the bedspace for more damaged bodies. They said I would be contacted in the next few days.

It was in fact the following day that I was informed of the outcome of my stay in the hospital. "Hello again," began the letter, which was typed on a plain, though waterstained sheet of paper. "I was so pleased to finally meet you in person. I thought your performance in our interview at the hospital was really first rate, and I am authorized to offer you a position with us. There is an opening in our organization for someone with your resourcefulness and imagination. I'm afraid things didn't work out with Mr. Spence. But he certainly did have a camera's eye, and we have gotten some wonderful pictures from him. I would especially like to share with you his last shots of the soft black stars, or S.B.S., as we sometimes refer to them. Veritable super-art, if there ever was such a thing!

"By the way, the results of your tests — some of which you have yet to be subjected to — are going to come back positive. If you think an intestinal virus is misery, just wait a few more months. So think fast, sir. We will arrange another meeting with you in any case. And remember — *you* approached *us*. Or was it the other way around?

"As you might have noticed by now, all this artistic business can only keep you going so long before you're left speechlessly gaping at the realities and functions of . . . well, I think you know what I'm trying to say. I was forced into this realization myself, and I'm quite mindful of what a blow this can be. Indeed, it was I who invented the appelative for our organization as it is currently known. Not that I put any stock in names, nor should you. Our company is so much older than its own name, or any other name for that matter. (And how many it's had over the years — The Ten Thousand Things, Anima Mundi, Nethescurial.) You should be proud that we have a special part for you to play, such a talented artist. In time you will forget yourself entirely in your work, as we all do eventually. Myself, I go around with a trunkful of aliases, but do you think I can say who I once was *really*? A man of the theater, that seems plausible. Possibly I was the father of Faust or Hamlet . . . or merely Peter Pan.

"In closing, I do hope you will seriously consider our offer to join us. We can do something about your medical predicament. We can do just about anything. Otherwise, I'm afraid that all I can do is welcome you to your own private hell, which will be as unspeakable as any on earth."

The letter was signed Dr. Theodore Groddeck, and its prognostication of my physical health was accurate: I have taken more tests at the backstreet hospital and the results are somewhat grim. For several days and sleepless nights I have considered the alternatives the doctor proposed to me, as well as others of my own devising, and have yet to reach a decision on what course to follow. The one conclusion that keeps forcing itself upon me is that it makes no difference what choice I make, or do not make. You can never anticipate the Teatro . . . or anything else. You can never know what you are approaching, or what is approaching you. Soon enough my thoughts will lose all clarity, and I will no longer be aware that there was ever a decision to be made.

The soft black stars have already begun to fill the sky. Ω

A DAY ON THE BOG
by Lord Dunsany

Ilustrated by Keith Minnion

There was gentlemen in Ireland in the old days, said Mickey Tuohey, such as you very seldom see now. Severals of them there were, and all of them great gentlemen. And I'll tell you what they used to do: when they'd go out shooting grouse on the bog they'd take silver flasks with them that held as much as a quart of whiskey. A quart of whiskey in one flask. Sure, you never see anything like that nowadays. The old stock are nearly all gone, more's the pity. I mind the time when Mr Fitzcharles (the light of Heaven to him, for he is dead long ago) went out on the red bog one day, and he takes me with him to mind the dog. And the bog went right to the horizon and over the other side of it. And we walked all day, and when it got neat to one o'clock, and we had a fine bag of snipe and a few grouse, he says to me, "What about a bit of lunch, Tuohey?"

And I says to him, "Sir, it was the very thing I was thinking myself."

And we sits down on the heather and eats a few sandwiches, and that sort of stuff, that I had in the gamebag. And then he says to me, "Did you happen to remember to bring my flask, Tuohey?"

Remember it! Sure I remember it to this day.

And I says, "I did, sir."

And I brings out the great silver flask that used to hold a quart.

"Then shall we have a little whiskey," he says, "to keep our throats from getting dry?"

And I had two tumblers in the gamebag, made of horn, the way that they wouldn't break. And our throats never got dry that morning. It was the best of old whiskey that Mr Fitzcharles used to have in those days, mild as milk, and did you no more harm nor milk, and a great deal more good. And Mr Fitzcharles gave me half of it for myself, and he drinks his half straight off, without taking a breath. That's the kind of grand old gentleman that he was. We sat there in the sun resting and feeling the good that the whiskey was doing us, and the red bog round us as far as they eye could see. And a leprechaun comes over the bog and he runs straight up to us, the only time in my life I ever seen a leprechaun close, though I'd often heard tell of them; a little brown lad not half the height of a man. And he stands there on a patch of bright-red moss and looks at us. And he says to us, "You are the two grandest men ever I seen."

And Mr Fitzcharles says to him, "Is there anything I can do for you?"

And the leprechaun says, "Sure, there is. Would your honour give me your soul, that I may become a mortal and go about on the dry land, and see towns and wear boots and a fine glossy hat?"

And I was terrified for the sake of Mr Fitzcharles, for he was the most generous-hearted man in the world, one of the great gentlemen, and he would never refuse anyone anything, and I was afraid that he would give up his soul and be damned. But he thinks for a moment before he answers, as a man should. And then he says to the leprechaun, "I'm afraid I'm only a Protestant."

"Ah, well," says the leprechaun, "what matter? But never mind now. Sure, I'll ask for it some other time."

And then I was more frightened than ever, for I was afraid he would ask me for mine. And I couldn't refuse him, if he did, in the presence of Mr Fitzcharles, on account of him being one of the most generous-hearted men in the world, as I'm just after telling you. I couldn't refuse anybody anything when I was out with him, whatever I might do at another time. So I sat there trying to look the other way. But the leprechaun hops round in front of the way I was looking, quicker nor I could turn my eyes away from him. And he says to me, "Will you lend me your soul?"

Well, you know the way it is when anyone asks you to lend him something: it is harder to refuse nor when he asks you to give it. But the result is the same either way. And I thought for a moment or two, the same as Mr Fitzcharles had done; and then I says to him, "I'll lend you my soul for so long as you like, if you'll give me your crock of gold."

And, mind you, it isn't that I valued the crock of gold more nor my soul. Sure, it would be a great mistake to do that. But I knew that he'd never part with his crock. And, sure, he wouldn't. And what he says is, "Sure, I wouldn't pay you all that for it."

"You and your crock of gold," I says to him. "Sure, you've not enough in it to buy a pig, let alone a good Catholic soul."

"Begob," he says to me, "I've enough in it to buy a herd of cattle, and your soul as well, and another one like it thrown in for luck. And you'll not find my crock, for I'm going to run away in the opposite direction from where it is, so as not to lead you to it."

Well, we hunted most of the evening for that crock in the opposite direction from the one in which he had run. But after a bit I says to Mr Fitzcharles, "Maybe he's not so simple as he appeared. What if the little devil has been telling a lie to us?"

"And so he might," says Mr Fitzcharles. "I would never trust a leprechaun.

And that was perfectly right, for there was nothing Mr Fitzcharles didn't know.

So we hunted in the other direction, the one in which he *had* run. But very soon the good that the whiskey had done us seemed to begin to run out of us, and there was no more left in the flask to keep us going; and it was like looking for a snipe, without a dog, that has fallen a long way off. Sure, the red bog has a great knack of hiding things. So we give it up. The cheek of him, saying that he wouldn't make the exchange! Ah, but those were the good days. You can't get enough for two shillings to moisten your lips now.

Ω

SEA WITCH

A voice of power carries over water,
from a tower in the bay, rooted in boulders.
No one knows whose lover or whose daughter,

or what chance or ill-chance brought her
to the hearth above the waves where she grows older.
A woman's voice has traveled over water,

up village streets where poorer women barter
with the bundles of the day upon their shoulders.
They do not care whose lover or whose daughter,

they say the blue-haired Mage of Ocean taught her;
that ghosts of all the drowned (or something older)
drove her and her spells across the water.

They tell of pirate ships that court her,
of amulets and cloth of gold they've sold her,
but no one knows whose lover or whose daughter,

or why, last night, she cried out to the water,
or what, in ancient language harsh, it told her.
A witch's voice has carried over water,
but no one knows whose lover or whose daughter.

— **Anne Sheldon**

A TALK WITH PETER STRAUB
by Darrell Schweitzer

Worlds of Fantasy & Horror: Your recent novels, such as *The Hellfire Club* and *Mystery* have no supernatural content. Your work in the past few years has turned away from the fantastic. Why?

Straub: What you're describing is a very conscious move on my part. After I wrote the novel *Floating Dragon,* and then collaborated with Steve King on *The Talisman,* it seemed to me that I had burned out on that kind of material. It was exciting for a long time to work on the kind of conventional metaphors of horror. But after *Floating Dragon,* in which I had deliberately shot my bolt and gone over the top, I felt that I had exhausted that material as far as I was concerned, and also exhausted myself when it came to using it.

It took me a long time to figure out what to do after that. I knew I wanted to work with matters that seemed more important to me, that seemed more central to my own life and self. Once I had started writing *Koko,* it was hard going. It took me at least a year to write the first hundred pages. But once I got into the swing, I saw that I was writing much better than I had been previously, and also that something new had entered what I wrote, which was a better sort of consciousness. All I mean is a deeper awareness of the motives of the characters I was working with, the reasons why people do things. People have different motives which influence behavior. Some are conscious; some are not. Part of the improvement that I noticed in what I was doing was that I was much clearer about the conscious motives and the unconscious motives. It all seemed to work quite well. I was very, very pleased with the book when it was finally finished. Since then I have been trying to stay at that level and explore whatever it is that comes to mind.

WoF&H: Is this immediacy or increased depth the result of your now writing about something that is *not* imaginary — that is, human psychology and motivations — as opposed to say, ghosts, which you and the reader both know to be made-up? So, are you gaining this new strength from simple realism?

Straub: I don't know that I ever really believed in ghosts, and I'm not sure that I don't believe in them now. So I want it both ways on that one. What was at stake was the quality of my interest in the material itself. I felt that I had done all I could with it, and so that was a way of saying I couldn't "believe" in ghostly matters, if you put the belief in quotes. It didn't suit my imagination.

WoF&H: Did your older books still mean as much to you, even though you could no longer work in that mode, or did your supernatural novels now seem to be on a lower plane, in retrospect?

Straub: I didn't lose any of the affection I had for my earlier books, and I didn't think they were any lesser accomplishments. At the time I was doing them, I was enraptured by the material of the supernatural, that is, ghosts and the various surreal elements of the supernatural category. I remember thinking that stuff was like blues. It was bottomlessly deep. You could swim down in it forever. That is probably true for a lot of people, but for me I just got to the bottom, and it wasn't so good anymore. I suppose the real point was that I saw that if I were to keep on doing that, I would just wind up repeating myself, which has never had much appeal to me.

WoF&H: This would seem to be an occupational hazard for horror writers, and a recently developed one. That is to say, prior to Stephen King, there was no such thing as a professional horror novelist, someone who made his living almost entirely from writing horror novels. The classic writers of the farther past, like Poe or Le Fanu or Edith Wharton, more recently, someone like E.F. Benson, were general men or women of letters. They wrote all kinds of things, including some horror. Not even Fritz Leiber or Richard Matheson wrote one horror novel after another. They got to vary their tone. I'm amazed at how well Ramsey Campbell has held up under the pressure of genre.

Did you find that editorial or marketing forces were trying to turn you into this new kind of writer?

Straub: In a way I think we all did become a new sort of writer. Remember that I started off about the same time as Steve. He was a new person when I was a new person. When I was writing my first books like that, I had never heard of him. I only heard of him because he gave a blurb to my books. He wasn't a phenomenon at that point. It never occurred to me that there was any trouble at all in writing decent works of fiction that were also horror novels. That seemed like a non-issue. I thought, of course you could do it, as long as you did it the right way. What I liked about King's work was that it was clear that he was doing it in what I thought was the right way. It took Ramsey a longer time, because he was doing mainly short stories. It was well into my acquaintanceship with Ramsey Campbell that he first started to do novels, and it took him a time to find his feet there.

Now, no matter I said before, if people are asked to describe me, the first thing they will say is I'm a horror writer. Whenever I publish a book, and it's reviewed, nearly the first words out of the reviewer's mouth is "horror writer." Often on the blurb, they say, "the newest work by the master of horror, Peter Straub," or whatever. This word comes in. It is inescapable. That's cool with me. I'm comfortable about that, because even if I'm writing a book about a woman who's kidnapped, as in *The Hellfire Club,* there is still plenty of actual horror in that. Really what I like about this is that it

by Darrell Schweitzer   39

pushes the definition, way, way out, so it overlaps with mystery and suspense.

WoF&H: This brings up a question I've posed before. What would happen if Stephen King wrote *The Sound of Music*?

Straub: It would be a horror musical.

WoF&H: Well, what if you wrote something that was as far removed from your usual horror novel as *Chitty-Chitty-Bang-Bang* was from James Bond? You can imagine that must have given Ian Fleming's publisher a turn. What would your publisher do?

Straub: I think we'd probably have to have a long talk. Of course it would depend on the actual strength of the manuscript. Because I am me, and my reflexes will always lead me down certain paths, the book would never be that far afield. It would never be a romance novel. It would never be a historical bodice-ripper. If it were, there would be lots of stuff ripped besides bodices. So you're talking about a case that would probably never come up.

WoF&H: We're in the age of the specialist writer, who is expected to produce just one thing. But look back at, say, E.F. Benson, who was a great ghost-story writer but is better known today for his social comedies.

Straub: Yes, Mapp and Lucia. It would be fun to do something like that. But it never occurred to me to think of myself as a specialty writer. I see myself as the sole proprietor of a plot of ground of certain dimensions, and my job is to tend that ground and see what will grow. It's all the same, because it's all my ground. There might be corn or peas, but they'd be my veggies. So I think that all of them have a distinct commonality. Even if they were as different as corn and peas, they would still be recognizable as mine.

That is indeed part of the point. If you pick up a book by Stephen King, no matter what the content is, you read a page and you know it's him. Either that or it's one of his imitators who happened to have a good day when he wrote that page. That's the real point. You are supposed to discover your voice or your manner and work it as hard and as well as you can.

WoF&H: Of course in *The Talisman* there are passages where each of you is deliberately imitating the other's voice in order to fool the reader.

Straub: That was a nice little joke. I'm sure it worked. I know I threw in allusions to things King liked, and several times I saw Steve put in allusions to Zoot Sims and Dexter Gordon and try to persuade people that I'd written that. There's also the matter of style.

The other day I looked at *The Talisman* because I got a lot of mail about it, and I opened up the book and thought, "that's Steve," and then I remembered that I had written that. I had deliberately used Steve King's cadences.

WoF&H: Surely in a collaboration a communal voice comes out anyway.

Straub: That's right. It coalesces, so that jokiness evaporated fairly early on, so we settle in to what was a pretty consistent common voice.

WoF&H: Would you ever consider doing it again?

Straub: I don't think so. I don't think anybody in his right mind would do it at all. ((Laughs.)) I don't want to collaborate with anybody again, ever, and I don't think Steve would, and I certainly wouldn't want to collaborate with anybody but him.

WoF&H: So everything is going to have to come out of your head —

Straub: It's supposed to. Those are the ground rules.

WoF&H: It's supposed to. Do you ever feel that you'll use up everything you've got that's based on your own life?

Straub: In the sense that I'll run out of invention and be unable to recombine matters in a way that wouldn't imtitate effects in earlier books? I don't know. That has never actually occurred to me. Part of the reason I think that it may be unlikely is that every character imposes a new world, a new set of circumstances. Every character brings with him his own world of complexities. So you have your own built-in freshness every time you begin again.

Now, having said that, I'll have to backtrack a little bit, because I am clearly always interested in certain things, which will go from book to book: complicated families, books inside books — people reading books, sometimes about other books — this is just something that I like. I might get tired of that, and then I'll stop doing it. I think I'd like to move at some point toward simplicity and have a good, straightforward book that begins with A and ends with Z. For me it is a lot more fun to work it the other way around and to put in all these layers and go back in time and uncover things that happened long ago that reverberate in the present. That really seems to be what my instincts do. But at some point I'd like to do a nice simple chase. That could be fun.

WoF&H: How much research into realistic matters do you do? Do you go to the locales and get to know people in the professions of your characters? I know that, for example, if I were to try to write a novel about military officers, I'd be in deep trouble, because I don't know how they think and act and what their lives are like.

Straub: In regard to places, if it's a truly exotic place, then I have to go there or I know I'll get it all wrong. So for *Koko* I took a long trip to Hong Kong, Singapore, Taipei, Bangkok, and so forth. I took careful notes and I took photographs, and, basically, I remembered how it smelled, how it looked. I also had maps of these places. I figured out where the characters were living, where they could meet to talk to one another, and all that. So that was very helpful. More generally, though, I just make it up. If you make up a town, you can't get it wrong, as long as, the first time a character goes to Jones Street and he turns left, he always turns left later on. I also make it fairly easy on myself by very often writing about writers. If I were to write about military people, I'd have to find some somehow and hang out and hear the way they talk. But because I have met and known people from a wide variety of professions, I can pretty well draw material from banks of impressions that I have stored. I should probably talk to more policemen. I used to know some cops in Westport, and I got a lot of stuff from them, but that's probably not too accurate anymore. The area where I feel kind of endangered would be if I were to try to write about people in their twenties, because I probably don't get at all how they think, and I probably don't know how they speak either. It would be lovely to write a story about a young guy starting out with a law firm or an ad agency and going to sports bars — the kind of people I see around New York all the time — but I would have to live in one's hip pocket for a week before I could get it right.

WoF&H: Or else you'd have to set it in the past, when you were twenty.

Straub: That's right. Set it back there with jousts and chain-mail.

WoF&H: Inevitably most of the stories that we see about childhood these days are set in the '50s or the '60s.

Straub: Certainly mine are. Or late '40s.

WoF&H: Let's talk about the beginning of your career.

Straub: I sold the first novel I wrote, which was called *Marriages,* and it did abysmally. I had been writing a second novel, which was much, much better, but the publishers I had at the time, Coward-McCann and Andre Deutch, rejected it. It thought it was because of the book, but of course it isn't. It was because they hadn't done anything with the first one. So if I had asked my agents to keep on trying to sell that novel, *Under Venus,* they would have eventually found a place to sell it. But I thought it was my fault, and I spent a great deal of time rewriting it, until I was hideously depressed. I spent a lot more time lying in bed thinking about not rewriting it than I actually spent rewriting it.

So the agent that I had at the time suggested that I write something new, and I thought that it might possibly save my life if I wrote something that had some kind of acceptability to it. So walked around Hampstead Heath when we were in London, and I had an idea that did something for me. It gave me a little chill. I thought that was what I ought to do. It was more of a horror idea, not especially an adventure thing. When I started to write it, it really worked. It was called *Julia.* It came out very nicely. There were no problems. I was satisfied with the writing. I didn't understand all the story when I started, but it all connected up. It connected itself to itself as it went along, so I understood, right away that I had found a subject and a field in which I was at home. So I had no problem with trying to work that a little more.

WoF&H: Had you grown up reading this sort of stuff, *Great Tales of the Supernatural,* Lovecraft, and the rest?

Straub: *Great Tales of Terror and the Supernatural* was one of my favorite books. When I was about twelve or thirteen, I remember carrying it around. I remember taking it to Boy Scout camp. I just loved that book. I don't think I read Lovecraft except for what was in that book, and I don't remember which stories. I think there were one or two.

WoF&H: "The Rats in the Walls" and "The Dunwich Horror."

Straub: Then I moved away from all that, and it wasn't until I finished writing *Julia* and had probably started writing *If You Could See Me Now* that Tom Tessier started telling me of the people I ought to read. So because of Tessier, I got a lot of Lovecraft, and I got some Richard Matheson stories, Bob Bloch stories, some Lovecraft Circle people, and so began to find out what was actually there, to learn who my grandparents were. It was wonderful. It was a great experience. I had a tremendous time, just wading in.

WoF&H: Horror, like science fiction, has some aspects of a club. But it seems that a lot of horror writers like yourself came in from the outside, and didn't discover the club until their first couple of novels gave them credentials.

Straub: Yes, exactly. In a way I'm glad I wasn't in the club. I had to invent a lot of things for myself. My attitudes hadn't been hardened by group opinion, and also I didn't waste a lot of time on fanzines, and other things they do in science fiction.

WoF&H: Fanzines may be a fine idea when you're sixteen years old.

Straub: In my case I would have been better off doing what I did, which was reading yards and yards of fiction.

WoF&H: When did you actually start writing?

Straub: I wrote in gradeschool. I wrote some short stories in high school and then didn't write much fiction in in college. In fact, I don't think I wrote any. I wrote a lot of other stuff. I really started writing seriously after I got out of Columbia, after I got my master's and started teaching. Then I began reading lots of poetry and, as if infected, I started to write it. I spent a lot of time doing that. It was only when I was about twenty-six or twenty-seven that I realized that I had always thought of myself as a novelist, and it was time to do something about it, or it would just be a fantasy. Whatever I had to be of use there would be lost. So, without much of a plan I just started to write a novel by hand in a big journal, and when I finished that journal, I just bought another one. There were two or three of those books. I wrote about five hundred words a day. It felt wonderful. I didn't know if it was any good or not. Then I typed it up and mailed it to a publisher, Andre Deutch, and some woman there — Jill Mortimer was her name — wrote to me to say that she quite liked the book and would try to convince the board to accept it. Three months later, they did. It didn't seem difficult then. The difficulty came later.

WoF&H: What were the difficulties? You seem to have been blessed at that point. Many people struggle for years to get a two-thousand word story into print.

Straub: The struggle happened when the second book, *Under Venus,* was rejected. Then I thought maybe I'm a one-book wonder. I had no confidence that I could repeat what had seemed a success, especially given the fact of a subsequent failure. But when I started writing *Julia,* I knew half-way through that book that if I could stick it out, everything would be fine. So we're talking about a period of somewhere like two or three years, in which my confidence was shattered and I was working blind.

WoF&H: I'm still impressed that the first substantial piece of fiction you attempted was a novel and you sold it. I always tell beginners that if it takes you thirty tries to get it right, that might take a couple years, but thirty *novels* is another matter entirely. Call this the coward's approach. You don't write novels until you're already selling stories, so that at least you know you're writing on something that approximates a professional level.

Straub: I told myself that I would actually give it three tries. If I wrote three whole novels and none of them were accepted, then I would go off and be a fireman or a brain surgeon.

WoF&H: Would you really have given up?

Straub: I don't know. I never had to learn.

WoF&H: Certainly *Ghost Story* was the one that made you a best-seller. It must have changed your life.

Straub: Incredibly. It changed my life enormously, in ways that were almost all positive, just enormously positive. I had to leave England, because of taxation, which was a bit of a blow. I had intended to come back to America anyhow, but not that soon. We had to do it fast. Apart from that, in the millions of readjustments that followed, it meant that publishers knew my name. The publishers' secretaries knew my name. The editors knew my name. It was easy. Suddenly people were asking me for work. That hasn't stopped. I still get all these requests for stories for anthologies. I could live comfortably. I could live at the level of comfort where you no longer have to ask the price of just about anything, which is a great spot.

WoF&H: Do you find your life market-driven, in the sense that there are thousands of people out there depending on you to make millions of dollars for them, and they won't let you stop?

Straub: To some extent that's true, but I'm not Stephen King. I try to resist that course, in that I am far more interested in seeing where I will go following my personal voices. I think I would resist if I were given instructions as to what the topic should be.

WoF&H: In essence you've become a brand name.

Straub: Dean Koontz is a brand name. I sort of was Dean Koontz once. If I had kept on writing books like *Ghost Story,* now I would be selling seven hundred thousand hardbacks. But I didn't do that and I didn't

move that way. I moved another way. Everything is still being taken care of very nicely. I think it would be nice to be a brand name, but I don't think that's quite what I am.

WoF&H: You are in the sense that, say, *Mystery* was not published as a mystery novel, but as a Peter Straub book.

Straub: That was my goal from the start. I know Steve King felt that way too, because we used to talk about this back in the days of our boyhood. He didn't want and I didn't want to be published as a genre writer. That seemed like instant death. It was like confinement or constriction. I'm not sure how or why, but it was easy for us to be published as mainstream novelists with a left-hand tilt. Speaking personally, I think that made it a lot easier for me to find readers.

WoF&H: Getting back to the idea of your writing the equivalent of *Chitty-Chitty-Bang-Bang,* don't you become your own genre, in the sense that everyone has their idea of what a Peter Straub book is?

Straub: That's the point. Right from the start, I thought that I wanted to be my own genre, a genre known and identified by my name. And by now I think I have done enough work so I just about have achieved that. People all have a general notion of what it is, and some will be curious enough to lay out $27.50 or whatever it is that hardbacks cost these days to see what the new product is like.

WoF&H: What are your writing methods like? I ask because I collect them. I've never found two writers who are alike. Some people write all sorts of notes on index cards and pin them to the walls, while others just plunge in.

Straub: I'm sort of a plunger. I spend about six months literally walking around making notes, and then when I have lots of notes and a firm notion of the characters in the story, then I write a long thing which I call notes but is in effect an outline, in which I describe what happens step by step. I begin by following this outline, a process which is like walking along a nice safe path through the forest. I have every confidence that I know what I'm doing and where I am going. Then the trees crowd in. The path disappears. It is night. The outline was lost long ago. The safe road that I thought I was following doesn't exist anymore, and I have to find my way through the forest unaided. When I started doing that, it was scary, but when I found it worked every time, then I felt I ought to do it that way, and it felt good.

WoF&H: Is your approach any different when the story contains fantasy — things that are impossible?

Straub: I don't think so. It is unusual now for me to describe something that I know is impossible. When I do that, there is a sort of pleasant imaginative tingle. I am conscious of having fun. There's a very sweet little buzz that I get from that. But that's more about the interior of my head than what goes on in the writing.

WoF&H: What kind of fan-mail do you get? Do you get strange mail?

Straub: No. The strangest mail is the stuff from prisons, usually. Sometimes that's kind of harmless and pathetic. Other times it's just guys who want help. They want money to fund their appeals. The rest of the mail is just kindly and appreciative. It's always very, very nice to receive. I answer all of it, unless somebody wants something that is unreasonable. If they want me to basically write their thesis about me, I write back and explain that they're on their own.

WoF&H: Do you get these ones where somebody has a great idea, and if you'll write it they'll split the profits fifty-fifty?

Straub: Yeah. I get those, about four a year, and I always write back and say I have too much to do to take on this project.

WoF&H: So you haven't gotten to the point that you get crushed by your own celebrityhood.

Straub: No. Mine is very tolerable.

WoF&H: I've heard that Stephen King's mail is screened to make sure there aren't any screenplays, novels, or stories in it, lest somebody say, "My novel has a ghost in it. Your novel has a ghost in it. You stole my idea. I'm suing for ten million dollars in damages."

Straub: He was sued two or three times on precisely that basis. I think the suits not only didn't go to court; I think they evaporated because the people who were bringing them were flakes. If I were in his situation, I'd have to be wary too.

WoF&H: Isn't it just the case that when you become that famous, you attract the attention of extortionists whose real idea is to sue for five million dollars and settle out of court for fifty thousand? It's a living.

Straub: I suppose. You're a target. But I haven't noticed this happening with me, so I guess I'm not famous enough.

WoF&H: What are you working on now?

Straub: I'm just in the very early stages of a book that I think could be called a doppelgänger novel. When I was beginning the process I've described and making notes, the point at which I got excited was when I realized that it was a classic doppelgänger situation. That instantly for me put a kind of magic in the heart of the story and it suggested all sorts of possibilities that I hadn't seen before. I don't want to say too much more about it.

WoF&H: It's a supernatural story?

Straub: I suppose it is. There is a hugely irrational element at work. It may be made up. It may be a lie. It may be an invention by the version of me who is in the book. The manuscript is passed from hand to hand until it comes to me, and I'm the person who presents it to the public. So I may have loused up the story and added it. But if you take it as literal truth, yes, there's a strong supernatural element.

WoF&H: So we're not quite done with the fantastic yet.

Straub: Obviously not, because I got so happy when I thought of it. All I can say is thank God it isn't vampires or werewolves.

WoF&H: There's a wonderful quote from David Schow who said that vampires have become the *Star Trek* of horror.

Straub: Exactly.

WoF&H: Thank you Peter.   Ω

THE CHAIR
by R. Chetwynd-Hayes

illustrated by Allen Koszowski

The old man in the second-hand furniture shop had a pointed grey beard, a mass of white hair and spoke with a faint foreign accent. "The chair came from a house with an unfortunate history."

This tantalizing statement was further enhanced when the old fellow refused to elaborate further; but I dismissed, as nothing more than a rather unique sales gimmick, for who can resist buying an item of furniture with a mysterious past?

"The gentleman will note," he said patting the winged-back, "the brocade, which is so marvellously well-preserved; the claw feet; the graceful curve of the arms. It is indeed a bargain at eighty pounds."

"Early eighteenth-century," I murmured, determined to appear well-versed in antiquarian lore. "Fifty pounds."

He shrugged thin, bowed shoulders. "The gentleman drives a hard bargain and as a sign of deep respect I will reduce the price to seventy pounds."

We finally settled for sixty-five.

The chair looked well against the wall that faced the foot of my four-poster bed. I had only to raise my head from the velvet-covered pillow and there it was — a relic from some long-dead yesterday. The brocade — as the old man had said — was in an excellent state of preservation: its pattern of tiny pink roses only slightly faded, the silver background still gleaming with a satisfying sheen.

One more item.

My bedroom was now a haven carved out of the rock of time. Tudor bed, early Georgian wardrobe and dressing-table, Queen Anne cabinet, Jacobean commode — and now the chair. I was not certain of its age. Maybe Queen Anne; most likely the first George. Certainly not later. Now I could sleep and dream of ladies in long, flowing dresses and of gentlemen in black velvet doublets and crimson hose. The realm of what-might-have-been was so much more interesting than a world of roaring machines, rustling income-tax forms and flickering television screens. Yesterday the great walked with earth-shaking steps; today the small scamper across an asphalt desert and leave a trail of corruption in their wake.

I lay in my vast four-poster bed, monarch of a kingdom that was born when the Tudors strutted the corridors of Whitehall. In my hands was a facsimile of a newspaper dated August 28, 1828. I experienced a thrill of delicious ecstasy while I read of the execution

of William Corder — he of Red Barn fame. A mere hundred fifty years ago, but a sufficiently long journey back along the eternal road to create a buffer of years between me and the age of mechanical confusion.

I turned a page. The paper acquired a crease — I shook it — lowered it — then raised it again. But the threefold action had been fatal to my peace of mind. For, as I had momentarily looked over the lowered newspaper, I had seen a woman seated in the chair. The tiny print became a jumbled mass of black lines, the paper trembled as I tried to dismiss that brief vision of a long white face and large dark eyes that had glittered — or maybe glared — from beneath slim, black brows.

I did not think that perhaps my faculties had become deranged, or toy with words — such as optical illusion, imagination, and other like clichés. One does not practise self-deception under these circumstances, for the human eye and brain are loyal servants and rarely attempt to deceive their master.

No — from behind my frail barricade of paper I knew there was a strange woman seated in the chair and she had not entered through the doorway, or crawled from under the bed, or slid silently from the wardrobe — but had suddenly come into being. I lowered the newspaper inch by inch and gradually unveiled the face of truth.

She was so still. A study in black and white. Black hair, brows and dress; white face, hands, and shoes. The long face might have been thought beautiful by those who like smooth unlined skin and thin red — so red — lips. I noticed that the hands — which lay one on each knee — were extraordinarily long; and on the left middle finger was a large stone, possibly a ruby, encased in a gold filigree setting.

We stared at each other; and her dark eyes did not blink, only glittered with a faintly mischievous gleam — or so it seemed to me, who sat upright, wrapped in the cold mantle of fear — and maybe there was a pale ghost of a smile twisting the thin red lips.

Then she raised her right hand and beckoned.

It was not an imperious gesture. Rather a coy invitation; a seductive bending of four fingers; a subtle command that it would be well to obey. But prolonged fear curdles and becomes anger. Suddenly I was yelling, mouthing obscenities, aware of a burning hatred for the seated figure, which did nothing more than beckon. My outstretched hand gripped a gilt bedside clock and I hurled it straight at the white face.

She vanished just before the clock crashed against the chair back.

I am a person who can come to terms with any situation.

I remember being interviewed by an Officers' Selection Board during the war, when a stupid old fool of a colonel asked me: "What would you do if you met a battleship walking across a field?" I gave the only possible, positive answer: "Find out why."

It was not of course the answer they wanted. I was supposed to smile and say: "Take more water with it," or some such nonsense. But I still maintain that such a phenomenon would have aroused the curiosity of a reasonably intelligent man, once he had mastered his quite natural alarm. I believe there are only two basic laws in the universe — Cause and Effect. Let us take the case of the walking battleship. One must assume the vessel had acquired legs. Were they formed from metal or flesh and blood? The gentlemen on the selection board, for some reason best known to themselves, declined to answer this simple question, and in fact, refused to pursue the matter any further.

But if I had been supplied with this basic information, there is no doubt in my mind that I would have solved the mystery and so demonstrated my gift for dealing with any untoward contingency.

Thus, on the morning after my disconcerting experience, I first admonished myself for having given way to alarm and despondency, then set out to discover why a ghost should haunt a second-hand item of furniture.

I examined the chair most thoroughly. The upholstery was not stained in any way; there was no sign of damage, repair, recent French polishing on legs or visible woodwork — nothing in fact that might supply even an irrational explanation.

The seat, back and arms were well padded — with horsehair I imagined, and which appeared to have lost none of its resilience. A good solid chair with plenty of room to stretch out, curl up, sleep in, read in, do whatever-you-like-in; but certainly not intended to haunt in.

The physical examination of the chair — if I may be permitted the expression — was now complete, and for all the good it had done me, I might as well have gone for a long walk. I then passed on to a line of reasonable conjecture: Sometime during the past two hundred years, a woman with a beautiful, long, white face, had sat in the chair and saturated the upholstery with her personality. On occasion, someone tuned in on the right wave-length had recreated her image. Last night that person had been me; and, when I threw the clock, the line of contact had been broken. It was as simple as that.

I felt quite pleased with my reasoning powers and did a little dance round the room. Within the space of ten minutes I had solved a mystery that would have had a normal person gibbering in the fireplace, or smashing a valuable chair to pieces with an axe. "Fear is the child of stupidity," I shouted. "Reason is the voice of sanity," and rejoiced in a feeling of superiority over the brainless ants that crawl over the surface of this planet.

Then I stopped and stared at the chair with dilated eyes. Wait a minute! The woman had beckoned to me! But . . . but had she? Could she not have been beckoning to someone long dead? A mere re-enactment of a scene that had taken place in the dim past.

I breathed a deep sigh of relief and again took pleasure in my keen deductive powers. Sherlock Holmes would have undoubtedly booted that fool Watson down the stairs had I been around at the time. I could hardly wait for nightfall and the possible reappearance of the apparition, which I could now watch with detached interest, completely free from brain-sapping, reason-freezing fear.

I went downstairs and cooked a meal of six fried eggs, three sausages and boiled mushrooms. Nothing like brainwork to give a man an appetite.

Not a sight or a sign of her did I see for three weeks.

It has been my unhappy experience that you can never rely on women, be they dead or alive, time-images or just whispers in a dark room. When you expect them, they never turn up; when you least want them — there they are, standing on the doorstep, armed with a nightbag and a seductive smile.

I sat up in bed and stared at that chair for night after night, and it remained as empty as a Russian church on May Day. I gave her every encouragement: "Come on, you silly cow. Don't be shy. Show yourself."

Finally, although I did not actually give up, I began to lose interest. Rather like a lover whose advances are not so much repelled as ignored. If a fire is not fed, it eventually dies down and becomes a mass of smouldering embers.

At the end of the third week I was forced to realize my mistaken assumption. We all think that ghosts can materialize only during the hours of darkness and that daytime is a kind of non-spook period, when the only spirits that are worthy of concern are kept in bottles.

At three o'clock in the afternoon, with the sunlight streaming through my nylon curtains, I walked into my bedroom — and there she was — seated in the chair and staring at me with those never-to-be-forgotten eyes. I stopped and was quite unable to subdue a sudden wave of fear. Then I remembered she was only a time-image; no more real than an old movie projected on a screen, long after the actors were dead.

I said: "So there you are!" and sat down on the bed.

I decided she was — had been — a most beautiful woman. The long white face would defy the cruel fingers of time until late middle-age, and then there would be a graceful wilting; a gradual transformation. I do not know how long we sat and looked at each other — only, of course, she was not looking at me — but presently her arm came up and the hand beckoned, inviting me — or someone — to come forward and possibly be suitably rewarded for walking a few, faltering steps.

I laughed. It was really remarkable to feel so fearless; to view this apparition as merely an object for investigation. I said: "I wonder, little lady, who he was? I take it you are beckoning to a man. Shameless hussy. Did he obey? He'd have been a fool not to, despite those glittering eyes."

The beckoning went on. Arm bending, fingers almost clenching, then opening — the continuous gesture was becoming a little boring. I decided to experiment. I got up and walked towards the fireplace, then looked back over one shoulder. Her head had turned and the eyes were still watching me — and the left hand — the non-beckoning one — was out-stretched, as though she were appealing to me not to go away, and fear came riding in on a wave of anger. I shouted: "Go away, damn you. I won't be badgered by a patch of coloured air. Go...o....o....o...o..."

She vanished. Left an empty chair and a man who cried out, "I didn't mean it. Come back. Please come back."

The summer died and autumn turned leaves to russet-brown, then sent a chill north wind to chase them along country lanes and urban pavements. And during all that time the chair remained empty.

Gradually I came to accept the awful truth. I had fallen in love with a shadow. A beckoning figure that had as much reality as the Mona Lisa, Venus de Milo, or — and I kept harping back to this theme — a beautiful heroine in an old film.

Do not think for one moment that I surrendered to this humiliating passion without putting up a soul-shaking fight. While I lay in bed, day after day, week after week, eating little, unwashed, unshaven, watching an empty chair, I cursed myself and the long-dead woman, and tried to climb back on to the throne of reason.

One night I moved into a spare room, determined not to look upon that cursed chair for at least three weeks, confident that it needed only will power to set me free again. But in less than ten minutes I was tormented by the thought that she might have returned, was sitting in a darkened room, beckoning, beckoning . . . and I would not be there. I unlocked the door, ran into the room that had been my haven in a world gone mad and sank down before the empty chair. My voice went screaming back along the misty avenue of time:

"Come back. Drive me mad — but come back."

At the end of the third month, tired of appealing to a recalcitrant shade who refused to put in an appearance, I decided on a course of action that was long overdue. I went back to the second-hand furniture shop.

The old man came out of the shadows and peered at me over a pair of rimless spectacles.

"How can I serve the gentleman?"

The mere sight of his silly goatlike face, his frail, bent body, made the smouldering rage that had been fed by months of humiliation blaze up into a searing flame. I spat the question at him: "The chair. Where did you get it?"

He shrugged, a helpless gesture that brought him to the threshold of death. "I have sold so many chairs, Sir. I cannot remember where they all come from."

I thrust my face forward until it was a bare six inches from his own. I saw the weak, watery eyes, the flabby, wrinkled skin and I hated him with a hatred that passed all understanding.

"You said it came from a house with an unfortunate history."

He sighed, then turned away and began to walk between an agglomeration of rubbish that littered the floor, and I had the ridiculous idea that if I took my eyes from him for so much as a single second, he would turn into a lamp standard or just disappear. His plaintive voice manufactured words:

"All houses have an unfortunate history, as the gentleman must be aware. Tragedy walks in every room."

I took three long paces forward and grabbed his shoulder, then swung him round. He did not appear to be frightened or even surprised at my aggressive action.

"Don't play with words. You know the chair I mean. Where did it come from?"

He eased his shoulder from my grip and stared wistfully out of the window. I had to strain my ears to catch the whispered words.

"It was pulled down as the gentleman will find out if he but walks to Bedford Park. Now a thousand little brick boxes cover its graveyard."

I said softly, appealingly, "The chair was in this shop. You must have seen her."

His eyes were faintly mocking when he looked up.

"I am a very old man. She had no power over me. I would suggest the gentleman go to the Twilight Home. There is an old lady there. A Miss Pirbright. She may remember."

The Twilight Home For Distressed Ladies — I was not aware that such places still existed — was an old house that loomed up from behind a curtain of high walls. I pressed the brass bell button and, trembling with excitement, although I had not the faintest idea what questions I was to ask or the kind of reception I would receive, waited for the grim, green door to open.

I was soon confronted by a tall coloured girl attired in a spotless white overall, whose face resembled a beautiful brown-tinted mask. She smiled gently and asked, "You wish to see someone, sir?"

I cleared my throat. "Yes, a Miss Pirbright."

Her smile deepened. "Won't you come in?"

I followed her along a path that was bordered on either side by flowering shrubs, then up a flight of steps and into the house. When we entered a spacious hall, she stopped and looked at me.

"Are you a relative, sir?"

"No — an old friend."

She nodded slowly. "I see. It is a very long time since Miss Pirbright received a visitor and she's very old. Over ninety, I believe. And — well — she's rather muddled. So do not be surprised if she does not recognize you."

I would have been much more surprised if she had, so did not comment, but followed the nurse down a long passage and out into an enclosed verandah. Here a number of ancient ladies sat in deep armchairs, some staring blankly out of the windows, others reading or knitting, while a few — a pitiful few — talked with thin, querulous voices.

Miss Pirbright was tucked away in a far corner.

Extremely old age can be beautiful. It can also be pathetic, frightening or repulsive. Miss Pirbright was all three: a bundle of skin and bones wrapped in a tartan shawl, a wrinkled monkey-face surmounted by a mist of sparse white hair. The nurse gently shook one boney shoulder and all but shouted: "Miss Pirbright . . . Miss Pirbright. You have a visitor."

The head came up and a harsh voice pronounced a single word. "What?"

"A visitor for you. Isn't that nice?"

The faded blue eyes examined me with faint interest, then the voice found another word. "Visitor?"

The nurse smiled at me ruefully. "It's not one of her best days, I'm afraid. Don't tire her. I'll be back in a little while."

I sat down on a nearby chair and tried to control my rising anger, for how could I possibly get information from this animated corpse, without shaking it until the toothless gums rattled? But I tried.

"Miss Pirbright," I said imitating the nurse's shout, "Did you once live in an old house in Bedford Park?"

I watched the tiny, clawlike hands pluck at the shawl fringe, and when it seemed as if there was to be no answer, repeated those last two words several times. "Bedford Park . . . Bedford Park . . ."

Her head nodded violently and the fingers became as tiny snakes writhing in a nest of wool.

"Aye, the house . . . house . . . sunlight and wallpaper and Miss Emily in the window."

"Miss Emily!" The name was a verbal gem and I grabbed it, rolled it across my brain, toyed with it, all but set it to music. "Tell me about Miss Emily."

The old head came up and the eyes were filled with gentle reproach.

"Everybody knows Miss Emily. Beautiful as a spring morning, she is. Aye. Going to marry Mr. Ascot, she is . . ." Again the violent nodding, the writhing fingers. "Was . . . was . . . only, he never . . . never . . ."

"Never what?" I prompted. "What was it that Mr. Ascot did not do?"

Now there was a shocked expression on the wrinkled face, as though I had spoken an unmentionable word, or unearthed a secret that had been locked away in that dying brain for seventy years.

"He never came . . . not when he should. Miss Emily didn't cry. Just walked from church and went back to the house. Aye, sat in that chair and waited."

I shuddered. A man who has spent a lifetime looking for gold and has suddenly stumbled into an untapped mine, could not have experienced the joy that momentarily robbed me of speech. At length I was able to repeat the one word: "Chair!"

The old brain had found another memory trail. "Chair — aye. Old it were, the covering all tattered and after — he never came — not when he should — Miss Emily covered it herself. Clever she was with a needle. Never know it weren't done by an expert. 'That be fine work, Miss Emily,' I said. And she laughed and laughed . . . until she cry."

So that was why the brocade was not very faded. It was not more than fifty — sixty — seventy years old? It was difficult to know the exact period the old woman was talking about, but it would seem to be somewhere back in her distant youth. I took a deep breath and dared to ask the final question.

"Miss Pirbright . . . did . . . Miss Emily ever sit in the chair and — beckon?"

I was not prepared for the look of terror that suddenly transformed the old face into a grimacing mask. The tiny mouth gaped and I could see a shrivelled tongue twisted up like a scrap of rotting leather, and a horrible sound came from the contorting throat as though a scream were being strangled at birth. I patted her back, muttered soothing words, but she jerked away, took two shuddering breaths, then asked in a shrieking whisper:

"How d . . . o . . . o yer know she beckon. Beckon . . ."

Before I could improvise a suitable answer, she went on as though I were not there, lost in some private nightmare that my question had brought back to life.

"I came into the room . . . moonlight it was . . . and Miss Emily was seated in that chair. I knew she'd done something dreadful . . . face as white as death . . . and God forgive me . . . I didn't want to move . . . just stand there and gasp . . . not scream . . . not then . . . and she beckoned to me . . . hand up . . . fingers bending . . . bending . . . bending . . ."

The harsh voice died away and I growled: "Go on. What happened?"

"I . . . went to her . . . eyes glittering like lighted candles . . . smell of almonds . . . bottle on floor . . . she said . . . said . . . I die in his arms!"

That was all I could get from the old crone, and presently the nurse returned and was none too pleased to find her in a state of near-collapse. But I walked down the bush-lined path on cushioned feet. I had solved the mystery. Miss Emily had committed suicide after being left at the altar. The truth was so farcical, so story-bookish, my ridiculous passion had died like a hothouse plant exposed to a winter's frost.

I was free.

I entered the house and ran upstairs to my bedroom.

Miss Emily — I had her name off pat now — was seated in the chair; pale, beautiful face turned towards me, eyes glittering, arm raised, beckoning — begging a young Miss Pirbright to come forward and hear her final nonsensical words. I stood by the door and laughed. Laughed until the tears ran down my face, stamped, pounded clenched fist against trembling legs, then screamed my contemptuous rage.

"If you had been there yesterday, my fine lady, I would have come to you. But not now. To die for love! You should have hated him. Died for hate. That would have been worth while. Hate . . . hate . . ."

I walked slowly towards her and the beckoning arm was more insistent now; sawing the air, jerking, the fingers opening and closing as though they were trying to grab a handful of departing life. I looked down into the pale face, once more confident, fearless, knowing exactly what must be done. I spoke gently as befits an intelligent man, dealing with an unusual situation. "Time-image you may be. But I can't have you sitting there beckoning away for the rest of my life. The one sure way of bursting a bubble is to prick it." And without wasting further time or words, I turned about and — sat on her.

It should have worked. It really should. A time-image can have no substance and once a sane, intelligent, fearless man has planted his posterior into its lap, there should be absolutely nothing. But, oh, most merciful God, in whose existence I have never believed, why were there solid legs beneath mine, and why did two arms crawl round my chest . . . and two cold hands seek my throat . . . and hot breath sear my neck? I kicked and screamed . . . tore at the confining arms and gradually — so very slowly — she melted. Became cold rubber, slimy flannel, tainted mist — then nothing. A bad dream dispersed by the first light of a summer morning.

I got up. Grabbed that damned, thrice accursed chair and smashed it against the nearest wall. I tore the brocade, pulled out the stuffing, broke the wooden frame . . . and then . . . a skull rolled across the floor . . . a skeleton hand caressed my knee . . .

No . . . no . . . there's no need for that. No need for strait-jackets, syringes or any of the other instruments of torture you've got stacked away. I'm quite calm now. But you do realize how she did it, don't you? Having killed him, she must have flattened him . . . or maybe dried him out. Then she stripped the chair down to its frame . . . and folded the body up. Ha . . . ha . . . ha . . . damn clever when you think of it.

Fold legs under thighs, shove him down into the chair, torso and head fit very nicely into the back, arms into arms — get it? Then she replaced all the stuffing, re-covered the chair with a nice piece of new brocade . . . then . . . then died in his arms.

But having done all that, why does she still sit there, on that plain wooden chair and keep staring at me . . . beckoning . . . *beckoning* . . . ?   Ω

THE CHAIR

SNOW WHITE TURNS 39

How to break a talking mirror: hammer
and earplugs. Seven years of bad luck? Peanuts
stacked against that Bette Davis cackle
every morning when I hit the sink
without my make-up. On that black dawn
I raise my cheekbones to the bathroom light
and a hundred watts are not enough to flush
these tear-track shadows, I smash the glass.

    No more clipping recipes for sauteed
    hearts of cheerleader, I can tell you that,
    or sending milkmaids out to feed the wolves.
    No more wolves to feed, or woodsmen either,
    in our tidy kingdom. My husband found me
    under glass. How I miss the woodsman.

— Anne Sheldon

STYX AND STONES

On the day that I died I performed suicide
With some cyanide pills and an axe.
As I chopped off my head, I just chuckled and said
"Now that *that's* come off, I can relax!"
But that Lucifer bloke, in a billow of smoke,
Took my soul down to Hell, locked in chains.
And, declining to burn it, he
Damned (through Eternity)
All my immortal remains . . .

    Now I shovel the coal down in Satan's black hole.
    (Hell has furnaces; I am the stoker.)
    And (bemoaning my fate) I must sweep out the grate,
    Then I polish the tongs and the poker.
    But for ten seconds (once every twelve million years)
    "Down tools, lads!" an Imp shouts. I burst into cheers,
    Rush upstairs to Heaven, take *one* desperate glimpse . . .
    Then back down to Hell, where I'm seized by the Imps.
    Twelve million more years 'til the next time! Ah, well . . .
    Except for the tea-breaks, this job is pure Hell!

—F. Gwynplaine MacIntyre

MY VAMPIRE CAKE
by Ian Watson

Illustrated by Denis Tiani

Aha, do you suppose that I intend to tell you a recipe?

What could the special ingredient of *Vampire Cake* possibly be? The blood of fresh hot healthy young virgins, of either sex, mixed with cherries or strawberries? Scarcely!

Would the cake be in the shape of an aluring alabastine neck of ivory icing decorated with two toothsome dimples of cochineal, from which thin ribbons of scarlet icing meander downward on to a snow-white shoulder of a base?

Oh no, not at all. The cake I made and decorated so serenely and classically — my masterpiece of the art of sugar, if I may say so — aluded to vampirism neither in its appearance nor in its contents.

I'm truly sorry that I cannot show you this cake. My client forbade any photographs. He was superstitious about visual images, in mirrors or lenses. And he did devour that cake entirely — with the consuming hunger of someone who had not tasted regular food for the past two hundred years. (Not that my cake was in any way routine!) He gorged himself on it with a spiritual as much as a physical appetite.

My cake was a *vampire cake* because it was made especially for a vampire's two-hundredth anniversary. I was about to say that this was Philippe Carnavalet's birthday cake. But that's misleading. The anniversary in question was that of his transformation from mortal man to undead person. So I might refer to the occasion as being his *deathday,* and the cake as his deathday cake.

We scarcely ever make death cakes, do we? Birthday cakes, wedding cakes, Christmas cakes, retirement cakes, oh yes. Yet seldom a celebration cake for the wake! At a funeral, bright wreaths and sprays of blooms sound the uplifting note. The sensuality and brio of a splendidly decorated cake would seem unsuitable. Ought the icing to be mournfully black — or angelicly white? If the dear departed succumbed to a heart attack on his favourite golf links, should the icing be correspondingly green (coloured, of course, with spinach juice)? Should there be a model of the golfer swinging his last club? If she was a businesswoman, should she be modelled sitting at a marzipan desk, with her in-tray empty at last?

Do I digress?

Not without a purpose! Philippe's death-day was intimately associated with sweet nourishment — indeed, the sweetest of all.

By his own account Philippe Carnavalet was born in 1770 some seventy miles east of Paris at the little town of Carnaval in the Plain of Champagne. Champagne, and carnival! That may sound like a jolly area, but as Philippe grew into adolescence taxes were steadily increasing to fund the national deficit. Tariffs were being piled upon taxes. The peasantry were suffering direly. Nor were the petit bourgeoisie any too happy. Response to protests all too often took the form of bayonets and gunfire. Revolution and Terror and the mass guillotining of the nobility were just around the corner.

What a mass of nobility and sub-nobility there were in France, all with their various privileges! Philippe's father had prospered by commercial speculation well enough to buy the modest but seigneural Château de Carnaval and change his name accordingly, becoming pseudo-nobility.

Then the shit, as it were, hit the fan. The mob stormed the Bastille. The rioters hoped to loot powder for the up-to-date guns they had seized elsewhere. In the process they freed all seven inmates of that gaol. What a heroic day. (I am viewing the event with Philippe's jaundiced eye.) Four of these prisoners were forgers. Two were lunatics, one of whom was an Englishman who believed he was Julius Caesar reborn. The seventh was a debauched aristo whose family had locked him up to restrain his rampant lechery. A few days earlier, and the mob could have liberated the Marquis de Sade — but Sade had just recently been transferred to an asylum. The governor of the Bastille surrendered so as to avoid massacring more of the crowd. He was repaid by being hacked to pieces.

Soon the Assembly abolished feudal rights, ruining twenty-thousand nobles. Many decamped to Switzerland. Although reduced in circumstances, others remained. Presently châteaux were being looted and burned (though not at Carnaval, where Philippe's father hung on). The King tried to escape. Overcome by a craving to eat pig's trotters, His Majesty broke his journey. He was arrested. As a result of this, the movements of would-be émigrés were strictly regulated — and the Terror began. Committees of Public Safety of the United Indivisible Republic conducted purges. Philippe's father couldn't get away. But by bribery he finessed a safe-conduct for his son.

Philippe de Carnaval guillotined the pretentious pronoun from his name, passing himself off as Citizen Carnavalet. It sounded as if his father and grandfather before him may have served meat at table for some noble family. In fact I think *carne* is slang for bad meat. Revolutionary guards at the frontier could only guffaw at this irony.

Here we introduce yet another gastronomic note — and a culinary delight was to be Philippe's downfall.

Philippe happened to be related to that genius of the dining table, Grimod, who produced regular volumes of an *Almanach des Gourmandes* during the first decade-and-a-bit of the following century. The transformed Philippe was to observe such foody enthusiasms with a bitter disdain since his own diet was by then restricted to human or animal blood. A couple of centuries later this connection (by blood, in the banal sense!) still preyed on Philippe's mind.

Was I aware, he enquired of me, "that Grimod was born deformed? His right hand was a pincer attached to his arm by a membrane just like a duck's foot. His left hand was a claw worthy of a bird of prey. He had false hands made for himself, constructed of springs and iron. Over these he would wear gloves of white pigskin."

"With these, he cooked?" I was rash enough to ask.

"Bah! How could he? This was the eighteenth century, not today. He never donned an apron in his life. His taste buds and his stomach were his tools. He was solely a connoisseur. A gourmet. Or a glutton."

Did Grimod eat to compensate for a ruined sex life? Because he was unable to bestow seductive caresses by means of springs and iron? Because ladies would be inhibited? Because he could not pleasure himself satisfactorily?

Not at all! Grimod acquired a fine mistress by promising to delight her with foreplay in the style of Tiberius in his grotto in Capri, where trained children swam underwater to nibble the Emperor for arousal. The lips, ah the lips! The gourmet lips. In those days classical references were appreciated.

We don't want to hear this, do we?

However, there's a point.

It's a point concerned with concupiscence — and with gourmet chocolate.

Presently the impoverished though elegant Philippe was employed as French tutor to a Bavarian count's children. In that lonely *Schloss* on the edge of the Alps, Graf von Helmberg jealously guarded the virtue of his family's name. This caused frustration to his bored eldest daughter, Johanna, a considerable beauty.

Philippe fell in love, or in lust, with Johanna. Now, in France Philippe had acquired a recipe for truly ravishing drinking chocolate, a silky melting sweet delight of a drink. He proceeded to obtain the ingredients. He courted Johanna surreptitiously with cups of chocolate. This appealed to her sweet tooth. She developed a craving.

We all know that monks used to be forbidden chocolate in case it aroused libido. We all know that Montezuma always swigged an extra cup of chocolate spiced with chilli before visiting a concubine. For the sake of decorum, Aztec women were forbidden the piquant beverage.

Johanna's craving led to copulation. Alas, Philippe was caught. Enraged, the Graf threw Philippe into the dungeon of the *Schloss,* pending appropriate punishment. Sparing no expense, von Helmberg obtained a large amount of chocolate from Vienna.

On his deathday, Philippe's wrists and ankles were tied. He was laid on his back in a coffin.

"If you can drink enough of the damned stuff, you'll live!" von Helmberg bellowed at him. Into the coffin, the cooks began to pour pot after pot of thick hot chocolate, made to Philippe's own recipe which had been extorted from him on threat of pain. He never confided the recipe to me. Yet I am sure, from his bitterness towards Grimod, that it originally came from that relative of his.

Soon enough the chocolate oozed up over Philippe's face. He craned his neck, to continue breathing. This was a mistake, since the Graf had ordered ample ingredients. From now on, the chocolate was decanted *much* more slowly.

Perforce, Philippe began to lap.

The Graf had no intention of allowing Philippe any real chance. The victim of this bizarre vengeance may have lapped for an hour or more until he was bloated. Remorselessly, sweet liquid engulfed the hapless prisoner. He was submerged. He choked, he drowned.

Yes, *death by chocolate!* We all know the name of the cake. Philippe was the filling.

In slowly congealing chocolate he was buried in the woods away from the *Schloss,* and his coffin covered over with a shallow depth of loam.

I do not know whether being embalmed within and without by chocolate made to his recipe was responsible for his metamorphosis into an undead person dependent on a diet of blood for nourishment — or whether another vampire on the prowl noted the disturbance of the soil and dug him up. Maybe this conjectural vampire simply sniffed him out from a distance as a pig sniffs a buried truffle! To a vampire's enhanced senses the sweet odour must have been conspicuous, and if not mouthwatering, at least piquing of his curiosity. Or of her curiosity. The whole episode left Philippe with a loathing for the smell of chocolate equal to the vampire's supposed dread of garlic.

Philippe assured me that other vampires walk the Earth, and what's more, that their transformation was often due to circumstances more peculiar than legends would have us believe. He is not the only one. But vampires are few and far between, and unsociable. The likelihood of encountering one is low.

So how did I meet Philippe, you are wondering!

Due to my constant involvement with icing, maybe my flesh smells sweeter than most. It was also *sweetness* which saved my life.

I had just returned from our Cake Decorators Convention of last year, held in that splendid Hotel de France in St Helier on the island of Jersey. For those of you who missed our stay in that excellent establishment, be it known that the basement houses a small chocolate factory. A shop in the lobby vends the products. Most noteworthy are the champagne truffles — but another popular souvenir last year proved to be the five kilogram chocolate bars, hefty enough to brain a mugger with.

The blessèd isle of Jersey boasts many attractions along its lanes so narrow and winding that the Lamborghinis only ever drive in second gear. To my mind the most remarkable is the neolithic burial mound at Grouville known as La Hougue Bie. *La Oooo-g Beee.*

Within the span of a couple of minutes you can step from Prehistory by way of the Middle Ages to the Nazi period when the island was occupied. Along a low stone tunnel you stoop your way to reach the Great Chamber roofed with twenty-five ton slabs. Here you are at one with the men of five thousand years ago. Atop the mound is a chapel where a fraudulent cleric set up as a fortune teller during the gullible Middle Ages. At the side of the mound is the entrance to an underground German bunker of the Second World War. What a juxtaposition of epochs side by side! What an epitome of the layers of history!

I had holidayed on Jersey previously. Consequently, for last year's convention, as you may well recall, I made a cake in the shape of La Hougue Bie, crowned by its chapel, and cut away to reveal not only the monumental passage grave but also the Nazi bunker.

In marzipan and in pastillage I made models of a few German soldiers and of some Neolithic men, and of the medieval cleric up above, and of a Viking scaling the side of the mound — for Vikings were there as well.

The exploration of fantasy is one of the delights of cake decoration, as our Caribbean colleagues demonstrate nowadays so flamboyantly and exuberantly. I fully expect to see a decorator from the West Indies occupy this place of honour next year or the year after.

The passage of a year has mellowed my chagrin at some of the adverse reactions to the décor of my cake. What I saw as virtuosity, apparently other people viewed as a jarring of styles. Perspectives must have shifted within the past twelve months. A re-evaluation has taken place! Here I stand today, before you.

It was on my return from Jersey, as I say, that I met Philippe de Carnaval. The house where I live, alone amidst my cakes-in-progress, is at the far end of a quiet close within a stone's throw — or rather, three or four stones' throws — of the local cathedral. When I pipe icing of an evening how the sound of bell practice thrills me, though my hands never vibrate.

It was late evening and dark when I arrived home from the airport. Floodlights illuminated the cathedral, a veritable Gothic wedding cake. I was so enchanted by the sight that I left my car (the luggage still locked safely inside) and strolled along the pathway linking my close with the cathedral green. I took my in-flight travel bag with me, since it contained documents. The bag also held one of those five-kilogram chocolate bars. I had packed half a dozen of these in a suitcase — then on last minute impulse just before catching the minibus to the airfield I bought yet another.

As I stood admiring the cathedral rising immaculately and luminously from the lawns, I became aware of soft footfalls along the pathway behind me.

I turned — to witness this slim figure of a sudden rushing towards me. He was dressed in a black velvet cloak. For a moment he seemed ecclesiastical.

Then I saw his twin fangs gleam, unsheathed.

Plunging my hand into my bag, I hauled out the heaviest object I had with me — that brick of chocolate.

My would-be assailant skidded to a halt. His nostrils flared. He quailed. The chocolate was wrapped in cellophane. With his acute night vision Philippe could recognize it for what it was. With his sensitive nose he could *smell* it. What to me was hardly a whiffer to him was a reek.

He recoiled just as if I'd brandished a silver cross smeared with garlic. He sank to his knees, and wept.

"What are you?" he demanded in a tormented tone.

And so our acquaintance commenced.

I shan't burden you with too many fussy details. Sufficient to say that Philippe was weary of his two hundred undead years. He dearly sought some form of purification which would release him appropriately and, if I may say so, *transcendentally*. He had lived by the tooth. What circumstance could liberate him from that Bastille of his undying body but something which evoked — in inverted form — the source of his present condition?

Is not the arctic whiteness of royal icing the very antithesis of the darkness of the chocolate which once embalmed him?

A well-iced cake takes many long hours to produce. Yet in essence it is ephemeral. It will be consumed — destroyed! It will vanish utterly in a spiritual affirmation. After two hundred long years, Philippe must likewise attain a climactic nullity.

My cake would be serene. It would possess a classical severity, restrained and dignified, sublime in its nobility. Its architectural sublimity would translate this anguished vampire from undead body into spirit — in the way that a solid sublimates into vapour. By the act of eating such a cake — so paradoxical a novelty after two hundred years — he would gain release. Don't mistake my meaning! My cake would not act upon him as some sort of toxic poison, but as a catalyst of deliverance.

At this point, I must pause to pay homage to Mr Ronnie Rock, icer extraordinaire.

Mr Rock's name is startlingly felicitous. A prosaic-seeming fellow in an old apron, what an archangel he was with the piping tube! Well may you applaud this departed hero of the common man. Not an aristo by birth, but a *sans-culotte*, although he wore trousers beneath his apron. Ours is a proletarian art in origin.

Once upon a time, as you should know, sugar was only the food of kings and of sultans. Hence the name *royal icing* for the mixture of egg whites and icing sugar — by contrast with the gum tragacanth paste such as I used to model my Nazi soldiers. Yet sugar was to become the very food of the proletariat, the main source of calories. And amongst the working class, who worked harder than bakers? By heaving those overweight sacks of flours and by bending over troughs to heave and tear and pummel the dough, shoulders grew huge and rounded. Feet were permanently splayed. Men's chests became barrels, asthmatic due to all the flour dust.

Within this harsh milieu of slavish labour, cakes were decorated gloriously as a statement of dignity and individuality.

Ronnie Rock: his Grecian columns soared tier above tier separated by entablatures, to a drum cupola. So would mine.

Much has been said of the tears and terrors — the sheer panic — of the novice attempting to pipe royal icing as perfectly as Ronnie piped it. In spite of my wealth of experience I confess to a similar initial qualm, to be piping for a vampire client.

Yet I prevailed. Or else, how should I be here this afternoon, addressing our very own *National Assembly* of cake decorators?

Sugar, of course, is a preservative. How should sugar serve to extinguish a person who had already been preserved far beyond his natural term?

Oh by its gleaming whiteness, by its angelic purity! This quality, incorporated into Philippe's undead body, would transsubstantiate him. It would transfigure him into a body of light, which would all be astral halo! I repeat that I am not alluding to any toxic effect such as a drug addict might experience from a surfeit of purest heroine or cocaine white as snow!

Finally, the night came when my Ronnie Rock cake was ready. With the night, he also came to me, barefoot and silent. During the daytime Philippe was sleeping high up in the cathedral in some concealed coign to which nobody else would dream of climbing without benefit of scaffolding. A week earlier, a courting couple found a lad's body deep in the acre of rhododendrons in the public park. That lad had expired due to loss of blood, although no blood stained his resting place. His injuries were compatible with a car crash, from which he had managed to stagger away. Not far from the park was a burned-out Toyota. Plainly the car had been stolen for joy-riding. Philippe had supped, yet he had not *eaten* for two hundred years.

By candlelight I uncovered the cake to his wondering gaze.

After studying it he said to me, "You have done well, Decorator." And I nodded, for I knew this was true; and here was the rightful homage of an aristo to an artisan. Actually, these were the last words he uttered — since the unveiling of the cake led soon enough to devouring and demolition.

Not so much a consuming, as a *consummation!*

A prodigious act of consuming, in itself, given the grandeur of the cake. In his own native era Philippe must have witnessed similar acts of gluttony. Many are the tales of gourmands who died at table from surfeits of oysters, salmon, kidneys, pheasants, lamb, dish after dish demolished with gusto. Yet I had eschewed any rich fruity filling, using only the lightest soufflé of a sponge mixture as substructure for the soaring columns and walls and entablatures of icing which were the true body of the cake.

A consummation, yes...

As Philippe violated his enforced fast and gorged upon the whitest of icing, such sensual and astonished tremors shook him. How exquisitely he trembled, with a terrified ecstasy.

He shed his cloak, beneath which on this night of nights he wore no other clothing. His limbs were radiant in the candlelight, phosphorescent. After a while I could no longer bear to look upon him. Almost in a trance I closed my eyes.

How long was I in this state of stupor, while his rapture intensified? A quarter of an hour? A half an hour? When I looked again, the icing had all disappeared; and so had he. Only crumbs of sponge remained, and his discarded cloak.

Ladies and Gentlemen, I shall say no more except to thank you all warmly for honouring me today. The cake which you admire upon this table — the Colosseum of Rome as it was in antiquity, recreated in royal icing — is undoubtedly a lesser achievement than my vampire cake. Alas, my vampire cake vanished utterly from the world — just as Philippe de Carnaval himself vanished, consumed in brilliant light. Ω

PRIME

Magic?
Is there magic?
To conjure up another world,
Where fishes sail
On translucent wings
In blue summer sky,
And the unicorns graze,
And felines fly,
Cat-birds,
On the south wind,
And the woman has a face
Of shining flowers,
And all the hours,
Timeless, float like butterflies
In the mellow air of summer.

Imagination is the prime; first mover.
The dream
Floats radiant on the fields.
Ghost galleons, cargoed with opals,
Captained by dragons,
Crewed by
Small mice, great lions, golden stallions,
Sail seas of mist,
Dream seas.
Drake would have known them,
And his Golden Queen.

— Margo Skinner

. . . and suddenly he heard the exultant squealing of the rats. He began to scream insanely but could not drown them out. For a moment he thrashed about hysterically within his narrow prison, and then he was quiet. . . .

"The Graveyard Rats" by Henry Kuttner

by Allen Koszowski

THE SORCERER'S GIFT
by Darrell Schweitzer

Illustrated by by Stephen E. Fabian

Lady Hansherat was already a phantom dwelling among ancient tombs, already dead in her own mind and in the minds of all who had ever known her, certainly mad when she came to possess her "child."

Her story is familiar. The tragedy based on her life, *The Fatal Stroke*, first performed at the court of Angzerab IV, will live long in memory.

Everyone knows how Hansherat's young husband, Valpetor, was murdered by certain great lords of the Delta, by hawk-faced Andraxes, silent Belphage, and mocking Ruaine; how his body was burned in secret without any rites, so that his soul was trapped in *Leshe*, the twilight borderland between dreaming and true death, whence it returned each night into Lady Hansherat's bedroom to shriek its despair.

But the murderers underestimated her. Somehow, steady-handed as any sorceress, she captured Valpetor's soul in a glass bottle, shaped the bottle in fire, and the slain husband seemed returned to life, to confound his enemies. How they scattered!

Thus Hansherat and Valpetor were restored to the Great King's favor, rising higher than before in his service, the Lady waxing ever more proud, always quick to remind Valpetor that he had *her* to thank for his rescue, until one day she forgot herself and struck her husband across the face with her fan in the midst of some trifling quarrel. The glass broke and his soul escaped, howling into the rafters and dark corners of the palace, from which it could only be exorcised, never recovered.

And Lady Hansherat, her clothing rent with grief, all hope and fortune lost, appeared one last time before the Great King, declining to kneel, merely saying, "When my son is at my side, I shall come again to this place." She did not know why she said this. The words seemed to be whispered into her mind by another and she repeated them, without any volition of her own.

Of course she had no son. Andraxes, Belphage, and Ruaine, now returned from exile, ridiculed her, saying, "Let the headsman clean this trash away, if he will deign to soil his axe with it."

"Because she is mad, she cannot be harmed," said the Great King. "That is the law."

Hansherat smiled at her enemies, perhaps slyly, then departed, "like a star fading at dawn," and there the poet ends his tragedy, the prophecy unfulfilled, an inexplicable mystery.

But that is not the end. Listen. There is more:

Hansherat wandered south. Soon she became a familiar figure glimpsed at the Great River's edge in the evening, her fantastically colored tatters trailing behind her. She spoke with spirits. She kept the company of ghosts among the reeds. She appeared many times in the dreams of the dying.

And she often knelt in the shallow water, or on the muddy bank, calling on Shedelvendra, the forgiving goddess, but also addressing certain other powers, even the dread Shadow Titans whom the gods themselves fear. In the night, she thought she saw the starry sky ripple like sea foam and part, revealing a deeper blackness within which the faces of the Titans slowly appeared. Perhaps it was merely her madness. Perhaps, too, she actually saw them.

More often, in her own dreams, she beheld the broken glass face of her husband and heard his soul howling like the wind in a ruined tower; and again the hawk-visaged Andraxes, the silent, cruel Belphage, and the mocking Ruaine returned to torment her.

"Where is your son?" they would ask. "Your son. Your son. Where?"

She would wake up screaming.

At last she came to that many-named place beyond the river's Great Bend, where the water runs straight again, and only rough grass and thorns hold the desert back from the very banks. There she took shelter among the ruined tombs of forgotten dynasties, in the company of ghosts, stone kings, and carvings of fabulous beasts. Offerings from river travellers sustained her. She learned to wade out as far as she could go, shouting praise or prophecies or even curses at passing vessels, then gather the baskets left floating behind. She became a kind of oracle, described in guidebooks, the subject of many stories, though few knew that this was Lady Hansherat, who had once been such a power in the court of the Delta.

Sometimes the gods truly spoke through her.

So she lingered, alone with her sorrows and memories, searching her dreams for her husband's soul, and for some trace of that son whose advent she had somehow foretold.

One night a cold hand touched her on the shoulder.

She shrugged, taking it for another dream, or a draught from some deep vault, and merely pulled her tattered garments more tightly around herself.

"Come," said a voice like the wind and sand whispering together. "Rise up."

She rose and followed what might have been a black vapor or an animate bundle of sticks and rags out into the desert, beneath a moonless sky. Possibly her guide wore an almost featureless mask cut out of black paper. She couldn't tell. The stars revealed nothing.

At last the hand touched her once more and the voice said, "Dig here."

She squatted down and dug with both hands, burrowing like an animal until her bony fingers clutched a marble casket so small she could lift it up in the palm of one hand.

"Your son awaits beyond this small door."

She thought she understood. What had been just one more dream suddenly became desperately, immediately urgent. Trembling, she unlatched the lid and dumped out into her other hand what felt like a dried, gnarled root.

She looked up at her guide, bewildered and angry, but at that very instant, in the first light of dawn, her husband appeared to her as he had been in life. Yet there was no pain in his expression, only a resigned sadness, as if he were now, somehow, at peace.

Then the sunlight shone through him and he vanished. Weeping, Hansherat cradled the shrivelled thing in her hands. Her tears fell on what might have been a tiny face. To her astonishment, two eyes opened, then a mouth.

"Help me," the thing said.

That day, among the tombs, her madness receded somewhat. She worked with deliberation, even cunning, as she drew from her stores a small flask of wine and poured out a few drops in libation to Shedelvendra and also to the righteous Nine Gods. But she also cut her finger with a sharp stone and offered her blood to the Titans. Then she dipped her bleeding finger into the wine and touched both blood and wine to the object cupped in her other hand.

That afternoon, she left it resting in the box while she searched for fish among the shallows. When she returned, the box was tipped over and the slowly writhing thing lay on the sand beside it, too large to fit back inside.

She picked it up and tried to nurse it at her breast, but she had no milk.

Each night, free of dreams now, her mind clear, her thoughts on the present and the immediate future. She tended her charge, easing wine or bits of meat or breadcrumbs between the tiny, cracked lips.

It was no infant, she understood soon enough. By the light of the waxing moon, delicate limbs rapidly lengthened, but remained skeletal, gnarled, like sticks of driftwood, the skin rough and hard to the touch, like ancient, cracked leather. It reminded her of an insect breaking painfully out of a chrysallis.

She measured its progress and made her plans.

But in the light of the full moon, the skin was smooth and the joints supple, and the face, at least, had filled out. *It* had become *he*.

She lay the boy out on a stone slab, regarding him.

He stared up at the sky, naked, shivering in the night breeze.

"Are you really my *son?* Truly?" She touched him gently on the forehead, then ran her finger over a white mark there, like a burn scar.

If only he could be her son, then, through him, something of Valpetor might live again.

He rose on his elbows, his back arched, rigid as he spoke in many voices, in many languages, addressing invisible presences in the air. She feared to listen, but she did listen, ever attentive as he called out Balredon and Talno and Lekkanut-Na and many other names, as many spirits seemed to contest the mastery of this single, small body.

"No, no," she said at last, shaking him. "Speak to *me*. Tell me who you are."

The fit passed. He lay still again, then clung to her hand with surprising strength. She eased him off the stone, onto the warmer sand. There they huddled throughout the night, while he sometimes wept, sometimes shouted in anger, and still spoke only to the unseen others.

At times, she was certain, voices replied out of the darkness.

But in the dawn's light he curled on his side and slept with his head in her lap. She could see him clearly now, narrow-shouldered and slender, paler than most people of the Delta, emaciated, every rib showing. He had a round, soft face. A tear streaked the dirt on his cheek. His age she guessed to be somewhere between twelve and fifteen.

She couldn't be sure. She wondered if he were a child at all, or some other being, in the form of one. Again, she was desperately afraid that all had been for nothing, that he was one more ghost among so many. He shouldn't have been alive, criss-crossed as he was by scars betokening wounds no one should have been able to survive, as if he had been torn apart by beasts and pierced through the body with spears. Part of his right ear was gone too. That, she thought wryly, reminded her of a tomcat who had been in one fight too many.

But he lay calmly in her lap, warm to the touch. He turned in his sleep, mumbling something.

She shook him awake. He opened his seemingly huge, dark eyes. She reached down to touch his chin. He struggled free of her and lay gasping from the effort, peering up at her inscrutably.

"I won't hurt you," she said.

He sat, and drew his legs up, trying to cover his nakedness. She noted, intrigued, that he was blushing.

"Give me something to wear," he said, speaking her own language, that of the Delta, but with a distinct upriver accent.

She had only her own rags, but offered him some of those. He did what little he could, then moved further away and sat still, hugging his shoulders, staring at her.

She couldn't meet his gaze for long. She shook her head and blinked.

"Shall I . . . name you?" she said, carefully focusing her eyes, not on his face, but on his knees. He looked so frail. His thighs were scarcely thicker than his calves.

"I already have a name."

"A name can be a powerful thing," she said. "Is it your soul's true name, or just a name?"

"I am called Sekenre."

"Which name is that?"

He shrugged, his expression seeming to say that none of this mattered. He seemed very young then, a genuine child. Then his face went slack and he seemed about to faint. She took him into her lap once more and folded her arms around him, rocking slowly back and forth.

Again he slept. Again she woke him.

She weighed her words very carefully.

"Sekenre, where did you come from?"

"From out of a dream inside another dream dreamt within a third. I am not sure where the dreaming stops."

She took one of his hands between both of hers, spreading his delicate fingers apart. The palm was seared a pale white.

"You've stopped dreaming, Sekenre. This is the waking world now." She squeezed his hand until he winced.

He made no reply, but drew away from her, sat up once more, then folded his hands together. When he opened them, blue flames flickered from his palms.

"Ah," she said, certain she had been afforded some profound insight, if only her thoughts could quite encompass it. It was like a distant mountain glimpsed through fog.

He closed his hands and the flames vanished.

"Sekenre," she said, once more considering every word with painstaking deliberation before speaking it. "I helped you this far, and I shall help you further. Will you, in return, help me?"

He affixed her with that almost hypnotic, wide-eyed stare, but with true child-like seriousness said, "Yes. I promise."

He opened his hands, revealing only scarred palms. Then he tried to stand up, but his legs wouldn't support him and she had to catch him before he fell.

So they lingered three more days and nights among the tombs. She fed him from her meager stores. Once she went off to the river to prophesy, and when she returned she found him writing something with his finger in the sand. At her approach, he quickly erased what he had written. She didn't ask about it. She knew how to wait. During those days and nights he told her scraps of stories about a childhood in the City of Reeds, upriver, as his accent suggested. It wasn't a happy beginning: a mother murdered early in his life, a father who deteriorated terrifyingly into a lunatic sorcerer who still claimed he loved his son while the house shook with thunder and corpses wandered the halls at night. But there were quiet moments too, games, mysteries, explorations among the forest of pilings that held up the city; even what must have been

moments of fumbling, boyish comedy, the occasional prank.

But at times Sekenre seemed to confuse his own life with others, with other times and places. Sometimes he lapsed into foreign languages.

But she never contradicted him, never questioned deeper. He gained strength quickly, almost by the hour.

On the third night, he slept huddled against her side for warmth, while she lay awake. She fancied that Andraxes, Belphage, and Ruaine sat nearby, playing a game with ivory pieces on a painted board.

They looked at her in sudden alarm.

"You! You are dead!" they said in unison.

"I am returned," she said, laughing, and her laughter was a mighty wind, upsetting the board, scattering the pieces, swirling her enemies away like dry leaves.

She awoke suddenly and realized she had been dreaming after all. She slid her arm over Sekenre's bony shoulders, running her fingers gently through his tangled hair. She was certain that *he* had sent her that dream. Yes, she was certain now, he was her own son, begotten on her by the ghost of Valpetor.

He was her treasured, secretly guarded instrument of vengeance.

In the morning, the two of them went to the river to bathe, made offerings to the benevolent gods, and began their journey north, following the river, resting every couple of hours because the boy still needed it. He collapsed at midday, prostrated by the sun. She carried him in her arms to the shelter of a grove of palm trees, finding him surprisingly light. She too was a stick-figure from her privations, but iron hard, she decided, made of metal rods. He was a thing of reeds.

So they rested again until sunset. He seemed content to listen while she told him of the royal court in the Delta, of the ceremonies and banquets there, the great spectacles performed before the gods, of the king and queen and their palace filled with riches, and of the splendid company who dwelt with them there.

She left out quite a lot, making no mention of her husband's murder, her own disgrace, of her three foes. As she listened to herself talk, her own account seemed far more fantastic and fragmentary than his, but he did not contradict her, nor question her any deeper.

They walked a mile or so further in the cool evening, then sat down, ate of their meager stores, and slept. She dreamed only of his wide, dark eyes, staring at her.

In the morning twilight, they rose and walked only a short distance to a walled town. The last stars were fading from the sky. Watchlights still burned over the barred gate. As the two of them approached, a guard shouted for them to go away, saying no beggars were welcome here. Caravaneers, encamped around the gate waiting for admission, stirred.

Sekenre made fire with his hands and held it aloft. The gate opened, whether of its own accord or because the warders feared him, Hansherat could not be sure. Like everyone else, the guards, the caravaneers,

by Darrell Schweitzer

sleepy-eyed townspeople, she merely followed the bluish white flame and the nearly naked, sunburnt boy who carried it through winding streets, beneath archways and leaning houses that nearly touched overhead, shutting out the sky, until they emerged into the central square of the town. There Sekenre dropped on his knees before an image of the god Bel-Hemad, the Lord of Spring and Rain and the Master of Sparrows.

Sekenre heaved the flame into the air, where it vanished with an audible pop, then turned and sat cross-legged at the god's feet, drawing strange signs in the dirt.

Quickly Hansherat elbowed her way through the crowd and stood over Sekenre, announcing that he would prophesy, holding out her cupped hands for coins.

A priest arrived, but said nothing. A whole company of elders with long silvery beards and ankle-length red robes stood between Sekenre and the crowd, to witness while the boy divined the futures of many citizens, and foretold strange things to come. All the while Hansherat could only think of her enemies, of Andraxes, slack-faced with terror, Belphage whimpering aloud with fright, and Ruaine, mocking no more.

Yes, she would help Sekenre and he would help her. Mother and son they were, and the firmest of allies.

The elders argued among themselves in urgent whispers. The priest made a sign, both as a blessing and to ward off evil.

Hansherat and Sekenre sat side by side in the upper room of an inn. Two lamps, dangling from the ceiling, swayed slightly, sending shadows drifting. Moonlight shone through the carven screen set in the room's only window. A gentle breeze blew. Hansherat listened to the sounds from the town below: voices, a cart rumbling, horses' hooves clopping on stone, an angry camel braying; unchanging, commonplace things, reminding her of the old life she had once lost and now hoped to regain.

She wore soft leather shoes and a plain dark robe, clean and comfortable. For now, she could imagine nothing better. Fine gowns and jewels, even crowns would come later.

Someone had given Sekenre baggy white trousers which had to be cut off at his ankles so he wouldn't trip over them, and an ornately embroidered silk tunic, also much too large, dropping down below his knees. He could hide his hands in the billowing sleeves or wear them rolled up. He seemed unduly fascinated by the design: birds and flowers and serpents intertwined on a black background. Hansherat wondered if there was something in it she couldn't see, some hidden, magical symbol.

She regarded him as he sat there fingering the silk, oblivious to her, his grubby feet dangling where he couldn't quite reach the floor. She still could not fathom the mystery of him. He seemed both an ordinary young man — closer to middle teens she

decided, just very short and thin — and completely inexplicable. He was her son. She was certain of that. She clung to that like a drowning woman clutching a floating log. But he had come out of a marble box two inches square. The ghost of Valpetor begot him, but he seemed to remember different origins, a Reedlandish childhood in some detail, and fragments of others. At times, she thought, he was still that shrivelled thing she had found, hard and dry and very, very ancient.

"Sekenre," she said. "What are you, really?"

His stomach rumbled loud enough for Hansherat to hear.

He shrugged and said, "What you see."

"What *can* I see? Only the surface. But inside, are you divine? Can you truly prophesy?"

He stared at her, his face expressionless. "Can you?"

After a moment of silent confusion, she spoke to him again with painstaking deliberation, studying him for any reaction.

"I think my powers of prophecy, such as I ever had, have left me now. The gods no longer find a voice in Hansherat."

Because Hansherat is no longer mad, she added silently, because Hansherat has recovered direction and a goal, because the gods speak through those who are lost, whose minds achieve the same randomness of clouds, or birds in flight, or the delicate contours of wind-shaped sand, from which, likewise, much can be divined.

That brought her one more moment of despair: what if Sekenre were merely insane, divinely insane perhaps, but still useless?

But he smiled at her, and his smile wasn't that of a mischievous child at all so much as that of an old and practiced rogue.

"I was just doing tricks. We needed the money, don't you think?"

"But you *are* magical." That was not a question. It was more of a demand.

He shrugged again, once more assuming that offputting aspect of a genuine child.

She got out the marble box and flipped it open, holding its emptiness up to him. "Remember?"

He reached over and closed the box, his movements now assured, even authoritative, as if, as quickly as that, he had become a different person. He pointed a finger at her as if he were the adult giving correction.

"Do not try to understand me," he said. "Merely trust and hope and be certain that I shall serve you as you have served me."

"Trust and hope," she said softly.

"And be certain." He paused, listening for something she could not hear. "Your faith may be tested . . ." Again he paused, listening. She heard only the town noises, coming in through the window. ". . . far sooner . . ." There. Yes. She heard it too. A footstep shuffling in the corridor outside. ". . . than I had expected."

The door to the room opened and a serving girl came in with a tray, which she set down on a small table in the far corner, then carried both table and tray over to where Hansherat and Sekenre sat.

"Your dinner, compliments of the master of this house," she said, bowing slightly, "who is honored beyond words by your holy presence here, Sir." She nodded slightly to Sekenre and curtseyed to Hansherat.

Lamplight revealed cups of wine and two fine meals. Hansherat realized with discomfort how long it had been since she had eaten anything like that.

"I thank you," she said to the servant, "and your master too."

Too hungry to wait any longer, she took a candied plum on her fork.

But Sekenre merely said, "Girl, come here. There is something I must tell you."

Holding the plum, Hansherat watched as the servant leaned down to hear what Sekenre would whisper into her ear.

With a sudden, violent motion, Sekenre grabbed the girl by the hair and yanked her down into his lap, while snatching a knife from the table. He cut off her head with a single stroke. Hansherat screamed. She froze in amazement at the sight of the girl's headless body, which did not fall, but righted itself, and stood before the table, swaying in a slow circle.

There was no blood.

Sekenre held up the still living head. Its eyes rolled up till only the whites were visible. The mouth muttered something unintelligible, but definitely spoke.

Now Sekenre addressed his captive as Hansherat had never heard him speak before, his voice breaking, like a boy imitating a giant, his thin chest unable to sound the thunderous tones, but the manner, the diction, the accent were *not* those of Sekenre at all, but of another speaking through him.

"So you have discovered my stratagem. My hiding place is found out. I had thought to attack. Now I am to defend. So be it. I am not afraid."

He breathed into the girl-thing's face and it blackened, smoked, and shrivelled, like a ball of crumpled paper at the edge of a fire. He threw it across the room, then stood up, reached around the back of the still standing body and snatched out a red, beating heart.

He held it up to Hansherat, still speaking in that harsh, fierce way. "This alone of her is alive. The rest is a construct, a fabrication, as you see, hollow behind, its flesh only covering front and sides, filled with air. When the *heart* dies —" He stabbed it with the knife. The heart exploded, splattering both of them with blood.

Then he dropped the knife and sat down. He seemed like an awkward boy again, unsure of what to do now that he'd made such an obvious mess and soiled his new, silken tunic.

The serving girl's body collapsed in on itself like melting wax.

"Well, you see what happens," Sekenre said in his familiar, soft voice.

Hansherat put down her fork even before she noticed that the plum was now offal and most of what she could recognize on the plate was mud and sawdust.

Suddenly, the two lamps dangling from the ceiling twisted wildly on their chains as if the room were filled with a whirlwind. But she felt no wind. Shadows flickered crazily. The wooden screen in the window rattled.

By moonlight she watched in horrified fascination as Sekenre stripped off tunic and trousers, neatly folded them under the bed, and began to trace intricate patterns on himself with the girl-creature's blood.

The air became so cold her breath, and his, came in white puffs. She could tell he was shivering and sweating at the same time. Still he worked steadily, covering himself with designs she could not make out. Then he made a circle in blood on the floor and wrote something around its rim, what might have been a single, long word in looping script which joined back into itself.

He made fire with his hands and touched the circle. The unbroken script glowed a brilliant white. The light spread up his arms, until the traceries that covered him glowed faintly blue, like luminous tatoos. The room grew ever colder. His whole body shook violently. His breath sounded hoarse, labored.

"Sekenre?"

He looked up at her.

"Sekenre, please tell me what is going on."

"My enemies have found me sooner than I thought they would. I can't explain now —"

"But later —?"

"Later. If I win."

Hansherat's first impulse was simply to run away, to get out of that room and forget about Sekenre and the Delta and the king and even Valpetor's ghost, and run screaming into the night, back to her tombs and madness and prophecies.

But she could not desert her son. Sekenre was her son, somehow, inexplicably. She stayed where she was, hugging her knees.

The two lamps went out, one after another, as if smothered by an invisible hand. The "wind" stopped. The lamps hung straight down on their chains, motionless.

Sekenre stood up in the bitterly cold air. Faint vapor rose from his skin. Delicate patterns of blue fire outlined his face, his front, sides, arms and legs; but he hadn't been able to reach his back, so he, like the serving girl, seemed hollow behind.

The circle on the floor burst into flames, roaring, but still giving off no heat at all.

"They're coming," said Sekenre. He shoved the table to the far side of the room. Dishes and cups clattered. Hansherat drew back onto the bed, her back against the wall, watching as a pair of eyes like deep red embers rose into the air within the burning circle and a dark form slowly took shape, something like an old, hideous man who was half insect. His shoulders gleamed, black and smooth as metal. Countless hairy, spiked limbs wriggled out of his belly. His pale face sagged to one side, like a mask of dead flesh clumsily stretched over something it would never fit. Only his arms, his bare blue-veined legs, and his narrow buttocks were completely human.

Sekenre paced around the circle, always keeping his back away from it. The thing turned to follow. Something else formed next to it, a horse-headed man, muscular, naked, covered like Sekenre with swirls and strange patterns, but set into his skin with red-hot bits of metal. Hansherat could feel the heat of them and smell the horse-man's searing flesh.

Still Sekenre paced. The two followed him, around and around. A third foe appeared, standing between the other two, a male dwarf no more than two feet high, either clad in or covered with feathers, his huge eyes aglow with reflected light. A human owl, Hansherat thought.

"Now is the time for Sekenre to truly die," said the owl-man. "Now shall Balredon and Talno and Lekkanut-Na and Tannivar pour out their secrets. Now shall even Vashtem be summoned into endless torment."

"Now," said the horse-man.

"Now," said the insect.

Still Sekenre paced in silence. The apparitions turned, angrily. The insect-thing noticed Hansherat on the bed and chittered.

"We'll devour Sekenre's wench."

"When we are done with her, yes," said the horse-man.

"Tear her apart while still she lives," said the dwarf.

The horse-headed one roared in a voice like raging thunder, shaking the room, deafening Hansherat, the force knocking her back against the wall hard, nearly squeezing the breath out of her. What followed was confusing. One moment Sekenre stood between her and the bed and the monster roared. Then she could not see him. She sat up groggily, *on the floor*, and drew her hand back in sudden terror from where she had almost smeared the scripted word at the circle's edge. That, she was certain, would have been fatal to them both.

"Help me," Sekenre gasped. She saw him now, on the floor, wrestling in the coils of what might have been an invisible serpent.

"What can I do?"

"Go to the window! Open it! Go!"

Hansherat lurched to her feet just as the horse-headed one roared again, sending her tumbling, away from the circle this time. Her head slammed into the wall below the window. She sat up, dazed, dimly aware of blood streaming from her nose and ears. She tried to rise, but got no further than her knees. The intricately-carven wooden screen still filled the window, but the light streaming through was blinding, as if the window looked out into the heart of the sun.

She closed her eyes as hard as she could, turned her face away, and fumbled for the screen, swimming in light and terrible heat, screaming in her own agony.

The screen came away in her hands. Fire poured into the room, washing over her. She had the brief impression of living flame, fiery birds, monsters without any shape she could define, and, at the end, an enormous face, the face of a god, gazing up at her from somewhere far below, from some universe of infinite fire.

And then, darkness. For the longest time she sat with her back to the wall, eyes too dazzled to make out anything but drifting splotches of light. Her ears rang. But there was no other pain. She wasn't burnt. The air was cold again.

Then some of those light-splotches moved. It was Sekenre. The blue light of his body markings drifted like clouds of fireflies. But the circle on the floor flickered with reassuring steadiness, its heatless flames no more than an inch high, like hundreds of tiny candles. A blackened horse's head lay smoldering in the center of it.

"Sekenre?" she whispered. "Is it over?"

He made no reply, but began pacing around the circle again, his bare feet padding, the floorboards creaking.

"Sekenre?"

She groped along the wall, keeping well clear of him and the circle, seeking the darkness and comfort of the bed once more. Her hand found a wooden leg. She hauled herself up. The room swayed around her. Sekenre was chanting or reciting something she couldn't make out. She let herself fall face-down onto the bed.

But its surface was alive, cold and greasy, heaving. Her right hand was inside a *mouth*, which closed on her like a vise, crushing her wrist. Another set of teeth fastened onto her chin, grinding from side to side. She felt a shock of pain as what might have been a clawed hand tore her robe from her shoulders.

She wriggled her face free and screamed. The second mouth had her by the hair now. She tried to pull her hand free. The whole mass oozed onto the floor, dragging her with it.

Then Sekenre was standing above her, commanding the thing into the circle. It released her, drifted like a cloud across the burning letters without smearing them, then sank down through the floorboards like a crocodile into river mud.

He helped her up. She stood unsteadily, vaguely aware that the whole back of her robe was sticky with blood, that she might be badly hurt, even dying. But Sekenre merely said, "Go back to the window and tell me what you see."

She staggered, caught hold of the windowsill, and leaned out, blinking. There didn't seem to be any town below, only the night sky, above and below both, filled with an infinity of stars. That was impossible, she tried to convince herself. But she saw. She lost all sense of up and down and felt sick, as if she were falling.

"Just stars," she said weakly, "Just stars."

"Good. Stay there."

So she clung to the windowsill for what seemed like hours, peering out into the firmament of heaven, while behind her Sekenre recited something very slowly, pausing for the count of four or five after every word. Once she glanced back over her shoulder and saw him tracing fiery symbols in the air with his finger.

And again, someone was in the room with them, a woman dressed in scarlet, holding a lantern and a sword. Then a clap of thunder. Then something hunched and massive like a lion with serpentine arms flailing, cracking in the air like whips. It reached out of the burning circle and caught Sekenre across the bare back, whirling him around, another limb sweeping his feet from beneath him. He fell, struggling as the monster dragged him toward itself.

She cried out, but he shouted, "Stay where you are!" and in another instant the lion-thing was gone.

She saw the stars ripple like luminous foam. She turned back into the room to tell Sekenre, but instead watched him confront a naked black man covered from head to foot in glowing symbols. Sekenre's own markings, she saw, were damaged, many of them smeared or gone altogether. The rest seemed to give off less light than before.

But she could only watch helplessly as the black man reached for Sekenre and Sekenre reached for the black man, neither touching the other, as if, Hansherat thought, there were an invisible barrier between them with equally invisible holes in it, and the winner was the one who found the way through first.

Sekenre found it, wiping the black man's chest clear, then reaching up and ripping out his throat with a single, violent jerk. Once more, blood sprayed over the walls and ceiling. The black man vanished.

And again, a bald, fat man in an iridescent blue robe sat cross-legged in the middle of the circle, writing on a tablet in his lap with a quill. Sekenre also had a tablet and pen. The fat man held up what he had written. Sekenre gasped, as if struck a heavy blow. The fat man grinned. Then Sekenre held up his tablet, and the other scowled, drawing back in fear. He scribbled some more; but before he had finished, he gave up, cast his tablet aside, screamed, and vanished, darkness closing over him like the cover of a book suddenly snapped shut.

It went on for hours, Sekenre's enemies appearing in countless forms, sometimes vanishing again too quickly for Hansherat's eyes to follow. Sometimes she wasn't sure it was Sekenre who fought them. His form, too, flickered into something else. More often he spoke or recited or cried out in voices she didn't know, in strange languages.

Fascinated, she watched, clinging to the windowsill, the view beyond the window forgotten, while frigid wind blew in over her.

"Look!" Sekenre shouted at last. "Look out again! What do you see?"

She screamed at what she saw, and her mind could not grasp, nor could her words describe as the rippling tapestry of stars tore apart like a curtain, the very heavens trailing in streamers against a greater darkness, and out of that darkness the Shadow Titans appeared, equal and opposite to the gods, whom even the gods feared. They opened their eyes and beheld her spying on them. They opened their mouths to devour her with their speech. She fainted.

"You have won, Sekenre. It's finally over."

Hansherat sat up in the darkness, leaning painfully against the wall beneath the window. It seemed that someone else spoke, not her.

"It's safe now. You can erase the circle."

The voice sounded so familiar.

Hansherat shook her head, forcing herself awake. She saw Sekenre on his knees before the circle, his back to her. He didn't seem to be in any ritual position, but, instead, too weak to stand. She could see the dark gouge across his back where the lion-creature had struck him. He was covered with blood. Very few of his protective markings remained.

Inside the burning circle stood a perfect replica of herself, a false Hansherat, duplicated down to the torn, bloody robe and lacerated shoulders.

"You are my son," this other Hansherat said. "I am your mother. Come to me now."

Sekenre lurched unsteadily. "My mother died," he said. "A long time ago."

"No, I am your mother. You are my son. Come." The false Hansherat held out a hand.

And he reached for it. "I want to stop," he said, sobbing. "I just want to stop."

"No! Sekenre! No!" Lady Hansherat screamed.

Sekenre turned, that lost-little-boy expression on his face. He held a long copper knife in his hand.

"Behold your final enemy!" said the thing within the circle, pointing at Lady Hansherat. "Kill it and you'll be finished. Don't you see? That's the only one left."

Sekenre crawled toward the window, the knife scraping the floor, his eyes wide, staring.

"No, Sekenre!"

He didn't seem to hear her. The apparition in the circle laughed. He was almost in reach when Hansherat found the strength to heave herself to her feet, easily evading the clumsy swing of his knife. The boy rose to his knees, trying to stand, turned to follow her, but fell over on his back with a yelp of pain as he hit the floor. Hansherat snatched the knife out of his hand, ran to the flaming circle, stepped inside, grabbed the false image of herself by the front of the robe with one hand while driving the knife through its back with the other.

The back was open, hollow. Meeting no resistance, the knife pierced the thing's heart, burst out through its chest, and cut Hansherat's own wrist. Startled, she dropped the knife. The false Hansherat disintegrated into fine, swirling dust.

The circle was empty now, and broken where Hansherat's foot had smeared it. The fires burned lower, then went out. Tiny trails of smoke rose in the freezing darkness.

She stood still, shuddering.

Sekenre coughed. "You're not finished," he said. She turned, startled, only able to make out a few glowing swirls and points of light moving as he approached her. Quickly she snatched up the knife again. "Victory can swiftly turn into defeat if you're not careful. Give me the knife. It's more essential than you can ever imagine."

She backed away.

He shuffled toward her. "Give it."

She clung to the plain wooden handle with both hands. How strange that she should notice such a detail in such circumstances: It was no magical implement, just a carving knife from the table setting.

"I'm afraid," she said.

He put his hands on hers. "Not of me. You should never be afraid of me."

He took the knife from her unresisting fingers. The remains of the impaled heart crumbled at his touch, dry and brittle and impossibly light, like an old wasp's nest you find in the winter.

"You see?" she said. "She was like that other one, the servant girl, hollow behind, just like you said."

She couldn't really follow what he was doing. It was too dark. He knelt down, back to her.

"You've ably destroyed the unliving *device,*" he said. "Now let's finish off the one who devised it."

Grunting, he drove the knife down through the floorboards. A shrill, warbling shriek sounded from below. For just an instant, a flabby, glowing face rose up out of the wood. Sekenre twisted the blade. Black blood poured from the screaming mouth. The face sank down and vanished.

Then it was Sekenre who was screaming, in the same warbling voice. He thrashed over the floor, clawing at the wood.

Hansherat crouched beside him, holding him by the shoulders until he was calm again. He was slick and clammy to the touch, but she felt his heart racing within his thin chest. When he spoke, he seemed barely able to form the words, but it was his own voice. She knew it was Sekenre and no one else who whispered, merely, "Thank you."

In the gray dawn, Hansherat looked out the window, over the rooftops of the town. Two soldiers of the watch strolled lazily below, their pikes over their shoulders. Somewhere nearby, a rooster crowed.

Hansherat called for the landlord, who came to her door, yawning, lantern in hand.

"Didn't you sleep well, Reverend Lady?"

"You mean you didn't *hear* anything?"

"Hear what?"

Then the man's eyes widened as he saw the burnt horse-skull in the middle of the floor, the smoke trailing from the magic circle, the knife still embedded in the floorboards, and Sekenre lying there, naked and bloody.

"Merciful gods! Oh merciful gods!" The landlord kept repeating that over and over. But Hansherat had to give him credit. He didn't run away. Instead he helped her carry Sekenre to the bed, and the two of them examined him. The wound across his back was huge and deep. He was going to have another massive scar from it, she realized.

The boy moaned and started to struggle. She held him firmly in place.

"Sekenre, you ought to wear armor while doing this."

"No," he said, his words muffled in a pillow. "If the sigils are covered up, they have no power."

His had been covered up with his own blood.

Calmly, methodically, she examined him, finding burns, welts, and gashes all over, but no deep punctures; a lot of bruises, and, she suspected, a one or two broken ribs, but nothing worse than that. His face was puffy and red, his lips split, one of his eyes blackened. She saw him right then as a child who needed her help and nothing more.

She sent the landlord out for water, ointments and bandages. He went, closing the door behind him, shouting to the servants to stay away.

When they had finished and Sekenre was sleeping peacefully, the landlord said, "Merciful gods, this will never do. It'll bring a curse on my establishment. You two must go *at once.*"

Angrily, Hansherat made what she hoped he would take for a magical gesture. "My son and I are both sorcerers," she said in a low voice. "You can see that. If you do not let us remain until he is able to travel, *we* will most definitely put a curse on your establishment."

"Oh merciful gods —"

"All that you have seen shall remain a secret. Tell the others only that the holy prophet and prophetess require seclusion, that no one may come up here."

"Oh merciful — I shall try —"

She made another sign in the air. The landlord flinched.

"You will *succeed.*"

Ten days later they left, secretly, in the evening just before the town's gates closed. Both wore plain, loose robes and sandals, carrying provisions, money, and extra clothes in satchels. Sekenre held his bundle in his arms, in front of him. It was still too painful for him to carry anything over his back.

In the darkness, beneath the clear and starry sky, somewhere along the river, they camped beneath a cluster of palm trees. Sekenre made an ordinary fire by rubbing sticks together. The two of them sat leaning over it for warmth. The desert night soon grew quite cold.

Hansherat finally said what she had been longing to say.

"Sekenre, you have a lot of explaining to do."

He replied slowly, almost solemnly, but in his familiar voice. She knew it was truly Sekenre speaking.

"Yes, I do. Very well then, know that I am Sekenre the sorcerer, called the Illuminator. I am nearly three hundred years old. For a hundred of those years, I lay in the box, as I was when you found me. Know, too, that we sorcerers fight strange wars, over the centuries, across many worlds, in *Leshe* among the ghosts, in dreams, in the sky and under the earth. In the course of these, my rivals became too strong for me and there was no other way to escape them but to lie in that box, to become a seed which might one day be replanted and grow again into Sekenre. In the intervening century, the others battled among themselves, and were weakened, but not as much as I had hoped. It was a near thing. You saved me, Lady Hansherat of the Delta. I owe you my life."

She wanted to weep. He still had that little-boy manner, the wide-eyed, innocent expression. She wanted him to be her son, but even she, even mad, ragged Hansherat knew that she could never be the mother of the three-hundred-year-old sorcerer Sekenre. That was impossible. That delusion was gone.

"But *why* do sorcerers do it?"

"Fight, you mean? Because they are afraid. They fight to be free from fear. They become disfigured, grotesquely transformed, but they can't stop. They mutilate themselves, becoming ever stronger in their pain. They carve signs into their flesh. I knew a sorcerer once who tore out his own eyes so that molten metal serpents could inhabit the sockets. They served him well until somebody poured a bucket of icewater over his head and they shattered."

He paused. Hansherat supposed he was remembering strange and terrible things from long ago, which even he could not bring himself to describe. "This wasn't even my quarrel, you know," he said at last, shuffling closer to the fire. "One of those within me, Balredon or Tannivar, one of them — they can still hide secrets from me — someone made an enemy, who was aligned with another, who betrayed a third. It goes on and on. I think you know this already. Whenever a sorcerer is killed, the slain one becomes *part* of the slayer. Thus we devour one another, filling ourselves with the souls and memories of our victims. Sometimes, for a sorcerer, death is a kind of escape, as it was for my own father, when he induced me to murder him. He hoped to hide from his enemies in the body of his own son. That was how I began. Oh, I contain multitudes and mysteries, Lady Hansherat. Everyone my father ever killed, everyone each of *them* ever killed, many more I've acquired along the way —"

For just an instant she felt absolute, abject terror. She covered her face with her hands, then let out a whimpering cry. "Do you mean . . .? If I had finished what you finished —?"

"Absolutely. When I drove the knife through the floor, I merely added to the number of the already varied company within me. But if *you* had done it, *you* would have become a sorcerer too. That I would never wish upon you."

He paused to untie his sandals, banging them together to shake the sand out. He lay back on the sand and stretched, wriggling his toes. He seemed, Hansherat thought, terribly, deceptively *human* when he did things like that.

She hardened her thoughts, recalling her own purpose.

"Sekenre, if you cannot stop doing what you do, it won't matter much if you do it one more time —"

"I am trying to find a way. More than anything else, I'd like to stop."

"But before you do, I remind you of your promise to help me as I helped you."

He sat up and remained silent again for a very long time. The fire burned down. He poked the embers idly with a stick. Hansherat shivered in the night air. Somewhere along the river, geese honked.

Sekenre sighed. "I won't do it."

Very coldly, she said, "Would you break your promise? Have you no honor, no gratitude? Should I have left you where I found you?"

"I have gratitude," he said. "Possibly even honor of some sort. But I will not do what you want."

"Then I have lost my only hope."

"Doesn't that depend on what you were hoping for?" Now he spoke, not like a boy at all, but like a wise old man who just happened to have a boy's voice. "Lady, I am grateful to you for saving me. You even, many times, tried to comfort me. You did that of your own will, not because I tricked you or magicked you into it. I still know what such things mean, despite everything I have become. But I also know what you want —"

"I haven't told you —"

"Let me guess. You want me to return you to the capital, kill all your enemies, restore you to power and riches, maybe even make you queen —"

"But I didn't tell you this. How could you know?"

"I'm a sorcerer, Lady. But, even if I were not, you are completely transparent."

"Then, yes, that is what I want. Let that be my reward for saving you."

He took her hand in his. He gazed into her eyes.

"Don't ask this. Please, don't. I performed such a favor for another exile once. She got to be queen, all right, but ended up with her head nailed over the city gate. In the process, a lot of people got killed, including several sorcerers, strangers, whose powers and old feuds I acquired. That is how it continues. Each new atrocity requires vengeance, each act of vengeance a fresh atrocity. As it is with sorcerers, so with queens. But the way to *stop* is by halting right here, right now.

You don't have to forgive your enemies. Merely live beyond the hurt they have done you. Vengeance might hurt you even more."

Hansherat struck the ground with her fist, feeling helpless and foolish. "But I swore before the king that I would return with my son . . ."

"And it was I who put that thought into your head. It was merely a stratagem. I wish it were not so. I wish I truly could be your son."

"You put —?"

"As I slept in the box, my spirit wandered in *Leshe*, among the restless dead. There I met your husband's ghost. He told me everything. I sent him to you, directing you to uncover the box. Then I whispered into your mind, and caused you to prophesy before the king."

It was too bewildering. It didn't make sense. "But, but . . . I spoke to the king *before* Valpetor's ghost led me to the box."

He smiled that disarming smile of his. "It was I, too, who entered your dreams and instructed you in the art of capturing a soul in glass. Remember? No, you do not. I covered over the memory, like drawing a curtain, before I left."

"Can you travel in time, then?"

"There is no time in sorcery, nor in dreams, nor in death. Therefore, once my purpose had been served, I led Valpetor into *Tashe*, the realm true death, where he is at rest, whence he cannot be recalled because he is beyond time."

Lady Hansherat wept long and hard. "For that, I am truly grateful, Sekenre," she said at last.

"Nevertheless, it is I who am in your debt, and I shall give you adequate recompense before we part."

He travelled with her for many years, wandering from place to place, working small miracles to sustain them. He was her companion who pretended to be her son.

They came into Reedland, to the quaint and tumbledown City of Reeds, a place of wooden houses tottering on stilts, of watery avenues, docks, and endless fish smells.

"This is where I grew up," he said. "I was a real boy here. But it was so long ago, no one will recognize me now."

So they dwelt there in one of the rickety houses. He spent long days in his sunlit study, wrapped in that oversized silk tunic (which he wore into rags; she used to chide him about it), working magic with parchment and pens and colored paints, painstakingly illuminating, symbols, words, the story of his life, and hers. He explained that it made him whole and real. He defined himself that way.

While in Reedland, he was her son in public, but in private, her husband. She was still young enough. He gave her a true son whom she named Tuolas, which means, in the Deltan tongue, "Autumn."

But a sorcerer, of course, does not age. He cannot change, except to die. Sekenre had to present his own offspring as his younger brother, then his elder, and finally, his father. When Tuolas married and the circumstances became too strange for the growing family, when Hansherat could not bear to look on Sekenre but would never say so, he went away, so the rest of them might live ordinary lives.

He visited Hansherat only once more, when she was very old, and Tuolas was nearly sixty himself. The sorcerer paid for their passage on a ship, and the three of them sailed downriver to the City of the Delta, where the ancient lady beheld one last time the palace of the king, the houses of the great lords, and the many temples of the gods. There had been a change of dynasty. Hawk-faced Andraxes, silent Belphage, and mocking Ruaine were long dead, executed for treason.

But Hansherat did not announce herself to the new king. No one knew that she had indeed returned to the capital with her son, as had been prophesied.

"Such is my parting gift to you," Sekenre said. "Don't you think it was better this way?"

The legend is very old, but that is how the story of Lady Hansherat really ends. I know it and I tell you, for I am Sekenre who writes this. Ω